Alex Cohen
Books 1-3

Leopold Borstinski

BOOK ONE

THE

BOWERY

SLUGGER

SATURDAY, JANUARY 19, 1918

1

THE GAME OF baseball has a long and fine tradition, dating back over a century when rival villages would resolve their differences with a bat and a ball. While similar in appearance to the British sport of rounders, baseball is an American game played under American rules.

Even though the rule book is thick, at its heart the game involves two teams: one tries to run round a square and the other tries to stop them. A member of the team who is aiming to complete circuits of the square must use a stick to propel the ball, lobbed at them by the opposition, as far away from the square as possible. That gives them sufficient time to run around the square.

The stick, or bat, is tapered and varnished to within an inch of its life so that the baseball travels unimpeded on its journey. The other advantage of this stick is that the wood, out of which it is made, comes from only the finest trees. Why should we care about such details? Because when you take a baseball bat to a man's skull, you can be certain you will cause him damage.

Fabian planted the end of his baseball bat firmly into the side of Sammy's cranium, causing a little rhythmic arc of red to appear from his ear. Fabian continued to clobber him with blows to his kidneys, chest, back and head. Power swings and a practiced eye ensured each swing hit its intended target with deadly force. At first, Sammy twisted himself into a ball, desperate to protect his sides and front from the rain of woody assaults smashing against him. Then the pounding took its toll and his energy waned until his body slackened and he ceased trying to defend himself.

"You'd better not get up from this, you *gonif*. Understand?"

Silence for a reply because Sammy lay on the ground, one leg twitching, with no other movement. Fabian poked him in the ribs once. Nothing. He took the hem of the guy's shirt and wiped his bat clean with it, like it was any old *schmatta*. He walked out of the alleyway, careful not to be seen by any passerby. Then Fabian slipped into the shadows of the Manhattan night.

5

Although he didn't waste time looking back on his life, if Fabian had bothered, he would have realized that night was precisely three years to the day after he arrived in the United States of America.

Fabian continued to flee the scene of his crime, slinking from one stall to the next as he made his way back home. The image of Sammy's skull, blood pouring out, lingered in his mind despite himself.

He pushed through the crowds south on Norfolk, turned right onto Heston and headed towards the Bowery before another right back onto Eldridge Street. His eyes stared a few feet ahead of his shoes, hat tipped forward to make it harder for people to see his face.

THURSDAY, JANUARY 21, 1915

2

THE FIRST TIME Fabian walked down Heston was a very different story. His young face stared up at the buildings, blinking at the lights and the market stalls which lined the street. He didn't notice the most surprising thing: he was surrounded by Yiddish speakers. Everywhere he wandered that day, the signs were in Yiddish, the shopkeepers spoke it. His world continued to be filled with the language of the Jews. The old shtetl lived and breathed in the middle of Manhattan.

His first time out of the tenement rooms by himself, Fabian sauntered with his hands in his pockets, enjoying the sights and smells of the city. He soaked in the familiarity of home despite this new place existing thousands of miles away from anything he knew.

On one side of the street were a string of shops: a kosher butcher, baker, cheeses and milk. All the things a person might need to sustain himself through the day. And his family. Then lined up by the kerb, but perched on the street, stood a series of stands and booths, selling everything else a young man dreamed of owning: chocolate, fruit and a whole lot besides. The same pattern of shops and stalls was mirrored on the other side of the street. And all about, people were charging up and down. Everyone was going somewhere, had a place to go—or a deal to make.

Away from the main thoroughfare, Fabian spotted the odd alleyway, caught in the shadows between the different buildings. He hovered near the entrance of one, curious to see what was happening in the darkness and seclusion next to the public hustle and bustle.

He leaned against the corner of the alleyway building, arms folded and legs crossed, whistling himself a little tune. That gave him the opportunity to glance back to check out what was occurring without appearing too interested.

A huddle of lads crouched near a wall at the far end. Occasionally they'd shriek with delight, but most of the time some would throw coins down while another would chuck some dice toward the brickwork. A whoop and

9

then a bunch of youths collected coins and occasionally one would walk away. Fabian witnessed his first game of craps.

Half an hour later, he found himself stood by the huddle, trying to figure out the rules and then Fabian spent another five minutes working out how to win. Within sixty minutes, he'd earned himself twenty cents on an initial three cent investment. Not the greatest return in the history of high finance but a good day's work for an unemployed adolescent.

Fabian took his leave from the assembled throng and returned to the hubbub of the main thoroughfare where the lure of freshly cooked gefilte fish wafted up his nostrils. He heard his stomach rumble as his body announced its hunger.

Like so many other occasions in his life, Fabian had a major problem— while he was surrounded by food, he only had twenty cents to his name. The winnings from the craps game was his entire estate. So he purchased a challah bread and some sugar for five cents each. Fabian sprinkled some of the sweet granules onto a piece of bread he'd torn off and chewed on it briefly before swallowing. Out of the corner of his eye, he spotted a cheese stall and sauntered over, whistling as he went. The owner was having an argument with a woman who was complaining about the quality of his produce and was demanding he refund her for a block she'd bought the day before, which had already gone off.

Fabian stood at the corner of the stall with his hand holding his bread and then he let his fingers wander until they could gouge out a piece of cheese. They ventured back into his pants pocket and he returned to his vantage point thirty feet further away as the fevered discussion morphed into a series of gestures and general shouting before the woman stormed off once her remonstrations fell on deaf ears. Fabian popped the cheese onto another piece of bread and enjoyed his bounty.

With the drama ended, Fabian stopped leaning against the wall and scurried on down the sidewalk. Until now he'd traveled south along Suffolk, but then he turned right on Hester, one block north of Canal Street. Why the turn? An instinctive move away from a cop who stood on the street corner, watching the world go by.

WHILE FABIAN WAS no jailbird in the old country, he'd had several brushes with the police and this was not the time for him to get acquainted with the local law enforcement squad. There would be ample opportunity in the months and years ahead.

Hester led him west, but Fabian only sauntered half a block along before he stopped and leaned against another wall. He liked people watching. He had a natural curiosity in others, but also a constant desire to spot his next mark. You can take the boy out of the Ukrainian criminal underworld but you can't take the criminal underworld out of the boy.

The recurring theme with all the men was the length of their beards and the strings or *tzitzit* hanging out from under their shirts as part of their religious observance. Fabian knew the streets were safe; no matter what may happen, there would be no hordes rampaging near his home swiping away at any Jew left standing.

A shiver ran down his spine as he recalled why his family had taken their possessions and spent almost three months in the hold of a ship. Then he turned back to Suffolk where he was drawn to the craps game, four hundred feet away from the cop on his corner.

With ten cents burning a hole in his pocket, Fabian strolled over to the mass of boys who were still surrounding the rolling dice. He paused with his hands in his pockets as the next few throws took place—to check how everyone's luck was going and also to make sure the same guys were running the game. Fabian recognized a fella from before, standing and surveying every move made by the younger ones as they laid down coins. Occasionally, the boy managing the game would pass coins up to the older one, who would trouser the fresh cash.

Fabian caught his eye and received a nod for his trouble. He nodded back and five minutes later, they stood next to each other and struck up a conversation.

"Good win earlier."

"Thanks… This your game?"

"Fancy your luck again, then?"

Fabian snorted out a laugh.

"This isn't a game of luck. It's a numbers game."

"All about the odds, for sure… What's your name?"

"They're calling me Fabian nowadays."

"Hi, Fabian. Today they call me Sam."

"Pleasure is all mine."

"Straight back at you. Most of our customers play and lose. It is rare to bump into a winner."

"A game of probability. If you have a head for numbers, you can make some sensible decisions."

"Quite, but most people don't get that simple fact."

Fabian smiled.

"I try not to play games I'll lose. Bad business."

"Oh, you are an entrepreneur."

"I'm just a guy making his way in this *meshuggener* world."

"I understand. This is a crazy town."

"Wouldn't know. We've only just arrived."

"We?"

"Oh. My family."

"From the old country?"

"Yeah."

"What do you know?"

"Some homespun wisdom and a bit of Yiddishe chutzpah."

"We all need a touch of that, for sure. You busy right now?"

"I'm back here kicking my heels, aren't I?"

"You seem a stand-up mensch. Can I get you to do me a favor?"

"No charge for asking."

"Would you mind the shop for me? Just for five minutes. I have a guy to meet about a thing."

"No need to explain."

"You've got a good eye. I can tell."

"I'll look after the stall, happily."

"Here's some seed capital in case of need but the idea is that you end up with more cash than less by the time I return."

"I got it. You meet the man."

They shook hands and Sam walked off. Fabian glanced at him as he departed, noticing Sam's brown hair, slightly curled, and the fact he was barely five feet tall.

Fabian stood with his legs apart and arms folded, staring at the boys throwing the dice and glaring at their hands whenever a bet was placed.

Fifteen minutes later, Sammy returned.

"*VUS MACHS DA*? What's up?"

"All is fine, thank you for asking. Any trouble here?"

"Nope. All's in order, Sam."

"Thank you for the help."

"My pleasure."

Fabian returned Sam's gelt, who held out his hand to shake Fabian's and as they did, Fabian felt a piece of paper appear in his palm. When he looked down before putting his hand back in his pocket, he saw it was a dollar bill.

"Very kind."

"Good to meet a trustworthy sort in this den of sin we love to call the Bowery."

"Thanks anyway."

"You mentioned you'd just arrived in town. Does that mean you need work?"

"Always interested in earning a buck," and he winked at Sam as he said it to acknowledge the fee he'd just received again.

"Perhaps we should go to my office to discuss the matter further. A man shouldn't do business on the street unless he's buying a hooker."

"Nicely put. When can we go? Aren't you busy right now?"

"Not really."

Sam clicked his fingers and a boy appeared from nowhere. He must have been in the alley all the time Fabian was there.

"Look after the game while I discuss business."

The lad nodded and surveyed the gaggle of players intently.

"Why did you ask me for help if you'd already got a hired hand?"

"Best way to see what kind of person you are."

"Take me to your office."

3

SAM AND FABIAN sauntered out of the alley chewing the fat. Up Suffolk and they passed a group of shoppers who had settled around a street vendor. He was telling some tale to sell tonic water. The huddle contained at least twenty people and they were intently listening to the spiel. Sam elbowed Fabian gently and they stopped and stood by a haberdashery shop, pretending to check out buttons.

Fabian watched as Sam soaked up all the information he could see about the schnooks in the audience.

"Are you thinking what I'm thinking?"

"Probably."

Sam smiled and nodded.

"Let's do this thing."

He moved toward the edge of the crowd, Fabian turned to the other side and mingled in Sam's general direction. As Fabian passed behind him, Sam's hand thrust into Fabian's stomach and he reached there instinctively. He felt handfuls of paper and a wallet so he stuffed his hands into his pockets. The notes and wallet deposited quickly, he took his hands out again in case there was a second delivery.

Sure enough, Sam had walked away to another part of the crowd and returned to stand in front of him. More cash in his pockets and Sam sauntered off back to the haberdashery.

Fabian waited a respectable amount of time then joined him.

"Keep walking. Stop in two blocks and not before."

Fabian nodded and did as he was bid.

"How'd we do?"

"Wait a minute."

They stood opposite each other, nice and close, to let Fabian take the money out and count it without passersby seeing what was happening.

"Ten dollars in notes and twenty from the wallet. Plus another dollar or two in nickels and dimes."

14

"Toss the wallet."

"Already done on the way over here."

"Good job."

Fabian made to shake hands with Sam so he could pass the notes over to his brother-in-arms. He took the cash and hugged Fabian, depositing ten dollars in his hand as he did so.

"Keep the coins or dump them. I don't care either way. Just don't jingle down the street."

"Understood. And thanks. You did all the work."

"Not really—and you know it. I left you as the fall guy with all the dough when I walked away from the crowd."

Sam smiled at Fabian, who responded with a wink.

"Guess you're right."

"We both took a risk and we've both been paid for our trouble. That seems fair to me."

"And to me, Sam."

"Call me Sammy. All my friends do."

"Okay, Sammy. Shall we go to your office and talk business?"

"For sure. We're practically there."

The two carried on until Sammy swung right into Forsyth and then north past Grand until they reached the corner of Broome Street. Sammy halted abruptly and Fabian almost walked straight into the back of him but braked just in time.

"Here we are. Welcome to my office."

Fabian looked round for any hint of a commercial property but all he could see were rows of shops on Broome and the same on Forsyth. His expression was quizzical and he looked askance at Sammy, who turned around and pointed at the entrance on the actual corner of the two streets. Fabian's eyes followed Sammy's finger and carried on up the side of the building until he saw a sign hanging above the door: The Forsyth Hotel. Sammy nipped inside.

The first floor comprised a reception with a bar and an open area filled with tables. A staircase on the far wall splayed out at the bottom as though this place had a grandiose past, but judging by the ruffians frequenting it today, the hotel's glory days had long since passed—if they had ever happened at all.

"What can I get you gentlemen?"

"Well, barkeep. I'll try out one of your beers if I may?"

"Coming right up. And what about your friend?"

"Same for me."

"Good choice."

The barman headed to a pump to dispense the drinks and Fabian surveyed the interior. The walls comprised floor to ceiling dark brown wood panels, which gave the place a gloomy feeling even in the afternoon's light.

This meant you could sit near a table only three feet away and have no idea who was sat there. Everyone could have their privacy in the heart of the crowd. Fabian understood why Sammy had chosen this venue. A person could do business here.

A man and a woman descended the stairs. He strode out as soon as he hit the floor and she waltzed over to the bar, eyeing Fabian up and down. She had long black hair and curves in all the right places.

"Wanna buy a girl a drink, handsome?"

"Beat it, toots. He's not a john."

Sammy bought her a shot anyway to show there were no hard feelings.

"Sarah, meet Fabian. The guy's new in town and we've some business to discuss, so forgive my rudeness just now."

"No worries, Sammy. We've all got work to do."

He slapped her on the ass as she took her glass of scotch and headed towards a man standing on his own at the other end of the bar.

"You two know each other?"

"We both work in the same establishment, so we're on the same side, you might say."

"And is her work any good?"

"Keep your eye on the prize and let's talk business. Okay, Fabian?"

"Sure thing."

Fabian reddened a little because he was surprised quite how brazen he was about his desire for a female body. Three months on a boat can do that to a fella.

SAMMY CHOSE A place away from Sarah's new hopeful and near the back of the establishment, far from the entrance. They sat opposite each other at a small table and Sammy hugged his beer glass, leaning forward with a low voice to force Fabian to do the same.

"We know you're a mensch. Do you have any other skills of a more direct relevance to the modern age?"

"Back in the old country I encouraged people to pay their debts and ran the occasional game of cards. Nothing fancy but I earned ten percent of the proceeds on departure from the table."

"Was there an entry fee?"

Fabian chuckled.

"The quality of my players meant I couldn't be too picky about who sat at the baize."

"I understand."

Sammy took a swig of beer and wiped his frothy lips on his jacket sleeve.

"We can use a man of your caliber."

"And who are 'we' exactly?"

"My friends and I, that's who. Don't worry about them right now. If matters work out well between you and me then you'll meet them soon enough. And if things don't..."

The life limiting prospects of failure became obvious to Fabian. Many individuals would have exited the building there and then, but not Fabian. As he had explained to Sammy, his time in the Ukraine had not been wasted on academic studies but he had learned how to read people and to persuade them to bend to his will. Sometimes he would use his voice and sometimes his fists.

Fabian's mind drifted to reminiscing about the old country where he had lived in the same village all his life until the troubles got too much and his family had to flee. He thought about the small wooden house they called home and the sounds and smells of their fire as it crackled in the evening.

Sammy's words snapped Fabian back to reality.

"Before we let you loose running a poker game, we'll start you off on something simpler. While I might have a good feeling about you, my colleagues will want to see a demonstration of your work ethic before we cut you into anything substantial."

"I'm fine with that. Right now, I want a way to earn a living and support my family."

"Very noble. We all have mouths to feed."

Sammy cracked his knuckles and outlined Fabian's duties for his first task: courier. In short, each morning Sammy would give a name and an address to Fabian who would go to the guy, collect a package and walk it to the next location. Repeat all day and come back to Sammy at The Forsyth Hotel in the evening. If all went well, he'd receive a stipend for his trouble.

"Sounds like a good plan."

"I'm sure you won't disappoint."

"Trust me, I'm a doctor."

They both laughed, shook hands, and Fabian left Sammy at the table. Just before he walked out of the hotel, he glanced round and saw Sarah's ass wiggling up the stairs with a man in tow. Everyone was working hard at The Forsyth.

TUESDAY, JANUARY 19, 1915

4

LIKE GENERATIONS OF immigrants before and after, the Cohen family had set off for America not speaking the language but hoping, beyond hope, this land of opportunity would deliver plenty to them.

Their desire was driven by fear. The Ukraine had been a wonderful home for parents, grandparents and great grandparents before them, but the world was shifting and turning. As so many of their extended family and neighbors had discovered, there was a time to stay and a time to go. And now was the time to go. Jews were no longer welcome in their own country as the Cossacks reached the small corner of the countryside they called home.

They schlepped to Hamburg by train with just the clothes on their backs and whatever they could stuff into hastily packed cases. Then they waited for a ferry to take them to Great Britain. With Europe behind them, their tears had stopped flowing because the gritty reality of immigrant exile was descending upon them at a tremendous pace.

At least they'd had the good sense to find someone who spoke the language well enough to know that when they walked off the boat, they weren't already in America. Some of their company wandered off after kissing the ground in the false belief they had arrived in New York harbor. Scotland's Leith was a more likely reality, which meant the longer part of the journey was ahead of them.

The Cohens sat patiently in the waiting area, which was just a massive hut filled to the gunnels with hungry and tired Jews. They had prepaid for their tickets to America and had spent a small fortune to have some English money so they could buy food during the long wait before their ship came in.

Forty hours later, Alex, his mother, father and three siblings marched up the gangplank and down into the bowels of the boat which would take them to the land of the free. No light was visible in steerage and fresh air became a memory shortly thereafter too.

THEY SHARED THE space with all sorts of people. Many were families, but there were couples and singletons too. Alex noticed lads on their own, presumably either joining family already in the States or they were the first of their kin to make the crossing.

At night, Alex heard groans and moans as husbands and wives did what came naturally, even though everyone was sleeping cheek by jowl with each other. The sounds made him extremely aroused but there was nowhere sufficiently private for him to do anything about it.

He saw two old men get carted off during the trip and rumor spread they had died in their sleep. The ship's representative told the assembled throng it was due to natural causes, but the mutterings afterwards painted a picture of them dying because of the conditions they were all living in. The filth.

Finally, a jolt and they could tell the ship had stopped. Tense excitement filled the air as a whisper went round: we've made it to the New World.

Before anything else happened, they waited three hours as all the first and second-class passengers had to disembark first. The Cohens just hugged each other and settled back down to wait in silence. Alex's father carried on reading his bible and his mother tried to keep his brothers and sister entertained using a five-inch piece of string and a lot of imagination.

As the hours passed, the feelings of hope and excitement which had engulfed everyone evaporated and people were left with a bitter sense of boredom and disappointment. Alex figured they'd waited long enough and couldn't understand that this was exactly how third-class passengers were treated. The fact they'd spent a year saving for the tickets meant nothing to the captain or the owner of the shipping line.

The Cohens told themselves they took a year to save up the money, but no one wanted to acknowledge or would ever mention the truth; that if Alex hadn't been involved in the black market then they would never have set foot on a boat—to Scotland, America or anywhere else. Instead, Alex had earned enough in six weeks helping to run a gambling house. Honest folks got their gelt in honorable ways and the New World represented an opportunity for Alex to amend his darker tendencies, so his parents hoped.

No one knew quite how long they had waited but suddenly there was a hush across the huddled throng as everyone noticed a burst of fresh air ripple over their heads. A door had been opened which must lead to the deck. Soon they'd schlep off the boat and start their new lives. The tension and excitement came back to the room.

ALEX'S HEART RACED ever so slightly and his sister's hand clasped his as her expectation and fear rose in equal measure. He smiled at Esther, who returned his grin with a note of caution and a quiver in her top lip.

"Everything's gonna be just fine. Don't you worry about a thing."

Esther could only offer a smile for a reply as she wasn't sure if Alex's words were true or just uttered to placate her. She pushed a few brown locks behind her right ear and squeezed his hand again.

"I'm scared," she said after three minutes silence.

"We're all in this together. And no matter what happens to us or where we go, you can be certain of two things."

"What's that?"

"You'll always be surrounded by your loving family."

"And the second thing?"

"No one will chase us out of our home because we're Jewish. This is the land of honey dripping on every street corner."

"I hope you're right."

"Sure am, sweet pea."

Five minutes later and the gaggle of passengers turned into a throbbing mob as doors down unseen corridors opened and the Cohens began the slow trudge off the ship. Half an hour more and they stood on the deck.

Alex inhaled deeply to suck in as much of the American air as his lungs could take. It tasted of freedom, reeked of opportunity.

5

ESTHER LOOSENED HER grip on Alex's hand, so life appeared to be more positive for her the more she saw the sky and smelled the seagulls. Meanwhile, the boys were getting restless and were pushing and poking each other to relieve their boredom. Aaron was only five and Reuben a mere ten months older. They knew the family was on the move, but no one had bothered to explain to them what was actually going on or why. Everyone treated them like babies and, up to a point, they were but if someone had mentioned they were heading off to a new continent to begin a fresh life away from the hatred they had encountered in the Ukraine, then perhaps they wouldn't have spent so much of the journey complaining. That's what Alex thought anyway, but he knew his parents had other ideas.

The Cohens believed their eldest boy and girl would be tainted by their memories and experiences of the old country, but if they didn't say too much then the younger pair might only know the peace and freedom America would deliver.

They were pushed and shoved onto the wharf and split into groups of thirty. Then each of these groups were pummeled onto a two-story barge; people on top and their baggage on the bottom. Once each vessel was full, it pulled away from the dock and headed out to sea—or at least that's what it felt like to Alex. In reality, they could tell they were leaving Manhattan; landmarks were visible to those who cared to look behind.

The barge forged its way along the sea lanes and turned a corner to reveal an image every passenger recognized: The Statue of Liberty. The boat chugged forward until it arrived at Ellis Island and they disembarked. This time it only took a few minutes from the tug master casting a line, to all the passengers stepping foot on dry land again. They followed the herd and went into a main building, having retrieved their baggage from the boat's lower tier first.

Then up a slope where they entered the customs hall. Despite the crush of arrivals, when Alex looked up, he saw that the place was enormous. The

24

vaulted ceiling allowed light to pour in through what appeared to be a wall of windows and Alex was able to see over people's heads and watch as everyone snaked round the room until, after two hours in line, the Cohens were face to face with a man in a uniform sporting a waxed mustache.

When he spoke, no one in the Cohen clan understood a word the guy said. Complete nonsense. As Alex's father stared politely but quizzically back at the officer, the guy turned round and beckoned for someone else to come over. A much shorter man appeared with no mustache and spoke to them in Yiddish which they all understood immediately.

Alex glanced around the hall again and realized all the signs were in a very strange language; none of the letters looked right at all. There was no Hebrew to be seen. He was shocked for a second and then figured he'd blanked out the signs from his vision because they meant less than nothing to him.

"What is your name?"

"Moishe Cohen."

The translator turned to the customs officer:

"Name: Moses Cohen."

The officer scribbled down the response.

"Your wife's name?"

"Ruth Cohen."

"Your children's names?"

Although Moishe was, by nature, a gentle man he lost his patience with the linguist. Perhaps the reality of what the guy had said to his colleague had somehow sunk into Moishe's head. Perhaps it was the way the translator looked and spoke to him in such a disdainful manner. Whatever the cause, Moishe turned to Ruth and critiqued the man accurately and with no wasted words:

"*Farbissener mumser.*" Bastard.

"Fabian Mustard," declared the translator and the customs officer wrote the details down.

"What about the girl and the two youngsters?"

"Esther, Reuben and Aaron."

"Esther, Ruben and Harry," was the translation offered, which was scribed perfectly by the gentile in the peaked cap.

Fabian Mustard was born. A strapping five foot eleven tall with black straight hair and a large nose—there was no getting away from those nostrils. He was big, but not for his height and he had muscles, not flab, to fill out his frame.

THE REST OF the interview carried on much as it had started. A series of staccato questions followed by a repeated response in English for the benefit of the long-suffering customs official.

Alex took to the name Fabian immediately. It felt right to gain a new moniker for a modern life in the land of opportunity. Fabian Mustard. He had no idea how ridiculous it sounded to a local. Not yet.

The officer inked his stamps and prepared the official documentation, three sheets of paper per adult and one supplementary sheet for each child. The translator muttered to him several times and occasionally they'd snigger or laugh with a roar. Then more scribbling and stamping until a signature was delivered at the bottom of the final sheet.

The interpreter took the pieces of paper and placed them into a folder. A single page was signed and blotted, then handed over to *Father* Cohen. He clutched the sheet as though his life depended on it.

They picked up all their baggage, such as it was, and hauled themselves across the enormous hall—to the far side where Americans exited. Out the tall doors and into a passageway. Alex wasn't too sure what he expected, but it wasn't that. A line of trumpeters offering a fanfare? Perhaps not, but some sense of genuine arrival would have been nice.

Instead there was a corridor filled with shuffling people who had just received their right to remain and were now trying to start their new lives.

This meant the Cohens needed to find some accommodation for tonight otherwise they'd be sleeping on the self-same streets they were hoping would be paved with gold. Alex might not have seen an American street that closely, but he reckoned the primary material the sidewalk would be made of was not a precious metal.

The good news was that at the far end of the corridor—before they exited onto the street—was an office run by a Jewish charity to give advice on temporary housing. The practicalities of their arrival in the promised land now became paramount and neither Cohen parent had spent any time thinking this bit through. All their energy had been spent on fleeing their old home and getting to America. Well, they had arrived, and they needed shelter, food and a way of earning a living.

Inside the office, the familiar sound of Yiddish echoed around the room and, for the first time since they'd left steerage, everyone could understand what was going on, even the children. Alex listened as a kindly middle-aged man gave his parents the address of a place for them to stay that night. He'd placed a phone call, and the shelter knew the Cohens were coming.

Then the family ambled over to a money broker in an adjacent room and they swapped all their cash for dollars. There was no turning back even if they wanted. Esther looked horrified as she witnessed one of the final totems of the Ukraine literally vanishing in her father's hands, but Alex relished the idea of destroying their memories. He enjoyed living in the present and found Esther's timidity annoying and tiring in equal measure.

Armed with greenbacks, the Cohens left the confines of the corridor, walked through the far door and spewed out onto a street near the edge of Ellis Island.

The first thing to do was to make their way to Manhattan and reach the shelter before nightfall, if possible. Then they could deal with whatever life had to throw at them after some rest and, with a bit of luck, some fresh food.

WEDNESDAY, JANUARY 20, 1915

6

FABIAN'S EYES OPENED wide, and he blinked in the American dawn. Basking in the safety of the New World, just before he'd lapsed into unconsciousness the previous night, he'd embraced this country by adopting his new name. He was now the American, Fabian Mustard.

Their temporary shelter was mainly dry with a single patch of mold in the corner of their solitary room. If they had planned to stay for any length of time, it would have been a problem, but they'd be fine for a night or two.

First thing, after a breakfast of nothing topped with hope, swilled down with fear of the unknown location they'd landed in, the family left the confinement of the room and headed out to find a proper place to live.

Moishe had been given the location of an apartment block with a landlord willing to rent out living quarters to Jews. The Cohens thought this sounded a positive thing as they didn't want to be surrounded by gentiles. This wasn't a prejudice but a result of their direct experience back home. Life had been wonderful within the shtetl and the only gentiles were the village police, who were benign apart from when dealing with Alexander, and the outsiders who were trying to kill them. The logical conclusion for the Cohens was that gentiles were not friendly types and should be avoided at all costs.

Suffolk Street was the right choice for them, in the heart of the Jewish ghetto in the Lower East Side. The street ran north to south in the Bowery, jam packed with narrow tall tenement buildings. As they only possessed the money they'd brought with them, Moishe spent little on rent because they could always move into something bigger once they got themselves settled and he'd earned some gelt.

Their apartment was on the fourth floor with a staircase running up the center of the building. There was a kitchen, a parlor and two bedrooms. All for eleven dollars a month, four weeks in advance. Furniture was included in the price as the previous tenants left New York in a hurry, so that would save the Cohens some cash. Moishe and Ruth saw this as an opportunity to get settled before having to buy big items like beds or a table.

31

Papa handed over the rent and they moved in the following day to spend their first Shabbos in America inside a place they might now call home. The flip side of this decision was that there was exactly one month for Moishe, Ruth and Alexander to find a further eleven dollars before the landlord would throw the family out onto the street. But that was not today's problem.

THE ENTIRE FAMILY experienced the joy of tenement life with its two bedrooms as soon as they arrived and closed the door behind them. While the old country had given Fabian his own room with the younger children sharing, he lost that privilege on Suffolk Street.

To make up for this indignity, his parents offered him first choice over the two beds. As there were no windows, the only real options were to be near to the door or further away. He chose to be far away: there would be less noise from the parlor, and he could do his best to hide in the furthest corner.

The landing outside their front door fed two other apartments containing one family each, both Jewish. At the other end, the Waghalters and halfway along was the Aaronovitch clan, with six children plus parents squished into a one-bed hovel. The only item missing was a bathroom. That was located on the floor below.

That story comprised another three apartments containing three families. Even though the stairway was immersed in semi-darkness, all floors contained spillover from the homes; doors were open and every inch of space within the building was occupied by people, young and old.

The family beneath the Cohens were the Grunbergs—Benjamin and Ora with their daughter Rebecca. As Fabian mooched along the landing, he glanced into each room. On his way back from the bathroom, he looked into the front apartment and there was the most beautiful sight good fortune cast before his eyes.

A girl in her petticoats was spinning on one foot, forming ballet moves as she rotated. He just about made out the curves of her hips and he most definitely saw the round shape of her breasts. Without realizing, Fabian stopped and gawped at the most perfect body.

"Finished staring, *boychick*?"

Fabian whistled his appreciation, while feeling ashamed at being caught out as a voyeur.

"*Bei mir bist du shoen.*"

"Kind of you to say so, but I'm not your floor show. Go back to playing with your toys."

Then she slammed the door in Alex's face. Dejected, he slunk upstairs and sulked in his bedroom for an hour after chucking out the rest of the kids to be alone and figure out what he was going to do about the vision now twirling beneath his feet. He wanted her and he wasn't prepared to let go of that dream.

JULY 1915

7

THE EVENING BEFORE rent day, Moishe and Ruth had huddled in the corner of the parlor while the children ate. He had carried on plying his trade as a tailor but instead of being the only one in the village, Moishe found the land of opportunity was the land of arch competition. He had received two suits for alteration but that was all. Ruth had taken in washing but the few cents she made per item added up to only two dollars across the month. Add that to the three Moishe had earned and prospects were not good.

Alex listened intently to their whispers and his mother's sobbing and gazed at his father's steely blank stare. He sighed, his hand in his pants pocket, and quietly, calmly asked, "How much are we short?"

"Six dollars."

He nodded, stood up and placed that sum on the table in front of his parents. Just before he replaced his roll in his pants, he halted and put down another five bucks.

"We'll need this for food, right?"

"*Oy vey mir.*"

"Where did you get this?"

"Do you really want to know because I'll tell you? Just be assured I'm not hanging around street corners. I work every day, and this is a fair share of my earnings back to the family."

His mother opened her mouth as if to ask her question again, but Moishe put his hand on hers to hush her up. The money was on the table and their rent problem had vanished in the space of two seconds.

"Whatever you're involved in, don't get in so deep you can't escape."

"I'm aware of what I'm doing and I'm getting good money for it."

"Let's not get into any *broiges* here; be thankful, Moishe, for the bounty we've received."

"Amen."

Alex at home and Fabian on the street. Either way, Sammy paid him two and a half dollars a week to shift packages around town and ask no questions.

NEXT DAY, FABIAN met Sammy at the Forsyth as he did every morning. As he entered the building, he nodded at the barman.

"Hello, Fabian."

"Hi, Nathan."

"Coffee?"

"Nice."

Fabian headed to the bar and then took his coffee over to Sammy, who sat at what Fabian discovered was his usual table at the back of the establishment.

"Hi."

"Yep, good day to you."

They sat in silence for a while as Sammy got his head together and Fabian downed a few glugs of coffee. Neither was a morning person, but they were both working stiffs who had a full day ahead of them before they'd meet up again in the evening.

"All okay?"

"*Alles gut.*"

Fifteen minutes later and Fabian had finished his drink and shoved down some bread and butter supplied by Nathan. One of Sammy's runners hustled toward their table and Fabian leaned backwards to give Sammy as much privacy as possible while the guy whispered instructions directly into his ear. Then he took his five cents and left without an audible word leaving his lips.

"First order of the day."

"Where and what?"

Sammy gave him the address and described the box Fabian should expect and the location of the drop. He stood up, shook hands and went off to collect the package.

The pickup was on Canal and Elizabeth, one block south and three blocks west of the Forsyth so Fabian expected the journey to take around fifteen minutes. One thing he had learned is that it's more important to get the task done and not get nabbed by the cops—or any other interested parties—than to get the situation over fast. Sammy let him sit at his table because he was careful and trusted. The other couriers stood on the street corner outside and Fabian hoped he was paid a little more for his trouble too, but he had never spent enough time with the others to be sure.

He dawdled over to his first destination and found the address provided by Sammy. Fabian knocked on the door with his knuckles as he couldn't find a knocker. Rat-a-tat-tat.

The door opened two inches and Fabian saw an eye squinting in the sunlight.

"Yes?"

"Sammy sent me."

No more complex a password was needed, and the eye opened the door sufficiently to enable Fabian to slip inside. By the time he'd closed the door behind him, the eye had walked the length of a corridor and headed into a backroom. Fabian checked there were no other rooms—or people—visible and followed the guy. His ears were pricked open in case of trouble and Fabian's eyes flitted left and right as soon as he stepped into what was once a kitchen before the building had been converted to its current use. Whatever that was.

Zilch. Just Fabian and the eye, who had taken a box out of a cupboard before Fabian had a chance to sit down.

"Here's the package. You know where you're taking it?"

"I was told you'd know that."

"That I do."

"Gonna tell me?"

The eye laughed.

"Sure thing, kid."

With the address firmly lodged in his brain, Fabian picked up the box and walked out the building. The box was made of wood and had a lid with a lock, tight shut. His destination was on Bowery and Stanton, six blocks north and one east. If Fabian wanted to melt into the crowd, he needed to go up Bowery but that was the most dangerous street in the city, as far as Fabian was concerned. Trouble was a boy with a box would stand out like a sore thumb on Elizabeth or Chrystie, a block to the east of Bowery.

Fabian propped the box on his foot outside the eye's door and pulled out brass knuckles, put them on and replaced the carton in front of his chest. He figured if he met with any issues, he could deal with them immediately by dropping the package and then carry on his way afterwards. No-one had told him it was a fragile cargo and anything as heavy as the contents should be able to withstand the odd knock or two.

The Bowery had received its reputation thirty years earlier as the roughest neighborhood in Manhattan—and for good reason. Along certain sections of the road in the Lower East Side, each building was occupied by either a gambling den, whorehouse or bar. Sometimes they combined to meet the needs of a man who had many vices to fulfill at the same time.

The fact there was such a high density of illegal establishments wasn't the issue for Fabian. He was made of sterner stuff. His problem was simply that such venues attracted fellows who might look for an easy mark and mistake him for that kind of guy. Under those circumstances, trouble would descend on him and that would get in the way of his doing business for Sammy.

HE ENJOYED THE rough and tumble of a good fight, provided everybody played fair and only brought a knife to the scrum and nothing more serious than that. In the old country, so few had been able to afford a gun the problem never arose, but Fabian understood matters were different in America. The way he was earning decent money for walking around the city every day showed this land of opportunity had a hardened edge to it. He understood the amount he was earning meant the packages he was schlepping were worth a tiny fortune because an ordinary courier made a fraction of his earnings.

And if he was being paid handsomely then others further up the chain were dipping their beaks in the trough and pulling out a tidy sum too.

The opportunities open to his parents were entirely closed to him—mainly because he refused to work for an honest day's pay when a dishonest day's effort generated more money than he could spend. There was no point trying to convince people to let him sew their trousers when he could get paid more for walking around the Bowery with a box in his arms.

As he made his way north, eyes and ears desperately trying to catch every nuanced sight and sound on the street, Fabian realized most of the route had closed doors; the place only really heated up in the afternoons and evenings —once people were liquored up and bumping into each other seeking the next good time.

Within ten minutes he finished his journey and arrived at the address. A rat-a-tat-tat on the door revealed a palace inside, comprising two rooms filled with plush sofas and velvet cushions, gold paint and an elaborate chandelier. At the far end was a doorway with a purple velvet curtain strung across the gap preventing curious eyes from seeing any further.

The goon who'd opened the door for him nodded past the drapery so Fabian took the box further inside the emporium.

He pushed past the curtain, as both his hands were full, and the material slid over his face until he'd got his entire body the other side of the damn thing. Fabian had closed his eyes when the drapes first hit him—part instinct and part because the fabric stank of stale beer and cigars. Then he couldn't stop looking no matter how hard he tried.

There were two men sat in wide armchairs with their shirts undone and the rest of the room was filled to the gunnels with women. Some wore stockings, and some did not. A few wore basques and some did not. A handful wore panties while some did not. All were vying for the attention of the two lucky men.

"This must be the best whorehouse in the whole of Manhattan," he thought.

"Better believe it, buddy."

Fabian twirled around to see the timekeeper smirking at him; the guy monitored all the johns and still had energy to mock him.

"I said that out loud, then?"

"Sure did, buddy."

Fabian shrugged with a broad smile ripped across his face and he had plenty to be happy about. He was a fifteen-year-old boy surrounded by nipples and asses. Died and gone to heaven. Or rather hell, because he could look, but he'd better not touch the goods.

"Where'd I find a man to speak to about this box?"

"No further than me, but let's go somewhere more private to finish our discussion."

The timekeeper led Fabian out of the room of many delights and into a side office, which was as drab as you can imagine and twice as stuffy. A desk, a couple of chairs and shelving filled the space.

Fabian put the box down on the desk after the timekeeper had made some room for it. The guy pulled a key out of his jacket pocket and opened the lid, but he ensured Fabian couldn't poke his nose inside.

"All in order. Any trouble on your way over here?"

"Nah. All good."

"Fine. Here's an envelope for you to take to the Grand Theater."

Fabian didn't need to ask where that was as he had been there many times with his family: Grand and Chrystie—not so far from here at all.

"And this is a little something for your trouble."

The timekeeper thrust a note into Fabian's hand and, even though there was no need for a gratuity, he gladly took it.

"When you have some spare time, visit us and spend your money here if you like."

"You can bet your bottom dollar I will."

"Oh, I never bet on a sure thing."

They both smiled, shook hands and Fabian walked out of the office and back into the cornucopia of female riches, just in time to watch a woman dressed only in stockings and suspenders lead one of the two men out of the room and off for some private attention.

FABIAN GRIPPED THE envelope in his right hand and considered putting it in his inside jacket pocket, but it was too big and too stiff to fold without potentially damaging the contents. And that was always a bad idea.

The Grand was a perfect description for the theater. Fabian had never seen as much gold leaf on the pillars or marble on the floor. The whole placed oozed opulence. He could hardly believe he was going to meet someone from behind the scenes. The Cohens popped into the cheap seats at least once a week and, even now he was grown up, Fabian continued to enjoy coming along and letting himself be engulfed by the magic of the stories and be transported back to the old country by the tunes the actors sang.

When he stood in the lobby, a footman advanced towards him and enquired what the hell he was doing there.

"I'm here for Ida."

"Miss Grynberg, you mean?"

"That's what I said."

The peaked cap took him back of house via an entrance hidden in the wall down to the stalls. From there, they traveled at high speed around the stage, past costumes and lighting rigs. All the bits and pieces you needed to put on a full show.

Rat-a-tat-tat on a door with a star on it and a female voice permitted them in. Fabian entered but peaked cap closed the door behind him.

Ida Grynberg sat on a chaise longue draped in a silk kimono, reading a book. She dropped it beside herself when she stopped looking at Fabian and noticed the envelope he held.

Her hair fell below her shoulders and with a twist of her head, she flicked one half behind her right shoulder and smiled at him. But Fabian had been at this game long enough to know she only appeared to be pleased. In reality she was smiling at his envelope.

"Do you have anything for me, young man?"

"Oh, I reckon I could find something."

She stared at him and scrunched up her expression, mildly repulsed, uncertain whether to take Fabian's remark at face value or to assume he was getting fresh like most boys his age.

"Perhaps it's in your hand."

He pretended to look quizzically at her, not understanding what she was driving at. Then he looked down and did a fake double-take, copying a comedian he'd seen at the Grand on the Sunday just gone.

"This? Yes, it's for you."

Fabian took one step nearer to the chaise longue to reach Ida and he proffered the envelope. She snatched it from him and then thought better of it and placed the brown packet next to her on the fancy sofa.

"Thank you. Here's something for your trouble."

She held out her hand and Fabian felt two quarters drop into his palm. Last of the millionaire showgirls.

"You shouldn't have."

"You're welcome. I'm sure you can see yourself out."

Fabian shrugged and wandered out the room. As he turned to close the door behind him, he glanced over as Ida opened the envelope to reveal a bag containing whitish gray powder, some of which she tipped onto a nearby table. Then she looked up at him and he shut the door and walked away.

8

LUNCHTIME. FABIAN'S WORKING life revolved around the Bowery—
there had only been three occasions when he had been sent to the furthest
reaches of the Lower East Side: once up to Second Avenue to deliver a letter,
once west to Pier 22 past Jay with a sealed box, and once over the bridge to
Brooklyn to collect an envelope that contained a roll of banknotes.

Now he was a handful of blocks away from home and as he had nothing
else in his schedule until three, Fabian headed to the apartment to get some
free food from his mother's kitchen—paid for by him—and put his feet up
for a while. Every other day he'd swing by the Forsyth to shoot the breeze
with some of the guys. Over the last month he had made a concerted effort
to get to know the other couriers. Being in with Sammy was important but
getting stabbed in the back because you haven't taken care of your own
makes you a *dummkopf*.

On the way over, he passed a cream confection stall. There were Danish
pastries and other sweet treats. Perhaps the heat of the day overtook him,
maybe he was plain hungry, but Fabian stopped and bought a piece of apple
strudel. A light white dusting of sugar was spread majestically over the top
and he could feel the stickiness of the confection easing around his fingers as
he held the delight between his first finger and thumb, careful not to crush it
in his stumpy grip.

The dribble was nearly cascading down his chin by the time he reached
Suffolk Street two blocks further on. Into the building and up the stairs. On
each landing, children and adults alike stared at his prize. Almost home.

The third floor, one below the Cohens, contained Rebecca and her
devastating curves. Fabian had found himself lost for words when he first
saw her; captivated by her intense beauty but also captured by his teenage
lack of social grace. But each day when he walked past their door, his head
would turn hoping to catch a glimpse of the soft curls in her hair or, on a
very rare occasion, even a half smile or nod of recognition. He would smile

43

back but he hadn't come up with a good enough reason to stop and chat, especially after how dismissive she had been the one time they had talked.

In a reflex gesture, Fabian turned his head as he reached the door and there was Rebecca practicing her ballet moves, holding onto a chair for balance—cheaper than owning a barre.

Just as his head turned, she stopped a spin and faced directly at him and smiled. The fourth smile he had ever received from her. Fabian halted in his tracks, smiled, and leaned against the door jamb, careful not to enter the apartment fully.

"Hi."

"Hello. You look like you're in a hurry. Don't let me take you away from your manly business."

"Home for lunch. A guy has to eat, you know."

"I'm sure someone as hard working as you surely must."

"Hey, we all have to earn our keep, right?"

Rebecca looked at him and shrugged, shoulders sagging as the reality of Fabian's words rang all too true.

"Yeah, Mama and I sew to help ends meet."

"My father is a tailor. If he ever gets too much work to cope with, I'll let him know he can call on you, if you like."

"Thanks."

"Don't thank me just yet. The man hasn't had a full day's employment since we landed here. Times are tough."

"They sure are."

By this time, Rebecca had edged towards the door, having been stood in the middle of their parlor room when Fabian first appeared in view.

"If you don't mind me asking," and she leaned against the wall only three feet away from Fabian, "if times are that tough, what are you doing with that?"

She pointed at the strudel and her eyes opened wide with envy.

"That's a little treat I bought on the way over."

"Sure looks tasty."

"Doesn't it so? Cost me a quarter."

"*Oi vey*! I don't think I've eaten anything like that since we arrived here."

They both contemplated the space between Fabian's thumb and first finger; the icing sugar, the syrup, the pastry.

"Want some?"

"Are you serious, Alex?"

She knew his name even though he hadn't had an opportunity to tell it to her. He thought for a minute, because he'd said the words—blurted them out —but hadn't thought about the consequences of Rebecca taking him up on the offer. Then he breathed in her fragrance from three feet away and felt a rush in the pit of his stomach.

"Yes, I am. Here…"

He proffered the strudel and leaned in to let her reach his hand. She got closer too, put her lips around the end of the pastry and bit into it. Her lips closed round the piece in her mouth, she chewed and then swallowed. All within Alex's touch. Then her tongue popped out to capture the icing sugar that hadn't quite made it inside yet.

"Damn, that is so good."

"Is it?"

"Try some now."

"You have more first."

She squinted at him to make sure he wasn't messing with her and, without asking twice, she took another mouthful, bigger than the original bite. Her eyes rolled and Alex noticed there was a small flake of pastry still clinging to her cheek beyond the reach of her tongue.

He raised his other hand to her face and, sticking out the back of his finger, he wiped the crumb away. Then he looked at the strudel and saw there was really only one mouthful left.

"Finish it."

"But you haven't had any yet."

"It's my mitzvah for the day."

Alex moved the remains of the pastry toward Rebecca's mouth until the confection touched her lips and she opened her mouth to consume it. Her lips covered the strudel and his fingers. Then her tongue licked his thumb and first finger to remove all traces of strudel from them. As she swallowed the last vestige of his prize, she smiled at him; a warm, kind sign of appreciation.

"Thank you."

Before he could say a word, Rebecca went up on tiptoe, holding onto his arm and planted a kiss on his cheek. Then she looked around the landing to check no-one had seen the chaste expression of gratitude.

"You're welcome."

"I need to return to my dancing."

"Sure." There must have been disappointment in his voice because she immediately added, "Visit again. You don't have to bring strudel, but I'd love to get to know you better. Word in the building is that you're mixed up with the local hoodlums, but anyone who gives away his only strudel can't be all bad."

"I have business associates…"

Rebecca raised an eyebrow at the phrase.

"…and my work pays the bills for my family. I wouldn't call them hoodlums if I were you as they paid for the strudel you ate just now."

These words could have been uttered with menace because Alex didn't like people questioning the quality of the men he worked for, but he spoke quietly and with a jaunty tone to his voice. As much as Rebecca's words irritated him, he remained dangerously attracted to her. Those curves under her blouse and her scent around his nostrils.

She appeared suitably chastised.

"Hoodlums. Schmoodlums. I liked your strudel."

She smiled again and returned to balancing by the chair in the center of the parlor room. Alex carried on upstairs to get some food as he noticed his stomach rumble. Bread. Cheese. Two slices of wurst.

Leaving the building, Alex morphed back to being Fabian by the time his right foot hit the sidewalk.

His first destination in the afternoon was to an office right on the corner of Bayard and Bowery. The unassuming frontage hid the significance of its contents in plain sight—and Fabian knew this as Sammy had warned him the previous evening how important it was.

Rat-a-tat-tat and the front door opened after a pair of eyes appeared in a slot and vanished again when it was slammed shut. No-one asked who he was here to see or about his business. Fabian was expected else he'd have been thrown back onto the street or beaten up and dumped in an alley somewhere. There were powerful people in this building.

Two hoods stood in the entrance hall checking him out and Fabian remained still, hands in pockets, leaning against the wall. There was no point doing anything; whatever would happen would come to pass in its own sweet time.

A guy sauntered down the stairs and beckoned Fabian to follow him up. When he got to the top, there was a landing and several closed doors. The man leaned against the only jamb with an open door, waiting for Fabian to catch up. He nodded and let Fabian walk past him then closed the door behind Fabian's heels.

A table and a set of chairs stood in the middle of the room and there was a smaller desk under a window. It had a potted plant on a doily trying to recreate a scene of domestic bliss. And failing.

Two men sat at the table and a third was standing, looking as though he was about to leave. None of them acknowledged Fabian, and they continued to talk in American for three minutes. Fabian only understood a couple of the words. It was all gentile to him. The guy who was standing made for the door. Sounded like his name was Monk—or something. After he left, one of the two at the table spoke.

"You come highly recommended."

"Thank you, Mr Moskowitz."

Sammy had briefed Fabian well.

"Call me Ira, everyone does."

Ira Moskowitz ran the largest Jewish gang in the Bowery on behalf of Waxey Gordon who was finishing off a stretch in Sing Sing and was expected back in the January. Sammy had not needed to labor the point that Ira was to be taken incredibly seriously.

"I have a job for you at 207 Bowery, just south of Rivington. Ask for Little Danny; it's his clubhouse."

Fabian had heard of Little Danny Riordan; the glory days of gang involvement with Tammany Hall had long since waned, but there was still a relationship to speak of otherwise why would Fabian be sent there?

"You need to collect an envelope—but only from Little Danny himself. Nobody else. Understand?"

"Sure, Ira."

"And bring it back to me as soon as you can."

"I got it."

"Good. Off you go."

WHEN FABIAN ARRIVED at the clubhouse, he got in easy enough, but then he had to negotiate his way to Little Danny with only three words of English to his name. Two of them were 'Little Danny'.

He was ushered into a room lined with shelf after shelf packed with hardback books. There was a plump middle-aged man flicking through some tome and Fabian guessed this was Little Danny.

"Little Danny?"

"Anyone follow you here?"

Fabian stared blankly at him as he had no idea what had just been asked of him. He shrugged and used his third word:

"Letter?"

Little Danny nodded and pulled out an envelope from inside his jacket.

"You tell Ira this is the last payment we will ever make, you hear?"

Fabian held his hand out for the envelope and Little Danny handed it over. With nothing to say to the guy, Fabian tipped his hat and left the room.

Back at Ira's, Fabian passed the package over.

"Any trouble?"

"None. He spoke to me and sounded like he was trying to threaten me, but I couldn't understand a word he said."

"Don't worry about it. He's always complaining about something. Never gives me a moment's peace."

Ira held out his hand and passed a note to Fabian as they shook hands.

"See you later, kid."

"Bye, Ira. And thanks."

After Fabian left the building, he looked to check what note he'd been given. It was a twenty. The next month Little Danny's youngest son was found dead on the Eastchester railway tracks in the Bronx. Killed by a train, they said.

JANUARY 1916

9

THE FORSYTH HOTEL was an oasis of warmth in the depths of winter. Fabian and Sammy sat at a table; hands wrapped around a Russian coffee each—a shot of vodka in each mug of brown liquid counting as breakfast. They were young and knew no better.

"You've been doing well."

"Thanks."

"No, seriously. Your ability to handle yourself hasn't gone unnoticed. Word from above is they'd like to see you involved in more... indoor pursuits."

"And what does that involve exactly?"

"Any fool with a pair of feet can walk round this city shifting packages and envelopes from one place to another. If you're dumb, you peek inside the odd box and stick your nose where it's not wanted but apart from that, a guy might earn an average living schlepping parcels around the neighborhood.

"You've been good to me, I know."

"You've been good to yourself, more's the point. As I said, we can find you work which involves staying indoors more."

"In this weather, I'm all ears."

Sammy laid out the plan for Fabian nice and careful. First, he'd spend some time in the background to watch and learn from the old masters. Then he'd get opportunities to work within a team where some of his other skills might be more useful to him.

Fabian had told Sammy back in the old country he'd had a reputation for bashing heads—quite successfully. At the time when it was first mentioned, Sammy had told him he was hired to shift envelopes and not bash skulls. But he'd remembered Fabian's words and acted upon them.

"Look there are a few opportunities in the organization where a steady head and a firm hand will be of use. The first task is to serve refreshments for

Waxey at a meeting he's having later today. Do you think you're up for the job?"

"Waxey's out of stir and you want me to serve drinks for him?"

Sammy smiled.

"Tea and coffee. You must have come across these refreshments here or back in the old country."

Now it was Fabian's turn to curl his lips.

"I'm just surprised Waxey wants me to be his waiter for the day. There must be better suited people."

"I think you'll find the coffees are an incidental. You make sure you're at Waxey's at one thirty sharp and the rest will become clear when you get there."

Sammy looked as though he had ended the conversation and there didn't appear to be any more information for him to divulge. But Fabian had another issue to raise before he poured tea for Waxey.

"Sammy, what consideration should I be expecting for this indoor work?"

"Always on the make. That's one of the many things I like about you Fabian."

"Well?"

"I'll leave you to discuss those kinds of matters with Waxey. If he's willing to pay you, that is. Now, get outta here."

Fabian couldn't tell how much Sammy was teasing him, but he didn't want to negotiate with Waxey because he was a formidable character with a powerful reputation. Fabian doubted his boyish chutzpah would hold any sway with a man in Waxey's position. On a positive note Fabian reminded himself the guys had treated him well so far and were unlikely to screw with him at this stage, but he had yet to see them ask for any real payback.

AT THE APPOINTED time, Fabian arrived at the corner of Bayard and Bowery. In the meeting room, Waxey issued his instructions to Fabian.

"There's a meeting which will take place here in an hour and I need you to serve teas and coffees to my guests."

"Okay, Waxey. You know I'm not exactly a waiter?"

He raised an eyebrow and the left side of his mouth curled upwards. This accentuated the strangeness of his expression: the man suffered from a *farmishte pisk*, lopsided lips with the left part considerably lower than the right. It was the main reason people saw him smile so infrequently; he was painfully aware of how grotesque he appeared when he was happy.

"I am supremely confident you'll be able to pour a cup or two without messing up. Besides, that's not the only reason I wanted you to be in the room."

"How so?"

"Ira tells me you started well, and I hear others have been satisfied with your performance. But now I want to see how you handle yourself."

"Will there trouble?"

"Trouble? I doubt it very much. I don't know what meetings you think I hold but there will be no problems with our guests. And you are going to make sure my words become truth."

Fabian soaked in Waxey's beady stare and stayed silent.

Just short of an hour later, the room had gained two attendees. Waxey was sat at the table with Ira next to him, leaving two spare chairs. Along with Fabian stood another young fella who had not spoken a word since he arrived ten minutes earlier. The guy looked the same age as Fabian but was five inches shorter at least. Stocky, no neck. Apart from that, Fabian had no opinion because the boy had given nothing away. He was introduced as Max.

Three minutes later, two men entered and shook hands with Waxey and Ira. To Fabian they looked middle-aged but were in fact only in their early thirties. All four sat at the table while Fabian and Max offered everybody drinks. The newcomers asked for a coffee each but neither Waxey nor Ira were interested.

"Thank you for coming today."

"We just need to get this *tsoris* behind us. There is no way we want any bad blood."

"We are glad to hear that."

Waxey glanced at Ira before continuing.

"You are late with your payments and I am informed you have intimated you don't intend to make good on what you owe."

Now it was the turn of the two guys to glance at each other. One took out a handkerchief from his pants pocket and wiped his forehead dry. Then he spoke.

"There was a misunderstanding a day or two ago when things were said in the heat of the moment which were not meant. These were reported back to you and here we are."

"Here we are. Indeed."

Waxey raised a finger at Fabian and he delivered a coffee cup. Until that point, Fabian and Max had stood against one wall to be as unobtrusive as possible given the small size of the room.

Waxey used the opportunity to stir the coffee and allow his words to hang in the air.

"So, did you bring any of the arrears with you now—as you want this problem to be behind you?"

More mopping of brows.

"Mr Gordon, the explanation of why we haven't brought any money today is the same reason we have fallen behind with our payments. Business has not been good these past four weeks."

"Spare me your sob story, please. I am a man of business not a person of excuses. Forgive me but I tire easily when someone bleats like a little lamb."

Waxey took a sip of coffee.

"Let me make this simple for you because you appear bedeviled by detail and complexity with your excuses and arguments.

"Either you deliver what you owe by sundown on Friday or we will take over your store on the Saturday morning."

"You can't do that to us!"

"My position is clear and unless you have money to offer me—and you've just told me you do not—then we have no further matters to discuss today."

"We can't get the gelt to you, but we need the *schmatta* trade to put food on our families' tables."

"This meeting is over. By Friday, our money or your business."

As the sweaty fellow rose, Waxey stood and the guy took one pace towards him. Fabian sensed the tailor's anger and didn't like the look of his advance. Having moved four paces forwards, Fabian placed himself between Waxey and the tailor. The guy put his hand back and formed a fist. Within a second Fabian had punched him squarely on the jaw, making him lose his balance and fall over. A tooth spilled out and landed on the wooden floor next to him.

"Gentlemen. The meeting is over and it is time for you to leave."

Fabian looked at Waxey and Ira, unsure if he had just blown his chances with his new mentors but they stared cold steel back at him. He felt his cheeks redden.

Ira waited for both men to be in a fit state to depart and hustled them out the room.

"I'm sorry, Waxey. I thought he was going to thump you."

"Don't worry about it, Slugger. Your instincts were fine. If you hadn't acted, I would have had to do something for sure."

Ira stepped toward Max and spoke in his ear; Max nodded and left without ever acknowledging Fabian's existence.

"Fabian. I hope you don't have a quick temper. That gets you nowhere in business."

"Not at all. I try to be as measured as I can and thought the guy was going to hit you."

"I don't mind a certain physical approach in my men, Slugger, but I don't want people around me who can't control themselves. Fellas who don't think through the consequences of their actions make mistakes. And their errors cost me dearly."

"That's not me. Don't worry on that account."

"I'm not worried, Slugger—merely warning you of what can happen if you don't behave the way I require."

"Got it."

"We will not mention this again unless you spend most of your time slugging people…"

Waxey smiled and play-punched Fabian on the shoulder.

"…and I doubt if that's going to be a problem. Now, is it? …Just remember one thing when you work for me. We work together, we live together but we die alone. Never turn your back on me and I promise I will never turn my back on you."

The following day Fabian returned to Waxey's hangout although he made sure he still had breakfast with Sammy.

Max was there again, and they were both given the address of a bakery behind with its payments to Waxey. He didn't offer too much detail why they needed to pay him, but they were most definitely in arrears—and it needed collecting.

THE BREAD SHOP was a mere two blocks east so Max and Fabian only took ten minutes to get there. Max demanded a detour to a fruit stall because he fancied an apple. When they arrived, the place was already open and doing a great morning trade. Women were buying challah and other breads, rolls and baked goods. Cash was flying into the till almost faster than it could be taken out of the hands of the customers. Fabian thought if trade was this good why didn't they just pay Waxey and be done with it.

The crowd quietened down to a trickle by nine thirty and the boys waited across the street to choose their moment when they'd have the full attention of the owner.

"Are you the manager?"

"Who wants to know?"

"Me. Are you the manager?"

Max's direct approach was confrontational; Fabian would have tried a more conciliatory manner first. But Waxey had made it clear this was the other guy's show and he was a supporting player.

"Yes I am. And you are…?"

"My colleague and I represent Waxey Gordon's interests in your establishment."

These were mighty fine words from one who had uttered absolutely nothing the last time Fabian had seen Max.

"Get outta my bakery. You and Waxey Gordon can go to take a hike."

"Far from taking a hike, you owe Mr Gordon money and we are here to make sure you pay it."

"You think I'll hand over fifteen dollars to neighborhood scum like you? Do me a favor."

With that, the baker laughed, delivering small globules of spit onto Max's jacket. Then he turned his back on Max and carried on with his bakery duties.

Max did not take kindly to being spat on even if it was by accident. He grabbed the guy by his shoulder and spun him round. Then he stepped forward so his face was only inches away from the baker's.

"Now you listen to me, you *ferdrayt dreck*, confused little shit. We have come for Waxey's money and you will give it to us."

10

MAX PUSHED THE guy away to regain his own personal space, and the baker stumbled over the corner of the stall and fell to the ground, grabbing at a basket of breads which came tumbling down over him.

The guy was certainly listening to Max, but his fight-or-flight reflex had kicked in with the surprise of finding himself lying on his own floor and he muttered something unintelligible under his breath.

"What did you say to me?" roared Max, and even though it was officially Max's show, Fabian felt the need to step in because they were going nowhere and, surrounded by all this freshly baked bread, Fabian was getting mighty hungry.

Now it was his turn to stride forward and place a gentle grip on Max's shoulder. To show him he wasn't intervening, Fabian winked at Max and put his palm out to help the baker to his feet, who was still chuntering away.

"We've got off to a bad start, haven't we? Are you all right?"

Fabian helped dust down the baker's clothes, placing a hand gently on his upper arm while he swiped at his overalls to remove the dirt from the floor. He continued flicking away at the clothes until the baker calmed down and was pointing out bits Fabian had missed.

With an arm still wrapped loosely over the baker's shoulders, Fabian walked them away from Max and towards the back of the shop where the cash register sat on a table.

"What you must understand is we mean you no ill, but we cannot leave here without some form of consideration. If fifteen dollars is too much, then why don't we agree on just one buck.

"We saw you did well this morning and I'm certain you can spare a single dollar for Waxey. The rest can wait until later for sure but that way you'll have shown willing to resolve this matter."

"A dollar you say? And you leave me alone?"

"For today. To give you time to get matters resolved as gentlemen do."

"Like gentlemen. You should tell your... colleague about acting like a gentleman."

"Let's not go back to the start of our meeting, eh? Would you consider a buck as a fair resolution of the matter for today?"

"A dollar then."

The baker let Fabian keep his arm around his shoulders as he pressed the keys on the cash register to enter a 'no sale' to make the cash drawer ping open.

Fabian's fist moved to the nape of the baker's neck and it slammed forwards, smashing his face on the register. When he recoiled backwards, Fabian repeated the motion and the bread man lay in a heap on the ground quivering. Fabian put his hand in the till and took out fifteen dollars, leaving the rest of the money untouched.

"Listen to me and get real close."

The guy shook and wept.

"When we come round asking for what you owe, what you need to do is to give it to us with no hullabaloo or bleating. Understand?"

The baker nodded but was still incapable of uttering a single intelligible word. Fabian slammed the register shut and strode to the front of the shop where Max looked on in disbelief. Fabian grabbed a loaf of bread from a pile in the corner, brushed past Max and left.

Max followed two seconds later and sprinted to catch up.

"I didn't mean to intervene, but I could see we were going to be there for too long."

"Sure thing, Slugger."

Fabian noticed Max kept glancing at him as they pounded along the sidewalk. He said nothing but a steely knot formed in his stomach and a sense of pride grew within him. Max was a useless enforcer, but he recognized Fabian's gifts readily enough. And that made Fabian smile inside.

Of course, Sammy must have seen some good in Max but his qualities were far from obvious right now although Fabian could imagine him holding a coat or pouring a cup of coffee. Probably too cruel. Possibly not.

They arrived at Waxey's to report back on their escapade. Max spoke first painting a picture of derring-do on behalf of Fabian and himself.

"And which one of you gents is carrying my money right now?"

Fabian put his hand in his pants pocket and pulled out the cash from the register.

"Excellent."

He counted the notes and placed the coins on the table. Then he whipped out some notes and shook Fabian by the hand transferring the money into Fabian's willing mitt. Then he shook Max's hand but Fabian couldn't see how many or what denomination had been handed over to the guy who had done little apart from watch Fabian carry out the assigned task.

When Fabian checked in his palm, he saw two Jacksons. He was so surprised at the amount, he looked askance at Waxey, who cocked his head sideways for a second and then righted himself.

"A good job well executed deserves recognition. Congratulations, boys."

Fabian smiled in response, but Max spoke.

"Thank you. Took some work to get that baker to pay up."

"Is that right, Fabian?"

He nodded in agreement and Waxey looked back at Max.

"Well enjoy your winnings then."

Max shoved his money into a pants pocket and headed out. Fabian turned to follow him but Waxey motioned for him to stay.

"What contribution did Max offer?"

Fabian was stuck with a quandary—tell the truth or show some loyalty to Max who was his teammate.

"It was his job, but he messed up at the start and I waded in to save the situation."

"Doesn't surprise me to hear. Max has done this before. You won't be seeing Max no more."

Good decision all round.

"People stay, people go."

"And this one's gone."

"So, is there anything else I can help you with?"

"For sure, Fabian. You wouldn't be here if Sammy hadn't recommended you."

"And was Max a recommendation?"

"There's more than one way to get to do a job for me."

"Only asking, Waxey."

"That's fine. You are right to ask me. It's the best way to learn. And the next job is another debt collection. This time you will be on your own now Max is seeking new employment on the street."

"Is there anything else you'd like to tell me about the job apart from the address?"

"No, not particularly. Let's see how you get on. Come back when you have my money or don't come back at all."

Waxey wrote down the details and passed the paper over to Fabian who bid him farewell and exited quickly.

FABIAN MADE HIS way to Bleeker and Broadway and found the frontage matching the address stuffed into the palm of his left hand. This was no baker's shop; from the outside it looked like a house but when he stepped towards the front door, the whirring noises inside gave the place an industrial or factory feel.

He walked inside and the whir became extraordinarily loud. Despite the volume, Fabian recognized the sound of sewing machines instantly. The rag trade was a wonderful business relying on cheap labor for its large profit margins. And if you don't pay your bills, profits rise even further—hence Fabian's presence in the building.

Leaving the entrance, Fabian entered a room with row upon row of sewing machines being worked on by a series of girls and women. He spun his eyes around the room and saw no one of interest.

"Where's Reuben, please?"

The girl nearest to him shrugged her shoulders without stopping. One step forward and same question.

"Upstairs."

"Thanks."

A stroll to the second floor and another room with a different bank of sewing machines. Behind each sat a female but at the far end of the room stood a man holding a bunch of papers in his hand, shouting at one woman and gesticulating. Fabian couldn't figure out what was being said because of the cacophony of the machinery.

"Reuben?"

"Who wants to know?"

"Waxey sent me to discuss a matter with you."

"I have nothing to say to you, my little *boychik.*"

"I never said you needed to speak. But you must listen. Either pay what you owe or you will incur Waxey's displeasure."

"Little man, I told you to go away. I'm not paying that *gonif* one solitary cent."

"This is not a negotiation. Give me what you owe."

Reuben the tailor stared at Fabian who stood resolutely still, arms at his side, relaxed.

"I am not negotiating. I am telling you what is happening. Not one red cent."

Fabian sighed and then landed a punch with his now-clenched fist, sending Reuben sprawling to the floor on the other side of the room. The women stopped sewing, looked at each other and stampeded out the door. By the time the last had left, Fabian had grabbed Reuben by the neck and was pounding his head on the floor.

"This is your final chance. Do you hear me?"

Reuben nodded, spitting blood.

"Are you going to pay up?"

"I don't have any money on the premises."

"Don't make me laugh."

He picked Reuben up and dragged his body towards a window. Using Reuben's own momentum, Fabian swung the man through the window and smashed an opening in the glass. Small shards stuck into his hair and neck. Blood was pouring from several cuts, but still he wouldn't capitulate.

"Don't make me do this, Reuben. I'm counting to three. Get Waxey's money or you're going out the window. Understand?"

"I don't have any cash in the building."

"If you did, would you pay up?"

Reuben's sobbing stopped for a minute as he pondered the question.

"No..."

Before he could utter another syllable, Fabian hauled him straight through the open space and watched him land in a crumpled heap on the sidewalk below.

A crowd had formed by the time Fabian got to Reuben, but he wasn't moving at all—apart from one leg twitching away as a nervous impulse. The man had landed on his head and his skull had cracked in two as soon as he hit the ground.

Fabian checked up and down the street for signs of trouble. Nothing. He bent down and took out a wallet from Reuben's inside jacket pocket, extracted the notes it contained, and dropped the wallet next to the now lifeless body. Then he walked away taking a circuitous route back to Waxey's in case anyone was following.

"How d'you get on?"

"Not as well as I'd hoped, Waxey."

"How so?"

"Reuben won't be making any more payments. He fell out of a window and died. But I did receive a small payment from him before his untimely demise."

Fabian handed over the greenbacks and Waxey counted the proceeds.

"Remarkable."

"How so?"

"You got nearly a hundred and fifty dollars here but the tailor's debt to me was only seventy-five."

Fabian smiled.

"Maybe the contribution was made post-mortem."

"Perhaps... I'll let you keep the surplus. I'm only interested in getting what's owed to me. Not a penny more."

They sat down at Waxey's table and shared a shot of vodka.

"I thought you'd be mad at me for the way Reuben ended up."

"Fabian, I'd rather he was still alive, but I won't be sitting *shiva* either. The man had refused to pay his debt for several weeks. Killing customers is not a viable long-term plan but making an occasional example focuses people's minds. We won't have any problems with collections for the next month or two."

Three more vodka shots each and Fabian agreed to work directly for Waxey and not have Sammy as his boss.

MARCH 1916

11

WAXEY CONTINUED TO give Slugger more responsibility until he was running his own numbers racket. With a team of four, Slugger Cohen took over a back table in the Forsyth Hotel where Nathan Milstein served beer or coffee and Fabian held court over his men and those seeking his benefaction.

The simple reality of the game was explained to him by Waxey's friend, Arnold Rothstein.

"We take the three numbers from the daily summary of takings from the tote and people place bets on this random number."

He proffered the description on the day when Waxey gave Fabian the job. At face value, this was a simple lottery and the minimum stake was a single cent.

And why would a gang leader like Waxey be interested in running the numbers? Those who wanted to lay a wager but didn't have a single cent were offered credit for their betting. Word on the street was that Rothstein had figured out a way of fixing the game, but Fabian wasn't too sure whether to believe that rumor.

A steady stream of men and women sauntered into the Forsyth throughout the day heading straight to Fabian with coins to buy a stake in the daily lottery. Every hour one of his crew would appear with a large handful of pieces of paper containing people's lucky numbers and a pile of cash. Fabian received a bonus if he also held promissory notes—IOUs that meant the gang could gouge the debtor for months to come. Unlike most of the guys running a pool, Fabian passed all that commission over to his squad. He figured the best policy to make Waxey happy was to get success from his team of hustlers. Fabian was paid a handsome salary to sit on his haunches every day and was prepared to wait for the cherries on the cake to arrive later with his next promotion—whenever that came.

At five he met the guys so they could decide which individuals to lean on; those who looked like they were turning into bad debts. Most of the time, he would send his men out to sort matters, but occasionally if there was a high roller who needed some special attention then Slugger would leave the hotel and make his way to convince a john to part with the cash he owed.

A woman rarely welched on a deal; it was almost always the men. Somehow, they believed their word was not their bond, but Slugger understood that's all you had—your word and the reputation to back it up. Everything else was cheap talk.

◆ ◆ ◆

FABIAN HAD BEEN running his book for two months and had picked up a reasonably large clientele, which meant there was also an inevitable buildup of poor payers. He had spent almost every evening the past two weeks discussing arrears with people old enough to behave better. By the time he left their premises they had gained a deeper understanding of the situation they had created for themselves. Occasionally this was exemplified by the dental treatment required after Slugger's visit, but Fabian understood this was no way to run a business.

While violent threats extracted any monies owed, there was a limit to how many people could be threatened each night. What Fabian needed was a reputation, so his name alone would create the pressing need to pay up what was left on the slate at the end of the week. The opportunity arose because of the greed and arrogance of his erstwhile gang mate, Max.

One Thursday, Fabian was laden down with the pool takings. Instead of putting it all in the Forsyth safe—Nathan was always obliging—for some reason best known to himself, Slugger took it home with him so he could go straight to Waxey's in the morning before breakfast. Why ignore his routine? He couldn't say but it was something he wanted to do.

He walked east along Broome Street soaking in the last rays of the sun as it cast its long shadows over the buildings before dropping into the river, below the horizon.

Slugger's peripheral vision was interrupted by the faint outline of a guy walking at his speed on the other side of the road. There were others on the street that evening but the way this fella carried himself separated him from the ordinary Joes. When he crossed Ludlow, he made a point of looking up and down the street and another guy was on his tail.

This wasn't good. Two against one was not great odds and when Slugger saw a third boy, he upped his pace in the hope he could make it home before anything kicked off, but all this did was to alert the three he was nervous.

Slugger slowed down again so he could steady his breathing and to buy himself thinking time. When he got to Norfolk, Max stood on the opposite corner of the junction and Slugger realized it wasn't about the money. Sure, they would try to take it off him, but Max wanted his blood. The cash was a secondary consideration.

He put his hand in his pants pocket and fitted the knuckledusters around both sets of fingers; he always kept them with him in case situations like this ever arose.

Slugger crossed the street and headed straight towards Max. The other three converged on him just as he arrived at the kerb where his erstwhile colleague remained standing.

"Long time."

"Been a while."

"How's it going?"

"Not bad. And you?"

"No complaints. Waxey keeps me busy."

"I'm sure he does. Do you enjoy being his lapdog?"

"A business partner. And, yes, I like my work. How are you earning a crust nowadays? Still trying to beat up bakers?"

A sneer left the corner of his mouth, enough to goad Max into action but he didn't rise to the bait.

"I have bigger fish to fry. I don't get involved in boys' games."

"Glad to hear it."

They stared at each other, not making a sound, each eyeing the other, seeking a weakness in their countenance. But nothing.

There were two ways this conversation would end: either he would walk away, or Max would. Before anyone could think about what to do next, Fabian threw a hook which jolted Max's chin and snapped his head backward. Max was not expecting Slugger to make the first move and staggered back. Slugger grabbed the opportunity to land a fist on one of the other three and sent him reeling to the floor, his nose spewing blood.

Max recovered his balance and stormed towards Slugger. As Max lunged at him, Slugger saw a stiletto knife poised in his hand. As the blade glinted in the light of the setting sun, Slugger stepped sideways, avoiding the blade altogether, and landed a slammed fist onto the back of Max's skull as he sped past. This time he connected fully, and Max hit the ground, face down, dropping the knife. Slugger bent down, grabbed the shiv and slit Max's neck from ear to ear. Then he looked up and saw Max's able assistants running for dear life. He plunged the blade into Max's heart, stood up and sauntered away, vanishing into the crowd.

A few minutes later he was home, sitting in the apartment giving his mother some spending money. If she had been looking carefully, she would have noticed a single drop of blood on the collar of his shirt. But she was too busy counting the cash Alex had just poured onto the table to care about red spots.

Mama Ruth hugged her son. He warmed to her affection and squeezed her in return, knowing how she'd have reacted if she even had an inkling of the money's origins. Back in the old country, his parents accepted his line of work because he had so few options, but they believed America represented a fresh start for him and the whole family. That idealism had soon been scraped off the soles of their shoes and now Moishe and Ruth understood the land paved with gold was a myth. The only people making real money were gang members and whores, many of whom could be seen, large as life, any hour of the day on Bowery—only a handful of blocks away to the west.

Was she ignorant of how Alex got his wealth? Probably not. Was she prepared to berate him for feeding and clothing her family? Definitely not. She understood that in this town you must do what it takes to pay your bills. Although he would have been furious, Ruth gave some of his money to Jewish charities recommended by their rabbi. This kept her conscience clean and meant she could sleep at night. With Alex's new position creating more gelt for the Cohens, for the first time since they had arrived, Ruth saved a few dollars each month.

By the summer, the family would have three months' rent in the bank which would soften the impact if Alex was thrown out of the gang for whatever reason. The greatest risk wasn't Alex leaving the crew but him departing this world altogether. Gang members died young—at least the dumb ones did. Ruth pushed those thoughts to the back of her mind as she enjoyed the moment with her son in her arms, towering above her. A provider.

Alex spent less than half an hour with her before he made his excuses and left. He slept at the apartment but spent virtually every waking minute somewhere else.

I should get my own place, he thought as he departed the building and headed back to the Forsyth. This notion echoed around his head as it did most mornings, but he had yet to do anything about it. While he yearned for personal freedom, he continued to hanker for the proximity of his mother and an opportunity to catch sight of Rebecca.

There was a girl who was worth living at home for even though he'd barely said three words to her since she ate the dessert out of his fingers. The memory sent a shiver down his spine and into his balls. Maybe at some point she'd dance for him.

When he arrived at the Forsyth, Fabian went to Sammy's table instead of his own for a prearranged lunch. Although they'd see each other every day, Fabian respected that Sammy was no longer his nursemaid and didn't need to listen to his daily worries, but he liked the boy and had not forgotten the opportunity he'd been given when they first landed in the city.

"Hi. Thanks for waiting for me."

"*Gar nichts*. Think nothing of it. All I've done is order myself a beer. Want one?"

"Yeah, that'd be perfect."

"Nathan! Another brew when you're ready."

Fabian settled into his chair and thought about his hunger.

"How's the steak today, Nathan?"

"Wouldn't touch it if I were you. The meatballs are fine though."

"Sold."

"Me too."

Nathan returned behind the bar to place the order with the kitchen.

"And business?"

"Can't complain, Fabian. And you?"

"All fine, thanks. There's always the rough with the smooth, but income is up every month since I took over the racket so Waxey's happy. And if Waxey's happy—"

"Then I'm happy," interjected Sammy, and they both laughed.

Soon after, Nathan appeared with two plates of meatballs which they gulped down like they'd not seen food before. Having fressed the entire contents plus sauce within five minutes, Fabian and Sammy sat back in their chairs and sipped their beers.

"I'm glad business is going well for you, Fabian. But sometimes I come across things which would make Waxey concerned."

"Then don't tell him and he won't be burdened by these worries of yours."

The hairs at the back of Fabian's neck bristled as he didn't appreciate the tone in Sammy's voice. He had given him a leg-up into the organization for sure, but he had no right to get all high-and-mighty with him.

"I won't tell him but others might. You know me well enough by now; telling tales out of school isn't my style, but you can't stop anyone else having a loose tongue."

"And what do you think you've heard?"

"This and that. You know."

"No, I don't. What's the gossip?"

Sammy stopped averting his gaze and stared coldly into Fabian's eyes. The smile vacated his expression and Fabian was left looking at a man who was pure business and no friend.

"How's Max? Seen him recently?"

"Not in a long while."

"Fabian. That's not quite right because there were witnesses."

"Witnesses?"

"You sliced him from ear to ear in daylight in the middle of the street. People saw."

"I'm certain they did, and I haven't had to chase a single payment since."

"For sure, but Waxey prefers his operations to be in the shadows, not played out in public. You understand, right?"

"Of course I do, but I didn't choose that fight. Max and his crew came to me and I defended myself. If it had been up to me, I'd have cut his throat in an alley and left him to the rats. Instead the *meshuggene momzer* was waiting for me near my home. Where my family lives."

"A bad business all round. That I don't disagree, but did you have to spill blood so publicly?"

"He was the one brought the knife to the party. I only had my dusters."

Sammy nodded.

"And he stood on the sidewalk and attacked me. He chose the street not the alleyway."

Another nod of understanding.

"And he got his in the end with no apology from me."

"I'm just saying Waxey won't be pleased."

"Sure, but my blood boils even thinking about the little turd."

"Yep. Remember this is business though. Max might have been a *shtunk*, a stinker and got what was coming but no-one wants the cops sniffing around our place of work, do they?"

Slugger said nothing for a spell, eyeing Sammy to glean as much as he could from his expression.

"I'll talk to Waxey and tell him what happened. Give him my side of the story before the wagging tongues lick round his earholes."

"Good plan, my friend."

Sammy exhaled what sounded like a huge sigh of relief, Slugger noted.

"Glad that's over with. So… you caught any tail recently?"

"A gentleman never kisses and tells."

"But you're no gentleman."

They both laughed and Slugger spun a yarn of *shiksa* ass whose retelling they both enjoyed.

12

BACK AT HIS usual perch, Slugger sat with a beer and waited for the world to make demands of him. The first arrival was Abraham Opler, one of Slugger's gang. Without asking, he plopped down and nodded, waiting to speak with him. He might not have been polite enough to wait for permission to sit but he recognized the need to not interrupt Slugger's train of thought.

"How're the streets?"

"Mighty fine."

"Any problems?"

"None. Everyone is paying up promptly—ever since… recent events."

A smile erupted at the corner of his mouth, but Slugger found nothing amusing in those words. With Sammy's concerns still ringing in his ears, now was not the time to be seen joking about Max's demise. Even though they were sat twenty or more feet away from each other, sometimes Slugger felt like Sammy registered every syllable of his conversations.

"Good. I'm glad to hear operations are smooth. Of course, I'm also interested to learn how you are increasing our customer base. Any new clients this last week?"

Abraham shuffled in his seat, showing the negative answer through his body language. Fabian took another swig of his beer.

"I thought you were my highflying guy?"

"It's difficult finding people who want to gamble and who aren't already using some other pool."

"Never said it was a breeze, but that's part of the job, isn't it?"

"Sure thing, but that don't make it any easier."

"Look, there's nothing wrong with going outside our normal streets, right? Even walking an extra block or two could mean you bump into fresh blood."

"Yeah…"

"And if you find there's a pool who might be ripe for a takeover bid…"

71

Fabian shrugged his shoulders and took another dramatic swig of beer. "…then we can talk through the best way of helping them volunteer to come under our wing."

Abraham giggled.

"Yeah, under our wing."

He had worked with Slugger for long enough to understand what a takeover meant: broken bones, smashed skulls and an instant pool of business maintained through intimidation, fear and the loser's belief they can beat the house.

A STRANGER HOVERED five feet away from their table and Slugger raised his head and beckoned him near. The man stood with his hat clasped between his palms.

"I've a good feelin' about my number."

"Glad you do. What's the size of your bet?"

"A dollar."

"Abraham, looks like we've got a high roller on our hands."

A big grin ripped across his face and then Slugger switched it off and directed his eyes back at the man.

"Only kidding with you, hope you don't mind, fella. Your money's good with us. Do you have it with you or would you like credit?"

"Oh, I got the money. No credit for me. Not today."

"Excellent news, my friend. Haven't seen you round here before. Breezin' through?"

"Nope. Landed a few days ago and here I am seeking my fortune with my dollar."

"Let me have your number otherwise you're just giving me a greenback. I appreciate the gesture, but it won't be winning you nothing apart from my friendship."

The guy stated his three digits and Fabian added the details to a little black notebook he kept in his jacket pocket. Fabian knew even if the book went missing, all the information was inside his head anyway but taking notes on paper supplemented the drama of placing a bet and offered a moment of closure on the transaction—until someone was lucky enough to collect any winnings. Fabian always paid up fast otherwise it'd be bad for business. Every loser who came to his pool needed to believe not only they had a chance of winning, but the money would be theirs within minutes. You could trust Fabian, the mensch.

As Ishmael shuffled out of the Forsyth and donned his hat as soon as he hit the sidewalk, Abraham bid Fabian good day and left the hotel himself. Fabian cast his eyes over the bar.

Nathan was cleaning glasses and stacking them upside down in neat rows in readiness for the late afternoon rush. Sammy was huddled at his table, deep in conversation with a man whose face was hidden from Slugger's view.

As his gaze swooped around the room, Sarah appeared waltzing down the stairs. A john had left a minute before Ishmael's arrival and, as usual, Fabian paid no never mind to their comings and goings.

This time, in the light of the midafternoon, Fabian thought he caught sight of the outline of Sarah's young body captured in shadow by the silky material engulfing her. He gazed at the curve of a breast and the point where her thighs met. Then she reached the bottom of the stairwell and the magic dissolved before his eyes.

He carried on staring at her as she wandered over to the bar and ordered a shot from Nathan. As he poured, she leaned her back on the metal bar and put both her elbows on the counter to check out the place.

"Like what you see?"

Fabian blushed because he'd thought he was appearing more casual than he actually was.

"You can be on a diet and still look at the menu, can't you?"

"And you're on a diet, are you?"

She smiled and for Fabian the whole room came alive. Her dressing gown slipped apart, ever so slightly, revealing two inches of the bare skin of her cleavage before Sarah wrapped herself up nice and tight again.

"If you buy this girl a drink, you can do more than stare."

"It's hard to tell but I'm working right now. Maybe later, hon'."

They both knew this was an empty gesture on his part. The number of quiet afternoons they'd spent together in this room was far too many to count and Fabian never made a move on her. Not because he didn't want to, but why should Nathan and Sammy time his exploits with Sarah down to the second as they did with every john who sauntered up the stairs with her?

At that moment Ben Werfel and Dan Schatzmann swung by to give up their takings for the first round of payments in the afternoon.

"Any trouble?"

"None. Clean as a rabbi's conscience."

"Any new business?"

"We're getting good regular bets from the usual bunch of no-hopers but there's no-one left to sell numbers to."

"You saying it's time to grab more territory?"

"If we want to make more money, then yes, I reckon."

Dan nodded at Ben's words and Fabian acknowledged he was right. Before he did anything about the matter, he needed to get the go-ahead from Waxey. There was nothing worse than going to war with another gang Waxey was tight with.

When Fabian came back from visiting Waxey, Isaac Polyakov had turned up and he was able to brief all his guys at once. The time for expansion was upon them.

APRIL 1916

13

MORE BY LUCK than good judgment, Alex bumped into Rebecca again when he was bringing his family's allowance over one Wednesday afternoon. He had yet another sweet dessert in his hand and allowed her to lick it off his fingers.

This time, before she hid herself back inside her apartment, he seized the moment and idly asked if she might like to visit Coney Island with him. To his surprise, she agreed almost instantly.

They took the ferry from downtown Manhattan direct to the Steeplechase Pier on the Electric City by the Sea. Alex had bought tickets in advance so they didn't have to stand in line. Straight on board and they sat down waiting for the shuttle to leave.

Rebecca was more conversational than she had ever been when in her apartment. Perhaps because he was taking her out for the day, or she was free from the shackles of being watched by her family.

They talked about her ballet and her aspirations for the future. Rebecca believed the more she practiced the better her chances of appearing in the legitimate theater. Despite her parents' misgivings, she didn't want to stand on a Yiddish stage and pirouette; she had set her sights on the English-speaking world.

Alex admired her strength of purpose. This was the first time he had been attracted to her mind and not just her alluring body. There was a warmth to his smile which had been absent before. Without thinking about what he was doing, he edged an inch or two closer to her until he could sense the material of his jacket nestling against the folds of her coat. There was a connection between them now, a bond.

"And does your family help you?"

"Help? Well… they let me spend time rehearsing every day."

"And?"

"And apart from that, Mama and Papa aren't happy. They want me to do something sensible and safe."

"Mine too."

"Yes? The rest of my time I sew for nickels. I live way too much of my life with a thimble on my thumb."

She sighed a melancholy breath and her hands flopped onto her lap, one over the other. Operating on instinct, Alex put his hand on hers and looked into her eyes.

"You'll get there. They'll come around, for sure. Talent always rises to the top."

Then a little squeeze and he moved his arm to its previous position. Rebecca returned his gaze, searching in his expression to see if he was ribbing her or if he was serious.

"Thank you."

She slipped her arm under his and they remained linked until the ferry arrived at Coney Island and they sauntered off the boat and back onto dry land.

AS THEY WALKED along the main drag in Steeplechase Park, Rebecca hooked her arm around Alex's again and he kept to her slower pace. They turned their heads slightly toward each other and let gentle smiles curl the corners of their mouths. Then they carried on walking and pointing out the attractions and sights of the park.

"Fancy going on a ride?"

"Sure, but nothing too scary."

"You decide. I'm easy."

Rebecca spun round and stopped to point at the Ferris wheel. Alex nodded and grabbed her by the hand and took her over to wait in line. She giggled to reveal the girl she really was, and talk faded into her plans to tour the world with her dance troupe. Like countless adolescents before them, Rebecca and Alex lived inside their own bubble and engulfed themselves in the excitement of all the fun of the fair.

A stream of people left the wheel, and they were first in line for the next batch. Four minutes later he helped Rebecca into a car, sat down himself, and the carny locked a metal bar in place to prevent them falling out. She nestled in beside him and he placed his arm around her shoulders.

The wheel started its rotation and soon they were high above Coney Island and able to see across to Manhattan. Magical.

"All the people look like ants."

"Crazy! I'm on top of the world, Rebecca."

She gave him a squeeze, and they proceeded to look around America until the wheel took them near the ground again and everyone became visible. Then it repeated its cycle, and the two regained their awe at the state of New York. At the bottom of the next rotation, she tried to touch a passing butterfly, but it flew past her fingers. Another smile from Alex and the car went on its upward trajectory.

At the top, the ride halted. Rebecca glanced at Alex and he faced her. This was not part of the planned ride. They had watched enough folk before they got on to have counted that you looped round for four or five minutes and then everyone was taken off in the space of another minute—maybe two at most. Now they were stuck and so was everybody else apart from the people on the opposite diameter of the wheel to them who were right at the bottom and had been released from jail by the carny.

The guy had found a bullhorn, and he told everyone to remain calm and the ride would start up again in a few minutes time.

Rebecca inched closer to Alex and, without thinking, he planted a kiss on her forehead for reassurance.

"I don't like this, Alex."

"It'll be all right. These things happen but they get fixed. There'll be someone with a monkey wrench adding some grease to the cogs this very second."

"Sure, but I still don't like it."

He squeezed her shoulder to offer reassurance, but he didn't think it was working. Rebecca's teeth began to chatter despite the afternoon's temperature.

"How long do you think we'll be stuck up here?"

"Can't be sure but the chances are it'll only be another few minutes."

"Keep talking. Your voice is keeping me calmed down."

Alex gulped.

"Every day I walk past your door, I turn my head towards your apartment hoping to catch a glimpse of you."

"Yeah?"

"And I've never forgotten the days when you ate my dessert."

"You didn't mind, did you? You said it was fine."

"Of course. I'm not complaining. Just saying you've had a bigger impact on my life than you might imagine."

"You're kind."

"You are the kind one—sewing and demeaning yourself when you are a true artist. Your creative soul deserves so much more and one day I'll make sure you have just that."

A momentary silence fell between them and Alex felt the need to occupy that space with his words.

"I mean, sometime. If you'll let me. That is… if we were ever more than neighbors."

Rebecca turned her head and pulled in the hand dangling over her shoulder and kissed it tenderly.

"Don't worry. I get what you mean and you're very sweet. From what I've heard, you are busy yourself but with more down-to-earth matters."

Before he could say a word, there was a jolt and the Ferris wheel kicked off again and they clung to each other until their descent was complete.

Back on the ground they hustled away and Alex bought them a cotton candy each to take their minds off what had just occurred. With the taste of wispy sugar tingling in their mouths, conversation soon moved on from Rebecca's fear of being trapped at the top of the wheel. Alex had offered her security, but she was so much more relaxed now the perceived danger was over.

He lightened the mood by asking more questions about her ballet dreams.

"Do you think you'll stay in New York once you're established as a dancer?"

"Well, I'd have to be here or in Chicago. I can't imagine being anywhere else. Those are the two cities of culture, wouldn't you say?"

"Asking the wrong man, I'm afraid. I know what great dancing looks like but that doesn't mean I've had the opportunity to find out much about where to see it—apart from one floor below my parents' apartment."

As they talked, they sauntered past the concessions until they stopped next to a toy stall.

"Gonna catch a bear for your gal?"

Alex looked at Rebecca who held both hands behind her back and nodded in a girlish way.

"Oh, do try."

"Sure I will."

The game was simple: shoot at a target and win if you hit the bullseye. Zip if you miss.

Alex positioned himself, leaning an elbow on the counter to steady his aim. He was no expert with a firearm, but he had a good eye. The first shot went four inches above the center.

"Squeeze the trigger, son."

The second shot traveled two inches below and Alex ground his molars. A deep breath, he relaxed his shoulders and closed the eye he wasn't using to look down the sights. The final pellet spat out of the barrel and landed squarely in the middle of the target.

"Bullseye!"

Rebecca squeaked with delight and chose a dark brown teddy bear which she hugged all the way to the end of the pier where they stopped to have a bite to eat.

ALEX WAS PLEASED he'd made her happy. He was besotted with her but had scant idea what to do about it. Of course, he'd managed to invite her out today, but he had no clue how far things would go—he knew so little about her.

She stood on her tiptoes and pecked him on the cheek as thanks for the bear. In return he put a hand on her side and squeezed gently. Given what Sarah got up to day in and day out, his time with Rebecca seemed childish in comparison but they'd formed a genuine bond over the last few hours. Or so Alex reckoned.

"You're welcome."

"Where did you learn to shoot like that? No. Don't answer that. I probably shouldn't find out the answer."

Alex's cheeks reddened as Rebecca's words reminded him of the person he was and the kinds of characters he spent his working days with.

"I'm teasing, silly. People tell me you're supporting your entire family and that makes you a great man in my eyes."

"Do they gossip about me then?"

"In the block everyone expresses an opinion. It's that or work and we all need a rest. Your name comes up now and again. Don't get big-headed on me."

"Just didn't imagine anyone talking about me before. Not what I'd expect. I wasn't fishing."

"It's nothing to worry about. After you arrived, everyone buzzed about what you were going to do and then your papa asked around for work. When we saw he didn't find any, but you brought in the rent, that made you the breadwinner."

"He's a good man, my father."

"Sure is. He helps everybody in the tenement but no-one pays him for any of that help do they?"

"Nah."

"Takes guts and determination to be responsible for a family's food, warmth and shelter. And that's what you do. You're quite a mensch."

Alex shrugged, not sure how to respond. He thought if he agreed, he'd sound big-headed and if he disagreed, he'd sound foolish.

"Fancy something to eat?"

Rebecca laughed.

"Good idea."

"What you want?"

"What ya got?"

Alex swiveled round and spotted a place fifty feet away.

"This way."

He took her by the hand and sauntered over to the *Steeplechase Diner*. They waited in line for five minutes until they were shown to a booth and they sat opposite each other.

14

AFTER ORDERING A salt beef sandwich and soda for both of them, Alex relaxed back into his seat. For a moment they were silent and gazed into each other's eyes, calm and happy in their contemplation.

"Penny for your thoughts."

"Nothing much. Enjoying the view."

Rebecca blushed and flustered around the dessert menu, pretending to be interested in cheesecake.

"Charmer."

"It's true. Your eyes are something else."

"Stop it."

Alex had no desire to embarrass her, so he obeyed her instruction and fiddled with the soda glass that had arrived at the table during their conversation.

"How's your sandwich?"

"Good. Yours?"

"Mighty fine."

The light in the diner gave Rebecca a halo effect just above her head. She was an angel. Literally. And here he was sitting opposite her, eating a roast beef on rye, watching a small red dot of ketchup on the corner of her mouth. She hadn't noticed so Alex stretched out a finger and wiped it back toward her lips. Just as his hand withdrew, Rebecca's tongue whipped out and licked the rest of her skin clean.

She grabbed his retreating hand and removed the ketchup from his fingertip with her tongue. Her cheeks reddened and she let go. Alex allowed a discreet smile to waft over his face as he pondered the meaning of her actions. Her flushed complexion expressed her realization of what she had done.

They continued eating in silence until only crumbs remained on their plates and gurgling noises emerged from the straws which the waitress had placed in their sodas. Alex paid and left a healthy tip, purposefully making it visible to Rebecca if she'd cared to glance at the table as they walked away.

REBECCA AND ALEX smooched along the boulevard some more, talking about nothing as they pootled. Her arm had returned to its resting place on his and he breathed in the aroma of her perfume whenever he turned his head toward hers. Then the inevitable happened.

"So, what exactly do you do for a living? There are many rumors about you."

"I'd be surprised if anyone has the time to waste talking about me. I'm just a guy trying to get by."

"No, you're not. There's no-one else in our block your age able to feed his family and pay the rent. That's what they're saying."

"Don't believe all you hear on a stairwell."

"I don't, believe me. If I thought everything they say about you is true, then I wouldn't be here with you now."

"I see. And what do they claim?"

"That you're a thug and a gangster."

"Thug?"

Alex laughed. How quickly the gossip spreads in this town.

"The women say you've beaten up shopkeepers to extort cash from them."

"Shopkeepers? Extortion?"

Another laugh.

"I work for a guy who lends gelt to people. Ordinary men and women who can't go to a bank for a loan. Because they're poor and have no collateral. Trouble is these are the kinda folk who don't keep up with their repayments, so some schmuck has to speak with them and help them make the right choice."

"I didn't think it'd be extortion. That didn't happen in the old country and I couldn't imagine it happening over here."

"There you go."

"But people have said your nickname is Slugger."

"That's because I used to do some boxing when I was younger. I was quite successful and the guys rib me about it."

"Have you hit anyone since you've come over here?"

"No-one that didn't deserve it."

Rebecca stopped them both and turned to face Alex. Her expression cold, concerned.

"What do you mean by that?"

"In my line of work sometimes folk do stupid things. Instead of handing over the money they owe, they lash out at the person who's reminding them they're in debt. That'd be me. So occasionally I have to defend myself. No more, no less."

She stared at him trying to gauge whether his words were truth or lies. Then Rebecca smiled and planted a brief kiss on his lips.

"Thanks for lunch, Slugger."

"You're welcome, but don't call me that please."

"Only teasing."

"I know, but that's a different part of my life and you're worth so much more than that... to me."

Another blush from Rebecca and she hugged him.

"I like you Alex Cohen."

"Straight back at you, kid."

"Let's go home, shall we?"

"Was it something I said?"

"Not at all. I've got work to do—and there's still dance practice too."

She took his hand to steady herself and performed a quick pirouette on the boardwalk.

"Come on then. Let's wait for the ferry."

Alex hoped Rebecca heard the disappointed drawl in his voice, but he thought too much of himself to plead with her for them to stay a while. He couldn't tell whether she believed him, but her expression showed genuine concern and he figured she'd agreed a return time with her parents.

They were lucky. The next ferry was already at the pier and passengers were walking up the gang plank and settling in on board. To Alex, it felt like only a moment or two had passed when the boat arrived in the Lower East Side and the couple wended their way back towards the Bowery.

"Do you fancy a quick snifter before we go home?"

"Well, I shouldn't... but I am having a lovely time. I suppose you know a local venue of fine repute?"

"Something like that, yeah."

They both giggled a little and Alex took Rebecca's hand and led her to the Forsyth Hotel. Sammy was sat at his usual table and Nathan was shining up glasses. Alex reckoned the man must've spent most of his life with a towel stuck inside a beer glass.

"What'll you have?"

Alex nodded at Nathan and turned to gaze at Rebecca who bit her lower lip, totally undecided. He leaned in until his lips were right by her ear and murmured:

"I don't suppose you've ever been in a bar like this before?"

"No. Not in my life," she whispered back.

"A small beer for the lady and a large brew for me, Nathan."

A nod of acknowledgement and the barman carried on about his business.

"You come here often?"

"Most days. Not for the drink, you understand. I use one of these tables as my office. People come and visit me to ask for my help."

"You must be important to have your own table and chair."

"Any schlemiel can sit in a bar. It's who comes to see you that sets a man apart."

Rebecca looked round and saw the individuals who frequented this roughhouse.

"Doesn't seem as though everyone here is a gentleman."

Alex laughed.

"There are women here too!"

"I don't mean that, silly. They aren't very refined looking."

"No, they're probably not but they make up most of the population round here so beggars can't be choosers."

"No, I suppose not…"

Rebecca leaned against the counter and surveyed the motley crew inhabiting the Forsyth's late afternoon. A few of the men eyed her back, coldly. Like they were judging her price—what she'd charge for a trip upstairs. She sensed their eyes and flipped round and faced the bar. Alex felt her hips touching his body as she sought physical comfort from him.

"Everything's fine, my little *bubala*. Have a sip of your beer."

The change in his tone got her to follow his bidding immediately, and she brought the glass up to her lips and took the smallest of sips possible. Alex knew she'd be used to kosher wine but doubted her palate had ever experienced a beer before.

Her scrunched up nose and disgusted expression reinforced his belief.

"That is horrid!"

"An acquired taste."

"You've gotta be kidding me?"

"No, it improves the more you sip it. The more you get used to it."

"Red wine doesn't suffer that fate."

"White wine's the same. Maybe it's because you brew beer but not wine."

"No idea. Do you have that often?"

"Now and again. I mean, I'm not a drunkard if that's what you're asking."

"Oh no. I wasn't trying to imply that, Alex. It just is so rank."

"I know. Would you like me to get you a different libation? A glass of wine?"

"Um, yes please. Sorry, I didn't mean to squander your money."

"Doesn't matter. I'm sure it won't go to waste. Nathan will resell it if we ask him nicely."

"Yuck."

"I'm kidding with ya."

They both laughed and leaned into each other again. This time, Alex planted a kiss on Rebecca's forehead. Then he swiftly repeated the action before she could move away.

Nathan had been listening to their conversation and placed a wine glass on the counter between them. She took the drink and glugged a third of it in one breath.

"Thirsty?"

"Wanted to get the taste of that beer out of my mouth."

Rebecca set the wine back on the bar and Alex put his fingers under her chin as she turned, raising her head towards his. He bent down until their lips touched and they kissed. This time there was no peck but a longer, much more satisfying experience.

Then he picked up his beer and took a swig, Rebecca reflecting his movements with her wine glass.

"You're a man filled with contradictions, aren't you, Alex Cohen?"

"I have my moments."

As he moved to place his arm around her torso, a fella staggered past them, ricocheting from one table to another. As he passed, he slapped Rebecca on the *tuches*, making her yelp with surprise at a stranger hitting her ass.

On instinct alone, Alex whirled round and planted a fist on the guy's chin. The drunk's body flew through the air as Slugger landed his punch and the guy fell onto the floor unconscious. Rebecca screamed and covered her mouth to stop any more sound escaping. Her eyes were wide with alarm, and she stared at Alex and then gawked at the man eating sawdust on the ground.

"Let's go, shall we?"

Rebecca nodded and grabbed his hand, keeping her attention glued to the floorboards so she didn't catch sight of any other unpleasantness in that building. She only looked up after they'd left the Forsyth and were heading home.

There was a silence between them until they were twenty feet from the tenement. Then Alex took her hand, and she trailed him into an alleyway.

"I just wanted to say I'm sorry about what happened back there. Didn't mean for you to get scared."

"I know. It was the surprise more than anything. I wasn't expecting anyone to lay a hand on me."

Alex's eyes cast downwards to the ground.

"Truth is, the way you reacted was very gallant. Very… attractive."

He looked up and straight at her. Her eyes had a twinkle rather than an angry fire and they kissed again. For much longer than the last time. Alex held her hips in his hands and she rested her palms behind his neck. They remained in that position for an eternity before Rebecca stopped and ran off to the tenement entrance.

"Pop by and you can meet my parents if you like."

Her voice caught in the wind as she entered the building and Alex was left on his own in a blustery alleyway. But there was a warmth in his stomach he'd never known before.

MAY 1916

15

OVER THE FOLLOWING weeks, Alex's thoughts lingered around the smell of Rebecca and the flow of her ballet skirt. This never impeded trade though —and business had never been better.

Fabian had spotted some action a few blocks south, just east of Chatham Square near the corner of East Broadway and Market. This was sufficiently far away not to be stomping on another of Waxey's outlets but not so distant as to be outside of his sphere of influence if heat descended on them.

For three days, each gang member spent an hour or two checking out the target headquarters. They were getting as much footfall as Slugger's game but all the johns were strangers. Perfect.

The other great thing about the setup was that it was relaxed—like they hadn't a care in the world. This meant Slugger's gang should have little trouble breaking into this merry band which pleased Ben, Abraham, Dan and Isaac. Alex was less heartened.

If they were this casual in their operations then who was to say they didn't have serious muscle backing them that didn't need to show its face every day? A good point for which he had no answer.

It's amazing what you can find out by hanging on street corners and asking the odd question of a passerby. Turns out Slugger had fixed his gaze on one of the few independents still functioning in the Lower East Side. These guys were confident because they thought no one had spotted them going about their daily grind of getting in cash and enforcing payments. There were no credit lines of any importance from these fellas—they didn't have the backing to offer anything more than a day or two's grace on a missed payment. Clearly they were taking the money but not wanting to put any of their ill-gotten gains at risk. Slugger respected people who believed in keeping hold of their gelt. Savings are important. Sometimes.

Other times saving your skin takes a higher priority. Slugger waited until the goons were out collecting their dues, leaving the big chief on his own in the bar where they operated. He was a large fella and sat with his back to a wall near the rear of the joint. Wise man.

SLUGGER ENTERED THE bar on his own—the other four were waiting around the corner and came in one-by-one over the next thirty minutes. Each of them propped up a different part of the counter. No-one acknowledged any of the others. Calm and relaxed, sipping their beers and a shot of scotch for Slugger. The barman headed toward the back of the establishment and that was when Slugger made his move.

"You got any action?"

"Who's asking?"

"Fabian Mustard."

The big chief laughed loudly.

"Who the hell are you?"

"I'm the guy who's enquiring very nicely if you have any action. Do you?"

"Away with you. There's nothing for the likes of you here."

"I'm feeling lucky with a number and I've heard you're the fella I can place a wager with."

"Maybe I am and maybe I'm not, but you need to come with a recommendation. I don't do business with strangers."

"I respect that. I want to arrange a bet for Waxey Gordon."

Now the big chief stared straight at Slugger, blood draining from his expression. His eyes darted left and right but all he saw was Slugger towering over him—he'd not bothered to sit down—and a bunch of guys quaffing beers at the bar.

"A bet, you say? How much and on what number?"

A nervous smile ripped across his face as he couldn't tell if this was a shakedown or just a peculiar bet from someone using Waxey's name in vain.

"I'll bet every cent I have."

"On?"

"No number. I wager you're out of business and need to take a long journey out of state. I don't care where and I don't care how but you must leave now and never turn back."

"Don't be ridiculous."

Slugger grinned down and the big chief smiled. At that point, he shuffled in his chair and Slugger seized the moment to pull his hand, adorned with one of his favorite knuckledusters, out of his pants pocket and slam the man off his seat, blood and two teeth fleeing his mouth as he hit the dirt.

Ben and Dan moved away from the bar and headed to the front to deal with any newcomers to the scene and Isaac and Abraham scuttled toward the back to keep the barman quiet. With no customers apart from the big chief, they had the place to themselves.

The guy got on all fours before Slugger kicked him in the kidneys leaving him reeling back on the floor.

"Listen very carefully, you hear?"

The man clung to his sides and moaned.

"You little *nudnik*. Either you leave this place and I never see you again or you'd better prepare to meet your maker. So help me I'll kill you now, you *pisher*. They call me Slugger and I have a reputation which might have traveled far enough south for you to have heard of me. Have you?"

The gurgling coming out of the chief's mouth seemed to confirm Slugger's claims.

"What's it to be? Don't make me wait too long."

"I'll go."

"Good decision, my friend."

Without taking an eye off him, Slugger called out to Dan. "Get this man a towel. He needs to clean himself up on his way out of here."

With a dishcloth around his still-bleeding mouth, the chief walked out of the bar. Then Slugger walked over to the barman and gave him a handsome tip and explained they'd be his new customers.

Over the next hour, the chief's two goons arrived back, and Slugger offered each of them a beer, which they accepted as much out of fear as anything else.

"Gents, I hope your boss didn't owe you any pay because you won't be seeing him again around these parts.

"But you will be seeing us. From this point on, you work for me. If that's not agreeable to you then that's fine but I need to know now."

The two looked at each other nervously.

"If you want to walk out on this racket, no harm'll befall you from my hand. You have not crossed me so I wish you no ill will. But if you join our crew then I expect loyalty just as I give it. So what's it to be?"

"I'm in."

"And so am I."

"Good decision, gents. Here's a small joining gift. The *schnorrer* probably owed you some money and I don't want you to be out of pocket."

So they wouldn't feel too overwhelmed on their first afternoon, Slugger left them in the capable hands of his four hoods and walked out into the bright sunlight. He visited the following morning and ensured the racket was running smoothly. After a week, he reported back to Waxey they'd broken ground below Canal and everything was sitting pretty.

"Good news and congratulations. Not everyone is ingenious enough to take a new business under their wing. And in case you haven't noticed yet, I like resourceful men around me. Helps put out fires and expand our reach. The more we have, the more we can share with our friends."

Slugger stood ever so slightly straighter in front of Waxey, entire body erect, the praise flowing into every one of his pores.

"Do you think any one of your fellas could watch over the racket for you if you were off somewhere else?"

Fabian thought for five seconds. Were they capable or did they still need hand holding?

"I'd like to say yes, but there's a doubt in my mind."

"A good honest answer. How long do you reckon it'll take for them to be responsible for the two rackets you're operating?"

"Three or four weeks before I'm completely certain. If I promote one of them then I'll need to get another pair of feet on the ground and getting that right takes time."

"There's no rush but once you are comfortable, I have a job for you. This will be on top of your current responsibilities. But to make this work, your guys must step up and pay tribute to you for the privilege of carrying on under your excellent leadership. That way, we free up your time."

"Understood. What for?"

"My boy, there's more to life than gambling—there's power in a union."

ALEX SAT AT the table, hands in his lap, surveying the bustling scene around him. There were the three younger girls as well as Benjamin and Ora, Rebecca's parents.

As was usual, Benjamin remained at the head of the dinner table and scowled at him throughout the entire meal. Alex couldn't tell if this was his natural countenance or whether the man refused to hide how much he loathed this fella who had taken his daughter to Coney Island.

In contrast, Ora talked to him constantly, expecting answers to her questions irrespective of the quantity of food left on his plate which she also expected him to eat with great rapidity.

"You haven't eaten your latkes."

"I'm getting there, Mrs Grunberg."

Benjamin stared at him, chewing the chicken stew, grinding at the meat with his molars like he was pulverizing one of Alex's arms.

"Look at you, so thin. You need to take care of yourself."

"Oh, I do, Mrs Grunberg. And might I say how this is a mighty fine meal, thank you. I hope you didn't go to any trouble on my account."

Rebecca giggled from across the table; Mrs Grunberg had ensured she and Alex didn't sit next to each other when they all sat for dinner.

He looked at her quizzically.

"Alex, of course Mama went to a lot of trouble. We don't have guests come and eat with us every day of the week, you know."

Ora Grunberg's cheeks reddened as the implication they might not have meat each dinner shone through Rebecca's words. Alex understood. Tenement life was tough for everyone. If it wasn't then you'd leave and find somewhere better and less squalid.

"Don't tease your mother so, Rebecca. This is a fabulous meal, and I am honored you were prepared to share it with me."

Benjamin stopped chewing for a second and threw his eyes up into the air. Clearly, he thought the boy was trying too hard. Soon he'd get a bout of indigestion from all these fine words.

"Alex, how very kind. Benjamin, wasn't that a lovely thing he has just said?"

Benjamin chose that moment to have a quick cough to avoid responding to the positive statement about Alex. He'd heard the rumors and believed most. And now the Bowery Slugger sat at his dinner table.

The little girls ate quietly, occasionally lifting their eyes to give him a glance to check he was still there and interested in their big sister. Beyond that, they contributed nothing to the evening—apart from a complaint about not wanting to go to bed this early. That family conversation only took place after the dinner was eaten and the washing up was completed by Alex and Rebecca while Ora and Benjamin sat in the living room waiting for their return.

"Grab yourself a dining chair," instructed Ora and he obeyed, placing it near to Rebecca's seat.

"And what do you think of Rebecca's *meshuggener* plans to become a dancer?"

"I think she's very talented and has the dedication to succeed."

"She spins round this room and kicks her leg up like a pair of scissors in a tutu. That you call talent?"

Benjamin's first words of the evening forced Rebecca's arms to cross and a huff to escape her lips. Alex knew a family argument brewing when he sat smack in the middle of it and wanted to have no part in the *broiges*. He turned back to Ora. "And in the meantime, I understand she's contributing to the family income by working the rest of her time."

Ora nodded and glared at her husband whose sole contribution had generated a palpable tension in the room. Only the girls were oblivious as they prepared for bed.

"Yes she is. Helps her family and has an interest."

"It's more than an interest, Mama. It's what I'll do with my life."

"We'll see, my love. I don't doubt your ability but I know it's so hard to make it big in high culture entertainment."

"You wait and see, Mama."

Alex smiled at Rebecca, pleased to have created some calm within this family discourse. Soon enough, he reckoned he'd outstayed his welcome and bid them all goodnight. She walked him the ten feet to the threshold while her parents stared at them and soaked in every syllable of their conversation. To give themselves some privacy, she followed him onto the stairwell and closed the door behind her.

"Thanks for coming down. It was good for you to meet my folks."

"Hey, it's always fun watching other people's families. And yours was no exception!"

"Don't. Mama means well, but she tries too hard. And Papa? The man hasn't smiled in sixteen years and he wasn't going to start tonight."

"He's all right. Just like my old papa, without the sense of humor but with a job. Swings and roundabouts."

Rebecca grinned and held his hand. They stole a chaste kiss, knowing there were eyes on almost every stair. Alex stroked her left cheek and walked up one flight to enter his family's home.

16

THREE WEEKS AFTER his meeting with Waxey, Slugger stood in front of Ira Moskowitz, waiting to find out what his new job was all about.

"There's power in a union."

Ira was stationed at his usual seat at the table in Waxey's headquarters. For a second, Fabian wondered if Ira ever left that position.

"Sit down, Slugger."

A boy came in and took their coffee order, returning a five minutes later with their respective brews. Ira had one sip and then stood up and headed to stare out of the window.

"I'm glad you're on board."

"Glad to be here."

"Sure, sure. Any idea what Waxey has in mind for you?"

"Nope. It's something to do with a union..."

Ira laughed and carried on staring out the window at the bustling scene below.

"You have gainful employment."

"A job?"

"You're going to be a union rep, working for the masses of the American Union for Factory Floor Employees and Sundry Workers."

"Huh?"

"Come across the AUFFE before?"

"Uh, yes I guess so."

"Well, now you're a union rep there. Congratulations."

"Thanks. I think."

A chuckle erupted from Ira's mouth.

"Relax. It's simple really. We have a link with AUFFE. A very positive relationship. They make donations to people in our circle and Waxey and I ensure nothing unpleasant happens to any member of the union. Like a strike lasts too long and the workers are out of pocket. Or a union leader gets pushed under a car or suffers a calamity such as an unexpected blow to the head by an iron bar.

"They are protected from all these things happening to them, if you get my meaning."

Protection.

"And so I will represent rag trade women who sew for a living?"

"Don't be ridiculous. Of course you're not. What experience do you have of the *schmatta* business?"

Fabian shrugged because the answer was *gornisht*.

"And don't forget: my mama, may she rest in peace, spent her entire life sewing and repairing clothes. When I was a kid, I thought she had a metal tip on her thumb, she wore that thimble for so long."

"Sorry. I didn't mean no offence."

"None taken. I just want you to be respectful to all the union people you meet. They take themselves very seriously and won't appreciate you dismissing them. More to the point, they make us a lot of gelt and help influence Tammany in our favor."

"Got it."

"Good. Right now I want you to get your face known in the union office. You'll get paid every Friday by the union finance department. Make sure they give you your payments. If there's ever any excuse, tell me. Don't argue with them, it's a waste of time."

"What do I do for the money to earn my keep?"

Ira chuckled again. This greenhorn entertained him.

"Nothing. That's the beauty of this racket. We do zip most of the time and occasionally we intercede in some wrangling or other. Sometimes we flex our muscles and they tell me you're very good at that."

"I can handle myself, it's true."

"And some… whatever happened to that boy Max?"

"Slipped on the sidewalk."

"Yeah, Slugger. And fell onto a shiv."

Ira winked at him, knowingly.

"Besides, when matters arise, you'll earn your wages for sure."

"And what should I do for the rest of the time?"

"Soak up the silence or get your gang to expand into more territory. Waxey says you broke in below Canal. You should carry on doing that."

Fabian nodded, more at ease in the knowledge there was some action ahead.

"But remember that independents are easier to deal with than pools run by bigger guns."

"I picked the first one out pretty carefully to avoid a big fight on my hands."

"Smart and handy with a knife. Stick with us and you'll go far, my boy. Any questions?"

"Just the one."

"Shoot."

"Where is the AUFFE offices?"

Ira sat down at the table and downed his coffee in one gulp. Then he laughed an enormous roar of a laugh.

"Slugger. You're sitting in it right now!"

The Slugger looked at Ira and got the joke shortly after. They had the perfect setup. The third floor of the building was given over to the union to keep the relationship tight. In exchange for regular payments, they protected it from the evils of Capital and funneled money into the Democrats in Tammany Hall.

At the top floor, Fabian introduced himself to the other union reps. He'd seen them all hanging around the building since he first arrived the previous year.

The thought of putting his feet up on a desk and sitting to wait for something to happen did not appeal. So Fabian left and headed south of Canal to scout out pools to take over. Also, he thought he'd pay his crew a visit in the afternoon. That way, they'd see they weren't forgotten and were being watched. Helped keep them on their toes.

As he was walking past the shopkeepers and their stalls, Fabian thought about the money he was earning and what he was going to do with it. His pay had almost doubled since yesterday and the more pools he opened, the better off he'd be.

Now was the time to smarten himself up. A trip to a tailor—maybe even give his father some work—would be a good place to start. He needed to dress the part if he was going to rise up the ranks of the organization. And then once his ego had puffed up enough, Slugger considered what gifts he would bestow on his family and on Rebecca.

SLUGGER FOUND THREE possible pools over the following two weeks just by walking round, looking and listening to what was happening on the streets. He rejected a further five potential setups as they were packed with gorillas—too many and too tough. He wanted low hanging fruit and two quick wins. Nothing more, nothing less.

Fabian sat at his usual table in the Forsyth with a beer in one hand and the other in his lap, watching the world go by—or the microcosm of johns and gamblers who frequented the venue of an afternoon. Sammy remained near the back dealing with a flurry of people who needed his attention. No voices were raised but Fabian had a sense there was tension in the air. Once the current batch wandered off, he took his beer over to Sammy.

"How's it going?"

"Don't ask. Everyone wants a pound of my flesh."

"Money lending is a fraught business, for sure."

"Tell me about it. No one is capable of thinking for themselves. They act like I'm the only person with any brains. Drives me *meshugga*."

"Apart from all your flunkies, how's it going?"

"What? Oh, fine," he sniggered. "A boss's work is never done."

"Too right, Sammy… Time for a quick chat?"

"Not really. There's things to organize this afternoon."

"No, I mean a business conversation. There's an opportunity I'd like to talk through with you."

"Pull up a chair, I'm all ears."

Fabian sat down and placed his beer on the table after taking a swig of it.

"Over the next few weeks, I will move in on some other pools. they're south of Canal so I'm not treading on anyone's toes."

"Got the all-clear from Waxey? You like to go full steam ahead sometimes. It's your virtue and your vice."

"For sure Waxey's good with it. I've already added one pool to my roster and now that's all sorted, I want to repeat the exercise."

"Nice job."

"Thing is, the wider I spread my wings, the less I see of what's going on."

"Ah, the perennial dilemma of the lofty general," Sammy smirked.

"Lay off, will ya? That's the problem but here is a solution: would you be willing to work with me looking after the new pools? We'd cut the pie up fair and square and we can trust each other. What do you say?"

"Very kind, Fabian. But I'm not too sure. Would we be operating together, or would I be working for you? Word on the street is that lately the numbers racket is not your only source of income anymore. You're in thick with Ira and that's a tier above my pay grade.

"Don't get me wrong, I wish you well in all your ambitions but I'm my own boss. Apart from the tribute I kick back to Waxey once a week. But he understands I just need to be left alone. I bring in his money and that's all I must do. If I worked for you, things would be different. Different between us for a start, but also, I'd get a boss who will be up my ass every day. And that's not what I want."

Fabian sipped his beer, perusing the highlights of Sammy's concerns.

"I trust you Sammy. More than anyone else in this world. The reason we are talking about this is because your word means something. A lot to me in particular. Would I be on your tail if matters go wrong? Yes. Would I expect you to fix things? No, I'd think we'd work together to sort stuff out. I'm suggesting a partnership based on my ownership of Canal Street pools and your oversight and management. We'd both share the spoils because we worked jointly to create those spoils."

Now it was Sammy's turn to lapse into silence and cogitate.

"And what if I want to expand my sphere of control?"

"If you get more pools for yourself then fantastic and I wish you well. If you do that by going south of Canal then I'd like you to talk to me about it beforehand. And if you do that by trying to take over one of my pools there, I'll slit your throat from ear to ear. I've got a reputation for that already."

The last two sentences were said with a broad smile but Fabian meant every word without a trace of exaggeration.

"Partners then?"

"For sure. Partners."

Fabian raised a hand and Sammy took it and they shook. The deal was struck.

"Thank you. Nothing's about to happen overnight. By the end of July there should be one or two more come on stream."

"What about your current crew?"

"I'm leaving them to manage the small crop I currently control. Once they've got more experience, we might want them to support you with the rest of Canal pools. One step at a time though. I'll make sure they're incentivized to help you. We're all in this together."

"And talking of which, did anything come out of your run in with little Max?"

"Not at all. Why? What's the gossip?"

"Nothing. Usually at least one civilian tries to rat us out and we encourage them to change their testimony or get a sudden bout of amnesia."

"Or a baseball bat to the temple."

"Exactly. But I hadn't heard anything about Max."

"The cops dragged his miserable ass to the morgue and did nothing about it. Seems like he owed some of the brethren kickbacks so as a corpse he was just a bad debt to them."

"Bad way to go. No disrespect."

"The boy was a *gonif* and couldn't be trusted."

"Amen to that."

They clinked their glasses and sipped their beers talking about nothing in particular for five minutes. Occasionally they'd discuss a mighty fine derrière that passed by on its way up to a room with a john.

Then Fabian returned to his table, knowing he'd secured a safe pair of hands for his ever-expanding reach. He said what he meant: he could trust Sammy.

JUNE 1916

17

FABIAN'S LIFE AT the union headquarters passed slowly the first month or two. Nothing happened, and he spent his time talking with the other fellas or jawing with the labor union men themselves. True blue union guys avoided Bayard and Bowery because of its close relationship to other elements of society. At least, that was the phrase Yonah Kulischer used to describe the situation.

He was the accountant and knew everything that went on with the finances. For that reason alone, Yonah was a good man to keep on side but he still didn't take himself too seriously. An unusual trait in a bookkeeper and they got on well.

Yonah understood the union could only succeed if its reach extended beyond the length of its arms; Waxey and Ira offered that extension. And he also knew those kinds of relationships were not for the fainthearted. These guys operated within the law only if it was expedient—and most times it was not.

Now and again, Ira asked Fabian to have a quiet word with a chapter head who wasn't toeing the line. In early June, Fabian visited Kaleb Ganz, responsible for Chapter 16, west of the Bowery one block north of the corner of Spring and Mott.

The building facade was regaled with union livery and Fabian read the letters AUFFE clear as day above the door and front window. He sauntered into the reception hall.

"Is there a Mr Ganz available, hon'?"

The woman looked at him and pondered a moment.

"Who should I say is enquiring?"

"I've important information about the chapter finances I need to discuss with him personally."

"I'll see if he's in."

"That'd be very kind, thank you."

Fabian relaxed his shoulders, stood and waited, while she walked through a door and he could hear voices on the other side; the woman's and a man's.

She bustled back momentarily, standing between Fabian and the door she'd closed behind her.

"I'm afraid he's busy right now and asks if you could book an appointment and come another day."

"Oh dear. You see I need to speak with him today. As I said, this is a vital matter and can't wait."

"Ah."

She glanced left then right, unsure what to do now. Her instructions were clear—don't allow the guy in, but her expression showed she didn't want to let the union down if something serious was taking place.

Fabian sensed her dilemma.

"Tell you what, why don't I pop my head round the door, for a second, and Mr Ganz can decide for himself."

"He can't be disturbed…"

Slugger had tried being nice, and it wasn't working, so he took a more direct approach, pushing past the receptionist and barging through into Ganz's office.

"I'M SORRY, MR Ganz, he wouldn't take no for an answer."

That was all she could utter as Slugger slammed the door in her face and stood in front of Ganz.

"Get out of here this minute. Who the hell do you think you are?"

"Waxey Gordon sent me and who I am doesn't matter. What I have to say is what you need to focus on. Right now."

He stepped forward, leaning his knuckles on Ganz's desk, towering over the union official.

"You are behind on your payments. You owe the union money and Mr Gordon isn't happy. When Waxey isn't happy, neither am I."

"What dues? We owe nothing. We're clean here."

"You misunderstood me. This isn't about your fine upstanding members. Their money has gone straight into the AUFFE coffers. I'm talking about you, little man. You owe the union your dues."

"My dues? What do you mean? I'm paid up like everybody else in the chapter."

"Don't call me a liar. If you had paid, I would not be here. You are not and I'm here to collect.

"I don't understand. What dues?"

Fabian sighed. Ganz had forgotten the first rule of running a union. Always pay your protection on time.

"In order for your chapter to remain safe—and your members to not get intimidated while they go about their lawful business—you need to make sure that your subscription doesn't lapse."

Ganz's expression twisted from sheer confusion to utter fear. The man had got to the punchline.

"Oh God."

Fabian allowed him the time to think. There was no point forcing him into a corner when all he wanted was for the man to put his hand in his pocket and supply the gelt.

"Oh God, I get it. A guy turned up five days ago, and I sent him packing. Thought it was a joke. If I'd known…"

Ganz was silent as his brain continued to think through what had occurred and the dangerous waters in which he was now sailing.

"How much do I owe?"

"Last week was a reminder about last month's subscription. I'm here to collect that and get this month's too. That's one hundred dollars today."

"I don't have that kind of money."

"Then you'd better find it—and fast. Soon I will charge you interest and then I'll lose my patience. You really don't want that to happen, I can assure you of that."

"No. I get it. I just don't have the dough right now. How much time do I have to pay?"

"I can loan you the money if it's easier for you, but you must pay me back —with interest."

"Right."

"Then all you do is make sure you have another fifty every month from now on."

"That's more than I earn. How am I going to do that?"

"Are you new to the job, Kaleb?"

"Yes, can you tell?"

"Well, Yonah told me you were. What most guys in your situation do is raise the dues a few cents and that way, we get our money, the men stay safe and you keep the use of your limbs. Everyone's happy."

"Everyone's happy," Kaleb intoned. "I have no choice. Let's take out a loan."

"The vig is five percent a month. I am here to do business with you. This isn't a shakedown."

"Five percent?"

"Take it or leave it."

"I'll take it."

They shook hands and Fabian wrote the details in his little black book.

"You'll need to make regular payments every week until you pay off the debt. I'll be at the union headquarters and you can find me there. Only repay me and no-one else, you understand?"

Fabian tipped his hat and walked out of the Chapter 16 building and into the midday sun.

IN BETWEEN HIS union work, Fabian kept on top of the numbers pools. Not only did it give him some useful spending money, but it delivered future earnings from his debtors' list. Now and again, a hapless gambler would be short his owings and Fabian would visit.

Stood in the doorway of *The Oregon*, a saloon on Allen and Rivington, Fabian sighed. He knew how the next ten minutes would pan out. A brief discussion with the owner three weeks behind with his payments, a firm but clear conversation with added menace. Either the guy coughs some cash or gets a beating. He preferred the former but was calm about the latter. Hence his ennui as he stepped into the bar and checked out what was going on.

To the left was the counter itself, a solitary man cleaning glasses like all bartenders do. There was a scattering of tables, and a flight of stairs at the back led up to the so-called private rooms. Two fellas sat at a table sipping a brown brew.

If there had been a musical instrument in the joint, the piano would have stopped playing. The barkeep eyed Fabian with suspicion, paid no never mind and carried on with his polishing. The two men went back to their drinking and conversation.

Fabian sauntered up to the bar and waited for the barman to come over. Even though he was the only punter seeking to quench his thirst, the barkeep took thirty seconds before he stopped work on his current glass and sidled over to Fabian.

"What'll you have?"

"Small beer… and some information."

"Let me get the brew and we'll see about the rest."

Fabian waited as Joey poured the oaty liquid and returned. Slugger threw down a few coins for payment.

"What d'you want to know?"

"Is Eli Blechmann about?"

"Who wants to know?"

"I just asked the question and I'm waiting for an answer."

"Who said anyone of that name is in this joint?"

"Don't make me ask again. It's a simple enquiry. Is he here or not?"

"Not being funny but Eli is usually not in if anybody asks that kind of question."

"Understandable. If I said to you I was his business partner, would that help you at all?"

"Then I'd tell you he was upstairs, first door on the right. But if you weren't his business partner then I'd lose a day's pay."

"You won't lose no money on account of me."

Joey nodded and turned his head to the staircase hoping to encourage Fabian to follow his line of sight.

AT THE TOP of the stairs, Fabian headed straight for the open door on the right and peered inside. A guy—presumably Eli Blechmann—sat at his desk with a pile of notes and coins in front of him, counting yesterday's takings no doubt.

"Eli, I'm glad you're in as I've popped by."

The man swung round and stared at Fabian, his jaw dropped in confusion.

"Huh? Who... who are you?"

"Me? The guy you owe money to."

"What money?"

"Eli, don't make me beg. You had a lucky feeling about the numbers and it didn't come good. Four times in a row if I recall. Each time you doubled up your bet until you needed to borrow gelt... from me."

Eli's confusion morphed into ashen fear. He knew who Fabian was and what he was doing here.

"So, Eli. Where's my cash?"

"I don't have it right now."

"You're kidding me? You sit in front of a pile of swag, but you don't have any cash. Do me a favor. You owe me three weeks' payments and I want it."

Eli put down the notes he'd been counting and acted as though they simply weren't there.

"This isn't my—"

"Don't give me that. You look like you were holding at least my fifteen dollars just then."

Fabian stepped forward and completely entered Eli's office, blocking any escape attempt by the guy.

"I can't give you this money. It's not mine."

"And the gelt you borrowed from me isn't yours either. Seems to me you've got way too much of other people's property on your hands. And you need to pay me back."

With that, Slugger lurched forwards, grabbed Eli by the neck and slammed his head down towards his desk. Coins and notes flew sideways as his forehead thumped onto them. Slugger pulled Eli backwards to reveal blood pouring out of his nose and a nickel stuck to his forehead, like a third eye.

"Give me my money," Slugger growled.

Eli Blechmann knew there was no arguing and counted out fifteen dollar bills, handing them over to Fabian.

"Next week pay up on time or you'll get much worse. Understand?"

"Sure."

"Stuff a handkerchief up your nose and you'll stop the bleeding soon enough."

Fabian turned round and closed the door behind him so Blechmann could get himself sorted out of sight from any busybody who might walk past.

18

INSTEAD OF A nosey Parker, Sarah appeared in view, causing Fabian to raise both eyebrows.

"Well, hello stranger."

"Hi, to you."

He opened his mouth to ask what she was doing on the second floor of Eli Blechmann's bar when he thought better of it. Sarah was wearing a black silk dressing gown and, by the looks of things, not much else. She was working.

"Up to much?"

"Looking after financial matters."

"Eli likes to wager."

"And doesn't like to lose."

Sarah chuckled and nodded.

"I haven't seen you at the Forsyth for a while."

She shook her head.

"Nah, business wasn't great there, and I thought I'd try a different venue."

Fabian understood this wasn't the entire story because she was far from an independent worker. Like almost everyone north of Canal, she worked for Waxey. Instead he nodded.

"Yeah, a girl's gotta do, I suppose."

"Sure thing."

A flash of memory engulfed him for a moment; the first time she'd sashayed past him in the Forsyth on the day he'd met Sammy. He recalled her perfume and the swing of her hips. The shape of her bust.

"Are you free now?"

"Yeah, there's no trade downstairs and let me check my diary…"

Sarah pulled her dressing gown away from her body near her cleavage.

"Nothing happening I can see."

"Then shall we spend some time together?"

Sarah eyed him quizzically.

111

"For a drink and a chat downstairs or upstairs for something else."

"Second floor, I was thinking." He gulped.

"Well come into my office, kind stranger."

She allowed her hips to swing along the corridor and he happily followed them until she arrived at a door and turned to check he was still nearby.

INSIDE, THE WALLS were painted red. There was a bed, a wardrobe, a dressing stand and chair, and not much else. Fabian popped his hat onto the table and just stayed there, unsure what to do.

"Let me help you with your jacket, dear."

Sarah stood right next to him and took the sleeves of his jacket off his arms, her hands lingering on his torso and massaging his shoulders as she hung the item of clothing on the back of the chair.

Then she undid her dressing gown and let it fall onto the floor, leaving Fabian to stare at her flesh for a while. There was a camisole covering her breasts, a corset and a pair of stockings. Her skin was pale and her black hair was long enough to reach her back. Only just.

He reached out and touched the straps and pushed them until they fell from her shoulders. First the right and then the left. With the second one done, the camisole began to slide off and landed on the ground on top of the dressing gown, but Fabian kept his eyes on Sarah's torso and the curve of the breasts he'd just revealed.

Once he gingerly placed a hand on one of her nipples, she undid his shirt and unbuttoned his flies.

"Be a dear and get me out of this."

She spun round and tapped the straps of her corset, which he slowly untangled while Sarah removed her stockings. When they were both finished, she stood up and let him hold her breasts in both hands.

"Come on, we aren't here to stand around, now are we?"

She led him into the bed and they started to get more intimate. All the while Fabian was kissing Sarah, the image of Rebecca played in his mind and he pretended that her stomach, thighs, breasts were in his mouth and not Sarah's at all. He liked Sarah's body, but he loved the idea it was Rebecca beneath the sheets with him instead.

Later when he was putting his clothes back on as Sarah lay in bed, still imagined how Rebecca would behave after they made love. Reality slammed in his face once Sarah spoke.

"Nothing personal, but you're going to have to pay for my time. It's five dollars, I'm afraid."

Fabian thought for a second as he didn't like the idea of that.

"Tell you what. Don't ask me to pay for your time and trust me instead."

Sarah looked at him, uncertain whether he was about to chisel her and not wanting to have any trouble with someone with Slugger's reputation.

"I trust you, Fabian."

He finished getting dressed and tied up his shoes. Then he pulled out ten dollars from his pants pocket and placed it on the dressing table.

"That's a present from me to you. Get yourself something nice."

Sarah smiled and understood. A five-dollar tip on top of the fee was huge. It meant Fabian was a man worth trusting.

"Will you be around again?"

"I hope so, Sarah. I might even make my own weekly collection from Blechmann if he's lucky."

He put his hand on her crotch and squeezed, then walked straight out the room, down the stairs and out the building.

ISAAC POLYAKOV WAS a wily old bird for someone who had yet to reach his sixteenth birthday. When he saw an opportunity, he would grab it with both hands and deal with the consequences later. As a life strategy, it had worked well for him ever since his family arrived in America when he was five. He had bummed around for a while once he was sent out to work but had found his feet with Fabian. Now he was at the heart of a numbers pool making decent dough.

Trouble was the boy didn't realize how to be satisfied—he always wanted more. Even though he was swimming in cash, he believed he was owed a little more and, given that Fabian wasn't doing anything about it, Isaac took matters in his own hands.

At the end of the week, Sammy totted up the takings and ensured what was noted matched the cash Waxey'd received. They were fifty dollars short. The first time this happened, Sammy was perplexed and doubted his addition skills, but he mentioned it to Fabian who sorted out the shortfall from his own pocket.

"Keep an eye on them, Sammy. Fifty is a lot to lose down the side of an armchair."

When the same thing happened the next week, he was less forgiving.

"Find out who's doing this, Sammy. I want the name before the end of the weekend."

SATURDAY MORNING, SAMMY met up with Fabian in the Forsyth, coming over to his table to give him the news.

"I think I've figured out the thief."

"Doesn't sound like you're certain."

"I'm not but I'm pretty sure."

"That's not sufficient. We need to be absolutely certain. This isn't a court of law. Reasonable doubt isn't good enough. I want to know."

"Give me more time and I'll get there for you."

"That's all I ask, Sammy."

Fabian remained in the Forsyth all day long, sipping the odd beer, jawing with Nathan and managing business. There was no union work on a Saturday, so he didn't bother popping over to Bayard and Bowery. Also, he stayed away from Waxey until he had solved the problem of the shortfall in his take. Even though Fabian had covered the loss so far, he preferred to tell Waxey what had happened as a past event rather than a current situation. Didn't want to appear out of control.

By three in the afternoon, Sammy returned.

"And?"

"And I know who it is."

"You want me to guess or you going to spill?"

"Isaac."

Sammy peered straight into Fabian's eyes to gauge the reaction inside his head but saw nothing but a cold glare and a clenched jaw.

"How?"

"Easy really. He's the one Ben put in charge to count the money. Everyone else just stuffs the cash into their pockets or into a tin. They all have a rough idea of how much they've earned, but it's only after Ben's finished counting that they are sure.

"Even though he tots up in front of them, he palms the odd note. Only five bucks a day but after a week, it mounts up. There's no big steal, just daily skimming."

"How d'you know?"

"I watched him. The others are too young to spot a grifter when they see one. I noticed immediately."

"Why?"

"Huh? Why what?"

"Why'd he do it?"

"Haven't asked him. Figured he'd fly off if he figured out we were onto him."

"Why d'you think?"

"Dunno. The money I'd guess but you've looked after those boys, especially when you went the other side of Canal. They understood you were relying on them to keep the old tram on the rails while you were building a new train."

"Where is he now?"

"Round the corner. The crew are meeting up soon for an afternoon count. You want me to come with?"

"No. Thanks for your help."

"That's what friends are for."

They both stood up and shook hands. Fabian let Sammy settle down at his usual table before leaving the Forsyth and walking round the corner to find his boys.

19

BEN, ISAAC AND the other two were sat at the back of another dive bar, huddled around the table. Between the four, you couldn't see what was going on, but the fact Abraham's head kept bobbing up for air showed there was business afoot. The afternoon count had begun.

Fabian stood over them, silently watching Isaac as the rest of their eyes stared at the paper and coins. Sammy was right—no-one bothered to check Isaac's hands as he skimmed two dollar bills while Fabian watched. That took quite some balls for the kid.

When the count was finished, they bagged up the coins and Isaac put the notes into their money tin. Then Isaac looked up.

"Hi, Fabian."

A single nod in response. The others joined in the welcome but Fabian said nothing, merely nodding acknowledgement to each of the boys.

"Mind if I sit down?"

"Sure thing. Make some room for the man, guys. Pull him up a chair."

Dan grabbed a seat, and they all shuffled round the circular table until there was enough space for him to fit. He made certain he sat next to Isaac.

"How's business?"

"All good."

"Pleased to hear it, Isaac. All good with the count?"

"Sure thing, boss."

Fabian glanced at Abraham who'd uttered that statement.

"And was everything fine last week too?"

"Definitely, boss."

He glanced at Ben who'd offered that pronouncement.

"Trouble is, boys, everything is far from all right."

All expressions appeared concerned, Isaac's more so than the others.

"Seven days ago, you were short fifty and yesterday you were short another fifty."

"What? How come..."

"Ben, I assumed there was some bad counting before, so I made up the difference before we passed the money off to Waxey. Once is a mistake. Twice is daylight robbery."

Fabian allowed the final phrase to sink into all their brains. Isaac blinked a little too rapidly. He knew exactly what Fabian meant, but the others needed more time to think through the implications of those words.

The three boys scanned each other's faces trying to tell who was skimming from Fabian—by looking at them. Fabian felt tension in Isaac's arm; they were sitting cheek by jowl. Before Isaac tried to stand and run, Fabian whipped his hand onto Isaac's wrist and smashed it onto the table.

◆ ◆ ◆

"SAMMY SAW YOU do it you *fercockte dreck*, you miserable shit. And you carried on doing it in front of me a minute ago."

Fabian picked up the arm and slammed it down again until Isaac released his fist and two dollar notes flew out of his grip. The rest of the crew were aghast. It was obvious they had no idea what had been going on.

Slugger opened the money box and took out all the notes using his free hand and crammed them into his jacket pocket.

"You've been caught with your fingers in the till, Isaac."

He picked up the wrist again and shoved it so that Isaac's fingers were resting on the edge of the tin and his other hand swooped in and slammed the box shut, trapping Isaac's fingers in the metal jaw between the tin's rim and the lid.

Isaac squealed with pain and Slugger stood up and leaned on the tin lid, crushing the fingers even more. Isaac screamed again and Ben put his palm over Isaac's mouth. Abraham looked around, but the bar remained empty. Another push down, another scream and blood pulsed out of Isaac's hand. Slugger opened the box and a finger lay at its bottom, as red liquid continued to pour from Isaac's hand.

Slugger leaned in, almost nose-to-nose with Isaac.

"If I ever see you again, you're dead. Go to the cops? You're dead. Complain about me to a doctor? You're dead. Do you understand?"

Isaac nodded as Ben's hand was still clamped to his face.

"Let him go, Ben. Do you understand, Isaac?"

The lad nodded again.

"Look me in the eyes and tell me, boy, or you'll be floating down the East River by this evening."

"Yes, I understand."

Slugger rifled through Isaac's pockets and pulled out a few notes and two coins. He threw the latter back at Isaac, although they fell onto the floor.

"*Gay avek, meeskait.*"

Isaac didn't need to be told twice. He took the end of his finger from inside the tin and did his best to run out the building.

"CLEAR UP THE mess Isaac's made before someone comes in. Start with the floorboards." Fabian instructed. He moved to a table near the counter and left the boys to follow his instructions. This allowed them a chance to think through what had transpired and gave him an opportunity to calm down.

All the blood cleaned away from sight, the three lads sat down, and he ordered a beer for each of them.

"Let's reflect on what took place, shall we? Relying on one person to do the count was not a good plan. So from now on, everyone does their own counting and writes down the amount they're passing on. If you can't write, get someone to help you but you need to know how much money you're putting in. That way we can add up exactly who's brought in what and see if there is any shortfall sooner.

"More importantly, you guys will do that for yourselves and deal with any problems before word reaches me."

"Sure thing, boss."

"Don't worry, Ben. It took an experienced eye like Sammy's to spot Isaac's sharp fingers, so I don't blame you. That said, you are all responsible for me having to provide a hundred dollars of my money to cover Isaac's bad judgement."

All eyes looked downwards.

"There are four of us sat round this table and I think it's only fair that all four take the hit. Seem reasonable?"

As he'd just sheared off one of Isaac's fingers, this was the most sensible proposition the crew had heard since they arrived in the joint an hour and a half ago. They nodded.

"And that means each of you owe me twenty-five. Unless you want to, you don't have to pay me now; I'll take it out of your wages over the next couple of months. I'm no *schnorrer*."

Fabian finished his beer in silence and left them alone to discuss the afternoon's performance behind his back. Before returning to the tenement, he visited the Oregon's bar for a shot of scotch and an encounter with Sarah who received another ten-dollar gift.

JANUARY 1917

20

THE TEMPERATURE BARELY hovered above freezing that year so Fabian spent as much of his time indoors as he could manage. Despite his fake silk drawers, once the chill got inside him, it took him hours to shake it off.

After the Isaac excitement the previous summer, everything settled down into a calm pattern with the boys, although they were fast becoming men. In the previous six months, Fabian had added four more pools to his roster—with help from Sammy—and he made a tidy bundle just out of that.

Then there was his day job at the union. Ira had described it very accurately. Most mornings he hung round the third floor talking to the other reps and to Yonah who was always up for a chat. His afternoons were spent checking up on the pools and paying a visit to Sarah when he couldn't get a sight of Rebecca.

His parents mistook his attendance at home as a renewed interest in family life, but he only popped over there to sleep and hoping to see Rebecca. They had dated off and on ever since Coney Island, but his lifestyle and her father's attitude made an ongoing relationship out of the question. At least for now, he thought.

One morning he was yakking with Yonah about nothing at all when Ira popped his head around the door.

"We need to talk."

Fabian sprang up and followed Ira down to his office.

"What's the beef?"

"There's a storm brewing and we must sort it out before the lightning flashes and the thunder rolls overhead."

"Right. Tell me the problem and what I should do about it?"

"AUFFE is organizing a strike at a nearby factory which'll close production. This means some friends of ours will be out of pocket and we don't want that to happen."

"And…?"

121

"So you and some of your boys must convince the union to not down tools or convince the owner to capitulate to their demands. Honest truth—I don't care which it is as long as there's no strike."

"Right. And when are they walking out?"

"Day after tomorrow."

"And we've only known about this since when?"

"Hey, don't get all high-and-mighty with me. It is what it is, and we need to deal."

"Sure, I was just a bit surprised."

"Keep it to yourself next time. And don't tell Yonah about this. He's leakier than a sieve."

"Understood."

Ira gave Fabian details about the factory, the local union rep and the owner.

"You still here?"

"Not me, I'm already gone."

THE FACTORY STOOD at Tompkins and Stanton right by Pier 52. A great location if you received goods by boat and needed to shift product around the country. Fabian took Ben, Abraham and Dan with him for this initial meeting. They had toughened up since Isaac's departure and had reached the point where he not only trusted them but he could rely on them to use their brains and their brawn.

When they arrived on foot, Fabian and the crew searched for Samuel Liliental. All they had to do was ask the first machinist they saw, and she sent them off to Samuel's office. It was a converted broom cupboard with barely enough space for a chair and a side table with a box full of papers in the far corner instead of a filing cabinet.

"Samuel?"

"I am he."

"The name's Fabian and I'm from AUFFE headquarters."

"Well, well. To what do I owe this honor?"

"Thought we'd pay you a visit and see how things are going."

"I would say come into my office, but we wouldn't all fit."

Samuel chuckled and Fabian joined in. Not because he was funny but to get the guy onside.

"Anywhere else we could go for a private conversation then?"

"Sure thing. Come this way."

Samuel led them through a labyrinth of aisles between sewing machines, mainly operated by teenage girls, and other clothes manufacturing plant. They traipsed downstairs and upstairs until eventually Samuel opened a door and they stood on the roof.

"For private conversations only, gents."

Fabian looked east and saw an expanse of water with the low skyline of Brooklyn near the horizon. West and north was Manhattan in all its glory and south was water again and more of Brooklyn.

"Let's get to business then."

"Of course, Fabian. What's headquarters worried about now?"

"We understand you're planning industrial action soon."

"News travels slowly doesn't it?"

"Day after tomorrow?"

"Very slowly... Yes, we've had enough, and it's time to take a stand."

"What are you striking for?"

"More pay, safer conditions. The usual complaints of the downtrodden masses."

"No need to preach to me. I'm with the union."

"You're with head office, which is different. Remember?"

The man possessed some steel, Fabian noticed. Samuel knew what that meant and was street smart enough to know if head office sent people over, it wasn't going to be just for a social.

"Don't preach. That's all I said. My father's a tailor and has been looking for work since we arrived in this country... There's no need to tell me about how hard it is for an honest man to earn an honest day's wage. How much more are you guys asking to put into your pay packet?"

"Two quarters a week. Amounts to a measly seventy dollars on the payroll but the old man won't listen to a thing about it."

"If you got the pay rise would that be enough to stop the strike?"

"Perhaps. See, when we are injured in this fleapit the old man won't even take us to a hospital."

"More gelt and better conditions. You want the Earth and the Moon, don't you?"

Fabian allowed a small laugh to leap out the side of his mouth, just to show there was no menace in mind. Yet.

"If you got the money, would that be enough to call off the strike? I mean, we could deal with the injuries later. We're not brushing them under the carpet. Just making it tomorrow's problem, not today's."

"Do you think you can deliver on the money? I've been negotiating for months and got nowhere."

"Appreciate that, Samuel. But let's say those of us from head office can be quite persuasive."

"If we get our money, we'll carry on working. If you don't, we're out. We're tired of being treated like a bunch of schlemiels."

Fabian nodded, and the crew followed him off the roof and back through the maze into the belly of the factory. On the first floor, to the right of the main door stood a reception desk and an office. When they arrived, they'd ignored the receptionist as Fabian had no desire to announce his arrival. Now was different.

"HI THERE. I don't have an appointment, but I'd like to see Jacob Krein."

"May I ask who's asking for him?"

"You surely can. I'm from AUFFE head office and hope to discuss an urgent matter with him. He'll want to talk to me for certain."

The receptionist popped her head around Krein's door and, after some discussion, she invited them in.

"Sit down, gentlemen."

"Thank you, Mr Krein. Don't mind if I call you Jacob, do you? You can call me Fabian."

"You said you were from AUFFE. Are you here about the strike?"

"Well, we're here to help you prevent it happening."

"But you are from the union, right? Aren't you backing your guys?"

"That's why we are here to meet with you. Discussions between you and Samuel have not borne fruit."

"He wants everything now and with no concessions from any of the workers."

"It's one perspective certainly. I don't intend to review the past conversations you've been having. They are of no concern to me. Instead I want to focus on the future."

"Right? How's that then?"

"Jacob, the future holds two distinct paths, as I see it. One path involves the factory ceasing output and then the place gets closed down and you lose everything you've spent your life working towards. The second path is different. Here you make a small contribution to the employees' emoluments and everybody is happy."

"Not quite everyone. I end up spending more money and get nothing for it."

"Apart from boosted morale from your workers."

"They can boost their morale outside the factory gates. You're offering me the same bull as Liliental."

"I'm sorry. I don't think you have enough detail to help you understand the scenarios well enough. With the first path, I said the business closed down, did I not?"

"Yes you did."

"But I didn't mention why the factory collapsed?"

"No..."

"The factory had to close because you were indisposed."

"Huh?"

"You see, you did not take out the necessary insurance."

"Insurance? What insurance?"

"Club-and-throat insurance."

"Listen, I pay protection. Don't you try to muscle in on something that's already in place. You'll get your throat cut."

"Sound advice, Jacob. You should hear yourself. I am very aware of the protection money you currently pay. If I was not, we wouldn't be having this conversation. But I can tell you that unless you supply Samuel with what he's asking, you will need club-and-throat insurance from me.

"These fellows sat in your plush office are a dab hand with a club. And if they don't persuade you to change your tune then I'll come along and slice your throat open from ear to ear. If you haven't come across my name before, ask around. Plenty of people know me and my deeds."

ABRAHAM GIGGLED SLIGHTLY and Fabian threw him an evil glance. Ben nudged him and he stopped immediately.

"The insurance will cost you a hundred dollars a week, but you will be perfectly safe. Alternatively, you can choose the second path and pay the workers here half a dollar a week more. The first path costs you more and puts your life in danger. Option two is cheaper and everyone carries on like nothing has happened. The choice is yours."

"I told you I already pay protection and I will not pay any more. Not to the likes of you."

Fabian stared into Krein's beady eyes, not releasing his view for four seconds.

"Jacob, you must remember I work for the people who protect your business from harm. I am authorized to make you this offer so we can stop the strike. You have until the end of tomorrow to reach a decision.

"Ask around about me. I want you to know I do not make a good enemy. If the cost of the pay rise is a problem, then you could take out a loan from me with excellent terms."

"Get out of here!"

Fabian stood up and headed for the door, followed by his crew.

"Until tomorrow night. Then your current level of protection won't be enough to keep you safe. Remember that."

The following afternoon, Fabian was sat in the Forsyth and Nathan had delivered a coffee to his table. Krein entered and scuttled straight to the bar. Nathan pointed to Fabian and the factory owner scurried over, fedora in hand.

"Hello. Good to see you."

Krein nodded and squeezed his hat harder.

"Sit down, Jacob."

He sat and fidgeted.

"Coffee? Tea? Something stronger?"

"No thank you. Um… a coffee would be much appreciated. If you don't mind?"

"Why should I mind? Nathan, another coffee here!"

The extra volume in Fabian's voice made Jacob quiver.

"So have you used the moments since we met wisely?"

"I did as you suggested and you sure are well known. I spend too much time holed up in my business, I suppose."

"Not to worry, Jacob. The good thing is that you picked up testimony about me."

"I certainly have the measure of you. And I'd like to apologize for my brusque manner yesterday. If I had known who was in my office, it would have been a very different conversation, I can assure you of that."

"You knew what you knew. And now you know. That's all good."

Nathan arrived with the coffee and Jacob piled sugar into it. Although his hand was shaking, he got the cup to his lips and sipped twice from the thick brew. Fabian allowed him the time to calm down enough to carry on the conversation.

"And?"

21

"WELL, FABIAN. I'VE given them girls a pay rise. Fifty cents a week."

"That's very generous of you. On behalf of Samuel, the workers and the union, I thank you for your kindness. This won't be forgotten. Not by me anyway."

"Don't mention it. I'm just trying to get by, weathering the storm against the rocks of financial ruin."

"You are a very fine captain, Jacob."

"Thank you."

Jacob sipped at his coffee and Fabian allowed him to do this in silence. Then Jacob's head perked up.

"Oh, I almost forgot. Liliental mentioned your father was involved in the schmatta business."

"This is true."

"Well, I have a position free for him if he needs it. Liliental said he was having difficulty finding employment."

"How very kind of you to offer. I'm sure you'll be very fair with whatever job you have available."

"I'll be generous all right."

Jacob grinned, knowing the last thing he was going to do was stiff Fabian's father.

"Is there anything more I can help you with, Jacob?"

"No, that's all I came over to speak to you about."

They shook hands on both deals and Krein left, uncrumpling his hat as he departed from Fabian's sight.

His primary concern was to let Ira see everything was fine; Samuel could wait. Fabian took a brisk walk the few blocks to Waxey's and up to the second floor to find Ira.

"That matter you asked me to look into?"

"Yes?"

"All taken care of."

Fabian was being circumspect as Ira had company—a guy Fabian didn't recognize.

"Excellent news. Thanks for wrestling that one to the ground. Any trouble?"

"None. Simple art of persuasion—and understanding what motivates people."

"The right motivation helps tremendously."

"Didn't want to interrupt you but good news is worth hearing firsthand."

"Don't worry about it—and I'm glad you popped by."

Now the conversation was ebbing away, Fabian had a chance to take a peek at the stranger. He wore a three-piece suit with a tie and matching kerchief in his breast jacket pocket. Some well-to-do fella for sure.

"CHARLIE, LET ME introduce you to Fabian."

They shook hands, although Charlie didn't get out of his chair.

"Charlie Murphy is one of our best customers, Fabian."

"Yes, sir."

"Ira, leave the boy alone. Fabian, good to meet you and I wish you well."

Fabian thought he recognized the name, just about. Charles Murphy was something to do with Tammany Hall and was in the papers as a social reformer. But the tenements were still liberally splattered around the Bowery and ordinary people like his parents and siblings were desperately trying to scratch a living out of nothing. So Fabian was none too impressed with the guy.

The gray-haired man offered Fabian a kindly smile but zip for his family, nothing for the folk who lived round here. And what would Ira be doing hobnobbing with the likes of Murphy, the Democrat heavy.

From what Fabian had heard Sammy and the others say, Waxey and Ira had been cigarette paper close with Tammany all their lives. Doing favors on election days and helping to stuff ballet boxes. In return, the cops kept off their backs and everyone was taken care of. Tribute didn't stop at Waxey Gordon—the chain traveled much higher than him—and he was a god in the Bowery.

There were times when they'd all be sharing a beer and Waxey would reminisce about when the Mustachio Petes ran the Bowery. These old fellas with facial hair worthy of note were tight with Tammany and did their bidding. The way Waxey and Ira told it, they weren't in Tammany's pocket like the old guard but from where Fabian stood, there wasn't much difference between any of them.

Waxey ensured Fabian earned a good living doing what he did best. No doubt about that. But he left cash on the table because he was comfortable where he was. If they pushed further out from the Bowery—in any direction really—the amount of money they'd earn and the sheer quantity of power they'd derive from that capital would far outweigh the short-term pain of gaining new territory. But Waxey and Ira wanted a quiet life and nothing more.

THAT WASN'T THE only way Waxey behaved the same as the Mustachio Petes. These old Italians always kept to their own and created a closed shop where no-one else could break in. Both Waxey and Ira were born in the US and, even though they had welcomed Fabian with open arms, they still thought of him as a foreigner. They spoke the same Yiddish language, they were born into the same tribe, but he was from the old country and they were born in the land of the free. Fabian could never escape from that and he understood he would never get into their inner circle.

Fabian said his goodbyes to Ira and Murphy and left to make sure he was home in time for the Friday night meal. He might be king dog on the streets but there was no way he was going to incur the wrath of his mother and be late tonight.

He was so focused on the job at hand, Fabian forgot to turn his head to glimpse Rebecca as he rushed up the stairs to the Cohen residence.

"Hi, Ma! Hi, Pa."

"Alex. You arrived at just the right time."

They broke bread, lit candles and prayed during the meal. Once they reached the end of the religious proceedings, Fabian spoke, "Papa, I met someone who has a job to offer you."

"Oh really? Who is this person with magical work for me?"

"His name is Jacob Krein, and he owns a schmatta factory near Pier 51."

"And what does he want with me?"

"I mentioned you were a tailor, and he said he was looking for good men like you to sew for him. I don't have all the details but go over on Monday and speak with him."

"Moishe, what harm can it do? Your boy might have found you a job."

"My boy! Has it come to this that a son finds work for his father?"

"*Zey shtil.* It sounds a great opportunity. Alex, it is a great opportunity, right?"

"Yes, Mama. Jacob will look after Pa, I'm sure. Treat him well and the income will be decent. I didn't ask exactly how much because I thought that should be left for the two men to sort out privately."

"See Moishe. You negotiate your salary. Alex has just made the introduction."

"That's right, Ma. I made the introduction. And Jacob is keen to take you on, Pa."

"How do you know this?"

"Because Jacob said it to me. He volunteered the question. I didn't ask him at all. Bolt from the blue."

Moishe was silent a while, ruminating on how a factory owner might have bumped into his son and what kind of deep water he would be in if he accepted the job. As his features softened, Alex could tell his father realized this was the first real job offer he'd received since the family arrived in the country. Beggars can't be choosers.

"OF COURSE, I'LL see this fellow, Krein. My son has found me an opportunity. Who knows? In a year I could run this factory of his."

"Way to go, Pa!"

"We should celebrate, Moishe. How about getting the good wine out?"

"Ruth, let's not put the cart before the horse. If this chap isn't lying to our boy, we can drink a toast when I get my first pay packet."

She nodded and bowed her head slightly as her enthusiasm seeped out of her. Her husband was right. There was nothing quite like the bitter taste of disappointment and the Cohens had been sucking on that teat for far too long.

"And how's my little Esther?"

"Fine. I help Mother around the house and with the cleaning."

"You still taking in washing, Ma?"

"Why yes, dear."

"I thought the money I contribute would mean you'd have no need for that."

"Well dear, your pa and I keep anything left over from the rent and food for a rainy day."

Alex slapped his forehead loudly with the palm of his hand.

"You meshuggeners. You drive me crazy. Money is meant to make your lives easier. Mean you need to do less work."

"We know what money's for, lad. Don't get too big for your breeches."

"Pa. How wet does tomorrow have to be before you enjoy today?"

"Truth is, son, soon we'll have enough to move into a bigger place. One where your brother and sisters might even have their own rooms. And that's thanks to you and your contribution.

"We are grateful, but we want to spend the gelt the way we choose to— not how you'd necessarily like."

Alex was quiet for a spell knowing, however reluctantly, that his father was right. He had told them the money was a gift, and they had thanked him at the time and taken the cash on good faith that it hadn't been earned from any dirty business. They'd had enough of that back in the old country.

THE OTHER REASON he fell into silence was the slow dawning that if the Cohens moved, the opportunities to see Rebecca would reach near zero. Forget his money and the flavor of Sarah's ass, Rebecca was the only thing that really lit up his day.

"I understand. My apologies. A bigger place would be marvelous. Just be a shame to leave the neighborhood. You've grown roots here."

"Sure we have," said Ruth.

"But let's not pretend you've not got some interest in this building beyond the bricks and mortar."

Alex scrunched his face up at her.

"You forgetting the Grunbergs?"

He blushed and experienced a flutter in the pit of his stomach.

"You think we don't see what's going on? Of course we do. That Rebecca is a lovely young woman. Head bit in the clouds, but a pretty girl."

"She's a great dancer."

"That may be so but her parents want her to learn a trade so she can support her family. Not flutter about twisting around the rooms like a dizzy butterfly."

"But she is lovely."

"No doubt about it, dear... So why don't you do something if you are so smitten with the dancer?"

Alex gulped. How could he tell his mother he didn't think he was worthy of such a beautiful creature? That he was so used to looking at her from afar, he got tongue-tied on the rare occasion they were together?

"It's complicated..."

"No it's not. You've already been out with her and met her parents but she's fabulous, we're not good enough for her to walk down a flight of stairs and break bread with us?"

"It's not like that, Mama."

"Alex. I'm only teasing you. But seriously, all you have to do is make an effort. She's a great catch. If you do nothing about her, there'll be others who do."

"Others?"

"Not this instant. I'm saying she's a good person and if you don't show a proper interest then her parents will find someone who does. These might be modern times, but adults still need to sort out some things."

"Have you been talking to her mother and father?"

Ruth Cohen was reduced to silence as she mulled over an answer to Alex's question.

"There have been words spoken. Sounding out, you might say. Benjamin and Ora seem to like you and are happy if you two get together. But if an engagement isn't discussed soon, they'll look elsewhere for their darling daughter's future happiness."

With that, Ruth shoved the last piece of challah bread into the sauce and munched on it until there was nothing left in her mouth but the fond recollection of the flavors from her cooking.

The rest of the night, Alex was monosyllabic and retired to bed early, thinking through all the implications of his mother's words.

FEBRUARY 1917

22

NOBODY COULD REMEMBER a winter as cold as this one in New York. Ice was everywhere, and the snow was thick as a mattress on top of the sheet of slippery evil which had spread across the city in January and refused to leave.

Even the hoods stayed indoors as there was no money to be made on the streets. They waited for their customers in bars, cupping their hands around piping hot coffees laced with hard liquor. Fabian was the same. He holed up in the Forsyth waiting for reports from Ben on his numbers games north of Canal and from Sammy to cover the south side.

One or two afternoons a week, Fabian wrapped himself in an enormous coat, scarf and gloves and trudged through the snow to visit Sarah in the Oregon. The rooms had added blankets to their roster to accommodate the needs of the by-the-hour guests. Most times, he made the trip after eating a hearty lunch at home and stopping to stare at Rebecca's dance practice through the doorway of her apartment. She was fast growing into a beautiful woman from the pretty girl he'd first met two years before.

Despite the temperature, the money rolled in and Fabian was sitting back, taking stock before another push beyond Canal in the spring.

Sammy sauntered over and sat down, holding his own mug of coffee like a muffler.

"Hey, you. How's tricks?"

"Mighty fine, Sammy. Mighty fine. You?"

"Going all right, thanks."

"Good to hear."

"Fabian, I need to ask you a favor and I'm not sure how you will take it."

"Say and we'll both find out."

Sammy couldn't argue with the simplicity of Fabian's statement.

"I'm looking to break ground south of Canal and I'd like your help to do so."

"South of Canal?"

"Yep. As I said, I don't know how happy you're gonna be even hearing my question."

Fabian sat up in his chair, having slumped down with thoughts of Rebecca's dancing and Sarah's naked body.

"When you first agreed to help oversee some of my pools, I suggested this might happen, so I'm not surprised. What kind of assistance are you hoping for?"

"Well, I think I've found some likely opportunities, but I'd like your opinion if they're any good. And also, would be great to borrow some of your men for the takeover. Mine are reliable but dumb. Yours are more handy under pressure, if you see what I mean."

"Oh, I do. Thing is, I was planning on my own expansion in a month or two, so it really depends on where you're thinking of going. I can't go around helping you take a place over when I could run the joint for the sake of cracking two heads."

"I get that, Fabian. So I've come to you early. I don't want you to think I'm stepping on your toes, but I would like to do more dancing. South of the Canal, that is."

"And have you spoken with Waxey about this?"

"Yes. He's happy provided you're happy."

FABIAN WAS PLEASED he'd been offered some respect by Waxey, although he figured the man was more concerned with preventing an internecine war between two of his captains.

"Then let's talk things through. I'm sure we can reach an accommodation."

The rest of the afternoon and the following morning, the two stretched their legs along the blocks the other side of Canal. Each time Fabian used his usual ploy of leaning against a corner of a building at a nearby alleyway to form a judgement. At first blush, all the locations found by Sammy appeared to be thriving concerns. If they were able to do business at this temperature, then they'd go gangbusters in the summer. Not a single one was on Fabian's shortlist for his spring offensive.

Back at the Forsyth, they sat down, and Fabian explained his thoughts.

"Sammy, an excellent selection. Congratulations on some good finds."

"Thank you."

"I have no problem helping with manpower but for a small difficulty."

"What's that, Fabian?"

"Every single one of those plump pools are on my list for taking over too."

Sammy's eyes hung heavy with disappointment and his shoulders sagged.

"But we can work something out. I don't wish to crush your American spirit. This country was built on enterprise, so I'm told."

"That and slavery."

"Whatever. I don't wish to stifle you."

"What are you suggesting?"

"This is my current idea. If I supply the people for the takeover and provide fellas to look after the pools once we're running them then you repeat what you've done for me and deliver the oversight and management. Over time, my boys move on and your guys run things for you."

"Sounds good so far."

Fabian smiled. He saw Sammy was waiting for the catch.

"But as I will lose out—I was planning for these places to be all mine until yesterday—we need to agree a fair share of the profits."

Sammy gulped because he realized the sting in the tail was about to land on his neck.

"When I asked you to help me, we had a fifty-fifty split of the profit, but on this occasion, you're coming to me seeking my help. This means I need a slightly richer stake, at least for the first two years. If I don't cooperate, I'll send my own men in and grab me one hundred percent of the opportunity."

"Right. And how much do you want your end to be?"

"Sixty percent, but only in the first two years. Then we can drop it down to our standard equal split deal."

"I see. You were going to go for them, for sure?"

"Yep. They are the juiciest of the low-hanging fruit."

"And have you got any wiggle room on the divide?"

"I could turn it to seventy-thirty if you prefer."

Fabian winked at him.

"Then I'll take the sixty-forty split and we're in business."

"Done."

And with a handshake, Fabian and Sammy agreed to gouge their way even further into the dark lands south of Canal.

THE FOLLOWING SATURDAY morning Fabian walked from the Forsyth to his parents' apartment. A block and a half away from his destination, he stopped for a second as he strolled past the local *shul* or synagogue. The service must have ended shortly before because a crowd of people spewed out of the front entrance.

As was the custom, the men wore long coats—not just because of the harsh winter—and the women were their *Shabbos* best. Shoes were polished and hair had been brushed accordingly. Among the sea of adults and children, one face stood out from the throng: Rebecca. Fabian's heart stopped beating for a second as he gazed on the rapture of her features. His focus was so intense. It was like the ending of a film: all black with a solitary circle of light casting attention to the single point of focus—Rebecca.

Then the spectacle playing in his mind drew further out and Fabian noticed her parents, her siblings and some guy who was at the heart of the family picture. That wasn't right. Who was this fella and what was he doing there?

With nothing else on his to-do list, Fabian watched as the group chatted to other members of the congregation until the cold got inside their bones a little too much and they said their goodbyes to head for home. Rebecca's arm was draped over this newcomer's and they seemed perfectly comfortable with each other. Fabian saw them laugh together, sharing a joke with her parents. He was wonderfully ensconced in the Grunberg circle to Fabian's annoyance.

They sauntered along the sidewalks until they got back to the corner of Grande and Suffolk—and home. Fabian carried on watching from afar, torn between rushing up to them to ask what was going on and staying put and witnessing the affair from two hundred feet away. No-one noticed his presence; they were all too caught up in their own world to bother to spot him on the other side of the street.

When they all strolled into the tenement block, Fabian had to decide between following them in or going on his merry way and accepting his fate. He would visit his parents for lunch. He waited ten-twenty-thirty seconds before making his move and entering the building. That way, the Grunbergs plus one would have enough time to get into their rooms and he could avoid bumping into them on the stairwell.

He trudged up the steps, his feet heavy on the wooden flooring. As he walked past the Grunberg apartment, he turned his head to peer into their place and saw what he feared the most. The new fella was sat next to Rebecca at the lunch table and they were giggling away while her mother served up the lunchtime meal.

Fabian noticed Rebecca turn towards their open door but he couldn't bring himself to catch her glance, so he continued to walk along the stairwell and up into his parents' apartment.

23

"HI, MAMA!"

"Alex! What a pleasant surprise."

"I was in the neighborhood, so I dropped by."

"Well, that's just lovely."

"Is there room at the table for an extra mouth?"

"For you, always, dear."

His siblings shuffled along, and Mama picked up a spare chair for him to use. Halfway through the meal, Alex interrupted the flow of conversation for his own ends.

"Have you heard how the Grunbergs are getting on?"

"They're doing well, so's I know."

A smirk from mama.

"Any reason you ask?"

"No. Have you seen Rebecca recently?"

"Not for a while but I was talking with her mother just the other day."

"Oh? And what was she saying?"

"Rebecca still wants to be a dancer some time but is thinking about becoming a teacher first. That way she can teach dance and earn money while she tries to break into show business."

"Sounds like a sensible plan. Do her parents prefer that idea?"

"Yes, but they'd rather she just did more sewing and took in more washing. Education is a marvelous thing, but it pays tomorrow's bills, not today's."

"I know, Mama."

"When was the last time you saw Rebecca yourself?"

"Not for a few weeks."

"Probably longer than that, I'd say. Mrs Grunberg told me she hasn't seen you for ages."

"Has been a while, for sure. I've had business to attend to, and it's been so cold out."

"Cold? Yes. But you've left it so long Rebecca has got herself a suitor. Or rather, her parents have found her a beau, more's the point."

"What do you know about him?"

"Why are you so interested in that piece of *longe lokshen*?"

Thin streak of piss: you said it Mama, Alex mused.

"No particular reason…"

"He's tall and thin and the son of a doctor. The family are quite refined—or at least they used to be before they came over to America, adjusting to life here has been tough for them."

"Been hard for us all."

"Well, they live in the block next door, just there."

Mama pointed north to the other side of their living room wall.

"Conveniently close then."

"Yes. They see each other quite a bit, so Ora was saying. He's over two or three times a week and she spends time at his place. Under the watchful eye of the doctor."

Ruth winked at Alex and his father chuckled.

"You didn't get far enough to need to be watched, my boy, now did you?"

Alex glared at the man, but he was right. The four dates had each been day trips, but he had never got more than the odd kiss from her. There was never a time he got a hand on her chest or a thigh.

"I ALWAYS BEHAVED like a gentleman, Father."

Moishe snickered again, only deeper and louder.

"I'm sorry to hear that, lad."

"Moishe! Don't talk that way. Not on Shabbos."

More chuckling and a wink from Alex to his father showed they both knew what they meant. A rare shared joke between the two men, which settled down into muffled giggles and reduced to silence after a minute.

"Do you reckon you missed the boat with that one?"

"I hope not, Mama, but it's not looking good."

"Not at all. Any idea how you will convince her parents to put you back in their good books and shift out this parvenu?"

"There are two options I can see. I need to figure out which one's best."

"Always scheming. That's my boy!"

He nodded at his father but didn't want to view this as scheming. He just wanted Rebecca and couldn't deal with the idea of someone else enjoying her company. Sat immediately beneath him as he chewed on his lokshen pudding, giggling with Rebecca when she could laugh with Alex.

Truth was he had no clue what to do. If her parents had welcomed the guy into their home, there was no chance they'd boot him out in preference to Alex. Son of a doctor compared to the son of an almost unemployed tailor. What's to choose?

These thoughts permeated his mind all the way through the weekend and into Monday and Tuesday. He was desperate to square the circle but anything he might do would drive her away from him. He was paralyzed with indecision for the first time in his life.

The quandary continued in his mind as he was slamming a debtor's head against a brick wall. So focused on the problem of Rebecca, Abraham put a hand on his shoulder.

"Hey, Slugger. We need him conscious so he can agree to more payments."

Slugger looked down and saw the scraped and bloody mess gripped in his fingers.

"Sure thing, Abraham."

He leaned into the bloody face in his grip until he could smell the blood.

"Do we have an understanding now? You going to make me a payment."

The poor sap dug deep into his pockets and fished out two dollars. Among spit and blood he claimed this was all he had on him.

"We'll be back at the end of the week and you'd better have more for us or you'll get more of this treatment."

The fella stumbled away, blood dribbling out of his mouth, coughing as he fled.

Fabian checked out his hands—there were cuts on the knuckles. A clear sign he hadn't been concentrating at the work at hand. He'd need to lay off any rough stuff for a day or two otherwise the wounds would open up. Should have worn his knuckledusters. So unusual he had not—almost like his mind was focused on other matters. Lust for Rebecca would get him hurt if he wasn't careful.

SINCE HEARING FROM his mama about Rebecca, Fabian found he was grinding his teeth more and that she was becoming something of a preoccupation, more so than in the past.

The next time he paid a call on a customer who was behind with payments, Slugger showed how one teenage boy could throw a grown man six feet in the air before he'd land on his back with a bone defying crunch. Slugger kicked him in the kidneys two, three times before Dan pulled him off.

"Jack gets the message, boss. Right?"

The crumpled heap on the floor grunted acceptance, although he didn't look as though he was intending getting up any time soon.

"Get the man a glass of water!"

Back at the Forsyth, Sammy broke bread with him on Friday.

"I hear you're proving yourself to be quite assertive nowadays."

"Can't have punters reckoning I'm a soft touch."

"No one thinks that of you, Slugger."

Fabian winced at the use of that epithet.

"I don't like people calling me that."

"Yeah, but you really are earning the nickname, aren't you?"

"Don't see that's true."

"Word on the street is you've turned into a hard nut lunatic. You prefer to kick a guy in the guts rather than collect the shekels and move on."

"And what do the kids on the street say?"

"Plenty. They're not always right, but the streets have eyes and ears. And mouths that pass on gossip to those who'll listen—like Waxey."

A grinding of molars.

"He's asked me to have a word with you."

"And this is the word?"

"He's concerned about you. Wants to check whether everything is fine with you and yours."

"Sammy, it's all good, but there's some things on my mind I can't shake off too easily."

"Anything I can do to help?"

Fabian spat out a laugh.

"It's personal, not business. So thanks for the offer but I doubt it."

"Women, booze or gambling?"

"Huh?"

"Always one of those three."

"Women, as you ask."

"Too much or too little?"

Fabian laughed and squinted at Sammy, unsure if the fella was poking his nose too closely into his private business.

"Very little as it happens."

"Extremely little of a particular broad, I'm guessing, because with your wallet, you can get any dame in town. Am I right?"

"Almost any woman and that's the problem. There's only one woman in the whole city I can't get…"

"…and she's the one you want."

Now it was Sammy's turn to laugh and Fabian joined in with a quieter snigger.

"That's life, sure it is. Man, you are caught, hook, line and sinker. I don't suppose some jewelry, a bunch of flowers and a swanky meal would do the job?"

"Blooms? No. Meal? Done that. No. Jewelry? There's only one piece of metal would make her happy—and her parents too."

"Let me guess. Would it be a plain gold ring by any chance?"

"You got it."

"And she's worth it?"

"That's the crazy thing. I can't be certain. We've spent time together for sure, but not those kinds of moments."

"Holy moly. You mean you've not..."

"Don't go there."

"Have I met her?"

"Not that I'm aware, but she is a neighborhood girl."

"Good clean young lady for a fine upstanding young man."

"Yep."

"If you're that sure, why not just ask her father for permission to marry her?"

"I'm too late."

"Does she have an engagement ring on her finger?"

"No."

"Then you're not too late."

Sammy shrugged. There wasn't much more he could do for Fabian. Good news was he could tell Waxey business was fine and there was nothing to worry about.

MARCH 1917

24

THE TEMPERATURE ROSE when March arrived, the rain replacing snow as the main meteorological menace. By the time you arrived at your destination, you were soaked through. The dampness on Fabian's body translated as a dark growl inside his mind. Every night he walked up the tenement stairs he imagined seeing Rebecca nestling with her fella on the apartment sofa. He'd shudder and carry on up to his room.

Perhaps all would be better if his family vacated the place and then he'd be removed from the constant reminders of Rebecca's existence. Maybe that's what he needed to get over her.

Try as he might, he could not bring himself to instigate that conversation with his parents and, even though they were saving hard with his money, they showed no sign themselves of wanting to move. In fact, moving was never mentioned again that Fabian noticed. If not for a bigger apartment then what were they saving for? The money was theirs to do with as they saw fit. He'd agreed that already and knew he needed to believe it. That was much harder to do, but he tried his best.

Despite all these jumbled up thoughts flying around his brain, Fabian kept a tight lid on all his business interests. Some argued he held the reins a little too short. If anyone was the least bit out of line, they'd get a whipping from the man. And that was inside his crew.

Any stranger late with a payment or who crossed him in the street received far worse. Waxey was right to be concerned and Sammy continued his watchful eye over Fabian. From a distance.

St Patrick's Day would have represented the usual turnout of Irish men on the streets of New York, but it was canceled in the morning because of a horrendous storm that washed Manhattan out. Angry Irishmen took to every bar they could find to console themselves at the lack of parade on the one hundred and fiftieth anniversary of the New York march. They even found themselves in the Bowery, mixing in with the Jewish ghetto occupants.

Two fellas landed in the Forsyth that Saturday afternoon, went up to the bar and ordered a beer each. Fabian ignored them although he noticed they were strangers with their weird accents, unusual colored hair and English language. Live and let live, he thought.

Four rounds later and the gents were louder and rowdier. They began to sing their songs to boost their sagging morale. Again, Fabian tried to ignore them as they were doing no real harm. The bar had filled up with the post-lunch trade and was fair heaving by the time the two had consumed a further three drinks each. They were loaded and singing at the top of their lungs.

◆ ◆ ◆

FABIAN GAVE UP his table to the sheer volume of humans pressed into the first floor and considered getting drenched to find solace with Sarah. As he made his way through the assembled masses to the door, he detoured to the counter to settle up with Nathan.

After five long minutes, he got his elbows to lean on the wooden surface right next to the two Irishmen. They stood with their backs to the bar itself, arm in arm, singing and gesticulating with their free hands, while also holding their beer glasses.

Fabian accepted their jollity for what it was: a pair of drunks having fun on a damp Saturday afternoon. But while he waited to speak with Nathan, he noticed a few drops of brew landing on his shoulder. He understood this was an accidental spill, but he still wasn't happy about getting wet while he was indoors. He took a deep breath and quietly, but assertively, held the nearest arm and told them to quieten down a little.

The one whose arm he had clasped, looked down at him, peering because his inebriated eyes found it hard to focus and also because the fellow had never heard anyone speak Yiddish before and had no clue what Fabian had said.

These two factors conspired poorly because the guy laughed and carried on his exuberant singing and swaying, causing Fabian the first real sense of annoyance. Hadn't the fella heard him ask for space and for them to quieten down? Who did they think they were ignoring him like that?

Nathan spotted him waiting patiently and wended his way over.

"Want another, Fabian."

"No thanks. Let's just settle up. It's too boisterous for me round here."

"You and me both. Love getting the money in, but I need a rest. I've been pulling chugs of beer all day long."

"Well, when you get the chance let me know how much I owe you."

"Give me a minute. Usually it's in my head but today's plain crazy."

As Nathan turned away to go to the cash register, Fabian felt an elbow slam into the small of his back, forcing him to stagger and his sternum to hit the counter. Thunk.

Fabian whipped round. The only culprit was the enormous Irishman swaying next to him. Everyone else was talking or queuing at the bar trying to get a drink. Anger overwhelmed him and he pushed the fella back.

"Watch what you're doing. I've told you once already. Have your fun but don't cross the line and push me around."

The force sent the fella straight to the ground because he was none too steady on his feet before Fabian had lunged at him. His friend was not happy and squared off against Fabian. The rest of the world ignored the man on the floor—people got drunk and hit the dirt in a Bowery bar. That was normal. And two guys having a disagreement was also perfectly natural, so no-one even gave them the space to have a proper set-to.

Instead, Fabian did the only thing that felt natural to him at that moment. In that place. He pulled out a shiv and stabbed the guy in the stomach. Yanked the blade out and then plugged him again, this time slicing from left to right. The guy fell to his knees and then hit the floor. Fabian looked each way but no-one was paying any attention. He took out five dollars and signaled to Nathan he was leaving it on the bar. The locals knew not to touch Fabian's money, and he left, placing the knife back in his pocket before he'd reached the door.

By the time he arrived at the Oregon, any blood had washed off his hands and out of his clothing. Sarah took one look at the bedraggled mess before her and dragged him upstairs to dry out. She didn't understand why he cried so.

APRIL 1917

25

THOUGHTS OF REBECCA'S curves and her holding hands and laughing with that guy permeated Alex's mind. The images stayed in front of his eyelids before he went to sleep and were the first thing he saw in the dawn. If he did nothing, he would regret his inaction for the rest of his life. So Alex hatched himself a plan.

He waited one Tuesday morning, leaving home half an hour later than normal. This would give everyone ample time to vacate the apartments—the Cohens and the Grunbergs. Alex sauntered down the stairs until he reached Rebecca's and stopped, leaning on the doorjamb. Sure enough, Rebecca stood by the dining table, holding onto a chair to practice her ballet positions. Over and over again. First position, second position—and repeat.

Alex enjoyed the view, transfixed by the movement of her body, the swoosh of her legs and the way he imagined her breasts wiggled under her dress. Pure unimpeachable pleasure.

After nearly five minutes, Rebecca stopped and turned round to see him staring at her.

"Enjoying the show?"

"Sure am. It's great watching you practice. You have such poise, such grace. I could watch you all day."

"Thanks for saying so, but no-one else agrees with you."

"How so?"

"Well, there are my parents to begin with. My family next. Even Amos."

"Amos?"

"Oh, he's just a fella I've been spending time with recently."

"I see. Just a fella?"

"Yeah… kinda."

Rebecca stared at the floorboards for a second and then looked back up.

"Alex, you must have a strong idea how I feel about us, but you only visit once in a while. What's a girl to do?"

"Wait longer?"

Rebecca laughed and walked towards him, placing a hand on his arm briefly.

"Longer? I've known you forever, Alex Cohen. My parents are talking about marriage and if I could see we had a chance then I'd fight for us. But…"

"I blow hot and cold, don't I?"

"Yes, you do. When we were going out, I thought you were the one. You were so attentive and gentle and kind. Then I'd not hear anything from you for months. I can't be like that. And my parents were tearing themselves apart watching me try to live vicariously through stories of your misdeeds."

"Misdeeds?"

"What people say about you. Those tales can't all be made up by gossips."

Alex sighed slightly. He'd clung to the belief that he had kept his work and his personal life separate this time. In the old country, he had failed at this with everyone knowing his business—even when it got bloody and unpleasant.

HERE, AT LEAST, he'd thought, the two worlds had no overlap. But this was a demarcation existing only in his head. When he left the tenement in the morning, he strode down the same streets whether it was to buy a bagel for his mother or to collect unpaid interest for Ira and the crew.

"Why not give me one last chance? I believe in you and in us. Only trouble is I've not been any good at showing you."

"I don't think so. We've got past last chances, I reckon. Another time, another place and we'd be together. But my parents are keen for me to get engaged to this son of a doctor. He's a good catch."

"Is that what you want? To nab a good catch and settle down? What about your dreams? What about your dance troupe?"

"As Mama has told me innumerable times, the dancing can wait. I need to start my adult life."

Alex grimaced at these words. He recognized the sound of his mother's voice in the turn of phrase and the cold attitude behind the scenes. Whatever happens, the family must create itself another generation of timid followers. But he'd seen times were tough and had found a way to carve his path through the treacle of existence. Sounded as though she was going to be sucked away from her hopes and squished into a box to keep her people happy—and some other family too.

"You could start your adult life with me."

Rebecca reached out and held his hands so they stood opposite each other, real close.

"Alex. You have faith in me, but Amos is safe and offers me a certain financial future. He will be a good provider for our children."

"Babies?" Alex whistled.

"Yes, for our children. I need to reflect beyond my own needs and focus on the next generation."

"Before another bunch of kids turn up, we must live our lives a little."

"You're wrong, Alex. It's different for girls. We have to behave differently about children in ways men do not."

"If Amos found someone else, would you consider settling down with me instead?"

"To be honest, we'd have a wonderful time together, but I'd worry every night you were out at your... work."

"Rebecca, I manage a bunch of fellas who offer services to local folk who can't get help from elsewhere. No more and no less. I'm a businessman."

"Maybe I would consider it seriously but Amos is most definitely around so this is all hypothetical. It's not real and I don't want you to think this is anything more than that. You understand?"

"Don't worry. I've got no *loch in kop*. I exist in reality, not some fantasy world."

He bent down and pecked her on the forehead, and she held his chin and kissed him on the mouth.

"If only things had been different between us, my little boychick."

"I haven't given up hope just yet."

"That's my Alex."

Rebecca let go his hands and twirled round so her skirt touched his legs as she wandered back into the living room to continue practicing her positions. He stayed a moment or two and continued down the stairs and out into the spring day.

THURSDAY. ALEX ASKED around until he found where Amos's father worked. His boy would be helping out so he could get a better measure of the guy. Only a block east from his home, the *schmendrick* was tending to the needs of his flock. Or rather his father's flock.

"One day all these sick people will be yours," must have been said to Amos before now but Alex was more concerned to observe how the boy behaved rather than make judgements about his therapeutic abilities. Although quite how the runt was going to pay for his medical tuition beat Alex. The family must be minted, he surmised.

Without allowing that opinion to leave his brain, Alex stood outside the surgery and watched. Amos's training was so complete, his responsibility was to help the illiterate patrons fill out their forms before they got aid from his father. Unqualified waste of space.

This lump of half-nothing was a good catch, according to the Grunbergs and Rebecca's mama should know, right? Meantime, Alex stared from across the street, leaning on the corner of a building—his favorite pose. The morning carried on in the same dull vein until he couldn't take it anymore and walked away to grab some lunch.

When he returned around two, the surgery was still packed to the gunnels with men, women and children desperate for attention. By the cacophony of coughs, sneezes and wheezes, the majority had lung infections. This wasn't a surgery for a medical emergency; this was a place where a family doctor could make a living.

Now Alex understood why Amos made a good catch. This was a guaranteed income for the rest of his natural life. All the boy needed to do was to have a prescription pad and some knowledge of anatomy and he truly was set forever. A career of coughs and flu. If Alex was running the joint, he'd open it up in the evening to tend to the needs of the local professional floozies too. You could double your income for only an hour or two's extra work a night.

Alex followed Amos home after the surgery closed as he sauntered the one-and-a-half blocks north. As he walked along, the lad kept his hands in his pants pockets and whistled to himself a jaunty tune. He was content in his world and Alex hankered after the certainty Amos luxuriated in. The boy knew the color of his future work and, no doubt once he'd started his medical training, he had his prospective wife too. Alex was jealous of this schmendrick.

THE NEXT DAY, Alex took a break from trailing Amos to maintain a firm grip on his own business activities but by one in the afternoon, Alex stood watching the surgery and again followed Amos home. As it was Friday, the place shut earlier and both he and his father made their way home—at a faster pace than the previous night.

Weekends were family time and Alex had no desire to witness Amos in the bosom of his family, especially as this would also involve watching him so close to the bosom of Rebecca too.

The next week, he returned to stalking the boy until by Wednesday, he felt he knew the longe lokshen's movements well enough. That evening, Amos took the same path home as he always did. Same tune whistling past his lips. Alex caught up with him after he'd turned the corner away from the surgery. He was one pace behind Amos and a small alleyway loomed ahead of them, just to the left of their sidewalk.

Once the entrance appeared, Alex yanked Amos by the back of his collar and swung him round into the dark alley, slamming him into the nearest wall.

"What the...?"

"Listen to me!"

"What…"

Alex slapped Amos on the cheek to get his attention. This sort of thing never happened to him, so he was completely disoriented.

"Listen carefully."

"I don't…"

Another slap.

"Don't think or speak. What you need to do is close your mouth and open up your ears."

The boy shivered with fear.

"Look at me, Amos!"

His eyes raised up slightly to focus on Slugger's entire face and not on his throat.

"Word around town is that you're spending time at the Grunberg residence. Is that correct?"

Amos squinted as though trying to remember or plain understand the words barked at him by Slugger. Then he nodded.

"Speak to me. Is it true?"

"Yes."

"Do you like working with your father at the surgery?"

A second quizzical stare. Slugger grabbed both shoulders and slammed Amos against the wall again.

"Answer me!"

"Yes, I do."

"If you want to continue to enjoy your life then you need to do one small thing else your world will come crashing down."

Yet another confused expression.

"What?"

"You need to stop seeing Rebecca Grunberg. Don't see her, don't speak with her. She is dead to you. Understand?"

"But why?"

Slugger took in an enormous breath. He was trying his best to keep his temper under control and warn the boy off. Nothing more.

"Because I'm giving you a healthy warning. You will not remain well if you see more of Rebecca."

Slugger glared, hoping to impress on Amos the importance of his words through this single gaze.

"You can't tell me who I can see and who I can't. Our families are friends. We spend time together. What you're asking of me is impossible. Besides, we will get married someday. It's all been decided."

Slugger gritted his teeth as a wave of anger burst from his belly and up through his chest. He clenched a fist and planted a blow into Amos's solar plexus. The boy crumpled to the floor holding his stomach, wheezing.

"You need to stop seeing Rebecca. Whatever has occurred in the past or plans you may have for the future are now void. Understand?"

The boy carried on attempting to regain his breath.

"But…"

Slugger kicked him in the kidneys. Two short taps. Enough to hurt, not enough to maim.

"But nothing. Do you understand?"

"I don't…"

Slugger kicked him between the legs. Amos grabbed his crotch and began to cry. Slugger adjusted the scarf he'd placed over his face a moment before he swung Amos into the alleyway.

"Listen, fella. You have two options. Agree to what I am saying, or I'll take a knife out and cut you into ribbons."

Amos's eyes widened as the tears continued to splatter onto his cheeks. Twenty seconds later, he nodded.

"Talk to me, boy. Do you agree?"

"Yes, I do."

"Good decision, little man. You don't know who I am but I sure as hell know you. If I hear you've visited Rebecca, spoken with her or even bumped into her on the street, I'll hunt you down and slit your throat from ear to ear. Do you understand?"

"Sure. Yes. No more Rebecca."

A stifled cry flopped out of Amos's mouth and Slugger let go of him and pushed him back onto the street. As soon as he'd done that, Alex ran in the opposite direction and turned the corner sharpish. There was no way Amos was going to have a chance to follow him. Scarf off, Alex took a circuitous route to the Forsyth where he downed two beers in quick succession.

"How long have I been here, Nathan?"

"You tell me, Fabian."

"At least an hour, I'd say. Wouldn't you?"

"Sure thing. Got here around five."

"Another beer and a vodka chaser."

"You got it."

26

SAMMY NOTICED SLUGGER'S mood change the following day. He had not been particularly upbeat the previous three weeks but now Fabian was in a dark place. Darker than anywhere he'd been before. There was no talking to him. All Sammy received was a nod or an occasional grunt. Nothing meaningful by response. He kept up appearances in front of his crew and was minimally civil with everyone—until he could switch off the fake smile and be himself.

He told his fellas to tell him sooner if they were having any problems with late payers. This gave him an opportunity to vent his anger about his life at the indebted patrons at his number pools. Factory owners were also in Fabian's line of fire. The union work was as sporadic as ever, but when Ira popped his head around the third-floor door, Fabian had to act—and without delay.

Benjamin Weinbaum owned a schmatta sweat shop at the sharp corner of First and East Houston. More bodies than you could count squeezed into an exceedingly small area with barely enough space to prevent the elbow of one sewer bumping into the arm of another.

The AUFFE believed Weinbaum was schtupping some of the women in his charge. If that wasn't bad enough, the union reckoned he was underpaying the ones he was banging. Some of the girls were only sixteen and seventeen years old but none of them were prepared to go to the police to make a formal complaint. Everyone understood: why would a nice Jewish girl want to admit to the *goyim* someone had raped her? The girls, their families and the union wanted justice. Ira explained the situation to Fabian who was dispatched to sort the matter out.

Slugger arrived at Weinbaum Tailoring Emporium and pushed his way into the reception area. Like every other building in town, the woman at the front desk acted as a good gatekeeper for the boss until Slugger broke the rules and barged through to the chief's office without knocking or asking permission. So much easier than making an appointment and coming back at the appropriate time and day, he found.

WEINBAUM WORE A shocking black wig on the top of his head. Perhaps he wasn't expecting company, but it looked like a guinea pig had landed on his bald scalp and instantly died. As he stood up to demand Slugger left immediately, he revealed his lack of height. Fabian understood why he needed to force himself on women because he was not a naturally attractive human being, especially when you included the globules of spittle forming around the corners of his mouth.

"Get out of here, I said."

"I heard you, Benjamin. There's no need to repeat yourself so."

Fabian smiled a broad grin hoping to put Weinbaum at his ease, but the smirk was too wide and ended up looking more threatening than anything else. Almost like he wasn't trying to hide his real emotions.

"Now listen, young man. You have no appointment and you need to leave."

"No. You listen to me old man."

Fabian stepped forward and around the desk to be intimidatingly close to Weinbaum—he towered over the upstart tailor.

"I am here on behalf of the union on a matter most grave. And you will listen to our complaint."

"Well, really."

Weinbaum was flustered and couldn't figure out in what direction Fabian was about to take the conversation. Now he understood this was about business and the gelt in his pocket, it was worth sitting down and taking a moment to listen.

"Complaint?"

"Yes. There has been a serious breach of both terms and conditions in this warehouse."

"What breach?"

The man gulped as if he realized what was about to be said but he couldn't believe what was unfolding, nonetheless. He sat in his leather chair, waiting.

"You've been underpaying some of the women here."

"Women?"

"Some of the girls here."

"I pay a piece rate. Some younger ones aren't as speedy as the more mature workers in the factory."

"There are other reasons they aren't as fast though, right?"

Silence as Weinbaum had a long hard think about what Fabian might allude to. Blank expression. And then; eyebrows raised, and realization flooded across his face.

"It is true some of them need my personal attention and that takes them away from their sewing machines."

"Are you kidding me?"

Fabian sneered at Weinbaum with unmitigated contempt. Those girls were the same age as Rebecca.

"I take these ladies with no experience and give them a living."

"What a great philanthropist you must be. But there's a world of difference between helping unemployed girls in the local community and ripping off their stockings and having your way with them!"

Weinbaum's cheeks reddened, and he placed his head in his hands.

"Oh no."

"The union needs you to do two things. First, you must pay all you owe to the women and girls you've *yentzed*. Second, you need to keep your sausage in your pants, man. Or I'll chop it off."

WEINBAUM WAS THINKING about the money he was being asked to give up and his fear of Fabian's violence. The two thoughts rattled around his head, bumping into each other, creating a vortex in his mind he was not expecting to find.

"Don't you go threatening me. I'll have the cops on you. Besides, I pay protection and there's no way you can treat me like this—not if you're really from the union."

This miniature man had grown a backbone in the last two minutes and Fabian was not impressed with this fresh turn of events. He pulled out his knife and leaned over Weinbaum who shrank back in his chair.

"You'd better believe I'm with the union, you *pisher*. The girls might be too afraid to go to the cops but one way or another, you have to pay for where you've been poking your putz."

"I'll offer them a stipend to make up for their time. That I can understand. But the other thing? I never did anything they didn't want to do, and I see no reason why you should be shoving your nose in my business."

"Benjamin. If you think I will let you carry on with those girls, you're very much mistaken. The choice is yours. Cease and desist or lose your favorite organ."

"You've got no right—"

Slugger had had enough and swung his hand towards Weinbaum's crotch, stabbing the knife deep into the guy's thigh. He wasn't so stupid as to castrate the momzer.

Weinbaum howled in pain and Slugger wiped both sides of the blade on Benjamin's pants.

"Deliver the payments by tomorrow and if I find you've touched up one of those women, I'll make you eat your own putz."

He slapped Weinbaum in the face to ensure the man had his attention. Then he walked swiftly out the office, out the building and zigzagged his way back to union headquarters before the Weinbaum receptionist did anything foolish like call the cops on him.

Yonah was sitting at his desk focusing hard on his adding machine when Fabian entered so he left the accountant alone. He grabbed a coffee from the kitchen on the floor below and plonked himself down at a spare slot facing the window.

The anger in his chest had abated and his breathing was back to normal. Fabian stared out at the street scene below, self-righteous thoughts flooding his brain. He remained in the same position for nearly an hour until Ira popped his head around the door.

"YOU GOT A moment, Fabian?"

"Sure thing."

They hustled into Ira's usual meeting room and both sat down. Ira's expression displaying a particularly furrowed brow.

"You deal with the Weinberg matter?"

"Yes, this afternoon."

"Good. Everything went well?"

"It only took me a few minutes conversation to get him to change his mind."

"Thing is, Fabian, word on the street is that Weinberg's been taken to hospital. Stabbed. Knifed in the thigh."

He saw Ira grinding his teeth.

"Yes. He wasn't prepared to play ball, so I helped him to recalibrate his attitude."

"What the hell were you thinking of? Why were you carrying a knife to a business meeting?"

Now it was Fabian's turn to scrunch up his face.

"Ira, we all take the tools of our trade out with us on a job."

"Take them, for sure. Show them, by all means. But go around stabbing people? Don't maim those we are extracting money from. That's bad business, Fabian. I have no problem if you must slap fellas about to get them to see sense. We all need a slapping now and again."

Ira stared directly into Fabian's eyes and let his last sentence hang in the air for the boy to mull over.

"But we are not violent men. We need our customers to be alive—and for them to come to us with their problems and not squeal to the cops."

"Is Weinberg squealing?"

"No. Not yet at least. From what my people tell me, the man's scared right now. Keeps babbling about eating his own dick. The doctors think he's delirious, but it smacks of you making a demand with menace. Did you threaten to chop off his putz?"

"Yes. Given what he was doing to those girls and his lack of interest in offering amends, it was the least I could throw at him. But I was never going to do it."

"So how come he's bleeding out on a gurney?"

"I cut him once in the thigh. Clean stroke in and out. I'm not a butcher despite how you're looking at me. Few stitches and he'll be fine. More importantly, the guy'll pay back the girls tomorrow for the money he stole from their wages and he won't be touching any of his female staff any time soon."

Fabian let out a small chuckle even though he was aware of the seriousness of his situation. The moment spent doing this gave Ira a chance to reflect.

"His thigh, you say?"

"Of course. I'm no *mohel*."

"Don't go threatening to lop off someone's putz. Not good for business."

"Sure thing, Ira."

"And keep to your fists and not that knife of yours. A slap or two, a broken bone or three. That's fine. Slicing someone from ear to ear—if your life is under duress. Not under any other circumstances. We need these people to fear us, yes, but they also need to do business with us every day of the year. Just because Wilson's declared war on Germany doesn't mean we all gotta garrote folk on the streets."

"I get it."

"I hope you do, my boy. You're a good operator. An excellent team player. We are pleased with your progress so far."

"What else can I do? I am ambitious."

"Fabian. You've shown yourself to be that. You need to show how reliable and level-headed you are before you take on any greater responsibility. We must be able to trust you to keep calm—even when some minnow chooses to ignore our requests for a fair wage."

September 1917

27

ALEX WAITED UNTIL Rebecca left to go shopping for her mother before accidentally bumping into her on Suffolk.

"Would you like some help with that?"

Rebecca's eyes darted open with surprise—she hadn't seen him approaching as she was busy testing the ripeness of oranges.

"Sure thing."

A half smile and she passed all her bags into Alex's hands, burdening him with the entire weight of her shopping to carry on dealing with the fruit. As she was about to pay, the shopkeeper looked up at Alex, who smiled in his general direction. Recognition spread across the vendor's face and he refused to accept payment. Rebecca insisted, trying to foist her money on the guy.

"I have an account here. Consider it as a gift from me to you."

"How kind, but the Grunbergs like to pay our way."

"Only if you're certain."

"Better believe it."

He nodded at the shopkeeper who agreed to take payment for the three oranges in Rebecca's hand. She placed them at the top of one bag Alex was holding and they headed back to the tenement.

"Fancy bumping into you during the hours of daylight. I thought you only turned up when it's time to eat your mama's cooking."

Her tone was a touch acerbic but he didn't notice. He was too busy inhaling deeply to catch the scent of her body.

"Don't be like that. Most men work during the week and I'm no different."

"You might go out to work, Alex, but you are so different from them. Don't pretend otherwise. The stories about you don't get any better."

"Don't believe half of what you hear and none of what you read."

"There's nothing wrong with reading, Alex. Reverse snobbery doesn't suit you."

167

"I'm only joking. Besides, I've missed you. Apart from a glimpse of you practicing your dancing some mornings on the way down the stairs, I haven't seen you for what feels like months."

"It's been ages, that's why."

"Well, I wasn't sure you wanted me around."

"HEY, DON'T GO there, fella. I told you my situation and nothing I said was about me not wanting you in my life. That's not fair."

"I guess."

"Yes, for sure."

"I meant I didn't expect I had much hope of us getting together—what with that guy hanging around you and your family. Sounded as though your mother's plan was coming good and there wasn't any space for me in it."

"Alex, there wasn't really, I'm afraid. But circumstances have moved on."

Rebecca's voice trailed off into silence as she delved inside her head and finished the thought alone.

"Oh?"

"Yeah, Amos's family decided against an arrangement with us."

"I'm sorry."

"Are you?"

"I want you to be content and if that was going to make you happy…"

"Right. Strange thing was he refused to speak with me. Would only let his father talk for him. Amos wasn't the outgoing type; more of a nebbish really, but he'd always been comfortable talking to me about anything. His innermost feelings. Suddenly he wouldn't even be in the same room as me."

They had reached Rebecca's door by now, which was open like every other day. Rebecca stopped and stared at Alex to read what was going on behind his expression. He let her because it gave him the chance to be close to her and to revel in the beauty of her face. Her eyes, those lips. After a while the bags started to dig into his fingers and he carried on walking into the kitchen to put everything down.

"Sorry, I forgot you were my pack mule."

"I'll always take your burdens."

Alex sighed and leaned on one of the dining chairs. Those last few words had taken a lifetime to arrive inside him and he'd let them go as though they were light as air. Rebecca put a hand on his arm.

"You're sweet, despite what they say."

"Back to made up stories about me?"

"I understand some of them are tall tales. Of course they are. But some of them ring a little too close to believable."

"Like what?"

"Amos. One day all was fine, the next he couldn't be anywhere near me. Sounded as though he was frightened by something—or someone."

"What have I done? What have the mysterious 'they' said I did?"

"You threatened him and told him you'd kill him if he saw me again."

Alex felt an acid warmth in the pit of his stomach and hoped his expression hadn't changed for the worse.

"THAT IS RIDICULOUS. How crazy does that sounds when you say it out loud?"

"I really have no idea what or who to trust any more, Alex. I mean, you need strong-arm tactics working in the gang and some on our own street say you even carry a knife—and they've seen you use it."

"This story is getting wilder by the second."

"Is it? Did you threaten Amos?"

She put her hand in his as she asked this question. As if she could tell whether he was lying merely by touching him.

"Of course not. Whatever happened with Amos is strictly between you and him. And if you don't know, I sure have no clue."

"Really?"

"On the souls of my grandchildren as yet unborn."

"That's good enough for me."

Keeping her hand in his, she leaned into him and they kissed. Alex placed his other hand around her back and stroked it gently, feeling her spine with his thumb. She was perfect in every respect.

After two minutes, she became self-conscious and let go, walking to the kitchen sink

"Would you like a drink of water?"

"No thanks, Rebecca."

"Coffee instead?"

"No, I'm fine. Just enjoying being in your company."

Alex had never spoken truer words in his life.

"You genuinely are a sweet man."

"And you are a beautiful woman."

Just as Alex was about to carry on speaking, Rebeca interrupted him.

"But as much as I think you are lovely—and I do—I don't think we can be together. Some of those stories might be made up but not all of them. You have a reputation and it scares me to be honest. You scare me."

"Me? How?"

"Sometimes when you look into the distance, I see anger and hatred. And I couldn't be close to a person with that much aggression inside himself."

"If I changed?"

"You can be a gorgeous fellow so, yes, if you weren't in the world you are in, who knows what might be between us. But until then..."

"Sure, I get it. The business I'm in is all I've got, and my family relies on me to put bread on the table. If I was on my own, I'd stop in a heartbeat."

"But you're not."

"No. I've got a lot of mouths to feed. I mean, don't tell him but the only reason my papa has a job is because of me and my business dealings. So if I walked away from that, he'd be on the street too."

A tear rolled down Rebecca's cheek, which he brushed away with his finger and wiped it off his pants.

"Don't be sad. Give me some time to sort my affairs out. We've still a got a chance."

"Have we, Alex?"

"There's always a chance."

Another kiss on the lips and he left the Grunbergs' to decide if he was prepared to turn his back on everything he'd built up since the day he'd arrived in this land of the free.

28

ALEX SAT NEXT to his mother that Shabbos night. The blessings over the food and drink were complete, and they were now consuming the fruit of his efforts.

"And are you ever going to settle down, then?"

"Ma. I've not even had a chance to eat a piece of challah before you start on me?"

"Who's starting? I'm only asking, is all."

Alex put a torn-off shred of bread in his mouth and swallowed.

"So, now you've eaten some challah. Do you have plans to settle down any time soon?"

"Yes, as you ask."

"Really? Tell. Who's the lucky girl that's won my son's heart?"

"Wait a minute, Ma. I said I was considering it. I did not say I had done anything about it."

"*Oy vey gevalt*. Now he sounds like he's becoming a lawyer with his clever speeches."

"Ah, give me a break."

"Are you going out with this girl or not? Is all I'm asking you, my love."

"Not at this precise moment, no."

"You raised my hopes. You with the talk."

"It's not as simple as you make it sound."

"What's to be complicated with? Either you're going out with someone or you're not. Where's the gray middle area?"

His younger siblings giggled at the verbal pounding Alex was receiving, content they were not the object of their mother's interrogation.

"We were seeing each other and now we are not. She'd rather I was following a different career path."

"You have a career too! This girl brings out hidden depths in my darling."

"Hey, I work. Real hard."

171

Moishe put his hand up to interject before his wife engulfed all the available air space.

"My child, your mother means it's not like you run your own business or work inside some American corporation. We appreciate all your efforts for the family. We do."

"That's all right then."

Moishe smiled at his boy and scowled at his wife but she ignored him—as always.

"IT'S NOT YOUR work I was ribbing you over, it was the phrase you used to describe it. That's all love."

"It is a career. I started out at the bottom of the ladder and made my way up. Now I run a team of guys and they themselves run groups under them. There is a kind of corporate hierarchy to the whole thing."

"My son the manager. I never thought I'd see the day... No, really."

Mama saw the look on her boy's face and she felt she was treading a thin line. The Cohens heard the stories of their son's exploits just as much as Rebecca did and Ruth believed far more of them than Rebecca. Alex had a history in the old country of which Rebecca was unaware.

"You reckon you can go further in this... career of yours? And do you think this girl will change her mind about you if you don't?"

"I dunno, Mama. From what she told me recently, I can't see her choosing me."

"And what do her mother and father think?"

"I've no idea."

"What do you mean? Are you and this flibbertigibbet not involving either set of parents? What has the world come to?"

"It's a modern century, Mama, and a new country. Folk do things differently here."

"Some people maybe, but not everyone."

Ruth emphasized the first word very carefully.

"Right now, it doesn't matter because we are not a couple."

"If you stopped doing what you do, would you be an item then?"

"Yes. I'd go round tomorrow morning and ask her father for permission to marry her—or get you to do it instead."

Alex looked to Papa at this point.

"Quite."

Moishe's contribution was pithy.

"But there is no other job for me to do and I am successful at it. Should I really give up everything I have achieved in this country just for a life with a dancer with no prospects?"

The corners of Ruth's mouth rose slightly and her eyes twinkled as she realized who they were talking about.

"She is a beautiful girl, my boy."

He turned to her and the edges of his jaw softened.

"Yes, she is but I have no idea how I'd support us all if I wasn't working for the guys I do."

"Sounds as though you're stuck, Alex."

"I am right now."

"I'm sure you'll figure it out. You always do. You are a bright boy… More latkes?"

THE OREGON DRINKING hole was in full swing; tables were packed, and they were two men deep at the bar itself. Beer was flowing like it was going out of fashion. Fabian stood at one end of the counter, not wanting to sit as the staircase obscured his view.

Now and again he was jostled, but generally he was left alone—he was not in anybody's way and the regulars were aware of his background and the extent to which he struck fear in the owner.

The barkeep was always friendly, but never over familiar; Fabian's reputation took care of that. Besides, he was a good tipper. Two beers downed and a third on the way, Fabian caught sight of Sarah coming downstairs, adjusting her kimono to reveal a glimpse of breast without giving too much away for free.

Having rearranged herself, she looked up at the scrum before her and sighed. When a large number of men gathered in the name of beer, they would rarely want to be separated from the brew for a sufficient amount of time for a girl to make any money. Even if she had curves like Sarah.

Fabian stood up straight to increase his height so as to be visible above the throng. She spotted him and raised an eyebrow at the scene she surveyed. He nodded at her, and using a series of hand gestures, offered to buy her a drink. Sarah shook her head. If she carried on to the floor all that would happen would be a large number of free gropes on her *tuches* and not much else. She beckoned to him to join her on the stairs. As soon as his beer arrived, Fabian did just that.

"They're packed in here tonight."

"Yep. No reason for it other than everyone's got a thirst at the same time."

"Fancy going back to your room. I can hardly hear you over all this hullabaloo."

"Sure thing. Here for a chat or here for some company?"

"Bit of both probably."

"Works for me, darling."

They wandered up to the second floor, along the corridor and into Sarah's boudoir.

"Pour yourself a drink or stick with your beer if you like."

A bottle of scotch stood on the bedside table but he wasn't in the mood for hard liquor.

"Beer's fine by me."

"It's your poison."

Fabian smiled a little and sat down on the edge of the bed. Sarah perched next to him but didn't do her usual strip beforehand.

"What's on your mind?"

"This and that..."

"You'll need to give me more of a clue."

She laughed and squeezed his knee, leaving her hand there and dropping the other on his shoulder so she sat facing him with one leg over the other.

"What do you think of the work I do?"

"How d'you mean?"

"Well, you see me hang out in the Forsyth and come round threatening Eli here. It's not what most would call an honorable life, is it?"

"I'm really not able to judge, now am I?"

"What ya mean?"

Sarah pulled her dressing gown off her shoulders to reveal her underwear.

"There aren't many people here would describe what I do as honorable!"

Fabian took in an eyeful of her body, soaking in the sight of her nipples and the curves around her belly button.

"Point well made."

He laughed and kissed her on the lips, briefly, squeezing a breast for good measure.

"But I would say you're honorable. You can tell the difference between right and wrong—where to draw the line. This is a stone-cold fact."

Sarah nodded.

"So is what I do so awful do you think?"

"Fabian. You help keep order in the neighborhood and I've only heard about you threatening folks who owe you money. That sounds straight and narrow to me."

"That's what I reckon, Sarah."

"I don't see why you're asking me about this."

She stroked his neck with her thumb to elicit a greater response.

"Thing is, someone's made me an offer, but I'd need to leave this life to get it. Turn my back on all I've created for myself since landing on Ellis Island."

Sarah stopped stroking his neck and pondered.

"It'd be a big leap and no mistake. Is it worth it? What's the prize?"

"You'll laugh if I tell you."

"No I won't. Trust me."

Fabian looked at her carefully judging her reaction.

"I'd win me a wife."

Sarah giggled then immediately covered her mouth.

"Sorry, love, but I wasn't expecting that. Besides, you can catch yourself a woman every night of the week and still keep your place with Waxey."

With that, she squeezed his crotch, playfully.

"Aw, don't. This is serious for me."

"Only teasing you... but I'm not the person to ask. Would drop this game in an instant if you said you were going to look after me."

"Huh?"

"Seriously. I do this for the money, not the company. You're the only fella I've come across who's acted respectful. You are literally one in a million to me. And you wouldn't need to step down from the life."

"That's..."

"...not on the cards. I get that; I'm just saying. Should you abandon this way of life for the love of a good woman? How the hell can I say?"

"Sorry, it was an unfair question to ask. I want someone to give me the answer."

"You'll know when you get it and not before."

"I guess so."

Fabian placed his hand on Sarah's thigh and they started to canoodle until they were both naked and under the covers. By the time he left the room, his beer glass was empty and a ten spot was lying on the bedside table.

DECEMBER 1917

29

FABIAN SPENT TIME with his boys. He hadn't been ignoring them, but he was aware his focus had been on himself and his own problems the past couple of months. He felt he owed them a boozy evening.

Nowadays the lads comprised his original crew, Ben, Abraham and Dan along with a newer member, Paulie. He came from south of Canal and had shown himself more than capable when under pressure even though he only spoke a handful of Yiddish words. They all did their best to practice their English—when they remembered.

"Beers all round, Nathan."

A slug of brew landed on the bar in front of them and the crew huddled around a solitary table—near the back of the Forsyth as ever. They quaffed their beers and told jokes that made little sense, as men do.

"Where are your women? Young men like you should occupy yourselves with more than money!"

Dan looked at Ben who turned to Paulie.

"We don't do too badly, old man."

"Less of the old, you surly knave. Well, I never see any skirt around you."

"You see us when we're at work. A twist is for the evenings, right?"

Paulie turned to Abraham and Ben who both nodded assent while Dan just chuckled to himself. The Forsyth was filling up with a mix of locals and strangers. Business picked up too for the *nafkas* as men walked up the stairs holding hands with scantily clad women. There was always a shapely calf to see but if you wanted a better view, you had to pay. After fifteen minutes, Paulie muttered something none of the others understood and took one woman upstairs. Some things need no words.

"How's Paulie settling in?"

"Just fine, Fabian. Can be hard to figure out his English, especially as it comes in a thick Italian accent."

They all laughed, knowing how little they'd understand even if he had the finest American pronunciation in the world. Despite their years in New

York, none of these come-overs had found the need to speak English regularly. Their families had fled one shtetl for another in the Bowery. The main difference between the two was that in the old country the Cossacks ransacked their homes, assaulted the men and raped the women. Here they were left alone by the cops and nobody saw a government official one year to the next.

"I LIKE WE have Paulie on our side. It's good to get a different point of view —once you can figure it out."

Another chuckle by all the group. As the laughter subsided, Paulie appeared at the bar with a smile on his face wider than the gap between his ears. Fifteen minutes well spent.

Fabian beckoned him over because he had clearly lost his bearings. The lad sat down and Fabian got them another round.

"You like this crew?"

"Yes. Is good."

"See guys, at some point, we must expand out of the Bowery. Not this year and not next, but some time and then Paulie will come into his own because the rest of Manhattan can understand what he's saying."

They nodded at the profundity of Fabian's words.

"I know it's hard but we should all practice our English now and again."

"What little there is between us at any rate."

Ben was correct. Fabian only had three phrases under his belt. He could order a beer at a bar and say please and thank you, but not much else.

"It'd help us get more respect from the likes of Waxey too."

Abraham's comment was on the money. Waxey Gordon was a native born American and his ability to straddle both stools—the Yiddish world and the American—explained how he'd got to where he had in this town.

Dan added, "Yeah, us come-overs always place second in the pecking order."

"Wait a minute, fellas. We've done pretty well for ourselves, I'd say. You can't go blaming Waxey for where he was born. That ain't reasonable."

"Course not, Fabian. But you must admit there are only natives in the high command."

Fabian fell silent, intensely aware Dan was spot on. Being a come-over had a major disadvantage in the current organization. At the back of the mind of every native was the thought that the allegiance of a come-over was to the old country and not to Americans. Until someone toppled Waxey himself, there would be no change to that. Was Fabian that man? Sure as hell no!

A scuffle broke out five feet away from their table. No-one seemed to know what was the source of the fury but the two guys pushing, pulling and punching were certain they had a beef. Those between the fighters and the bar grabbed their drinks and hightailed it to the other side of the Forsyth but those sat at tables had less room to exit the vicinity.

The men punched their way to Fabian's table and one pushed the other onto his chair, making him spill his drink. All his crew's eyes landed on Fabian as he ground his molars and chose how to respond.

Slugger stood up, turned around and grabbed the guy who'd fallen on top of him by the scruff of the neck with just a single hand. With the other, he slapped the man on the right cheek and then the left. A knee to the groin and the man dropped to the floor clutching himself.

Meanwhile the other one stood frozen with panic in his face. Now, facing him, he knew exactly who Fabian was and the trouble he'd created for himself.

"Sorry, mister. Sure didn't mean to disturb you."

"That's as may be. You disturbed me and my friends here." Fabian waved in the general direction of his crew, all of whom were standing in case the scene escalated into an ugly brawl. The guy spread both palms to show he really wasn't looking for the trouble he'd landed for himself.

"Apologies to you all. No offense intended, like I said."

"Offense has been taken though. I don't judge a man by what he intends but by what he does. And you and your friend spilled my drink and interrupted a fine conversation. Isn't that right, lads?"

All murmured agreement apart from Paulie who nodded his head several times instead.

"What's your name?"

"Huh?"

"What is your name?"

"Jeremiah. Jeremy."

"Well, Jeremy. I'd say you need to offer us some compensation before we extract it ourselves."

Jeremy's eyes darted left and right as everybody in the bar stared at him, wanting to see what happened next.

"Beers all round for everyone at your table?"

"Good start, Jeremy."

"Um. Sorry?"

"For what?"

"For disturbing you."

"And anything else?"

Fabian's eyes looked towards Nathan to offer some clue to what was going on inside his head.

"Oh, and apologies to you for messing up the bar."

"Your apology to me and my fellas is accepted. I'd expect you want to provide better compensation to Nathan than just words."

"Of course."

Jeremy stuffed a hand in his pocket and put a five note onto the counter. Fabian nodded.

"Nathan, a round of beers and vodka chasers please!"

"Would you say that's enough satisfaction, Nathan?"

"Sure is, Fabian."

"Jeremy, well done. Now I suggest you and your friend leave the Forsyth and don't come back in a hurry."

"Thank you."

"You're very welcome."

Jeremy picked his friend up off the floor by the armpits and dragged his ass out of the building. A cheer arose the moment the door closed behind them.

Fabian raised his glass, necked the vodka shot and slammed the glass on the table. The others copied him, and the night carried on with beer and chuckles in equal measure.

THREE DAYS LATER, Alex was in the Forsyth bar again but under very different circumstances. On this occasion, he sat as far away from the entrance as he possibly could, a long way from the counter too. Instead of a gaggle of boys, a solitary girl perched opposite him, her back to the rest of the room. Rebecca sipped her white wine and he tinkered with his small beer.

"Thanks for coming out with me tonight."

"My pleasure. It was nice of you to suggest it."

"How have you been?"

"Just fine. I'm sewing more for my mother."

"So less time for dancing?"

"Yes."

A sadness in her eyes and another sip of wine.

"I'm sorry."

"Me too."

Rebecca giggled.

"But it doesn't mean I've given up hope. I'm just biding my time."

"Pleased to hear it. I'd hate to think you stopped doing that."

"Me too."

A smile.

"And are you going steady with anyone?"

"Not yet but my parents are on the look-out. They spoke to your father at one point."

"And I didn't make the grade?"

"Apparently not, else we'd have jumped the broomstick by now, I'm certain."

Alex considered that prospect briefly and realized he liked the idea.

"Given much thought to what we said before?"

"Sure thing. I know you won't believe me but it's not as easy as it sounds —leaving this life."

Alex gesticulated around the room. The Forsyth was buzzing by now even though it was a weekday. Rebecca cast a glance behind her shoulder to soak in the atmosphere.

"There's more to your world than a bunch of men drinking beer at night. Don't pretend to me, Alex."

"I know. There's money collections and debtor meetings. Then there's figuring out strategies to expand our activities."

"You sound like JP Morgan."

"Not quite, but the stories you hear are about us cracking heads and that's not really what we're about. It is so much more mundane than that."

"Life is, isn't it? But we all make difficult choices to get through the days, don't you think?"

"Of course. It hasn't been easy for you to push your dancing into the background."

"No. It hurts. Every day."

Alex put his hand on Rebecca's and she cupped it with her other palm. They sat there for five minutes, soaking in the connection between them.

The noise level increased as a bar scuffle took place well away from their table. Choosing a space far from anywhere had been a good decision. The sound of raised voices broke the spell and Rebecca looked around again.

"This isn't a nice place, Alex."

"It can be. See that seat over there?"

He pointed to his usual perch.

"That's my office. People come from all over the neighborhood to seek my advice and help from that chair there."

Rebecca leaned her chin on her hands, elbows on the wooden surface.

"You sure are somebody in this town."

"Small acorn but I'm hoping to grow into something more significant."

"You'll be somebody. That energy behind your eyes. I can tell. A will to succeed."

"I recognize that same drive in you too. That's what makes us two pieces of the same jigsaw."

"You reckon?"

"I do."

"Trouble is, Alex, while you're comfortable in this room, I feel totally vulnerable. The only reason I'm sitting here is because I trust you not to put me in harm's way. But I want you to understand this is not my world. This is not a place I can be."

He sipped his beer.

"And it's not that this is a drinking hole, although my parents'd be horrified to know I'd been here tonight. And it's not the whores taking men upstairs for sex. You put me with my back to proceedings, but I'm not that naïve, Alex. It's that you are so inured to the goings on here, you think it is all normal."

He was silent for a while and they carried on sipping their drinks, both enjoying the moment as the conversation morphed to lighter topics. Alex and Rebecca stopped thinking about tomorrow and reveled in each other's company for that night alone.

The bottom line was clear—if he wanted to be with her then his time with Waxey was over.

30

FABIAN WAS UNDER pressure from Ira and Waxey to deliver on his union interests. The problems of AUFFE was one thing—and Fabian always supported the rights of their members. But there was more to the world of unions than ensuring the workers' dues came in each year. This was a business like any other and the more representatives in AUFFE, the bigger the kickback to Waxey for protection and other services.

This need to expand the membership trickled down to the likes of Fabian. There were two sources of member: those who had joined a different union and those who were unaffiliated. Neither group was easy to encourage and Fabian calculated picking out a handful people represented a huge amount of effort with little to show for it. So he played things smart.

Fabian waited until there was a problem with a different union and then swooped in to take advantage of their woes.

Waxey mentioned to him there was trouble in a dockside factory. The owner had a large order to fulfill with a short deadline but was refusing to pay any extra to get the job done on time. There were only a handful of AUFFE workers and they had complained to the shop steward who had passed the message up the line until Ira was informed.

"Fabian, can you put some pressure on the factory to do what's right?"

"Yeah, Ira. You know me; happy to help."

He leaped out of his chair and bounded off to sort matters out. Honigsmann Wholesalers was located at Mangin and Third, facing Pier 53 and the Houston Street ferry. The warehouse entrance looked the same as all the others on the dock. The only distinguishing feature was a sign with the words: 'Honigsmann Wholesalers. Proprietor—David Honigsmann'.

"Is David in?"

Fabian's encounters with receptionists always followed the same pattern and today was no different. Into the Honigsmann office, Fabian apologized for the intrusion and asked only for a few moments of the man's time. The guy looked stressed, but that was his state before Fabian had opened his mouth.

"I've got no beef with the AUFFE. There's only a handful of you guys working for me and we get on okay mostly."

"I understand, David. Obviously, I'm concerned about the extra pressure you've been putting our people under recently."

"Look, we've got a massive order for dresses to ship out to Boston by the end of next month. If things go to plan, we'll hit this year's sales target early."

"David, I understand the problems businesses like yours face. I see these sorts of things every day in my line of work. And I am not indifferent to your difficulties. Far from it."

Fabian enjoyed this more conciliatory tone and wondered if it would generate a better result than slapping the guy senseless with brass knuckles and a blade.

"Without wishing to be rude, Mr...?"

"Mustard. But call me Fabian. Everyone does."

"Without being rude, Fabian, your words are wonderful to hear but have you come into my office unannounced to help or to offer tea and sympathy?"

Fabian smiled and emitted a small chuckle.

"Great point, David. How would you feel if I could guarantee your workers will do their utmost to get the schmatta made on time?"

"Guarantees are fabulous. Workers operating at their best doesn't necessarily get me anywhere though."

"David, I was not trying to be clever with my words but there are matters outside the control of your staff that could jeopardize the consignment. That's all."

"I get it. What's your guarantee worth and how much is it going to cost me?"

"I like a man who asks sensible questions, David. The guarantee is my word and in some parts of town, that's a highly prized commodity. You can ask around to assay its value."

David Honigsmann nodded. Fabian's name meant little to him, but he was prepared to listen further.

"The cost? Not a single dime to you but I'd need to come and go as I please in your factory until the shipment is sent out. No questions asked."

"Looks like I have nothing to lose. How can I refuse such a request? You got a deal, Fabian, but if it goes south, every one of my AUFFE workers will be out on the street. Understood?"

"I'd expect no less from you—if that were to happen. As I'm doing you a favor now, in the future I might ask for some help in return. Sound reasonable?"

Fabian put his hand out, and they shook to seal the agreement. Then he tipped his hat and hurried out to get things rolling.

He had no interest in whether the shipment was completed on time and with only four AUFFE members in the building, his enthusiasm in protecting their rights was minimal too. Fabian's eye was on the real prize—there were nearly three hundred representatives of the American Tailors' Union stuffed into this sweatshop and Fabian wanted them all. Every last one.

The local ATU convener was Italian and came from south of Canal. Fabian's plan was to ignore him completely as he would report back to his bosses what was going on. Instead, he wandered round the warehouse, talking to the women sewing and told them if they joined the AUFFE he'd get them a bonus for their work. He fluffed it up with talk of how much better his union was looking after workers' rights but he dangled hard cash at them in ten days' time if they moved now.

THREE DAYS LATER and most were onside, so that on the fourth day, a reception party was waiting for him near Pier 53. This was no surprise to Fabian as he'd been expecting them ever since he started his campaign inside Honigsmann Wholesalers. Each morning, his crew and a few helpers, had waited round the corner in case of trouble. And today, trouble had called in early.

As Fabian walked to the warehouse entrance, he tipped his hat to the three goons leaning against the wall. They stood upright and stepped towards him.

By the time he was ten feet away from them, his fellas had reached him, holding baseball bats. Paulie carried an iron bar. The tip of the hat was Fabian's signal.

"The ATU ain't welcome here anymore."

Before any of the thugs could form a sentence, Abraham and Dan had scored a home run and Paulie was demonstrating superior skills on a pair of kidneys and spine. Fabian grinned at his men as they sent the goons packing.

"Excellent job! Stick around for a while in case they come back, will you?"

Then inside to collect dues. He'd seen many faces stuck to the few outside windows as the action unfolded and knew word would spread about the superior forces of the AUFFE within minutes.

The next day, the ATU goons returned in greater number but Fabian enlisted Waxey's help and brought along twenty of his own. The following morning, Fabian walked into the building alone and mopped up the rest of the membership.

One shipment completed on time, he booked an appointment with Honigsmann.

"I believe you hit your deadline, David."

"Yes, Fabian. Thanks to you everyone knuckled down, stopped complaining and worked flat out."

"I did my bit. The women are the ones you ought to thank. It was their sweat and tears that's made your money."

"A great bunch of workers, for certain."

"Yes, and I think you should show them some thanks for all that effort."

"Do you?"

"For sure. Why not award them each a three-dollar bonus?"

"Now, Fabian, that's a lot of my cash you want to spend."

"Sure, but if you give them something they can buy food with, you'll get more out of them the next time Boston places an order. Besides, we both know you can afford it."

Fabian smiled at David and relaxed into his chair. The knuckleduster in his pocket was itching to come out of hiding but Fabian continued his experiment.

"That may be the case, but they delivered for me this time with no extra cash."

"David. Do me a favor and throw them a couple of dollars to show your appreciation. Do me that favor."

He emphasized each of the words in the last sentence until David's expression indicated he got the message.

"I did as you suggested, Fabian, and asked around about you. I will do you this favor for sure. A dollar each as a bonus!"

"One dollar?"

"Two dollars then. You are right. I made decent money out of Boston thanks to their efforts."

"Two dollars?"

"Fabian. If I pay them three each then my profit margin gets too tight. I will share my good fortune up to a point but I am not a Communist."

"Two dollars is a wonderful consideration. Thank you. And the women thank you too."

"I've been told I now have a warehouse filled with AUFFE members."

"Is that what they say? Great news travels fast, doesn't it?"

Fabian smiled and left Honigsmann's office.

SAMMY SAT IN the Forsyth at his usual table, Fabian at his as he sipped from his coffee mug and contemplated his recent success at Honigsmann Wholesalers. Halfway through, Sammy sidled over next to him.

"Hey, you."

"Hi, how goes it?"

"Fine."

"We're not doing badly south of Canal, are we?"

"No, Sammy. Things are going well. It's been a good business arrangement."

"Sure has. Do you think we can expand even further?"

"Well, we operate eight pools together, right?"

"Yep. That's the count."

"And I've got a similar number under my direct control."

"So where are you thinking we should go next?"

"Well, between us we have a strong presence across East Broadway, Henry and Madison but we could head southwest to Spruce, Beekman or perhaps as far as Maiden and Derty. Who knows, we could even end up at Pine or Wall Street in a year or two."

"Big dreams, Sammy."

"Nothing wrong with a strategy. I'm certain you've told me that in the past."

"Sure have."

"So how's about it?"

"About what? If you want to take over more territory, don't let me stop you."

"Come on, Fabian. I can't do it without you."

"Sammy, you think too much of me. You don't need me. I'm sure Waxey would be happy to support you."

"Sure he would, but if I did that, the pools would always be seen as his and not mine. Our agreement is different. I'd get my own pools after a time."

"If we followed our last arrangement that would be so but the wider the territory we run, the thinner my guys would be spread. And they would be the ones getting baseball bats slammed on their heads. Your people would quietly count up the cash."

"You haven't complained in the past."

"And I'm not complaining now, Sammy. Just saying how our deal works out on the ground. The profit share is fine for me, but it costs my people in cuts, bruises and physical pain."

Fabian wondered why Sammy wanted him as a backer for his ventures. Waxey had the muscle and the right connections. Sammy was talking about a place where there were Italian gangs and the last vestige of the Irish too. Fabian was calm about pushing out other Jews from pools but there was a bigger game at stake when you pushed around the Irish and Italians. He had nothing against Paulie—he was a good guy—but he was an outsider, nonetheless.

So why would Sammy want Fabian as his right-hand man and not Waxey? How could Sammy benefit from not getting direct support from Waxey?

Fabian sipped more coffee, pondering those questions. The answer was simple—Sammy wanted him to fail.

JANUARY 18, 1918

31

FABIAN, SAMMY AND Waxey Gordon sat around a table, jawing and chugging coffee. Five minutes of chat later and Waxey cleared his throat. Fabian knew what was happening next because he'd done nothing since his conversation with Sammy four weeks before.

"Thank you both for coming over today. We need to iron out an issue that's arisen."

"Fine by me."

"Me too."

Waxey took a glug from his coffee to create a dramatic pause. It worked.

"You have been two of my finest troopers these past three years. Our reach has expanded thanks to you—and others—and money has poured in. You have managed debtors effectively and the usury business has thrived within your wards."

"Sammy and I work well together."

"Sure do."

"But recently I've noticed a slowdown in your expansion into new territory. I'd be interested to understand why this occurred."

Now it was Fabian's turn to take a dramatic sip of brown liquid. He looked at Sammy to give him a chance to open his mouth first but Sammy was staying schtum.

"Waxey, it's simple. This past year, Sammy and I agreed to partner over new pools. I provide the muscle and he provides the day-to-day management. As we all know, this has proved a good model. We share profits straight down the line and after a while, I move on to fresh pastures. That way, Sammy builds up a solid business and I take my, ahem, talents and apply them elsewhere."

"That has worked well. But why the slow down then?"

"My crew is small but tough. We are strong and get the job done but chiseling into foreign turf is different from breaking fresh ground. Waxey, you know better than any of us how my fellas must stay close to the new pool for weeks after we've turfed out the old inhabitants. I've got to where my men can't support any other pools while monitoring all the current activities."

Waxey stirred his coffee for no discernible reason, all the while looking at Sammy, who remained silent.

"Fabian, isn't the answer for you to expand your crew?"

"It is one of the possible answers, but we must remember I lose my interest in Sammy's pools after a year and then I need more funds to pay my gang."

"Your agreement with Sammy was very generous. You should always look after each other otherwise we are nothing but vermin."

"We were both happy with the terms, weren't we, Fabian?"

"Yes, we were. But I thought there would be a handful of new locations and then I could go back to my usual business. I was helping a friend who had helped me only a few years before."

"All laudable stuff but what's done is done. History is a marvelous thing, but we live in the present. What's to do now?"

They all looked deep into their respective mugs, seeking the answer in cold coffee. Fabian had prepared for the meeting since Ira asked him to come in and see Waxey the previous day.

"The partnership between us works well, but it's the impending closure of the agreement that's having knock-on effects which aren't helping."

Sammy's expression morphed from calm to concerned.

"If we continued with the profit share then I'd have guaranteed funding to expand my crew. That way, we could go deeper into other territories for you."

He was aware this also meant he would maintain his fifty per cent stake in the shared pools. Fabian's original plan was to make a quick turn out of Sammy's efforts but the pools south of Canal had proved to be highly lucrative.

Another reason for wanting to keep the stakes was Sammy himself. Fabian clung to the thought Sammy was trying to oust him; push him so far that he'd end up spreading his crew too thin or wind up in a fight with a knife in his jugular. He needed Waxey's support during these dangerous times.

"Are you agreeable, Sammy? Maintain the partnership on the same terms with existing units and expand on the same basis?"

Sammy's eyes widened; he'd already spent Fabian's share though he hadn't received it yet. But Waxey had asked the question, not Fabian and Sammy had to respond.

"That's fine right now but I think we should reassess in, say, a year's time. A lot can happen in twelve months. America has joined the war in Europe. Our community might have less money to spend and that could hit profits and the dynamics of our businesses."

"A year is a long time in the Bowery. Of course we can have another sit-down next January."

"Are you both agreed then?"

Fabian and Sammy nodded and then they shook hands to show Waxey how their partnership was back on solid ground.

"We can all make a lot of cash out of this, you know that?"

"Sure do, Waxey. The Italians and the Irish are a different bunch though to tussle with."

"They are, Fabian. But at heart they are exactly like us—interested in making money. Territory is of secondary importance."

"But you need space to operate in."

"Yes but partnerships can work in this situation too. Don't be so quick to grab land when you should focus on grabbing cash flow."

Fabian listened to those words and filed them for later. He assumed Waxey wanted the territory that was the Lower East Side, but would be happy with the money from the Lower East Side instead.

Sammy was a slippery fish. He had set up Fabian to be forced to carry on being Sammy's muscle on the ground. Fabian wouldn't forget how the man had maneuvered him the last twenty-four hours.

January 19, 1918 10 AM

32

AS A SIGN of the renewed business relationship, Sammy joined Fabian the following day at their first gouge into a new territory under the recent rules.

"For once he's putting his nuts on the line."

And there was some truth to that. Sammy always preferred to let Fabian use his fists than lay a hand on another. Usually he was somewhere in the background—to the point where Fabian felt Sammy was just holding everybody else's coats. But not today.

On the corner of Oliver and Madison, Fabian surveyed the scene before him. He reckoned they were too far from Canal for his own comfort. They might only be two blocks south east of Bowery, but they were deep into Yake Brady land, a ruthless Irish gang with connections to the boxing fraternity.

Fabian sank back into the wall he was leaning against. The more he glanced around, the more conspicuous he felt. They were in a different ghetto for sure judging by the looks they were getting from passersby.

"Two on the door and who knows how many inside."

"Let's watch some more. An extra five minutes might make all the difference."

"You said it, Fabian."

An occasional customer would pop in for a minute and then saunter out. Everything looked relaxed but Fabian knew Sammy scouted well. This place was a goldmine otherwise they wouldn't be stood in the middle of a new Dublin planning to knock over the joint. Whatever Fabian thought of Sammy, the fella was tip-top when picking out prime sites. Couldn't take that away from the fox.

Three more heads appeared from inside, talking to the bouncers on the door. The bulges in their coats showed they were carrying more than a woolen jumper under there. This was not going to be a walk in the park.

Fabian beckoned Paulie, who was trying to vanish in a crevice between two buildings, towards him.

"Listen to me carefully. I want you to go in there and place a bet. Understand?"

"Yes."

"Tell me how many goons there are and the layout of the venue. Yes?"

"Yes."

Paulie understood more Yiddish than he spoke but his English was second to none. He was the perfect choice for this job. Hands in pockets he walked in the opposite direction and three minutes later he reappeared from around the block. Paulie was a smart boy. Into the building with a nod to the goons.

Fabian tensed, putting his hand in his pants pocket and feeding his fingers into his knuckledusters. He counted slowly in his head. Paulie had around a minute before the cavalry would charge in and things would get messy fast.

He had around fifteen seconds left when he exited the building, whistling and returning using his same circuitous route.

"And?"

"Five in total. They're carrying iron bars and at least two knives in there. Appear tough but they look flabby to me."

"Good work."

Five of them and six of us, if you included Sammy. The odds were better than Fabian might have hoped. He sent word down the line they'd hit the place in ten minutes. Paulie first as a recognized face, then Ben, Abraham and Dan, followed by Sammy and himself. They'd wait for him and follow his lead.

Before eleven, they stood inside surrounded by the goons. Fabian sensed the tension in the air and hoped this was only his imagination. The last thing he needed was for everyone to smell of starch and fear.

"Looks like a rabbi convention."

Paulie smiled, but the others didn't understand enough to either get the joke or take offense.

"Hey, buddy, what're you doing round these parts so far from home?"

The challenge was addressed to Ben, but he had no idea what they were on about, so remained silent.

One goon punched Ben in the shoulder, half playfully.

"I asked you a question, buddy."

Fabian saw the guy's muscles tense in his arms and knew trouble was about to start. Always better to take the initiative. He swung a fist into the face of the nearest thug who flew backwards onto the floor.

Before the first goon landed, the guy aiming at Ben pulled out a knife and slashed him in the neck. Blood spurted and Ben crumpled to the ground. Then merry hell broke loose. Abraham and Dan used their fists and blades to attack the other goon while Sammy went for the door. Slugger let him, so he'd be able to surprise the bouncers while Slugger stayed to hit the others.

A bench stood between him and one of the Yake Brady gang, a boy around fifteen but steely enough, despite what Paulie had said. Slugger lunged at him, but his arm wasn't sufficiently long to reach. He feinted left then right, but the kid had no intention of playing that game. So Slugger grabbed the bench and threw it out the way. The lad froze for a second, not expecting Slugger's move which gave him the opportunity to bury his knife in his chest, yank it out and repeat the process. One very much down and out.

Slugger swung round to see a red-haired goon slash at Dan's belly until he fell on the floor. Slugger bounded over and grabbed the guy from behind, lifting his head up and back to reveal his throat. A parabola of crimson gushed out and Slugger slammed him onto the ground. Abraham and Paulie remained standing with Irish and Jewish blood mixing on the floor. Ben's left foot twitched sporadically while Dan screamed, clutching his stomach, which was a dark pool of red.

"Help him!"

Abraham bent down to tend to Dan as best he could while Slugger headed to the open door. Five feet away, Sammy was lying in the dirt cowering as the two bouncers played with him, kicking him in the kidneys or slapping him around the head. Sammy must have sped out the building so fast, they didn't have time to see what was going on inside and just chased him down the street.

Slugger grabbed one of them and smashed his face into the brick wall. The other saw the menace in his eyes and made the only intelligent choice— he ran away. Slugger ran back inside.

"How's Ben?"

"Dead."

"Leave him then... Dan?"

"Not good. Needs a doctor."

Abraham and Fabian grabbed one armpit each and dragged Dan onto the street with Paulie by their side.

"Come on!"

Sammy looked up and saw what was happening, picked himself up and joined them as they tried to get back to safe turf. Dan's toes scuffed the road as the two hauled him along, a trail of red liquid in his wake.

As they caught sight of Bowery and East Broadway, they knew they only had a handful of blocks to go. Dan was screaming in agony and every single person they passed stared at the bloody mess of men storming along the sidewalk.

Fabian spotted a barrow lying next to a grocer's shop. He flung out its contents onto the ground. Rotating it backwards so they could drag his carcass onto the cart, Fabian and Sammy flew down the streets with their makeshift stretcher with Paulie and Abraham in front pushing people out of the way.

"Where are we going?"

"Ira's."

"He won't be pleased with us arriving in this state."

Sammy was right. There were witnesses along every street to show where they'd come from and where they were going. Even a bent cop would be able to follow the trail from corpse to bleeding Dan. They couldn't go to Bayard and Bowery. Think, Alex, think.

Fabian recalled the only doctor he knew although he had no idea if he could trust him: Amos's father. They hightailed it over to his surgery, flung the door open and pushed their way into his room.

The man took one look at Dan and took them next door where they laid the poor boy down. All the guys left the doctor to do his work apart from Fabian. He stayed so the lad would have a friendly face to see—if he ever opened his eyes again.

Adam Feierman ripped off Dan's top to investigate the bleeding. Fabian saw a puddle of red where the boy's stomach ought to be. The doctor placed some gauze over the open wounds and gave the boy a shot of morphine. A minute later and Dan was still for the first time, in hours, so it felt. Feierman took Fabian out of the room, leaving the door ajar.

"What are the chances, doc?"

"Of him surviving, you mean? Next to none, I'm afraid. You've seen the wounds. They are many and deep. If the boy were in a hospital then maybe, he might have an outside chance if someone could stitch him back together."

"That could be done?"

"If you have the money and he has the time. And even then, it'd still be fifty-fifty whether he lived."

Fabian looked askance at the doctor who stared at him.

"It's not my place to ask how this happened but we both know this was no accident. I would have thought you'd worked out this is the price of the life you lead."

"I didn't come here for a sermon."

"No, I'm sure you did not, but that's the truth. I'm just pointing out what is staring you in the face."

"Let's get back to Dan. How much money would we need and how soon to get it?"

"Over a hundred dollars and in the next thirty minutes. At best. The boy is dying on my gurney as we speak."

33

THEY BOTH PEERED back into the room and although Dan was quiet, the red lake had already spread across the entire surface of his bandages.

"And if we don't have that money?"

"We wait until the end."

Feierman left Fabian alone and returned to his other patient. The guys huddled around Fabian.

"What's the story, boss?"

"Dan ain't gonna make it. He's sedated but hasn't got long."

"Should we get his ma and pa?"

"And let them see him like this? No."

He led them into the room and each said their goodbyes to their companion. Then he sent them back to Waxey to report on this morning's events.

"Stay with me, Sammy."

"Sure, Fabian."

Despite what had happened and how he felt about Sammy, Fabian still needed his long-time friend near him as he watched Dan go to meet his maker. They grabbed two chairs and sat near him, just in case he needed anything from them. The morphine was giving him everything he wanted— some peace and rest.

Twenty minutes later, Fabian looked up and Dan's head had flopped to one side. He nudged Sammy who was caught up in his own thoughts looking out the window.

"Is he…?"

Fabian put his ear to Dan's mouth and heard no breathing and felt no air on his earlobe. He called in Feierman who pronounced Dan officially deceased and then they reached an accommodation over his costs and the need to inform Dan's parents.

Sammy and Fabian walked out the back of the building.

"We better get you cleaned up."

"Yeah, I look like I work in an abattoir."

Sammy wasn't wrong; there was blood on Fabian's hands, sleeves and all over his body. Sammy only had a few flecks of his own innards splattered around his collar.

"Let's go to the Forsyth."

Sammy nodded and as they strode down the street, Fabian whipped off his coat, rolled it up and threw it into a passing dump truck. As they carried on, Fabian had the feeling everyone was noticing his red doused cuffs.

"Give me your coat, will you? I stand out with all this filth on me."

Sammy handed over his jacket and three minutes later, Fabian swiped a hat from a table in front of a bar they walked past. He kept the brim firmly over his eyes in the hope no-one would recognize him if asked by the cops later. At the back of his mind was the possibility that the Yake Brady gang might come seeking them too. There were Irish corpses left when they ran north of Canal.

EVENTUALLY FABIAN AND Sammy reached the Forsyth and, without asking Nathan or looking directly at anyone in the bar, made their way straight to the kitchens where Fabian began to wash himself down. Ten minutes into the process, Nathan came back of house to check on what was going on.

"You guys want any help?"

"Not right now, Nathan. Thanks."

"Spot of bother, I see."

"And then some. Do you have any spare clothes? I need to get out of these things. They're in a complete state."

Nathan eyed the crimson to rust colored clothing draped on Fabian's body and agreed they needed dealing with. An advantage of being a whorehouse and a bar is that gentlemen are wont to forget all their clothes in the rush to get back to their wives and the hotel had a fine selection of outerwear for Fabian. They both swapped their bloody shirts for fresh ones and Nathan gave them a bag for their dirties. Fabian knew Nathan shouldn't be saddled with destroying that much evidence. Not fair on him and too risky if Nathan were caught.

"Given the mayhem we left behind, we will need some personal protection. Got anything that'd help?"

Nathan smiled because this was the latest in a long and familiar line of similar requests Waxey's men had made over the years. He beckoned them with a single finger and they followed him to what looked like an office. Desk, chair, shelves with paperwork strewn all over them. And a box about six foot by three foot in the corner. Nathan opened the lid and inside was a collection of knuckledusters, iron bars and bats.

"No knives in here. Too easy to cut yourself when you grab something."

He had thought of everything. The blades were in a separate box sitting on the shelves. Fabian grabbed a baseball bat, knuckledusters and a short-bladed knife. Sammy took a single brass knuckle; they both knew he wasn't much of a fighter as this morning's events amply demonstrated.

By the time they walked out the Forsyth, the sun had set. It was five thirty.

"Quite a day."

"Yes, Sammy. We lost two good men and we'll be licking these wounds for some time."

"Yeah. Do you think we should hit the Yake Brady's place again?"

"Not without serious help from Waxey. Those Yakeys were tough. Real determined."

"You said it. But our guys fought hard. They earned their money this morning."

"Those who are still alive to get paid."

Silence descended as Fabian calculated how big a donation he should make to Ben and Dan's families. This was the first fatality in the line of duty he'd faced this side of the Atlantic. Fabian decided to get advice from Ira.

Then he realized, after all the attention on the boys he still needed to report back to Waxey. They'd need to go there now and hope he wasn't too mad at being the last to know.

Fabian led them along the street and noticed his stomach rumbling. With adrenalin pumping and blood and guts to sort out, he hadn't eaten since breakfast. He bought some bread, cheese and an apple on the way.

As they strode towards Waxey's, they passed an alleyway—one Fabian remembered immediately.

"Hey, stop for a second."

He led Sammy into the alley. It was long and much wider at the other end than at its entrance.

"Know this place?"

Sammy looked blankly around and slowly a flicker twitched across his face as he squinted into the darkness in front.

"The day we met."

"The craps game over there."

Fabian pointed to the far wall. For the first time that day, they both relaxed. He reminded Sammy how he'd pretended to put Fabian in charge of the game and now he was running his own crew.

"See, Sammy. You were right to put your faith in me—a great judge of character."

"You're not so bad yourself, Fabian."

"I have my moments but I also have times of weakness. My biggest failing is I need everyone to be happy. No, really. So I end up doing things which I don't wish to do or go against my instincts because it will benefit others. I'm soft like that."

Sammy leaned against a wall and snorted in disbelief as Fabian regaled him with this claim; it had been a long day and Sammy reckoned he could mouth off this once.

"You know I never wanted to expand that far south of Canal but I could see you felt it was the right thing to do. So when Waxey asks me to help, what do I do?"

"You helped me."

"Exactly correct. Despite thinking it was a dumbass idea, I went along with it and supported you. What have you lost? A shirt and a coat. What am I down? Two good men and the respect of my crew, because I'm the one that got Ben and Dan killed.

"To your credit, Sammy, you are great—at getting other people to do your dirty work. It's a skill. I looked after your craps game back then and here I am still looking after your interests in the numbers racket. You are unbelievable.

"But I have learned my lesson. From this moment I will change. I swear on the souls of my grandchildren as yet unborn. From now on, I'm not going to look after your concerns anymore. It's time I looked after my own and stopped helping you feather your own nest, you putz."

Slugger gripped his baseball bat and with a single swing struck Sammy on the side of the skull. A parabola of blood spat out of his ear as his body hurtled downwards. Then a rain of blows cascaded out of Slugger all over Sammy's torso, head and back.

Sammy cowered in a ball and tried to shrink into nothing, but Slugger continued until Sammy gave in and slumped, body flaccid.

"You'd better not get up from this, you *gonif.* Understand? Two of mine are dead because of you."

Sammy's leg twitched. Fabian looked down and saw the blood specks on his coat. Today was not a good day for his tailoring. He wiped the baseball bat with Sammy's shirt tails and left the alleyway. Time to talk to Waxey.

JANUARY 19, 1918 6:30 PM

34

FABIAN POURED HIMSELF a coffee and stretched out at the table in Waxey's meeting room. The familiarity of the chairs, their position far from the window and the peeling paint on the walls gave him a comfort he'd never thought he would experience again. Tough day.

Waxey walked in and sat down, a glass of beer in his hand. His expression was serious: eyes cold, jaw stiff.

"So, talk to me."

"Things went south. Big time. And they've been getting worse as the day's gone on."

"Start at the beginning and let me know everything. Then we can figure out where to go from here."

Fabian described the attack on the Yake Brady numbers game, emphasizing the bravery of his men and omitting the fact Sammy ran out as soon as the fighting began. He told how they took out two of their guys but at the expense of Ben and Dan.

"Good fellas, both."

How they flew through the streets dragging Dan along with them until they reached the doctor. Fabian focused on the details of Dan's death, still heavy in his heart. As he spoke, he realized the boy's body was only two hours cold. This lulled him into a silence and Waxey left him absorbed in his thoughts for three minutes.

"And what happened next? Where's Sammy?"

"I'm hoping you got to hear the news around then because I sent the boys round here."

"Yes. They were highly excited and eventually I pieced together the story. Then I gave them a bonus and told them to get out of town until the middle of next week. Let the dust settle in case the cops investigate a death in the Bowery for the first time in their lives."

"Thank you for dealing with that, Waxey."

"Don't give it another thought. We work together, we live together but we always die alone."

Fabian let that thought drip inside his brain.

"Once Sammy and I finished settling matters with the doc, we left to head here, but we looked dreadful, blood all over us. So we fled to the Forsyth to clean ourselves up. Couldn't think of anywhere more discreet; Nathan is a good man."

"Known him since I was a kid. Same class at school. He's a stand-up fella."

"He got us some new threads, and we washed. Then we left to see you."

"But there's only you and me in the room."

"Yes, well. That's when the day got worse. Three of the Yake Brady mob must have followed our trail or something. But we were heading here when we saw them following us. Right or wrong, we ran and split up. Sammy headed east toward the wharfs and I ran west to Bowery. One came after me and two followed Sammy.

"I waited round a corner and bolted out at my guy. He jumped a mile high. I took a swing at him and he was out cold. So I left him where he fell and tried to find Sammy to help him."

"Did you locate him?"

"No. I looked all over but there was no sign."

"Them Yake Brady got a lot of answering to do."

Fabian nodded in agreement. Lying to Waxey wasn't the greatest plan in the world but telling the truth was worse.

"What should I do?"

"You? Now? Nothing. Leave it with me. Carry on as you normally would. Don't break your usual routine."

"Business just carries on?"

"Times like these; for you, yes. I've got the Yake Brady situation to deal with but it's not your fault. This has been bubbling for a while. It's why I wanted you and Sammy to hit them today. Figured we'd kick at their heels and gauge their response. Well, now we know, and I'll respond when the time is right.

"You need to keep your head down and carry on with your work. Your crew might not be with you for the next three days but tomorrow I'll send you some guys to do collections. Don't get too aggressive with any late payers. We mustn't remind people about that swing of yours, Slugger."

Waxey used that nickname carefully. He wasn't goading Fabian or teasing him; just wanted him to be very aware of his reputation and how it might make it easier for any cop to come calling on the off chance.

"Got it, Waxey."

"When Sammy gets back, we can talk about what you will do next, but if those two caught up with him... he was never much of a fighter."

"We should have stuck together."

Waxey eyed him up and down.

"Yes, you should."

"I peeled off left, and he careered off rightwards before I could do anything."

"It happens. People decide in the heat of the moment. We've all been there."

Fabian nodded, barely able to make eye contact but knowing he must if wasn't to reveal his lie.

"Go home, freshen up. Get rid of all the clothes you're wearing. But I don't need to tell you that."

"It's all right, Waxey. Good to hear solid words after the day I've had."

"And don't pop round to Dan or Ben's family. Yake Brady can easily ask around and find where they live. You don't want to be found there if they do. Leave the rest to me."

January 19, 1918 8 PM

35

AFTER A LONG soak in the tub, Alex put on fresh clothes and bundled his old things up to throw away later. Images from earlier in the day flashed into his mind. When the knife went into Dan. The slashing of Ben's throat. Sammy lying still on the ground buried by the shadow of the wall into absolute darkness.

He needed to escape from this blackness into the light. So he flew down one flight of stairs to take in the glow of Rebecca. There she sat in the bosom of her family, an evening meal waning into conversation and washing up.

Alex stood and watched, focusing his entire attention on her and all that she did. The warmth of the lighting inside the apartment gave her hair an angelic hue. Despite all that had gone before that day, this was a perfect moment.

She turned her head toward the right and noticed him in the doorway and beamed.

"How long have you been standing there?"

"A minute, no more."

"Why don't you come on in."

Her parents smiled to invite him in and finally her mother beckoned for him to enter. Alex sat down with the Grunbergs and tried to follow their conversation. He hadn't been eavesdropping. Only staring.

They had shuffled their chairs round so he could sit next to Rebecca, but he'd have preferred to be opposite her so he could bathe in the sight of her. This way, he could only catch a glimpse when he turned his head, without being obvious about his intentions.

Alex helped by cleaning the dishes with her; he washed, and she dried. They stood next to each other like any couple would, although they were far from being together and he had done nothing to extricate himself from the numbers or labor racketeering.

"Do you fancy going out for a drink?"

"Like last time?"

215

"I hope not. You can choose where we go. I just want to spend some time with you this evening, is all."

"If Mama will let me. There should be a chaperone nowadays."

"Why?"

"We are both of an age where parents need to look after the interests of their daughters."

She winked because Alex might be many things, but he was always honorable. At least with her. She touched his arm and giggled.

"Mr Grunberg. Will you permit me to take Rebecca out for a promenade or even a small libation?"

"My boy, so polite. Of course you may. But she must be home by nine."

"That doesn't give us much time."

"Then stop talking with me and leave the apartment."

Papa Grunberg issued a sardonic curl of his lips. Alex nodded, and they bustled out the building and down onto the street.

"Where d'you like to go?"

"There's a coffee shop not too far from here where respectable people sit down for a slice of cake."

"Take me to your jam sponge."

He followed her as they zigzagged around the Bowery ending up five or six blocks away from home. For reasons best known to her, Rebecca'd taken them on a circuitous route to Delaney and Columbia.

"Are you trying to confuse me where we are?"

"Not at all, Alex. I just wanted to make sure all my friends had time to see me out at night on my own."

"On your own?"

"Yeah, without my parents, silly. Men have it easy. Women spend their lives under the watchful eyes of their mama and papa."

They walked inside and sat down. Five minutes later a waiter appeared to take their order. Alex told her she could have anything she wanted.

"Coffee and walnut cake, please."

"For two."

Alex waited for the waitress to leave the vicinity.

"So how's life without dance?"

"I'm not without it. Just not much of it. And it's fine."

"I'm only asking because I think you deserve more."

Rebecca patted him on the hand.

"I know but sometimes you have a funny way of saying things. Makes you sound very antagonistic."

"It's frustrating knowing you can help someone you really like but they won't let you."

They stared into each other's eyes and he rested his hand on hers until the order arrived. They drank a couple of mouthfuls of coffee and tucked into their cake. There were walnut pieces stuck onto the icing and Alex savored the intense flavors rolling around his palate. The harshness of the day faded inside his head.

"And have you done anything about what we spoke of last time?"

"Not yet. It really isn't easy, even if you see it as a simple task. Honestly, if I don't do what I do, I have no idea from Adam what I could do instead."

"A day's work for an honest day's toil."

"Hey now. Who's being antagonistic?"

"Sorry. You could be so much more than you are right now, but you have to believe in yourself. I believe in you, Alex, and I know I can't live a life the way you do. Nor could my parents. So it is down to you to change."

Alex swallowed hard. The last thing he needed now was a sermon on the perils of the life in the gang. Not after today. He gritted his teeth and inhaled deeply through his nose. Also, he didn't want to have an argument with the one person who delivered goodness into his world.

"I am not a tailor or a doctor. I am not my parents. This makes it difficult to find a fresh direction to my life, but I am trying. You need to give me a chance."

"Sure, Alex. I'd offer you as much time as I can but I'm not in charge here. My parents are—as you know. Each minute of every day they are talking with a matchmaker to get me married off now that Amos..."

Her voice faded away as she rekindled thoughts she wished would not resurface. Alex gave her enough time to dwell but not linger on Amos Feierstien. Then he thought about the boy's father and what he had done this afternoon to give Dan peace in the last moments of his existence.

"Today has not been a great day for me, Rebecca. Might be the best for you though. For the first time I am not sure I can stay involved in my business."

36

"WHAT HAPPENED?"

"I can't go into details and, if you knew, you wouldn't want me to. Just, my world is turning upside down. If it carries on in that trajectory, I will have no choice and will have to turn my back on it—even if I have nothing else to do."

"Sounds gruesome."

"Like you wouldn't believe."

Rebecca opened her mouth to speak, but no words escaped her lips. They finished their cake in silence, both mulling over their conversation.

Alex got the check, and they left for home, holding hands as they sauntered west along Delancey. They kept the chat light and breezy, not wanting to delve into the fundamental chasm between them. They both reveled in each other's company and the feel of the other next to them. He knew this is what he wanted and relaxed into imagining it become his reality.

They'd just passed the sign for Ridge Street, four blocks short of Suffolk, when two boys walked up to them. They couldn't have been older than fourteen, dressed scruffily and from the neighborhood.

"You got money?"

One was three inches taller than his friend and did all the talking while the companion stood with a menacing scowl on his face.

"We're not looking for any trouble here, guys."

Rebecca held onto Alex's hand a little tighter than before.

"Good and you won't get any. You got money?"

"Don't see it's any of your business. Be off with you and find a different patsy."

Alex stood tall, straightening his back despite the weight of the day bearing down on him. The last thing he needed right now were two tykes hustling him on the street. Sounding like his father, he wondered why they weren't tucked up at home in their beds.

"Give us some money and we're away."

Alex fished around his back pocket and pulled out two nickels.

"Here it is. Take it or leave it. That's all you're getting from us."

His eyes bored into the kids, glaring at them. He hoped they would pick up the sense he was not the right person to mess with tonight, but the implication of his gaze appeared to wash over them.

"Not enough. We want some proper money. If you're offering us nickels, then you've got more to offer."

Rebecca squeezed his hand more and whispered: "Give them what they want so we can get out of here. Please."

Alex ignored her pleading. Too many people had been hurt and died for him to concede so quickly to the pair of half-nothings stood before him.

"Be on your way and be glad with five cents each. It's more than you deserve."

"Same again and we're outa your face."

Alex laughed.

"If you're only worth a couple of dimes, you'd better get away from me now or I might change my mind and do you some serious harm."

Rebecca's hand tightened even more over his. Alex knew this was scaring her, but he wasn't in the mood to get played by a pair of kids. His male ego was at stake too.

"We can look after ourselves, mister. Give us another dime and we're gone. You and your girl carry on with your walk."

Alex glanced at Rebecca and resumed staring at the two boys. He threw a dime onto the sidewalk and returned the remains of his cash to his back pocket. The silent companion bent down and picked the coin out from the grime of the street.

As the negotiator turned to watch his friend pick up the coin, Alex took the opportunity to tap him in the side with his foot, making him lose his balance and knocking him over. Alex laughed again.

"Tip for you—never take your eye off your mark. Now off with you before you get into some real trouble. Tell your friends you chiseled two dimes out of Fabian and see what they say."

Both boys were on the floor and looked quizzically up. They sprang up, glanced at each other and raced away. Rebecca's hand began to relax in his.

"Who's Fabian?"

"Has no-one in the block told you? When we arrived here, I was named Fabian Mustard by customs and it's kinda stuck as my street name."

"Fabian. Sounds so old American."

"I know. I'm about as far from that as anyone could be."

They both chuckled and Alex pulled Rebecca in toward him to kiss her on the forehead. He wanted so much more but wasn't sure she'd let him. So he played safe. Ever the gentleman.

She placed an arm around his back to stop him from moving away and kissed him on the lips. Her leg touched his thigh, and he felt like he'd won today's numbers.

"Let's go home, shall we?"

"If I'm to keep my word to your father then we'd better."

He put his arm over her shoulders, and she clung to his waist. They walked in unison over to Suffolk and then the two blocks south to the tenement. Although he hadn't considered their location in this way before, Alex realized they lived only six blocks north of Cherry, the front line between Waxey Gordon and Yake Brady territories.

Into the block and up the stairs until they stood outside the Grunbergs' apartment with its door permanently open to the world.

"Thank you for spending time with me tonight."

"Isn't the girl meant to say that at the end of the night, Alex?"

"Sometimes I guess, but I mean it."

"You're welcome. If you can sort out your work, then I think you should get your father to speak with mine."

"I will do my best. Today was so strange, I still can't work out it out. I don't want to talk to you about it—best you never know—but once I figure things out..."

"Oh, Alex. Be careful: only make promises you can keep. If you're work is so difficult to leave, then so be it. Tell me and we can be friends and have an occasional slice of cake and a coffee. It's up to you, but you've spent months not doing anything and I'm not getting any younger and my parents haven't occupied a day of their lives without looking for a suitor for me. The longer you leave it, the less likely we'll be together."

"And you couldn't accept me for what I do?"

Rebecca looked at him and turned her head to one side as if judging his words through her eyes.

"The fact you cannot tell me what has happened to you today is proof I want nothing to do with such a life—or anyone who lives it. Dirty gang bums."

She snorted the last syllables and an image flashed through his head of Ben's body lying on the floor surrounded by his own blood. He was no bum.

"Don't say that!"

He raised an arm and let the back of his hand slap against Rebecca's cheek, causing her to spin around and grab the door to steady herself.

"Get out of here!"

Alex scurried down the stairs before he could apologize. What had he been thinking? Why on earth had he hit her so? Not for the first time this evening, he launched himself into the shadows and hurtled along sidewalks hoping to vanish into the nothingness of the night.

JANUARY 19, 1918 10 PM

37

WHY? THE QUESTION rattled inside his skull as Fabian ricocheted along the streets. Once he'd bumped into three people on the trot, the rest of the passersby on the sidewalk gave him a wide berth.

Everything had got on top of him today and Rebecca's comment was the last straw. The disappointment of not breaking into the pool. If he couldn't hustle what was left for him to do? Nothing. And without Sammy to mind the shop, what would happen to his mini empire. Not only that, but half the boys were gone who ran the pools each day. Even Mama's chicken soup wouldn't be able to make this mess any better for him.

The pressure? Fabian wanted to spend his life with Rebecca, but his head was so intertwined with Waxey's crews. Seeing her again had reminded him how far away he was from living out his dreams. His hopes lay in that beautiful woman who probably wouldn't speak to him again. The twin weights on his shoulders, how to recover from this morning and to win Rebecca's heart tore him asunder. He had lashed out like a little babe.

The frustration? Fabian knew he was caught between two stools and didn't know which way to turn. To have power and riches on the one hand or his love on the other.

There stood the Oregon in all its finery. The late-night crowd appeared to have already arrived and the place was in full swing. It wasn't bursting, so much as groaning at its edges.

He pushed in and reached the bar after a long struggle. Fabian didn't have the energy or inclination to use his physical strength against these lowlifes.

"Beer. Large. And a vodka chaser."

With both glasses in his hands, he followed a path toward the outskirts of the mayhem, perching himself at the corner of a table.

"Don't mind if I sit down, do you?"

The two men shrugged disinterest and Fabian sat down, regardless. If they had objected, then he'd have thrown them out without a moment's hesitation.

He knocked back the hard liquor and took a swig from his beer. Fabian surveyed the Oregon's first floor and saw only carousing, drinking and a couple in the corner pecking at each other's lips. All the Bowery's diverse community was here—apart from the children. Presumably, they were tucked up in bed, all cozy and asleep.

He played his game of guessing which of the women were whores and which of the men would pay to go upstairs with them. He was better at judging the nafkas than picking out the willing johns. Half the time he couldn't see the men's faces but he could always see what clothes the girls were wearing. And he was right. The uniform of a Bowery nafka looked as though it had been handed out by her pimp, though Fabian knew this didn't happen.

As his mind wandered away from his game onto a feeble attempt to see all the way up the legs of a particularly attractive girl perched not four feet from him, one eye kept guard on the staircase. Fabian was hoping to catch Sarah, but he hadn't seen her since he came in.

The black-haired prostitute sat on the lap of a hulk of a guy and a hand was journeying up her leg and toward her thigh. Each time it went past her knee, she'd grab it and place it lower down. She sure was teasing him because there is no way on this earth a woman would have walked into here wearing nothing but a dressing gown and basque. Fabian couldn't figure out why she wasn't taking him upstairs to earn better money than a cut of the drinks profit.

That said, he sure was packing it away. Fabian had seen three large beers go down the guy's neck since he sat down and then the john ordered a bottle of champagne. More money than sense. He didn't recognize the nafka. She must be new—well done to her for milking the fella dry. Even if she didn't part her legs for him, she would still have made a tidy sum out of him, now the sparkling wine was flowing.

Her gown was black silk and her corset was red, in the grand tradition of working women around the world. Despite his efforts, Fabian failed to see much more between her legs than the occasional flash of white thigh. That was how she wanted it—the mark needed to stay keen but shouldn't peak too early—for all the obvious reasons.

Another girl came down the stairs, but she wasn't the person he was seeking. Fabian returned to the bar and filled up both glasses.

"Sarah in tonight?"

"Yeah, she's busy right now."

"Figured that out for myself."

"She won't be long, I'm sure."

A return to the table and he knocked the vodka to the back of his throat. Then a sip of beer and further staring in front of him. A second bottle of champagne had arrived for the nearby couple. The guy knew how to drink and must have hollow legs because Fabian couldn't hear any slurring in his voice.

Once the bubbly was empty, she took him by the hand and led him up the stairs. He teetered on his feet but made it safely until they vanished from sight. The girl was smart. With that much alcohol inside him, there would be no problem finishing him off in a few minutes then she could be back to woo some other customer.

Still no Sarah though. Fabian was bored waiting. He'd soaked up about enough of the atmosphere in the bar as he was prepared to. The place was noisy, smoky and filled with drunks. They always thought they were funnier, cleverer and stronger than the next guy and the last thing he wanted tonight was more fighting.

He finished his beer, ordered a shot of whiskey and sauntered upstairs. With the glass in one hand, he passed his fingers casually along the wall of the corridor on the second floor. He counted the doors as he walked past them; they were all shut and he had no desire to walk in on strangers unannounced.

FABIAN STOOD OUTSIDE Sarah's door and leaned his ear against the wood. Nothing but muffled noises, although they sounded more like words than moans. The client was paying for one long conversation, he thought. There was a high-pitched laugh as Sarah chortled at something the john said. Fabian ground his molars, unhappy at the prospect of some other man enjoying her company. He didn't mind sharing her body—he knew that was an inevitable consequence of her job. But he'd not imagined anyone else talking to her like she was a human being.

He knocked on the door. Even if there was conversation taking place, Fabian had little desire to see the guy if he was naked.

"Not now, I'm busy."

"Here are the refreshments you ordered."

"No drinks for here. You've got the wrong room."

"Definitely here. Champagne: two glasses, one ice bucket."

He reckoned the lure of an expensive bottle to charge the client might be sufficient to tempt her out—and he was right.

A rustle inside, the door opened a crack and Sarah slithered out the room.

"Fabian. I thought I recognized the voice. Why are you messing about? I'm working."

"I know but I've been waiting for you and I thought you'd be done soon."

"Gonna be a while. Isaac likes to take his time and I charge him by the quarter hour, so he gets no complaints from me."

Fabian looked down at her and saw the open gown, loosened corset and both nipples peeping out the top.

"Your eyes'll fall off their stems."

She squeezed his groin and smiled up at him.

"It'll all be over in the next hour for sure, but he's a regular."

The disappointment in Fabian's face must have spread from one ear to the other.

"Don't look at me like that. A girl has to earn a living. By the time I pay the rent on this room, I've got to hustle my ass simply to get some food on the table."

"I know. It's just… it's been a rough day."

"For you and me both, kid."

Fabian placed a solitary fingertip on a breast and circled a nipple without making contact.

"Your time will come. Patience, my dear."

She kissed him on the cheek, went back inside and shut him out. Fabian was not impressed. Waiting for her to finish with some john was too much for him to process. On the other hand, if he smashed through the door, Sarah would not be in the right frame of mind no matter what dough he splashed on her. He was trapped.

A swig of his whiskey and he crumpled down on the floor. He couldn't return to the fray downstairs and, if he wasn't going to be in the room with Sarah, the best thing for him was to wait outside. Fabian had had enough. He was spent, so he closed his eyes and let the back of his head touch the wall. His legs were apart, and he held the glass in both hands in front of his stomach, nearly touching his groin. Aside from an occasional sip of his drink, he remained still for what felt like an eternity.

Other doors opened; some closed. Each time he received a strange look, but nobody said anything. The men were more concerned about going back downstairs and that their buttons were all done up. The women recognized him, in the main, and figured if Fabian wanted to sit on the floor, that was his right and no one should argue with him.

Finally, when he looked up, he saw his glass was empty and lying on its side. Sixty-five minutes had passed since Sarah stepped out to talk with him. The time for waiting was over.

Fabian stood up, turned to face the door, grabbed the doorknob and barged his way in. She was seated on the bed, no underwear on her and just her gown draped like she'd cast it off at some earlier point and not bothered where it landed. Averill Dikla sat next to her, still wearing all his clothes.

"Fabian!"

Sarah stood up, surprised, and then grabbed her silk cover and wrapped it around herself.

"You need to leave now."

He assumed she was speaking to Averill, who made no attempt to act on the instruction.

"Fabian, I haven't finished here yet. Please. I'm asking you to wait."

Fabian's eyes were fully focused on Averill, who just sat there looking at the floor. His eyes were red like he'd been crying. There was a half full glass of water—or vodka—at his feet.

"I've waited long enough. It's been more than an hour now and your friend needs to be the one who goes."

Sarah turned her head to check on Averill who hadn't moved a muscle since Fabian's entrance. Then she edged towards Fabian and whispered in his ear.

"Please don't ruin this for me. Averill's in a bad way and I'm the only person he trusts to talk to. When he's gone, I promise you we'll spend the whole of the night together. But this is work now and I can't let him down."

"I want you."

Fabian's hands had attached themselves to her hips, and she placed her fingers on his.

"I'd prefer to be with you too. But after Averill's gone. Not until then."

Fabian darted from Sarah's face to Averill's. Could he strong-arm Averill out the room? What benefit had there been for any of his aggression today? His shoulders slumped, and he released his grip on her pelvis.

"I'm sorry."

"Hey, I always like a man who's interested in me."

He headed for the door. Then Averill stood up.

"It's time for me to go, Sarah."

"Please don't. Fabian's leaving now. He was just a bit impatient, right?"

"Yes, sure thing."

"No, I should be going anyway."

Averill shuffled to the bedside table and put some money down. Then he bumbled over to the door, having kissed her on the cheek on his way past, and closed it as he left. Fabian and Sarah were finally alone.

38

"HOPE HE DIDN'T shortchange you."

Sarah walked over to the cash and counted it.

"No, the sap paid me for another hour. Guess I owe him next time."

"And he sits there and cries?"

"Pretty much, yes. Twice he's touched my knee and once I took his pants off but that's about as far as we've gone. Just a lot of talking and a bunch of tears."

"Like my parents' marriage."

"Not just them from what I can tell."

A smile and a wink.

"I've been cooped up in here for hours. Do you fancy going someplace?"

"Where were you thinking?"

"Dunno... How about a dance?"

"Dancing."

"Yes. Move from one foot to another? In time to some music?"

"Sure. Why not?"

Fabian had hoped for a quiet moment with Sarah, nuzzling under the blankets while he poured out his heart to her, but he understood she'd suffered enough of that from Avrill. She needed a break.

"I'll put some clothes on and we can get out of here."

"Got anywhere in particular in mind?"

"There's a place round the corner from here."

He sat in the chair and watched as Sarah opened the wardrobe and threw clothes onto the covers. Then underwear, dress and make-up at the dressing table and she was ready. He'd never noticed the mirror and the table before in all the times he'd been here. His mind always focused on the bed. He smiled inside at his own tunnel vision.

"Let's go. What're you waiting for?"

As they made for the door, Fabian slapped Sarah's behind playfully, then grabbed her round the waist and planted a kiss firmly on her lips.

"They'll be plenty of time for that later, dear. Now we dance."

She led them out the Oregon and round to *The Portland Hotel* which used its wooden floor as a dance area three times a week; even had a four-piece band and not merely a fella on a piano.

Fabian insisted they settle into a table early on. When the barman saw her, he nodded at her and took her order. Then his line of sight traveled to her companion and his eyes widened a little when he recognized Fabian. Their first drinks were on the house and the barkeep had a quiet word with the maître d' so a location was found in a good position.

The liquid hardly touched his lips before Sarah grabbed his hand and dragged him to the dance floor. There were already half a dozen couples shuffling along to the beat of the music. No-one was ballroom standard, but all toes appeared safe from stamping and Fabian's skills perfectly matched the requirement.

Luck was on Fabian's side because no sooner had they arrived on the floor than the band shifted down a gear and played a slow number. The existing couples got all smoochy and three more pairs joined them for a slow move around the space. Sarah put her arms around Fabian's neck, and he wrapped his arms around her waist. Then she rested her head on his chest and he let himself sag slightly so his chin touched the top of her head and he could breathe in the perfume of her hair. In that moment, he was relaxed. Totally at peace with the world, despite the day's hardships.

One song segued into the next and they slowly rotated their way around the dance floor, over and over again. Even when the music picked up and a fast beat was on offer, they remained at the same pace, much to the annoyance of some other patrons. But Fabian didn't mind, and Sarah seemed in no rush to change what they were doing.

The Portland maintained a policy of providing music until all drinking customers had departed from the building. By one in the morning, they were the only ones on the dance floor and there were only the usual quantity of barflies stuck to the honey of the bar.

"The band will pack up after the next song."

Fabian nodded acceptance and showed his appreciation by leaving a tip for them. He knew they'd overstayed their welcome, and the musicians had been forced to play longer than they wanted by the maître d'.

"I enjoyed that. I'm glad you made the suggestion."

"Full of good ideas. That's me."

They held hands as they ambled to the Oregon, legs in sync as they sauntered along the sidewalk.

Back in Sarah's room, they stripped and got into bed. She got frisky but Fabian stopped her as he still had matters he wanted to get off his chest. Instead, they lay down with Sarah on top of him, so he could try to control the vixen. Her legs were splayed apart and her thighs hugged his, so the truth was he was unable to move without her permission. But he perceived he was in charge and that was important to him.

"My crew's been decimated today. We hit a Yake Brady numbers racket and ran away with a bloody nose—guys dead and maimed."

Sarah kissed him on the neck in response.

"I've lost a bunch of my people and Sammy's missing. The Yake Brady crew came after us this afternoon and the last time I saw him alive he was being chased down the road, two against one."

Fabian chose not to give Sarah the truth about Sammy because her loose talk could cost him his life. 'We work together, we live together, but we die alone.'

Another kiss from her to ease the pain.

"I've no idea how I will face tomorrow. I really don't."

Two kisses on the neck and one on his upper torso. Sarah ran her fingers through his hair.

"To cap it all, I saw Rebecca this evening."

Sarah's body stiffened at the mention of that name.

"And I've screwed that up completely. She was taunting me over doing nothing about quitting the business and I slapped her to shut her up. It's all *fercockt*."

More kisses and she moved her hips around his pelvis.

"Hope you haven't come to me for any answers."

"Just want to say it all out loud. Not much more."

"I understand."

Sarah continued to rock her body over his, kissing him as she did so.

"Fabian. I'll tell you again because it is still true. If you wanted us to be together, I'd do so in a heartbeat. That's not what you want, but with me you could keep your life and I reckon we'd make a good pair."

"You're probably right but there's too much going on in my head for me to do anything about that."

"Seems to me you want change without doing anything about it. To get your woman, you must leave the business. But you are not prepared to do it. If you were, it would've happened by now. You don't procrastinate like this."

"Is that what this boils down to? I want to have my cake and eat it?"

"Pretty much, wouldn't you say?"

"I guess."

Fabian fell into silence as he mulled that thought over in his mind. She was right. He was intoxicated by a beautiful woman, but he had no interest in doing anything about getting her. *Gornisht*. Didn't stop him wanting her though.

"Do you think she'd wait for me?"

"Until when?"

"Until I'm a success."

"Sounds like a long time to me."

"Yeah, but if I made it, I could stop this line of—"

"Fabian, listen. You will not solve your problem by talking about it. If you want the girl, you know what you need to do. If you're not prepared to do it, let her go. Either way, you must stop driving yourself meshugge over this woman. Stops you from concentrating on matters at hand."

Sarah slid down his torso, kissing him until his attention was turned to their bodies and they frolicked for a while.

Afterwards, they spooned, with Fabian curling around Sarah's tuches, fingers draped on her breast, stroking and playing with it mindlessly.

"I once asked you what you thought I should do, and you didn't answer me properly."

"Not true. I did offer you a response, just one you didn't want to hear—that you should forget about Rebecca and hook up with me."

He was quiet because, more or less, she was right. That had been what she said. He enjoyed his time with Sarah and she was certainly easygoing. But did he feel about her the way he felt about Rebecca? No, not at all. Over their years together, he had seen every inch of this woman's body, but it was Rebecca's he craved, as unknown today as it was the first moment he yearned for her.

"Fabian."

"Yes?"

"Can we please find something else to talk about instead of Rebecca?"

"Sure."

"Can't speak for you, but I enjoy our moments together and having a third person in the bed cramps my enjoyment."

"Kinky."

"That's you, my dear. You're the one who brings her into our bedroom and won't let her leave. Like you're chaining her to the bed."

"Very kinky."

"And I should know. I've had all sorts in this place. The good thing is I charge extra for weird."

"Am I weird?"

"You are a very different kind of weird. Besides, you don't pay."

Sarah wriggled deep into Fabian's curves and he laughed.

"Oh, I pay all right! Just not with dollars."

He tickled her, and she turned round to tickle him back. They squirmed and giggled until Fabian had Sarah pinned down, hands on her wrists and legs on top of hers. She chuckled.

"What you going to do about it now?"

He bent down and kissed her, and they made love again. Afterwards they fell asleep in each other's arms. Like a trysting couple but with none of the emotion between them.

Fabian awoke around five, mouth dry and tasting obscene—a strange mix of beer, liquor and sex. His belly rumbled loud enough to wake the dead, and he remembered he hadn't had dinner. He twisted round and looked down to see Sarah's ass. Cute.

His stomach made a noise again although she didn't stir. He could do far worse than stick with that butt and forget all about Rebecca. She was nothing but trouble for him; messed with his head and refused to put out until they were married—or at least engaged.

Sarah let the world flow around her and was a great lay. She knew more than most women because of her line of work. And he was the beneficiary for sure. What she'd taught him these past few months would take a lifetime to convince Rebecca to even try.

Still sleeping, Sarah pulled the blankets up and over her shoulders. With only her head peeping out from under the covers, Fabian stared at her ear and at her hair. Despite his hunger, he was at ease beside her. There was a calm emanating from them.

Another gurgle from his midriff and he padded out the chamber in search of something to eat. Downstairs was a crate of fruit, so he grabbed an apple and a banana and strolled back upstairs, consumed the stolen goods, hunkered down and returned to sleep.

JANUARY 20, 1918

39

FABIAN'S EYES OPENED again at just gone eight. Sarah's heavy breathing might have been described as snoring by anyone who felt so inclined, but Fabian put the blankets back over her chest to keep her warm. He hopped out of bed and threw on his things.

A brief detour to his parents' apartment and a quick change of clothes before he headed straight to the Forsyth to prepare for this brand-new day.

Nathan poured a steaming mug of coffee as soon as he entered the bar and Fabian collected it before he sat down at his table. Sammy's absence hovered over the room as loudly as if he'd been guffawing in Fabian's ear.

"How're you doing?"

"Not bad under the circumstances." Fabian attempted a smile but the best he could achieve was a grimace.

"Tough day all round." Nathan's eyes flickered to the missing Sammy's table and back onto Fabian.

"You said it."

"If there's anything I can do, Fabian."

"Appreciate it. You helped yesterday just when we needed it, so you've already made your contribution. I won't forget."

"Was nothing. Believe me, if two of your friends scamper into your place gushing blood, you'd do the same."

A genuine smile.

"Not everyone would step up, Nathan. Really."

"Like I said…"

Nathan walked away rather than taking the compliment. He was a good guy. Kept his nose clean and never asked unnecessary questions—or made any demands. Poured you a drink and helped when assistance was needed. Fabian had never heard him ask for zip. Waxey looked after him, but there was never a demand for anything more than his usual share. No bonus, no chiseling anyone. It was probably how he'd survived all these years with all sorts of hotheads walking through his life.

Meanwhile Fabian sat at his table waiting for Abraham and Paulie, all that was left of his crew. This morning he'd need to visit each of their pools so the foot soldiers felt there was a sharp eye aimed directly at them even though Ben and Dan weren't around to run things. Their funerals would be today or tomorrow—but Waxey had instructed him not to go anywhere near the families.

Paulie arrived first and sat down opposite Fabian. Nathan rustled up a cup for him, sugar but no milk. The boy looked tired, which was far from surprising. Fabian called him a boy, but he was only a year younger than himself. They were both men and, irrespective of age, if you're old enough to fight and risk dying then you're old enough to be described as a man.

"Get much sleep last night?"

"Some."

"Good."

"Took a while though."

"Yes, it's not easy."

They spoke in a strange mix of Yiddish and American as both had learned each other's language the past few months. Fabian noted he should learn more English. If he'd known what the goons were saying yesterday, he'd have been able to judge a better time to start their attack. Ifs and maybes were the stuff of dreams though.

This thought was stymied by the twin arrivals of Abraham, looking like death warmed up, and a boy with a message from Waxey. Nathan supplied coffee to Abraham and Fabian gave a nickel to the boy who handed over his note and left. Time for the day to start.

A FLURRY OF people in and out of Waxey's office was the first sign for Fabian business was not running as usual today. There were unknown faces swarming all over the place but familiar folk were visible too.

On the second floor, Fabian stood silently, patiently, for Waxey to get around to him. Yesterday's mayhem headline appeared to have slammed into page two by nine this morning. Everyone was rushing, no one was talking.

"Good to see you, Fabian. Sleep okay?"

"Not bad. Been better."

"Sure thing… Here's the deal: today we are hitting the Yake Brady turf."

"Over a pool hustle gone wrong?"

"Course not. The Bowery needs a shake-up and your misadventure was the overture—whether or not you'd succeeded."

The words sank in.

"We were just a pawn in a bigger game?"

"Wheels within wheels. We're always a hamster in someone else's cage. I have people I report to. No-one is independent, Fabian. Don't be naïve."

"Yeah… So how did yesterday's escapade cause today's ruckus?"

"We tickled the Yake Brady chin yesterday and today we slam them in the face with an iron bar."

"Lots of fresh faces here."

"That's because an operation like this takes plenty of muscle. More than I had on my own. We're working with some Italian friends. We'll be carving up the territory south of Canal in a matter of days."

"I've an Italian, Paulie, in my crew. What's left of it."

"Good guy?"

"Yes, I'd say so."

"Trust him?"

"Sure. I mean, it's hard to get quite what he's thinking sometimes because my English isn't good enough."

"And his Yiddish is rubbish too."

"True, but he's been good for us."

"Last night I promised you fresh blood in your crew and I'm gonna keep my word but probably not in the way you were expecting. I've got some young Italians for you. Two for today and we'll see what happens later on. These guys come with high recommendations from my friends so you should have no problems with them. You can use Paulie as a go-between until we all learn to speak native."

There was a smile on Waxey's face and the joke was on him. The guy flopped out of his mother's womb on American soil and was more than able to communicate with the locals.

"Are we going to join in the attack today?"

"Hell no. You guys can have a break for now. Lick your wounds and keep everyone calm. While the advance party marauds its way around the Lower East Side, we need the rest of the organization to work like clockwork. Your job is to ensure your crew keeps vicelike control over all you own. And while we wait to find out about Sammy, watch over his assets too. Vicelike grip, Fabian. Understand?"

"Sure do."

"All right, Slugger. Get going—and well done for yesterday."

"Congratulations?"

"You gave the Yake Brady a bloody nose. Some of ours might be done but so are some of theirs. Who'd be crazy enough to kill someone over a game of numbers? Now they know we are and that's down to you."

"And the crew."

"They followed you, but yes, and the crew."

Waxey put out his hand for a shake and Fabian experienced the firm pressure of a man who was comfortable with his power.

AT THE FORSYTH, Fabian's table was pretty crowded before he even arrived. Paulie and Abraham had settled in nicely and there were two olive-skinned guys sat next to them. Fabian didn't care they were Italian, but he had an inbuilt distrust because they were not chosen by him. He also knew this was a problem entirely of his own making—or rather of his and Sammy's. Waxey had forced him to back up Sammy's expansion plans into Yake Brady territory.

This morning it looked as though the plan was more Waxey's than Sammy's. If Sammy was so close to Waxey, Fabian needed to play everything very carefully over the next few days and weeks. He had been corralled into helping Sammy but he had assumed this was just Sammy using Waxey to get his own way. Didn't appear like that was the case anymore.

They shuffled round to make space for him, and Nathan brought a mug of coffee without being asked, as ever. The two new fellas introduced themselves: Gabriele and Lorenzo.

Gabriele was the taller and, presumably, the elder. Fifteen, probably sixteen, definitely not seventeen. Black curly mane and deep dark-brown eyes. Something about his manner told Fabian he could handle himself in a fight. Lorenzo had a pointed nose and a missing tooth. Not the prettiest boy but had clearly been in his fair share of scraps. Dark brown hair. A scar near his right eye leading toward an ear. Paulie translated as Fabian gave instructions.

"Our job now is to let everyone see it's business as usual. If anyone owes us money, get it. If someone's late with a payment then deal with them accordingly. Today is not the day to allow our customers to get away with anything. We are holding a firm line across all the pools."

"Even with our regulars?"

"Abraham, manage your locations with common sense. If you have prior arrangements with people then honor them for sure. But if a stranger asks you for another day, force them to take out a loan or break a limb. Either is a good result right now.

"Paulie, you must walk Lorenzo and Gabriele to their stations and help them get the lay of the land. Then report back to me as soon as you are able. By lunchtime, I want you all to have been seen in all pools. That way, everyone gets the message that we are unbowed by anything they might have heard about yesterday."

"Tongues are already wagging."

"I'm sure they are. Enough people saw us dragging Dan through the streets, blood and guts 'n' all, to have formed an opinion about how we did. But they also need to remember that we work together and we live together. We carry on no matter what."

"Will you be here if we encounter any problems?"

"Here or checking over Sammy's locations, Paulie."

He nodded. There was a heap to do to maintain order across Fabian's realm.

"And let me be the first to tell you guys in case you hear anything on the street."

All their ears pricked up to get the gossip firsthand.

"This morning Waxey is hitting the Yake Brady gang hard. He's working with some Italians to heap eternal damnation on those Irish bastards."

Again, Fabian didn't care if a fella was Italian, Irish or Jewish. What counted was whether you could be trusted and if the fella kept his word. He had found where you came from gave no hint whether you were a stand-up guy.

"Any questions?"

"No, boss."

"Finish your drinks and off you go. This will be a long morning for all us. But keep your eyes out for any Yake Brady goons looking for trouble, especially when you are south of Canal. Their headquarters is on Cherry Street so be real careful if you're anywhere near those parts."

Paulie took his new charges off first leaving Abraham alone with Fabian. His cup was empty, but he didn't budge.

"Can I ask you something?"

"Of course."

"How bad is it going to be?"

Fabian laughed. What a question given all that happened the day before.

"In a week, we'll be back on an even keel. We might be spread thin but all the wheels on the bus will carry on turning."

Eyes darted at Sammy's table.

"And what about Sammy?"

"Still don't know. When I saw him, he was fleeing Yake Brady guys and that looks like the last time any of us saw him alive. So it's not looking good."

Abraham continued to stare at Fabian with no response.

"But we've got to keep on going. If Sammy turns up in a day or two then we need to protect his territory for him."

"And if he doesn't?"

"Then we need to secure the self-same area for Waxey and he'll be the one to decide who he gets to take care of it in the future."

"You've got a claim on it though, right?"

"Why d'you ask, Abraham?"

"Because if it works out Sammy's gone, then I'd like to step up and partner with you… if I can."

Trust Abraham to sniff out an opportunity before any corpse has been placed in the ground. Excellent eye for business, though.

"We'll discuss all this as and when we need to, but, sure, I won't forget we've had this conversation."

"Thanks, Fabian."

"Now get outta here."

Abraham kicked back his chair and sprinted out the door. Clearly, he wanted a bigger piece of the action and wasn't embarrassed to grab it while stomping on someone's grave.

Fabian stayed at the Forsyth for an hour then he traveled to each of Sammy's pools locations to lay down the law. At each site, he was the first person to offer direction to his people so Fabian came across like Moses coming down from the mountain. By the time he returned for lunch, everyone had seen he was alive and still very much in charge. Two broken arms and a blooded nose took care of that and Slugger wasn't even trying.

40

ANOTHER EVENING IN the Forsyth with Fabian and his crew as the sun set and there was no word from Waxey how the day had gone. Fabian spent the afternoon splitting his time between being rock steady at his table and roaming around Sammy's pools to settle people down and to keep an eye out for the man to show. Zilch—on both counts.

Beers were flowing, and the guys relaxed into the evening.

"Hard day, Fabian."

"I know, Paulie. I had to slap some of Sammy's crew into line..."

A curl of his lips and the others giggled.

"...but nothing they couldn't handle. Besides, if Sammy is taking a few days off holed up somewhere, they still need to know it's business as usual."

"Any news how it's going in Yake Brady territory?"

"Nope. Not a word, but that just means everyone is busy. Also, if the move is as big as I think it is then the fighting won't be over for the day."

A kid was scuffing his heels by the bar and Fabian called him over.

"Go to this address. Tell them Fabian wants to know if Waxey or Ira are back yet. Got it?"

The boy nodded.

"When you return with an answer for me, there'll be gelt in it for you. What are you waiting for?"

"Funny thing, Fabian, is that most of our marks acted like there was nothing going on."

"Abraham, that's because for almost everyone outside this outfit, nothing has happened. What's important to you can be irrelevant to the rest of the world. Any issues with your folk today, though?"

"Nothing. Everything was peachy smooth, boss. All money arrived that was due in. No new loans out but that's not surprising. An ordinary day."

"The more of those the merrier, right?"

Nods all round. They'd talked about baseball, the war in Europe, the cost of a challah but the one item off the list was what happened yesterday.

Nobody wanted to relive the past so soon. Nobody could face talking about Sammy, Ben or Dan. There was still grief behind their eyes.

Another beer finished, and the kid came back, wide-eyed and panting—he'd run all the way.

"A man told me Waxey was back but not Ira. They said you should come over when you're ready."

"Good work, little fellow."

Fabian tossed him a nickel, and the kid returned to scuffing his heels.

"Sounds as though we're done for the day."

"Sure thing, Fabian."

"Paulie, how have Gabriele and Lorenzo got on?"

"All okay. Took charge quickly and bashed a few heads but proportionate. Did nothing you wouldn't have approved."

"Good news. Looks like we've survived the day unscathed. Well done, everyone. I doubt if any of us thought I'd say that this evening."

The tangential reference was sufficient acknowledgement of the horrors of the previous day.

"It'll get better. Take one thing at a time but don't take your eyes off the ball. That way madness lies."

Fabian ordered another round from Nathan and took his leave to head over to Waxey, as instructed. At Bayard and Bowery, there was a flurry of activity. Men came and went at a great pace and Fabian forced a path among the throng. He overheard stories of today's fight from a dozen different perspectives. In the main, it sounded like Waxey had the upper hand but the cuts and bruises on display showed this was no easy land grab. But Fabian knew that was the case before he entered the building.

Waxey was holding court up on the second floor and Fabian waited at the back of the room. Many people wanted his attention and the fella was flagging even though there were tens of men to deal with before the day was done.

An hour later, Fabian sat down in front of him and smiled.

"Long day?"

"This morning we hit every numbers racket Yake Brady owned. By eleven, we controlled two-thirds of them and burned the rest to the ground."

Fabian's eyebrows raised.

"There was some low-level resistance but nothing major."

"Every knuckle in the building must have a scrape to show for it."

"The men did well but we couldn't have done it without the Italians."

"Which Italians, Waxey? You've not told me who we're doing business with."

"No? Not intentional, just a lot going on. We have an alignment of interest with Charlie Lucky, who wants to expand his gambling operations, just as we do."

"Makes sense. For what it's worth, I've had only positive reports from my two today. And thanks for the men."

"I'm glad they've been pulling their weight."

"Sure have. I'd have lost my grip without them."

"And any word of Sammy?"

Fabian felt his cheeks heat and tried to control his physical reaction to his friend's name.

"Nothing. Maybe he's in hiding."

"That is possible, but unlikely."

"What about the two who were chasing him?"

"They vanished in a puff, Fabian. No sign, north or south of Canal."

"Not a dicky bird. You'd think someone would have seen something."

"Just because a citizen saw somebody from the corner of their eye doesn't mean we'll bump into them the next day."

"True. Besides, Sammy'll either appear or he won't. We shall deal with whatever happens."

"Yep. Sure will."

"What about tomorrow? Want any help?"

"Keep the numbers rackets rolling around the neighborhood and make certain your crew remains tight."

"You don't want me in the front line?"

"Appreciate the offer but Charlie Lucky's men made most of the play today and tomorrow you can bet your last dollar Yake Brady will come over and hit us hard. We need people like you on home turf when that happens. Tool up, you will need more than your fists by tomorrow night."

Fabian nodded and Waxey slipped into silence indicating he'd had enough and Fabian should leave.

WRAPPED UP IN blankets with Sarah, Fabian relaxed into the bedding, knowing the Yake Brady fight was hurtling at them. Thoughts of Sammy faded from the front of his mind and were replaced by the touch of Sarah's hands on his body.

The hairs on his leg were moving in response to Sarah's thigh and she rolled over on top of him.

"Penny for your thoughts."

"Nah. Just thinking about what happened today on the streets."

"Another tough day?"

"Not as bad as yesterday."

"Of course not."

"But without Sammy…"

Sarah gave him a squeeze as though he would feel better, but it was the thought that counted. He appreciated her effort to ease his distress.

"Thanks, babe."

She always relaxed him. She understood how he ticked and worked to make him the center of her world—apart from when she'd forced him to dance last night.

"Gonna be rough again tomorrow."

"How so?"

"Waxey's taken the fight to Yake Brady south of Canal today. They'll bring the war to us in the morning."

"You be careful. You've already put your life on the line once this week."

"I know, but you can't walk away from a battle. Not when you're defending your livelihood and the people around you."

Sarah was silent, and he felt her breathing as her chest heaved in and out against him.

"Take good care of yourself anyway."

"Yes, ma'am."

They laughed out loud and rolled around some more. Memories of his men's blood left his mind for the evening but when the time came for him to go to sleep, the images floated before his eyes and Fabian could only remain unconscious in fits and starts.

The following morning he kissed Sarah goodbye and, as he left the room, he realized he hadn't taken out any money for her bedside table—the first such occasion since they'd met. He almost returned but knew that would be as strange as walking straight out, though he wasn't too sure how she would take it—and what she'd infer from the missing cash.

Fabian concluded he didn't have time to figure this out now. Yake Brady would hit them hard and they'd need as many of Charlie Lucky's men as possible if they were going to survive the onslaught.

January 27, 1918

41

A LONG WEEK had passed since he'd left Sarah's bed, but Fabian had no chance to think about anything. He spent each day keeping a firm grip on his crew and the expanded territory including all Sammy's pools. When he wasn't attending to business, he was beating Yake Brady people to pulp.

Fabian showed his mettle time and again, leading various attacks on the Irish gang. He also found working with the Italians easy—the biggest hurdle was the language barrier but Paulie proved an invaluable interpreter despite his still-limited grasp on Yiddish.

In the morning Fabian visited one of Sammy's pools. There had been a discrepancy with the previous night's count, and he showed everyone what happens when mistakes got made. Echoes of his trouble with Isaac rebounded between his ears and his brutal response to the new situation was entirely predictable. Four broken fingers later and there would be no further errors in adding up the money.

Walking west along Grand, Fabian arrived at the corner with Jackson and knew he was only two blocks north of Cherry, right by the Yake Brady headquarters. His muscles tensed and he tried to stretch out his senses in every direction because trouble was, literally, round every corner.

He bounced into an alleyway knowing his approach was too casual and he spotted two fellas who were heading towards him from the Cherry side. They could have been anyone going about their business, but Fabian noticed one was clinging to a metal bar he'd hidden under his coat. He stayed in the alleyway waiting for them to pass, sinking back into the shadows by a wall, not wanting to deal with the fellas on his own. After seven days constant fighting, he was tired of never letting his guard down, never being certain he was safe, even on his own streets.

Although not strictly necessary, he'd warned his family and the Grunbergs not to be outside in case they got caught in the crossfire. Only Waxey and Ira owned firearms, but you never knew with the Yake Brady gang. No pistols had appeared so far, but they'd stop at nothing to beat Waxey Gordon and Charlie Lucky.

Once the two goons passed the alleyway, Fabian slunk to the front entrance and checked which direction they were heading—east toward the wharfs. This suited him as he was off to the Forsyth. To be absolutely sure nothing was amiss, he popped into a bar to keep an eye on the street.

The place, on Grand between Sheriff and Willett, was nothing to write home about. There were two barflies attached to the counter itself and all the tables were empty apart from one old man. In case of trouble, Fabian perched at the table next to the solitary drinker. The guy had pushed the brim of his hat down hard so Fabian couldn't make out his face until he'd sat down with his coffee.

A flicker of recognition and Fabian tried to place the fella. He was fairly sure he'd come across the guy before but couldn't say where or when. The man looked back at him and nodded with a half-smile. Now Fabian was unsure if the guy knew him or was just being polite, given he'd sat down right next to the guy in an almost empty establishment.

"Hello."

Fabian played it safe.

"Morning to you."

Nice and neutral.

"How's it going?"

"Just fine, mac. And you?"

"Holding my own."

"YOU REMEMBER ME? Because I recall you."

At least Fabian wasn't mistaken even though the man remained a stranger to him.

"Vaguely, to be honest. We've met before but I'm not sure when. Sounds like you know though."

The guy smiled and held out his hand, which Fabian instinctively shook.

"Monk Eastman. We were in Waxey's place. You were green. Back then."

Eastman eyed Fabian up and down with a knowing and withering look.

"Yeah? Couple of years ago?"

"I'd say."

"Was green then."

"Reckon you were. But I got a good head for faces and yours is one of them."

"You still working with Waxey?"

"Never said I was running with him then, did I?"

"Uh, no, suppose not."

"I'm messing with you. Old timer's prerogative. No, I'm not with Waxey anymore."

"But you used to be?"

"Yeah, you could say I worked with him."

Eastman chuckled to himself with sadness and regret in his eyes. A hollow man sat in front of Fabian. Then the name came shimmering into Fabian's brain; Eastman used to be somebody. He ran one of the Lower East Side gangs but fell by the wayside before Fabian even landed in the country.

"Mr Eastman, apologies. It's taken me a few minutes to put the pieces together."

"Don't worry about it. Most people your age haven't heard of me."

He sighed heavily and sipped his coffee.

"What are you up to now? I mean, are you out of the business?"

Eastman's turn to laugh again.

"You'd better believe it. They let me out of jail in October. But guess what I'm doing tomorrow?"

Fabian's mind went blank—no idea.

"I give up."

"I'm shipping out."

"You're leaving Manhattan?"

"I joined the army and basic training starts for the war in Europe."

"You are kidding me."

"No, why would I joke?"

"Dunno."

"Back in Europe, we can't let the Cossacks win control, can we? So someone has to go over there and help the Allies. And I aim to shoot me some Austrian-Hungarian ass now that President Wilson's declared war on them too. Didn't care too much for a fight with the Germans, but those Prussian bastards are different."

He winked at Fabian who was still taken aback by Eastman's plan.

"The army?"

"Yes."

Eastman stared straight into Fabian's eyes, making him blink. The guy was deadly serious. He had been in charge of one of the most powerful gangs in the five counties and now he was set to don a uniform and fight for his country and not for his wallet.

"Why are you fighting for strangers?"

"They are our brothers and sisters."

"Huh?"

"Were you born here?"

"No."

"Fled from Europe?"

"Yes."

"Did you leave any of your kin behind?"

"The extended family, yes."

"And who is protecting them right now?"

Fabian thought for a minute and realized—nobody. He contemplated the implications of that answer.

"That's why I'm off to the war. They need our help. If we do nothing then they'll die. The Jews of Europe will perish because you know no one else will look after them. Who cares about a bunch of poor Semites?"

He offered no response to this rhetoric. Instead, Fabian bought Eastman a drink and shook him by the hand again. Then he left the bar and carried on back to the Forsyth.

AFTER LUNCH, WAXEY sent word for Fabian to drop everything and come help. Yake Brady had surrounded the headquarters and there was only a finite amount of time before they'd run in or smoke them out. Neither was positive.

When Fabian arrived with Abraham and Paulie—he didn't want to risk the new fellas on this—they saw ten or fifteen guys stood on the street. After a quick scout round the back, Abraham reported a similar number were waiting at the rear entrance, which ran into an alley. The goons were armed with a mix of iron bars, knives and lead pipes. All those weapons were dangerous enough but no-one was sporting any guns, which meant a hand-to-hand counterattack was on the cards.

Fabian held back wanting to see who else appeared. His crew were three, and they were twenty or thirty—the odds were not in their favor. The goons just stood there, jeering occasionally and waving arms now and again, but they were in no hurry to do anything more. Either they didn't know who was in the building or they were putting the frighteners on the occupiers. He caught a glimpse into a fourth-floor window and believed he saw Yonah staring down at the street scene.

Half an hour later and the goons had hardly moved. They were splayed out around the front, several feet apart but at the other side of the building, they remained huddled near the back door. Fabian wondered who or what they were waiting for because at the current rate, they'd be there all night.

From his perspective, the good news was that handfuls of Waxey's other men had positioned themselves along the nearby street corners, front and back. They numbered around twenty to thirty, so the two groups were relatively equally matched. Word spread among them to attack in ten minutes.

The plan was simple—someone had purloined a jerrycan filled with gasoline and another fella had rounded up a box of bottles and torn up a couple of shirts. By the time everyone was ready, Fabian and the others were holding bottles filled with gasoline, stuffed with a rag soaked in the stuff. As soon as he saw one streak of fire enter the street, he lit his first bottle and threw it directly at a bunch of the thugs. Then the second, swiftly followed by the last.

Flames streaked across Bayard like the Fourth of July. Two of the bottles landed on a goon, the glass cutting him and the gas burning his skin off. Those that missed the goons created puddles of fire, scaring those stood nearby into running in random directions.

When the chaos appeared to be at its height, Fabian stepped out into the street and made a dash to the nearest goon who was fleeing the flames and heading straight at him. At the last moment before they met, Fabian swung back, and Slugger smashed his iron bar into the goon's face. The fella flipped backwards, hitting the ground headfirst. Slugger bent down and landed the metal squarely between the guy's eyes and moved on to his next victim.

42

WHEN HE SPUN round to see who to attack next, the entire frontage was filled with men he knew, and others being pummeled and kicked to near death. Slugger moved two steps forward and stuck a knife into the side of a guy who was squaring up against Paulie. He plugged the fella twice more, once in the small of the back and once in the kidneys. As he dropped face down to the floor screaming, Slugger grabbed his head and sliced the throat wide open. And then onto the next. And the next.

Within five minutes, the front of the building was cleared. All but two were dead, and they were lying in pools of other people's blood. And fire.

The second wave came running onto the street from the back. This bunch stood facing a line of Gordon troops but hadn't taken into account the fact that the building was filled with their foe. The front door was flung open and out spewed a horde more guys, trapping the goons and reeking unholy revenge on all that had happened before. Fabian and the other men joined in a few seconds later to mop up what was left breathing.

The battle of Bayard was over. Waxey, who'd made the first kills as soon as he arrived on the scene, congratulated everyone and reminded them to grab any weapons they could find and then to make like the wind. The cops would have to turn up to sort out this massacre—and they didn't want to be here to be interviewed when they did.

Fabian saw Abraham walking toward him and looked for Paulie, but he was nowhere to be found.

"Paulie?"

Abraham spun round and shrugged.

"Help me find him!"

The effort took about three seconds in total. Paulie was hidden from view because he was kneeling next to one goon, rifling through clothes and pockets for anything of value. Fabian saw him grab a wallet and a knife with a silver and bone handle.

"Not now, Paulie. Time to go."

The Italian looked up at him as if to plead to carry on. There was cash left behind, but some things are worth more than money—like your freedom and a bunch of questions from nosey cops.

"Let's get outta here."

Off they headed to the Forsyth for a much-needed drink to calm nerves and take the edge off their emotions. The fight hadn't lasted long, but it had been incredibly intense.

"Well done, you two."

"Will they come back?"

"Not today for sure. We left no one alive to tell their boss what happened."

They laughed and sipped their vodka until Nathan delivered beers for everyone.

"Soon there'll be a truce—or Waxey will take out Brady himself."

"I heard they got a lotta guns."

"Paulie, that's the word on the street but we haven't seen any yet, have we?"

"No, Fabian."

"That makes me think the talk is bigger than reality. I'm not saying Waxey shouldn't go packin' but the last week would have been different if there were firearms among them. Yeah?"

"Sure, I guess."

"For definite, Paulie. There's no way I'd have walked into today with a knife and a piece of pipe if there was a six-chamber aimed at my heart."

They nodded in agreement as Fabian's logic was faultless. Another round of drinks and he left the guys to get slightly drunk and then slap some heads about in the numbers rackets. Collections don't make themselves. Meantime, he had some business of his own to take care of.

MONK EASTMAN RETURNED to Fabian's thoughts as he was sitting in the Forsyth. The man had been top of the pile only a few years ago. He'd owned the Lower East Side. Then the ground crumbled beneath him ending up in a three-year stretch in Dannemora. Now he was nothing but a vague memory in the history of the Bowery.

Big whoop. What caught in Fabian's brain was how the guy was operating way beyond himself and into the lives of people the other side of the world. That made him a mighty man again. Eastman was born in the United States and so you'd guess he felt no connection to anyone in the old country. But unknown Jews were closer to him than the fellas in the next-door tenement.

When Eastman asked him about the rest of his family, Fabian realized no-one had even mentioned them since the day they landed. It was as if they'd ceased to exist. As if everything and everyone to do with old country plain vanished in a puff of smoke like a magician's trick on a vaudeville stage. Only these were real men, women and children residing in actual houses and living in perpetual fear of death.

And who would stand up for them when the Cossacks or the Prussians came? They were his kith and kin, his flesh and blood. If Eastman could do something so should Fabian.

He walked north to Second and Third Avenue until he reached a Selective Service Department building. The Star-Spangled Banner flew and flapped above the entrance. Two men in uniform stood in front, one sitting on the facade steps, another talking to him with a foot on the third step and his elbow leaning on that leg, smoking a cigarette.

Like almost everyone in the gangs, Fabian had ignored the calls to register for the draft over the previous six months and the lottery to be called up had passed him by. Europe was in the midst of war, but he hadn't engaged with what that meant.

Fabian stepped indoors and found a large area with a set of desks at the far side and a bunch of army uniforms mingling with the civilians in the room. Some chatted among themselves or moved pieces of paper from one table to another.

He walked up to the first desk and used the best English at his disposal.

"I want to fight."

"You've come to the right place, bud."

"Here. Fight?"

"Yes, bud. Do you speak English? Can you understand me?"

Fabian looked at him blankly. He had no idea what the guy was saying to him. This was going to be harder than he'd thought. He'd forgotten the rest of Manhattan was a different world than the Bowery.

"Italian? German? French?"

Silence.

"Polish? Yiddish?"

Fabian nodded.

"Polish?"

Nothing.

"Yiddish?"

Another nod.

"Hang on a moment."

The guy the other side of the desk stood up and came back with a friend, slightly taller with greased-back blond hair.

"You wanting to fight, mac?"

Relief to hear Yiddish again after only a few words in a foreign language.

"Yes in Europe. The war…"

"Got it. Did you register for the draft?"

"What draft?"

The man threw his eyes upwards like he'd heard that story a million times before.

"You were meant to register for the draft lottery. There was one last June… Doesn't matter."

"I've not come here for a lottery. I wish to volunteer to fight."

The irony that the Selective Service might want to put him in a number lottery was not lost on Fabian and he smiled.

"What's funny?"

"Private joke, don't worry about it."

"I won't."

"How old are you?"

"Twenty-one."

Fabian looked directly into the guy's eyes as he spoke, hoping he wouldn't see through that lie.

"Let me get this straight, you want to volunteer to go to basic training and ship out to France?"

"That's right. And the rest of Europe."

"The rest can wait. Right now the Allied forces are pushing the enemy back in France."

"So can I leave now?"

"Kidding me, right? There's a process to follow, mac. You register today and you'll get a date later to go for training."

"But I won't be put into the lottery."

"The draft? No. You will be overseas in a few months."

"That's what I want."

"It's what you're gonna get, bud."

"Good news."

The man smiled at him and went off to grab the right forms, filled them in —and helped Fabian complete the rest.

"I don't have much English. Is that a problem?"

"No, but the more you know, the easier it'll be."

"Look, there are an abundance of immigrants in this man's army and we wish to win this war. So we're all working together in this. New York's a melting pot so there'll be a lot of languages in the platoon."

That made Fabian feel better. He didn't want to be the isolated Jew. He spoke Ukrainian, although he was rusty, but that wouldn't get him much further than Yiddish.

"How long before I go to fight?"

"Admire your enthusiasm, bud. Hope you've got the stomach for the real thing."

Fabian smiled; last week's escapades were a mere handful of blocks south of here.

"I can hold my own."

The man eyed him up and down, noticing the sinewy upper arm muscles and the way he sat in the chair.

"Reckon so. Where d'you live?"

"The Bowery."

"Like I said, reckon you can take care of yourself."

"Better believe it."

"Ever fired a gun before?"

"Nope. But I've been handy with a knife if the need arose. These are dangerous times we are living in."

The man stared at Fabian again, trying to imagine quite how he filled his days.

"So, how long before I ship out?"

"Oh, it'll take four months to train you so late spring or early summer. Depends when you're called. Check in here once a week."

"Sounds like a plan."

"You've signed an agreement with Uncle Sam. The only way to get out of it is if you're insane or dead."

"And if I'm meshugge, you'll just wait until I stop being crazy?"

"You better believe it."

"No problem. Not for me. I aim to fight in Europe."

"Not everyone in the Bowery is of your mind."

"The come-overs would be more likely. The kids who were born here feel less connection with the old country."

"You're probably right but our trouble is that many of... your kind... appear to have missed the calls for the draft completely."

"The Bowery is a nation unto itself. If you wanted to speak to men there, you should have got a visa. I needed one to visit you today."

They both laughed at the truth in Fabian's joke. The Bowery was a closed community and sticking a bunch of English posters on some walls wouldn't reach the people who'd spoken and read Yiddish all their lives.

Alex Cohen walked out of the Selective Service Department with his head held high and a stiff back. The two soldiers on the steps were still smoking and talking. But he knew he was going to fight. If not for America, then to save the old country.

JANUARY 28, 1918

43

FABIAN'S CHEST WAS still puffed up when he got the news that Yake Brady had agreed a ceasefire and Waxey wanted him immediately. Another boy barely out of diapers received a nickel and Fabian headed straight for Bayard and Bowery.

There was a bustle and energy to the place which hadn't been evident a month before, but the tension had eased from the building.

Fabian waited in line for his turn to speak to the boss.

"So is it all over?"

"Yep. Yake Brady agreed we'd run the numbers for them but I'm giving them a small slice of the action to keep them sweet."

"Nice."

"And they influence unions we had no reach into and they're kindly letting us dip our beaks in that trough too."

"How generous."

"And we'll be lending them some men too as they've lost so many in the last seven days."

"How did we do in that regard?"

"We suffered losses too, but far fewer than them. That's what made Yake give up. He worked out he'd run out of fellas. Our work with Charlie Lucky has already paid dividends."

Fabian knew little of the Italian other than he had a fierce reputation and that was probably all the information he needed. While the Irish and the Germans before them had always stayed with their own, Charlie Lucky had a different strategy and operated across the ethnic divide.

Certainly it worked. A share of a bigger pie with greater longer-term security was working well for him—and those he collaborated with. Waxey had expanded his universe in the last week precisely because he had the imagination to work hand in hand with Lucky.

"And is that only the start?"

"What do you mean?"

"Well, between the two of you, you control most of the Lower East Side, all territory east of the Bowery and south of First Avenue."

"Guess so."

"How much further do you think you'll go?"

Waxey chuckled.

"We are still licking our wounds from the last fight and you want to move onto the next."

"Not tomorrow, but there's plenty of Manhattan up for grabs with the right men by your side."

"Good pitch, Slugger."

"Yeah, I'm looking to put more bread on my family's table, but things take time to plan, don't they? When the next push comes—and I hope it does— remember I'm up for the challenge."

"Chaos is opportunity?"

"Well, yes, now you mention it."

"You're all heart, Fabian."

He didn't know when he was going to be called up so the more money he could make beforehand, the more his family would have in his absence. If he played the game right, Waxey might even give them a little support each week until his return from the front. Maybe.

"Anyway, what do you want me to do over the next few days?"

"Couple of things. Keep a close eye on your crew and ensure they don't slack. This is not the time to make mistakes in the numbers or labor unions. Everything must proceed nice and easy. No slip-ups.

"Second, I want you involved in some of Yake Brady business. I know you're minding Sammy's locations and soon we must decide about a permanent solution because he doesn't appear to be coming back any time soon."

"No. No-one's seen hide nor hair of him since that night."

"Well, on top of that, I will want you to supervise some Yake locations too."

"Numbers?"

"Initially, yes. You can assert your influence, shall we say?"

"Like I'm doing with Sammy's crews?"

"Yes. Don't feel the need to handle them with kid gloves."

"Really?"

"Firm but fair. I don't want you spoiling for a punch-up but if any of them steps out of line, you should deal assertively."

"Don't bash heads unless they are asking for a bruising."

"Well put. Ira will be on the front line with union work and he'll need your help in a few weeks' time. Right now, he'll introduce himself to the factory owners and explain our range of services."

They both smiled because Ira was no door-to-door salesman.

"I don't want to talk about money. Let's take stock of all the new assets and we can decide the details later."

"Fine by me, Waxey."

"If I'm right, we doubled our interest in the numbers and possibly trebled our involvement in, ahem, union business. There's change in the air, for sure, Fabian. We need to bed down all these new activities before we expand again. Me and Lucky have big plans but we ain't talking about them now."

"Onwards and upwards. Provided that's our destination, I'm on board."

"Nicely put. I got a bunch of other fellas to see and you need to visit a lot of sites."

"I'm outta here, Waxey."

"We work together, we live together."

"Sure do."

A handshake and Fabian left for the Forsyth; he had good news to deliver to his crew, but they'd face some hard graft the next few weeks.

FABIAN TOOK A different route than normal from Bayard to the Forsyth. No reason, only he felt like a change. There are only a few ways to walk from one location to another, so he shouldn't have been surprised to find himself at the alleyway where his time in America had started—and where he'd tried to end the life of his friend Sammy.

He popped into the alley to soak in what Waxey had said and also to allow a tinge of nostalgia to enter him, knowing as he did, he would be in a training camp before long.

The narrow entrance hid the large space behind, which contained crates, rubbish and anything else the wind had blown in or a person had dumped. At the furthest corner was a pile of boxes leaning against the wall. Fabian couldn't say why but there was something about the way those crates were positioned that made him take a second look. The breeze hadn't shifted them so someone must have done it and that's what smelled like something was awry.

Fabian strolled over to the cartons to investigate further. As he approached, he got the sense of a flicker of motion inside. He tensed slightly ready for action, but he knew it could be rats. To Fabian's eye, the crates were walls leaning against the brickwork and a layer of canvas material lay on top to form a ceiling. The whole thing acted as protection from the elements and a hiding hole for anyone wanting to stay in the Bowery without being visible.

A pair of shoes peeked out a corner and one of them twitched. The movement Fabian saw wasn't a rat.

"Who's in there?"

No reply. The footwear vanished and shrank inside the makeshift wooden tent.

"You just moved your feet."

Silence.

"Come out or I'll huff and puff and trash your hovel to pieces."

Legs appeared, and the guy shuffled out until his whole torso and head was visible. When Fabian saw his face, somehow, he wasn't surprised. It might have been dirty, caked with mud but there sat Sammy in front of him.

"How are you, Sammy?"

"Why do you care?"

"Things went sour between us, but I've calmed down since. I wish you no more ill will. I was angry about what you did to encourage Waxey to force my hand and help you. Then when the guys died…"

Sammy nodded, understanding at least some of Fabian's perspective.

"That's no excuse, Fabian. You left me for dead. All I could do was crawl into this corner and collapse."

"No-one's seen you since, though. How have you survived?"

"I stole scraps early morning or late at night. And I begged midtown for cash."

"Why didn't you just quit the area? Why stick around?"

"You've stripped me of everything. I reckon you owe me before I run away from the only world I know."

44

"IS THAT WHAT you want?"

"Do I have any option? I mean, you didn't trust me and now I can't trust you. Seems to me we can't work with each other no more, Fabian. You're not going anywhere, which leaves me with little choice. But you've taken everything from me."

"You did it to yourself. Sammy, you set me up to put my balls on the line so you could expand away."

"You indicated you were happy with our arrangement, Fabian, and I just saw extra pools as a natural extension of that."

"No denial you didn't throw me into the firing line… So what will it take for you to go and not come back?"

Sammy glared at him.

"And what makes you think I'll be the person who goes? Waxey'll be none too happy when he finds out you did for me. We work together…"

This turned Fabian's world upside down. Sammy had always been the passive one and he was not expecting Sammy to fight back. Presumably, he'd reckoned if he met Slugger again, he'd be dead. Yet here they were face-to-face, and the man was still alive. The idea flashed through Fabian to plug him repeatedly with the knife in his pocket but he couldn't stomach it. Knowing he was leaving the Bowery in the next few weeks had changed his perspective.

If Waxey knew Fabian had attacked Sammy, then Fabian would be found floating down the East River. As always, he came out fighting.

"What makes you think you'd survive to the end of the day if you spoke with Waxey? I'd hunt you down and kill you. Hope you understand that I wouldn't care about the consequences."

Sammy's cheeks reddened and Fabian could see the truth of his words sinking in. But the last thing he needed right now was to lose Waxey's trust. Everyone had to be onside.

"I'm guessing we both want to separate our paths and live to tell the tale."

"That would be good."

"Sounded as if you'd be open to moving out of Manhattan if you had a financial cushion, that is."

"You give me enough to seed a new life in Boston or Chicago and I'd be all right with that."

"And you wouldn't feel the desire to speak with Waxey if we reached that deal?"

"No. And you'd leave me alone?"

"If you moved away, I'd have no need to hunt you down like a dog, no."

Both men sat by the crates and pondered their futures.

"How much money would you want, Sammy?"

"Three thousand means I could be comfortable living in another city."

"Tell you what, it's Monday. Give me until the end of the week and I'll get you at least that amount, if not more. When we part, I want both of us to know we got a good trade. Sour grapes can cause heartburn later."

"If you throw me the money, we'll be fine. If not, Waxey will deal with you."

"Agreed. But we can't have you living in a crate for the next week."

"I don't want that either."

"Why don't we find you a place outside the Bowery where you could hole up but stay off the street?"

"Works for me."

"Let's get you into a hotel. I know one on Twelfth Street where they won't ask questions. I'll organize some credit and you can order any room service you want until Friday."

"Get it set up. Let me know when it's ready."

Fabian agreed and left the alleyway. As he returned to the street, an idea repeated in his mind. "I'm gonna kill that man."

FABIAN HAD TWO tasks for the afternoon. One was to secure a room at the Hotel Blackhawk on Twelfth and Broadway. A walk over and a quiet word with the proprietor meant Sammy had a comfortable bed and all the food and drink he might want until Friday.

On the way downtown, Fabian stopped in the alleyway and gave Sammy the details. They agreed he'd go over that evening under cover of dark. The other job was to speak with Waxey.

At Bayard and Bowery, Fabian walked up to the second floor and found Waxey in his usual location, sat at the table with a drink in his hand. The man never stopped. Probably the secret of his success—that and an unnerving ability to handle himself in a fight no matter what the odds.

There was a rumor turned folklore that back in the early days, when there was a different gang running each street corner, Waxey had risen through the ranks because of his prowess as a bare-knuckle fighter. But, so the story went, he shot through to be top dog on the day he was sparring with a guy who'd messed with some female acquaintance. Waxey was so enraged he picked the fella up and snapped his spine on his own knee as he flung the body downwards. Old wives' tale or the God's honest truth—either way he'd never looked back and no-one crossed him twice and lived to talk about it later.

"Waxey, there's some news about Sammy but I don't know if I trust it."

"Oh? What've you heard?"

"A man I know reckons they saw him at the station taking a train to Boston."

"Do you believe him?"

"No idea, but it's the first positive word I've come across since that night."

"How'd this fella of yours know it was Sammy?"

"They had a business relationship by and by."

"And you know him, how?"

"Sammy introduced him to me early on when we first met."

"And you bumped into him, when?"

Fabian cocked his head to one side. Waxey didn't usually ask so many direct questions. If he said something, Waxey took it at face value. Until now.

"I've put the word out to loads of guys this past week. He heard I was after finding Sammy and when he saw him at Grand Central at the Lexington entrance… Where else was he going?"

"You didn't answer my question, Fabian."

"Huh?"

"When did you bump into your informant?"

"Earlier today, he found me as I was leaving the Forsyth this afternoon."

"And even though you were looking for Sammy, this fella didn't rush to stop Sammy getting on the train?"

"He was at the station entrance, Sammy was running into a carriage, the whistle blew and off it flew. So he said."

"Are you going to go to Boston to find him?"

"Huh?"

"He's your business partner. Don't you want to catch up with him, make sure he's fine, look after him if he's been injured?"

"Well, I'm concerned for him, but if he's well enough to board a train, he's okay to hop over to the Forsyth. So I reckon he doesn't want to see me."

"Now why would that be, Fabian?"

"Maybe he's embarrassed about running away. Maybe the kicking he got was enough to send him away from this business. He was never one to run toward a fight, was he?"

"No. Good strategist, lousy with the rough stuff."

"There you go. If Sammy wanted any part in the business, he'd have come round the Forsyth."

"So you've said. Twice. The idea Sammy would walk away from the money from his numbers games. Something doesn't add up, does it?"

"People who are terrified do strange things."

"Sure, Fabian. Sammy might have been scared a week ago, but do you really reckon he was so transfixed in horror that the fear in his stomach has lasted over seven days? That, my friend, is where this story of yours falls apart."

"Waxey, my guy may be mistaken. If it wasn't Sammy, there's no mystery to unravel about the fella who boarded the express."

"That's true. The phantom train passenger would be of no concern to us, but we'd still be left with the question of where Sammy has got to."

"There is that."

"I'll put out word in Boston for people I know to keep an eye out for him. And you carry on looking in the Bowery. I'd like a body or a buddy."

"Me too."

"Are you intending to meet up with your station informant?"

"Not in particular."

"Well, go back to him and get him to check his recollection. If he's lying, hoping to get some reward, make sure you prepare a special payment from me."

A steely glance into Fabian's eyes told him Waxey was in no humor to be lied to and Fabian hoped his cheeks weren't reddening as he sat there. But he couldn't tell.

"Anything else?"

"That's enough for one day, Waxey."

"Your story is thin, Fabian, and it seems to me you've been played like a bassoon."

"I'm no buffoon."

"Get outta here."

JANUARY 29, 1918

45

FABIAN SPENT THE evening at the Oregon as he preferred to sleep somewhere safe—for yet another night in a row. He and Sarah had spent as little time together as the days when Fabian first came in to chase Eli's debt. He wasn't taking her for granted but he was relying on the fact he could spend time with her whenever he wanted. She listened to him, understood him and she appeared to love him for who he was, not what he might become. That was reassuring in a woman, especially as he no longer left her any money on the bedside table. They behaved almost like a regular couple.

They woke up and got dressed as normal and popped downstairs for breakfast. Sarah had free run of the kitchen and always rustled up coffee, bread and jam. Once she stretched to a cheese blintz, but Fabian noticed she stole that from a tray. Like himself, she was no angel with an oven.

Having eaten, she said she'd got some chores to do, so they left the Oregon together. This was a new experience as usually Sarah would go back upstairs and ready her room for the first customer. She said nothing but he understood the woman and the world she inhabited.

Out the hotel they turned right. At the corner they went their separate ways, but she gave him a peck on the lips to say goodbye. Cheeks flushed red as he wasn't expecting any outward display of affection from her. The most she'd ever done before was hold his hand on the way upstairs.

"See you later."

"Reckon you will, Fabian. Same time tonight?"

"Hope so, yes."

"Bye."

He stood watching Sarah sashay away from him, her hips working overtime because she knew she was visible to his eye and the entire world. Like she was intent on making heads turn. She couldn't help herself. He remained in that position until she turned the corner at the next block and vanished from view.

"She's pretty."

Fabian swiveled round to find the owner of that voice but he knew the female tones before he faced her.

"Rebecca. I'm surprised to see you in these parts."

"Not as surprised as I am to see you coming out of a hotel holding hands with a woman. You told me you only had eyes for me."

"My heart is for you and sometimes my eyes wander."

Rebecca giggled.

"Good answer for a man who's on the spot."

"It's true."

"But you're still doing the work you do."

"For now. But in two weeks, everything's gonna change."

The distrust in her expression stretched across her face. He had made the same claim so many times he knew she couldn't believe him.

"You'll see. When it happens, you'll see and then hopefully we can…"

"Don't repeat it, Alex. If what you say is true, I'll see and if your words are as empty as before then at least you won't have lied to me."

Alex nodded. His promise of a better tomorrow never seemed to materialize. Rebecca was nearly correct. He hadn't deceived her, but the truth had ebbed out of his mouth every time he failed to deliver on his assurance to her that he'd leave this life behind. The only difference was that Alex knew he was right on this occasion, but he had nothing to show for it apart from some forms he'd signed for the Selective Service Department.

"It's hard but have faith in me."

"That's a big ask—especially from someone like you."

"Me?"

"You work on the seedier side of town."

"Nowhere in the Bowery is exactly clean."

"Don't play games with me, Alex Cohen. You lend money to families who can't afford it and get people to threaten them if they can't pay the exorbitant interest you charge them."

"It's not seedy, just unpleasant. If it wasn't me, it would be some other guy. At least I look after my territory too."

"And what about the street battles the last week or two? You told my parents not to go outside. It was that dangerous."

"I advised them there was trouble brewing. I didn't want any of you to get hurt. Would you rather I'd said nothing?"

"That's not my point, Alex, and you know that. If you weren't engaged in that kind of business then we wouldn't need to be afraid to walk along our own sidewalks."

"The gangs will go up against each other whether or not I'm involved. It's the natural flow of things. There's always territory to be won somewhere."

"Listen to how you talk to me. These streets aren't territory; they are people's homes, shops, places to meet, work and fall in love."

"And when these self-same people run into problems, they don't go to the authorities, the rabbis, the cops. They come to us and we help them out. We sort out their difficulties and give them the opportunity to live their American dream. To continue their lives, fall in love and build a safe future for their families. We provide security."

"Alex, keep telling yourself that. If you actually believe what you've just said, then why would you want to leave that life? For me or for anyone else. That nafka, for example."

"Sarah?"

"The whore has a name."

"Hey, no need for that."

"Don't be so defensive, Alex. There's nothing wrong with sleeping with a woman and paying for the privilege."

"I don't pay."

Rebecca laughed.

"I bet you do. One way or another."

He glared at her. She didn't need to drag Sarah into this. And Rebecca was so condescending in how she spoke about Sarah too. That was what stuck in Alex's craw.

"I gotta go."

"I'm sure you do."

"Take care of yourself. Despite what I just said, I still wouldn't want you to get hurt. Underneath it all, you're a nice man."

She pecked him on the cheek and walked away. Fabian turned in the opposite direction and headed to the Blackhawk.

AS FABIAN LEFT the Bowery, he took a zigzag route just in case anyone was following him. His paranoia levels had risen only because of his conversation with Waxey. There was a doubt in that man's voice—and words —for the first time since they'd met. Naturally, this concerned Fabian because he relied on Waxey being a rock, a reliable constant in an otherwise ever-changing unpredictable world.

So instead of walking north up Bowery itself, he trebled his journey length by heading west, north, east, north, repeating the pattern until he'd got as far as Eighth Street. Fabian figured that anyone still following him would not be shaken off anyway, so he might as well not bother. To check there weren't any stragglers, he popped into an occasional alleyway and waited a few minutes so anybody behind would end up ahead of him.

Nearly two hours after he left the Oregon, Fabian arrived at the Blackhawk entrance. This was a tired hotel, whose better days had long since faded away into crumbling plasterwork and peeling paint. The floorboards in the vestibule were sticky underfoot. While the venue might not have the bright cheer of the Oregon or Forsyth, it made up for its weaknesses with the absolute discretion of its owner.

Aaron Clenovitch had several hotel interests downtown, of which the Blackhawk was his first and most loved. Fabian had come across him a year before when Aaron placed a bet or two he couldn't cover. Money lent, they got talking because Fabian sensed this guy was no ordinary gambler—and he was right. Clenovitch played the numbers for fun but he derived his amusement by the size of the wager. This led him to have occasional cash flow issues.

The man had principles. He'd gamble huge sums but didn't approve of prostitutes using his premises for sexual congress. So he never rented a room by the hour. If a hustler could afford to hire a room by the week, Aaron viewed her as a businesswoman and not a nafka.

In exchange for not being a slut, Aaron let you be. More than that, because his buildings were far from chic, there were seldom visitors, which meant his clientele were individuals who wanted to be left alone and didn't care about the state of the corridors. And when a visitor appeared, they were studiously ignored. The lack of staff at the reception desk announced this respect for client privacy louder than any notice ever could.

Fabian knew which room Aaron had allocated to Sammy, so he stepped in the elevator and got out on the sixth floor. He walked down the corridor and stopped outside suite 609. Knocked on the door and waited.

46

TWENTY SECONDS LATER, Fabian heard someone the other side of the door and assumed Sammy was using the spy hole before he opened up. Fabian felt for the knife resting in his pants pocket and walked inside.

Under the circumstances, the place was good—and way more comfortable than a pile of crates in an alley. A bed, table and chair, armchair and a view of another hotel twenty feet away.

"This isn't bad. Better than I thought it'd be, to be honest."

"No complaints. The maid appears once a day and room service is second to none."

"Pleased to hear it. I'm paying them enough to wait on you hand and foot."

"I would say thank you for looking after me but that would stretch a point."

Fabian snorted a half-laugh.

"Understood. I hadn't been in any of the rooms so I wasn't too sure what to expect. All I knew is they'd look after you."

"Thanks for not jerking me around."

Fabian's fingers wrapped themselves on the shaft of the knife. Ready.

"Despite what you may think of me, I couldn't bear the thought of you hiding out in an alley for a week. That wasn't right and you don't deserve it."

"I agree. How are you getting on with the money?"

"It's going fine but these things take time. There are stashes hidden all over the city and I don't want anyone to notice I'm making a series of withdrawals."

"Is that why you asked for so many days?"

"Yes. One afternoon is all I'd need if you'd demanded a hundred bucks, but this is a huge amount of money to pull together. You'll get it. Don't worry this isn't the start of a sob story, but I want you to appreciate I'm acting slow and careful so both our throats can stay in one piece."

Sammy soaked in Fabian's words.

"Has Waxey asked after me?"

"Every time I see him. You're missed for sure. I mentioned someone saw you on a train to Boston so Waxey's putting out some feelers over there to find you. And it won't be good for your health if you converse with Waxey—Chicago will be a much safer bet."

Fabian's fingers tightened on the shaft. This boy was getting on his nerves.

"Fabian, a deal is an agreement only if both parties carry their load. And I will hold my end of the bargain if you keep yours."

"Good news, Sammy. By Friday, you'll be on a train with a bagful of cash and the knowledge we can both sleep soundly at night."

"Sleeping through the night would be wonderful."

Sammy sighed and Fabian almost felt sorry for him but then he remembered why they were stood in a dilapidated room in the Blackhawk and his fingers gripped the knife firmly. Then Fabian realized he already slept fine at night—at least with Sarah's body by his side.

"I'll pop by in two days' time. In the meantime…"

"I won't open the door to strangers or paint the town red either."

Fabian nodded and squelched down the Blackhawk corridor. Those floorboards sure needed a clean.

"WOULD YOU LIKE to go for a hot chocolate?"

This was the best Alex could think of on the spur of the moment. He had taken up his position leaning against the doorjamb outside Rebecca's apartment on his way upstairs. The swoosh of her dress had caught the corner of his eye and he stopped to watch and stare.

Rebecca grinned and licked her lips.

"You know how to charm a girl, don't you?"

"I sure do, but do you want to get a hot chocolate, anyway?"

He smirked, arms folded, relaxed, knowing he had saved himself from eradicating Sammy—at least for the time being.

She held both hands behind her and swung her shoulders back and forth in a girlish manner.

"You persuaded me. Let me get my jacket."

Two minutes later, she appeared wearing a different dress and her hair was tied back. A coat wasn't the only thing she'd sorted out.

"Where were you thinking of taking us?"

"The cafe round the corner. They make a good cheesecake."

Rebecca nodded, knowing where Alex meant, and he was right, the dessert was to die for. They arrived, placed an order with the waiter and settled into their conversation.

"You going to tell me about the woman from this morning?"

"I wasn't planning on it. Just as I didn't ask you about your fella before he upped sticks and ran away. Sorry, that sounded much harsher than I meant. I have never asked you questions about the boys you've dated, so I figure it's only fair you do the same."

"I guess. But I know you kissed her and none of the guys I hooked up with got close to touching lips. Apart from Amos but my parents were watching, so that doesn't count."

"Nope, definitely does not."

Alex winked at her and she laughed, embarrassed but knowing a chaste peck on a cheek was not in the same ballpark as a kiss on the lips from Sarah.

Conversation ebbed and flowed as their drinks arrived along with a chunk of cheesecake to share. Alex offered to get a piece each but Rebecca said she wasn't all that hungry so they went halves. Chomping on the soft cheesy cream and crunchy biscuit base kept them quiet for five minutes. They were both more in need of food than either realized.

"Tastes good, huh?"

"Yep. A fine selection of venue."

"Why thank you kindly."

"Thank me by telling me you're leaving your ghastly business behind you."

Alex put his fork down and looked at Rebecca, one hand on each of his knees.

"You won't let this go, will you?"

"Too much depends on it, Alex. You say you want to be with me more than anything else in the world and I've told you the only thing I want you to give up to show me you mean it. That your word is true.

"And have you done that? No. You carry on as though you don't care about me—because if you cared, you'd stop and allow me what I crave, which is you and me in a safe place without me worrying every night whether you're coming home in a wooden box."

"I've told you to give me just a few more days and you'll see."

"Really? I'm not being funny, Alex, but if you believed you were out of that business in only a few days would you really be leaving a whorehouse in the morning with a nafka?"

"But…"

"Are you honestly telling me you think it acceptable to sleep with a whore and two weeks later propose marriage to me?"

"I…"

"Because if you do, be clear young man; I'm not that kind of girl."

"Wait a minute, won't you? You are so quick to jump to conclusions. The owner owes me money and I make personal connections, they serve a good breakfast in that hotel."

"It's a whorehouse, Alex. If I know that, surely you do too."

"Some rooms are available on an extremely short-term rent, you are right, but there are longer staying guests too."

"Really?"

"Yes. I'm not saying you'd want to introduce them to the rabbi, but they are ordinary folk with a discerning eye... for a cheap room over a whorehouse."

They both laughed because it was true, not because it was particularly funny.

"And over the years visiting the place, I've got to know some people who work there."

"The women who whore there, you mean."

"Most are women I know there."

"And these girls sell their bodies, don't they?"

"Yes, some do. And some customers only pay the girls to listen and nothing else."

"Right. Sure they do."

"You'd be surprised."

"I'm certain I would be shocked by what goes on inside that place and I have no desire for you to tell me, Alex Cohen."

"There you go. The fact Sarah kissed me goodbye after having breakfast isn't that awful, is it?"

"If that's all that has happened between you two."

"Well then."

"This morning you said you'd slept with her."

"No, I implied I'd slept with her as a joke because you jumped to a conclusion about her."

"I saw you holding hands with her and I described her as a whore which she is. And now you tell me all you did was have breakfast with her. Why would you touch that woman if it was only breakfast you'd had?"

Alex was tired of Rebecca's questions and needing to defend himself against her puritanical assumptions.

"Sarah is a whore, and we held hands walking out the door as friends. That's it. Like it or lump it but that's all there is."

Rebecca sipped the last dregs of her hot chocolate and patted the corners of her mouth with her napkin. Then she sighed and stood up.

"Whores, gangs, racketeering. That's the world you live in and you've given me nothing to believe you're going to change. We are through. Don't bother popping your head around our door again. I have zip to say to you. Ever. Whatever we might have had or might have hoped for, the truth is we are nothing, Alex Cohen. I never want to see you again in my life."

Rebecca stormed out the cafe before Alex had a chance to calm her down. He threw a dollar on the table and went after her, but she was walking at a terrific pace. She reached the tenement, but Alex was too far away to run up to her and say a word. She reached her apartment before he caught up with her. And then she closed the door. He slumped down on the floor and cried, sobbing tears for ten minutes. He stood up, out the building and headed for the Oregon and the rapture of Sarah's willing flesh.

JANUARY 30, 1918

47

THE FIRE IN Rebecca's eyes haunted him through the night and into the following morning. After he kissed Sarah goodbye outside the Oregon again, Fabian looked round in case Rebecca was on the corner, but she wasn't anywhere to be seen.

He felt the overwhelming need to go to the Selective Service building and see if his translator friend was there. The guy was just another army pinhead, but he had shown some humanity and an interest in his wellbeing —more than anyone else beyond the Bowery had ever done for him.

Outside the building, it appeared the same two guys were talking on the steps, but Alex knew that was his imagination playing tricks on him.

Inside were the same set of desks, the same men in uniform standing or sitting just as they had done when he first came in to sign up for the war to end all wars.

He noticed his translator filing papers in the corner of the room and went up to him.

"Hi."

"Hello."

"How are you doing?"

"Just fine, thanks."

The guy glanced at him with a puzzled expression. Like he was wondering why Alex had come into the Selective Service Department for a chat. And he wasn't wrong. Alex knew he wanted company and Jim was the only person he could think of to give him that companionship right now. Jim's name was on a badge attached to his jacket breast pocket. The last name looked Polish and Alex couldn't figure out how to pronounce it.

"What you doing here?"

"Come in to talk to you to be honest."

"About what?"

"Well, I know no one who will go off to fight. I mean, I saw one fella, but I didn't know him. Just bumped into him over a drink."

"You signed up because you spoke with a guy in a bar? You're kidding me?"

"No, not at all."

"Most people are running away from something. Is that you? Are you running from troubles at home?"

"Problems in my backyard. I guess so, yes. I mean…"

"Look, I don't want to be rude but I'm not here to chat with you. I turn up so that guys like you can understand what's going on in here. That's how I'm doing my bit for my country as my lungs aren't up to much. They declared me unfit to fight so I contribute to the war effort this way instead."

"Hadn't thought about that."

"Why would you? Besides, it's not your problem. You're fighting fit. Ready for action."

"Do you know what it'll be like over there?"

"You'll get American rations so no need to worry about the food."

"Hadn't crossed my mind."

"Oh, then…?"

"The fighting. Will we be shooting at each other from a long distance or will it be hand-to-hand skirmishes seeing the enemy face-to-face?"

"The British and the French have spent most of their time facing the enemy down in fields. The countryside is where the battles have been fought —just as they always have. Yes there's hand-to-hand fighting when it comes down to it. If there's a bridge to be taken and so on. But much of the time there's long lines of troops, hiding in trenches waiting to take a shot at some of them German soldiers."

Alex had thought little about what fighting in a war really meant. He imagined it would be like the battle on Bayard only with everyone in uniforms wearing helmets. And even if it were nothing like that—and it sounded like it would not be—he didn't mind. The fight was the thing, not the method of combat.

"How long do you think the war will last?"

"Over by Hanukkah maybe. Every year since it started the British have been promising it will all be over by Christmas, but it has kept going on. Now that the great United States is involved, we should be able to beat them Germans soon. We are a young fresh nation and the Brits and the French are old tired empires. They need our get-up-and-go."

"Do you think we'll save many Jews?"

"What do you mean?"

"In the Ukraine, Poland, Russia. If we fight in Europe, we can stop the Austrian Hungarians and save Jewish villages."

"Doubt it. Not in France."

Jim chuckled.

"But the bigger picture. I'm talking about beating the Prussians and that'll stop the pogroms, wouldn't you say?"

"Dare say it will. But we are over there to win for Jew and Gentile alike. This isn't a Jewish crusade."

Alex's turn to chuckle.

"I know what I'm getting involved in. It's just… the fella I met in that bar I mentioned, he told me he's gonna fight to help protect the Jews that didn't make it and come over to America. And that sounds mighty fine to me."

"Sure is, but I want you to understand this isn't a Semite war."

"Of course it's not. Don't be ridiculous; I'm no fool."

"Only checking. If you are fighting in Uncle Sam's army, it's for everyone. No-one gets left out."

"We work together, we live together but we always die alone."

"That sort of thing, yes, but don't go filling your head with worries. Enjoy your time before you ship out. And take care of yourself when you're over there."

"Any word on when?"

"Look on the board over there and see if your name is down."

Jim showed Alex where to look and, sure enough, he saw he was on the list with January 31 as the date to go for basic training. The reality of tomorrow bit into him. He turned to speak with Jim, but he was already standing next to a desk translating for another young guy seeking to kill himself a German. Alex swallowed hard and breathed deeply, staring at the words on the wall.

Before he left, he still had one or two loose ends to take care of and not much time to get it all done.

FABIAN'S FIRST INSTINCT was to go round to everyone he knew to say goodbye, but that wasn't a viable option. He would tell his family tonight over dinner and somehow explain to Sarah. As for his crew? Whatever he said and however he explained the reasons for his absence they would jostle for position to take over and there was nothing he could do about that. Letting Waxey know was high on his priority list but there was still the problem of Sammy.

To keep him quiet, Fabian had lied about getting him his money, thinking he could manage matters if needs be or plain kill the guy if things got out of hand. Now he found himself in neither camp.

As he needed to deal with the situation head on, Fabian made his cautious way up to the Blackhawk. This time he was less paranoid but decided not to take any unnecessary chances. Into the building and across the sticky corridor to Sammy's room. Rat-a-tat-tat and wait.

"Come on in."

"Are they still looking after you all right here?"

"Sure thing. How's the cash coming along?"

"Fine, but I still need another couple of days. I told you Friday and today is only Wednesday, so I still got two days."

"The sooner you get me my gelt, the sooner this whole affair is over."

"I am very aware of that, Sammy. You asked for a lot of money. I'm not arguing against it—don't worry. But large sums take time to pull together."

Fabian thought about the cash he'd stashed in various parts of the Lower East Side: his rainy-day money. It would only take an hour or two to gather enough to hand to his parents to give them a very comfortable buffer while he was away, but Sammy didn't need to know that.

"I brought some cards. Wanna play a few hands?"

"What? Yeah, it's very dull being stuck in a hotel for days on end."

"You might have spiced up your time with a woman or two."

"Huh? No, I didn't want to take the chance they might recognize me."

"Makes sense but the room is under my name, Alex Cohen, so if you change your mind later on, I'd go ahead if I were you. Have a party and get some beers in."

Sammy's eyes lit up. Fabian saw the isolation was making Sammy crack up. He fingered the knife in his pocket then sat down to play cards.

48

AN HOUR LATER and he'd lost count of the number of hands they'd gone through but Fabian was bored. Conversation had been minimal apart from the occasional shared joke relating to the luck of the cards. He figured it was time to go, so he stood up.

"Are you leaving so soon?"

"I've got things to do and places to be. I can't spend my entire day in hiding in this hotel. People would suspect something if I melted into thin air."

"Are you trying to be funny? I vanished and where was the search party for me?"

"They searched, Sammy. Waxey looked but no-one was stupid enough to check under a bunch of crates."

"I sure can hide."

"Vanished like a magic act on Coney Island."

"Will you come over tomorrow?"

"Don't think that will be possible, Sammy."

"Sure would be nice to have some human company again."

"Call room service for a nafka if you're lonely."

"No need to be like that. I'm saying I've enjoyed our time today and would like to do it again tomorrow."

"And I'm saying no, Sammy. I will spend the day getting your money in readiness for your final and permanent vanishing act."

Fabian started to head for the door, but Sammy stepped forward and gripped his shoulder. Pure instinct made him shrug it off instantly, but his friend immediately clasped his shoulder again. Fabian grabbed Sammy's fingers, bent them back and carried on twisting until Sammy was kneeling on the floor clinging to his arm in the hope his own shoulder wouldn't get dislocated and his wrist bones break. He squealed with the pain.

"I said no, Sammy, and that is what I meant."

"I thought…"

"That's your trouble, Sammy, you try to think but you're not very good at it. Are you?"

Slugger continued to twist Sammy's arm, bearing his weight down onto the guy's elbow. They both felt it was about to snap and then Sammy let out a belting scream.

"Shut up!"

A constant whimpering replaced the gut-wrenching howl and Slugger leaned down on that elbow. Sammy could only fast breathe through his nose, bubbles of mucus appeared and dripped out of his nostrils onto the floor.

"Please..."

"Too late for that."

"Listen..."

Slugger couldn't take it anymore. He regretted what he'd done to Sammy but what was done was done. He had to judge Sammy on the here and now. With a glance down at the pathetic sight before him, another wave of anger welled up inside him.

One punch to the throat and Sammy was no more. He gurgled a little but slumped onto the floor less than a second after Slugger had acted.

Slugger took four deep inhalations and calmed himself down. It's what he should have done in the alley but back then he couldn't find the heart.

Room service supplied a large sack and Slugger dragged the corpse out the hotel, but first he opened the registration book. He spotted the name 'Alex Cohen' and tore that page out and stuffed it in his pocket.

The head bumped down the backstairs and carried on slamming against the ground until Fabian located a decent hiding place—an alleyway round the corner. He tipped the body out of the hotel-labeled sack and threw some rubbish on top of Sammy's corpse. Then back to the Bowery for lunch.

FABIAN GRABBED SOME bread and salt beef on his way through the Bowery even though his destination was the Forsyth and lunch with his crew. His energy levels were at an all-time low and he needed a pick-me-up to keep him going.

As he walked down Second Avenue, Monk Eastman framed into his consciousness and the plain simple force of his argument for fighting echoed in Fabian's mind. Who else is left to look after the Jews who didn't flee?

At the Forsyth, Fabian covered lunch for his gang, and they paid him his tribute for the week. One thing he'd learned from the trouble with Yake Brady was to vary the dates and times for drops. So each time he chose a different day to receive his kickback from the crew. If you can't predict what you will do, then how can anybody else? Made perfect sense even if he was about to skip town.

He stayed for a beer or two, but time was pressing.

"Come on, guys. There's work to be getting on with."

"Sure thing, boss."

He left them to it and figured they'd finish the drinks he bought and then get back to the numbers. If he was wrong, there'd be little consequence for him, anyway.

A detour before heading to Bayard and Bowery. There was another of his alleyways which was safer than a bank. It was halfway along Second Street between Avenue A and Avenue B—the north side. There was nothing special about this narrow gap between two buildings other than the loose brickwork at the far end, round the corner from the front, and out of sight from passersby on the street.

Fabian removed three bricks which were hidden behind a pile of mesh and debris. There was a gap between the outer wall and the inner boards. And in that space was a sack tied up with a piece of rope. And inside the bag was over five hundred dollars which he had saved over the years since he landed from the old country. This was the gelt he was leaving for his family to tide them over until his return. It was one of four such bags he had secreted around the Lower East Side. If he gave his parents all the money, then they'd spend it with nothing to show for it—other than some new furniture and a home that cost more rent.

He took the bag and raced to the Cohens' apartment as quickly as he could. No good could come from him dawdling along the street with a sackful of cash in his hand. With the money safely stashed under his bed, Fabian strolled over to Waxey's to talk to him about the future.

They both knocked back a shot of vodka before any conversation ensued. Waxey was in a strange mood.

"What was that in aid of?"

"Just two friends having a drink."

"Sure, but you usually say hello."

Waxey snorted with laughter.

"True, but the first tribute from the Yake Brady gang arrived thirty minutes ago and we will be swimming in cash."

He filled their shot glasses, and they slugged back the liquor, slamming the jars down on the table for dramatic effect. Waxey moved to fill the glasses again.

"Wait. Not for me. I've got more business to take care of this afternoon."

"What is so important you can't drink with me?"

"I'm preparing to go to Boston tomorrow to see if I can find Sammy."

Waxey put the vodka bottle down and listened.

"I said I wouldn't bother, but he deserves me spending some time there, doesn't he?"

"Well, I told you I'd send word, and no-one has spotted him if he was on that train of yours."

"Sure, it might have been wrong information, but it's the only thing we've got."

"Why the change of heart?"

Fabian was dead if Waxey ever discovered what he had done to Sammy. And he also knew Waxey would not approve him going off to the war, so the truth held no sway in his arguments.

"It's been long enough that if he was in the city, we'd find him or have heard of him. So he must be somewhere else. The best guess is that he's in Boston."

"I'll wire some people to expect you."

"No."

"No? Why wouldn't you want any help with this?"

"Because I've made the trip to Boston up, but I can't lie to you. Only the truth will disappoint you."

Waxey straightened in his chair, tensing his back and clenching a fist.

"A lie? Why lie to me?"

"I'm going to fight in the war."

An enormous guffaw erupted out of Waxey Gordon, the most powerful man in the Bowery and partner in crime with Charlie Lucky.

"You're kidding me."

"'Fraid not. I knew you'd be disappointed."

"I sure am but if that's what you think you wanna do, who am I to stop you?"

"Thank you. This sounds crazy, but I bumped into Monk Eastman and he talked sense about helping the Jews who hadn't fled to America."

Waxey held up his hand to stop Fabian in his tracks.

"Fabian. Monk spent nearly three years in the can and since he's come out, he's not been thinking straight."

"Made sense to me."

"And you're sure there's no other reason to fight other than the wisdom of Eastman?"

"None."

Waxey's stare bore through Fabian's eyes, distrust and malice in his expression. Fabian realized the whole story about Sammy had been a mistake, but he would live with the consequences. Or die from them if necessary.

"So I was wondering, Waxey."

"What?"

"Will you look after my family while I'm gone?"

"Of course. We work together, we live together. Don't you ever forget it."

Fabian was unsure if those words were a gentle reminder or an absolute threat. Waxey was giving nothing away.

"I won't and thank you."

"When you come back, there'll always be a place for you. You've worked hard and delivered much for me. You and Sammy both."

The sentence hung in the air and Fabian wasn't sure how to respond.

"I reckon he's dead. How about you, Fabian?"

"Must be. I just don't want to say it out loud. We've been together since my first days in America."

"I understand but, Fabian…"

"Yes?"

"If I ever find out he wasn't killed by Yake Brady's two men. If I found one of mine had done for Sammy instead…"

Waxey took a shot glass and, staring at Fabian all the while, crushed the glass in his hand until it shattered into a hundred pieces. He stared back at Waxey.

"You won't find out it was one of ours, Waxey."

He stood up and left Waxey's office, not wanting to outstay his welcome and aware of the implication of what Waxey had said to him. Almost like the man knew and the way Fabian responded implied he was right.

January 30, 1918 11 PM

49

THE COHEN FAMILY dinner was filled with tension that evening, as Alex predicted to himself before they sat down to eat. His mother knew something was up because he appeared expecting to be fed; her son spent almost all his time outside the apartment and the only guarantee she had was his appearance for the Friday night meal and that he'd sleep in his bed that one evening. The other certainty was his disappearance before the family went to shul.

He had the smarts not to ruin their digestion too much by waiting until after they'd finished dessert. Then he took out the pin and lobbed the grenade to break his mama's heart.

Alex explained his reasons as best he could, but he couldn't be heard over the crying and wailing. His father, as insipid a man as he was, shook him by the hand and wished him well. Then for the first time since Alex was a little boy, they hugged. That brought a tear to his eye. He had avoided saying goodbye to everyone apart from Waxey and this show of feeling from the most emotionless man in his life touched him more deeply than he knew was possible.

Thirty minutes later and Mama had calmed down to a level of constant sobbing. The rest of his siblings stared, not understanding what was going on—other than family grief without a dead body and the tearing of shirts. It made no sense, so they carried on playing.

He hugged his mother again until her tears created a soggy pool on the left shoulder of his shirt.

"I want you both to listen to me very carefully."

Mama and Papa looked at him, wondering what other terror was about to befall them.

"Under my bed is a sack for you to use in my absence. Try to hang onto it as long as possible because none of us knows quite how long I will be away. I reckon you should have enough for about a year."

At this point, Mama wailed again but Alex continued.

293

"And that doesn't include any gelt Papa earns so it should last longer than that—unless you go crazy."

His father nodded. The man might have ceded all conversational rights to his wife, but he was still the head of the house and supervised all expenditure. The cash would not be squandered on his watch.

"Put it somewhere safe."

Alex decided not to mention the help Waxey had promised in case it didn't transpire.

"If any of my business associates come calling, welcome them in. They'll only appear to check on your welfare and nothing more. So be friendly, Mama."

"When am I never friendly?"

"To individuals you don't like and to strangers who turn up at your door unannounced."

"Apart from that, when am I not friendly?"

A tiny smile curled up on her lips.

"Time for me to go."

"You're not staying the night. I thought…"

"I have other people to see before I ship out, Mama."

"But you'll be back later…"

"Leave him be, Ruth. The man is off to war tomorrow."

More tears but Moishe was correct. The last thing Alex wanted to do tonight was sleep alone in his parents' apartment.

FABIAN LAY NEXT to Sarah, enjoying the warmth of her torso against his. One of her legs was splayed on top of his thigh and the heat of her crotch touched his hip. Casually, he kept his hand on her tuches, stroking it occasionally as the mood took him.

"You're quiet tonight—even for you."

"Just thinking, that's all."

She giggled.

"Well think about this instead."

She scurried down his torso under the covers until all his focus was on her lips and the intense waves of pleasure she gave him.

That night he hardly slept a wink, alternately soaking in the balm of Sarah's body and fearing the horrors that awaited him overseas. The unknown was a dreadful prospect.

JANUARY 31, 1918

50

IN THE MORNING they had breakfast together. Fabian's eyes were heavy with tiredness but it was too late to conserve his energy now. They held hands outside the Oregon and kissed before parting. This time he grasped her tight and kissed her repeatedly. All through the night he'd been unable to tell Sarah where he was going.

Not because he loved her because he did not. It was almost as if he was unable to tell her because the most he could say was that he liked her. Or rather enjoyed her company and her attention—and the fact she asked nothing of him because she expected absolutely zip from him in return. They were the perfect couple—totally physically intimate with no emotional connection, at least as far as Fabian was concerned. He had never considered the possibility Sarah might feel anything for him despite her repeatedly telling him she'd spend the rest of her life with him.

"See you later."

He kissed her again and squeezed her butt cheek. Then he walked away without saying another word. Fabian wiped some moisture from his eye and headed north for Penn Station.

With the Bowery behind him, Fabian's senses intensified. Walking along unfamiliar streets made him nervous. Years of always needing to keep one eye over his shoulder had honed this instinct keenly. So much so he halted in front of shops automatically just to cast a glimpse back the way he'd come. He could not help himself.

In the distance, about a block away, he thought he spotted a guy looking like Paulie. Fabian stayed where he was to see if he could get a better look at the fella's face but no luck. He carried on strolling but after another half block, he pulled into a building vestibule and waited. Two minutes later, Paulie went past. Not any old Italian lad, but Paulie. This was not good. Waxey'd sent him and it wouldn't be to give him a bunch of flowers as a send-off.

Then twenty seconds afterward, Abraham sauntered by. If there was a flicker of doubt about Paulie's trip out the Bowery, there could be no coincidence with both crew members on a separate journey on the same morning as he was leaving town.

Fabian gulped and noticed his breathing accelerating. They were in front of him now so if he waited, they wouldn't be able to get to him. Only problem was they'd have figured precisely where he was heading: Penn.

He peeped his head out the building to spot the two on the sidewalk. There they were, ten shops ahead of him. Fabian sprinted one block west and four north, hoping this would put him sufficiently ahead of the boys to get to the station before them. He stopped to catch his breath and take stock.

Twentieth Street. Another dash four blocks and then he jogged one block east to make sure he had lost them. There they were. How? How had they done that? A run west and seven blocks north. He couldn't keep this up. No way. Back to Eighth Avenue and Paulie's face was clearly visible on the same side of the road, but Abraham was nowhere to be seen.

This was ridiculous, he was only a block away from Penn. Fabian turned around and there was Abraham, knife out, aimed at his heart. Somehow, he'd snuck behind him. Paulie appeared round the corner and lunged at him.

Slugger stepped aside, grabbed Paulie's lower arm and twisted it, forcing him to drop his blade. With his other hand, he took the back of Paulie's neck and pushed downwards.

"Don't make me do this. Tell Waxey you didn't find me. I don't want to hurt you, but you are giving me little option."

"Do what you need to do, Fabian."

Abraham stood, legs apart, waiting. Fabian threw Paulie into him and made a dash for it. Once the two picked themselves off the floor, they chased him hard.

Fabian slammed one foot in front of the other, desperate to keep as fast a pace as possible, knowing that to glance round would slow him down. The only thing to do was to run, run, run.

Penn's frontage loomed ahead of him and as he pelted inside, he allowed himself half a neck turn to check on Paulie and Abraham. Two heads bobbed above the ordinary passersby about three hundred feet behind.

Into the station, he hauled himself along, stumbling on his own shoes until he reached a guy with a peaked cap and the uniform of a station employee.

"Which way to the army train?"

"What?"

Fabian grabbed him by the lapels and in his best English said, "Army train? Where?"

"Platform four, fella."

"Four?"

"Yessir."

Fabian looked round and thought he recognized Abraham at the main entrance. No trace of Paulie this time. He searched for a platform sign, spinning around until the station guard pointed to the far corner. Fabian nodded and catapulted himself towards his goal. As he neared the platform, he twisted his head round and witnessed Paulie launch himself in Fabian's direction. Ten feet behind was Abraham.

At the platform he barged past the guard demanding to examine his papers and hurried as fast as his legs would carry him over to the carriages. First, second and halted at the third whose door was open. As he stepped up and into the carriage, the extra height allowed him to see both Abraham and Paulie stopped by the station security, who was calling a solider over to help him deal with these reprobates.

Alex Cohen slumped down in the first seat he found and let himself be engulfed by the safety of joining the American Expeditionary Force into the trenches of the Great War. Dysentery, shrapnel, hunger and trench foot would be his only friends, if he was lucky. Death would come as a welcome break from the horrors that awaited.

THE END

BOOK TWO
EAST SIDE
HUSTLER

JUNE 1919

1

ALEX COHEN TRUDGED along the road until he reached Bay Parkway and McDonald Avenue in Brooklyn, home of the Washington Cemetery. The damp patch in his shoes did nothing to take the piercing chill out of his spine. For a second, he recalled the trenches in France where he'd nearly died more times than he cared to remember.

He shut his eyes and stuffed his hands in his pockets. Ever since he'd returned from the war, a gnawing emptiness had settled in his stomach and refused to go away. The only reason he trudged on was the sure knowledge that many of his comrades had fallen in the Saint-Mihiel attack. That was September 1918 and nine months later, the sound of shells bursting around his ears kept Alex awake at night. And here he was, walking through this garden of stones, hoping to spot one particular slab.

Down the aisles, past decades of death organized in neat rows. He had no clue quite how he would find his objective, but no matter what, he'd have to get to the stone before nightfall.

The disgusted looks flashed at him from various people visiting their loved ones made Alex feel more alone. Like every other cemetery in the world, there was a cold wind blasting across the landscape. He looked down at his clothes and understood why the glances were so judgmental.

A shuffle down another path as leaves flew past him. It was summer and his heart was frozen. Then he stopped and turned to face one stone. Alex read the inscription, a mix of English, Yiddish and Hebrew: Fabian Mustard. The joke name given by a customs officer when he arrived in Ellis Island, like so many other immigrants hoping to find sidewalks paved with gold.

What was going on? How come Fabian was laid to rest here? Alex was confused because the coffin under that tombstone was empty for the simple reason that he was Fabian Mustard and had reverted to his original name when he left for the front.

Some other bums in the Bowery told him his parents bought the plot when they were informed by Uncle Sam that he was dead, but even though he felt like a corpse, he was alive. A tear dripped out of his right eye. The bleakness of seeing his own grave filled him with dread. That gnawing in the pit of his stomach made Alex wretch, and he slumped to the ground, vomit and phlegm mixing on the smooth slab.

When he'd regained his composure, he stood up and slunk out of the cemetery. Before he left, he placed a pebble on Fabian's grave—in the Jewish tradition. In that moment when he hit the dirt, Alex realized he was alone in the world and was a ghost, though still among the living.

After the journey from France, he'd been dumped on the street and told to sort himself out. Three months later and he was no better off than that first day he'd returned to American soil. This shadow-man previously ran a string of gambling pools, extortion rackets and protection across the Bowery and here he was, a nobody with a freshly-dug hole in the ground and a thirst in his throat. Alex trudged back to the Lower East Side and prepared to take his position in the land of the free.

2

EVEN THOUGH ALEX wanted to get back to the Bowery as quickly as possible, the sheer exhaustion he still experienced whenever he put one boot in front of the other prevented him from making much progress. Each time he slumped down to catch his breath or have a nap, the stink of rotting flesh filled his nostrils. When he shut his eyes, he would glimpse someone's head being blown off or the flash-bang of a shell landing.

Nothing would ever be the same again. And when he came back, he couldn't face hanging with his old crowd because they hadn't been there, seen the things he had been forced to see. The taste of the air in his gas mask. The stench of a gangrenous toe. How might a civilian understand the unmentionable acts of survival Alex had endured?

So he kept himself apart from the hustle and the bustle of Bowery life, hunkered down in alleys at night; taking out a begging bowl when the streets filled with normal people. If he was lucky, he'd pick up a few bits; enough for a loaf of bread. The rest he stole.

July segued into August and Alex remained in the gutters around Broome and Columbia. Most days his stomach rumbled but no matter how awful he felt, there was nothing to endure as bad as the war. Those trenches. The mud. That constant foreboding, never knowing if the next moment was your last. Then the whistle would blow and you'd fly over the top and wait to be mown down by enemy fire.

The only thing he was good for was begging. The pitiful looks he received from passersby reflected the physical state he was in. Despite the poverty of the ghetto, there were enough mensches to keep Alex in bread and jam. Sat on the sidewalk with his bowl prominently in front of him, he watched housewives buy food for dinner and saw men pop into cathouses. If they came out thirty minutes later then they'd gone straight upstairs to sample the fleshy wares. If they fell out of the entrance after an hour and staggered down the road, then booze was their vice.

Only once did he imagine he saw his mama and papa but before they came even close, Alex got up and shuffled to another street corner until he was certain they were not heading his way. To bring himself to think beyond the here and now was impossible; the current minute was as far into the future as he could cope with.

ALEX LAY IN an alley with no idea where he was. Somewhere in the Bowery. Curled in a heap, one image repeated in his head: a solitary girl performing a pirouette in her family's living room.

She lived immediately beneath his parent's apartment and her name was Rebecca. She was the most perfect and incredibly beautiful woman Alex ever met. Before basic training, she told him she never wanted to see him again as long as she lived. All he had was the memory of her ankle-length skirt swirling around, lifting until he glimpsed a calf.

Then his thoughts turned to her words, and he wished he could afford a bottle of vodka to drown out the sounds from his head. Instead, he wrapped his arms around his torso as tight as possible and waited for the morning to arrive.

When it did, that skirt continued to spin across the wooden floor and he recalled the gentle touch of her fingertips against his cheek. Having taunted himself to near destruction, Alex got up and shuffled to the main drag to panhandle his way through another day.

Every hour he changed his pitch and tried a different corner. Along the way, he grabbed any scraps of food lying on the floor. In his state, Alex wasn't fussy. He never knew where the next husk of bread would appear, so he paid no never mind if the piece he found was baked in mud or worse. In the trenches, they ate whatever they found to supplement their meager rations. So these morsels almost felt like luxury–only they weren't. He had a sufficient but slender grasp on reality to know how low he had got.

This self awareness fed the grinding ache in his belly and Alex realized he needed to find some way to leave the gutter life, but there was nowhere to go. Then he spotted a flyer fluttering down the street and for no reason at all, he reached out and grabbed it. It was in English but having spent time outside the Jewish shtetl, he now understood what it said.

HE PICKED HIMSELF up and shuffled over to the address on the paper. Having shlepped fifteen blocks, Alex found the place quickly. A charity was offering a warm meal and a bed for the night to veterans. At the door, Alex hesitated, but a woman took him by the arm and brought him in. She knew better than to ask a barrage of questions but a quiet calm oozed out of every pore.

Without a word, she led him to a series of tables where a man ladled soup out of an urn and into white bowls.

"There you go, soldier."

"How do you know I'm not just some bum off the street?"

"Are you?"

"No… I once was somebody round here."

"That's good enough for me, Mac."

The guy held a bowl and offered it to Alex. He shrugged and used both hands to carry the steaming broth to the next table where a kindly face added some bread, bobbing on top. For the first time, he checked out the room to see a set of benches in rows for the veterans to use while they ate.

There were huddles of guys talking to each other and a sprinkling of loners. Alex found a bench with nobody sat near it, flopped onto the seat and devoured his meal in record time. The flavors of the soup lingered on his tongue and he considered bargaining for a second portion, but realized his body wasn't equipped for that volume of proper food.

INSTEAD ALEX REMAINED seated and cherished the warmth of the room. He had forgotten the simple luxury of being indoors and relished it now. A hobo came over and sat opposite. Alex couldn't decide whether to be annoyed at this imposition on his world or glad of the proximity of another human being. He started with a noncommital grunt, which was mirrored back to him.

The guy concentrated on his soup and enjoyed using his bread to mop up some liquid along the rim of his bowl. Once the meal was over, he raised his gaze to Alex and smiled.

"Tastes good, doesn't it?"

"Yeah."

Despite his best desires, there was nothing else Alex could muster. There was a connection between them—both had lived through hell, but that was their problem. The one thing which bound the two men was so terrible that words failed them. The most they managed was to smile at each other once in a while.

"They serve coffee here too. Want some?"

"Good idea."

Alex followed the regular to the tables and collected a mug of hot brown liquid and the two men returned to their bench.

"Come here often?"

"Couple of times a week. You?"

"First time."

"Thought so. Didn't think I recognized you."

"Been back long?"

"A while, I guess."

"Sorry, don't know why I asked such a stupid question."

"Don't worry about it."

"Just wanted to have a normal conversation, but it was a dumb thing to say."

"I've heard a lot worse."

"The name's Alex."

"Mayson."

"Native New Yorker or never went far from where the boat landed?"

"Born and bred in the island."

"Lived here all the time I can remember."

With that statement, a yawn ripped across Alex's mouth and Mayson grinned.

"They'll shift these benches out of the way soon and bring out the camp beds."

Alex nodded and waited to be enveloped by the warm embrace of unconsciousness.

JULY 1919

3

ALEX VISITED THE soup kitchen once a week, but never more frequently. He knew not to treat the hot meal and warm bed as anything more than a luxury. That way, he didn't get weak.

Bowery streets were the same throughout the neighborhood. Tenement apartments crushed together, families living cheek by jowl. The sidewalks were peppered with stalls and stores offering the usual range of products people need to live a normal life: food, pots, furniture.

Nestling alongside this slice of American civilization was the other face of the area: the bars, cathouses and gambling dens that catered for the many adult vices. This Jewish neighborhood was filled with men and they are the same the world over.

From the safety of his alley, Alex would watch the rats come out in the evening. Some headed for the bars for conversation with friends and an occasional fight with a stranger. Others would nip into a whorehouse but stay for a drink on the first floor afterwards. He recalled the Forsyth Hotel and the Oregon, where his Sarah used to ply her trade. He would sip a beer and wait for her to be free before climbing into her bed and spending the rest of the night in her company. By the end, he didn't even pay for it, although he always left some green as a gift for her.

Her body was a lifetime ago and, despite how hard he tried, he no longer recalled the scent of her neck or the salt of her skin. Those were the memories that had kept him alive in France—and that image of Rebecca spinning round.

The sight of all the offal of humanity degrading and debasing itself every night and most afternoons filled Alex with even more despair. There really was no hope. Not for him, not for anybody. This place was a cesspit and everyone inside it was in a quagmire of depravity. Himself included.

ALEX FORAGED AROUND the back of a bakery one afternoon, hoping to uncover a heap of discarded loaves. Although he only found a crust or two, something about the aroma from the store reminded him of Friday night and his mama's *challah* bread.

In that instant, he crumpled to the ground and cried, tears soaking into the dry earth as soon as they landed. For a moment, he thought about going to the corner of Grande and Suffolk, up onto the fourth floor and wallowing in the joy of his mother's embrace, but he knew he didn't deserve it. Couldn't trust himself around such lovely normal people.

The truth was that despite his medal, Alex was ashamed of what he'd been driven to do in the trenches. What the generals described as bravery, he saw as nothing more than abject cowardice caused by the sheer need to survive. There was no way to bring himself to look Papa square in the eyes.

Somehow he imagined the man would see through him and know the barbarous acts he'd performed to be honored as a hero. What a ridiculous word. An enormous lie. Then Alex recalled the money he'd stashed before his hurried departure to France—as though his brain was trying to drag his attention away from his own thoughts. His own disgust.

All he remembered was shoving five hundred dollars into a sack and carving out a brick from a wall in an alley in the Bowery. If he could've remembered where it was, he'd have grabbed the cash and left New York far behind him. Whenever he concentrated on the image of that hole in the brickwork then his mind's eye would fill up with the whizz and bang of shells landing around him. He cowered waiting for the nonexistent barrage to stop.

Alex knew he could not continue living this way. He considered hitching a ride on a freight train out of town, but the thoughts in his skull would follow him wherever he traveled. He had to do something else, and he'd figured out exactly what that was.

4

ALEX SHUFFLED OUT of his alley and passed down the sidewalk, stealing some apples as he went. They crunched loudly in his head and he almost choked with the amount of juice in his mouth. He continued on his way, grabbing items off stalls as he walked. He even popped into a store or two, but found beady eyes staring at him, making it impossible for him to rob from the glaring owners.

In the end, his pockets were full, and he squatted at the corner of Bayard and Bowery. Alex shoveled some bread into his mouth and chewed the pieces until there were only crumbs left on his fingers. Then he devoured his last apple and threw the core into the gutter. Still savoring the taste, he leaned back against a wall and soaked in the scene surrounding him.

There were the usual scurrying housewives and men weaving around the sidewalks. Some guys drank from dawn to dusk—and beyond. In France, he'd gulped down whiskey when he had the chance, but there was never enough to remove the memories in his head—just sufficient to help him fall asleep. And the same images would haunt him again when he awoke.

Alex pulled out the knife from his tattered coat pocket. He had found the garment on the corpse of a hobo two weeks before. When he first wore it, the garment stank of death but he'd got used to the stench and stopped noticing by the second morning.

With the blade in one hand, he pulled back his sleeve to reach his wrist. He knew he'd never be able to slice his throat open but his wrist…

Alex gripped the handle tightly and moved the sharp metal onto his skin. Then he inhaled deeply, knowing the next moment would be decisive. Just as he was about to cut deep into his flesh, a hand came from nowhere and prized the knife out of his grasp.

He growled and turned his head up to see this interloper. The face scowling down at him was familiar but he couldn't quite place it. The man was from a time before France. When the trenches were just a phrase uttered by a sergeant at boot camp.

The fella continued to grimace at him as Alex stared back. Schmendrik. What was his problem and why did he think Alex's life was any of his business?

"Dear boy, we thought you were dead."

The Yiddish sentence floated into his ears and the voice almost sounded concerned. He continued to sit with his blank expression. Gar nichts.

"How long have you been back?"

Alex focused hard on the mouth, nose and eyes of the speaker until the face became familiar.

"Waxey?"

The gang boss smiled and held out his hand. Alex took it and stood up.

"Let's get you cleaned up. I'm guessing you haven't eaten in a while and I have to tell you, buddy, you stink. *Verstinkener schlemiel.*"

WAXEY GORDON LED Alex into his clubhouse on the corner of the street. The place had been decorated since the last time he'd been inside and a bright red-and-white sign adorned the frontage. The man didn't feel the need to hide his whereabouts; he was king of the heap.

Alex followed his former boss up to the second floor and flopped into the old meeting room. A couch had been added to the roster of shabby furniture but nothing else had changed. Even the stale smell of sweat and coffee still lingered in the air.

A steaming mug appeared in front of him and Alex placed a hand either side as though to warm up, but his body wasn't cold. Just his aching head. He looked up and found he was alone so he remained sat at the table and enjoyed the sensation of being inside a building. The walls, floor and ceiling offered a comfort—their very solidity giving him some of the security and certainty he craved.

Ira Moskowitz entered the room and approached him.

"Waxey said it was you, but I couldn't believe my ears. How are you doing? Don't answer that. I can see exactly. We need to get you some new clothes and introduce you to the dark art of a bath. No offense, friend."

A light squeeze of the shoulder was all Alex could cope with before he edged his torso away from Waxey's right-hand man. Ira wasn't offended and relaxed on the couch, spreading himself out and enjoying a moment's tranquility in an otherwise hectic day.

Alex barely recognized the man, but despite his overall caution built up from months living on the street, he felt no ill will toward the guy who seemed harmless enough. Waxey returned to explain that he'd made a few calls and found a place for him to go. There was an unnecessary smile on Waxey's face but Alex was in no mood for any games the fella was playing.

Fifteen minutes later, Alex stood at the entrance of the Oregon Hotel. The bar stretched along one wall opposite a smattering of tables. Alex dug his hands deep in his coat pocket and tensed his arm muscles as he recognized the interior and remembered who lived here.

As if on cue, Sarah trotted down the stairs and a smile ripped across her face as she caught sight of him. She bundled him in her arms and took him upstairs for a long soak in a bath and the chance to lie on her bed.

If she'd been planning anything more for their reunion, she would have been bitterly disappointed. As soon as Alex's head hit the feathery down of the pillow, he fell fast asleep.

SMOKE. MUD. BLOOD. Alex popped his eyes above the rim of his foxhole long enough to see the flames around the sniper's rifle in the distance. Maybe sixty or eighty feet away. An incredibly loud whizzing sound made him cover one ear with his left hand; his right clutched his weapon and nothing was going to separate him from that. His ears still ringing, he leaped out of the slush pit with a single aim to reach the sniper before the German spotted him and fired. Bobby was screaming in agony somewhere in the no-man's land ahead.

ALEX WOKE TO find himself naked and under layers of blankets. He covered his face with the sheets and inhaled, taking in Sarah's aroma and the smells of her bedroom. Sex mixed with sorcery. A chair creaked, and he saw her sit up, eyes barely open. She must have given up her bed.

Strange, because they'd shared this bed for months before he went to war —not that he had the strength or any inclination to do anything more than lie in the same room as Sarah at the moment.

"Do you fancy a bite to eat, Fabian?"

"Don't use Fabian: he died in France. My name is Alex Cohen."

"Seems peculiar to change what I call you."

"Believe me when I tell you that fella is dead. I've visited his grave so it must be true."

Sarah rolled her eyes and looked around for a smoke.

"Your parents are sentimental types."

She offered a cigarette and he accepted it. Since his return to America, the only cigarettes Alex had found were discarded butts. The luxury of his own tobacco overwhelmed him and salty water dribbled out of his eyes, splashing onto the white sheets. Sarah moved on the bed and wrapped her arms around him.

Alex hugged her and cried for what felt like a lifetime, but eventually his tears dried up and he was able to let go.

"Some lokshen soup?"

"And a coffee if there's any going spare."

"I'm sure we can stretch to a hot drink. Do you want anything stronger?" He shook his head.

"That'd just knock me out. I've not had much to eat these last few weeks. Not since I returned…"

"…from the fighting?"

"From France."

Sarah nodded and left to get the food, leaving Alex sat up in bed with a half-view out of the window. He didn't want to leave his sanctuary and slid back down under the covers. When she returned with a tray, Sarah found him snoring away but the smell of the soup roused him from slumber.

She spooned the hot liquid into his mouth and Alex allowed her, even though he was more than capable of feeding himself. This was the first time he'd been able to trust the world long enough to let his guard down and subsume himself into somebody else's protection.

And it was his Sarah. When they'd seen each other last, he'd kissed her on the lips and said goodbye as though that day was like any other. But it was the morning he shipped out of New York after volunteering to fight the Hun.

He'd forgotten his reasons for going and he doubted if they'd made much sense even then. No matter how much training you receive, nothing prepares you for trench warfare.

Then he allowed his mind to wander and he remembered the times he and Sarah had spent in that bed. The things they'd got up to and the conversations which had taken place. Hopes and dreams laid bare. An honesty between them that he'd torn apart when he scurried away to France without telling her either that he was going or what was his destination.

SEPTEMBER 1919

5

OVER THE NEXT two months, Alex spent his time with Sarah and for the first three weeks he didn't leave her bedchamber. His strength returned once his body got used to eating ordinary food again and the atrocious images flying across his head seemed to wane. At least for now. This gave him an opportunity to rebuild bridges with his former lover.

"You never explained why you didn't tell me you were going off to fight."

"I couldn't find the words and was afraid of how you'd react."

"What did you imagine I would do?"

"Not really sure anymore. Then, you were my bedrock, my anchor, and if you had turned your back on me, then I can't imagine what I'd have done."

Alex stared out of the window, not daring to make eye contact. Sarah put her hand on his.

"You weren't listening to me in that case. I said I would change my life around to live with you. To be your wife."

He darted a glance in her direction and nodded

"Yeah, but I was stupid enough not to hear your words. All the trouble with Sammy and what was going on with Rebecca…"

"Complicated, but it doesn't have to be like that. When you recover, you'll leave this room and maybe return to see me. The important thing for me is that you understand one message: I would drop my current life in an instant if you said you would commit to me."

"How would we get by?"

"We'd earn like everybody does—only there'd be nobody else either of us would sleep with. This would be our bed—in every sense."

Alex sandwiched Sarah's hand in his palms and squeezed gently.

"I'm not disregarding what you've said, but I can't deal with that right now. Not because I'm not interested in you—far from it—but because I'm finding it hard to focus on the future; I have spent so much time only concentrating on where the next meal will come from. Long-term planning is thinking about tomorrow, for me, and anything bigger than that has to be put on ice."

SARAH SIGHED, NODDED and withdrew her hand. Alex wondered if he'd said too much. He was amazed she wanted to spend her time with him and hadn't considered the practicalities: if she was with him all day and all night then how was she paying for the room and board?

A moment's reflection by Alex and he would have realized that Waxey was paying the bills. Who else would be that generous or have deep enough pockets? No one that Alex knew. Instead, he kept his existence wrapped inside a tiny ball comprising his next meal, staying warm and enjoying Sarah's company.

"This isn't where I ever imagined we'd be."

"What do you mean, Alex? I'd got used to having you around before you skipped town. I took ages to fill the Fabian-sized gap in my life."

"How d'you do that? With someone?"

"No need to be like that. You left me—remember that before you try to take any high moral ground."

"Says the *nafka* to the former gangster."

"And less of the whore, if you don't mind. You sound like the rest of them, judging me."

"Oh no, Sarah. I'm not being snarky."

"You sure sounded like it. You have no idea what I go through every moment I walk along the sidewalk."

But he did. Not before France, but Alex had spent enough time on the streets to appreciate the dangers the nafkas put themselves through as they went past ordinary men with lustful ideas.

"Sarah, did Waxey tell you what I've been through since I got back from the front?"

"This isn't about you. I'm the one you just insulted."

He was silent for a spell, mulling over what she'd said and how arrogant his response had been to her. He hadn't meant to be like that, but his paranoia about what she had done while he was overseas had overtaken him.

"Look, I'm sorry. It hurts me that you survived okay without me and my tongue lashed out just then. Nothing more than that."

Sarah uncrossed her arms and there was a silence between them for a minute.

"LISTEN TO ME, Sarah. This is important. I appreciate all you've done for me these past couple of months and I've been remembering our time together before…"

Alex's voice trailed off as his mind wandered to France, but quickly he snapped to the present.

"We were good together, weren't we?"

Her nod confirmed his belief.

"And I was wrong to push you away. Back then and now, although since Waxey found me, I've not been my full self."

"When you first were brought into this room, you were like a small child. So frail, so needy. You couldn't feed yourself, you were so weak."

"I'm stronger and ready to face the world again, but not alone. I want you with me."

Sarah leaned over to kiss him firmly on the lips and Alex responded by gingerly placing his palms on her cheeks to engulf her head in his hands. She made him happy—he realized that now—and he didn't want them to be apart.

He stood up and encouraged her to follow him until they reached the side of the bed. Then he removed her clothes, and they clambered under the sheets.

Later when they were sharing a cigarette, Alex stared at her body and wondered what would happen now.

"I've big dreams, Sarah, and this time I want you to be a part of them."

"You've heard my answer too many times before."

"I'm listening this time. You have to trust me when I tell you I choose to be with you. And we are going places. I will never be in the position I've just recovered from. Not again so long as I live and that's a stone-cold promise. I shall go back to work for Waxey until I'm so filthy rich that money is never a problem again. I will never have to panhandle for food or shelter. And neither will you. That is my commitment to you today. Right now we are surrounded by the scum of the Bowery, but one day we'll live the high life in the best part of the Lower East Side."

Sarah sat up, smiled and kissed him on the forehead. She'd spent enough time in bed with men to know when they were lying to her and deep in her heart she knew that Alex was telling the truth.

"One day, you and I will be on top of the world."

"You'd better get some sleep, Slugger."

"That's not my name anymore. He died a long time ago in a foreign field."

"Sure thing, honey."

They rolled over and soon snored loud enough to wake the dead.

6

THE NEXT DAY, Alex hopped out of bed, kissed Sarah on the forehead and made his way out of the Oregon. He blinked in the early morning light and stormed off to the corner of Bayard and Bowery. A nod to the guard on the door and up the stairs to find Waxey and Ira.

He discovered them eating breakfast over a newspaper in their favorite room. His boss beckoned him to join them and he poured himself a coffee and offered the two men a refill, but both declined. Alex waited as long as he could but the fellas were too engrossed in their reading matter to bother to acknowledge him any further. A polite cough achieved nothing.

"I've got a question to ask you."

"Dear boy, I'm all ears."

Waxey winked at Ira over his lowered paper and pretended to lean toward Alex to hear him better.

"I have known you two ever since I came to this country some five years ago."

"And every day has been a pleasure."

Ira smirked at Waxey's interruption but said nothing.

"Thanks, Waxey, but we both know that isn't entirely the case... Anyway, I was a good earner for you for quite a while but I am very aware I haven't paid my way since you helped me back on my feet."

"We're not asking for payback, Alex. We live together, we fight together..."

"...and I nearly died alone."

A silence descended as the three mulled over the implications of Alex's words. He'd been part of a tight crew and had run his men with an iron hand and a fair tone to his voice. That said, each knew he had run away from the Bowery and Waxey's gang.

He might have told Waxey what he was planning to do, but he most definitely hadn't asked permission. There was something in Waxey's expression which echoed those thoughts. No one had implied it but everybody was thinking it.

"I walked out of this room like a *schnorrer*. I was running away from my problems and didn't know which way to turn."

"The army wouldn't have been my first port in a storm."

"The boy left the thighs of one of our best nafkas to fight strangers in a far-off land."

"I thought I was going to save the Jews who hadn't made it to America. The ones who were still facing the pogroms."

"And did you?"

"Nope."

"Did you see any Jews when you were over there?"

"Only one."

"Oh? What was he like?"

"Devastatingly handsome and real funny, told brilliant stories, but no luck with any of the local ladies until he learned some American and a few French phrases."

"Where d'you see him, this raconteur?"

"In the shaving mirror every morning."

They laughed, and the chuckles carried on coming out of Alex's mouth long after the joke wasn't funny anymore. The whole point of him going was to follow Monk Eastman's advice and free the Jews who couldn't escape. Eventually the laughing subsided.

"Waxey, you were right. Monk was a washed-up has-been by the time I spoke with him. What the hell was I thinking?"

"Don't be overly hard on yourself; you were young and naïve. Thought you could rule the world and had all the answers."

"You're too kind, Ira. I was dumb and arrogant—a dangerous combination."

"Before you left, you took care of business. Don't be too harsh on yourself —leave that to others."

"Thank you. How are what remains of my crew?"

"Surviving, but safe and well."

Alex recalled the last time he'd seen Abraham and Paulie as they chased him onto the platform and his locomotive stole out of the station to take him to basic training.

"Still want to kill me?"

He savored a long mouthful of coffee just in case it was his last. Waxey must have issued the order, and the guys were merely doing what they'd been instructed. Would the tsuris with Sammy ever go away?

"The boys bear you no ill will, you can be sure of that."

"And how about you, Waxey?"

"I told you, Alex, that if I ever found out that you murdered Sammy then I would have you killed, but you are alive, standing in front of me so there is no way that I ordered a hit on you."

"So why were they chasing me? They certainly intended to do me harm."

"Perhaps they had their own agenda to follow. Maybe they felt betrayed by your sudden unannounced departure…"

"…or they didn't believe your story about Sammy getting set upon by the Yake Brady gang and vanishing in a puff. We never found his body."

Alex eyed Ira's expression to discern why he was mentioning all this detail like it was yesterday. Like he wanted Alex to know he was the one who ordered the hit and hadn't forgotten. Alex swallowed and moistened his lips with his tongue.

"What's done is done, though. Right, Ira?"

"So they say, Alex."

Alex glanced between the two men, unsure how much they were playing him. Sarah had explained to him that Waxey had gone up in the world and now had his fingers in most pies in the Lower East Side. Along the way, he'd picked up some mighty powerful—and dangerous—friends.

"Are we good, Waxey?"

"As I see it, Alex, when Sammy met his maker, he left this world with nothing of any material value. When you arrived at my front step, you possessed nothing too. You balance each other out and there is no more to say on the matter."

"Ira?"

"What Waxey says is fine by me. Sammy's dead and you're alive. And a war hero too."

"I wouldn't go that far."

"Sarah says the *goyim* gave you a medal."

Alex stared at the ground and tapped a boot. He recalled scrabbling up a mound with sniper fire all around. For that they handed out medals.

"You've embarrassed the boy, Ira. Let's talk of happier matters. Alex, when will you be well enough to run your own crew?"

THEY SAT AROUND a solitary table, a beer in front of every man. Alex surveyed the scene and tried to judge how things were going. Abraham seemed the most happy to see him and Paulie appeared to sulk almost before Alex entered the joint. Then there were two new guys.

Ezra Kohut had lived in the tenements of the Bowery all his life. He blended into the bar, looking like any other customer who ever ordered a beer. His family had come over at the end of the last century and Ezra had been born within a spit of their table.

Massimiliano Sciarra, Massimo for short, was Italian and had joined up with Waxey at the suggestion of Charlie Lucky around the time of the trouble with the Yake Brady gang. Having proved himself as an excellent fighter, Waxey asked Charlie if the fella could stay on the team and Charlie agreed.

Alex sipped his brew and allowed the other fellas to take control of the conversation. Besides, he wasn't feeling supremely confident inside himself. The guys talked about the neighborhood and their most recent sexual conquests. There was no mention of anything that happened more than two weeks ago and they referred to Alex only twice in the first thirty minutes. He reckoned this was his punishment from Abraham and Paulie, while Massimo and Ezra had no idea of the game being played.

The four men gave Alex the strong impression that they ruled their territory with an iron fist—Abraham and Paulie had learned well from him. Waxey had explained how their previous gang leader had met with an unfortunate accident—a knife plunged deep into the small of his back. Unlucky for him but great news for Alex because he could work with some fellas from before the war even if they weren't too happy to see him.

"Sure is good to see you guys again."

Grunts for replies and sipping of beer.

"When I left in a hurry, we didn't get a chance to say goodbye properly."

"That's because you ran away."

"I needed to leave, Abraham. And you chased after me. Remember?"

"Do you think either of us would forget that morning?"

"No, Paulie, but there's been a lot of time between then and now."

All five stared into their glasses but Alex was the first to look up and glance around.

"I knew that if I told you guys what I was planning on doing…"

"Fight for the goyim?"

"Fight to free the Jews who hadn't made it over here."

"Now you sound like Moses."

"I took advice from Monk Eastman."

"You knew him?"

"We only met twice but he made a big impression on me."

Eastman was a legend. An ox of a man who ruled the Lower East Side at the turn of the century but couldn't reinvent himself for the modern world. Alex understood that now.

"I made a mistake. More than one, to be honest. I shouldn't have just walked away. I was wrong and I apologize to you."

"Takes a big man to admit when he's wrong."

Paulie stood up and shook Alex's hand. Abraham shrugged and repeated the gesture. The other two downed their beers because Alex wasn't really speaking to them, anyway.

"Let me get another round. You guys look thirsty."

"I'll buy you a beer with a whiskey chaser."

"Thanks, Abraham."

For the first time since he'd sat at the table, Alex felt accepted—if only by one of the squad. Paulie's eyes remained transfixed on him but he didn't utter a single word for another five minutes. Then he sprang up, teetered gently because of the alcoholic effect of the brew and slurred an announcement.

"To the past and our future! To Sammy and Alex."

Two years ago and the shrewish Italian wouldn't have had the confidence or the audacity to speak up that way. All the while, his eyes pierced through Alex like a sniper's bullet.

He stared back at Paulie and raised his glass before taking a swig of beer that caused him to wipe away a white foam mustache with his sleeve.

"Brave and true words, my friend."

The rest of the group went silent as soon as Paulie fell back onto his chair. Alex continued maintaining a calm voice which possessed only a whisper of malice.

"Sammy is dead, for sure, and I was one of the last people to see him alive. I have witnessed many deaths in my short time on this earth. Young lives lost in battle abroad and at home. The Yake Brady war might only have lasted a week or two but it was brutal and blood was shed on both sides— theirs more than ours. Sammy is gone and Waxey has made his peace with this. If any of you cannot do the same, then you should speak here and now."

Alex took a sip from his beer and eyeballed each of the fellas, leaving Paulie until last. No one raised any objections and their eyes attempted to drown in their glasses.

"That settles the matter then. I loved Sammy and I am very sorry he's gone but tears won't bring back the dead. There were rumors I killed him but anyone who knew me then would attest to how I dealt with guys: a blade across the throat or a fist into your face. From what I understand, they never found Sammy's body, and that really isn't my style."

Paulie ground his molars but said zip. Whatever he thought happened back then, he could do nothing about it today. Alex was here and Sammy was not. *Shoyn.*

"To the future, Alex. I'm glad you are here and let's look forward to a prosperous tomorrow."

A clink of glasses all round and the men settled in for an evening's drinking. When the fellas wanted to move upstairs and sample the fleshy delights on offer at the bar, Alex bid them well and returned to the warmth and comfort of Sarah's bed.

DECEMBER 1919

7

LAST NIGHT'S BAR became today's office as Alex had yet to earn himself a slot in Waxey's headquarters, let alone winning back his old job as a union convener. To achieve that, he'd need to deliver something special, and the opportunity came knocking that morning.

The Mercury Hotel's drinking area led straight from the street. Any hapless individual who thought they wanted to stay the night would check in with the barman. Most of the residents were regulars who flouted the no-fraternization rule hourly. *Nafkas* popped downstairs with the sole purpose of picking up their next john.

Alex and his crew sat near to the rear of the establishment and he made sure he had his back to the wall. After he'd downed his first coffee of the day, a boy shuffled in and headed for Abraham. The kid whispered in his ear, Abraham nodded, smiled and gave the boy a nickel for his trouble.

"Something's up at the docks, according to my *boychik*."

"Worth standing up for?"

"There's gelt to be made if we play it right."

"Then stop sitting on your *tuches* and let's get over there."

THE FIVE MEN strode east from Columbia and Broome until they reached Pier 47 and then pushed north to Pier 50 and Rivington Street. A large warehouse faced the East River with gates the height of four people—at first glance. When they looked again, they noticed there was a normal door embedded in the right-hand portcullis. The words above the wrought-iron fence were rusted but told them everything they needed to know: Clinemann Clothing.

Rat-a-tat and they walked straight in. There was a dingy entranceway with an office on the left side, seats on the right and a wall up ahead. They could feel the sound of factory machinery in their rib cages. A constant judder like an impending earthquake. Alex entered the room without knocking and instructed his men to wait.

"Where is Mr. Clinemann?"

"Do you have an appointment?"

The secretary behind the desk was unimpressed by Alex's brusque manner but he continued, anyway.

"My name is Alex Cohen and Clinemann needs to speak with me."

"*Mister* Clinemann decides who he sees and not the other way around."

He stood still and played with the change in his pocket, making sure the woman heard the jangling over the hum of the factory. Then he waited some more.

"I asked where he is and I recommend you answer my question. You wouldn't want anything unfortunate to befall you."

Alex's gaze wandered over to one wall which comprised glass windows all along and a curtain to hide the workers busy at their toil. Then he returned his gaze to Ravid Gardner. Her cheeks reddened to a pink as her eyes followed the trajectory indicated by Alex's look. Was he going to throw her through the window? Very unlikely. Did she know that? Not at all.

There were two doors in the wall behind Ravid, one either side of her desk. She leaned her head to one side and glanced in one direction long enough for Alex to understand. He nodded, breezed past her and entered the inner chamber to see an average man in a black suit with a narrow mustache sitting behind a large oak desk.

"I'm so sorry, Mr. Clinemann, he barged his way through."

Alex let Ravid's lie hang in the air because it stopped Clinemann concentrating on more important matters until Alex cleared his throat to get Clinemann's attention.

ALEX CLOSED THE door on Ravid's protestations and waited to discover how this pinhead would react. Clinemann leaned back in his chair, fingertips pressed together and stared at Alex. He separated his fingers long enough to beckon Alex to sit down but remained silent.

"Thank you for taking the time out of your busy schedule to see me."

"You have forced yourself into my office without permission, but my guess is that you didn't visit my premises alone."

"Correct."

"And this is why I am not making a fuss. I imagine we have business to attend and you are not a fellow to take 'no' for an answer."

"Right, again. As you are showing remarkably clear insight, tell me why I am here, invading your day and disgruntling your employees?"

"I have my suspicions, but in matters of business, I do not play games. Explain why you are here and we can proceed further in our discussions."

Now it was Alex's turn to lean back in his chair to leave Clinemann hanging for a response. To stretch out time Alex lit a cigarette and cupped the lit end in his palm, a habit he'd gained in the trenches.

"You owe us money and we are here to collect."

"Forgive me, Mister…"

"Cohen."

"…but I don't hand my money over to any old hoodlum who comes bustling along. Panhandlers can take a walk."

A drag on his cigarette and, as Alex exhaled, a plume of smoke erupted from his month, mixing with his words.

"Mr. Gordon would not be impressed if he learned you were welching on a deal."

The color drained from Clinemann's cheeks. For all his bravura, he'd no idea what Alex was doing until he heard the name of the boss of the Lower East Side.

"I meant no disrespect."

"Apology accepted. I have been overseas until recently and you probably didn't recognize me."

"Sorry, but your name is not familiar to me."

"I used to be known as Fabian Mustard."

Although Alex hadn't thought it possible, Clinemann's complexion went a paler shade of white. Alex remained silent as he stubbed out his cigarette.

"So now we've introduced ourselves, let's get down to business. Perhaps your secretary can bring us a coffee to lubricate the conversation?"

"Of course."

"My men would appreciate something too."

Clinemann rang a bell and Ravid scurried in to do her master's bidding.

"I KNEW SOMEONE would visit me eventually."

"And you chose not to preempt this inevitable situation by seeking out Mr. Gordon?"

"To be honest, Mr. Cohen, I didn't see the point. From what I've gathered, if you don't pay up, the visit occurs no matter who you speak to beforehand."

The guy had a point, but nothing would shift Alex from his perch on top of the high moral ground. He'd lived through this routine too many times before.

"You don't seem to understand the difficult position you've put yourself in."

Clinemann shrugged, as though he knew what was coming next and had resigned himself to the whole shebang. Alex might not have hustled anybody for protection money for a year or two, but he didn't think he'd seen anyone behave this way before.

"How much gelt do you have on the premises?"

"Chump change. If I had what I owed, then I wouldn't put myself in this situation. Don't misunderstand me. This is a problem I don't want to have, but here we are."

"Where's the money? I understood your business is doing swell."

"Don't believe everything people say. Listen to the machines."

Alex strained his ears and discerned only the clatter of metal on metal.

"What am I supposed to notice?"

"The sound of non-union labor operating slowly. At the rate these guys take, I'll be lucky to get any garments packed and out by the end of the week."

"Scabs. What's the trouble with the unions?"

"Pay and conditions; the usual. Seems we aren't treating them fairly."

"Are you?"

Clinemann shrugged with the same level of detachment as his talk of money earlier. Could he really be playing things this cool and bluffing Alex?

"So you have two problems. My money and your workers. Resolve the second and the former appears."

"That's the long and the short of it."

BACK AT THE Mercury, Alex sipped a drink and considered his options while the other fellas went about their morning collections. Capital and labor were always at odds with each other, but he had never been on either side. To him, there was no right or wrong in this battle. The average working Joe was a *schnook* in his eyes and the bosses were no better.

Naturally, his ambivalence was masked to both sides by his apparent desire to help them. This strategy had worked over and over again in the past, but he was less certain it would succeed this time. To begin with, the modern world included a Russia where a people's revolution had taken place and unions knew they had strength behind them.

Abraham arrived first and grabbed a beer from Uriel Menahem at the bar. He slumped onto his seat and chugged back half his brew in one swallow.

"Thirsty?"

Abraham smiled and nodded.

"How do you think we should convince the union to play ball with Clinemann?"

"Find the local convener and grab them by the balls until they see sense. People overthink these problems, but we live in simple times and deal with simple folk. Arrange an appointment, will you?"

8

THE LOCAL CHAPTER of the Machinists and Sewers Union had its own offices in a building close to the Clinemann warehouse, two blocks north, because the docks always offered the cheapest accommodation due to the stench of the East River.

Guys played cards, sipped drinks and talked to each other. An untrained eye could be forgiven for believing that Alex had stumbled into an ordinary bar. But he was here to see one particular person and no other. Up to the barman and a simple question.

"Marvyn Beck?"

A solitary finger pointed at an individual in the far corner seated by himself. Ten seconds later and Alex sat opposite him, although Marvyn refused to acknowledge his presence. Alex waited as long as he could to give the guy a chance to behave like a man but Marvyn chose not to.

"I believe you've been expecting me. My people got in contact yesterday."

"Yes, but that doesn't mean I must be happy about it, given your... provenance."

"I come in peace and I'm hoping we'll be able to talk matters through to everyone's advantage—including your members."

"What has Clinemann sent you over to say that he couldn't tell me directly?"

"Marvyn, I represent a separate set of interests to your boss. Your concerns and mine are perfectly aligned. The only difference is that you care about the welfare of your members and I don't. They can live or die and I will sleep equally soundly tonight."

The guy looked straight at Alex all this while and had shrugged off his sullen disposition.

"What does Gordon want? And how much is it going to cost us?"

"No need to drag Waxey into this. You and I are talking; that is who you are dealing with. You know who I represent and have done your research on me. Congratulations. If my reputation precedes me, we can conduct

334

ourselves in a constructive manner and get everything resolved before lunch. I assume the food here is decent?"

"Good enough for a working man."

"That's more than a recommendation for me."

Alex ordered a coffee and returned to the table.

"What do you want from Clinemann?"

"More pay. Better conditions."

"And in exchange for the moon, you'll go back to work?"

"Of course. Everybody wants to earn a crust. We strike because we have no other option. We demanded paid sick leave for six months, but he didn't budge, even though people's lives were put in danger every day. Women are losing limbs, and their children starve to death because he won't spend the money to service and repair the machinery. The *gonif*."

"ARE YOU TELLING me this whole mess could be sorted out by getting a maintenance crew out to the factory?"

"If only it was that simple, Alex. The problem isn't just about the repairs. Clinemann has no respect for any of us. We're cogs in his machine, not people with families, hopes and dreams."

"What does that mean? You're there to work, not to have him finance your life."

"He acts like he doesn't trust us. If anything goes wrong, he blames the workers first before finding out the real cause, which is usually his managers. Pay peanuts and you get monkeys."

"I gotta tell you, I knew this was coming. When all's said and done, every union rep I've met bleats on about conditions, but what they always really want to talk about is money. No disrespect intended, Marvyn."

"None taken. And I want to improve the welfare of my members. That's why the union exists."

Alex had heard it all before, but beneath every union official was a grifter seeking fresh ways to make a turn. Some were brazen and asked for a slice of the action whereas others played around, not wanting to be seen to be conniving, money-grabbing charlatans. Marvyn fell into the latter camp.

"How can I help? A crew could fix the machinery in the morning; say the word and I will organize it. If there's anything else I can do, let me know. I want the strike to be over and your workers to be back, happy and churning out product."

"Schmatta to be precise."

"Whatever. What do you need to return to work? Tell me and I shall make it happen."

Marvyn sat back in his chair, thought for a minute, chugged some of his drink and leaned forward with both elbows on the table. Alex mirrored the move to add to the conspiratorial atmosphere.

"Fifty cents an hour for my people and fifty dollars a month for me and each of the reps at the factory. And the repair crew."

"Anything else?"

"No, that's all. Can you deliver that for me, Alex?"

"That is well within my grasp. Let's finish our conversation as we walk you home."

Marvyn nodded, and they sauntered out after Alex paid the bar bill.

THEY STOPPED WHEN they arrived at Marvyn's tenement and almost without thinking, he invited Alex inside. By the time they reached the fifth floor Alex was out of breath. He might be on the mend but he had not yet fully recovered. He rested, leaning on a wall, as Marvyn brought him a glass of water.

"Do you think I could sit down for a short while?"

Marvyn led him inside and he slumped onto a dining room chair. While he regained his composure, Alex used the time to look around. The place was the usual mix of cheap furniture and screaming children, who were old enough to sew but still too young to keep quiet in the evening when adults were talking.

Near the kitchen door stood his wife, one baby clasped to her hip, peering round the doorway at the stranger in her home. He smiled and walked over to make a fuss of the little 'un in her arms.

"You haven't introduced us, Marvyn. I'm Alex—and you are…?"

"…Rachel, and this is Samuel."

Without a word, Alex reached his arms out and Rachel placed Samuel in his care. Alex bounced the boy up and down until he gurgled playfully. Within two minutes he'd put the babe down. Samuel was too young to scuttle off by himself and remained on the floorboards where Alex had rested him.

He shoved his hands in his pants pockets and looked embarrassed to be surrounded by such an adorable family. An instant later, he pulled out a shiv, grabbed Rachel by the wrist and planted an arm around her torso. The blade stood ready, an inch away from her throat.

"Now I have your attention, Marvyn, it's time for you to hear my terms."

"YOU MISUNDERSTOOD HOW this all works. As you can see, I hold your family's life in my hands and you thought you should shake me down for fifty bucks a month."

Marvyn's eyes darted from Alex to Rachel and back again. He gulped hard but remained silent.

"So this is what we will do. You send everyone to return to work tomorrow. As a sign of appreciation I will not kill your wife or your children."

Marvyn swallowed again and licked his lips while Rachel carried on whimpering. Alex stared straight at Marvyn.

"If you do this for me, I shall ensure that Clinemann gets the machines repaired and I will look to getting your members a better rate of pay. I am sure he will see reason. But that is all that will happen. Your workers' lives will be improved because you have told me that is important to you."

To emphasize his point, Alex pushed his blade close to Rachel's throat, all the while staring at Marvyn.

"The only outstanding matter is that your family is clearly not safe; look at what you have allowed to happen here."

A tear rolled out of Marvyn's eye and he rubbed it away.

"You must get some insurance to protect yourself."

"Protection?"

"Yes, you will need to pay me to ensure your family stays safe. How you secure the fee is up to you. Pay it from your own pocket or raise your members' dues. I don't care. If you don't settle with me, harm will inevitably befall your kin. Give me my money and they live to a ripe old age. The choice is yours."

Marvyn nodded consent and Alex relaxed his grip on Rachel who felt as though she was about to crumple onto the floor. The knife remained by her throat because Alex couldn't be certain Marvyn wouldn't try something stupid. The pathetic lump of humanity before him showed no signs of being dangerous, but Alex knew how quickly calm situations can turn into bloody mayhem—in France or in the Lower East Side.

Alex lowered his knife hand and kept his other on Rachel in case of need.

"Stay where you are and I shall let go of her. Do you understand?"

A nod from Marvyn and yet another whimper from his wife. All the time, the kids were playing or simply gurgling on the floor as though everything was completely normal. They ignored the adult world this evening as they did any other night.

Twenty seconds later and Rachel grabbed their youngest in her arms and hustled the children into the bedroom where they remained, door shut.

"I shall leave you to decide what is an appropriate amount to pay each month to keep your family from harm. Naturally, if the sum ever falls short of what is needed…"

"…then you'll hurt them."

"You understand completely. Make the first instalment tomorrow morning. You'll find me at the Mercury. You can provide the second payment six weeks later and monthly thereafter without fail."

Alex called goodbye to Rachel, but all he achieved was to make her cry again. He shrugged and left the Beck apartment.

THE NEXT MORNING, Alex waited to receive his payment before heading off to the corner of Bayard and Bowery. He enjoyed the walk, not just because he was bringing his first contribution to Waxey since coming back from the war, though that helped.

He stopped at one of the many stalls on Bayard and bought bread and a chunk of cheese nearby. The pleasure of making the purchase and consuming the simple fare made his cheeks glow red.

Inside Waxey's headquarters, Alex recognized Anthony on the door. His olive complexion and pointy nose hinted at his Italian ancestry. Charlie Lucky sure was tight with Waxey and Ira. He might only have been absent a year, but the landscape of the Lower East Side had completely changed. None of the old Irish and German gangs had survived the onslaught of the Italian arrival and where they worked with the Jews, money appeared to fly out of the storm drains.

Onto the first floor and a rat-a-tat until a voice signaled for him to enter. Alex nodded at both Waxey and Ira sat in their usual seats with a coffee each in front of them. A boy stood in the corner, hands behind his back, just like Alex had done when he'd first arrived in Waxey's orbit.

As Alex sat down he stretched out a hand and placed a roll of green into Ira's palm. He counted the notes, smiled and whispered the amount to Waxey.

"Welcome back, Alex. Feel good to be earning again?"

"Yep. Back in the land of the living. Or rather, I'm getting there. I still get flashbacks and that darkness hangs over me until I eventually shake it off…"

"Don't be so melodramatic. You survived the war and you'll survive the peace. All you have to do is recall one simple truth…"

"…We live together, we fight together, but we die alone. Waxey, you don't need to remind me and I am grateful for all you've done for me."

"Have a rest. I understand you are not fit yet. That is not a criticism, merely recognition that you deserve some recuperation time. By the new year, we will enter a different world. The Protestants convinced the president to ban the sale and consumption of alcohol. Charlie has some great ideas and so do I. Together we will take over the world—and you can help us if you're well enough."

Alex wished to find out more but knew better than to ask. When the time was right, he'd be fully briefed. The only problem was Alex's place wasn't to be on the receiving end of Waxey's plans. He wanted a seat at the table where the planning happened. Perhaps Waxey's new world might offer Alex opportunities to step up inside the gang.

9

ALEX DID EXACTLY what he was told and popped back to the Mercury, remaining at his table until the evening customers began to pile in. Then he winked at Uriel and slunk home still tired from the previous day's exertion. Threatening an unarmed woman had been more energy-sapping than he might have imagined.

Just as he entered the Oregon bar, he stopped and balanced himself with a nearby table. White light across his vision. A deafening zing split his head open and then his sight returned to reveal a stranger's face melted into his skull beneath an army helmet.

He closed his eyes, swallowed and raised his eyelids to see a roomful of drinkers and two nafkas leaning at the counter in search of a fresh john. A zigzag to the bar and Alex downed a shot of vodka in a single glug. He left a quarter on the counter and wended his way to the stairs and off to his room.

Sarah sat at her dressing table with a hairbrush in her hand. He walked over, kissed her on the forehead and then fell back onto the bed. She turned her head at the sound of his body hitting the covers.

"You all right?"

"Good enough. The war's still haunting me."

She put the brush down and sat next to him, a palm on his chest as a sign of comfort, but Alex felt no better. The images were one thing, but what really drove him to the edge were the relived emotions. The fear and panic in the pit of his stomach. No matter how long the fighting lasted—a minute or a day—that dread took root for the duration.

SARAH LEFT ALEX inside himself and then returned to brushing her hair. Thirty minutes later, he woke up and stared at his woman silhouetted by a streetlight. The dark cloud in his mind had evaporated and instead he soaked in the beauty before him.

"You left me."

"I'm back now."

"For how long, though?"

"I don't know what you mean. There's nowhere I'd rather be than with you."

"But you walked out on me before, so how can I know you're not off again whenever you fancy?"

"I'm not the man I used to be. The war put paid to that."

"You're different, I'll grant you that, but you've been in the neighborhood a few months and now you're back under Waxey's influence, doing his bidding. At some point, you'll need to escape again. That's fine for you but I don't want to invest my time creating a life with you if you could vanish at any moment. I tried being patient with you while you got Rebecca out of your head and all that gave me was an empty bed and countless nights crying into my pillow."

Alex thought for a minute. She was right; he'd treated her so poorly. When push came to shove, he'd kept her at a distance. Her last memory of him must have been a kiss on the lips that morning and the sight of him bumping into Rebecca.

"I'm sorry. I was a selfish man, but I promise you I will stay true. You are my rock—the only person in the world who has offered me any genuine affection. You've been loyal when I haven't deserved it and tended to my physical needs when I was almost dead. I can never repay the debt of gratitude I owe you."

"Alex, I want to believe you but what have you offered me in the past? Empty words, ten dollars left on a bedside table and dust at your heels when you walked away."

"Whatever I said to you, I meant at the time and I never lied. If you remember, I said I couldn't commit to you because my head was filled with Rebecca and you told me you would wait and spend the rest of your life with me if I tired of yearning after that woman."

"Shall I strip off and get into bed because you make me sound like a whore? Lying around until her john gives her some attention and cash."

"Don't say that. I never treated you like some nafka. Respect—that's what you have always got from me. I am not those other men. You are my companion, my friend, my lover. You are my everything and I do not want us to be apart."

"Cheap words, Alex, because you left me to fight in a foreign land. And for what? *Gornisht*. Nothing."

Alex had not been expecting this onslaught and couldn't figure out what had caused it. He had come home for a rest, not an argument, and he was doing his best not to let his temper get the better of him.

"I thought I was saving the Jews who hadn't made it to America."

Sarah snorted and stared out the window.

"You put your life at risk for the goyim. Strangers."

"Monk Eastman…"

"…is a decrepit man, punch drunk, who'd hit the skids before you met him. Why did you listen to that *fercockte meshuggener*?"

He shrugged, sat up and swiveled his legs off the bed. She was right. Eastman had made sense at the time but only because Alex had wanted an excuse to flee his problems with Sammy in the Bowery.

"Well? Is this your idea of how to treat your companion? Silence."

"I'm not saying anything because you are right. I made a terrible mistake and have paid the price by nearly dying several times, and I almost lost you. I am sorry, Sarah. All I can offer you are my words and the hope that some day you will forgive me."

"Come here, you lummox."

She opened her arms and Alex stood in front of her and they hugged. Not the casual hug of occasional friends, but the deep comforting caress of two people who care deeply for each other even if they don't have the words to express it.

ALEX AND SARAH ate at the bar having given themselves some time to calm down.

"We should do something special instead of just spending another night here, Sarah. Where would you like to go?"

She smiled and giggled. One finger twirled her hair around itself while she considered her options. She untangled her digit and stroked it along Alex's arm.

"Can we see a show?"

"Anything in particular, hon'?"

"No, something with a few songs and laughs."

Alex's knowledge of the theatrical world was extremely limited. He'd only been inside a playhouse once, when he first came to New York and had been couriering opium packages around town for Waxey, and he had delivered a brown parcel to Ida Grynberg at The Grand on Second and Tenth Street.

A quick check of his watch, and they grabbed a taxi to the theater. At the box office, they had ten minutes before the show started—a vaudeville revue featuring the world-famous diva that Ida had become. They settled into their seats in the stalls and a minute later the curtain rose. The opening act was a big musical number to wake up the crowd, followed by a comedy double. And so on.

Alex and Sarah sat one hand in the other's lap for the entire first half, only separating to clap the performers.

"We should do this more often, Alex."

"I didn't know such things existed. We never had this in the old country."

"You can take the boy out of the Ukraine…"

◆ ◆ ◆

THE AUDIENCE ROSE and applauded when their beloved Ida opened the second half. She stood alone on stage at the start of her song and as the emotion and drama built up, she was joined by the chorus. Perhaps because his memory of Ida was of her shooting up in the dressing room, Alex was less impressed than anyone else in the auditorium and his eyes wandered around the stage.

For one instant, he thought he recognized a face and then it vanished into the back of the stage to emerge again two minutes later. Slightly older with longer hair, Alex reckoned he was staring at Rebecca Grunberg, the love of his teenage life.

His stomach tightened and a bead of sweat appeared on his upper lip. He wiped it away with his spare hand and hoped Sarah did not notice the change in his demeanor. All the good words he'd spoken that afternoon expressing his feelings for the woman by his side and one glance at someone who might be Rebecca had consigned it all to the trash. Or so it felt at that moment.

Alex blinked and tried to see his Rebecca for a third time but the song wound down and everyone exited the stage. He did his best to concentrate on the remaining acts but his mind returned to the memories of Rebecca practicing her ballet moves in her parents' apartment and of him at the door watching and marveling at her purity and beauty.

MARCH 1920

10

ON JANUARY 17, 1920 the world turned upside down with the arrival of the Eighteenth Amendment to the US constitution, usually known as the Volstead Act or Prohibition. Those who owned bars were the first to be impacted as there was not much money to be made selling coffee, although the brothels continued to make a roaring trade.

Illegal gambling was also unaffected by Prohibition because most people still believed they could beat the odds. Many johns had bought a couple of cases of beer or whiskey before the ban on the sale of alcohol had come into force but by the end of February many ordinary Joes were thirsty and, like everyone else on the wrong side of the law, Waxey saw an opportunity.

"Alex, this is the scoop. As you know, we've been shipping in rum from the Bahamas and while it sells, margins are tight and we see little long-term future in it. North is where the money lies."

"Upstate New York?"

"Canada, dear boy. We will drive whiskey over the Detroit river and bring it straight to our warehouses in the Lower East Side. The water is at its narrowest between Windsor, Ontario and Detroit, so that is where we shall cross the border. And because there's a river border, it's difficult for Uncle Sam to patrol."

Alex sipped his coffee and wondered why Waxey and Ira were giving him a lesson in economics. The three said nothing and Alex shuffled in his seat. A lifetime later, he decided he should break the silence before it overpowered them.

"Sorry, but why are you telling me about this?"

"Because you are fit and well now and we have a job for you and your crew."

Waxey smiled at Alex and glanced at Ira.

"We need someone tough we can trust to bring the shipment home, Alex. That's you."

His jaw dropped. Ever since Prohibition had been announced, talk across town had focused on how to make money out of this *goyishe* nonsense. Here was the answer.

"Get your men and head off to Windsor. You do this right and we'll look after you well. The days of running a street gang will be far behind you."

"Brilliant. Thank you… what's the catch?"

Waxey was the first to laugh, quickly followed by Ira, his old business partner.

"I like your attitude, dear boy. Straight answer to your straight question— you can end up dead. The Canadian and US customs will shoot you on sight if they find you smuggling liquor across the border. Then there are other interests—inside and beyond the Lower East Side who want control of this supply line and who'll do their damndest to stop you."

"Anybody else looking to see me dead?"

"Not that we've noticed."

"Better get started then."

VANNI BORGNINO SAT behind his desk and busied himself with some papers as Alex approached him. The guy looked up, smiled and reached out a hand to greet him.

"Any problems coming up here?"

"None. The border was quiet, and we pretended to be tourists. Is everything set this end?"

Borgnino was a stocky man but Alex wasn't about to underestimate him. If Waxey trusted him with an entire shipment of whiskey, the fella must be on the up and up.

"Pretty much ready. We are waiting on another six guns and then we can go."

"When are they due?"

"Tonight. Unless your men need a longer rest, I'd prefer to leave as soon as possible."

"Why the rush?"

"Not so much a rush as I'd like to get some kind of edge. Everyone knows everybody else's business, so we assume that word has got out about our travel plans. I have loudly told anybody within earshot that we are leaving tomorrow."

"I have heard there could be trouble along the way."

"And then some. The cops have informers and know we are going to take a shipment over the border but they don't know where we will cross…"

"…because you haven't told anyone."

"But even a bunch of cloth-eared Mounties will be able to follow the trail of a dozen trucks traveling at high speed across their country."

"They'll want our heads on a plate."

"You betcha. And assuming we get to the river safe enough, the fun's only just begun. We do not control anywhere in Detroit."

"And we have little influence between there and downtown New York."

"So I hope you guys are ready because this will be one hell of a ride."

"We can take care of ourselves."

"Sure you can, but how many times have you protected twelve vehicles, their drivers and a cargo that's worth more than gold?"

"We come bearing sawn-off shotguns and a reputation in the Bowery. Some of us have experience of fighting on foreign shores and lived to tell our loved ones about it."

Vanni smiled and whipped out a bottle of whiskey and poured two shots. They clinked glasses and swigged their drinks down. Another slug for the road and everyone was ready to blaze a trail through hell.

ALEX SPREAD OUT his men along the convoy, with Paulie leading the trucks and the rest of the gang two or three vehicles apart with Alex himself in the rear. He considered putting himself in the first pickup but decided it was better to see everything that happened.

The only thing in their favor that night was the new moon. The pitch black which enveloped the convoy made seeing the road difficult although they banked on the Mounties having an equally tricky job of spotting them.

Vanni stayed with the trucks until they set off from the far end of Dougall Avenue, two miles away from the river and the American border. Under cover of the inky darkness, Alex and the crew kept their eyes sharp and trained on the road ahead and on the tree lines to the left and right.

Five minutes later, a motorbike zoomed out of nowhere and Alex nearly blew a hole in the rider's chest, but fortunately held back half a second because it was Paulie. With the trucks still forging ahead Paulie warned there was trouble ten blocks in front. Despite Vanni's best intentions, word had got out and a local gang was waiting to intercept them.

Alex hopped onto his truck's tailboard and jumped behind Paulie on the bike.

"Hit the gas, Paulie. We need to show these hobos not to mess with the Bowery boys."

The wind buffeted Alex's face as Paulie drove them ahead of the convoy and toward the locals. If Alex strained his ears, he could hear the engines of the convoy less than a minute away to their rear. While time was against them—there was no opportunity for a complex plan—the stupidity of their opposition fell in their favor. For no obvious reason, the gang had positioned itself under streetlights with two men behind each car and maybe three stationed on the corner of each building at the junction. There was no time to even count heads accurately.

"Let's do this."

Paulie and Alex jumped off the bike and split up, one on each sidewalk, then scurried along to get close enough to be sure their shots would cause maximum damage. When he got so near that he thought he could see the whites of their eyes, Alex squeezed the trigger on his shotgun and caused a large and bloody hole to rip through the chest of the nearest guy to him, but still two hundred feet away.

The gang responded with a hail of bullets but they had no real idea where the attack had originated—just somewhere up ahead. Paulie took out a pair on the corner and Alex knocked out three behind one car. The sound of the convoy had become a roar.

MORE SLUGS WHIZZED past and a pane of glass shattered behind Alex's right ear. He responded by ducking down for a second and pumping three slugs into his assailant's body. It crumpled to the floor and Alex tried to figure out how many were left.

Paulie took out a handful more as Alex totted up the living among the carnage. As the lead truck came to a stop next to him, Alex saw a solitary gunman with his hands above his head.

"Paulie, take a look-see and let me know when the area's clear. Everyone else, stay inside."

The barrel of his shotgun aimed squarely at the guy's heart, Alex strode toward the dude until he was only ten feet away.

"Where are the others?"

"Please, don't kill me."

"Answer my questions and you will walk away from this and have a tale to tell your grandchildren."

"There are no others. You've slaughtered all of us."

A shot rang out, echoing between the sides of the nearby buildings. Alex clasped his piece tighter.

"You lied. Are there any more?"

The guy's eyes were wide and fear oozed out of every pore. He'd been banking on that other fella to get reinforcements. Alex walked forward until the barrel pressed against the fella's chest.

"Talk to me, little man."

"There are none left here. Frankie was the last one."

"Where was he heading?"

"Back to our headquarters on the other side of town... I got a wife and kids..."

"How long before they get off their tucheses and pay us a visit?"

"Ten, fifteen minutes. You weren't expected until tomorrow so we didn't have much time to get ready. But the others will be over soon."

Alex smiled, pulled the trigger, and the guy's body flew backward with the force of the bullet scorching through his flesh. Ezra and Massimo arrived to clear the cars from the street and the convoy trundled through Windsor and headed for the river.

As Ambassador Bridge came into view with its twinkling lights, they turned left to avoid the customs post on the Canadian side. Half a mile later, they took a right onto Morton Drive and reached a large sandy area in the middle of nowhere.

Moored at the water's edge was a wide flat-bottomed boat, big enough for all the trucks. Alex's guys jumped out of their vehicles and maintained a line surrounding all this activity, facing outward, shotguns in hands. A silence fell all around as everybody's ears were keenly stretched for impending trouble. The rest of the Windsor gang could appear at any moment.

The locals knew what they were doing and after ten minutes, the boat was loaded and Alex's crew boarded. A vessel that size was never going to be speedy, but it felt as though every inch took an hour. Eventually, the Canadian shoreline faded and Motor City beckoned on the other side of the river.

11

GUNS IN HAND, Alex and his crew were the first to get off the barge to
protect the trucks as they disembarked and the drivers got themselves
prepared for the long haul to New York. Twenty minutes after the boat sailed
back to Canada, everyone was ready to hit the road.

Just before Alex called for the first truck to begin, he saw a light in the
distance. The speck of white got bigger until it became two dots and fifteen
seconds later, the two dots became four and four became eight until Alex
heard engines approaching.

"Get ready!" he warned, but they all knew this was make or break; the
Windsor gang was only the start. The vehicles neared and Alex saw a guy on
the tailboard of each car. Then two hundred feet away, they stopped. One
man opened a door of the lead saloon and walked toward Alex until he was
fifty feet away. All the while, his hands pointed to the floor, palms open. His
coat flapped in the breeze as he slowed to a halt.

"My name's Abe Bernstein. Is Alex Cohen with you?"

Alex stepped forward and raised a hand.

"What brings you to this piece of dirt?"

"Waxey Gordon. Does his name ring a bell?"

"I reckon. You with the Sugar House gang?"

"Yep. Waxey mentioned you might be popping by."

The men walked toward each other so they didn't have to shout and
could have a more private conversation.

"You're traveling through our territory so the least we can do is to see you
have safe passage."

"Much obliged."

"We have received a consideration from Waxey so don't be so grateful."

"It's still good to see a friendly face, especially if this is the first of many
runs."

"Let's not get ahead of ourselves."

"No, sure thing..."

Abe took Alex and the entire convoy to a secluded warehouse a few minutes away from their crossing place. This gave them an opportunity to freshen up and grab a bite to eat. With only two hours driving done, the worst of the journey was before them.

There were locked iron gates at the entrance and a pair of fellas carrying machine guns. That was security enough. Once within the confines of the building, everyone was given free rein although Alex stayed with Abe rather than gorging himself on food and women like most of the men.

"Waxey speaks highly of you, young man."

"Kind of him. Your reputation speaks for itself."

Alex was being polite. The Sugar House gang had made a name for themselves in Detroit as a hard-nosed bunch of fellas who ruled their territory with a ruthless determination and a large dose of chutzpah.

What none said but everyone knew was that they were lucky to be living in Detroit. Its location so close to the Canadian border made it the ideal spot to haul liquor into the US. And whoever controlled that town would dip their beaks into every bootlegging run. Abe understood it, New York knew it and Chicago wanted a piece of the action too. Everybody wanted to be friends with Abe and his brothers. Waxey had briefed Alex well. The two men jawed over a coffee and a bowl of chicken soup. Then he checked the time and decided they should get going.

"The new moon'll help us stay invisible tonight before we have to peel off the main road at dawn. The longer we last without attracting the attention of cops or local hoods, the better."

"My men will accompany you out of the city and then you're on your own."

"I appreciate all your support. We've got twenty hours driving ahead of us and we'll barely have time to stop for a piss along the route."

"Good luck—until we meet again."

ON THE ROAD, they stopped for a five-minute break every two hours which gave the drivers a chance to rest their eyes and his men seized the opportunity to stretch their legs. No one wanted to be cooped up inside those vehicles for that long.

Physical discomfort was the least of their worries. Even though Alex had planned a route away from anything like a main highway, word was out that a convoy was heading east and there was a greeting party in every town they tried to skirt past.

Waxey had given Alex simple instructions: pay off as many guys as he could but those who were not motivated by money or who didn't see reason should be shot on sight. Alex did his best to keep his bankroll in his pocket, preferring to fight than hand over any green.

As they avoided the cities, the only trouble that came their way was from smaller gangs and an occasional family that ran a town. Alex figured that if he was going to make this trip on a regular basis, then he didn't want to pay off some goyishe hoods every time their trucks rolled by.

Besides, Waxey had been vague about Alex's cut so keeping some of his boss's spending money was an easy way to make some gelt out of the jaunt. He'd deal with the consequences of disobeying Waxey if they got back in one piece. Handling the yokels was one thing. They had to force their way through New Jersey and then across downtown Manhattan before they could raise the flag of victory.

◆ ◆ ◆

ONCE THEY SAW the first road sign for Jersey City, everybody relaxed. Everyone apart from Alex who knew the worst was yet to come. The Elizabeth family controlled a huge swathe of New Jersey, headed by Stefano Badami, a mean fella who was as tough as the reputation that preceded him. To top it all, there was bad blood between Waxey and Badami as they'd been vying for supremacy ever since Waxey had fallen in with Charlie Lucky.

The outskirts of Jersey City beckoned in the mid-afternoon sun and Alex wondered if they should take a detour further north but realized this would only burn more gas and not solve the fundamental problem that they were thundering through Elizabeth territory without permission.

So he kept to his original plan and aimed for Weehawken which had a ferry terminal, although Alex wasn't intending to take the liquor on to Manhattan using official means of transportation. Paulie's bike pulled up next to Alex, and he warned there was trouble ahead.

"There's a welcoming committee of around thirty guns. Time to find an alternate route."

"Any suggestions?"

"Make a run for it north. You'll find a bunch of derelict buildings a quarter of a mile in that direction. We could barricade ourselves in and defend ourselves from there."

"And then they can pick us off one-by-one. No deal. I've got a better idea but I'll need one brave soul to pull this off."

"You looking straight at me?"

"You volunteering?"

"Apparently so."

Alex outlined his plan and Paulie hopped into the lead truck. Its engine roared as the driver over-revved and it sped off aiming directly at the Elizabeth gang. As soon as the vehicle's smoke had cleared, the rest of the convoy zoomed south.

Two minutes later, they heard a volley of gunfire and then silence. Alex spat three times for luck and made a mental note to look after Paulie's family when they arrived home—assuming they made it back in one piece.

The trucks trundled along the residential roads on the edge of the city. They were only a handful of minutes away from a confrontation with the gang. Each revolution of the truck's wheels took them closer to a bloody end.

More gunfire in the distance. Alex couldn't tell quite from which direction it came or how far away either. But if the gang was still shooting, then Paulie was alive and drawing the Elizabeth crew away from the convoy. They turned a corner and screeched to a halt. The road was blocked by three large trucks and at least ten fellas waving machine guns. There was nowhere to go except to meet your maker.

ALEX HALTED THE convoy and swallowed hard. The Elizabeth gang were eight hundred feet away but there was no way the trucks could turn around and flee before being caught by the faster Elizabeth cars. Stand and fight was the only option.

He heard Abraham and Ezra's footsteps with Massimo trailing behind them. By the time all three reached him, Alex had hatched a plot. With a pair of binoculars, he counted the enemy numbers, twice.

"Listen real carefully. They know we are here and they can afford to wait. Remember, they want the liquor, not us so they will keep their eyes fixed on the trucks. We'll send one truck slowly down the street and they will assume it has come to negotiate. They won't shoot up the booze else they'd have ripped us to hell by now.

"Meantime, you three make your way along the street. Take your time. It's more important you get close enough to do some damage with your shotguns than blast at them ineffectively. Our truck will stop four hundred feet from the Elizabeth gang and you will not fire until I give the signal."

"What is it?"

"Ezra, when one of theirs collapses on the ground with a bullet between his eyes then keep firing at them all. Chances are the only thing you guys do will be to cause confusion, but that's precisely what we need to improve our odds. I'll do the rest."

His men spread out and scattered along the sidewalks, ducking and diving behind streetlights, parked cars and anything else that gave them protection from being seen by the machine gun toting Italian crew.

Alex grabbed a rifle from his truck, ran behind the nearest building and scaled the fire escape to reach the roof. His pockets were stuffed with shells, and he made his way from rooftop to rooftop until he was close enough to pick a vantage point where he could aim his scope at the heads and hearts ahead.

Thirty seconds later, their truck stopped on its cue and Alex watched the Elizabeth gang turn to each other as they wondered what was going on. He inhaled deeply and gave them his answer when he squeezed the trigger and a fella in a fedora fell down, crumpling onto his knees.

A burst of gunfire scorched across the nine remaining men, slugs ricocheting off their cars, windows shattering and mayhem all around. They responded by strafing anywhere in front with bullets, but Alex could tell the guys had no idea where to aim.

Another shell flew from the barrel of his rifle and a second fella discovered a new red hole in his body. And so this continued with Alex-the-marksman taking the kill shots while his Bowery men gave him the perfect cover. With only one fatality on their part, the East Side crew had done well, but that still meant Abraham's lay face down in a gutter. Two minutes after their truck had rolled into position, the Elizabeth crew lay in a bloody pool of their own liquid.

"Ceasefire!"

The four-second silence was punctured by whoops from the drivers. A quick check on the bodies to make sure no one was left alive, and they continued on their way to the Weehawken waterfront where two boats were waiting to transport the whiskey across the Hudson.

On the other side, the trucks sped across town until Alex recognized the streets. They were back in the haven of the Lower East Side.

12

WHEN HE GOT back to the Oregon, he took a shower to wash the grime of the interstate roads off his skin. Then he sat with Sarah at the bar and enjoyed a coffee. This was no ordinary hot drink as it was laced with a double shot of whiskey. It was known as an Oregon Coffee to those who frequented the joint regularly.

"You look tired, Alex."

"Like you have no idea, my *shayner maidel.*"

"Was it bad out there?"

"Had its moments, but we all got back in one piece, unlike some of the fellas we met on our travels."

Sarah shrank slightly away. She tried not to think about Alex's business too hard. She was occasionally on the receiving end of violence in her line of work and she avoided it at all costs for obvious reasons. On the other hand, bloodshed was drawn to Alex like flies to a midden and he usually shrugged it off casually. His manner showed her how tough this trip had been.

Alex was touched by Sarah's recoil. She might act as though she had a heart of stone but she was far more fragile than she would ever reveal in public. He reminded himself that his efforts to become somebody in this town were so he could take Sarah with him. She was his rock and his crutch. He needed her to get through the day, especially during difficult times like the ones they were living in.

"I'm glad you're back, safe and sound."

"It's great to see you; I'll be secure in your arms again tonight, hon'."

"So pleased to hear it, but I've got to warn you that you won't be happy in a minute or two."

Now it was Alex's turn to sit back as he girded himself for whatever bad news was going to descend from Sarah's mouth.

"I saw your mother this morning."

He couldn't decide if the world started spinning round or if he misheard.

"Mama?"

Sarah bit her lip, eyes gazing downward, and she nodded.

"Mama came here? To this place?"

"Oh no. We bumped into each other a block from here when I was out buying some food."

Alex understood this was no accident despite what Sarah thought. Ruth Cohen would not have wandered into this part of town just to purchase a slab of cheese. They might only be a handful of blocks away from the Cohen apartment but they were worlds apart and his mama understood that.

Besides, Alex hadn't spoken to her since the night before he left for France. In fact, he hadn't seen his father, Moishe or his brothers and sister either—apart from that moment when he'd watched them from afar in a near-dead funk. Esther would have grown up to be a woman by now and the little ones' ages probably cracked double digits.

"How are they all?"

"Fine, so she said… but she worries over you. Have you thought about visiting her?"

"Yes and discounted the idea. I can't imagine they'd want to meet this lump of disappointment again."

"She's your mother and she still cares about you."

"Or is it how much my business drags down her reputation in the community?"

"You're lucky you have a mother to worry over you and who's brave enough to walk down these streets of shame until she found me."

"Why now, do you think?"

"You are asking the wrong person. Pop over to Ruth and you'll find out."

"I'm not sure…"

"Listen, Alex. You have two options. Buy a challah tomorrow and visit them for a *Shabbas* meal or I'll drag you over there myself right now and you can deal with your mama's embarrassment at having a nafka grace her home."

"You don't leave me any option."

"Better believe it, pal. Watching you be apart from your family hurts me inside because I don't even know if my parents are alive or dead. You are a lucky man and are totally unaware of it."

Alex's cheeks warmed, and he agreed to buy some bread on the way over the following evening. He thought he might get some strudel too.

"Shall we go upstairs?"

"Does talk of your mother make you want to sleep with me?"

Sarah chuckled at Alex's expression, a mix of shock and confusion. They finished their drinks and returned to their room. Alex rolled over in bed as soon as he got under the sheets and was sound asleep, snoring loudly after a long, hard couple of days on the road.

◆ ◆ ◆

ALEX STOOD ON the corner of Grande and Suffolk staring up at the tenements before him. They looked the same as every other bedraggled building on the street with its overcrowded apartments and the sounds of Jewish life zipping through the air on Friday night. But this tenement was special; on the fourth floor lived Moishe and Ruth Cohen, Alex's parents. He gripped the challah tightly and entered.

A slow walk up the stairs and memories of the smells and colors fogged his brain. Alex had forgotten quite how many steps there were and took a quick rest on the third floor right by the Grunberg apartment. He thought about the number of hours he'd stood in the open doorway admiring Rebecca's twists and turns. For a second, he glimpsed inside to spy on her parents, Max and Rosa, intoning blessings at the start of their meal.

Just before he thought he might make eye contact with them, he moved on to the fourth floor and the place he'd called home from the time his family arrived in the land of opportunity to the day when he left to join the army. Even as he said these words to himself, they were a lie. For months before he went off to fight, he'd been spending his nights with Sarah and only coming back to this place for a dutiful Friday night meal.

Alex knocked on the door and listened intently to the muffled voices and sound of shoes on wood as somebody approached. As the man opened the entrance, he spoke without looking up.

"Whatever you're selling, we are not buying."

As his eyes made contact with Alex, Moishe's jaw dropped and his arms slumped by his side.

"Who is it, then?"

His mother's voice floated to the entrance where the two men stood. Alex pushed the challah into Moishe's hand and rushed on through. With no idea what to say, he chose simple actions instead. His mother screamed at the sight of her prodigal son and Alex was home.

As he stepped into the front room, the younger kids stared at him while sister Esther stood up, sashayed over and gave him a hug.

"So good to see you again. We were told you were dead and paid for a grave and everything."

With those words ringing in his ears, Alex stepped toward his mother and planted a kiss on her cheek. This act of love extinguished her screams, and she began to sob at a much lower volume. He turned round to give Papa a handshake, but the man picked his jaw off the floor and followed Esther by giving him a lingering hug. A solitary tear rolled down the old man's cheek. Alex had never seen him cry before.

Then he felt hands pushing them apart and there was Mama wanting her turn to embrace him. The kids remained in their seats and chewed their bread, not knowing or caring about this stranger.

"Sit down—unless this is a flying visit."

"No, Mama. I'm hoping you'll let me stay for dinner."

"And why wouldn't I want my eldest child to break bread with the rest of his family?"

Alex shrugged and waited until Esther sorted out a chair for him as Mama shuffled the kids round to make enough space at the table. Only when he was sat down did he notice how quickly he slipped back into speaking Yiddish.

The family put their hands together, closed their eyes and Papa recited blessings over their food and drink. Alex recognized the sounds of the Hebrew words but understood virtually nothing that was said. His interest in religion had ended with the presents he received when he was Bar Mitzvah. And that was a lifetime ago in the Ukraine before they fled the pogroms.

A thousand questions descended on him and Alex had no idea who to answer first. So he opted for silence and eating instead. Then once everyone settled down, he spoke.

"Sarah told me you came looking for me, Mama."

"What's a mother to do when her own son goes off to fight, comes back and doesn't even bother to return home, check we are safe, enquire after our wellbeing."

Alex ground his molars and knew this was just her manner. Mama wasn't really angry with him. From what Sarah had told him, the woman was fraught with worry. This aggressive stance was her way of dealing with her mixed emotions—relieved to see him alive but annoyed he hadn't been round sooner.

"Things weren't easy for me when I first returned to America. Physically… and mentally…"

His mother dropped her silverware and covered her mouth with her hands.

"…but I'm fine now, more or less."

"Boys go to war but come back as men."

"Exactly, Papa. It took me a while to be at peace with what I'd lived through. And during that time I was too ashamed to let you see me, although I spied on you all one evening."

"We didn't see you."

"Even if you had, you wouldn't have recognized me. I was not in a good shape."

"Well, you look fit and well now, that's for sure. Pour Esther a small glass of wine, Ruth so she can join in the toast."

His wife did as Moishe bid and he raised the red wine in his hand, followed by the other adults.

"*Lekhayim*. To life."

A clink of glasses and everybody ate with Alex who was pleased to be accepted back in the family without further interrogation. Later when Esther and the other kids were clearing the table and washing the dishes in the kitchen, Alex and his parents had a more earnest conversation.

"Are you and that woman a serious item?"

"Yes, her name is Sarah and we care for each other. She nursed me through my darkest days and stayed beside me."

"You trusted that… woman more than your own mother?"

"She lives in a different world than you. I love you so very much and for that reason, there are some parts of my life I can't bring into this apartment."

"And you believe you can trust her?"

"I have trusted her with my life, Mama. Just because she was a prostitute doesn't mean she has no moral compass. Far from it."

"You spoke in the past tense. Has she vowed to stop being a whore?"

"Papa, she hasn't made a solemn promise to me, no. But she has been waiting for me for years and while we're together, I shall provide for her and she will have no need to obtain money from other sources."

His parents stewed on Alex's comments and he looked around the room. Every item of furniture—chairs, table, sideboard—were exactly the same as he remembered them. Nothing had changed one iota.

"What did you do with the money I gave you before I left?"

Ruth glanced to Moishe, who sighed.

"Your mother gave it all away."

Now it was Alex's turn to sigh. "That was to keep you safe."

"Didn't feel right, Alex. You know how we both feel about how you earned your living."

"I do—and that hasn't changed. Did any people pop over and check on you in my absence?"

"Yes and I sent them packing but every week they turned up with groceries, which was very kind."

"Did you accept the food?"

"I didn't want it to go to waste, but I never took the money."

Waxey had kept his word to Alex despite his mother's attempt to remain on high moral ground. This reminded him that somewhere in the city, probably on the Lower East Side, were bundles of cash hidden in a wall where he'd stuffed his hard-earned gains before he went off to war. He still couldn't remember where the hell he'd put it.

13

ALEX STAYED TALKING for another hour and then his mother began to yawn and Esther asked permission to retire for bed. He took that as his cue to go, but he promised to visit again as soon as he was able. He considered offering to host a meal at the Oregon but thought better of it. Back at the bordello, Alex joined Sarah at the bar and ordered an Oregon Coffee.

"How was your family?"

"Well, thanks. It was like nothing had changed all this time—apart from the fact that Esther, Aaron and Reuben were older. Especially Esther; she's become a woman since I've been gone."

"I'm glad you went. Family is important."

They clinked mugs and finished their drinks.

"You know something, Sarah?"

"What?"

"I learned a lot this evening, thanks to you."

"You're welcome."

She tilted her head to one side trying to figure out what he meant, but nothing appeared to come to mind.

"I know what's important in my life. Seeing my mother and father together content in their unhappiness. They help to keep the other on track. My mother with her perceived slights and prejudices. My father and his pompous belief in working hard and doing the right thing. One would be nothing without the other."

"Your mom seemed a bit lost when she was scurrying around the market yesterday—as though she was missing something."

"She was away from Papa and was not comfortable in these surroundings."

"Nicely put. She could barely bring herself to speak to me, a mere nafka."

"Let's not focus on that, please. Forget my mother for a minute, I've been trying to do that all my life."

They both laughed and Alex sandwiched Sarah's hand in his palms.

"I'm nothing without you and I don't want to lose you. In the dim and distant past, you told me you'd drop everything in your world to be with me. So tonight, I'm wondering if that's still true."

Sarah was silent. She smiled at him and soaked in the moment, but Alex realized he hadn't asked *her the* question and that was why she hadn't replied.

"Will you marry me, Sarah Fleischman?"

"Mister Cohen, I will."

JUNE 1921

14

FIFTEEN MONTHS LATER, Alex walked into the Richardson Hotel, holding its keys. Waxey had asked him to run the blind pig as a reward for shipping whiskey from Canada since the start of Prohibition. Now he'd passed on the day-to-day responsibility of the bootlegging to some Italian dude and was going to concentrate his efforts on this speakeasy.

There was more than one way to make money but Alex knew where the profit lay. And it was in those cups of laced coffee. Gambling and women were available for the unaccompanied man, but couples were welcome to just drink themselves under the table.

To keep customers entertained while they slurped, there was a stage with dancing girls singing their lungs out and a small house band to maintain the party atmosphere until the early hours. While Alex might not have been too familiar with many of the staff, one face shone through.

Alex recognized Nathan Milstein as the barman from his old haunt at the Forsyth, where Alex held court all the years he had used that cathouse bar for an office. Sammy and he had met there, and he'd cleaned himself in the backroom when there'd been too much blood to hide. He could trust Nathan with his life.

Alex wandered over to the counter and waited for Nathan to serve him.

"Waxey told me you'd be coming. What can I get you?"

"Straight coffee. I don't consume my own merchandise. Reckon that's bad business."

"You're right. Mighty glad to find you here. This dive needs a firm hand."

"Let's talk more after closing time. For now, I'll sit in a corner and watch how the place runs. Don't tell anyone about me."

Nathan nodded and took his drink to the back, away from the stage where Alex could monitor the bar and who went up and down the stairs for a spot of female companionship. He also checked out which customers were let into the adjoining room to play cards or take the roulette wheel for a spin.

AT THE END of the night, Alex had seen enough. He gathered everyone to sit at the customer tables and he stood on the stage so everyone could see him. First, he introduced himself and then he explained the new house rules.

"Just because the johns are tipsy, don't assume that I'm drunk too. When I work here, I am sober as a judge and there must be no skimming of any cash register. Please don't act aggrieved, I saw it happening throughout the evening and almost everywhere."

General murmuring as waiters, barmen, croupiers and nafkas all felt like they'd been personally accused. From what Alex had seen, Nathan was the only one of them who'd not dipped his beak in the trough.

"The next thing on my list is the games room. Many people are let in but appear to leave within a minute or two. We will not have timewasters in this joint. If we attract serious gamblers, then heavy drinkers will follow."

Alex kept his eyes trained on the doormen who he'd seen receive several tips just to be let in the room. He didn't mind people earning a living, but not at the expense of annoying hardened gambling men.

He surveyed the group of tired staff, who clearly would rather he had not walked into the Richardson at all.

"We will turn this into the most talked about speakeasy in the Lower East Side, if not Manhattan itself. Get with the program and you'll know riches beyond your wildest dreams."

"And if we don't?" asked a muffled voice somewhere near the back.

"Then you won't have to dream at all."

Once everyone else departed, Alex and Nathan walked round to check each room was ready for the next day's work. Just before they switched all the lights off, Alex offered Nathan a drink. They remained in a back room and Nathan took a bottle of whiskey out from a cupboard.

"What do you reckon, Nathan?"

"This place was being run into the ground. Chances are we'll lose people over the next week or two, but that's okay. You don't want thieves working for you."

"Do we get many highflyers visiting our gambling den?"

"I thought Waxey had told you all about this joint."

"Apparently not."

"About once a week, the Big Bankroll swings by and the house makes enough not to worry about who else plays cards for the rest of the time."

Alex's eyes opened wide. Waxey had neglected to mention that detail when he'd handed over the keys. He'd told him about the poor state of the whores and how he wanted Alex to sell more booze but he'd omitted to inform him that Arnold Rothstein gambled here.

THE RICHARDSON WAS located on Broadway and Twenty-sixth, just around the corner from Madison Square. Over the past year, with more than a little help from Charlie Lucky, Waxey had spread his wings north, out of the Bowery and toward midtown, leaving the Lower East Side behind him. He maintained control over every aspect of criminal activity south of Canal but there was a world of possibility away from the docks and piers.

While Charlie's reach was bigger than Waxey's, there were still areas which were not controlled by either of them and the Richardson was two blocks away from the edge of Charlie's territory. Next door was Salvatore Maranzano's turf and ever since Charlie started working with Rothstein, Maranzano had been chiseling at the edges of his empire.

Two weeks after he pocketed the keys to the joint, Alex unlocked the main door as he always did in the morning. With his newfound responsibility had come a discovery of mornings, something he and Sarah had habitually avoided, preferring instead to enjoy the early part of the day in bed and asleep. They enjoyed their married life.

When Alex arrived at the entrance, he knew something was wrong before he'd even got to the door. To begin with, it was ajar, and he'd locked up tight the night before. As he stepped across the threshold, he drew his revolver expecting trouble.

There was devastation wherever he looked. Tables were upside down or smashed into pieces. The bar was a pile of firewood and the stage had deep axe gouges all over it. Gun still in hand, he headed to the games room— whoever had worked over the joint had spent time here. More tables strewn and destroyed and the four roulette wheels lay buckled on their sides on the floor.

A quick run up the stairs showed the bedrooms were in a similar state. Back downstairs, Alex went to his office. The door had been kicked in and was hanging on one hinge but nothing had been touched inside. Not a single piece of paper had been moved. That was a clear message.

This was no robbery by amateurs but a calculated attack by people who knew what they were doing and wanted to maximize impact—paperwork was not the target of this raid.

With the phones ripped out of their sockets, Alex went to find one that worked in a neighborhood store and told Waxey to send some men uptown. Then he waited until the fellas showed up and he organized them to keep watch at every entrance to the building.

Nathan arrived thirty minutes later and Alex told him the story of his morning.

"Get the word out on the street that we are closing for a refurbishment. We'll open again in a week come what may. In the meantime, I need to find Paulie and the rest of the crew. We've got an errand to run."

15

ALEX LAID OUT his plan to the boys in the Mercury and they asked questions until everything was clear. Then they downed their drinks and headed off to Maranzano's territory.

They walked north on First Avenue until the crew reached Twenty-sixth and on past the Richardson. Everyone put their hands in their pockets to keep a weapon on standby as they crossed Fifth then Sixth Avenue and reached Maranzano's turf.

The air tasted the same but the people on these blocks looked different. The massive reduction in Yiddish signs and language. More Italian spoken— and the clothes everybody wore. All these elements told the gang to stay tight and be ready for anything.

Pregnant with expectation for two more blocks, the crew straightened their backs at the sight of the Speckled Hen, a bar long-since vacated by Irish gangs at the turn of the century and now occupied by an altogether different clientele interested in a healthy mix of hooch and whores interspersed with an occasional bet on the turn of a card or the spin of a wheel. It was the Richardson with an Italian accent.

Thirty feet away from the entrance, Alex halted his gang, and they pretended to stop for a conversation. A fake laugh emphasized the ordinary state of this group of fellas if anybody had been bothering to notice them. They were just strangers in town, which meant they were potential johns but of no more interest than that to the casual observer.

The men entered the building and sat down at a table until a waiter swung by and offered them a drink. Paulie did all the talking as he had an authentic Italian accent, although the entire conversation was in English.

While the coffees were ordered, Alex scanned the joint. With a bar at the back end of the room and a stage on one side, there was an unmarked door which must lead to offices and an unknown number of guys with weapons. On the opposite side to the stage were drapes which Alex guessed led to the gaming area. One fella was all that separated them from the tables beyond the curtain.

"There's not much to see here. Paulie and I will pay a visit behind the scenes while you two play a few hands. Keep your eyes peeled but don't make any moves until we have announced our arrival. And remember, we are here to damage property and not to harm civilians. If anyone is going to serve up revenge, it's me, because the Richardson is mine."

Alex and Paulie waited near the staff entrance for fifteen seconds until they were certain no one had spotted them. Then they skipped into a corridor and closed the door behind them. There were muffled voices up ahead but they couldn't be sure quite where the noise came from. They pulled their revolvers out and slunk along the poorly lit space until they reached the far end and were faced with a choice between two doors.

Alex pressed his ear to both but the only sound came from the right-hand room. He signaled for Paulie to open the left-hand door and sure enough, there was nothing to see except filing cabinets and desks piled with papers. When they kicked open the other door, they were met by two surprised expressions belonging to a pair of fellas sat at a desk counting money.

Before they could respond by standing up or asking a single question, Alex had whipped the nearest guy around the chin with his pistol and Paulie had punched the other in the face. Paulie muttered something menacing in his native tongue and both fellas put their hands on their heads and kneeled on the floor.

A quick check of their pockets and the desk drawers revealed three pistols which Alex and Paulie stuffed into their pockets. Then Alex decided to clip the guys around the head because they had nothing to tie them up with and they would only be troublesome if they were allowed to wander the building. Paulie shrugged and he and Alex returned to the other end of the corridor and back into the auditorium.

EVERYTHING APPEARED CALM so Paulie and Alex wended their way to the gaming area. The fella in charge of the drapes eyeballed them but made no serious attempt to check them out. Poker was nearest and four roulette wheels were on the far side of the room. Cheap copies of Italian masters adorned the walls which had been painted a powder blue.

Alex saw Massimo and Ezra had separated and he caught their attention so they knew to be ready. Apart from the tellers who were unlikely to give them any trouble, there appeared to be just one fella running the room. Paulie sauntered over to be near him and Alex waltzed into the middle, halfway between the card tables and the spinning wheels.

He fired his gun into the air, causing a pile of fractured plaster to fall on nearby customers, who screamed in surprise at the sound of firearms and because it felt as though the ceiling was caving in. Alex fired again, and the gamblers stormed for the exit.

The nominal head of the room had been thumped at the base of his neck by Paulie as soon as the first shot left the barrel. Massimo and Ezra seized the opportunity to upturn tables, smash chairs and destroy green baize and roulette wheels as quickly as they could, transforming everything into firewood.

While the crowd continued to surge through the single door space, the four men joined the throng to hide among the johns. They reached the auditorium and scattered in separate directions. Two fellas stood in the middle of the room to calm down the mob spewing out of the building.

In less than a minute, the place was empty, apart from Alex's crew and a number of fellas who had appeared from a hidden door in one wall. Suddenly this was no longer a fight Alex thought they could win as they were clearly outnumbered.

Seven guys spread themselves out around the room with Paulie, Massimo and Ezra feeling the squeeze before anything had even happened. Alex eyed all the dudes as best he could, trying to figure out who needed to be taken out first and how to wend his way through the table chicane to reach them.

The stand-off lasted half a minute until Paulie spoke in Italian using the most commanding voice in the world. All heads turned to connect the sounds bellowing across the auditorium with a head containing moving lips. And this was the moment Alex attacked.

He lunged at the nearest fella who was only ten feet away. As he rushed forward, dodging past two tables, he raised his pistol arm and aimed squarely at the guy's chest. Then Alex reached him and saved a bullet by slamming the gun into the fella's face. Blood spurted out of his nose and eye, causing him to drop to the floor in agony. A kick to the groin ensured he wasn't getting up soon.

On cue, the other three zigzagged around the white linen-draped obstacles and punched, gouged and pummeled their way through as many of the guys as they could. In less than a minute, three of theirs were felled, and the match was even.

Everybody stopped for a second to take stock. Ezra glanced at Alex and smiled, pleased with their efforts. Then a crack splintered the air and Paulie flew over a table, spraying a red arc onto the tablecloth. He was dead by the time he landed on the floorboards.

ALL THE MEN hit the deck and Alex pushed the nearest table over as bullets started to fly across the room. Massimo popped up his head for a moment and seized the opportunity to aim a slug into one of the Maranzano gang.

Now there were three of them and three of Alex's crew so they had a chance, although Maranzano's fellas were in a better position. Alex's guys were nearer the center of the room and were facing off against men stood by walls so there was only one side from which they could be attacked. This wasn't going to be easy.

Another hail of bullets and Alex was pinned to the floor, face down. He heard the zing of a slug as it entered human flesh but had no idea who had been hit. A quick check to the side of his hiding place and he just about made out a body slumped to his left: one of the Maranzano goons.

"You guys good?"

Positive noises from Ezra and Massimo gave him cause to breathe easier for a few seconds. Italian spouted from Massimo and there was a moment's lull as whatever he'd said was given due consideration.

"What did you say to them?"

"I told them we made a terrible mistake and asked if they'd let us leave if we put down our arms."

"Seriously?"

"Why not? They're standing between us and the door, aren't they?"

Massimo was right. Alex had been so focused on attacking the men, he hadn't given a thought to how they were going to get out. He'd figured they'd walk out once the others were dead, but Massimo had calculated their odds differently. One fella shouted something back.

"The guy in charge—the one to the left—says we can walk free if we stop right now."

"That's mighty fine of him. Let him know we appreciate his kind and respectful consideration. Tell him we came here hot-headed from the Richardson and should have thought through our actions a little more clearly. We will pay for the damage to his premises too."

As Massimo translated Alex's good intentions, Ezra scurried along the floor and under a table to get a better vantage point. All that remained visible were his feet sticking out. Alex checked the chambers of his revolver and found he only had four bullets left.

"Do your new friends understand any English?"

"Not that I can tell."

"And how's your Yiddish after all these years?"

"Nicht so schlecht."

"Then listen carefully."

Alex told Massimo and Ezra exactly what they needed to do if they were to triumph that afternoon. Besides, Alex knew that they would never be allowed to leave this place alive no matter what some blind pig boss might promise. Heroes or in a coffin—those were the only ways they would exit this building today.

From nowhere that Alex could see, a stream of bullets came flying over his head—the goon had got himself an automatic machine gun. With his lips almost sucking the ground, Alex counted pairs of feet through the table legs and realized that one more man had appeared through the invisible door. The machine gun must be his.

All they could do was wait for the onslaught to finish because so many bullets were flying thick and fast only a fool would have raised his head out from hiding just to get off a single lucky shot. After a minute, there was a sudden silence as the guy had to reload and then they grabbed the chance they'd been waiting for.

Massimo fired a shot into the shins of one fella, who dropped to the ground enabling Massimo to fire off two more slugs, but this time one entered the guy's chest and the other coursed through his eye and out the other side of his head.

Ezra rolled out from his hiding place and threw a knife into the neck of the goon with the machine gun. He spat out blood, gurgled and flew backwards. Alex hadn't known Ezra had brought a blade to this gunfight.

This left the boss who stood and stared as both his comrades fell within seconds of each other and Alex rushed towards him while he was focused on the destruction surrounding him. Alex squeezed the trigger but nothing happened; the mechanism had jammed. Instead he kept on running, hoping that the guy wouldn't expect him to do anything as crazy as he was attempting.

He reached the fella and landed an enormous punch to his chin before he had registered Alex was stood in front of him. Luigi fell to the floor with Alex sat astride him, punching and slapping him around the face until there was nothing left but a bloody mess. He carried on raining blows upon the corpse and only stopped when both Ezra and Massimo physically dragged him away and waited for him to calm down.

Once Alex had caught his breath, he surveyed the devastation. Blood sprayed on himself, the walls, floor and tables, along with enough bullet holes to use the plasterboard for a sieve. Dead bodies and destroyed drinking and gambling equipment. Paulie lay still surrounded by a red pool of liquid.

"Let's get him home—after we burn this joint to the ground."

1910 ··· **1920** ··· 1930 ··· 1940 ··· 1950 ··· 1960 ··· 1970

16

THE NEXT DAY, Alex paced up and down the hallway in Waxey's headquarters all too aware that Ira and Waxey were talking about him on the other side of the door to their second-floor office. After an eternity, the hinges creaked, and they invited him inside.

As usual, they both sat in exactly the same location with almost the identical posture too. It was as if the furniture was so used to their weight and the position of their bodies that the wood had warped to match their lumps and curves.

Today there was one significant difference—a new fella sat with them, Benjamin Siegel. Thick jaw and haunted bugged-out eyes but nothing else out of the ordinary about him. Alex had seen him with Waxey before but had never been this up-close to the guy who was making a name for himself as a gun for hire. As Alex sat down, Benjamin rose, tipped his hat and left.

"See you around, Alex."

"Bye, Benjamin."

"Gentlemen…"

And he was gone. This left Alex being stared at by Ira while Waxey stirred the spoon in his coffee. This was pure affectation because the man never added sugar or cream so there was no need to have the spoon in the drink in the first place.

"Yesterday, some misfortune happened at the Richardson, dear boy."

"Yes and I heard that a speakeasy burned down on the other side of the tracks."

"That news came my way too. I assume they were connected."

"Stranger things have happened, Waxey."

"Was anyone hurt?"

"Not in the Richardson. Maranzano hit us overnight."

"And then you responded in the cold light of day."

"More or less."

Alex felt uneasy because he could not be sure what Waxey thought of the previous day's exploits. Should he have done nothing? Sought permission before acting? Kept Maranzano's crew alive?

"I would have done the same, dear boy, and my boss would have reprimanded me for not seeking permission before I had gone over there and blasted a hole in the head of every single one of them. How did you know the perpetrators were in the Speckled Hen?"

"I had no idea. It was the first Maranzano place we found. An eye for an eye, so it didn't matter to me which joint got blinded."

Ira snorted to hide his mirth and Waxey grinned.

"For the record, you should have come to me first and agreed a hit on Maranzano's territory. I have spent much of the morning preventing an all-out war from erupting. The good news is that they struck us first and we were only retaliating, although turning the place to ashes was hardly a like-for-like response."

"Sorry about that. I saw a red mist by the end. All those bullets flying brought back memories from less happy times."

Alex stared into the middle distance and Waxey gave him a moment to return from France to the Lower East Side.

"The good news is that Charlie Lucky interceded on our behalf and took the heat. We've done good business together over the last year or two, especially with booze…"

"…and prostitution."

"Yes, Ira."

Silence for a second as Waxey lost and regained his train of thought.

"So, Charlie spoke up on our behalf and smoothed matters over. We are fortunate because Charlie and Maranzano are rivals, but Lucky has fingers in so many pies that he can't afford for us to fight among ourselves. And he is right; there is way too much money to be made these days with hooch, gaming and women. You'd almost believe the days of union infiltration and protection were a thing of the past."

All three men laughed at that joke, because they understood that Waxey was the man who controlled every pier and every dock on the Lower East Side. There wasn't a union in the area that didn't pay a weekly subscription to the man.

"Seriously, Alex. Send a token of appreciation to Charlie for stopping this from getting out of hand."

"I'll also need to look after Paulie's family."

"Leave that honor to me. A small lump sum to his favorite nafka is not something with which you need to concern yourself. Focus on what is important. Aren't you expecting your first child sometime soon?"

"Today, Waxey. Sarah went into labor a few hours ago."

"Get over to the hospital then so you can stand idly by while she does all the work."

Alex nodded and rushed to leave. As the door closed behind him, he heard Ira's voice offer some practical advice.

"Don't forget to buy a large box of cigars. You are going to want to celebrate once she's done all her pushing."

MOISHE ISIAH COHEN was named after his paternal grandfather and what Sarah remembered being told was the name of her father. The labor had taken six hours and the little man screamed a lungful as soon as he entered the world—so much so Alex heard his first cries from the waiting room where he immediately handed out cigars to anyone willing to receive one. Ira had been right.

Over the following year, Sarah, Alex and Moishe did their best to learn how to be a normal family. They were so very happy. Of course, there were many occasions when Alex had to be away from home but he did his best to make sure he always looked in on his *bubbala* before he went to bed.

His relationship with Sarah ran the gamut of high pleasure—Moishe's first crawl, first word, first anything—through to harsh crises. While Sarah wanted Alex to succeed, she loved him too much to want to see him get hurt and she knew his work would kill him eventually.

For Alex, if Sarah wanted to enjoy the trappings of his success then she would have to accept that this much money came at a price. She told him she only wanted to be happy but she wore the fur coats with a little too much relish.

SMOKE. MUD. BLOOD. Sweat poured into Alex's eyes as he hauled himself out of his foxhole and up the slope toward Bobby. No more than five feet on, he hit the dirt as shells landed all around. His friend continued to scream in pain and that damn sniper had him pinned down so he could hardly move. Fear in the pit of his stomach knotted until tears dripped out of his eyes.

INSTEAD OF LIVING in a room above a flophouse, the Cohens had moved into an apartment of their own on Avenue A and Second. While still a rented tenement, it was a place of their own and the landlord was Ira. While Alex created sufficient wealth for him then the rent was never going to be something they'd need to hand over.

Alex didn't notice it, but for the first time in his life he knew some contentment. It wasn't happiness, because he spent the summer of '21 living through the daily grind of bootlegging, union bashing, running numbers rackets and organizing cathouses. But the peace he experienced at home was new to him and he enjoyed it more than words could say, despite the hours spent awake in the middle of the night.

Sarah shouldered the greatest share of the burden of looking after Moishe —changing diapers, preparing and feeding the little man—and Alex did the things he was most comfortable with. Playing with Moishe after dinner if he was back in time or taking a family trip to Coney Island on an occasional day off.

The Cohens settled into a routine of domesticity with Alex the breadwinner and Sarah ruling the household. If he'd put his head above the parapet for even a second, Alex would have realized that he had become his father, although Moishe senior was a tailor and not a member of an organized crime gang.

As summer turned to fall, Waxey continued to tighten his grip on the flow of alcohol into the Eastern Seaboard—with no small help from Charlie Lucky and his connection to financier and gambler, Arnold Rothstein.

No major criminal activity on the East Coast took place without Arnold's approval because he was the go-to guy if you needed seed capital for any illegitimate venture. He had funded the first whiskey run through Detroit and had assessed the risks when Waxey and Maranzano had nearly gone to war. The man might have operated from the back of Lindy's Restaurant in midtown but he owned the world.

FEBRUARY 1922

17

AS THE IMPACT of the Volstead Act deepened, Waxey secured his position as the lynchpin of East Coast booze. High class and rich customers demanded quality product and Waxey obliged by ensuring safe passage for Canadian whiskey, authentic scotch and English gin. His long-time associate, Charlie Lucky worked with him on these supply lines.

Behind the scenes stood Rothstein, who was rarely mentioned but the movers and shakers knew of his presence. If there was a deal to be done or a business venture to make money, then the Big Bankroll had his manicured hand in the action.

Meantime, Alex no longer operated out of the back of a brothel. Nowadays he rented an office on Avenue B and Fourth with the name of a fake company on its glass door. Along with a desk and a potted plant, a coffee table, a couch and three easy chairs. All black leather.

A filing cabinet stood in the corner but if you'd taken a moment to open any of the drawers, you would have found them completely empty. Alex kept no records because none of his business dealings were legal and he saw no reason to create a paper trail for any nosy cop to find.

One cold Tuesday morning, Alex sat at his desk, while Ezra and Massimo hung around waiting for their men to report on the day's collections. The guys laughed and talked about nothing, and occasionally Alex would dive back into his newspaper.

A knock on the door made him look up and eyeball the other two. They both shrugged and Alex indicated for Ezra to get off his tuches to welcome their unexpected guest. Once all three were poised with a hand on their piece, Ezra let the visitor in. As soon as his face was revealed, they gave a collective sigh of relief—it was Benny Siegel.

Alex recognized him as one of Waxey's heavy-hitting associates who would drift out of view when Alex appeared.

"Come in and sit yourself down, Mr. Siegel."

"Call me Benny like all my other friends."

Alex walked round his desk and the men shook hands. Alex scooted Massimo out of his seat so Benny could remain close to his desk.

"Would you care for a coffee?"

"No, thank you. I'm good."

"Ezra, Massimo, would you be so kind as to pop out and buy me a cup of java?"

"Both of us?"

"That's right."

Alex scowled until they both got the message to leave so he and Benny could have a private conversation. Once they were gone, Benny drew a deep breath and described his problem.

"Waxey recommended we speak as I have a delicate matter and I need your help."

"What would you like me to do?"

"I have a friend in Chicago who has asked me to do him a favor and usually I would be happy to oblige."

"But not this time."

"My face is too well known in the Windy City and this matter requires a stranger. Somebody we can trust to do a good job who won't make a fuss and will move in and out of the city without causing a ripple."

"I'm flattered my public profile is so poor in the Midwest that you'd want to approach me for the task."

Benny smiled because both men understood Alex's position as the go-to guy on the Lower East Side.

"If I were to agree to offer my support, what would you have me do?"

"A simple act of persuasion. My friend is having difficulties maintaining his whiskey supplies from Canada because a certain individual is expanding his activities on the north side of town."

"You want me to go to Chicago to ask a guy to not block a whiskey convoy?"

"Insist, not ask."

"How strongly would I need to insist?"

"Whatever it takes to ensure the flow of booze into the south side."

They agreed Alex's fee with no negotiation as Alex understood this could be the start of a significant relationship and he didn't want money to get in the way. Also, he knew that Benny Siegel was not the kind to appreciate some gonif trying to haggle with him.

"Does your friend have a name?"

"Just ask for Alfonse."

Benny supplied an address and walked out, just as Ezra and Massimo returned with Alex's drink.

"What was all that about?"

"I'm going on a little trip."

THE REASON CHICAGO is known as the Windy City is lost in the mists of time. Many thought it referred to the Hawk Wind that squalls off Lake Michigan while others believed it was a reference to blowhard politicians from the previous century. Alex didn't care much about such issues. He wrapped his coat tight around his body as he stepped off the train. It was damned cold, and the breeze cut through him like a knife.

He was greeted at the station by a tall thin guy wearing a similar black coat and a fedora. Alex had never met him before but knew exactly who he was and followed the fella out of the station and onto the sidewalk for a five-block walk which led to a speakeasy. At the back was the entrance to a much larger room with gaming tables and girls aplenty.

The guy headed straight to a particular white tablecloth at the edge of the action and sat down. As Alex approached, the guy's eyes stared at another door and so Alex entered alone. Down a corridor and into a busy anteroom where fellas talked, moved bits of paper around desks, and generally appeared to be fiercely occupied.

With everyone ignoring him, Alex stayed at the entrance and waited. He knew he was expected and someone would have to deal with him otherwise he'd hop onto a return train sooner than planned.

Twenty seconds later, a plump man left his adjoining office to look at his people scurrying around like bugs. He took one glance at Alex in the doorway and pounded over to offer him a handshake.

"Come in. I hope they haven't made you wait too long. Nobody has any manners in this town."

"I'm Alex."

"Of course you are and I'm Alfonse Capone."

"I don't mean to be rude but how do you know I am who I say I am?"

"If you weren't, you'd be dead, young man. In case you hadn't heard, this is my town—or soon will be once you help me clear out the riffraff."

"Is there somewhere we could go that's more private? We have a few details to iron out."

Alfonse explained how difficult Alex's prey would be to kill while they sat in his office. They had slumped onto a massive leather couch and Alex sipped on a scotch on the rocks he'd taken more out of politeness than any desire for liquor.

"Brady Madden is no fool. He keeps off the streets most of the time and when he ventures out, he surrounds himself with foot soldiers."

"From what I read in the New York papers, the Chicago way involves the shooter swinging by in a car and letting rip with an automatic weapon. I wouldn't be hanging around street corners if I were Madden either."

"So how are we going to nail the Irish sonofabitch?"

Alex had a long hard think and hatched a plan that would enable him to kill the guy in broad daylight. He told Capone what he needed and took a swig of his drink.

"I like your thinking. I can see why Benny wanted to send you. You've got a long day tomorrow. I have organized some discreet accommodation for you. Would you like a skirt to keep you company?"

"Thanks, but I'm a happily married man."

"I didn't ask about the state of your marriage, but whether you wanted some tail tonight."

"I'm more concerned to know the food's going to be to my liking."

"No bacon or ham. I understand."

"That's not what I meant. I've heard strange things about Chicago pizzas."

Alfonse laughed and shook his head.

"Don't go believing everything you read in them papers. You can have a steak, some pasta or a nice piece of fish. Whatever you fancy."

CAPONE WAS AS good as his word; Alex ate well and slept soundly. The housekeeper woke him up, and he hustled out of the joint without paying, because Alfonse had made clear he would take care of the bill for his East Coast guest.

A brown paper package had been left for him at reception which he collected before making his way to offices one block away from Madden's favorite daytime haunt. Alex's plan relied on Madden following his usual daily routine. So Capone had called off all the fellas he'd hired to keep vigil over Dean O'Banion's underboss.

Alex took the stairs up to the fifth floor and idled along the corridor until he reached the location Alfonse had found for him at very short notice. As promised, the door was unlocked, so he walked inside and locked it in case of any unexpected visitors.

Three windows overlooked the street with a terrible view of more buildings opposite. There were many workplaces with a more enjoyable aspect, but this was perfect for Alex. By standing next to the right-hand window, he had a clear line of sight to the joint where Madden was holed up.

The gangs in Chicago were populated by young guys who had not learned their craft on the battlefields of Europe or the mean streets of the Bowery. Instead they relied on the scattergun effect of a hail of bullets to mask the fact that their aim wasn't very good. Hence the need to drive by so close and the notoriety achieved by the Chicago mobs with so many civilians slain without an apparent care in the world.

Alex unwrapped his parcel and summoned up all his army training to see him through the day. Among all the paper nestled a rifle and scope with a box of slugs. There had been no time to organize a tripod to steady the gun but Alex dragged a low cabinet over to the window to rest his elbow and maintain a clean line between the barrel and the building facia some four hundred feet away.

Just as he had learned to do every day as a sniper on the Western Front, Alex kept both eyes open as he stared through the telescopic lens. Meanwhile, his first finger stayed away from the trigger in case an accidental twitch ruined proceedings.

Two hours later, he licked his lips for the hundredth time and regretted not bringing a drink with him. His stomach rumbled too, but he knew he couldn't quit his position. The moment he did that, Madden would leave and not come back for another day.

Alex scrunched up his face to take his mind off his hunger and thirst. When he opened his eyes, he saw Madden standing by his office window. Although the view was far from perfect, he recognized the guy from the description Alfonse had provided, right down to the mole on his right cheek.

One inhalation and Alex placed his finger so that the tip was touching the trigger. The crosshairs on the scope were aimed straight at Madden's heart and Alex prepared to fire. Then a flurry of movement and Madden was through the door, out onto the sidewalk and ambling toward him, flanked by four guards, two front and back, one left, one right.

Alex's breathing increased as he did his best to keep the barrel of the rifle moving to match Madden's pace. Trouble was that the goon in front of him always stood between Alex and his target. This was getting desperate. At any minute Madden could cross the street or a car could pull up and he'd get in and be gone.

Then Madden stopped and looked down at his feet. Loose shoelace? No idea, but nobody told the goon up front who carried on walking for two paces until he noticed he no longer had company. And those two steps made all the difference. With no one there, Madden was unprotected—as naked as the day he was propelled into this world, despite the three guns surrounding him.

Alex inhaled and squeezed the trigger as the air began to leave his lungs. A bullet landed neatly in the upper right sector of his torso and the guy fell backwards, bumping into the gun behind. The two fellas either side twisted round and whipped out their weapons, but they hadn't figured out where the assailant was hiding. Alex sent a second slug into Madden's head, making a hole in his chin and a red mess as it left the other surface of his skull.

With both shell casings in his pocket so he didn't leave the joint in an untidy state, Alex used a cloth to wipe down the barrel and other surfaces of the rifle. Then he returned it inside its brown paper packaging, shifted the cabinet to its original position and left the office via the stairs.

A crowd was rushing to the slain body nearby but Alex strolled in the opposite direction and deposited the package in a dumpster at the back of a hotel. Then a long walk to the station and a relaxing train journey home.

18

WHEN ALEX'S TRAIN finally pulled into New York, he went straight home to freshen up and change his clothes—traveling light meant wearing the same suit for three days in succession. Once he'd sat down with Moishe for a few minutes, Alex found Sarah and gave her a peck on the cheek. He placed his palm on her round belly and smiled.

"What have you got to be so happy about?"

"You look so beautiful when you're pregnant, hon'."

"Fat and ugly, more likely. Men have it easy. You swan in here having been God knows where the last three days and act as though nothing has happened. Meanwhile, I'm stuck looking after our son and sweating like a pig with the second bundle of joy coming our way."

"My work takes me places…"

"Tell me about it."

"We got you a housekeeper to ease your burden."

"You hired a maid I don't trust not to steal our silver."

"She's a thief?"

Alex ground his molars and stiffened his back.

"Rosa is fine. She's reliable and Moishe loves her… I've missed you, I'm tired and I want you to be home more. Even with the hired help, I still crave adult conversation. When you're away, I'm left with baby talk and a servant stuck in this small apartment."

"It felt big when we first moved in."

"Anything seems large compared to a single room in a flophouse, but the family is expanding. If you were home more, then you'd know for yourself."

"I'll see if Ira has a bigger place for us."

"Instead of receiving handouts from your friends, maybe you should get a place by yourself. I don't know what you get up to anymore and I haven't asked, but I understand that in your business everyone has their day. They shine and then they fade—and Waxey's star has been shining for years."

As much as he was annoyed with Sarah for climbing on his back as soon as he'd entered the apartment, deep down what she said rang true. The only trouble was that now was not the time.

"WE'VE BEEN TALKING about you while you've been away."

"Nothing too rude, I hope."

Waxey and Ira looked at each other and smiled as Alex sat down at his usual perch in their meeting room.

"That accommodation you made to Benny has got you attention all the way back here on the East Coast."

"Amazing how the New York papers covered another guy dying on the Chicago streets."

"It wasn't in the press. Not here. Benny Siegel was extolling your virtues to Charlie Lucky, who had a conversation with me."

"I'm surprised anything got done when I was away with all this talking."

"Don't be fresh. The work you did was a test of your mettle. Madden was an O'Banion underboss, so it is only fit and proper that one underboss is killed by another."

Alex didn't quite understand what Waxey meant. It had just been another hit. Nothing special.

"We are giving you control of all the Lower East Side operations—still reporting to me."

"Sure, Waxey... I mean, thank you. This is more than I ever dreamed possible."

The lie dripped off Alex's tongue because he wanted much more than the Lower East Side but this was a very good start and he needed Waxey's continued support.

"Show your appreciation by making us more money and doing favors like in Chicago. It takes a steady hand to shoot someone from a block away."

While Alex walked the men through the mechanics of what he'd done, the rest of his mind raced through what he had just been given. He was now responsible for all the drinking, gaming and women fraternization south of Fourteenth Street and east of the Bowery. Not to mention all the union and protection rackets.

He controlled the juiciest docks in Manhattan but even in his moment of triumph, Alex wanted more. He already had his eye on the area north of his neighborhood and wondered how he could take a bite out of the other side of the Bowery. How to eat into Maranzano's territory would wait for another day.

One of his first acts as underboss was to pay a visit to a house on Forsyth and Stanton, a short hop from his old haunt as a teenager. After a brief discussion with its owner, Alex acquired the deeds to the place overlooking the parkland, and the Cohens moved in before Moishe's brother David was born.

THE SUCCESS OF the Italian and Jewish gangs in New York and America's other major cities created a response from the authorities. Ordinary citizens looked to the police to do something about the scourge of crime which blighted the urban sprawls from east to west.

The Big Apple was not immune from this increased interest in upholding the Volstead Act and word on the street was that times were about to become a whole load tougher.

"What we need is to get an inside track on the department of booze."

Ezra and Massimo nodded agreement as they sat around Alex's coffee table in his paperless office, but they had no suggestions or ideas of their own to offer.

"There's too much money to be made out of bootlegging to let the cops destroy all that we've built up. Any of you got an in with any of the beat flatfeet round here?"

Silence and shaking of heads. Ezra scrunched his face as though he was concentrating hard but left Alex with a faint impression that he needed to hit the head.

Alex restated the problem: "Tammany Hall is funding a group of out-of-town shoe leather to find the stills and put us out of business."

"And the distribution. With enough men, they could impound our trucks and destroy the booze in our warehouses."

"Exactly, Massimo. So we need to do something now before they get out of hand." Alex let out a heavy sigh.

"We can't bribe or kill gumshoes if we don't know who they are," stated Ezra.

"And how are we going to do that then?"

Alex was getting annoyed because he'd thought his top fellas would be more attuned to the problem at hand. Every day there was some story about how the so-called department of booze was readying itself for a big push. The Bureau of Prohibition was closing in and Alex could feel them breathing down his neck. His surprise was that the other two couldn't sense the black shoes and shaved sideburns too.

"I might know a guy…"

"Ezra, I'm sure you do. Why should I care?"

"This one works in the police department in the day and plays poker at night. He's good at catching thieves but terrible at judging a hand of five cards. Given how much he owes me, I reckon he might be prepared to spill his guts. One more bad day and I was planning on rearranging his kneecaps, anyway."

"Don't lean on him too hard as he'll be more of use to us if he's not laid up in hospital. I'd rather we suffer the loss of a few hundred dollars..."

"...four thousand, Alex. I've been mindful to be generous..."

"...a few grand lost now could be enough to save our entire bootlegging operation. That's a trade worth making. Let's pay a visit to this gentleman and see what we can agree.

EZRA AND ALEX waited at the back room of the Stars and Stripes, one of the many speakeasies under Cohen control. It was way too early for a cop to come calling so they spent an hour reminiscing over old times and propping up their optimism for the future despite the dire circumstances the operation was facing.

Then Ezra nudged Alex and shifted his glance to stare at a guy in brown pants and a white shirt. And a haircut that screamed cop. They waited for him to settle into his seat and sip his Irish coffee before they sauntered over and Ezra made the introductions, Ezra flanked to his left and Alex to his right.

"How's Lady Luck, Frankie?"

"Some you win, some you lose. You know how it is."

"Lately it's not been much of a winning streak, has it?"

"Not so's you'd notice, but every hand is a fresh chance to win, right, Ezra?"

"Spoken like a true winner."

"I wonder if you can help me. Would you be able to do that?"

"Of course, buddy. Always happy to lend a dime if I can."

"All I need is a conversation."

"Okay, Mac. What you want to talk about?"

"Call me Alex. And I want to know all about what you do for a day job."

"Nothing much, Alex. Keep the peace. Try to stop people from hurting each other."

"That's what I heard. I admire guys like you who put their lives on the line every day for a handful of green."

"Thank you. What's this really about? I mean, Ezra, with all due respect, you didn't come down to this dive joint just to introduce me to a friend to blow smoke up my ass."

"Smart fella, isn't he, Ezra?"

"I told you, Alex, he's a sharp one."

"Sure did. Why don't we go somewhere more private to carry on this conversation...? Take your drink."

19

FRANKIE DIDN'T APPEAR too worried as they meandered around the tables to reach Ezra's office. Once inside, Alex walked over and sat in Ezra's chair behind the desk, leaving the two others to seat themselves facing him.

"Ezra tells me he holds several of your markers and he wonders how you will make good on your debt."

"It's only a turn of a card away. I'm sure of that."

"I admire your faith in this uncertain world, Frankie, but sometimes self-belief is not enough. Do you have any collateral we can hold until the repayments are complete?"

"Collateral? I'm just a beat cop with a wife and kids. I ain't got nothing fancy like that."

Alex let those words hang in the air. He needed Frankie to think beyond his blind hope that he could double up his bets to get himself out of the deep hole he'd dug for himself. Besides, Alex already knew Frankie's apartment was rented, and he barely found enough dough for Mrs. Lando to buy groceries for the week.

The bright lights behind Frankie's eyes faded as he too realized today's meeting was more than a chat. Ezra had allowed him to amass the debt. At any point he could have stopped Frankie's line of credit, but he hadn't. Now, he was in hock to these serious men.

"Don't undersell yourself, Frankie. You don't have any collateral to offer me but you are still of value."

"Nice of you to say, but I don't see how."

"Ezra tells me you recently got a promotion. You're no longer walking the beat."

Frankie nodded but his expression showed no understanding.

"You're working at the Bureau of Prohibition nowadays. From what I hear, the pay's not much better than wearing a uniform."

"I get by."

"You need to do more than that, Frankie. Think of Eleanor and your kids. Don't they want a better life? Pretty clothes and somewhere safe to live."

"We live in a good neighborhood, Alex. Queens may not be fancy…"

"…but are they really safe there? That's what you must ask yourself."

Again, the implication of Alex's words slowly sank into Frankie's thick skull.

"What do you want from me?"

"The conversation we are having right now. Tell me more about what you do at the bureau."

THE FOLLOWING NIGHT, Alex and his men took a trip to Harlem. They had a bite to eat at the Club Deluxe and then went west until they met up with some of Massimo's guys on the corner of 145th and Riverside Drive. Two blocks north and the gang reached their destination: an unassuming warehouse with a pair of bored guards at the main entrance and nobody inside. Just as Frankie had described.

A truck pulled up on the opposite side of the street but the driver remained in the vehicle. One guard investigated this suspicious occurrence because he had nothing better to do and trucks rarely parked out this way in the middle of the night.

Alex watched as the guy approached from the passenger side and promptly vanished. His pal, still stood at the gate, had seen none of this because at the same moment, he was offering Massimo a light. To thank him for his act of kindness, Massimo cracked the guy's skull as he turned away, with just enough force to knock him unconscious.

The instructions from Alex had been very clear—despite how you might feel about these guys, don't hurt them. We want the contents of the warehouse because it is our liquor they have seized, and we are also showing Uncle Sam not to get in the way of our business. And our enterprise is making money, not homicide.

The bonded warehouse contained over a hundred thousand dollars of booze, almost all of which had been taken from the Lower East Side and, even if it hadn't been, the hooch was now in Alex's hands. Before the break of dawn, enough trucks had driven uptown to ensure there was no alcohol inside the building apart from a small flask they had left in the locked room where they dumped the two guards.

Later that morning, Alex visited Arnold Rothstein to let him know in person about the recapture of his assets. Whereas almost every businessman had an office to conduct private meetings, the Big Bankroll chose a rear table at Lindy's Restaurant on Broadway between Forty-ninth and Fiftieth.

Amid the hustle and bustle of patrons eating cheesecake, pastries or even a full meal of *gefilte* fish and *latkes*, Rothstein held court, although there was never more than one other fella at his table. That way there were never any witnesses to anything that was said. Like Alex, he wrote nothing down. What Rothstein couldn't remember wasn't worth knowing.

"Thanks for your time, Alex. We shall ensure we show you some appreciation."

"Very kind, Arnold, but let's just make sure we take care of my guys."

"Don't be noble. It is a *mitzvah* for me to thank you. A blessing and you should not take it away from me."

HAVING DEVOTED THE morning to Arnold, Alex headed downtown to speak with Waxey; his life spent in the orbit of the Big Bankroll had been exhilarating. The man had ideas that spread beyond the here and now, but he was always focused on the next deal. His gambler's mind reassessed the risks of any venture each time some new piece of information came to light. Alex relished being in his company and not solely because everyone he worked with made a ton of money.

By the time his cab dropped him onto the corner of Bayard and Bowery, Alex was fired with excitement at the prospect of working with Arnold on his next project, whenever that might be. His heart shrank to the size of a nickel once Waxey briefed him on the next task for his boss.

"Let me get this straight; you want me to crack some heads in a *schmatta* factory?"

"There's been some unrest and we need some calm in there. You know how to handle union hotheads, which is why I'm asking you to intercede on my behalf."

"Why do you need me? Surely this is something one of my boys could take care of. My time is better spent elsewhere."

"For sure, but my niece will need careful management and I am relying on you."

"And she is the union convener, Waxey?"

"She is, so no rough stuff. Convince her to do the right thing for her workers but there should be no bruises, no scars. Lean on her only if you must and only as much as is absolutely necessary."

Waxey hadn't explained why his niece spent her days sewing for a living but Alex knew that even with that blood tie, Ezra could have been trusted with the task. Because he had been their gofer for so many years, they might have given him more authority, but Waxey and Ira had yet to show him the respect his new position commanded.

When he arrived at the factory—one of the many peppering the piers near the Williamsburg Bridge—Alex found Raymond Cooper Inc to be the same as any other warehouse in the block, with one exception. It was the only building that had strikers marching in front.

Alex sighed. It was always easier to get both sides to see reason before anyone did anything stupid like withdrawing their labor or sending in scab workers. Tempers would be frayed and emotions would be higher than Alex needed them to be.

"Can you tell me how to find Noga Spencer?"

The guy with the banner pointed at the far side of this huddle of twenty folk. Alex walked around the group rather than push through the crowd, his natural impulses restrained by the necessity to keep everything cool.

"Noga?"

"Yes, bud."

"I'm here to help your cause."

"Pick up a placard and join us. You work round here?"

"Not anymore. I meant to help you end the strike. I'm not one to stand on street corners complaining."

"Who sent you and what do you really want? Are you one of Cooper's men?"

"Not at all. Why are you striking?"

"Cooper is paying us a pittance and fails to look after the girls when they are too ill to work."

"So more pay and a day off to recuperate once in a while."

"Something like that."

"And Cooper thinks he pays you enough and doesn't see why someone can't spend six days a week in front of a sewing machine and live through the winter."

"Pretty much, bud. Who did you say you were with?"

"Just a concerned citizen. Which is more important to you, the extra money or the time off?"

"The gelt but we want both."

"Your sort always does, but you'll settle for less. And if Cooper won't give in to your demands?"

"Then we'll stay outside until he does."

"Is there scab labor inside?"

"Yeah…"

"So he has no need for you anymore. If you walked away from this place and didn't come back, Cooper would never even notice."

Noga stared straight at Alex for the longest time. Like she knew deep down he was right but didn't want to admit to him or herself that she'd led her people out of the promised land and onto the unforgiving streets of New York.

"How long have you been out here?"

"A week."

"And the scabs?"

"Second day."

"Let me have a word with Cooper."

Alex knocked on the door and was eventually let in. He waited in an anteroom until Cooper was prepared to receive his unexpected visitor.

"Thank you for seeing me without an appointment. As I said to your assistant, I'm hoping to help end this ridiculous strike."

"All the girls have to do is come back inside. One of them was sick, and I didn't complain while she was off for a week, but when she returned, she spent most of her time coughing her lungs up or in the bathroom. So I let her go. The next day, the rest of them refused to come in."

"What can I say, Raymond? I am not here to defend their actions but I would like to see this matter settled."

"You and me both."

"Quite. Is there anything you could offer them to bring them back in, no matter how empty the gesture?"

"I don't see why I should. I've got others doing their jobs right now. My plan was to get the police to clear the street tomorrow."

"In the past, the local law enforcement haven't much cared how they treat strikers during such operations. I wouldn't want anybody to be hurt."

Cooper looked at Alex while he stared directly through this upstart tailor. The cops would break heads if they had a chance and Noga was not to even suffer a bruise.

"Let the workers back in and I'll make sure your factory doesn't meet with any unexpected accident—like a fire suddenly sweeping through your premises tonight."

"Don't threaten me, mister. I already pay protection to stop those kinds of events from happening. You should have done your homework before trying to hustle me."

"Raymond, your protection money won't save you, because you need to make extra plans. I am asking you for some consideration, a personal favor if you will."

"You never gave me your name."

"Alex Cohen."

20

ALEX CAME UP with excuses to visit Arnold Rothstein from time to time. He made the Big Bankroll aware of his plans and sought his advice on matters. This was the first man Alex had met who he respected. Waxey was and remained a really great guy, but they understood each other too well and took each other for granted.

There was a tract of land immediately north of Alex's territory which looked ripe for picking so Alex asked Arnold for his thoughts.

"Gramercy is tempting, don't you think?"

"Are your eyes bigger than your stomach?"

"How so?"

"Who controls the park area now?"

"It's Italian."

"Don't be coy. Be serious in business always. If you don't know the answer to that question then don't start the conversation."

"My apologies, Arnold. We both know I am hemmed in north and west by Maranzano. From my perspective, north is easier to punch into than heading toward Mulberry and the heart of the Italian community."

"That much makes sense to me, but you might like to consider a different approach than brandishing your muscle."

Alex looked puzzled as brute force had got him to his current position. Before the war, he'd been known as the Slugger.

"Collaborate, my friend. When the pie is big enough, taking a share can still earn you more than owning all of a single cookie."

"I'm not too sure."

"Whatever you decide, you will need to discuss matters with Meyer Lansky. His interests and mine are closely aligned, and he does much more direct business with Maranzano than I do right now. If you are to succeed, you need his support. Let me make the introductions."

MEYER LANSKY WAS a stubby young man; what he lacked in height he made up for in girth, but Alex was no fool. Just because the guy appeared mildly comical—like a beach ball if you squinted—didn't mean you should treat him with anything but the utmost seriousness. The fella had Rothstein's ear and worked on a daily basis with Charlie Lucky. No one else in New York City could make that boast stick.

"Thanks for meeting with me, Mr. Lansky. You sure have a swanky apartment."

"You're welcome and thank you for your kind words. I hope you don't mind but I have no office. Those sorts of places attract undesirable kinds of people."

"I'm surprised to hear you allow panhandlers to get within fifty feet."

"They don't. I was referring to the cops and assassins. A gentleman should be able to conduct his business without worrying about who is coming through the door."

At that moment, a fella appeared in Lansky's living room, and walked over to whisper in his ear. Alex jumped out of his seat for a moment due to the unfortunate timing of Lansky's words. The near-silent conversation lasted only a minute then Alex was alone with Lansky again.

"Our mutual friend suggested I speak with you."

Alex explained his current situation in the Lower East Side and how he was looking to punch north provided he had appropriate support.

"And you are seeking my help?"

"Mr. Rothstein is on board if you are."

"I don't care either way and that is a statement of pure neutrality. I say this because I own no territory so your control of some blocks in Manhattan are immaterial to me. I mean you no offense."

"None taken."

Alex let that lie slip from his tongue because he understood that Lansky saw this as a business matter, so literally nothing for him was personal.

"My interest is piqued by any fresh opportunities you create by running that part of town. While Arnold was kind to send you my way, he knows there is someone else whose approval you need to seek: Charlie Lucky."

Alex's heart sank with those words. As much as Charlie had backed him since Prohibition made them all rich, Alex knew that Charlie preferred things the way they were. Change was bad for his business and right now there was a tension bubbling under the surface between Italian factions and Charlie wouldn't want anybody to rock the boat.

"So you're saying 'no' then."

"I'm saying 'not yet'. Charlie has other plans that need to be put in place before we do anything between the Lower East Side and Times Square. Your moment to shine will come—just not today."

ALEX RETURNED TO his office with his tail between his legs. No matter how much he wanted to push hard uptown, he would die trying without the support of Rothstein, Lansky and Charlie. The next best option before him was to make more money with what he already controlled.

"What I'm looking for," he explained to his crew, "is something we've not done before that'll earn us plenty. Don't give me an answer now—go away and come up with an idea. There's a two-thousand-dollar bonus to anyone with a suggestion we can turn into reality."

There had never been so many blank stares at the ground in the entire history of Manhattan.

"No rush. Give me any of your thoughts some time this week."

He wasn't expecting much from his men but he figured he'd give them a chance to come good. Meantime, Alex wandered the streets hoping a money-making scheme would pop into his head just by breathing in the same air as the johns who came to his bars and whorehouses.

The common problem with their flophouses was that the cops mapped exactly what they were and where they were. This entailed spending unnecessary amounts of cash on kickbacks just to keep the uniforms away.

Then there were the johns themselves. They always wanted to spend as little time in the joints as possible, which was good for the nafkas because they could move on to the next customer, but this was a nightmare for the owner. You spent your whole life desperately finding the next man to push through the front door.

When the nafka trade went well, the bars groaned in their emptiness like a stomach starved of bread. And the trouble with barflies was that their behavior would go downhill the more time they spent in the establishment. Even the arrival of the speakeasy did nothing to deal with the drunks. Alex introduced dance nights to many of his blind pigs and this meant a few more women showed up but takings were rarely up; they just didn't slump.

Alex continued musing on this dichotomy as he leaned against a wall and noticed he'd wandered over to the Forsyth Hotel. As his eyes focused on the building in front of him, he recalled his early days in the city and the number of times he'd watched Sarah's soft curves float up and down the main staircase.

His eyebrows raised and the flicker of an idea spread across his mind. They would create a modern version of the Forsyth as a speakeasy and whorehouse. The riffraff would not be allowed into the joints because they'd have gatekeepers on the door—that was normal for speakeasies. And the men who turned up could have a drink at a table, a show, and female companionship in equal measure.

Gaming tables in the back might even attract a different john. They could add those at a later date if they thought it would increase profit. The advantage of this idea was that Alex could choose his locations carefully and whichever street corner he chose, the owners would be sure to agree to sell to him. That much was certain.

21

AS MUCH AS Alex disliked giving handouts to cops, he knew cash was the oil that greased the machine. Once the new venues were running, the beat uniforms would only know the closed front doors, but that didn't mean there'd be no itchy palms before that point.

He sent a lad over to the Thirteenth Precinct station house on Clinton between First and Second Streets to request the company of Captain Mort Frye at his office. When the boy returned, he looked downcast.

"What happened?"

"Took me ages to find the fella and when I did, I told him exactly what you said. Then he clipped me round the ear and kicked my butt clear out the station."

"Something for you to learn about cops, son; unless you're dangling them by the ankles out of a twenty-story building, they'll show you no respect at all. Here's some shrapnel for your troubles."

He handed the kid a dollar because there's nothing worse than being publicly humiliated when you are ten years old. Besides, the boy had spunk to get inside the place and fight his way through to the big man himself.

This left the question of whether Frye had taken the message seriously. Alex remained behind his desk all morning and just before lunchtime, the squeak of leather could be discerned even before the office door creaked open and Frye stood surveying the scene.

Ezra and Massimo shuffled out with no word from Alex. No one wanted to stay in a room with a precinct captain.

"Sit down, Captain Frye, and I appreciate you traveling all this way to see me."

"I don't like being summoned, Cohen, especially not by your sort."

While he wasn't expecting a warm welcome, Alex rankled because he couldn't decide if Frye was objecting to him because of his business connections or lack of foreskin. The former was part of the job, the latter was prejudice and Alex had no time for that in his life. Whatever the reason, Alex

400

told himself to keep calm because he wanted this jackass onside—else it would cost him in the long run.

"If my office is not to your liking, then I am more than happy for us to relocate to a place of your choosing."

"In an ideal world, you'd be in the precinct with handcuffs behind your back."

"We don't always get what we want, Captain Frye, but sometimes we can benefit from life's twists and turns. Sit down and let's talk... would you like a coffee?"

"If you are a legitimate businessman—and nothing I've heard about you indicates you are—then you wouldn't seek a private meeting with me."

"And if you were a legitimate police officer, you wouldn't be sitting here questioning my provenance."

"Well, I..."

"Your sort shouldn't take offense. I'm calling the situation as I see it. There's no need for either of us to get upset. I notice you have a taste for expensive shoes. I'd warrant they cost more than a month's pay, so please don't become indignant with me when I ask one of New York's finest to pay me a visit."

Frye glared at Alex until the fire ebbed from his eyes, while Alex enjoyed his drink.

"What would you like to talk about?"

"Soon I shall invest in local real estate and I'd like you to help me secure my investments."

"That's what the police are here to do."

"I figured. During the acquisition and preparation phases, I'd like your lads to keep a watchful eye on the properties."

"That can be arranged..."

"And after that I want to be left alone."

"Also within my reach."

"Pleased to hear it. For the first piece, I will make a donation to the Police Benevolent Fund and give you the money to pass on to the proper authorities."

"Thank you for your contribution and happy to oblige."

"And with the second part, let me be clear about what I want. There should be no unpleasant interference from any criminal element..."

A smile trickled from the corner of Frye's mouth but he understood that Alex didn't want the local kids robbing from him.

"...and your officers shouldn't come round snooping for a handout either. If you and I take care of business, then I need not pay anybody else."

"That can also be arranged and you have my personal guarantee that none of them boys will bother your people."

"Good news. Again I will use you as a conduit to the Police Benevolent Fund, assuming that is acceptable to you."

"Mighty swell, Mr. Cohen."

"Call me Alex; Mr. Cohen sounds like you're talking to my father."

November 1922

22

THANKS TO THE payoffs to Frye, all the new speakeasy brothels opened on schedule with a minimum of fuss and little or no interference from the cops. Alex marveled at how you could get anything that you wanted in this beloved country, provided you paid for it.

On some occasions Ezra would hand over the gelt and sometimes Alex would be the one to make others' dreams come true.

Voting in America had always been a lynchpin of the New World's democratic principles and the situation in New York reflected this. Manhattan naturally found its own way to express the power of the people with Tammany Hall, which exerted a stranglehold on election results.

Alex's new role on the Lower East Side meant there were certain duties to perform on the day of the state elections, which dated back at least a century to the time when the Democratic Party first interfered directly in the results of the people's vote.

"This is the deal." Alex issued his final orders in his office before the polling booths opened.

"We have identified which wards need our special attention. Make sure you have a copy of the list before you leave."

Heads nodded, but no one moved because they could tell the briefing was not over.

"We may come across individuals who do not take kindly to our approach in dishing out democracy. They are entitled to their opinion, but that does not mean they should express their views in public. Feel free to discourage them using any appropriate means necessary. They must all still be breathing when you leave them—with no exceptions. The only accidents I want to hear about are unintended stuffing of other ballot boxes. Is that clear?"

Tammany Hall had been the center of Democratic Party influence in New York for as long as people could remember and during that time, men like Tammany's boss Charles Murphy paid immigrants like Alex Cohen to fix election results. There was no other explanation of how the Democrats maintained their stranglehold on power for so long.

Alex didn't care much for politics or politicians. These were the people who had taken the country into the Great War and had allowed soldiers to die in the trenches over there. But, despite his dislike for those involved in electioneering, Alex's desire to acquire wealth and power meant he was more than prepared to do business with Murphy and his ilk.

Besides, he might think they were scum, but politicians had influence which he knew was a useful commodity and his newfound friends, Arnold and Meyer, recognized the importance of keeping these fellows onside. It was good for business—and Alex sure understood that.

DECEMBER 1922

23

THE END OF 1922 was a blessing and a curse. Overall, it had been a good year for Alex, his men and his business associates, although he was concerned that the hard-fought success he'd achieved would get swept away. This reflected Alex's lack of security and confidence as opposed to any identifiable threat.

"You fret too much."

"Sure, Arnold, but..."

"But, nothing. Once you've played your hand, the only thing left to do is to see how the other cards land. It is too late to worry at that point and you must accept your lot. You cannot change the past, only shape the future."

Rothstein was right and Alex knew; he just wasn't satisfied until he picked at the scab and made it bleed. He was grateful for the invitation from Arnold to join him and his wife for a New Year's Eve celebration at the Waldorf Astoria Hotel on Fifth Avenue and Thirty-third.

While he might have worried he was punching above his weight, Alex accepted his seat at the table almost before the offer had been uttered. How could he refuse such a kind invitation from the Big Bankroll?

The evening began with champagne cocktails in Arnold's suite. Alex and Sarah were introduced to Lansky and his wife, Benny Siegel and a brunette, and Charlie Lucky with his wife. Waxey and Ira were nowhere to be seen and Alex was confused for a moment. He'd assumed he would have been invited to a large party, not to an intimate gathering of the Big Bankroll's close business partners.

Sarah kept a tight grip on his hand and only after she'd downed the second glass of bubbly did she relax enough to allow their palms to separate. "I really don't feel like I should be here," she whispered, and Alex knew how she felt.

Once the cocktails were consumed, the party moved downstairs into the Grand Hall where their table was waiting. To book a spot inside that room on that night meant you were either rich beyond most people's dreams or incredibly powerful—or both. Both Alex and Sarah did their best to use the right silverware, and the waiters acted polite but haughty.

At some point when Alex was wrestling the bones of a salmon out of its flesh, Charles Murphy wandered by to pay his respects to Rothstein and stop for a conversation with Alex. He eyed Sarah almost the entire time he spoke —she had lost none of her allure in the five years since Alex first glimpsed her ankle.

"We appreciate all your efforts last month, Alex... and who is this ravishing creature?"

"Charles, let me introduce my wife, Sarah."

"Charmed, dear lady."

"Likewise, I'm sure."

"You and your husband must visit some time. We'd love to have you over for tea."

"That'd be lovely. Why don't I leave you men to make all the arrangements?"

Sarah might have believed she was a fish out of water, but she was familiar enough with the men to recognize trouble when she saw it. You didn't need to be a follower of politics to sense that Murphy's intentions would not be honorable. She knew a john when one walked up to her.

The rest of the meal passed without incident and when everyone in the room had finished eating, the orchestra stopped playing and were replaced by a jazz band. Sarah grabbed Alex by the hand and, not for the first time, she dragged him onto the dance floor. Within minutes they were joined by twenty or more couples until the place was heaving. She leaned into Alex and stretched up so her lips were nestling by his right ear.

"I'm glad we came. Are you having fun, because I am. I thought these people would be too snooty but Arnold and Meyer are cool guys."

"They sure are, hon'. Benny's okay too but he always has a different twist on his arm, so that can be kinda awkward. The guy can't settle down."

"You socialize with Benny often?"

"Not really, but he's the only one of us who doesn't have a steady."

At midnight, a thousand balloons descended from the ballroom ceiling and Alex shook hands with Arnold, Meyer and Charlie Lucky. Then he turned to kiss and hug Sarah.

"We've made it, honey. This is the life, don't ya think?"

"Sure do. Just remember, it's not the money but who you are that makes me love you though."

Alex looked at her quizzically but before she could explain, they were separated by the tide of revelers wishing everybody and anything a Happy New Year. The dancing continued and everyone carried on drinking their coffees laced with liquor until the small hours.

How did a respectable establishment get away with serving high-grade alcoholic beverages? Because there were enough judges in the room to throw out any court case and the providers of the booze were in the joint too.

By six am, the party was fading, and they called it quits. Arnold, Meyer and their spouses returned to Rothstein's suite—Benny and his squeeze had slunk away several hours earlier. This left Alex and Sarah to walk through reception and stand to wait for a taxi.

Despite the early time of day, a yellow cab swung by within seconds and halted in front of the hotel. Alex let Sarah get in first and she shimmied over the back seat to make room for her husband.

As Alex bent down to join her, a bullet zinged past, missing his head by inches. If he'd been standing upright then his brains would have been mixing with the white walls of the entrance.

Out of sheer instinct, he slammed the cab door shut and hit the dirt. The vehicle sped away with Sarah screaming as the driver exited the area at high velocity. This left Alex exposed although he had no clue where the assailant was located. He scurried to the revolving doors and rolled back inside. Uniformed cops appeared less than a minute later but, even if he'd wanted to help, Alex could tell them *gornisht.* When he finally made it home an hour later, he checked on the kids who were already awake and then lay on the bed and fell asleep within seconds.

24

IMAGES AND SOUNDS appeared to Alex from the depths of his subconscious while he slept. An alleyway in the mist. One stocky figure shuffled into view. Bruises and blood around his head and neck. Alex recognized the guy despite his disfigured features.

"Sammy?"

"Who else do you think it could be?"

"How are you after all this time?"

"I'm surprised you care... I'm not too bad under the circumstances."

"Huh?"

"How are you and how is Sarah?"

"Someone shot at us earlier today and I haven't seen her since then. You seen her passing by?"

"No, not that I noticed, but no one wanders into this alley. I was surprised to see you, to be honest."

Alex looked at his surroundings and realized where he was. This was where he'd first met Sammy when he arrived in town and the same place where he'd nearly clubbed his friend to death three years later. He turned his attention back to Sammy; more bruises had appeared around his eyes and his neck was discolored.

"Are you certain you are okay?"

"Don't worry about me. Focus on Sarah. You said you hadn't seen her."

"Not since the shooting."

"You might want to think about how you treat her."

"What do you mean?"

"You allowed someone to fire a bullet within a foot of her head. That's not exactly protecting her from harm. Does she deserve that?"

Alex looked down to his feet as his cheeks heated. He shoved his hands into his pants pockets.

"I do my best to provide for her. A roof over her head; I buy her pretty things. She tells me I'm a good provider."

"But you didn't take care of her today. She nearly died by your side."

"Have you seen her? She ran off in a cab and I haven't seen her since."

"She'll be back eventually. You need to do a better job of keeping her safe."

"Yes, I intend to."

"I hope those aren't empty words—you made me many promises and didn't keep them. Can she trust you?"

"Of course."

"If you want her to continue to trust you, then you must tread carefully."

"What do you mean?"

"The life you lead; the people you meet. This criminal world you inhabit is filled with opportunities to do the right thing and the ever-present possibility of making poor decisions."

"I don't understand what you're saying."

"Alex, you run prostitutes the length of Manhattan. Are you telling me you've never considered sampling the merchandise?"

Sammy's statement was met with a blank expression.

"Not once. There's only ever been one nafka I slept with and that was Sarah. At that time, she wasn't one of my girls."

"How noble, Alex. But you need to make sure you do the right thing by her."

"We are married, Sammy, and she has given me two boys."

"Just remain on a straight and righteous path or you will lose that woman. All the shiny expensive jewelry in the world won't keep her by your side if you veer from the one true road."

The mist thickened, and it seemed to Alex that Sammy was floating away. Then in an instant he was back, inches from Alex's bulbous nose.

"And one more comment before I must leave. How much longer will you stay with Waxey? When will you fly away?"

"Waxey saved me."

"Are you duty bound to sit by his feet until the day he dies?"

"That's not what I mean. I owe him some allegiance but I'm not shackled to him in the way you are implying."

"The secret to a successful career is knowing when it's time to go."

"And is that what you think I should do?"

"My opinions don't count. Do you think there is more to learn from Waxey?"

"He saved my life," Alex mumbled under his breath to emphasize how little he believed his own words.

"Eventually that debt will be paid and then you must decide whether Charlie Lucky or Lansky will make a more interesting business partner."

"Or Arnold. I could learn so much from that man."

"Before you make your selection, you'd need to leave Waxey and find out which of those gents would be prepared to have you come along for the ride."

"I'm happy where I am."

"Don't lie to me, Alex Cohen. You've found so many ways to create an excuse to see Rothstein and you even had a secret meeting with Lansky. So don't pretend to be all innocent with me."

"How d'you know about that?"

"I know everything you know. And more besides. Who's it going to be? Charlie Luciano or Meyer Lansky?"

"Arnold Rothstein?"

"You'd like to be him, wouldn't you? But he's too refined a gentleman and you are too much of a street fighter. Know thyself, Alex."

The mist grew thicker again until Alex was forced to close his eyes to prevent them from stinging. He clenched them tight for over a minute and when he opened them again, he found himself on top of his bed with all his clothes on. Sarah lay next to him asleep. He slipped off his pants and shoes and clambered under the covers without waking her. Alex leaned in to smell the perfume of Sarah's body and drifted back into unconsciousness with the comfort of knowing she was safe and sound, despite her snoring.

JANUARY 1923

25

TWO DAYS LATER and the dust had settled on the attack. Waxey appeared unconcerned. "It's the life we lead," was his comment, but he did not pass a thought on how Sarah might feel. This was not the world she was living in. Not at all.

From what Alex could see, she was shaken but not frightened. While she understood the hit was meant for him, she remained angry, whereas he got that this was business and nothing personal.

In part driven by Waxey's indifference and partly in response to his dream, Alex spent his time with Arnold. The man had shown real sympathy, even offering the Cohens the opportunity to remain at the Waldorf as his guests for a few days.

"That's very kind of you and much appreciated, but we are going to stay put. Sarah doesn't want the kids' lives to be disrupted and my best men surround the place day and night."

"I understand. If you change your mind, then you just say."

"What I would like to do is chat with whoever squeezed the trigger."

Lansky sat back on a couch, comfortable in the surroundings of Arnold's hotel suite. Charlie Lucky had joined them and Alex was pleased to be in their company. He was punching well above his weight.

"We are making discreet enquiries on your behalf. This was not a random act; some coward attacked you in front of your wife while you were attending my party."

Charlie sat next to Lansky and nodded; they had grown up together and continued to work closely together. The Italian sipped his coffee before passing comment.

"We will find the dog who did this and make an example of him, for sure, but right now let's return to business. We need to talk more about our supply lines…"

◆ ◆ ◆

417

A WEEK LATER, Alex received a phone call in his office.

"Charlie here."

"How are you?"

"All good. I'll be quick. The fella you're looking for is ready for a conversation with you."

"Which guy?"

"The one who tried to kill you."

Alex fell silent for three, maybe four, seconds.

"Hello. Are you still there?"

"Yes, I was thinking."

"My men are holding him until you arrive but take your time because this fella ain't goin' nowhere."

"Thank you. I owe you one."

"Nah. We live together, we fight together..."

"But we die alone, I know."

"Not for a very long while unless some chump tries to whack you when you're leaving a party: scum."

The phone went dead and Alex sat there, letting the buzz of the office engulf him. Then he blinked, swigged his coffee until the mug was empty and turned to Ezra.

"Don't wait up. I may be gone some time."

"Let me go with you."

"No need. Charlie's found my unknown assailant."

Despite Alex's protestations, Ezra drove him over to the hideout and strode inside the westside warehouse. The cavernous space at the heart of the building contained a table, a few chairs, and five men, one of whom was tied to a chair.

As they walked nearer to the huddle, Alex saw the fellas standing around doing nothing in particular. The guy with the ropes round his wrists was bruised about the face and had two small pools of blood by his shoes. Luciano's guys had been professional throughout the encounter.

When he got within twenty feet of the group, the men stood straight like they knew who he was, even though Alex didn't recognize any of this crew.

"Anyone know the name of this *farbissener momzer*?"

"He's a neighborhood kid. A few of us have seen him around, but nobody knows the little *schmendrick*."

Alex nodded and turned his attention to the boy. There was a gag in his mouth and Alex heard every inhalation and exhalation clear as day. After he approached, the breathing got more frequent and louder.

"Let's get these straps off your head, so we can talk."

He bent over the guy and undid the knot so the binding loosened and fell away from the boy's face. He then spat out a mouthful of muslin which had been forced past his lips earlier in the day. Alex looked round until Ezra supplied a chair which he placed opposite the lad.

"Before we start, I want you to listen carefully to what I have to say to you. Can you do that for me?"

"Yes, but this is a terrible mistake."

Alex put a solitary finger across his lips.

"We will talk about any mistakes in a minute. First, what is your name?"

"I'm scared that if I tell you, then you will harm my family."

"You have nothing to fear as I intend your kin no ill will. What is your name?"

"Savino Raneri."

"Why did you try to kill me and my wife?"

"I never aimed at her. Did she get hurt?"

"Bit late to worry about that now. No, she did not but you need to explain to me why you hid in the bushes and fired a shot at me."

The boy stopped talking and licked his lips. Alex indicated for one of the men to bring some water over. A few sips later and Alex repeated his question. Nada.

"Understand this. Either you answer my questions and you die an easy death, or refuse and these fellas will take their sweet time as they make you experience pain you can only imagine from your darkest nightmares. This is the only choice left."

Alex stared at those young eyes as they filled with fear, but no hate. There was nothing personal in the attack.

"This is my guess. You decided you wanted to skip working your way up and thought that whacking me would win you some friends in high places."

The boy's expression morphed from incredulity to panic to acceptance.

"Who do you work for, little man?"

The kid looked up but said nothing.

"I admire your chutzpah but you make terrible choices."

Alex stood up and nodded to Ezra. The boy's screams pierced Alex's ears until the gag was replaced. The next day, his corpse could be seen floating down the Hudson. He took four long hours to die and his body was a mess of bruises, cigarette burns, and cuts from various blades.

BOOZE IS A peculiar commodity; sometimes people are thirsty and other times not. January was one of those months when every bottle that arrived in Alex's warehouses shipped out the same day. Manhattan became a desiccated husk and Alex seized the opportunity as it presented itself.

He hightailed it over to Lindy's Restaurant and waited in line—not for a seat; that was easy to get—but for the table at the back of the establishment to be occupied by only one man: Arnold. When his turn arrived, Alex stepped forward with his coffee in hand and sat down next to Rothstein so neither would need to raise their voice much above a whisper.

"Thanks for seeing me."

"You didn't need to be here, Alex. We could have had a meeting in my suite."

"I understand, but I wanted you to know that I am not seeking any special favors, just a fair hearing."

"Talk to me."

As Alex inhaled, a waitress came over and delivered a large piece of cheesecake, forcing him to wait before pitching Rothstein.

"I'm moving every ounce of alcohol I can lay my hands on and it isn't enough. I need more territory to expand my storage capacity and to increase the number of locations to sell product. In short, I want to head north and reach out as far as Times Square eventually."

"Good to see a young man with fire in his belly and ambition coursing through his veins."

"And I'll need your support, Arnold, to do this. It'll cost hard gelt and your political protection. The Italians will not be impressed if I stomp over their territory."

"You are right to come to me again and I appreciate the respect you are showing me. Before I can decide whether to offer you the support you seek, I must ask you to do me a small favor."

"Name it."

"I'd like you to take a trip to Windsor for me."

26

THE TRIP TO Canada went smoothly but when Alex arrived in Windsor, the streets felt different to his last visit. The sidewalks were deserted—not just sparse but completely vacant—no one was out and about.

By the time he'd made his way to Arnold's contact on the far side of town on Dougall Avenue, Alex wondered whether the Spanish flu had descended on the inhabitants of this place. Its sole value to anyone beyond its civic border was its location so close to the US that you'd be forgiven for thinking you were still in America.

A rat-a-tat-tat on the door and a stranger let him in without even checking his credentials. He wasn't impressed with this lapse in security but bit his lip and followed the fella into an office.

"Wanna drink?"

"Coffee would be good."

A nod and the guy left, only to return three minutes later with a cup and a friend who introduced himself as Stefano Perisi, a thick mop of black hair upon his head.

"Thank you for coming, Mr. Cohen. We are living in troubling times."

"With no one guarding your front door, I'm not surprised you are troubled."

"Huh? We knew you were showing up and no one else would have turned up at this hour apart from you. Baggi holds the entire town in his clenched fist. Didn't you notice how few people were on the streets? The ordinary citizens are too scared to come out of their homes. No local would have knocked on our door out of the blue. So it had to be you."

"Who is this Baggi?"

"Fabiana Baggi is backed by friends from the East Coast. Nobody knows who but they have muscle and money. In only a handful of weeks, they've taken control of every place you can cross the river by boat. And, as you know, Windsor needs its supply lines, or it is nothing. Once they did that, all they needed to finish the job was to hit our warehouses. Within a week, they had the liquor, the boats, the trucks. Everything. And we were left holding our dicks."

"Stefano, Baggi might have borrowed this hick town for two weeks, but I am here to convince him to return what is not his."

"Not being funny, but good luck. Baggi's brought an army with him and they take no prisoners. You are with them or dead."

"I shall have a word with Fabiana Baggi and see if we can reach a businesslike arrangement."

STEFANO GAVE DIRECTIONS to Baggi's headquarters and offered to send one of his men to accompany Alex but he refused. There was no point putting another life in jeopardy, he'd said. Truth was that Alex didn't want to be associated with the local hoods any way at all. He wanted Baggi to see him in a different light.

Before he'd opened the door of his car, he felt a thousand gun barrels aimed at his head, so he eased himself out of the vehicle, careful to keep his hands visible at all times and to adopt a casual air as he sauntered to the building.

The clunk of bolts being unlocked met him as he approached until a voice called out from the inky blackness of the interior for him to stop in his tracks and assume the position. Alex halted and raised his hands above his head, thinking the phrase the guy had used made him sound like a cop.

The fella stepped out of the shadows, frisked him, and led him inside with the cold steel of his shotgun square between Alex's shoulder blades. This was just another tumbledown bar in a part of town which couldn't remember it had ever seen better days. He was pushed into a side room and waited ten long minutes before anybody returned. Even with no introduction, he sensed the guy before him was Baggi. The two stared at each other until Baggi broke the silence.

"What do you want?"

"A conversation with you."

"Baggi is listening."

"I represent some business interests from back east who had been using Windsor for a profitable enterprise until you arrived and prevented us from carrying out our commercial activities."

"Why should Baggi care about this?"

"These interests would like to reach an accommodation with you so that we may continue to ply our trade and you may still do… whatever you do here."

"Make money. Baggi is here to look after his friends' business interests."

"We need not be in conflict. We all want a clean supply of liquor from Windsor through to Manhattan and can work together to protect this route from outside interference."

"Baggi needs no help from a Jew."

Alex ground his molars but knew better than to respond with fist-thumping violence, his first impulse.

"Until now, the Sugar House Gang in Detroit has been under strict instruction not to attack your trucks once they've crossed the Detroit River because we wanted to give you the opportunity to work with us."

"Baggi is not concerned about a handful of bad-blood Jews. You are not offering Baggi anything of interest."

"Then I shall take my leave and remind you that I came here today with open arms and a desire to negotiate a deal."

Baggi stood up from his chair and let one of his goons march Alex off the premises. As he crossed the threshold, Alex turned his head around and smiled. Baggi had followed him out. Despite the Italian's bold words, he was worried, otherwise he'd have returned to whatever he'd been doing before Alex had appeared from nowhere.

Alex jumped back into his car and traveled at a sensible pace to his hotel —the joint had been warned of his impending arrival the previous day. Sure enough, John Smith signed into his room and called down for service as soon as the bellboy had pocketed his quarters and left.

Then Alex took off his shoes and stretched his toes before he picked up the handset by the bed and asked the operator to place a call to New York. A brief conversation and everything was sorted, so he savored every mouthful of his steak, knowing there was nothing more for him to do that night.

Despite himself, Alex slept until seven but made sure he ate a full breakfast even though there were no bagels or blintzes. By nine he was sat in his car and a black suit approached him, hat brim positioned to hide his eyes.

"Good to see you, Massimo."

"Likewise, boss. Ezra and the crew are ready and waiting."

"Did you bring everything I asked?"

"Of course. We're looking forward to this party."

"Hop in and you can direct me to the fellas."

ONE HOUR LATER, Alex had issued instructions to the twenty men who had driven from New York on his command. A similar number had positioned themselves outside the warehouses which were crammed full of Rothstein-funded whiskey. They were to do nothing unless anybody tried to leave and then their orders were simple: kill anyone who moved. The horde with Alex were to wait until he gave the word.

"How can we be sure that Baggi is inside?"

"He's locked this town down tight and hasn't bothered to protect his place properly otherwise we wouldn't be talking right now. So, he's happy in his flophouse with all his guys on the inside."

Ezra smiled at his boss's cold logic and understanding of how his enemies thought.

"Let's show this Italian what Jews are capable of."

Ezra hustled off to speak to his men and a minute later, four metal projectiles flew toward the door and windows of Baggi's headquarters. As soon as the first one landed, immediately by the entrance, a blinding flash and ear-splitting roar erupted as if from nowhere. Then another, then a third swiftly followed by the fourth.

Dirt and debris flew into the air, some blasted into the nearby windows causing glass to shatter and implode, some hurtled up and cascaded on parked cars and smashed onto the ground. Alex saw the craters formed by the grenades and flashed back to France. Limbs strewn next to the bodies of his fallen comrades, faces skewed in distorted death stares.

Machine guns punctured his reverie and his men picked out Baggi's people one by one. Some made the mistake of fleeing the scene and they were the first to die. Over the course of the next five minutes, Alex's crew shot and killed every man who appeared at any window or door of the building. Then there was silence.

Alex listened to the wind and indicated for his men to do nothing. A hand gesture to Massimo and three guys scurried across the street and stood either side of what had been the main entrance. They popped their heads inside and another volley of gunfire followed.

More gesticulation and Alex ran over with ten men; the rest held back in case of further trouble. Alex looked around at the rubble and blood, trying to spot Baggi among the dead bodies. No joy.

He signaled two fellas to hop upstairs. One burst of gunfire and twenty seconds later, both returned. Time to check out the room he'd visited the previous day. Alex pushed the side door open and prepared for a dramatic response, but nothing. Along the corridor and he turned a handle to see what would happen. Zilch.

He kicked the door, and it flung wide to reveal the same furniture as before but no Baggi. At least, he wasn't visible but Alex could hear deep breathing instead. He pulled out a revolver and pointed it at a desk. The sound seemed to come directly from it. Sure enough, Alex found a man's ass protruding from under the oak.

"Get up, Baggi."

A whimper and the man shuffled out and rose to his full height, hands on his head. Alex edged forward and moved sufficiently close to push the barrel of his gun past Baggi's teeth and into his mouth. The Italian mumbled something but none of his words could be understood because of the metal by his tongue. Alex didn't care precisely what was said because he could guess the general gist.

He shook his head and squeezed the trigger. Baggi wouldn't be getting an open casket funeral.

27

UPON HIS RETURN to the Big Apple, Alex had swung by Lindy's to report to Arnold. This time he didn't wait and headed straight to the front of the line to whisper the good news.

"Windsor is back under our control. I left some of my guys there in case there is any further trouble but that won't come from the Canadian end."

"Excellent. My friends north of your territory have agreed not to send any more of their associates over the border."

"We were fighting Maranzano's men?"

"Yes. Don't look at me like that with your puppy dog eyes and hurt expression. This is business. Occasionally I reach commercial arrangements with people you would prefer dead. That is the way of the world and nothing more. If you can't make peace with that stone-cold fact then you and I can no longer work together. That would be a shame because I think you could go far and we might both enjoy your success…"

"Because I'll need funding to get there?"

"Boychick, one day you'll be a *gantse mensch* at this rate. Of course I'll be there to prime the pump. We don't work as hard as this for the benefit of our health. Not me, for sure."

"Before I went off to fight in the war, I just wanted to survive. When I came back, I vowed I must never be in that situation again and money will protect me from returning to the gutter."

"Until it is our time to meet our maker."

Arnold fake-spat three times to ward off evil spirits and Alex didn't even blink, it was such a common occurrence among his people.

"Despite their assurances to you, when my men leave Windsor what'd stop Maranzano from moving back in?"

"Alex, they gave their word but I agree that this might not be enough."

"Although I wouldn't want to keep Ezra or Massimo stationed there, I could maintain a presence for a while."

"That would be helpful. The recent crisis has shown us we need to protect our assets more carefully. Would you be willing to run the Windsor end of the operation?"

"Sure."

"Then you should receive a percentage of the proceeds all my friends generate by you delivering them safe passage. Ten percent seems fair. Is that acceptable to you?"

"Of course. A very reasonable share, but I want you to know that my two best fellas will move back home soon."

"That is your business, not mine. All you must do is keep Windsor open for us. Who achieves that goal is down to you."

ONE DAY'S WORK had netted Alex a small fortune—not just today but far into the future. He understood that there was more to the deal than the removal of Fabiana Baggi and a grenade attack. That was the final piece of the jigsaw which had secured the offer but it meant he'd spent enough time in the presence of Arnold, Meyer and Charlie to gain their trust.

With the warm glow of pride ringing across his cheeks, Alex hurried home to Sarah to tell her the good news. He also needed to pack a bag and return to Windsor to put a more permanent solution in place than having Massimo and Ezra holed up in a fleapit hotel.

He took a train to Detroit and paid a visit to Abe Bernstein and the Sugar House gang. They sat in a private room at the back of a blind pig under Abe's control.

"Thank you for seeing me at short notice."

"Always good to see a friendly face. Word on the street tells me you were the other side of the river earlier this week."

"I'm glad your informers are earning their money. Yes, I had a little business to attend to, but that's all resolved."

"So I hear. Congratulations. We benefitted from that momzer's removal."

"His absence has certainly helped the flow of liquor to New York and our mutual friend sends his regards."

"Tell Arnold he should pop over here himself. I know of at least a dozen players who would chop off their mother's right arms to sit at the same green baize as the Big Bankroll."

"I'll tell him, but I make no promises."

They jawed over their previous encounter and Abe remarked on Alex's rise within the ranks. What the man didn't mention was how his position had improved too. When they'd last met, Abe and his brothers had taken control of most illegal activities in Detroit. Now thanks to Prohibition and the accidental location of Detroit so close to the Detroit River, no liquor survived the journey to Ohio without prior approval of the Sugar House gang.

"Alex, while it is truly wonderful to see you, were you doing anything more than merely passing through?"

"Ha ha. I respect you too much to pretend. I came here to discuss some business."

"Here we are. Speak."

"We both know the supply line from Manhattan requires Windsor to be under our wing and for you to extend safe passage to our transport. And you have always been kind enough to deliver that to us."

"For a price, Alex."

"I understand, Abe. You and Arnold have an agreement which both sides honor. But I'd like to suggest a supplementary arrangement on top of the existing deal."

"I'm listening. What do you have in mind?"

"Until now, if our trucks arrived in Detroit, you let them through. Our recent difficulty with Baggi has left me running Windsor with Arnold's backing. So what I'd like us to agree is that if an issue arises in Canada then you'll sail over and assist."

"And for risking my men's lives when you are in trouble...?"

"I shall split my earnings with you fifty-fifty. That's five percent of the total revenues from real whiskey coming into New York."

"Alex, I am happy to help as our interests are mutually aligned in the success of the bootlegging operation. And while I admire your offer, I must refuse."

"But..."

"Hear me out. Your split is too generous. If I take your terms then in a year or two, you will resent the amount I get. We both realize that most of the time the Sugar House shall receive money for virtually nothing. Eventually, you will decide there is too much green heading our way and do something about it. Blood will be shed and one of us will be dead. I like you too much to want to kill you, so why don't I only accept two percent and then the problem won't arise."

"That is incredibly generous. I feel as though my offer was cheap and foolish."

"Not at all. I prefer business partners who are breathing and we will both make a large amount of money out of this venture no matter how we share out the proceeds."

28

A FIRM HANDSHAKE with Abe and the deal was secured. Alex then popped over the border to discuss his plans with Ezra and Massimo. The former stayed in Windsor while Massimo found a suitable permanent replacement. No sooner had Alex dropped into his chair in the office when a call came through from Charlie Lucky and he was back on his feet and out the door.

"Transportation. That's my problem, Alex."

Charlie and Alex stood in a warehouse near Pier 57 at the outer reaches of Fifth Street. The difficulty was in front of their eyes. Alex knew this prime location was usually full to the brim with people and contraband but today there were just the two of them and their echoes.

"I can probably get you five to ten trucks within the next day, Charlie, and more if I have longer."

"I'd appreciate that, but it's not my immediate concern."

"Don't take this the wrong way but why is a man like you coming to a guy like me for a handful of vehicles?"

"Never undersell yourself, Alex. The reason we are having this conversation is that last week the cops were all over me like a rash and I've got a shipment approaching our shores that needs a safe home with someone I can trust."

"You require boats, not trucks. When will the goods arrive?"

"Day after tomorrow, so you don't have much time to prepare."

"How safe a haven do you need, Charlie?"

"The twenty-pound shipment contains uncut opium."

Alex whistled, appreciating the audacity of Charlie's plan. A quick calculation off the top of his head showed there would be nearly one hundred pounds of heroin hitting the street.

"That's quite a party."

"The cops know the shipment is on its way and want to get their grubby hands on it, but I need you to find a secure location away from prying eyes where we can stash the brown powder until I offload it."

"I've got some ideas for storage and after a couple of phone calls, the boats won't be a problem either. The advantage to running booze from every direction into Manhattan is that there's always someone who will lend me a hand."

"Good news. Arnold thought you'd be the perfect man for the job."

Another discussion over money and a firm handshake. Now Alex was getting a piece of both the booze and the heroin action. As they left the empty warehouse together, he had every right to smile.

THE FRENETIC PACE of his life meant Alex hardly saw Sarah and his boys the following few weeks. His next port of call was Florida. While many might head south for the winter, Alex was arriving in March but he still appreciated the warmth compared to home.

Arnold had asked him to take the trip because he had a need for a combination of muscle and management. There was a financial institution where a local gang wanted to make an unexpected withdrawal. The First Bank of Florida was based in Miami but its branch in Boca Rotan was of greater interest.

While the area was filling up with members of New York and Chicago's criminal elements, there was still a large amount of old money that screamed to be liberated from the clutches of the Florida banking system.

Pete and Frank Bunyan had made overtures to Arnold who had shown an interest in financing the deal and handling the tricky job of laundering the ill-gotten gains. The robbery itself required a small group of tough guys to hit the joint with an almighty bang and to make good their escape before anyone noticed the money had left the building.

The brothers had secured a local driver for the getaway and Alex was there for crowd control. He would also monitor Arnold's investment, although the Bunyan boys didn't realize quite how close he was to Rothstein and made the mistake of thinking of him as just New York muscle.

"Are we clear about everything?"

The four erstwhile robbers sat at a table in a gambling den owned by Pete. Pete had run through the plan twice to make sure everyone knew what to do.

"Apart from the security guard, are we expecting anyone to be packing any heat?"

"There's no one else who we know has a gun on them, Alex. How Joe Public responds when we enter the joint is another thing altogether."

"For sure. Nothing personal but the way you describe it, this job is like taking candy from a baby, but I've been sent halfway across the country so something must make the task harder."

"It's what we're stealing. Gold bullion. We are not to touch any cash or jewelry. Only the gold in the safe. Mr. Rothstein was very clear that we are authorized to steal the yellow bars and nothing else."

Alex raised an eyebrow and he solemnly nodded his head to acknowledge Arnold's intentions. Pete explained how they'd handle the precious metal.

THE NEXT DAY, three men wearing scarves over their mouths and noses stormed into the First Bank of Florida, one toting an automatic machine gun and the other two sporting revolvers.

Pete shoved his pistol into the security guard's stomach and he raised his hands. Having removed the guy's pistol from its holster, Pete slammed the butt of his own revolver against the officer's temple and the uniform slumped down. Meanwhile, Frank and Alex scooted across the main area and over to the tellers.

Alex leaped on top of the counter to get a better view of all the citizens and made sure he brandished his weapon for everybody to see.

"Everyone on the ground, face down."

Within fifteen long seconds, the four men and three women had complied with Pete's instruction. The bank staff had hit the deck immediately because they knew that heroes die in robberies and besides, the bank was insured. Now the Bunyans could get to work.

Pete and Frank headed over the counter and scuttled to the safe leaving Alex to keep control of the johns. Two of the women whimpered, but from his vantage point, Alex could see all the customers and staff were frozen against the marble floor.

All except one. The guard had roused himself and Alex noticed the man was moving along the ground, slowly shuffling toward the main entrance. Alex couldn't tell if the uniform was planning on making a break for the door or if he wanted to get to his stool. The answer came quickly as the guy lost patience and rolled over to reach his perch, grabbing a pistol which was hidden under a shelf right by the door.

Alex straightened his arm and took careful aim. A single shot rang out causing everybody to jump six feet in the air. By the time they landed back on earth, a ripple of red cascaded from the guard's knee. Alex wasn't stupid enough to kill the fella even though that was his gut instinct. They were here to rob gold and not assassinate bank personnel. Pete popped his head out from behind the staff-only entrance. A nod to Alex and that was his signal to leave.

"Count to one hundred. If anyone moves before you get to the end or tries to follow us then we'll shoot you dead."

More whimpering, but nobody was fool enough to do anything other than carry on kissing marble. Out the rear, Alex caught up with the brothers and exited out of the back entrance. The wheels were there right in front of him but something was missing.

"Where's the gold?"

"Let's get out of here first and we'll deal with the bullion later."

Alex had little choice but to follow the brothers' lead. That the gold had vanished was not a good sign and all his senses were on high alert. The escape from the bank went smoothly and twenty minutes later, they stopped in a car lot in the middle of nowhere. The fellas poured out of the vehicle and the wheels sped off leaving Alex and the Bunyans stranded on their own.

He scanned around and saw nothing but three black cars, all seemingly empty. If this was an ambush—and it felt like that to Alex—then it was most peculiar because the boys already had the loot. Two long seconds and no one moved a muscle.

"What are we doing here?"

"Alex, we're waiting for a truck. Everything is good."

He eyeballed Pete and Frank, who returned his gaze with an icy expression. He ambled over to one car and leaned against a passenger door, partly to check the vehicle wasn't hiding any machine-gun shaped surprises and partly to move away from the center of the lot. If trouble came calling, Alex didn't want to be surrounded.

Hands in pants pockets, he whistled and waited, watching both brothers for any move they might make. Five minutes passed and nobody had appeared.

"You sure we're in the right place?"

"Funny, Alex. Real funny."

Ten more minutes and still bupkis. Alex couldn't tell if the men were sweating because of the weather or nerves. The mysterious truck was taking its time. Frank whispered something into Pete's ear who nodded in reply. They both glanced at Alex and continued their conversation. He wondered if he should place a hand on his gun but bent down to tie up a shoelace instead. This gave him the opportunity to palm a piece before standing up again. Now he was ready for whatever came his way.

Almost at the same moment that thought flashed though his head, a vehicle approached in the distance. First, they saw the dust on the road and then they heard the rumble of its engine. The truck finally drove into the lot and stopped in between the brothers and Alex so they vanished from view.

He dropped to the ground to stare at visible feet beneath the chassis. A third pair appeared and Pete called out for Alex to come round. Gun poised, he walked over. If they were going to attack, now was the time.

29

PARANOIA IS A wonderful thing and Alex's fears mounted in his head, justified by events, but they were misplaced. The boys had just not told him of a last-minute change of plan and he supervised the removal of the gold from Florida with no further incident.

This meant he, Sarah and the kids could enjoy the first night of Seder, the Passover meal. The Rothsteins invited them over and they could hardly refuse such an offer even though neither of them were exactly religious. That said, Alex did feel a nostalgic twinge for his early childhood amid the memory of the stress of reading out a prayer in front of his entire extended family.

When the Cohens arrived, maids hustled the children into a playroom while Alex and Sarah were taken through to a dining room and Carolyn Greene, Arnold's wife made all the introductions. There was Benny Siegel with a floozy by his side, along with Mr. and Mrs. Lansky, Waxey Gordon plus one, and even Charlie Lucky.

"He's the stranger I couldn't leave at the door," explained Rothstein to the assembled throng, referring to one of the many Passover traditions. Sarah smiled as if getting the joke and Alex nodded like the comment meant something to him.

After cocktails were served and consumed, the children were brought in and everybody sat down at the dining table. There were the two Cohen boys and three Lansky kids but no Rothstein kin. Waxey's adult daughter put in an appearance just before they settled into their seats.

Arnold led the prayers and made sure the children received enough time to hide a piece of Matzah from the adults as generations of youngsters had done before. The mix of food and religion carried on for the next three hours until the group had eaten their way through the story of Exodus.

Alex found almost all the Hebrew difficult to follow, although Sarah seemed to fare better. The only element he recognized was the *Ma Nishtana*, the prayer from the youngest child past Bar Mitzvah age.

Arnold's fluency reminded Alex of his business partner's Orthodox origins, not that he showed any religious fervor on an ordinary day. Why was this night different from all other nights? Because Arnold was spouting Hebrew.

Once the meal eventually wound down, the women sidled off to talk among themselves and to leave the men alone.

"Freedom is a wonderful thing. We are lucky to live here and now."

Everyone nodded at Arnold's words and stared into their drinks, slowed by the volume of food consumed that night. Alex compared the life he would have experienced if his family had remained back home. Chances were, he, his parents and his siblings would have been killed by now.

The men did their best not to break the magic of the evening and avoided talking business. The trouble was that their work was the glue that kept them together. Alex found it hard to imagine sharing a meal with any of these guys if they didn't have a common interest in bootlegging, prostitution, gambling and drug running. These were happy days for them all.

30

ALEX SPENT MUCH of his time when not in the office back in the Richardson, almost as if he hankered for the simpler life of his early days in the country. In another compartment of his mind, he knew that spending time with his men in a speakeasy meant he was choosing not to spend it with Sarah and his boys.

Once the joint had been refurbished after the Maranzano attack, business returned quickly—its reputation was strong and locals knew it was backed by Alex and his associates. Word soon spread about what happened to the fellas who'd brought mayhem to the place.

Each night the venue buzzed with the sound of coffee cups clinking, filled to the brim with high quality hooch. The Richardson band played the latest tunes for dancing couples and the gaming room at the back occupied those who wanted to play cards while they drank themselves into oblivion. Meanwhile, the second floor unleashed opportunities for the man seeking company and a brew. Every male taste was catered for somewhere in the building.

Alex and his guys hid themselves away from the main room, separated by a two-way mirror so they could keep an eye on customers in case of trouble. Police raids were rare and almost always prearranged but drunks have a habit of escalating disputes into anger too quickly and can scare other johns away.

Ezra had the smarts to realize that the band needed improving. Why would couples go to a show on Broadway if they could come straight to the Richardson? So he paid singers from the most popular shows to do a stint at the club. When word spread, customers arrived two hours earlier and takings soared through the roof. After a few months, Ezra found he could pay the second-rank performers to sing instead and still the tables were full from eight in the evening.

ALEX SPRAWLED ON his favorite chair overlooking the Richardson's drinking room. His crew were still out making collections, having arranged to meet him later. He considered popping home for a short while, but knew the minute he announced his departure, an argument would follow and he didn't have the energy to have another row with Sarah.

The band tooted through some jazz numbers and then a singer took the stage and the mood changed. As soon as she appeared in front of the musicians, the audience applauded and that's what grabbed Alex's attention. As he peered into the darkened auditorium, he saw the sparkling white sequins of a shimmery dress until his eyes followed the contours of her body upwards as he reached her shoulders and head.

He squinted and looked again, then he scowled for a second. Alex didn't waste his time following show business, but he thought he might recognize the singer. His memory flicked through the female faces he'd seen over the years and stopped at one person he'd only observed twice in his life.

Ida Grynberg was a star of the Yiddish theater and had been onstage when he and Sarah had hit a show when he was recovering after the war. He'd also met her before France when he'd fed her opium habit. Both these events felt like ancient history now.

He flipped a switch on the wall and the sounds of the performance rattled through a small speaker near the ceiling. Alex had no ear for music, but he thought she sounded good and the response from the audience showed he was right. Two songs later and he moved to the back of the auditorium at a table of his own.

Now he was able to hear the lilt in her voice properly and could see her curves more easily. Both made him smile, and he noticed a warmth in the pit of his stomach. Alex doubted if Ida knew he was even there so he called a cigarette girl over and asked her to pass a hastily written note to the performer.

Twenty minutes later and she left the stage. A quick change into something more comfortable and Ida appeared at Alex's table, gliding in from nowhere.

"Thanks for the invitation, but have we met before?"

"Yes, but a long time ago under different circumstances. Forgive me, but I have always been an admirer of your work and would be so pleased if you'd do me the honor of sharing a drink with me."

"How could I refuse you, Mr. Cohen?"

"Call me Alex and, please, sit down."

◆ ◆ ◆

THREE DAYS LATER and Alex let himself into Ida's hotel room. She lay on the bed, fully clothed, with a pipe resting on the carpeted floor. He smiled, sat down on a chair to remove his shoes and messed about with the pipe until a plume of smoke escaped his lungs. Alex slumped next to Ida and allowed the intense joy of the opium to consume him.

After an hour unconscious, he opened one eye and saw only Ida's back. He raised a hand and touched her side but had no energy to do anything else. She was still asleep anyway. He closed his eyelid and returned to the inky blackness of his mind.

When he woke up again, Ida had vanished. Alex sat up with a start but relaxed when he saw her standing at the other side of the bedroom in only her underwear. A smile ripped across his face.

"I'm hungry."

"For me or the steak on my fork?"

"Both. Come here."

She did as she was told and brought the room service plate over. Ida fed him while he toyed with the straps on her camisole. He hadn't been so relaxed with a woman in a bedroom since he first slept with Sarah. And that was years ago.

Alex enjoyed spending time with Ida—she possessed that freewheeling indifference to public opinion, common to those who tread the boards. Her single-minded focus on her career kept her distant from long-term relationships, but that didn't mean she shunned the company of men. Far from it, but she used a pipe to take away the loneliness she felt at the end of every performance.

They remained next to each other until Ida stepped back, removed her clothing and slipped into bed. Alex did the same and thoughts of Sarah fizzled out of his mind.

ALEX PUT ON his clothes and glanced at the naked, sleeping Ida. She kept him alive with her wild carefree approach to life. She cared about her audience when onstage but the moment she walked down the steps, she focused entirely on what was important to her: hedonistic, raw experience. Back home, the contrast couldn't have been more stark as soon as he stepped into their hallway.

"I won't ask you where you've been because I am sick and tired of hearing your lies. Just tell me that you spoke with the consultant about David's knee."

The kid had tripped on his own feet the previous week and fallen on the sidewalk. Since then he'd been complaining about a pain in his right leg.

"Not yet but I'll get it sorted. It's been crazy busy at work."

Sarah faltered, pattered up to him and delivered a peck on his cheek. Then she recoiled with anger in her slits for eyes.

"Next time you sleep with someone behind my back at least have the decency to wipe her lipstick off your collar and not stink of her when you enter your family's home."

Alex let Sarah's fists pummel his chest until her energy abated and then he grabbed both her hands and pulled them down by her sides out of the way. This meant they stood inches apart, lips almost touching, staring into each other's eyes.

"I wouldn't be home so late if you showed some interest in me beyond complaining. And the streets are dangerous enough without you trying to hurt me. You need to treat me better before I want to spend more time with you and the boys."

Sarah fled upstairs and Alex heard her sobbing. He popped his head into the playroom and smiled as he watched the boys messing about with the nanny. He didn't interrupt them because they seemed so happy.

Alex hustled over to his bedroom, grabbed a change of clothing and rushed back out. All the while, Sarah's crying echoed around the house.

Over the next four years, Alex and Sarah were intimate four times. Once, the following day, when Alex returned to let Sarah know he had organized a doctor's appointment for David and three other occasions, each of which created another male heir–Asher, Elijah and Arik.

NOVEMBER 1927

31

WHEN THE HOLLAND Tunnel opened on November 12, cars lined up for nearly a mile to pay fifty cents to travel between New York and New Jersey. As vehicles trundled through the darkness of the world's longest road tunnel, Uncle Sam's Treasury was gouging its way through the money made by the Chicago outfit.

The US government's response to the bootlegging industry had been slow, in part because gangs operated beyond state lines and the cops did not. But that didn't mean there was no reaction—the Bureau of Prohibition had been formed and had hired bright men to bring down the hoods who were well organized and making money out of their illegal liquor enterprises.

Much focus was aimed at Chicago because of its relative proximity to the Windsor-Detroit supply line. This hit Alex and his friends square in their wallets, but they also understood that what happened first in the Windy City would be repeated closer to home in Manhattan.

Distilleries were smashed by federal agents and bootleg liquor poured down the drains. None of this was good for business. When the ordinary Joe popped over to a blind pig, they realized they were doing wrong, but surely did not consider themselves engaged in a criminal conspiracy with a bunch of cut-throat gangsters. The newspapers said otherwise. Takings were down and the fellas headed over to Arnold's suite for a meeting.

"We must do something about these bureau pinheads."

"What do you suggest, Meyer?"

"Pay them to look the other way. We've done that with the local cops all over the country. These guys out of uniforms need to feed their families, don't they?"

"Alfonse tried what you suggest and still they interrupt his work regularly. There's no reason we'll be more successful."

"Some of us, Alex, have a lower profile than Alfonse. No offense intended, Arnold."

"None taken, Charlie. Reporters seek me out and I respond politely to their questions in the hope they'll go away. Alfonse loves the publicity and the attention he gets from it."

"So what can we do about it?"

"Alex, perhaps the trick is to let them catch us."

"Are you out of your mind, Meyer?"

"Steady, Alex. What I mean is that if we allow the cops to find the odd warehouse or still, then they get the opportunity to call in the press hounds and show them how they are beating us to within an inch of our lives..."

"Meanwhile, we carry on in other locations and everyone is happy."

"While the main heat is in Chicago, we can probably get away with that here. But we need a different solution to protect our Detroit interests."

The men fell silent because Arnold was correct. They could hoodwink some dumb flatfoot with a half-empty warehouse but if the bureau sent any significant manpower over, they'd have a real job to keep all the speakeasies supplied with booze.

Alex decided to find a different place on the Canadian border to ship the booze over. He'd work with Abe Bernstein as they had a common interest in keeping the greenbacks flowing.

The men ironed out several details of the liquor business, as well as a few other matters and eventually they stood up to leave. Arnold asked Alex to stay a short while longer.

"There's something I'd like your assistance with, but I'd rather the others didn't find out."

"How can I help, Arnold?"

"The only thing I ask of anybody who works with me or for me is complete and utter loyalty. Without it, we are nothing. You and I understand this otherwise we would not be in the fortunate positions we find ourselves in."

"For sure. We live together, we fight together, but we die alone."

"Waxey was right. Trouble is that one of my associates has forgotten this simple truth. I have been informed he intends to share his knowledge of our operations with the cops."

"That's easy. A call to a captain in my pay and I can make the whole problem go away."

"If that was all that was required, I would have picked up the phone myself. This fellow is going to the Feds and I need him to be stopped, no matter what."

"Okay. We need to get to the guy before he makes his move."

"Exactly right. He mustn't sing, but whatever you do needs to be conducted without fuss. None of our mutual friends must hear about this or we will unnerve them and our circle of trust will get shattered. Also, we wouldn't want the Feds to come sniffing around later on."

"So he vanishes without trace or dies by natural causes. There aren't any other options that pop into my head."

"You are the right person for this, Alex. Just be aware he will be taken in for questioning tomorrow morning."

"That's not much time."

"Do whatever you need to stop Shlomo Tzvi squealing. Everything else is secondary to me."

THE BUREAU OF Prohibition had told Tzvi they'd collect him by taxi under police protection. Alex reckoned the speed of all this activity was designed to get a signed statement before the fella changed his mind. He was the first guy Alex had known who was prepared to rat on his people.

The ever-reliable Captain Frye furnished Alex with all the details he needed, so he was able to put together a plan before he went to bed in Ida's arms.

Ezra had borrowed a cab and uniform from their haulage interests and had stationed the vehicle outside the bureau offices at just the time Frye had said the Prohibition investigator would head out to meet Tzvi. Alex followed them in his own saloon.

They convoyed across Manhattan and went through the newly painted Holland Tunnel. Tzvi had been smart enough to lie low away from anyone who might have recognized him. Then they headed back the same way until the car sped past Fifth and Seventh Avenue and the Prohi investigator realized something was up.

Too late for him because Ezra locked the passenger doors and didn't stop until they reached the heart of Brownsville, deep in what the locals called Little Jerusalem, but the rest of the world knew as Brooklyn. Ezra stopped the taxi at the corner of Riverdale and Chester Avenue and the two men bustled Tzvi and the Prohi into a nearby building.

Ezra stuffed a gag into each of their mouths so that no one could hear any screams. This precaution was unnecessary because the joint was as empty as sin and the walls were thick and made of brick—no crummy tenement partitions here.

Alex and Ezra slapped Tzvi and the Prohi around a bit to get their attention and to disorient them slightly. Hands tied behind their backs, they were thrown into separate rooms and left lying on the floor in the semi-permanent half-light. With the doors slammed shut, Alex whispered his intentions to Ezra.

"Let's find out if Shlomo has anything to confess. He's on a one-way ticket to hell—and I don't even believe in hell."

"You're a good Jewish boy, of course you don't. What about the other guy?"

"Let's wait a while before deciding whether to kill him."

Alex entered Tzvi's room and kicked him in the kidneys. Then he picked him up by the armpits and slung him onto a chair, the only piece of furniture in the place.

"Why d'you do it, Shlomo?"

"Don't know what you're talking about. I ain't done nothing."

"If you treat me like a fool, then I'll become angry. You were sharing a cab with a Prohibition investigator who was taking you to his headquarters. Explain to me how you got yourself into this situation."

Three short, sharp breaths and Shlomo Tzvi unburdened himself.

"Money was tight and I had to cut a few corners, otherwise there was no food on my family's table. So we get pulled by a Prohi with a truckful of booze and they said they'd throw the book at me—I couldn't afford the fine. Or we could give them some information. Nothing much at first. The location of a truck we'd be using or the address of a warehouse. Then they wanted more and I didn't know what to do. I'd got in so far that I couldn't see a way of getting back. They told me I'd get a subpoena if I refused to cooperate. And here I am."

Alex allowed the dust to settle on the man's words and nodded his head. He understood the fella's situation only too well. If it wasn't for money, we'd all live immaculate lives. Alex shrugged and put his fingers deep into his pants pocket. His right hand retrieved a gun and he whipped the barrel out until it touched Shlomo's forehead. A single crack rang out as Alex squeezed the trigger once and Tzvi's brains blasted over the wall behind him in an almost perfect circle.

Ezra popped his head round the door to check that all was well. Alex signaled everything was fine and walked into the neighboring room. An acrid smell of urine hit his nose as he stepped inside. The man must have wet himself at the sound of the gunfire.

"Help me shift this guy out of here. The stench is unbearable."

Ezra dragged the Prohi out by his hair and along the corridor. At the far end was another empty office with white-painted brickwork and no furniture. Alex brought in three chairs so they could all get comfortable.

"What's your name, cop?"

"William Forster and I'm a Prohibition investigator."

"I asked for your name, not your life story, Bill."

"My name is William…"

A punch to the sternum from Ezra to shut him up and Bill crumpled in two. Alex stood up and sauntered toward the wheezing sack of humanity. He took a grip of the back of Bill's hair and pulled up his head so the guy could look him squarely in the eye.

"Bill. I want you to listen to me carefully. Can you do that for me?"

"Yes."

"Excellent. I need to find out what you got on our mutual friend next door. I'm guessing you were his handler otherwise he wouldn't have trusted you sufficiently to take the ride to your HQ."

Eyes darted left and right as Bill tried to think straight enough to figure out what to say.

"Yes."

"So what do you know, Bill?"

"Nothing. I mean, he was a reliable source and had come good for us five or six times. We leaned on him a bit and he folded like a cheap suit. We hadn't interviewed him yet. There's not much else I can say."

"Did he tell you who he worked for, for example?"

"No. We asked, but he was too scared. He demanded protection before he'd squawk."

"I believe you, Bill, because Shlomo was a coward and a family man. He wouldn't have wanted to put his wife and children in harm's way. As you heard, his family has lost a father, husband and provider. Do you have kith and kin, Bill?"

"A wife. We were planning on having children next year."

Alex smiled and Bill returned the expression. Then he blasted a hole in Bill's chest; he gurgled briefly and slumped onto the floor.

"Call some reliable guys to get this mess cleared up. I'm going back to the city. I'd forgotten how much I hate Brooklyn."

SMOKE. MUD. BLOOD. One moment his lips were pressed against the soil, the next Alex was scurrying along the ground, hauling himself forward by the elbows. Five feet, then ten. All the time he altered his direction based on where he could locate Bobby's screams.

Another five feet and bullets zinged across the muddy space between Alex and his friend. Eventually the strafing ceased, and he made it to lie by Bobby's side. The guy was blubbering and screaming alternately.

"Bobby, you'll be fine. I'm here now."

Alex said those words before he'd raised his head to assess how Bobby was doing. The man's body was a pool of blood surrounded by limbs. How could something as small as a bullet do so much damage to one person?

More strafing and when the sniper rested, Alex looked up again. The German was only forty feet ahead and Alex had seen enough flashes from the soldier's rifle to know precisely where he was. When he turned to look at Bobby, his friend was silent.

"Bobby?"

Dead. Alex felt a tear drip off his cheek and then he dug in, using Bobby's corpse as a shield. Training his scope on the location from where the sniper had been firing, Alex waited. He saw soil, grass trampled underfoot, mud and then a slight glint which told him the guy was still there, getting ready for another assault.

Only this time, Alex aimed at where that reflection had been and squeezed off a round. Then he stood by. For ten, twenty, thirty seconds but nothing. He raised his head slightly but nobody fired at him. He shuffled his way over and found the German corpse with a bullet in his skull. Seventeen years old, Alex reckoned, and a leg blown off in some earlier skirmish. They gave him a medal for taking so long to murder the cripple that he let Bobby die...

32

ARNOLD THANKED ALEX when he reported back later in the day, having cleaned himself up and dusted himself down. He made a mental note to share Arnold's financial appreciation with Ezra, who had done all the hard work with virtually no notice.

The consequences of their journey to Brownsville lasted much longer than the trip back to the Lower East Side. Bill's disappearance took two days to get noticed. By the time his superiors had filed a missing person report, Shlomo and Bill's bodies were propping up the foundations of a building in the Bronx, a residential block being constructed by one of Arnold's investments.

That meant the cops had to resort to breaking down doors and generally making a nuisance of themselves. Funny thing was that the Prohis were not taking bribes—for the first time since the Volstead Act came into force. The orders came from high up and landed on the heads of the low-paid investigators with a very clear message: get the scum who attacked one of our own. Nobody spoke for Tzvi, whose widow received a pension from Arnold on account of his mysterious vanishing.

Then the retaliation began. Every warehouse the Prohis thought might contain a crate of liquor was raided. Heads were cracked and fresh supplies were met at the bridges or tunnels into the town.

There wasn't a gang on Manhattan that didn't suffer. From Harlem in the north to Wall Street at the tip of the island, business was down and prospects were bleak. The Italians, the Jews and what was left of the Irish and German gangs were finding out what happened when federal investigators joined forces with local flatfeet. Not even Frye would answer Alex's calls.

"HOW LONG DO you think we can take this heat?"

"Alex, the cops aren't letting up. I can't see how we'll survive this for very much longer."

"Let's not get alarmist, Meyer. The Feds bend with the wind. All we do is wait for something to happen at the other end of the country and then resources will be flung over there as a knee-jerk reaction to some other calamity befalling this once great nation."

"Easy for you to say, Arnold, as you possess the reserves to lean on beyond anything the rest of us can muster."

"Tell your people to lie low. Keep a skeleton staff at each of your speakeasies and soak up any income from prostitution, gaming and union protection. The Feds understand that if they remove gambling, sex and alcohol from the law-abiding Joe then there'll be riots in the streets. Even the goyim won't stand for that."

"These problems would vanish in an instant if they found the guy who offed the Prohi."

"Let's not talk like that, Charlie. They want to divide us but we will always be stronger than that. We are a union."

"We live together, we fight together and we die alone."

Charlie Lucky sipped his drink and the others fell silent too. Arnold and Alex were the only two who knew what had really happened and how close all the guys in the suite had got to serving hard time if Tzvi had spilled his guts, because the chain of command led straight to the four fellas.

"That may be so, Arnold, but the other gangs are fit to burst. They might not prove anything but word on the street was that Alex executed the hit on your orders. I'm not saying they're right or wrong. Doesn't matter either way, but they are acting like it's true."

"Let them bleat."

"Easy to say, Alex, but Maranzano has put out a hit on you both. Others are holding fire, but you two have unfinished business from a few years back and he's fixing to sort everything."

"Charlie, is that for certain?"

"That's straight from reliable sources. I got dealings with Maranzano so I learn things I probably shouldn't. From what I can tell, it's a matter of days before a rifle is trained on you or you're found hanged with a knife in your back outside City Hall."

Alex cast a glance at Arnold, who threw a worried smile in his direction. The vultures were circling.

ARNOLD ROTHSTEIN LEFT for a vacation in Florida under Charlie's protection. Everyone figured the Big Bankroll would be safer if he laid low for a while and Miami-Dade county seemed the best place for him to rest. There were enough of Charlie's business partners operating casinos there for

Arnold to not only remain far away from any trouble but be entertained along the way.

Alex could not say the same. Although nobody said it, he felt they blamed him for their current troubles, even though he was only acting on behalf of the Big Bankroll. Arnold had coached Charlie since he was a boy so it was the Italian who explained how Alex should stay in town and face the heat else the gangs would follow Arnold south and who knew what would happen.

Charlie was right; they needed a worm to catch their fish but Alex wasn't happy about being left to dangle on the line. Maranzano alone had proved himself to be a formidable foe who would stop at nothing to see him dead. Their altercation over the Richardson was small potatoes compared to the revenue loss they were suffering now.

What Alex didn't want to admit to himself was that his ego drove him to remain in Manhattan too. There was no way he was going to allow himself to be sent packing by a bunch of hoods. This was his city and he would live in it until he was good and ready to leave. And not a moment before. This hubris almost made him forget those around him.

"You and Massimo should take a vacation in Windsor or somewhere safe. If they come gunning for me, there's no need for you to get caught in the crossfire."

"We'll be okay, Alex. I've got informants listening in every drinking hole from here to Central Park. As soon as they do anything, we'll know about it."

"And we're bringing in some fresh blood from Chicago and Detroit. These old men have enjoyed the easy life for too long. Typical, they feel a little heat down their necks, they panic. Their days are numbered. The moment has come for a new generation to step forward."

For the first moment in a week, Alex headed home to check on his family. Sarah sat in the living room and the kids played somewhere in the apartment. She glanced up from her book, half-smiled and returned to her story. Alex squatted on a stool next to her and placed a hand on her knee. With that, she looked straight at him and closed her novel.

"What's the matter, Alex?"

"I can't be sure, but things might get ugly."

"How bad?"

"There are business interests aligning against us."

"You don't need to talk to me like I'm one of your people. What's happening?"

Alex stared into her eyes and saw concern reflected back.

"I did some work for Arnold which meant the police have descended on the city. He's off to lie low for a while and I need to take the heat for him."

"You're fighting the cops?"

"Oh, no. It's the other bosses. They are losing money hand over fist and blame me."

"Will they kill you?"

"They'll give it a damn good try but I have too many people looking out for me to let that happen, hon'."

"I don't want to start an argument with you, honestly, but why suddenly come back here to tell me this?"

"Because I don't want you and the boys to get hurt. For your own safety, I think you should move out of the city until this has blown over."

"Where? For how long?"

"I don't want to be too dramatic, but Canada. There's a town called Windsor close to the border. It's only a few hours from here and it's under my control."

"Should we pack for a weekend?"

"Assume weeks rather than days, but it could all blow over in a short while. This is a precaution. Nothing more."

"And I suppose we should leave tonight? I mean, that would unsettle the kids most, wouldn't it?"

"Tomorrow. The day after at the latest. Give them time to get used to the idea, but go. I need to focus all my energies on sorting this out and can't afford to become sidetracked worrying about you."

"I never knew you cared."

33

THREE DAYS AFTER Sarah and the children traveled to Windsor, Maranzano made his first move. His men attacked the Richardson and, when Alex stepped inside, he experienced a terrible flashback but had learned enough in the intervening years not to retaliate but to sit and wait instead. His hours with Arnold were not wasted and the spirit of the street thug, Waxey was receding.

Alex spent the time preparing for the inevitable attack. The next day, he opened up a new venue on the other side of Madison Square, with metal bars over the frontage and a steel door, all hidden behind wooden fencing, until now. Clients entered easily but it could be closed down to outsiders immediately—unwelcome gangs or the cops alike.

Within a day, his old customers had found their way over to the new Richardson. The stage was smaller and Ida was none too happy, but a fur coat changed her countenance and Alex and his fellas carried on business as usual.

Two days later and the beer stopped flowing. No matter what route they used, Alex, Meyer and Charlie couldn't get their trucks into Manhattan. They even looked at using trains but as soon as they sent the first haul down the tracks, Maranzano's men robbed the train leaving blood on the line. Ezra and Massimo hit back with three groups of fellas who headed backstage at a number of Maranzano cathouses and slashed the face of every nafka they saw.

The response was swift and brutal. The old Sicilian sent his guys to ransack warehouses and trucks, shooting at any fella in the vicinity. This was a bloodbath on the New York streets which even the politicians were unable to ignore. Headlines screamed for the authorities to take action and Alex decided it was time to oblige.

"WE MUST CLIP this Mustache Pete. The old timer has gone too far."

Ezra and Massimo nodded in agreement, sick and tired of sitting on their hands the past week.

"Maranzano has been taking liberties at our expense."

"True. The fault lies at our door for the heat that's raining down on our fair city but I have tolerated this for long enough. Today we take the fight to Maranzano."

Alex described his plan until the two men understood what they needed to do and how they would win the war and not just the next battle. With everyone clear, they set to work.

Mulberry Street lay three blocks west of the Bowery and you would be forgiven for thinking you'd moved country if you took a walk along Grand Street. From the warmth of the shtetl to the cold winds of Little Italy in the length of twenty paces. The Hebrew lettering on the signage vanished and was replaced with the language of southern Europe.

Onward they marched until Massimo's gang arrived at Maranzano's headquarters at Mulberry and Broome. Within thirty seconds, Ezra's men appeared from the north and they waited for the signal. Right on cue, Alex appeared in his car, screeched to a halt and let rip with automatic gunfire, each slug tearing a little more away from the frontage.

By the time the vehicle zoomed off and Alex pulled in round the corner, a hail of bullets was erupting out of the building, aimed at nowhere in particular. Everyone kept their heads down and waited again. These fellas knew better than to make a move with so much death flying around the streets.

Eventually the Maranzano guns fell silent but Ezra and Massimo did nothing. Alex sensed the tension in the air he breathed as his men were itching to respond. Instead they waited for an eternity. Each inhalation and exhalation took a lifetime.

With every civilian having fled the neighborhood as soon as the first shot rang out, there was nothing to hear except your own lungs. Then the astute men in the building would have sensed a low rumble, which built in volume over the following five minutes. Before they realized where the noise was coming from, they found themselves surrounded—not just by the twenty guys who walked over with Ezra and Massimo, but by at least sixty more.

From where had these troops come? Chicago and Detroit. Alex knew the difficulties in the Lower East Side were hurting Alfonse and Abe as much as Meyer, Charlie and Arnold. So he'd placed two phone calls and asked for support. And here it was.

Having pinned Maranzano down inside his headquarters, Ezra's men cut the phone line and then the power cable too. Now the head of the snake was isolated, some of the Sugar House gang peeled off to ransack Maranzano property. Alex had previously furnished Abe with a list of venues and Abe picked professionals who could be guaranteed not to lose their heads and go on some kind of rampage. For Alex, this was a military campaign.

Abe's men returned at dusk at which point Alfonse's fellas took their leave of the main scene and assaulted the places on their list. As the sun rose, there were still forty fellas surrounding Mulberry and Broome with the remaining number taking a rest. They were in this for the long haul and Alex had prepared his guys to expect the siege to last for days not hours.

The one group Alex normally would have relied on was the cops, but because they'd created this situation by not turning their usual blind eye, he'd put in place a different plan for them.

While Tammany Hall's influence had reduced over the decades, the powerhouse still held sway and the politicians earned their kickbacks. Arnold helped Alex meet the right guy to have a quiet word. The cops would spend their time attending to the venues which were attacked and somehow Maranzano's corner of paradise would be left alone.

By noon, a voice shouted out that they wanted to have a discussion and one by one, the streets were vacated with only hundreds of empty shells on the ground to remind anyone that there had been any action there at all. That and every wall and pane of glass being shot to hell.

The military campaign turned Little Italy into a war zone for a day but the truce held, not just for the next few nights but even after Alfonse and Abe's men had gone home. Past Chanukah and on toward Passover.

APRIL 1928

34

THE DUST SETTLED on the street battles of the previous year but no one was foolish enough to believe that everything had been forgotten. Arnold returned to the city in time for his traditional New Year party and Alex brought Sarah along, despite her misgivings. And who could blame her?

As soon as the Passover festivities were over, Charlie updated Alex on the latest news from the Maranzano crew.

"Word on the street is that Maranzano wants you dead."

"There's bad blood there, for sure. I thought Maranzano might have let things go as we are all making money again and it was only ever business."

"Don't take this the wrong way but you do not understand because you are Jewish. The Sicilian in this Mustache Pete will never forget and never forgive. It's not in his nature."

"It's a vendetta; I get it."

"Like you have no idea. The trouble is that I can't help protect you. My position is supported by Maranzano even though Arnold and I do a lot of business together. You must find another way to take care of this problem."

"If you find out more, will you at least let me know?"

"Naturally. I just need to be careful that Maranzano doesn't get wise."

Alex needed to get some muscle behind him—and something that had more influence than a bunch of fellas with machine guns. He'd done that before but the old Sicilian was like a wasp in his ear.

Half a century before Alex arrived in the land of the free, the Democratic Party had wrestled control of New York though a simple cocktail of intimidation and bribery; both delivered by the gangs that ran the street corners. The center of the Democrats in Manhattan was Tammany Hall, so that was the natural place for Alex to head. If he could get the politicians behind him, then Alex could use their sway to keep Maranzano off his back.

George W. Olvany had become boss of Tammany Hall four years earlier and had instituted a series of grifts to line his pockets and those of his friends and business associates. Arnold mixed in his circles so, by extension,

Alex secured a meeting with the man who decided who would be Mayor of New York.

"I understand your problem, Alex, and there is nothing I would like more than to help one of Arnold's friends."

"That is great news. No one in Tammany looked good during the November troubles. Who wanted to celebrate Thanksgiving with so much blood on the street...?"

"...and liquor flowing down the drains."

"Exactly right. What a waste all round, but my sources tell me that certain individuals are planning to settle old scores and I hope you agree that this fine city has no need for that bloodletting."

"This is not Chicago."

"So can you help me clip Maranzano's wings?"

The former judge sipped his tea laced with gin and considered his options.

"The question isn't whether I am able to give you the assistance you crave; of course I can. Tammany Hall and your kind have been doing business for years. You and I need to reach some accommodation to grease the machinery to resolve this matter in your favor."

Alex sighed as quietly as he could muster. With these men and their municipal and government job titles, it always boiled down to how much gelt they would get today. They could never see beyond the end of their noses. Their beaks were buried so deep in the trough, they could barely breathe.

"Do you have a figure in mind, George?"

"Well, a one-off donation would be appreciated and enable me to mobilize appropriate forces at my disposal."

"The payments we make every month aren't enough?"

"Alex, you sound as though you begrudge our arrangement."

"Not at all. I'm finding it hard to understand what I get for my money."

"Peace of mind. You sleep soundly in your mistress's bed at night knowing the cops won't burst through the door and take you away with your shorts around your ankles."

Olvany scribbled on a piece of paper, folded it and pushed it over to Alex, who opened it and stared at the handwritten number. It was ridiculously high. Greed oozed out of every digit. Alex allowed himself a snort of laughter. He didn't like this Tammany boss and his Waspish manner.

"I appear to have wasted both of our time, George. I asked you for aid and you've offered me a trade at a price I am not prepared to pay."

◆ ◆ ◆

"ALEX, ONE OF my men tells me Maranzano has brought in a Jew to his crew; that's never happened before."

"Any idea about this guy, Charlie?"

"None. I haven't seen him and Maranzano never mentioned the fella, but my informant has never been wrong."

"Should I be worried?"

"The Mustache Pete has never had any time for Jews. The Sicilian only trusts people from the island."

"Until now, it would seem. Looks like I will have to take the fight to Maranzano once and for all."

BACK IN HIS office, squirreled away inside the depths of an anonymous building, Alex took stock of the situation with Massimo and Ezra.

"If we do nothing, then one day soon they'll discover me with a bullet in my head."

"We've got you covered. There's an extra security detail in place and we have eyes on every street corner."

"Ezra, that's good to know but I can't live my life like this. We need to know the threat is over."

"How do you want us to do that?"

"Massimo, I wish I had an answer but I don't know. Short of driving over and shooting the guy, my mind's a blank."

"You want me to do it?"

"No! Such a direct assault on the man won't solve anything. There'll always be another Maranzano. What we need to do is figure out how to remove his sort from the world. One bullet is no solution."

They were silent for a spell as each of the three did their best to square the circle. At one level, Alex wanted to get Chicago and Detroit behind him again and annihilate the Maranzano clan but he understood how Abe did business with them, as did Arnold. So that would never be acceptable to his many partners. There had to be a way though; he couldn't take the thought of sitting in that room waiting to die.

"Why don't we call for a meeting to clear the air, then whack everyone who shows up?"

"And, Massimo, what's stopping anybody who survives that slaughter visiting us the following day? If you're going to make a suggestion at least think it through first."

"Sorry, boss."

Then Alex's phone rang, and Arnold's voice requested the pleasure of his company in his suite at his earliest convenience.

"One of you guys come with me. I've got to visit a friend."

ARNOLD, MEYER AND Charlie were sitting down, slowly sinking into the leather seating when Alex walked in. Benny Siegel paced behind the couch housing Arnold and Charlie. The man never stopped walking the whole time. His continual movement added a sense of urgency which would otherwise have been missing from the room, given their discussions.

"Thanks for popping over, Alex. We've got some matters we need to discuss."

Alex chose a comfortable chair and lounged in it, conscious that all eyes were aimed at him and knowing this casual request had to have something to do with Maranzano. Charlie found it particularly hard to maintain eye contact with him; a sure sign of trouble ahead.

"What's on your mind, Arnold?"

"Just some business we need to put in order."

Benny barged into the center of the group forcing Alex and Arnold to break eye contact.

"Can we please get to the point? Alex, you must stop gunning for Maranzano as it's bad for all our businesses."

"How about stopping Maranzano? From what I understand, the Mustache Pete has put a hit out on me. Arnold, you've invited the wrong fella over. You should tell Maranzano he should stand down."

"That won't happen, Alex. Maranzano is a made man and is untouchable."

"Charlie, I know. And that's why Benny wants to cut to the chase. He can smell the Italian outfit breathing down his neck."

"Don't be like that, Alex, and Benny stop wearing a hole in my rug and sit down."

Siegel walked over and slumped in a spare chair. Throughout this time, he spun his hat round the fingers of one hand. Meanwhile, Arnold did his best to keep the atmosphere calm even though Alex looked daggers at anyone who spoke.

"We understand you've been talking to Tammany Hall, and that isn't good for business. Politicians are only interested in grifting and not in anything else."

"I was checking out what options I have. You are right, Arnold. All that happened was that Olvany tried a shakedown, so I walked away."

Then the phone rang, and all heads turned to the sound of its bell. Arnold sauntered over and picked up the device from the receiver. Within a minute, he'd replaced the handset and walked over to Alex. Then he tapped him on his jacket shoulder.

"You need to get home. Looks like someone has taken your youngest."

35

"THEY TOOK ARIK an hour ago."

"Tell me exactly what happened, hon'."

"I was shopping and the kids were out with Leah."

"Who?"

"Leah Rinat, our maid."

"Is that normal?"

"Yes, Alex. The three youngest go out with her most afternoons, weather permitting. Anyway, they were in the park and some guy rushed up, grabbed Arik and ran off."

With those words, Sarah began to sob again and Alex held her in his arms until the tears subsided.

"Do you trust Leah?"

"Of course. What a question."

"Have a think before you answer me, Sarah. Can we trust Leah?"

She remained silent for several seconds before responding.

"I thought I did, but now you're asking me with that voice, I'm not certain. She brought references and has been nothing but helpful. Maybe she's just been biding her time."

"Don't worry either way. I'll get Ezra to have a quiet word with her and we'll check out her story."

"What are you planning to do?"

"Just talk and nothing else. You need not be concerned. She won't be harmed no matter what. Chances are she's clean."

"Promise?"

"I do. The most important issue right now is to find out where Arik is and to bring him home."

"Do you know who has done this terrible thing? He's only two years old."

"Not yet. We will and I shall get him back."

Alex met Ezra in the kitchen for a private word. While he had no clue who might have physically kidnapped his son, you didn't need to be a genius to see the person pulling the strings was Salvatore Maranzano. From the way Arnold touched him on the shoulder, Alex knew that his trusted friend had figured it out too before he'd even put the phone down.

"Make some enquiries, Ezra. Find out if our maid was involved. Be very gentle with her because she may be completely innocent."

"And if she's not?"

"Extract all the information you can from her and ensure she meets with an accident. Sarah must suspect nothing, so let the calamity happen next month."

"Understood, boss. You reckon this has anything to do with business?"

"Of course. Any normal kidnapping and we would have received a call by now demanding a ransom to be paid. The fact the phone hasn't rung screams out who is the culprit."

"Maranzano."

"Yep, but that doesn't tell us where they are holding Arik. I have to know and fast."

"I'll ask Charlie Lucky if he's heard anything today."

"Okay. Get Massimo to send out his men. Scour Central Park for witnesses and I will see if Frye can earn his fee this week."

An hour later, Alex had calmed down Sarah enough so that he felt he could leave her alone. He left one of his foot soldiers at the apartment and hightailed out of the joint. For all that time, no call came through, which confirmed Alex's belief that Maranzano was behind this.

He returned to his office and did his best to wait. Alex knew his men would do their jobs and get him an address, but he wanted it to happen now, so he could regain the sense of control that Maranzano had snatched away from him along with his child.

Ezra passed him a coffee but all he could do was to stare at the drink until it got cold. Alex ground his molars and did his best to get Arik's image out of his mind. Then Massimo popped his head round the door and whispered in Ezra's ear, all the while his eyes peered at Alex. More whispers back and Ezra uncrossed his legs.

"We have news."

"Spill."

"Two of our guys spotted three Maranzano fellas with a kid matching Arik's description."

"Where?"

"Washington and Vestry."

"West side. Near Pier 29?"

"That's the one. A warehouse like any other on the street."

"And not in Maranzano's territory. That means he's getting protection."

"Let's not worry about those details right now and focus on bringing him out safely."

"I know; just expressing a thought. Time to go fishing near the Hudson."

TWENTY MINUTES LATER, Alex, Ezra and Noga Menahem stood on the opposite side of the street from an unassuming entrance with a sign above the door announcing 'Reilly Parts Inc'.

"Any idea how many more beyond the three you saw go in with my boy?"

"No one has come in or out since I arrived here. It looks like a disused husk of a building. Used to be a printing press back in the day."

"In that case, let's pay them a visit."

Alex sent Noga round the rear while he and Ezra searched for a way to get in without knocking on the front door. On the side, facing the river, was an open window on the first floor. Ezra pushed his arm through the gap and unlocked the adjacent pane of glass. A kick through the adjoining strut created a big enough space for both men to get through.

They crouched in the room, an office with desks, chairs and all the usual crap of a normal business that had gone bust. A thick layer of dust formed a patina of dirt across everything they touched. Alex listened at the door but heard nothing on the other side so gingerly he turned the creaking doorknob and popped his head into the corridor. No sign of anyone or anything.

Ezra and Alex crept along the empty passageway, checking on every room they went past. Out into a main reception area which led onto more offices on the other side. Still nothing. A set of stairs headed up to the second floor and another down to the basement. Ezra gestured up or down to Alex, who responded by pointing to the second floor. A nod and they scampered upstairs.

The stairwell opened up into a vast space filled with derelict printing machines. Some had paper inside them as though they had been abandoned halfway through publishing the local newspaper. Others were plain empty.

From nowhere, Alex's ears pricked to attention as he heard Arik's muffled voice. It sounded frightened and Ezra grabbed his shoulder to offer him support—and to prevent him from dashing off and doing something foolish in the heat of the moment.

Ezra's eyes flitted to the far side of the plant and Alex nodded. Still silent, they scurried over until they caught sight of a more open area near a window. With his hands bound by string and a gag stuffed in his mouth, Arik sat whimpering. Three men stood nearby, towering over the little boy. Alex felt the muscles in his arms tense and he gripped his gun even tighter.

ALEX COULD SEE the three guys were carrying pieces and there was no way he could guarantee Arik would survive if he started shooting. At this point, Noga arrived on the scene to even up the numbers. Despite his appearance, there was still too much danger in firing at will. They needed to get closer.

Noga edged ahead using a printing press as cover. Alex followed on behind, realizing he had a good idea. By the time Noga stopped shuffling forward, Alex had a clear line of sight on two of the three kidnappers, but that was not enough. One bullet was all that it would take to kill his little boy.

Meantime, Ezra had positioned himself the other side of the printing press and Alex espied the top of his head bobbing just above the machinery. Arik kicked off, whimpering more, and Alex snapped.

He squeezed the trigger and a slug spat out of the barrel and landed squarely in the chest of the nearest guy. Before he had the chance to crumple onto the ground his companion straightened his shooting arm and inhaled before firing his piece, and that was his mistake. Noga sent a bullet to his heart and a third shot rang out.

For a second, Alex couldn't tell quite what had happened. He blinked and saw his son sitting still in his chair but he had no idea if he was alive or dead. A blur of movement and the third guy ran past and away. Ezra and Noga gave chase leaving Alex to leap forward and wrestle Arik free from the handkerchief stuffed into his mouth and to undo the ropes tying his wrists and feet.

Alex picked his boy up in his arms and ran him down the steps and out onto the sidewalk. Into his car and back home so Arik could bask in the warmth of his mother's embrace. Before anyone could say a word, Alex smiled at the scene before him, turned and walked out to return to Pier 29.

Ezra stood on the street corner but Alex couldn't see Noga anywhere.

"What's cooking?"

"We chased the guy into a building half a block from here. Noga's keeping watch."

"How can one man cover all the entrances?"

"You'll see. It's fine, we've cornered him."

They hustled along the street while they spoke until they reached a low wall, behind which was a single-story construction. A door, a window and not much else to make it stand out, it looked as though it used to be an office but like the Reilly printers, the joint had seen better days.

"Noga said there's no back entrance. He hung round this neighborhood when he was a kid. He robbed from these places so he knows what he's talking about. Our guy has fled into a dead end."

Alex grinned and pulled out his gun. Ezra followed him until they caught up with Noga.

"You wait here a short while; it's time for me to have a conversation with this man."

The two men readied themselves in case of trouble, but kept their hands in their pockets because they couldn't imagine Alex needing any help.

He stormed toward the door, checking left and right for any sign of his quarry. A kick and the wood ripped off its hinges, then he trained his gun into the gloomy darkness ahead of him. A crash and Alex ran down the hallway and arrived at a far room whose door was wide open. Pointing his pistol into the space in front of him, he edged inside and stopped at the sight of a man standing by a desk, staring back at him like a rabbit caught in the lights of an oncoming truck.

Alex aimed his gun low and fired at one ankle causing blood to splat outwards just as the guy fell down and squealed with the pain of the bullet tearing through his flesh. Alex rushed forward and slammed his foot on the guy's wrist, forcing him to let go of his own firearm.

Then Alex dragged him by the scruff of his neck out of the room, down the corridor and out onto the street. Ezra and Noga grabbed him by the arms and led him away with Alex in tow. They bundled him into the back of the car and bombed across town until they reached the other side of the city and a quiet empty warehouse on home turf.

"WHY?"

Brunello Masi stared at Alex but remained silent.

"Why did you steal my son?"

Nothing. Cold eyes bored into Alex's skull.

"Who told you to do it? There's no way it was your idea."

Still no response, which made Alex well up with anger. He lunged forward, fingers forming a fist, and slammed a punch into Masi's face, so forceful that two teeth flew out and landed on the floor, causing a trickle of blood to drip out of the corner of his mouth.

"You'd better understand one thing. You tried to harm my boy and the only reason you are alive is because I know it was not your idea. So what you need to do is spill your guts before I cut you a new hole."

"I'm not giving up nobody."

Alex pulled out a blade and stabbed the knife deep into Masi's thigh; he released a bloodcurdling yelp that subsided into a whimper. Alex kneeled down so his mouth was next to Masi's left ear and whispered, "Who?"

The guy clenched his teeth and tried to purse his lips as best he could. No name was forthcoming so Alex stood up and smiled.

"Watch him."

Then he walked out of the building and returned thirty minutes later with a bag. Masi looked quizzically at him, beads of sweat falling from his forehead. His eyes opened wide when Alex swiveled round to reveal a screwdriver in his hand.

"The choice is yours. Tell me what I want to know or take the consequences."

The man's irises reflected his inner conflict. If he didn't give up a name, he faced a long period of pain and almost certain death from his inevitable injuries or Alex's anger. If Masi ratted his boss out, then he had a chance of living today, but the only way he could survive until morning was to skip town and never return. Even then, he'd spend the rest of his life not knowing if his next breath would be his last.

"If I tell you, will you let me live?"

"Speak the truth and I'll not only spare your soul but I shall give you some scratch and a train ticket to New Jersey. That way you'll be able to get out of town and vanish."

His eyes flitted side-to-side again as Masi weighed up his odds. He swallowed hard and tried to clear his throat but choked instead. Alex indicated to Ezra who took out a bottle and poured a few drops onto Masi's awaiting tongue. A smile briefly appeared on his face and vanished almost immediately as he remembered where he was and why he was there.

"Shmuel Hayyim."

"Who the hell...?"

"Shmuel Hayyim. He's in with Maranzano."

"Never heard of him and since when did that cockroach work with Jews?"

Without waiting for an answer, Alex dug the screwdriver into Masi's stomach and then yanked it out with a twist.

"Make me believe you."

"It's the truth. Maranzano has let a Yid into his outfit. None of us know why but there it is. If I give up an Italian, you'll find out and I'm a dead man for sure. You gotta believe me."

Alex eyeballed Masi and then turned to face Ezra, one eyebrow raised. His friend nodded and glanced at Masi who winced. There was a river of blood pouring out of the guy's body.

"I believe you. We'll take you to a medic we know and then get you out of the city."

"Thank you."

Those were the last words Brunello Masi uttered because Alex took his gun out of his pants pocket, shoved it next to Masi's temple and squeezed the trigger.

"Clear this mess up. I'm going back to be with my family."

36

ALEX WAS NO sooner through the door than Sarah stormed towards him, anger in her eyes and her body language. Before she opened her mouth, Alex could see how she felt.

"What the hell is going on, Alex?"

"How's Arik doing?"

"Just fine under the circumstances; no thanks to you."

"I got him home safe and sound."

"Don't talk to me like I'm some kind of moron. Yes, you brought him back but the only reason he was taken in the first place was because of you... and your business."

Sarah spat out the last two words with utter disdain. She stood at the other side of the hallway, almost as though she couldn't bring herself to be physically near him. Alex attempted to maintain his authority but she had a point, even though he had no intention of admitting that to her.

"The money I make means we can afford a place like this. Don't sneer at our success."

He stared Sarah down and clenched his jaw.

"Has he said anything about what happened?"

"Nothing. Hasn't spoken since he came home."

"Eaten?"

"A slice of *matzah*, but nothing else. He's hidden himself in his bedroom."

Alex nodded and sighed. He knew this conflict would get them nowhere. Instead, he walked toward Arik's room and Sarah followed without trying to stop him. Her fight wasn't with him at all, just frustration at not being able to keep the children safe.

Arik sat on the floor, playing with a fire truck. When his parents entered, he looked up for a second but carried on rocking the toy back and forth. Alex plonked himself next to his son and Sarah went the other side.

"Scary day, huh?"

Arik nodded and continued to move the toy round the floor.

"You were very brave. The way you handled yourself with those men."

Alex casually put an arm around his son and dangled his hand on the boy's shoulder. He leaned into his father with both hands still gripping his toy. Sarah reached out and planted a palm on his leg to show she cared too.

"Can you remember them saying anything to you while you were with them?"

Arik shrugged in silence. A minute later, he asked: "Did you kill them?"

"You don't have to worry your pretty little head about anything like that."

"Will they be back?"

"No, you'll never see them again, you can be certain of that."

Sarah's body stiffened as the conversation turned to what had happened in the warehouse. Arik had said nothing and Ezra had skated round the truth, clearly not sure how much he should impart.

"I saw blood come out of the men."

"We had to get you away from those no-goods because they wouldn't let you go."

"Is that why your friends and you had guns?"

"The most important thing was to make certain you were safe. What happened to them didn't matter."

"Are they dead?"

"That's why you don't have to worry about them coming back."

"Did you kill them?"

"Are you hungry? Your mama said you haven't eaten much since you got home."

"Shall we get you some lokshun soup?"

Arik's face lit up at the mention of his favorite food and Sarah took him by the hand to the dining room while the housekeeper heated some up from her earlier mealtime efforts. Alex followed the two out of the bedroom and made a quick phone call before he joined them for some lokshun. It reminded him of being a kid back in the old country. Now he had his own children to feed.

Once Arik had consumed as much as his stomach would allow, Sarah took him to bed. The boy was exhausted and didn't know it, so there were tears before he eventually settled down to sleep. Alex moved into the sitting room and lounged on a couch, the fingertips of one hand spread out resting on his forehead.

"You tired?"

"Yeah, rescuing children takes it out of you."

"Did you find out who organized the attack?"

"Yep. They'll get theirs, don't you worry, hon'."

"Before you kill them, make them hurt."

"I didn't think you liked the way I resorted to violence."

"I don't but Arik just told me how frightened he was until he saw his daddy standing in the gloom. Why did they take our Arik?"

"A foolish man attacked my family when he should have just gone for me. He will pay for that mistake."

"Make him scream for mercy. Let the momzer learn about pain and anguish."

"Stop talking like that. You've never once acted as though violence was the answer to any of our problems and you shouldn't do it this time. It's turning you... ugly."

Alex didn't have the right words to describe how she made him feel but it was unsettling. She abhorred his aggression and the way he'd achieved his success. For her to speak like that unnerved him. He had to get away, so he stood up and walked out of the apartment, leaving her dazed and confused on the couch.

AND INTO IDA'S arms. Alex's first thought was to check into a hotel but then he realized he wanted to be apart from Sarah but not alone and he was not prepared to spend money on a nafka. She might not have been expecting him—he didn't call ahead—but Ida hid her annoyance reasonably well.

She had readied herself for bed before Alex's arrival and clung to a dressing gown wrapped tightly around her body. Alex walked past her and headed straight for the drinks cabinet. He poured himself a vodka tonic and offered Ida a Cosmo, although he didn't have the energy to mix the cocktail.

Luckily, Ida declined his offer and accepted a vodka tonic instead. They settled down on the couch in her suite and she let him talk himself out of his anger about the day. She sat there and smiled. Eventually, she relaxed her shoulders and uncrossed her arms. Once Alex had wound himself down, Ida offered a few soothing words and pointed out that she had to get up early. He shrugged in complete disinterest but took the hint when she got up and padded over to the bedroom door.

"You coming or have you only turned up at my doorstep to complain about your wife?"

FEBRUARY 1929

37

MEYER, CHARLIE, BENNY and Alex sat in a back booth at Lindy's to commemorate the seven-month anniversary of the death of their close friend and business partner, Arnold Rothstein. He'd been shot and killed after a gambling argument. Arnold figured the poker game he was playing was rigged and once he'd amassed a six-figure debt, he'd asked for some time to pay and at a subsequent meeting, tempers rose until a piece was drawn and fired. Arnold stood no chance and took two days to die. All that agonizing time, he refused to name his assassin to the cops who turned up. He was a stand-up guy to the end.

The four men were all shocked at the news when they heard it, but they understood the world they all lived in.

"We work together, we fight together, but we die alone."

And without Rothstein's ability to find a win-win for all business ventures, cracks began to appear between the various parties who ran chunks of New York, Chicago and the many other cities within Arnold's sphere of influence.

While the four men agreed to eat cheesecake in memory of their dead friend, their need to discuss the state of their precarious empire was pressing on their minds. Meyer spoke for them all when he commented, "Times have been tough without Arnold. He was the ghost in the machine that kept all the parts moving."

"If he was still alive, I would have been able to track down Hayyim."

"Maybe, Alex. But you can be certain that when I find out who put the drop on Arnold, I'll hunt him down and kill him slowly and painfully."

They all knew Charlie meant exactly what he said. He was the closest to the Big Bankroll, and the rumors ran that Arnold had been the first to encourage Charlie into a suit and to dress like a businessman and not a street thug. Hot on his coattails was Meyer who was always smarter than Charlie but lacked the Italian's physical ruthlessness.

Benny's leg constantly twitched as his impatience oozed out of his shaking limb. The man could never sit still, with a constant eye on the next big thing, whether that was a deal in progress or a skirt.

There had been many encroachments on everybody's territories since Arnold's death with no sign of this letting up. Every two or three weeks a hail of bullets and a fresh pile of bodies would head to the morgue.

"The trouble is that the old world order has crumbled away with Arnold's passing and nothing and nobody has taken his place," Alex mused.

"We've got it bad and so has Alfonse."

"What's his problem? I thought he was milking it with booze and gaming."

"Alex, Chicago is still a split town. Alfonse controls the south side but that Irish gonif, Bugs Moran runs the north side."

"Hadn't they worked out a way to keep the peace, Meyer?"

"For a while, they stopped using slugs on each other but there has always been bad blood between them. Now, Alfonse wants to clear the air and put Moran in a body bag."

"Good luck to him, Charlie. From what little I've heard and read in the papers, Moran is no fool."

"You're right, Alex, but Alfonse has a plan up his sleeve and has sought our help."

Meyer and Charlie glanced at each other and then Luciano carried on.

"He asked if you'd be willing to pop over to the Windy City for a day or so."

"Is it necessary? I don't fancy being an assassin for hire, especially for such a high profile hit. Couldn't we send Massimo or Ezra?"

"This needs to be you, Alex. You might not acknowledge it, but you have quite a reputation in the Midwest. Besides, it'll be good for business. Alfonse will owe us a favor and our ties with his Chicago operations will get stronger."

"There's no money in this?"

"I'm sure you can claim your expenses."

Benny spoke for the first time and Alex ignored his sarcastic contribution. This was no laughing matter. Moran was a supremely big fish and his death would have repercussions. That said, Alfonse was doing very well for himself and would be a great partner to have.

"If I get my train fare paid, then I'll do it."

A quick wink in Benny's direction and Alex gouged a huge piece of cheesecake onto his fork and swallowed the large mouthful in one gulp. Benny smiled and his leg stopped twitching for almost five seconds, then resumed its motion.

"That's settled then. When you come back, we'll all be able to enjoy the closer tie with Alfonse. His men are ruthless and have helped us in the past."

"Wire Alfonse that I'll take an evening ride out of town and will see him tonight… Gentlemen, enjoy the rest of your cake, I'm going home to pack."

"Don't spend so long at Ida's that you miss your train."

The three men laughed at Benny's joke.

"No need to worry on that score. She spends too much time with that pipe of hers. Always has."

"You going to replace her with a new model?"

"At some point, Benny. I'm in no rush but I can't see us being together at the end of the year."

With that comment lingering in the air, Alex got up, shook hands with his friends, and headed to Chicago via Ida's bed and his family's apartment.

A CAR MET Alex at the station when he arrived in Chicago and took him to a nondescript hotel. The manager greeted him without introduction and led him to his suite. Ten minutes later, the phone rang and an unknown voice requested his presence in the lobby. Alex agreed and after a short journey, he was sat with Alfonse and several others.

The Italian had chosen a private room at the back of a blind pig in his control. Although it was late, he offered his guests a bite to eat and Alex asked for some sandwiches. The rest of the crew acknowledged they were hungry too and a mound of food was ordered. More predictably, a large round of drinks was requested also, which arrived within minutes.

Alfonse thanked everybody for coming and each man in the room eyed the others up, wondering quite what they were expected to do. Alex recognized only one face: Abe Bernstein, so he knew he was in good company. Next to him was Ron Boaz, a stocky fella with a carefully manicured black beard. There was Fred Burke, thin with wire-rimmed glasses, and a guy introduced as James Morton. Alex got the feeling everyone else knew each other but he couldn't be sure.

"The hit on Bugs Moran will take place tomorrow morning. I would like to thank our friend from the east for joining us. You all know Abe. Thanks for your support in these difficult times. The Sugar House gang has always been a tremendous business partner and I hope our association continues long into the future."

Chicago had been split between Irish and Italian interests since before Prohibition, but the easy money and location of the place conspired to attract the most entrepreneurial fellas from across the region. Alfonse had forged alliances with Detroit and the Lower East Side and Arnold had recognized his talent early in his career.

While Alfonse eyed cute deals, he was prone to erratic outbursts. So when the Irish boss on the north side started to make inroads into Capone's territory, he responded by whacking the guy. That was five years ago and each boss since had died due to excessive quantities of bullets in their brains. No one could say for sure, but word on the street was that Alfonse ordered every hit.

"Abe is supplying the vehicles and other assets for the job but won't be joining you."

"Four of us. How many of them?"

"Can't be precise, Alex. At least five, but there might be ten turn up."

"Those aren't great odds."

"You'll be more than fine. First, you are the most reliable fighters in the country. Second, if your sheer grit isn't enough, I have given you a little edge along the way. Two of you will carry Thompsons."

Alex let out a whistle to show he was impressed. He had used many munitions in his life, but those sub-machine guns had gained a name for themselves in the short time they'd been available on the street. A man could do a lot of damage to another human being with one of those bad boys.

"I'm sure you all have a thousand questions but let me go through the plan before anyone asks me anymore."

Once Alfonse had finished his explanation, he sat down and sipped a whiskey. The others discussed potential weaknesses and Alfonse was open to making any necessary changes. He didn't care about the detail of how Moran died; he just wanted a corpse.

For his part, Alex liked the vision of the plan, but wasn't sure it would work. It was clever—he couldn't deny it—and that was its potential downfall. In Alex's experience, simple always won out over complexity. Given he'd be in the thick of it, he hoped he was wrong. Under normal circumstances, he would have headed straight to the station and back to the safety of New York.

But Alex knew that wasn't an option because they all needed to keep Alfonse happy as there were deals to be done. What worried Alex most was that they had called him in the first place. This was a local problem that could have been handled locally. Alfonse had a reputation himself and Abe and the Sugar House gang were renowned as well.

Had they brought him over from the East Coast to be their fall guy? The idea that he might be their patsy sent a shiver down his spine. If he was right then Meyer, Charlie and Benny had sent him down the river. For the first time since Waxey had plucked him out of the gutter, Alex felt he was closing in on his own death.

38

THE NEXT MORNING a car picked up Alex and brought him to a building near the corner of North Cleveland Avenue and West Grant. They might have been well beyond the safety of Alfonse's reach but there they were inside an office with its windows boarded up, right on the doorstep of Bugs Moran.

Alfonse had supplied a range of firearms for the guys to choose from and two Tommy guns as promised. Alex and Fred were responsible for looking after them and having to take charge of an outfit each. They disrobed and changed into their new clothes while everyone waited. A lifetime later and the phone in the outside corridor burst into life. Fred stood up and hurried to pick up the call. A few words and he hung up on whoever had dropped a dime to this empty building.

"He's been spotted. It's time."

All four strode out onto the street and headed east two blocks until they reached a passageway at the bend of the road which led to North Clark Street. They walked southeast, parallel to the park, and less than five minutes later they halted one hundred feet away from a garage.

As Alex and the crew headed toward the entrance on the other side of the street, he checked up and down the road before he reminded himself of precisely the location of his Tommy inside his long coat and the pistol in his pants pocket. The police uniform felt strange, but he understood that it was an essential but unusual part of Alfonse's plan. No words were spoken, but each man looked at each other for reassurance that all was good. Alex pushed the door open, and they stormed into the garage just as he and Fred whipped out their revolvers and Alex inhaled deeply before he announced their arrival:

"Hands up. This is a raid."

Three guys sat at a table playing cards and four others stood near a vehicle. The hood was up and one of the men wore overalls and had his head stuck into the engine. He was the first to raise his hands and must have

477

been a civilian mechanic. Tough luck on him because he'd chosen the wrong place to work.

Fred headed toward the table and brandished his weapon. Two of the card sharps instantly put their hands on the wooden surface while the one nearest Fred hesitated for a second. Without saying a word, Fred whipped the butt of his pistol sideways, smashing it into the side of the fella's head. The force of the blow caused him to fly off his chair, and he landed on the greasy floor. A woman's revolver lay next to him.

James ran over to pick it up and withdrew a police badge from his inside jacket pocket just before he bent down to collect the piece. The other card players took the hint and dutifully put their hands on their heads. Fred and James continued to train their guns on them.

Meanwhile, Alex and Ron marched over to the truck. By now the mechanic had stepped to one side to separate himself physically from the others.

"We don't need no funny business from you chumps. Put your hands up and face that wall."

Alex's free hand pointed at a long wall at the far end of the garage. It had been painted some time in its life, but you'd be hard pushed to figure out when. The seven men sauntered over, knowing that these cops would frisk them and then seek some financial compensation for not dragging their sorry asses over to the precinct. Police across the country were the same—always after an extra buck and happy to take it from any criminal with the green to supply it.

"Face the wall and assume the position."

Alex's instructions were short and to the point, just like one of Chicago's finest would have said. With Fred and Alex still aiming their pistols at the seven, Ron and James passed down the line to remove any firearms from the assembled throng.

"All clean?" checked Alex.

"As my conscience."

Ron nodded to Alex who glanced at Fred. They took out the Tommys and before any of the Moran crew could respond to the sound of the safeties coming off the submachine guns, Fred and Alex strafed the wall, causing each man's body to drop to the floor within an instant.

A red spray covered the surface and beads of red trickled downward, crisscrossing the rough surface of the paint until it joined the pools of blood pouring out of the corpses. To make sure there were no mistakes, Ron and James fired two shots into each head.

"Time to go. Which one was Moran?"

"Second from the left, I think."

Alex nodded at Fred who smiled back. The smell of death and cordite was in the air, reminding Alex of the trenches. Only for an instant, but long enough for him to want to swallow hard to control his memory of Bobby and the beating of his heart.

"Let's get outta here."

As soon as they got onto the street, they all knew something was wrong. The getaway car was nowhere to be seen.

ALEX'S EYES DARTED around the road again in the hope he'd missed the automobile on this empty scene, but nothing was there. So James and Ron put their hands above their heads while Fred and Alex pointed their revolvers into the small of the civilians' backs. They walked south down the street looking to any casual passerby like two cops taking a pair of felons to the station house.

Sirens wailed in the distance and Fred eyeballed Alex but said nothing. The real flatfeet could be heading straight for them or there could be a bank stickup to attend. No one could tell quite what was happening.

"Where the hell is that car?"

"No idea. Makes me worried we're about to get hung out to dry."

"True, Fred, but Alfonse has always kept his word until now—to me at any rate."

"Same for me, but there's still no getaway in sight."

Two blocks and they carried on walking. There were no cars parked on the street, so no opportunity to boost one and escape. Alex thought he saw the scurrying ants of people five or six hundred feet ahead. They'd need to get off the sidewalk before then.

"Any ideas?"

"Break into an office and lie low?"

"Great short-term solution, Fred. Only problem is that if anyone spots us going in, then we're trapped."

In between the clip-clop of their footsteps came a new sound. It was louder, and therefore nearer, than the sirens but there was nobody on top of them. Alex quickly swiveled around and thought he saw someone vanish into the shadows. He peered into the middle distance but there was no one there, or so he thought.

The four men sped up slightly, all sensing their time would soon be up. The sound of the footsteps behind them increased in volume too. Whoever it was, he was certainly getting closer. Ron was twitchy.

He might have been walking with his hands on his head pretending to be in police custody, but he twisted one way and turned the other as he tried to get a fix on their potential assailant. Then a shot rang out and hell broke loose.

A bullet whizzed past and all four men scattered, each heading in a different direction. The slug had come from behind them and Alex used a trashcan for cover. Fred was on the other sidewalk. Ron and James had lucked out and reached the entrance to an alleyway. This gave them time to yank out their pistols and take aim.

Alex didn't have that luxury, but seeing the general direction of fire, he pulled out his Tommy gun and let a magazine empty into the air. One man collapsed to the floor, twitching.

"How many, Ron?"

"One down. I haven't spotted any others."

"Me neither," added James.

"You reckon it's safe?"

"For now."

They gathered themselves together and dusted their clothes down.

"Should we take a long route round and swing by the safehouse?"

"That was the original arrangement, Alex, but now I'm not so sure."

"We can't stay dressed as cops all day. And you're right, Alfonse's plan bit the dirt the minute some schmendrick forgot to pick us up."

The four men stood at the back of the alley in silence as each weighed up the best way to proceed. Alex was the first to speak.

"You two should get out of town immediately. If you're quick, you might even make it to the train station before the jig is up. Fred, you and I need fresh clothes unless we can steal a car and hightail it out of the city. So I suggest we head over to the safehouse. If we get a vehicle along the way, excellent. If not, we change back into our civvies and blend into the crowd more easily."

"Agreed, but these streets have eyes everywhere. We are deep inside the North Side with no cover. One fella has already found us and who knows how many more will follow."

"And your point is…?"

"Alex, we're dead meat if we stay on the street."

Fred was right. They were sitting ducks on the sidewalks. Then Alex had an idea.

"Good luck, you two. See you soon, I hope."

Handshakes for everyone then Ron and James popped their heads round the alley entrance and Alex heard their footsteps scampering into the distance. Once they were out of sight, Alex turned to Fred and said, "Follow me."

Over to a derelict house on the other end of the alleyway and Alex jumped up and grabbed at the fire escape ladder until he was able to pull it down. They clambered up the side of the building until they reached the top.

From one rooftop to another, the two men sprinted over the blocks out of sight from any nosy civilian who might have wanted to rat them out. The only present danger was leaping from one building to the next, but they were densely packed in this part of town so the jump wasn't too big.

Every so often, the two would drop to the first floor, scurry across a street and then back up to the skyline. Eventually they arrived at the safehouse and waited to check what was happening before they went in. All appeared calm with no one coming or going for a full ten minutes. They took their lives in their hands and hopped inside.

SIX HOURS AND three stolen cars later, Alex and Fred arrived at the outskirts of Detroit. They had taken turns behind the wheel with the other riding shotgun. With Fred at the wheel, they didn't take long to drive over to Abe's headquarters where they were met by Ron and James who'd got in by train some two hours earlier.

"Any word from Alfonse?"

"Yeah, by the time we arrived, he'd already apologized to Abe. The getaway car had a flat."

"You're kidding me."

"Nope, nothing more sinister or complicated than that. That's life."

Abe entered the room and gave Alex and Frank a manly hug each.

"Good to see you both again. Sounds like you had an adventure from what James was saying."

"It had its moments."

"You can tell me over dinner. Please stay here as my guest before you go back east."

"With pleasure. I'll just need to make two phone calls, if I may."

"Of course. You can use my office."

The next morning, February 15, Alex picked up the newspaper which had been delivered to his hotel suite along with his breakfast. As he munched on his toast, the front page was filled with details of the previous day's massacre in a Lincoln Park garage in Chicago. Seven had been slain but Bugs Moran had not been one of the dead.

MARCH 1929

39

DESPITE FAILING TO whack Moran, Alfonse sent word to Alex of how pleased he was with the efforts of the assassination squad. Several of Moran's inner circle were dead and the man himself was scared that Alfonse would make another attempt on his life. While the fella hit the mattresses, Capone took advantage and rampaged through Moran territory.

Alex had lost count of the number of times he had swung by Meyer's office, but now he found himself sat with Charlie, Benny and Lansky in the same comfortable armchair as before.

"Ever since Arnold passed away, God rest his soul, financing our ventures has proved difficult. The stability that Arnold's business relations delivered has floated off too."

"Charlie, you are right. The time we spend chiseling at territory or defending our own turf could be better spent making gelt. We are all losing out."

"While all this chaos is raining down on us here, we should seek fresh opportunities in other parts of the country."

"Benny, you forget we don't have any solid financial backing no more. Breaking new ground costs money."

Benny stared daggers at his old friend and compatriot, Meyer. They had grown up together and, despite some of their differences as adults, they respected each other—even when Meyer started doing business with the Italian, Charlie 'Lucky' Luciano.

"Arnold believed in bringing people closer. We wouldn't know each other if it wasn't for him. Perhaps we should follow his lead."

"Alex, Arnold only worked with men of honor. None of the momzers trying to hem us in can be trusted further than I spit."

Meyer was right. The various gang bosses north and west of their territory couldn't give their word on Monday and still mean it on Tuesday. They would never become partners. Maranzano and his Jewish friend would need to be taken out. The only question was when, not if.

"Meyer, Maranzano knows we do business together, and he tries not to encroach on your operations."

"You are right, Charlie. But don't pretend he shows me the same courtesy. Time and time again, he and his lieutenant have targeted not just me, but my family as well."

"And that was unforgivable. As I told you when that happened, Maranzano claimed he did not authorize that action."

"You believe him?"

"From the expression on his face, yes. But that doesn't mean he did anything to find the culprit either."

"Damn straight."

Just as every other occasion when the kidnapping came up, the men fell silent. While they all believed Maranzano should have routed out Hayyim and punished him appropriately, everyone did business with him and wanted the situation to fade away. Charlie was in a more complex state because Maranzano offered him protection. Charlie worked with Meyer and Arnold despite Maranzano, whose dislike of Jews was well known.

With only the sound of the clock ticking in the background, Alex returned the group from their collective reverie.

"We have men bleeding in the street and liquor being stolen from our warehouses. The cops are standing back to let each of our outfits tear a pound of flesh from the other. What are we going to do about it?"

"Take the fight to them."

"Benny, we've been doing that for months and nothing changes."

"Then we need to be more targeted. Why don't we cut off the head of the snake?"

"Whack Maranzano?"

Charlie looked askance at Benny. The Italian had known his friend from when they ran craps games in short trousers. Maranzano had taken care of Charlie all his adult life and given him power in his organization while he earned vast sums thanks to funding by Arnold. With the Big Bankroll dead, Charlie didn't want to face the prospect of sending his second father to the morgue. Benny continued outlining his logic out loud:

"So, if we don't target the boss then let's figure out which operations or people will cripple him the most and attack them now."

"Without his warehouses, he is nothing. If we squeeze his supply lines, then he'll be on his knees in a flash."

"Meyer is right. A two-pincer movement should do the job. We hit his warehouses and any route into the city that he uses. Until now, we thought scaring his customers away would do the trick."

◆ ◆ ◆

FIRST, ALEX AND his crew launched a series of attacks on every known storage facility run by Maranzano. Ezra and Massimo made sure that anyone fleeing the scene was gunned down and left to bleed to death on the sidewalk. After two days, Charlie informed the group that Maranzano's speakeasies were running dry and they should expect some mighty retaliation.

Second, Alex asked his out-of-town connections in Windsor, Detroit and Chicago to refuse to do business with Maranzano by promising to buy any goods they usually sold to the Italian on at least the same terms. Abe Bernstein and Alfonse understood what Alex was up to and looked the other way at this Manhattan squabble.

On the third day, Maranzano retaliated. A fire ripped through Alex's office building in what was a clear warning for him to back off. Civilians ran in all directions as the flames tore through each floor. Alex arrived late that morning but Ezra had made a lucky escape.

"The smoke, Alex. It took over the place in just a few minutes. For a second there, I didn't think I'd make it out in one piece. The screaming and shouting. There were women getting trampled in the rush for the exit. I mean, I don't blame anyone for wanting to get out quick, but..."

"...there's no need to kill someone along the way."

"Right."

"Pour yourself a drink and check on your men. If Maranzano has left his mark here, he's no doubt done the same in other parts of the city."

Ezra nodded and walked away to clear his lungs and follow Alex's orders. Massimo arrived on the scene with his jaw at his knees and Alex filled him in on the day's events.

AN HOUR LATER, Alex sat with his two lieutenants in Ida's apartment. There was nothing to link him directly to the residence, and he figured it would be safe for now. On hearing about her visitors, Ida made herself scarce.

"Abe has told me that he won't sell liquor to us for the moment. Seems like Maranzano's guys have attacked every convoy that's left Detroit since yesterday afternoon. Abe's caught between a rock and a hard place. All he wants to do is ship booze out of his town, only his two biggest clients are swinging at each other from beyond the county lines. He can't win."

"Neither can we, Alex. It'll only be a day or so and our blind pigs will be dry. And without a well from which to draw more gin, we lose our customers and they'll move somewhere else."

"Massimo, where do you think they'll go? Off to the Bronx or Queens? I doubt it. No one wants to leave the neighborhood for a brew. It's not losing johns that's the problem; we can't defend every speakeasy, gaming joint and brothel from attack. The cops can see we are on our knees and they appear good to Joe Public by watching us scratch each other's eyes out. What we must do is to avoid hurting any civilians. That never plays well in the papers."

"And when are we going to take out Maranzano? He's the canker."

"That is one mighty powerful man. Before you put a bullet in his brains, you'd better make sure that his business partners are comfortable with your actions. And we've not even started that round of negotiations. He has connections in Sicily and I need not tell you, Massimo, what that means."

Ezra remained unimpressed.

"He's just a man. Any sniper could take him out with a single slug. Nobody would know who had pulled the trigger."

"You understand it's never as simple as that. The killing is the easy part— it's keeping the world from falling apart afterwards that's difficult."

"I guess…"

"Besides," continued Alex, "Charlie tells me that Maranzano's hand is not behind this, anyway. It's Hayyim. Maranzano supports him, but he is the driving force for these attacks. The old Italian has deep pockets and is prepared to wait out the storm. Hayyim is baying for blood, mine in particular."

"Does Charlie know why you're in his crosshairs?"

"Nope, but the guy doesn't just want me dead. He wants me to suffer, my family to suffer and for my business associates to suffer too."

"Nice piece of work."

"He'll get his. That's a stone-cold promise to you. In the meantime, let's figure out how we will make some money tomorrow."

40

FOR THE BRIEFEST of moments, a calm descended on the Lower East Side, which was precisely when Alex got a call from Alfonse who had issues of his own.

"Do you remember my North Side problem you helped me with last month?"

"How could I forget?"

"Well, that itch still needs scratching, and I was wondering if you could visit Chicago and bare your claws."

"We are facing our own problems in New York but things are quiet—for now at least."

"So when can you get over?"

"I'll take the first available train, but I might need to dash back with little notice."

"That's as much as I might ask."

"Just no more dressing up."

The fight with Bugs Moran had continued ever since Alex had fled the Windy City and Alfonse was tired of wasting time on the Irishman.

"We have problems. I need you to show your face and put some fear into those Irish hearts. They've grown so accustomed to my men that those fellas aren't rattled anymore."

"And they should be. You know me, Alfonse, I'm always here for my friends."

ALEX AND CAPONE sat opposite each other at a convenient drinking club deep in the South Side. They'd spent only thirty minutes together since Alex's arrival in town at lunchtime the same day.

"With Moran pushing hard, would you be willing to walk into one of his blind pigs and put on a show?"

"Anything to entertain the troops."

"I'm more interested in scaring his customers and men."

"That's what I meant."

IT TOOK NO time to equip Alex with some firearms and hustle him twenty blocks north, where he and two of Alfonse's guys stood outside the Black Rabbit, looked at each other for less than a second, and walked inside.

They sauntered past the doorman and headed straight for the bar where they ordered a coffee and gin. Drinks served, the fellas wandered round the room until they found an empty table among the crowd. The place was packed—a large open space filled with men and women sitting at tables and chairs barely big enough to sustain their weight.

"This will not be easy."

Alex eyed the location of every fella he could see. His biggest concern was that there were so few guys on the floor. If he was lucky, Moran's gang was cocky and if Alex was not, then the cockroaches would come out of the woodwork as soon as he fired the first shot. The guy remained at the door and there were only two others, one at the far end of the bar and the other positioned on the opposite wall.

"Follow my lead. Let's get this done."

His two new colleagues nodded and gave Alex the space to stand up. He judged the right moment and wended his way over to the counter then moved down as though he was trying to avoid the crowd. Eventually, Alex stood next to the Moran bouncer.

"Got a light, Mac?"

The brown eyes stared at him like he hardly existed. Alex averted his gaze and mumbled something about needing a book of matches. A heavy sigh and a lighter was procured. Then Alex leaned in to enable the end of his cigarette to reach the flickering flame.

Just as the guy fumbled around putting the lighter back into his pocket, Alex pulled out a Barlow knife and plugged the guy in the stomach. A quick twist and he removed the blade then propped up the fella to glide him over to a chair in the corner. The body slumped onto the item of furniture, which enabled Alex to drag the corpse through a nearby door.

Alex held his breath until he found out if his gamble to move a body into an unknown place had paid off. The room was pitch black and Alex scrambled round to find a light switch. When he succeeded, he exhaled and looked around; boxes everywhere, some on the floor, others on shelves.

With one of the three guards taken care of, Alex returned to the main room and his eyes darted around to check everybody's position. Alfonse's men had stationed themselves near the two security guards he'd spotted before. The trouble was that a pair of new fellas had appeared from nowhere —or, more precisely, from a door on the other side of the tables and Alex had no clue how many more were waiting in the wings.

The clock was ticking until the barkeep noticed his watcher was missing, so Alex had little time to think or weigh up his options. He planted both feet firmly on the ground, whipped out a pistol and aimed at the chest of the guy at the door.

A red spray burst out of his back and people began to scream at the sound of the gun and the results of the slug's trajectory. As the other two of Moran's men drew their revolvers, Alfonse's guys had already taken aim and shot at them. Each body flew backwards from the proximity of their assailants. Lots more screaming so Alex fired several bullets into the ceiling.

By now, many people had hit the dirt and were cowering under their tables. Others sat where they were, frozen by fear and indecision. Alex moved around them, continuing to fire into the air, until he reached the entrance. Only then did Alfonse's guys follow him out. As they ran over to him, another fella appeared from the far-side doorway.

"This is it."

Alex aimed and squeezed the trigger. Click. The chamber was empty. He took his second pistol from his other pants pocket, smiled and blasted a hole through the guy's forehead. Alex tutted to himself because he was supposed to get the chest. Either way, the fella was bleeding out on the floor, red seeping through the cracks in the floorboards. No more of Moran's guys showed so the three men turned round and hopped into a waiting car. By the time Alex got back for a drink with Alfonse, a message had been left by Abe Bernstein and Alex was heading to the station and over to Detroit.

"THE COPS CALLED in the Feds and have cut off our liquor supply from Windsor."

Alex's eyes dilated at the news, as he understood why Abe had made him schlep all the way to the dung heap of the world. If he hadn't seen Abe's lips with his own eyes, Alex wouldn't have believed him. The amount of bribe money he'd spent greasing the palms of the local gumshoes over the years would bankrupt an ordinary guy, but Alex was no normal businessman.

He had enjoyed the benefits of being bankrolled by Rothstein, who had advised him to always oil the machine and to keep the little man happy. Arnold might have had huge ideas for the future, but he knew he stood on the shoulders of men who worked harder than he did.

"Why now?"

"You know better than me, from what I hear. Things are hot at home and I had to get you in Chicago. Sounds as though the whole damn country is ready to blow."

"These are nothing more than a few local difficulties. They are just turning up at the same time."

"Keep telling yourself that, Alex. Meanwhile we must secure our boats' safe passage across the Detroit River. We're receiving three big shipments over the next week. If we don't land that hooch then there'll be dry throats coast to coast."

"Find me a long black coat, a fedora and a pair of cop shoes. Time we got closer to the flatfeet, who are kicking at our heels."

Alex grabbed an old jalopy and headed for the river. With no plan in his head, he figured he'd try to sneak near the Feds and see what he could find out. He didn't need to wait too long before he bumped into two guys with cop haircuts under their hats, hanging on a street corner with nothing much to do. One was noticeably taller than the other and Shorty had blond hair.

"Borrow a light?"

Longe Lokshen nodded and passed Alex a book of matches.

"Thanks, Mac. How long you been out here?"

"Since lunchtime, like the rest of the detail. Who are you? Our relief?"

"You're joking. They drafted me in and told me to help, but no one's briefed us properly."

"Ness believes in keeping his cards close to his chest. Doesn't trust anyone."

"We sure live in dangerous times... How long's this operation been running?"

"Three days so far and man it's cold in this city."

Shorty dug his hands deeper into his coat pocket but the wind's chilly bite still cut through him. His companion juddered as a fresh gust sliced through the back of his neck like ice.

"We'd better get used to it. I hear there's another five days of this bull before we have even a chance of going home."

"Yeah, as if we'll walk round the corner and catch the bootleggers red-handed."

Alex enjoyed the irony of his statement. If only these schmucks knew how close they were. Instead, he wished them well and carried on toward the river. The number of times he'd made the crossing meant he knew this part of Detroit like the back of his hand.

Over three blocks to the shoreline and he came across a huddle of men, hiding behind a wall. One was surrounded by the rest and Alex could tell by the body language that this guy was in charge and issuing orders. He sidled up and stood near the back. The inspector was taking questions.

"We have strong intelligence that the Purple Gang are expecting a delivery any day now. We are working with the Mounties on the other side of the river to prevent that from happening."

The Purple Gang was the goyim name for Abe Bernstein's mob and Alex's jaw tightened at the sound of the insult.

"So Mr. Ness we're staying here until the shipment shows?"

"That's the plan, boys."

In that moment, Alex considered following Ness away from this group once they'd finished their pep talk and whacking him. Bury the momzer in the sand by the waterfront.

Then he hatched a simpler plan to send this schmendrick out of town— with a lot less fuss. He vanished into the shadows and returned to his jalopy and drove around until he found a pay phone. Then he dropped a dime.

"Abe, we can get these Feds off our backs before morning."

"How the hell do you propose we do that? You know we don't have the men or the weapons to kill them all?"

"Not one drop of blood needs to be shed."

"I'm listening."

"Send two boats across the river half-full with booze. Make it the good stuff. They are waiting for a massive shipment. If we show them that their rat was only right about the timing but not the quantity, I bet you they'll go home with their tails between their legs. None of the gumshoes on the ground have any appetite to spend the next week standing around the shoreline of Detroit."

"It's worth a try. Who do you think made the call to the Feds?"

"That I don't know, but when I meet the guy…"

41

WHEN ALEX RETURNED home, New York was in turmoil. The number of attacks on his real estate had rocketed in the last day.

"Appears they are hitting us somewhere every hour. It's crazy out there."

"Massimo, do you agree with Ezra?"

A simple nod confirmed Alex's worst fears—just as he was getting someplace in this town and building up proper security, somebody was grabbing at his ankles to drag him back into the gutter.

"Are the cops earning their fees?"

"Not at all. They've turned their backs on us. I tried leaning on them but they don't seem to care. It's like someone has put a fix in with them."

"Ezra, I think I can guess who. The best move right now will be to hit the mattresses. We will always find other venues for our speakeasies and there won't be any liquor hitting the city for at least a week. So let's lie low and wait to see what roaches crawl out from under the floorboards."

Massimo and Ezra agreed with Alex, but their expressions showed that hiding did not sit comfortably with either. He offered them a drink from his desk drawer which they declined. After they had departed, Alex locked up the office and traveled home to spend an evening with the kids before he too checked into a fleapit hotel under a false name.

AS EVER, AS soon as Alex stepped into the hallway, his boys appeared as though they'd been waiting all their lives to see him. Sarah held back, leaning on the living room door jamb, to allow sufficient hugs to be extracted from their father. Then she stepped forward, placed a gentle hand on his shoulder and stood on tiptoe to give him a welcoming kiss on the cheek.

He struggled to respond but the boys' excitement overwhelmed him and he moved the herd into the sitting room and had almost succeeded when the housekeeper announced that dinner was served. Sarah hustled the kids to their bathroom for some hand washing and led them over to the dining table.

Alex enjoyed these hours and admitted to himself he'd forgotten how much he enjoyed being with his family. They made him laugh out loud and Sarah made him smile inside when her hair was caught in a certain light. Eventually, all the food was consumed and all the silly jokes had been said.

He helped Sarah bundle the boys into their pajamas, teeth brushing, face washing—including behind the ears—and a hop under the covers in time for their papa to read them a bedtime story. As the kids dropped off to sleep, one after the other, Sarah and Alex returned to the sitting room and shared the couch while they both stared into the flames of the fire.

They said little to each other, choosing to spend their time together offering simple physical companionship. Alex found comfort in feeling the warmth of Sarah's body next to his. With Ida, he knew she only remained interested in him for the gifts he bestowed on her. With Sarah, she only expected him to care of her and the kids. It wasn't that she didn't take great pleasure in the beautiful trinkets and pretty clothes. But, if they weren't there, she wouldn't mind, and that was a big difference between her and Ida.

As the clock on the mantelpiece struck ten, they stood up and headed for bed themselves. Under the sheets, they cuddled more and, despite himself, Alex began to feel a renewed lust for his wife. He was about to take advantage of these fresh emotions when a hail of bullets erupted through the bedroom.

Driven by pure instinct, Alex rolled over Sarah and thudded to the floor. He grabbed her arm and dragged her down beside him. Slugs whizzed past them for a further twenty seconds and then silence.

"You okay?"

Alex saw Sarah nodding in the gloom.

"Stay here and don't move. Keep your head down in case they start up again."

He shuffled out of the room and rushed to the children. Even though they all had windows facing the same direction, the assailants had only targeted the master bedroom. The boys were whimpering but completely unharmed.

Alex drew a deep breath and tried to calm them down. This had all the trappings of one man: Shmuel Hayyim and he would have to pay for putting his family in danger yet again. This was an outrage. No matter what beef you had with a fella, you always kept it strictly business. And this was personal.

Alex stormed out of the apartment and over to his office where he made some phone calls. Ezra arrived first, but he only lived a block away. Massimo took another fifteen minutes as he had to travel east from Little Italy, Maranzano territory.

"Was it Hayyim or Maranzano who gave the order?"

Massimo looked straight into Alex's eyes, and said the single word…
Hayyim.

"He's not been seen near Mulberry for weeks, but tonight he appeared at
Tony's, between Broome and Grande. It's family owned and nobody bothers
anyone there. Very discreet. As I walked over here, I saw him sat at a
window seat."

Either Hayyim was getting careless, or he was setting himself up as bait.
Whichever it was, Alex put a hand into the bottom drawer of his desk and
pulled out two revolvers.

"What do you want us to do?"

"Massimo, walk back to Hayyim and request a meeting in thirty minutes
time. Let him choose the location, only it must be a public place and on
neutral turf. We will wait here so you can call me with the address."

His instructions issued, one of his most trusted allies vanished into the
night and the other sat down until the phone rang. Alex repeated the
location and told Massimo to leave Hayyim as soon as he was able. Then
Alex stood up and headed for the door, followed by Ezra.

Hayyim had selected a cafe on Fifth, a block away from Lindy's. As Alex
and Ezra approached the Diamond, they surveyed the area. Ezra elbowed
Alex who cocked his head in the general direction of two fellas leaning
against a wall on the other side of the street to the cafe entrance. They
stopped for a second so Alex could light his cigarette from a match in Ezra's
cupped hands, which allowed Alex to circle round without drawing too
much attention to himself.

"You see any others?"

"Nope, but who knows how many might be at the back of the place."

"Why don't you find out. I'll wait a while to give you a chance to go
round the rear and then I shall go in. After that, we do what we need to do to
kill Hayyim and get out alive."

AS ALEX STRODE to the Diamond's entrance, the fellas stiffened. Out of the
corner of his eye, Alex thought he saw them put their hands in their coat
pockets ready to draw their guns. Through the window, he spotted a pair of
tables, each with two men sipping coffee. When he walked in, a fella from
each table stood up and approached him. While one stared right through
him, the other patted him down and found one revolver.

"I'll look after that until you leave."

Alex raised one eyebrow and said nothing. Then the guy led him into the
middle of the room by a wall. There was a table set for four but only one
man sat alone. He took a swig from a glass of red wine, noticed Alex
standing five feet away and beckoned him nearer.

He stood up as Alex stepped forward and held his jacket open to show he wasn't packing any heat. Then both men sat down, opposite each other.

"Shmuel Hayyim, stories of your deeds precede you."

"And the name Alex Cohen carries considerable weight in some parts of this town."

Alex gritted his teeth, wanting to reach out and throttle this *farbissener pisher*. Instead he glanced to the back of the cafe but Ezra was nowhere to be seen. Meanwhile, his two escorts had returned to their seats at the front.

"You caused my wife and children much distress earlier today."

"I wish them no harm. The message I sent was aimed only at you."

"But you caused them upset and the matter will need to be resolved."

"Now is not the time for petty squabbles. You and I have plenty to talk about; we have a long history together."

"Only in a way. You have been chomping at my heels for five years."

"I have been following your career for longer than that, Alex."

"Oh?"

"You don't know who I am, do you?"

"A business partner of Salvatore Maranzano."

"Yes, but you knew my uncle."

"Did I?"

Alex was tiring of this man's arrogance. He was circling around but getting nowhere, although this last statement was intriguing. From the moment Alex had seen Hayyim, he felt as though he had met him before, despite Alex knowing this was impossible. He stared at the guy's face until Alex's jaw dropped and he recognized the family resemblance.

"Sammy Levine."

Those two whispered words, now spoken, provided all the explanation why Shmuel had expended so much energy attempting to bring about his downfall. His mind raced back to the days just before he left for the war and Shmuel completed his thoughts.

"You killed my uncle Sammy, stole his territory then ran away before Waxey Gordon could punish you."

"It wasn't like that. Sammy wasn't innocent. He set me up…"

"I don't wish to hear your excuses. I want reparations."

"Before we get round to discussing how to right the alleged wrongs of the past—and of the present—I need to take a leak."

"Do what you must do."

Alex sauntered as casually as he could to the rear of the cafe and into the john. Just before he opened the door, he looked back and saw one goon rise up and walk toward him. The guy would stand guard while he was inside.

Closing the door behind him, Alex pushed at the three cubicle doors. Two swung open and the third was locked. He pursed his lips and let forth a triple whistle. The occupant responded by opening his door and there sat Ezra proffering a pistol.

"There's three at the front, one outside here and Hayyim on his own."

Alex opened the john door and grabbed the guy still standing on the other side. Before anyone in the cafe could notice, he dragged the fella into the john, one palm over his mouth and the other on his wrist, twisting his arm behind his back.

A crack as Alex broke the bone and Ezra popped out from his hiding place to lend a hand. With a silencer on the barrel of his gun, Ezra shot the man at point blank range in the chest. Red gushed onto the floor but the guy was most definitely dead.

A nod and Alex stepped out of the john and headed beyond Hayyim and straight to the three by the door. Shmuel spoke to him as he walked past, but Alex didn't register what he said. His mind was focused on one thing only.

Twenty feet. Ten feet. Five feet. He pulled out his pistol and sent a bullet flying into each of the men in quick succession. He was so fast and the move so unexpected that not one of them had a chance to even draw his weapon, let alone doing anything else about it.

As soon as the other customers in the joint heard the violent retort of the handgun, bedlam let rip. Women screamed, men hid under tables; some even tried to flee. Alex swiveled round and marched to Hayyim's table. The young upstart hadn't moved an inch, transfixed by surprise. How had Alex smuggled a gun into the joint?

"Sammy and I learned one important lesson from Waxey Gordon. We live together, we fight together but you die alone."

Alex straightened his arm, pulled the trigger and a new hole opened up in the middle of Shmuel Hayyim, nephew of Sammy Levine, the man who had given Alex the education he'd never received in the old country and had betrayed him for a handful of dollars.

Ezra tapped Alex on the shoulder and brought him into the moment. People were fighting to escape from the cafe and the two guys outside had reached the entrance.

Alex followed Ezra out the rear and waited in the back alley for the goons to arrive. In a matter of seconds, both lay dead and Ezra led the way for them both to flee. Within an hour, Alex was lying next to Sarah in their bed although she refused to let him touch her.

MAY 1929

42

THE DEATH OF Hayyim sent shockwaves across the city and, the next day, all hostilities stopped as Maranzano saw no reason to continue Hayyim's fight because there was no money in prolonging everybody's misery. The ceasefire persisted for days then weeks. With supply lines freed up, booze flowed from coast to coast and the various mobs and gangs returned to their daily business routines.

As the months passed, Charlie began to piece together a plan to prevent any future infighting. To seal the deal, he invited everybody to Atlantic City to lay out his stall. To Alex's immense pleasure, he was included on the guest list too.

"Tomorrow will be a big day, Sarah."

They sprawled on the couch in the sitting room. The housekeeper had already put the kids to bed and settled in for an evening's knitting.

"I'm glad you're doing well. Passover was too much. All the shooting—and you spent so much time away from us..."

Sarah's voice trailed off, as though her thoughts continued but she didn't want Alex to hear them. This was usually when he reckoned she imagined him with Ida. Since the business with Hayyim, Alex had hardly seen his mistress. An occasional night here or there but nothing more than that. So Sarah's concern was no longer justified.

"You know I'm leaving town tomorrow. I should be back by the evening, but I can't be sure just yet."

"I was only saying... Do you ever think about the times we spent together when we met?"

Alex inhaled and recalled the scenes of him and Sarah holed up in the whorehouse. He'd paid her ten dollars even though he didn't need to. Then he stopped paying, and that was when you might say they first became a couple.

"Feels like a lifetime ago."

"It was—before you went off to war, and I still owed my debt to Waxey."

"Simpler times… before France."

"It changed you. When you came back, you'd hardened."

Alex stiffened, not because she was right, but because he didn't want to think about what he gave up to be the fella to go to Charlie's business meeting. And he resented her for reminding him of that piece of himself long gone.

That was what she did nowadays; be a constant reminder of who he used to be. He might not be with Ida anymore but he wondered if he should still be married to Sarah.

"War does that to you."

"You must have experienced unimaginable horror over there, but that's not what I meant. You've focused so much on the money, sometimes I think you forget the boys and I exist."

"It was never anything like that."

"Don't be so quick to deny it. I'm not accusing you, just saying."

"Everything I have done has been to put bread on the table for you and the kids. Nothing more."

"Yes, you have been a wonderful provider and I am incredibly grateful for that. But you didn't do all that for us. You did it for yourself and we were lucky recipients of the spoils of your personal war."

Alex ground his molars. Right or wrong, Sarah shouldn't speak to him this way, especially the night before Charlie's meeting.

"You're not sounding grateful. From what I remember, you'd still be in the Oregon if Waxey hadn't paid for you to look after me. I cleared Waxey's debt for you from the money I made on the streets. You weren't no angel."

"Alex, don't twist my words. All I'm saying is that you had your own reasons for doing things and we know each other well enough and have been through so much together that you can be honest with me. It's not what you do for a living that bothers me—I've never judged you, nor could I, given my old profession—it's the lies. When you can't bring yourself to tell me the truth, that's when you hurt me."

He felt the heat in his cheeks and noticed his fingertips were buried in the couch arm. He tried his best not to allow his anger to take over. If it did, he might do something unforgiveable or irreversible. He packed his guns early that day, in his briefcase, which was sitting in the hallway, awaiting his departure. Deep exhalation.

"I hardly see her anymore. Almost never."

"The fact you weren't open with me about that girl… it's not that I wanted you to be with any other woman, but I tried to understand that you needed to do so. It was the lying about it…"

She stood up and floated out of the room leaving Alex alone with his thoughts.

ALEX CLOSED THE apartment door behind him as he left for Atlantic City the following morning. Sarah exhaled deeply, then opened her eyes and jumped out of bed. Two cases full of clothes and she dashed into the boys' rooms to stash their things into bags too.

She rummaged around Alex's study until she found where he'd hidden a stack of green bills, knowing he wouldn't care about the gelt. She phoned for a taxi herself so that the housekeeper would have no clue where they were heading.

The boys got dressed, with a little help from Sarah and she cajoled them out of the apartment as calmly as she could. Although Alex shouldn't get back until tonight or tomorrow, she couldn't face what would happen if she bumped into him on the way out.

Five minutes later, the cab pulled out and headed for the tunnel. She was certain what she would do in the next twenty-four hours after they got to New Jersey but anything after that was a blank sheet of paper.

43

ALEX'S CAR SPED away from the apartment and he reminded Massimo that they had plenty of time and there was no need to rush. Ezra sat in the front too to give Alex extra space to stretch out. Everybody understood the importance of today's meeting.

They headed a few blocks south and, without warning, Alex demanded Massimo pull in, then he jumped out of the car and ducked into an alleyway. Ezra and Massimo looked at each other and shrugged.

"Nerves?"

"Maybe."

They were right and they were wrong. A knot contorted itself inside Alex's stomach but it was nothing to do with anxiety. As he'd stared blankly out of the automobile, he shook himself out of his reverie long enough to recognize where he was when he shouted for them to stop.

He ran into the alley at Norfolk and Broome and stopped at the far end round the corner, hidden from view from the street. A smile and he kneeled down by a wall. Behind boxes and muddy dirt, he used one finger to draw a rectangle around a brick. Barely able to get a purchase on it, he dragged the block out of its position.

Alex shoved his hand into the gaping hole and rummaged around until his fingers found their quarry. He hauled the sack onto the ground with a grin on his face, happy and amazed that his stash had survived untouched for over ten years. No one had spent his savings since Alex banked his money before he skipped off to the Great War.

He stuffed the wad of notes into his jacket pocket and hopped back into the car.

"You all right, boss?"

"Couldn't be better. Let's get out of here."

"Sure thing."

CHARLIE AND A fella called Johnny Torrio had hired a banqueting suite so that workers could join together and hold a union meeting, according to the hotel records. Alex knew Alfonse, Meyer, Benny and, of course, Charlie. As everybody sat down at the boardroom table in the middle of the vast space, Torrio introduced Frank Costello, Joe Adonis, Dutch Schultz, Louis Buchalter, Vincent Mangano and Albert Anastasia.

Each of these men owned and ran territory on the Eastern Seaboard or in Chicago. Who was missing? The Mustache Petes, the old fellas who'd formed the Italian gangs after they sailed over from Sicily.

Alex flanked Charlie and Benny, knowing he was in the company of the most powerful men in America. Before he could reflect on the implications of this thought, Torrio stood up and tapped a spoon against the side of his water glass, clinking his makeshift gavel to get everybody's attention.

"Thank you all for coming here today. I need not remind you of what we have achieved over the past ten or twenty years. We have gone from small town hustlers, with all due respect, to business owners with thousands in our pay and influence. Congratulations to you all."

A polite ripple of applause broke out across the assembled Italians and Jews. They quietened down as Torrio continued.

"But we have reached a junction. Since Arnold Rothstein died, we have been fighting among ourselves so much that the Feds have found enough time to organize an elite squad to break our bootlegging operations. We cannot allow them to succeed and I have a proposal which Charlie Luciano and I have put together."

Alex knew Charlie's idea because they'd talked about it at length since Alex proved himself with Hayyim. Each gang leader would join a single syndicate and there would be no more infighting. Each boss continued to own his existing territory and earned an equal say as a director of the board.

If a situation arose that meant one fella wanted to whack someone in a different crew then he would need permission from whichever boss controlled that gang and its territory. If consent was not granted then the syndicate members would listen to both sides and make a final decision.

The genius of the plan was that if the hit was authorized, then a special outfit would carry out the task. That way, there would be no bad blood between gangs as everyone would have already accepted that the Murder Corporation was untouchable.

After much discussion even Benny Siegel, the group's natural maverick, saw the benefits and agreed to join the syndicate as founder members. The meeting broke up and Alex sidled over to Benny and Meyer while Torrio and Charlie worked the room. Eventually, they reached Alex and took him to one side.

"We want you to consider working with Buchalter and Anastasia to form and operate the Murder Corporation."

Inside, Alex glowed, but he didn't know either of the fellas. Obviously, their reputations preceded them but there was no personal connection with them.

"Can I think it over and tell you in a day or two?"

"Of course. The offer is out there."

Alex's chest puffed up and felt like it was ready to explode. He was on the top of the world.

THE FOLLOWING DAY, Ezra parked outside Alex's apartment block. Both Ezra and Massimo had spent the entire journey excitedly discussing the heady realms their boss had reached. He wished them well and entered the building, heading up to the apartment.

In the elevator, Alex reminded himself of the heights he had achieved and that the security his status would give him meant he could focus on rebuilding bridges with Sarah. His desire to see Ida reduced to an all-time low. Key in the lock and Alex stepped into the hallway. He shut the door and called out to Sarah. "Honey, I'm home. Wait 'till I tell you what's happened. It's all going to be different from now on."

THE END

BOOK THREE

MIDTOWN HUCKSTER

SEPTEMBER 1931

1

THE NEW YORK Central building stood on Park Street between Forty-fifth and Forty-sixth. The place was built to be the heart of the city, resplendent with its marble lobby which stretched an entire block. Before nine in the morning on weekdays, you could guarantee the joint would fill with people hustling into and out of the thirty-five-story building.

On September 13, stood by the red elevator doors were four men in suits and long brown raincoats. One of them pressed the elevator button and they waited for the cab to return to the first floor. The tallest checked his watch while his nearest colleague commented under his breath, "Relax—we have plenty of time to get him. He won't be going anywhere for a while."

A nod and a sigh. Immanuel was right, but that didn't mean hanging around was any easier. If anyone had bothered to cast an eye over them, they would have seen the coats, the short haircuts and the black suits and shoes and thought they were looking at a bunch of government agents. Listening to their conversation, they would have assumed they were about to make an arrest.

The bell rang when the doors opened up and a herd of people belched out. The guys waited politely until the cab had emptied and they stepped inside. Immanuel asked for the ninth floor and the elevator operator acknowledged the request. When nobody else showed any interest in entering the car, the shutters slammed shut and the men stared at the ornate moldings and paintings of clouds on the ceiling.

THE THIRD MEMBER of the group had a bulbous nose and pulled out a handkerchief as he appeared to cough and splutter his way during the upward journey. The rest of them ignored him, but the elevator man kept shifting his eyes toward the ill guy.

Two women got in on the third floor, chatting away to each other and ignoring the men standing in the same confined space.

"So do you think Hank's interested?"

"He asked you out for a drink and he seems very attentive around you. He doesn't give me the time of day."

"I don't even know if I like him that way."

"Have you seen the size of his expense account...?"

The elevator opened onto the sixth floor and the girls left before the men could find out whether Faye would be in Hank's clutches before the weekend.

Immanuel glanced at the other three as they all calculated how many seconds it would take from the time the door closed to the point when they'd be facing their foe. Almost as soon as they had blinked, the elevator bell pinged and the operator announced, "Ninth floor."

Immanuel, bulbous nose, and the other two stopped in the hallway to read the register of businesses and to figure out which corridor they should walk down. Eyes scanned the alphabetical list across all four columns until the *Castellammare Trading Company* popped out from the rest.

Next to the name was a three-digit number, 924 and to the left was a sign indicating that suites over 920 were along that corridor. Immanuel pointed in the correct direction and the guys checked themselves in a mirror hanging opposite the board.

Whenever an occasional person traipsed past them, the men turned round in a huddle to discuss some weighty matter and resumed their journey once the stranger had passed. Down the aisle and left through a set of double doors. Then they stopped outside suite 924. Immanuel looked at his compatriots.

"Are we good?"

"Let's do this thing," muttered bulbous-nose, as much to himself as to the group. Immanuel tapped on the door and the fellas entered the Castellammare Trading Company offices.

THE PLACE DIDN'T look like much—the anteroom comprised a desk, filing cabinet and secretary, along with two couches and two men sat there making the whole office look messy. They sprawled across the furniture as though they owned the joint, but a door to the right of the assistant showed there was another room where the leader of the enterprise resided.

"Hello, miss. Is the boss in?"

"Do you have an appointment, gentlemen?"

"I can't rightly say that we do, but we have an urgent matter to discuss."

The slouched men had sat up straighter as the conversation ensued. These flatfeet had appeared unannounced and the chances were that they didn't have a warrant.

Immanuel flashed a badge and explained that he needed to insist on getting to the inner sanctum.

"Sorry, but I am under strict instructions not to disturb Mr. Maranzano."

"So he is in, then?"

Claudia Valenti's eyes flitted to the guys on the couches and looked back at Immanuel. The fellas stood up, one facing the three guests and the other looking directly toward Immanuel.

"That is none of your business, mister. You need to listen to the lady and come back some other time. Make an appointment, why don't you?"

"As we are here, we might as well wait until Mr. Maranzano has a spare couple of minutes."

He nodded at the other three—bulbous-nose leaned against the office door and the other two squeezed past and sat on the couches, one on each. Maranzano's fellas shifted around the room to avoid having their backs to any of these agents. Immanuel sidled next to one of his guys on the couch who whispered to him, but he kept his eyes on the secretary all the while.

"I do hope we are not getting in your way."

"No, but I really have no idea how long you will have to wait."

"Why don't you start by letting Maranzano know we are here?"

Claudia sighed, knowing Immanuel was right but aware that she was about to get into trouble. She looked askance at Maranzano's men, who showed no interest in intervening.

She held down a button on her squawk box and spoke clearly into the microphone, "Mr. Maranzano, there are four gentlemen to see you without an appointment."

"Tell them to go to hell."

"They are from the police."

"What the..."

The voice trailed off and three seconds later, his office door opened and Salvatore Maranzano, mob boss appeared. He was annoyed that he had been disturbed, but despite his lofty position, he realized he should show the detectives at least a small amount of respect if he were to rid himself of these annoying insects. He eyed the four men and shrugged.

"I guess you'd better come in, then."

These words were aimed at Immanuel, and bulbous nose followed him in. As they walked, Immanuel gave the other two a simple instruction: "Keep our friends here occupied and make sure they don't leave the premises."

Before he passed the threshold of Maranzano's office, Immanuel cast his glance over to the whisperer, who nodded but remained silent.

"I SUPPOSE YOU have a warrant, or is this one of your friendly shakedowns?"

"We wanted to have a conversation to alert you to a problem you will shortly face. Of course, if you make any donations to the Police Benevolence Fund, that's entirely up to you."

Maranzano tutted and sat down. He'd heard all the excuses in the world from a thousand cops who wanted a little extra in their pay packets at the end of the week. It wasn't the request which annoyed him; he just didn't like being disturbed before his second cup of coffee.

"Spare me the sob story and get to the point. I've better things to do with my time than listen to the likes of you."

"What you got against cops?"

"Nothing that fifty bucks or a bullet don't fix. It's Jews I can't stand and I reckon there are a couple in my office right now."

Immanuel turned to his companion and laughed.

"What you know, Alex, he doesn't like us."

Alex guffawed back and clung to the edge of Maranzano's desk to stop himself from falling over with mirth. Meanwhile, Immanuel had moved to the other side of the old Italian, chuckling as he did so.

"The truly funny thing is, *Mister* Maranzano, that we have come here to give you something, not to ask for anything at all."

"What? You've brought me a gift?"

"Nah, a message."

"And what has a Jew-boy like you got to say to a man like me?"

Alex Cohen took one step toward Maranzano, whipped out a knife from his pants pocket, bent down and plugged the blade in Maranzano's stomach. The Mustache Pete didn't know what was happening until he looked down and saw a river of red leaving his guts.

Immanuel launched himself at the guy, pulling out his own shiv and stabbed him two, three, four times.

"Charlie Lucky says you will die like a dog."

Alex sliced at Maranzano's torso. Blood gushed out of every wound and the body slumped to the floor. The head banged on the corner of the desk on its way down, but it didn't make a difference because the self-styled Boss of Bosses was unconscious.

Immanuel popped round the door to see how the men were doing. They were standing over two corpses, but the girl was nowhere to be seen.

"Where is the secretary?"

"Immanuel, we told her to go for a long walk and buy herself a large coffee. She'll be out for the rest of the day."

"Should have killed her anyway, Vito."

"Claudia won't squeal. I know where she lives and she knows I do. Even if the real cops come knocking, she'll suffer a terrible bout of amnesia."

"You'd better be right."

"It'll be fine, Alex."

Back in Maranzano's office, the corpse was surrounded by a red lake. To make a point to those who survived him, Alex took out a revolver with its silencer, placed the muzzle in Salvatore's mouth and squeezed off one slug. There would be no open casket for that cadaver.

The men left the Castellammare Trading Company and headed back along the corridor. Near the board listing the companies on the ninth floor, they checked themselves in the mirror before calling for the elevator. When the red doors parted, the four members of Murder Corporation got in and Alex requested the lobby. As they descended, he thought how pleased Charlie would be to know that the last of the old guard in the Italian mob was no more.

2

CHARLIE LUCKY AND Johnny Torrio had formed the syndicate two years before, along with the elite squad known as Murder Corporation. With Louis Buchalter and Albert Anastasia, Alex was responsible for the smooth running of the group that killed other gang members at the request of the bosses of the organized crime gangs that ran the Eastern Seaboard as well as far-flung places like Chicago and Detroit.

The three men had seats at the syndicate table and, for better or worse, they had muddled along without treading on each other's toes too much. Charlie Lucky was the joint head of the syndicate, but you would be forgiven for thinking it was his entire show. Johnny Torrio preferred to spend his time counting his money and focusing on his own operations.

If Murder Corporation had a headquarters, then it was situated in the Jewish enclave of Brownsville within the confines of Brooklyn, east of Manhattan. While it was Louis' home from home, Anastasia preferred somewhere a little more Italian and was more comfortable in East New York or midtown. Alex always enjoyed staying on the island and had a distrust of the bridge and tunnel club.

Albert called a meeting of the directors and Alex suggested Lindy's Restaurant for a coffee and slice of cheesecake. He'd had a soft spot for the venue ever since his time spent there with Arnold Rothstein before his mentor's untimely demise. They sat in a booth at the back, feet away from Arnold's old table.

"So what are we doing here?"

"Alex, first I hoped we would start with some pleasantries and then cover our latest contract a little later."

Louis laughed and winked at his old-time friend, Albert. "Ever in a hurry, Alex. You should learn to take things easy."

"Sorry, but there's always another buck to make and as you know, I don't like to hang around."

Albert turned to Louis, "How's the family?"

"No complaints, thank you, Albert."

"And the kids?"

"I imagine they are doing just fine. I don't see them that much, what with work and so on."

The two men maintained broad grins throughout this exchange.

"And how's your mistress? Is she well and looking after you?"

"Albert, I would say so for sure. You might be right if you figured the reason I don't spend enough time with my children is because of the excessive hours I enjoy in Ruth's arms."

Chuckles from the two men and Alex felt a bit of him die inside.

"Come on, guys. Enough is enough. All the people we love, sleep with, or pay maintenance for are in great health. Who's on the kill list?"

As soon as the words left his lips, Alex realized he had overstepped the mark—no direct references to the work they did should ever be uttered within earshot of strangers or anybody who didn't need to hear.

"My apologies, gentlemen. I let my impatience get the better of me."

"That's all right, my boy. We forgive you and you are right—business before pleasure."

Albert cleared his throat and spoke in a more businesslike manner.

"First on the agenda is a message from our friend, who thanks you Alex for the recent conclusion to the matter of our older acquaintance."

Charlie Lucky had worked for Maranzano almost the entire time Alex had known him, although the tension between them only became intolerable after the syndicate was formed back in '29. At that point, the old Sicilian guard refused to acknowledge there were fresh ways to function in the modern century and that Italians and Jews could work together for mutual benefit. In contrast, Charlie was the first to see that the New York melting pot applied to the criminal underworld as much as anywhere else in the city. He seized the initiative, helped in no small part by Rothstein, and figured out a way for every gang boss to dip his beak in the trough without pecking out anyone else's eyes.

"I'm glad everyone was happy with the outcome. The primary targets of our operation were all met, although I want you to be aware that a young woman fled the coop."

"Should we be worried about her, Alex?"

"No, as I am assured she won't squeal, Albert."

"Are you relying on the word of Tommy Lucchese?"

"Yes..."

"As much as Tommy is a good fella to have with you when the going gets tough, his desire to trust a skirt has put him in deep water previously, Alex..."

"And it would be a shame for him to sink to the bottom of the Hudson over this dame."

"Exactly, Alex, especially as we'd be the ones who'd fry."

"I shall take care of this oversight."

"Thank you, Alex. Let's not forget that loose talk costs lives."

"We live together, we love together, but we die alone."

They tucked into their cheesecakes, oblivious to the fact they were holding this meeting in broad daylight in a busy diner. The difference here was that Alex's lieutenants, Ezra Kohut and Massimo Sciarra stood guard near the entrance to prevent any unwelcome visitors inside the premises while they were there.

"Now let's move on to item two…"

CLAUDIA LIVED IN an ordinary tenement in Bed-Stuy, just north of Brownsville. Her time as secretary with Maranzano meant she knew far too much for a woman her age, but what was certain to her was that if she breathed a word to anyone about the four men who entered that office then she would sleep with the fishes.

She considered leaving town but figured she'd be too easy to find. So instead she holed up in her apartment and waited for everything to come good. Her best hope was that they had let her go in the first place—why release her to only kill her later? That idea permeated her mind until the following day when there was a tap on the door.

Claudia froze for a second because she wasn't expecting any visitors and, again she thought, it must be safe. What hitman would knock politely when they could kick the door down and murder her in her sleep? She peeked through the spyglass and saw a besuited guy, who seemed a bit like one of the four from yesterday. She shrugged and undid the latch.

"Come in, why don't you."

Alex doffed his fedora and strolled across the threshold and, with no further invitation, sauntered into the living room, quickly followed by Claudia.

"Thank you for seeing me, Claudia. I'm sure you must be at a loose end now your boss has met an untimely demise, so I hear."

"You know who I am."

"Tommy sends his regards." Alex knew the Lucchese name would offer the girl some comfort and put her at her ease.

"I understand it's an imposition but do you think I could have a coffee?"

"What? Sure, yes…"

Claudia wandered off to the kitchenette and busied herself with beans and her percolator. Although she hadn't noticed, Alex stood at the far end of the kitchen leaning against the refrigerator. She swiveled round to get some milk and jumped when she saw how close he was to her.

Despite her concerns, she carried on and waited for the water to boil and then she let the coffee bubble away in the upper chamber of the percolator. Alex remained still for the entire time.

A LIFETIME LATER, Claudia poured the steaming brown liquid into two cups and put them on a living room table next to her couch. Alex unbuttoned his jacket and sat down at one end, giving her more than enough space without feeling hemmed in. As a precaution she sat in her armchair instead, a few feet further away.

"Thank you, Claudia."

"You're welcome, but I doubt you have come all this way just for a cup of coffee."

"Correct. Recently you found yourself in a situation and I wanted to check my people didn't make you feel the least bit uncomfortable."

"Oh no, not at all. They were very nice about it—suggested I went out to get a drink before any trouble started."

"Good. I'm glad. Sometimes my boys can behave inappropriately and forget how they must be respectful around the fairer sex."

"There's nothing to worry about on that score, Mr. Cohen."

Alex stirred his coffee and stopped as soon as Claudia mentioned his name. Then he continued and took a sip before speaking again.

"You know who I am."

"I didn't recognize you, if that's what you were wondering. One of your guys used your name and I put two and two together."

"You're a bright girl, Claudia. Have you been back to the office at all?"

"I figured you told me to scram, so I did just that. Yesterday evening's paper told me all I needed to know."

"Did they say who did for Maranzano?"

"No, only that it was gang related."

"And what do you guess happened?"

"Mr. Cohen, Salvatore paid me to do what he asked, not to think."

"Call me Alex. How well did you know Salvatore?

Claudia blushed and her eyes cast down onto her lap—the rumors were true and that she was one of his many conquests.

"My apologies, it was wrong of me to ask you such an indelicate question. Can you forgive me?"

"Of course… Alex."

"Perhaps you'd be interested in carrying on a bedroom arrangement with me instead of Salvatore. You're a fine-looking woman, after all."

Claudia's eyes flicked from left to right. She couldn't believe what Alex was suggesting, but it would explain why the gentleman had come calling.

"Well, a girl has to earn a living…"

"Why not start our new relationship now? Hop into bed and I'll be with you in a minute—I need to freshen up first. I hope you don't mind."

"Not at all. It's pleasant having a man around who cares about such things."

She showed him the way to the bathroom and once she'd headed to the bedroom and undressed, Alex popped by the sink and waited a count of sixty. Then he flushed the toilet, put his hand in his inside jacket pocket and strode toward the bed.

Claudia lay under the blankets with her clothes strewn around the room. She smiled coquettishly at him and Alex returned her grin. He pulled out his pistol and shot her in the head. Then he stuffed a pillow over her face and squeezed the trigger again. He threw ten dollars on her bedside table and walked out into the fresh air.

3

A WEEK LATER, Alex sat opposite his good friend, Alfonse Capone, slurping spaghetti in a restaurant controlled by the man who ran Chicago.

"I'm surprised you came over to do this job yourself. Surely you have minions to carry out your every whim by now?"

"There is a network of associates—and you have known that for years—but any excuse to visit a pal."

"Too kind. I suppose you've been reading about my difficulties?"

"The papers are full of them. How d'you get into this mess?"

"Alex, the simple truth is that I listened to my accountant. He told me I should keep records of legitimate business dealings so I'd have something to explain my income. Turns out, he was wrong. The disparity was too great between what I bought and the money I officially brought in. The court case has only got another couple of weeks and then it'll all be over."

Alex grimaced because Alfonse was likely to face prison time and every law enforcement agent in the country had been working night and day to bring the man to his knees. To them, he represented the worst excesses of organized crime.

"Do you think you have a chance to get off?"

"Only if I am able to apply some leverage to a couple of the jurors. I have the brightest tax lawyers money can buy, but I'm guilty and everybody knows it."

They continued eating their pasta course, but by the time the last of the tomato sauce had been mopped up with the final piece of bread, neither of them wanted to talk about courts and jail.

"The reason I am here, Alfonse, is to explain about the contract. The target is your underboss, Grimaldi, and I want you to know this is strictly business for me. There is no personal malice involved whatsoever."

"I appreciate your concern. If he must go, then so be it. He has made a mistake and will pay for his misdeeds."

"I'm glad you understand the situation, Alfonse."

"Alex, the fact you have taken the time out of your day to talk to me on this matter speaks volumes. Besides, I agreed to the hit otherwise Murder Corporation wouldn't have been given the contract."

They smiled at each other because they both knew Alfonse was right. Any hit between gangs was approved by the syndicate members, and only then did anyone engage the services of Alex's group. A silence grew between them, but they were comfortable in each other's presence. There was nothing more to say. Grimaldi was a dead man walking and Alfonse would soon be incarcerated for who knew how long. That'd be down to the judge, but the chances were, he would not receive a slap on the wrist and a couple of months behind bars. And this might well be the last time the two men would get to see each other for quite a while—neither wanted to express it, but they knew it. You could detect it in their eyes.

PEPE GRIMALDI WOKE up in a blue funk—he should remember not to drink so much. He looked around to find he was in his apartment and the snoring next to him showed he was not alone. Pepe turned to face the broad and admired his taste in women. He eyed her naked body and wondered if he wanted to wake her for some more fun. Before he could reach a conclusion, there was a knock on the front door. Probably the boys come to pick him up. He checked his watch and discovered that he was running a few minutes late.

A grab of a towel and Pepe opened the front door and headed into the living room without looking back—an icy blast of air hit his chest and he didn't want to hang around welcoming his guys.

Alex stepped inside and followed Pepe until the fella halted and saw the stranger in his apartment.

"Anybody else here?" Alex snapped.

"Huh? A skirt in my bed, but no one else."

"Tell her to stay there and she won't have any trouble."

"She's asleep—she'll be no bother to anyone for a while."

"Make sure it stays that way. And you'd better put on some clothes—we're going for a ride."

"Where to?"

"Does it matter? Capone has issued an order."

Pepe shrugged and clung to his towel, which was lurching toward the ground. He shuffled off to the bedroom and threw on pants, shirt, and jacket—the first items he saw because he'd got a sense from Alex that the guy didn't want to be hanging around while he attempted sartorial decisions.

OUT IN THE hallway, Pepe made to walk down the stairs, but Alex pointed upwards.

"I thought you said we were going for a ride."

"Yep, but first I want us to have a private conversation and you have a guest in your apartment."

"Okay."

Pepe wasn't sure he believed the guy, but his argument made a certain level of sense. Besides, Capone ruled the roost and if that's what Alfonse wanted, that was what he got. Six long flights of stairs later and they ran out of steps—just a door leading to the roof. Alex sidled past Pepe and tried the handle. It was locked but a quick push with his shoulder and they stood outside, on top of the world.

Alex sauntered across the asphalt and stopped to lean against the balustrade at the far end of the building. Pepe dutifully followed in his wake until they were facing each other. Silence for a second and then Pepe decided enough with these antics.

"So what do you want to talk about?"

"How are things going with you, Pepe?"

"All right, I suppose. Why?"

"I hear things. People chat, you know how they do."

"Don't believe everything folks say."

"I check the facts before I reach a conclusion, which is why you and I are having this conversation."

"And what do you think you have found out?"

"Do you like a drink, Pepe?"

"As much as the next guy, I suppose."

"From all accounts, more than the next man. You like to party, wouldn't you say?"

"Yeah, but I'm not the only fella in Chicago to drink and have a bit of fun."

"No, you're not. That is true. Would you say you can hold your drink?"

"U-huh. Every now and again I get a bit wild, but most of the time, I handle myself just fine."

"In a speakeasy, having a coffee laced with gin."

"Or vodka. I prefer vodka if I can get hold of it."

"Me too, Pepe. That's something we have in common."

"Nice."

"And when you bring a lady friend home with you, like you did last night, do you always treat them with respect? Offer them a drink from your private collection? Show them a good time?"

"Why yes, what's the point of bringing a woman back to your place if you're not going to have a fine time?"

"Pepe, that's my point. I asked you if you always show the broads respect and you told me you did, but we both know that isn't true, don't we?"

For the first moment since their arrival on the roof, Pepe understood where the conversation was heading. He gritted his teeth and steeled himself, back straightened.

"Like I told you, don't believe everything people say."

"And let me remind you I check the facts. Pepe, your mistake wasn't to rough up Erika Pisani, but you raped the girlfriend of an underboss and left her alive."

By this point, Alex had circled Pepe several times during their conversation and as he spoke his last words, he ensured Pepe stood between him and the balustrade. Alex stepped forward in an instant and punched Pepe in the solar plexus. He crumpled immediately, giving Alex the opportunity to grab him by his collar and throw him off the roof. Pepe Grimaldi had left the building.

4

HOBOKEN WAS NOT Alex's idea of a great city, but he knew that the easiest way for him to maintain some contact with his sons was to visit them rather than expect their mother to bring them into Manhattan. When Sarah walked out on him, taking their five boys with her, Alex's men found her within two hours of their search. Thirty minutes later, he knocked on the door of the hotel suite where they were staying. Her ashen face spoke volumes as he stood there and demanded his children back, which she refused.

Alex considered dragging their sorry asses to what was once their home, but deep down he knew he wouldn't be able to look after them better than their mother. So instead, he let her go and asked that he still have access to the kids. Sarah's initial reaction was to refuse and that made Alex dig his heels in.

Rather than overtly threaten her as was his instinct, he held in his anger and waited. Her original response morphed over the following weeks into the realization that the boys needed a sturdy father figure in their lives and there wasn't any man much stronger than Alex.

Ever since, each week when Alex was in New York, he would take time on Saturday afternoons to head off to Hoboken and play with Moishe, David, Asher, Elijah and Arik—in the park when the weather was good and in a hotel suite hired for the purpose when times were cold, wet or both.

The youngest three knew him as the strange guy who'd appear in their lives now and again, but they didn't feel a close connection to him. Moishe would never forgive his father for letting Arik get kidnapped, although the boy couldn't help but be grateful to his papa for saving him from the bad men who stole him away.

ALEX PUSHED ARIK on the park swing while Asher and Elijah played make-believe in a playhouse at the top of a small ladder attached to a set of monkey bars. Moishe and David sat on the grass a few feet apart from the others, too old for such juvenile pursuits as climbing or messing about. They would soon be teenagers and it showed in their behavior if nothing else.

The little one was having a wild time as Alex pushed him higher and higher until Arik believed he was flying over the world. His father smiled at the simple pleasure the youngest of his men was experiencing. It seemed good to do good.

All was calm in Elysian Park and the male members of the Cohen family were only thirty feet away from the corner of Hudson and Tenth Streets. Every few minutes, Alex would look around to check on his charges, but there was no danger apart from hurt pride or a scuffed knee. The pleasant thing about this recreation area was that when Alex looked east, he saw Manhattan on the other side of the Hudson and that made him feel closer to home than he actually was.

He gave Arik a countdown for his return to earth and picked him up high above his head and helped him to land on both feet.

"First one to Moishe wins."

Alex slammed his foot down for his first step and ensured that Arik arrived at the two lads before himself. Neither David nor Moishe seemed pleased to greet the runners. Alex hopped over to a bag he'd brought along, took out a baseball and shouted over to Moishe: "Catch!"

Despite himself, the eldest leaped up to grab the ball, positioned himself so it landed in his cupped hands, and rolled on the floor to increase the drama of the moment. Alex pulled out a bat from the same bag and organized a mini tournament. When it was his turn to face the bowler, Alex made sure he didn't put too much swing on the baseball bat and, for a second, a memory flashed across his mind of the days before the war. The blood-smeared recollection over, he spent the rest of the day focused on squeezing every valuable minute out of his time with his sons.

5

SARAH ARRIVED LATE at the diner and blamed the housekeeper for her delay. Alex didn't care who was at fault, he just wanted to see his estranged wife again—there were matters to discuss with her. From the day she walked out on him and his lies, Sarah knew there was a gulf between what he said and what he meant. Over the intervening years, she got used to this, but every time she found Alex was departing from the truth, another nail dug into the coffin of their relationship.

She had made a pleasant life for herself away from New York but at heart she was a city girl, so had no desire to run off to some rural village to weave baskets or live through the Depression in abject loneliness and discomfort.

Alex might have lied about his involvement with his mistress and allowed his family to be put at risk as a result of his many dubious business activities, but he always ensured that she and the boys wanted for nothing of any material value.

By the time she arrived, Alex had ordered her a coffee with cream just how she liked it. This rankled with Sarah because it was down to her to decide what she wanted, but of course he had made the correct decision.

"Thanks for agreeing to see me, Sarah."

"That's okay. You're still the father of my children and we love them enough to want what's best for them, right?"

"Why, yes."

"So I'm guessing this has something to do with them."

"Well, indirectly, for sure."

Sarah stared at him, unsure what he meant. If it wasn't the boys, what could they possibly have to chat about? Alex started by asking how she had been and small talk persisted for an interminable five or ten minutes. She did her best not to appear impatient because she knew he operated at his own, usually brisk, pace and did not appreciate being thrown off his plan. So she chatted and waited for the payoff.

"SARAH, I NEED you to know that I'm not seeing anybody."

"Thanks for telling me, but it is none of my business anymore, Alex. You see who you want and the same goes for me. We aren't together and haven't been for two years."

"Two long years."

"We've had our difficulties, but we're in a decent place now, don't you think?"

"Yes, Sarah, I do. And that's what I wanted to talk to you about today."

"I'm listening, but I have absolutely no idea what you're on about."

"Sarah." Alex put down his cup and peered directly into her eyes with so much intensity that she too placed her cup back on its saucer. "I've been working hard ever since you... we split up to get on the straight and narrow. To do the right thing. I have been successful in my business dealings and have set aside a reasonable amount of money. That's how I have been able to afford to keep myself in clover and to ensure you and the boys have been looked after properly."

"I appreciate the house, the maid and all the other things you have done for us. It hasn't gone unnoticed."

"I'm pleased, Sarah, but I want more."

Sarah laughed, "You haven't changed. You were never satisfied with anything you had."

"But that's my point. I believe I have changed. If you would do me the honor of getting back together with me, I would walk away from my enterprises. If that is what it required to get you to return, then that is what I would do."

Sarah placed her hands on her lap.

"I want you fully in my life, Sarah. I have missed you and I yearn for your company again."

Sarah said nothing and sipped from her drink. Now she wished she'd agreed to add a splash of gin.

"As I've told you before, Alex, it isn't what you do for work that meant I had to leave. I was a *nafka* when you met me and you were a slugger. A whore and a street thug were a perfect match, right?"

He allowed a smile to erupt out of the corner of his mouth and then his lips subsided back to the usual countenance.

"You make money the only way you know how and I accepted that a long time ago—probably before we even got together. The problem I have with your work is that the people you deal with threatened the boys and me. I want to live in a world where my children can be safe. They should be able to go to bed and believe they will still be alive in the morning and not wind up riddled with bullets."

"For you I would quit the business—I've sufficient money as I said."

"Alex, you also know that isn't enough for me. When I left, there was one other thing that drove me away from you…"

"I don't see her anymore. I'm not seeing anybody."

"That was not the issue, Alex. The fact you'd slink out at night and spend time with that actress wasn't your finest moment, but I could have forgiven you. Your lying did us in the end. If I can't trust you to be honest with me, then we have nothing. Bupkis."

"Do you believe what I am saying to you?"

She sighed and shrugged.

"Now, of course you mean what you say, but that is not the issue for me. The question is whether you will still mean it this evening, tomorrow or any day in the future. That's what is so tough for me to accept. There have been too many times in the past when you have said all the right things and then done the opposite."

He swallowed hard.

"And, Alex, I would love to believe you. The idea we could make all this better between us would lift my heart. But do you mean it? Is Ida really in the past now? And would you give up your famous, dangerous friends just for me and the boys? I'm not seeing it, you know?"

"I'd do it in an instant if you'd really come back to me."

Sarah finished her coffee and dabbed her lips with her napkin.

"Let's leave things for now—give me a chance to think through what you have said. And it means we won't end in an argument. I know how you are when you don't get your way immediately."

She stood up and walked out of the diner, leaving Alex to stew on what she had declared and for his men to escort her to the waiting taxi.

March 1933

6

ALEX HAD FIRST met Charlie Lucky shortly after his arrival in the country, but they did not work closely together until after Alex's return from the Great War and his move away from his first mentor, Waxey Gordon and into the orbit of the Big Bankroll.

Now they were both members of the syndicate, an organization created by Charlie who acted as its chief executive. The Italian succeeded by thinking beyond the moment in which he lived. Tomorrow's problems were today's discussions, and this morning was no different.

"Alex, our world will change shortly and we need to be ready."

"I saw the papers too—they are giving up on Prohibition."

"The Protestant experiment had to end at some point and it looks like it is this month."

"So soon and so suddenly, Charlie."

"Don't sound too surprised. Any time such a dumbass idea ends up being law, you can bet it'll be repealed when everybody wakes up and smells the coffee. This was doomed before it began."

"We've made good money out of it though. I can't see honest folk visiting our speakeasies to buy watered down booze when they could pick up the real deal from some reliable Joe down the street."

"Alex, I reckon you're right, although we need to think what we will do with all that real estate. Sell it? Turn it into… I don't know what."

"We might not have all the answers now, but we'll figure it out. Besides, Roosevelt is signing the paperwork and it'll take several months before every state gives up on the whole sorry mess."

"There are enough individuals who dip their beaks in the trough who'll want it to last as long as possible."

"Yeah, Alex, there are sufficient cops and politicians on our payroll; it'll still be around until the end of the year."

"And at that point we require a fresh source of revenue."

"Correct, which is why I wanted to speak with you today."

"Go on, Charlie. I'm always interested in your plans, especially when we can both make some gelt along the way."

"Okay, this is the deal. I need not tell you how much green we've made from booze, but there's another commodity we must get into that'll make liquor money seem like chump change. And that is… heroin."

Alex's eyebrows rose toward the roof. Until now, he had known Charlie was importing the brown powder from North Africa using his connections in Sicily. Over the years, he had even helped his friend when the fella had the occasional transportation issues, but it was another thing to get involved directly.

"I don't know, Charlie."

"What's not to know? We buy the raw material through my friends in Palermo, ship it over here—we already have the transportation network thanks to moving all that Scotch and gin from Scotland and England—cut up the product with other powder and peddle it on the streets for a crazy profit."

"Heroin is different, Charlie."

"How is that, Alex?"

"We provide girls, we take bets, we sell liquor. Those are all things that men crave and whether or not we were there, they'd keep looking until they found them. But heroin… ordinary Joes don't need that stuff. We'd be selling them something they have no interest in. Do we really want our business to be based on forcing people to buy our goods? That sounds difficult to me and not what the politicians we have currently in our pockets will want to be involved in either. They'll run a mile from us when they find out."

Charlie looked at Alex all the while he spoke, a wry smile fixed upon his face. He let Alex say his piece and nodded occasionally to show he understood and respected his good friend.

"I understand your concerns, Alex. So tell me, do you like a pipe?"

"Not for a while. Haven't had a toke since Sarah left me. I went on a bender for a week and not a puff since."

"Alex, there's nothing wrong with an occasional opium pipe. The Chinese have been using them for generations, right?"

"Sure."

"But heroin is just processed opium. They are the same thing. If you are okay with opium pipes, then you shouldn't object to heroin. They are made from the same poppy."

Alex stared at Charlie and blinked. He hadn't thought about it that way before. He had no direct experience of heroin and didn't know anyone who used it, whereas the showbiz types who Ida mixed with always had a pipe in tow. Opium was normalized for him and heroin was something the Jews of Brooklyn did, but not the sophisticated guys in Manhattan.

TWO DAYS LATER, Alex found Charlie in his hotel suite and carried on where they left off.

"Why would we want to get involved in heroin trafficking when it's only in the last couple of years that the government has banned the stuff?"

"Alex, it is the law of supply and demand. If nobody wanted heroin, then there'd be no need to prohibit its use. Uncle Sam has basically announced to us that there's a business opportunity to seize."

"And if we don't do it...?"

"Some other guy will. You can bet your last dollar on that. So many fellas have the transportation infrastructure and distribution networks thanks to booze. Almost every syndicate member has the capability—and then there are guys in other parts of the country who could just as easily head east as any other direction. Either we find some other use for what we are sitting on or we start from scratch with I don't know what."

"I guess it's the same as the stuff they put in patent medicines."

"And who doesn't like a bottle of cola?"

"Or cough syrup."

"That's my point, Alex. The drug has been accepted for decades and now they are opening the floodgates on booze, they need something else to control people's lives over. Politicians are the worst. Pure scum. We should know because we bribe them enough."

They shared a chuckle, as they understood all too well how true that comment was. Alex fell silent for a spell, eyes cast downward, and felt Charlie watching him. When he looked up, he saw the guy's broad grin.

"So you in?"

"In principle. We haven't talked about gelt. If I move into the heroin trade, won't I have to give up on the Murder Corporation?"

"Not necessarily—at least not initially."

"Charlie, explain to me how I can have my cake and eat it."

"Well, I still need you to work with Albert and Louis. Albert might be a made man, but he nevertheless needs to listen to sensible advice—and he and Louis don't always see eye to eye."

"Okay...?"

"Bear with me. What I am proposing is that you and I go into business together, but as a side project, at least at first. You keep your current interests, as do I, and if I'm right, then we'll be awash with heroin money before the end of the year and can make some changes then. And if I am wrong, then we have lost nothing."

"Apart from our time, energy and investment capital."

"Yes, of course. But that's America, isn't it? You put your cojones on the line and see if you still have them in the morning."

"God bless America."

"Yeah, whatever."

"And will you inform the rest of the syndicate about our arrangement so everything is open, Charlie?"

"Why should we tell them about a private deal? It doesn't affect them and besides, the best way to kick-start a new venture is to keep it all small until you can expand. When we do, we'll cut in all our friends. If this thing is as big as I think it will be, then everyone dips their beaks in this trough and we'll need them to keep up with demand."

"Could it really get bigger than booze?"

"The profit we make? For sure. We watered down alcohol by ten or twenty percent. We'll dilute the heroin from Sicily by ninety-five percent. To my mind that makes it a better commodity because you can ship less across the Atlantic and still generate more money."

"With liquor, you take it from the boat, stack it in a warehouse and drive it to a bar. For heroin, don't you need somewhere to process the drugs and then a bunch of guys to hit the streets and sell the powder?"

"Right—and even with those extra costs, it's a better market to be in. Alex, you know I have worked this angle since the mid-twenties. Not in a big way, but I've been experimenting on how best to make this business work and I think I've found how to do it."

Alex looked deep into his friend's eyes. Charlie Luciano sure was enthusiastic over packets of brown powder, in a way he hadn't seen for a long time.

"Why me?"

"Alex, you have built up an impressive transportation network. Don't pretend Arnold didn't entrust you to create the principal route from Canada to New York for hard liquor. And you then protected it against other gangs, the cops, the Feds—the list goes on. You will have that transport system idle very soon and we can put it to excellent use. And if I haven't stroked your ego enough, I trust you, and you know how to handle yourself. I'll need a fella like you before this business is over."

He thought through all the angles and reckoned Charlie was right. Alex stuck out his hand and they shook to seal the deal.

7

ALEX HAD FORGOTTEN how old Ida looked—he hadn't seen her for months and the thought of her only appeared in his head the moment he disavowed her to Sarah. They had spent New Year together because he couldn't think of anything else to do and she had been available.

Despite the widening gulf between them, Alex continued to pay for her hotel accommodation and imagined that he always would. He felt no malice toward her—the truth was, he thought very little about her at all. That was the trouble. As much as he yearned for some form of companionship, Ida had stopped offering him that quite some time ago. Even before Sarah left, he had been talking of ditching the skirt, but had never been bothered enough to do anything significant about it.

Once or twice a month, he'd pop over and spend a night in her bed. A couple of years before, they had gone to the theater and he had spent time with her acting buddies, but those opportunities had fallen away.

Nowadays, they'd call room service for food, then Alex would satisfy himself with her, sleep, and leave before she woke. So Alex forgave Ida's surprise when he phoned and asked if she was free that evening.

HE OPENED THE door to the suite with the key he'd kept all these years and called out a quick hello.

"I'm in the bedroom. Make yourself a drink and I'll be with you in a minute," came the disembodied voice. He smiled and wandered through the hallway and dropped his coat on a nearby armchair.

"You want something?" he bellowed but received no reply. A shrug and Alex pulled out a bottle of Scotch from a closed sideboard. Ida hid the bottle because Prohibition was still in force in New York and she wanted no trouble from inquisitive maids. Two cubes of ice in the glass and he dropped onto one end of the couch.

She left him waiting for countless minutes before appearing in a red housecoat covering a pair of gold silk pajamas. For such a simple set of clothes, she had spent a ridiculous amount of time putting them on. She smiled as she rustled toward Alex and bent down to peck him on the lips before swishing round to fix herself a cocktail.

Once the cosmo was complete, Ida returned to the couch and sat next to him—all this while she had said not a word.

"Good to see you, Ida."

"Marvelous to see you too, darling."

"How have you been?"

"Oh you know how it is. I've been in between parts for so long now, I can barely remember my lines."

"I thought you were enjoying being the shining star on the cabaret circuit."

"Of course, my dear. Every week, there's somewhere I can sing. That meets my material needs—as well as your generosity, darling—but it doesn't feed my soul."

Alex listened to Ida's words and believed very few of them. By the time they dated, she was washed up, which was why she was taking jobs in upmarket speakeasies and not spending all her days in the Yiddish theater. There was nothing about her subsequent lifestyle that would have endeared her to off-Broadway producers.

They settled in and sipped their drinks. He listened to her reminisce about her glory days and Alex shared what little he was prepared to say about his business dealings and associates. While they chatted, he couldn't decide if he'd had enough of this woman or whether he wanted to grab her by the hand and take her to the bedroom. His ambivalence was difficult to measure.

"Then Larry took me to one side and whispered into my ear as he cupped my breast to tell me that the chicken feathers had left the room…"

Ida lived in the past and Alex was more concerned with what lay ahead in the world, but, she offered him the comfort of knowing what he was like and making so few demands of him that she was barely noticeable altogether. He blinked and focused on the curves of her body again—at least the ones visible through her housecoat. Despite the ravages of the intervening years, she still created flutters in the pit of his stomach. No other woman apart from Sarah could make that claim, other than Rebecca, whom he'd dated only a couple of times before the war.

Not that he had only slept with those three women—in fact, he'd not even got to first base with Rebecca. But there had been many others he had shared a bed with. Whenever he hit the nightclubs, a gaggle of girls would beat a line to his table, dropping handkerchiefs for him to pick up, or just walking straight up to him and starting a conversation.

Sometimes, he would invite the prettier ones to join him and on other occasions, he would feign ignorance and let them pass in the night. These conquests didn't mean much to him and he felt that was his problem. No woman could give him what he wanted—safety for the future and a calm place to sleep in the evening.

IDA STOOD UP to get herself another drink. "Want another?"

"I'm good, thanks. Why don't you throw on something warmer and we could go out for a meal?"

"Really, darling? I thought we might enjoy the rare moment we spend together nesting here."

"Ida, I thought we could try that new restaurant that's opened up opposite Lindy's. Then I reckon there'd be enough time to catch a show."

"I'd prefer to nest, Alex, but if you really need to be surrounded by other people, then let's go out to eat, but I have no desire to watch some hack annihilate a playwright's work. Even a second-rate writer deserves better than what's on offer on Broadway nowadays."

"I've read that theatreland is filled with Yiddish stars performing their old shtick for a *goyishe* crowd. I suggested it because I thought you might know some of the hoofers."

"Dear Alex, you are sweet, but really any of my peers has left the mainstream years ago. I mean to say, the travesty that calls itself theater is not worth even a cursory glance."

Alex sighed. This is what Ida was like. When she wound herself up on a topic, there was almost no way to talk her down from her high horse.

"Ida, it was only a suggestion. Forget about a show, but let's at least escape this place and go to a restaurant for some fine dining."

"There was a point when the only thing you'd want to do was to beat a retreat to my bedroom and never fly."

"And there was a time, Ida, when you had fire in your belly and a love of the crowd. Those days are gone, wouldn't you say?"

"We've all got older, Alex. That's all. Times change and you have to either accept the new ways or rail against them."

"Seems to me that you've done neither. Instead you're clinging to the banks of the river and hoping that everything will plain sail away. It's why you don't like leaving this suite I pay for."

"Let me go and change, Alex, before the conversation turns too acrid."

He had no idea what that meant and knew she was smarting from what he had said—Ida used difficult words whenever she wanted the upper hand. She knew he'd done little book work back in the old country and absolutely none after he arrived in America—unless you counted learning English when he was in base camp before he went off to fight.

IN GROSSMANN'S RESTAURANT, Alex had secured a table near the window because he knew Ida would enjoy the attention from an occasional passerby. He booked the spot just after Ida agreed to get dressed and when he was initially told they had no places free that evening, he explained he was Alex Cohen and wondered if the maître d' would be kind enough to check the bookings again.

"This is a delightful place—I'm glad you persuaded me to try it."

Ida's chin appeared briefly above the menu and he caught a smile. Alex always could make her head spin by spending gelt. Despite her bold thespian flourishes, Ida was a simple girl at heart who would follow the glitzy and shiny things until the end of the world.

"They say the steak is very good, but I doubt if there's anything abominable on offer."

"I'd prefer some grilled fish. Will that be a problem?"

"Shouldn't be. You ask and if the waiter kicks up a fuss, then let me handle the situation, but he won't."

Ida picked up the frosty edge in Alex's voice with his last few words. Her smile vacated her face for a second until she forced it to return. This was a dangerous man to cross and she knew it all too well.

Alex ordered two gin coffees with their meal and wondered if he would ever regain a taste for wine. Since Prohibition had started, there had been bottles of champagne to consume with his friends, but nothing as simple as a bottle of red to go with a bowl of pasta. He laughed to himself—he was becoming more Italian by the day. *Lokshen* soup and a glass of white—that'd be better.

In the taxi on their way to Ida's hotel, she got fresh with him, but he wasn't interested. The alcohol coursing through her veins was making her frisky, whereas the same liquor inside Alex made him want to withdraw from the world in reaction to her hotter advances.

When they got back to the suite, she responded to being spurned by ignoring him and stripping off in a last-ditch attempt to attract him to her. When that didn't work, the only thing left for Ida to want was her pipe. Alex walked out as she lapsed into a stoned silence as the opium fumes reached the depths of her lungs.

8

THE NEXT MORNING, Alex sat with Albert and Louis in a nondescript second floor office in Brownsville. The other two spent much of their time in this place, but Alex was far from comfortable. If he ignored the fact he had to leave Manhattan, then he was stuck with the peeling wallpaper and the ever-present sense that roaches could crawl out of the skirting board at any moment.

Albert offered the other two men a cup of coffee which they both accepted and only once he had settled back into his chair did matters progress.

"We have a contract to carry out."

"What's the story, Albert?"

"Looks like a young guy has overstretched his reach and whacked a fella without due authority, Louis."

"And did the fella survive?"

"No, Alex. This a hit and we should ensure the guy knows what has happened to him before he dies."

"So let's ask Abe to find a local gun to get this matter sorted."

This was a simple plan—Abe Reles was a reliable fella who had a vast network of contract killers. Sometimes Alex thought the whole of Brownsville must be stuffed with assassins, but he knew there were some ordinary citizens somewhere in the area.

"Good idea, Louis, other than the hit needs to happen in Atlantic City."

"Don't we have any contacts who could sort this out for us?"

"Why don't we just save ourselves the hassle, Albert, and I'll pop over tomorrow and get the job done."

"If you're sure, Alex."

"I fancy a day by the sea, so why not?"

ALEX STOOD ON the main boardwalk in Atlantic City as water droplets from the sea mingled with his hair. There was something refreshing about being battered by the wind next to a beach.

While he'd said he was looking forward to a day out, this was not entirely true. What he really wanted was to grab a break from his beloved New York. The city kept him alive, but it felt like it was dragging him down—his women troubles and the threat of losing all he had earned thanks to the onslaught of Prohibition weighed heavily on his shoulders.

Hands in pants pockets, Alex wandered along the wooden slats, passing diners, casinos, and other places of ill repute, all of which were owned by syndicate member, Enoch Johnson. The reason Alex was in town was because of Enoch's complaint against smalltime hood, Ziv Quigley, a mixed-race mongrel with an Irish father and Jewish mother.

This was not why Enoch had raised an issue with the syndicate. His beef was with the way the boy comported himself around town. Specifically, Ziv would often be heard badmouthing his boss, Enoch, in the late-night drinking establishments where the guy held court.

Ziv boasted about the money he was making—no sin in being proud of your own success—and of how he was skimming from the take at the casino where he worked. This was two mistakes rolled into one. First, he shouldn't have been doing it at all and, second, don't tell people you're stealing from your boss, especially when he is a member of the syndicate.

Alex continued his promenade until he reached the last storefront but one before the wooden walkway vanished into the sand of the beach. He looked up and down to check nobody was paying him any attention and entered the nearest building, The Lucky Nugget.

On arrival, he was greeted by a young woman who took him to the bar so he could buy a coffee before being shown through a curtained door and into a gaming room filled with a mix of roulette wheels and card tables. Alex judged the lay of the land by playing a few hands of blackjack.

He had a rudimentary description of Ziv and the rest he would make up as he went along. Just by chance when Alex entered the room, most of the baize counters had female dealers so he headed to a young male, who was the likeliest candidate of all the current crop of people running the card games.

A few hands later and Alex was twenty bucks up—at the expense of the two others sat at the table. One folded and stood up to find a luckier dealer and the other guy swapped out more green hoping the fortune of the cards would change just because he wanted it to.

Alex carried on hitting and sticking almost randomly to see what happened and, sure enough, he continued to win–he knew he was being played by the dealer. Alex glanced at the name badge on the guy's chest and read: Z Quigley. He'd found his mark.

He let the game carry on until he figured out all of Ziv's moves. The boy had practiced well, but a keen eye could see when he was palming and dealing from the bottom of the deck. Ziv didn't do it every time he supplied a card, but several times a round—and consistently so. They reached a point where Alex was now losing more than he was winning.

"Lady Luck has slipped off my shoulder."

"Never mind, Mac. I'm sure she'll come back and visit ya."

The accompanying chuckle had an edge to it that made Alex think Ziv was a little too cocksure. He smiled but let the rest of the hands play out and when his gelt ran out, he decided there was no need to feed the boy any more notes.

"I'm out and off to the bar. Can I get you anything?"

"Mighty upright of you. An Irish coffee would certainly hit the mark—if that's not too big an ask."

"Sure thing. And call me Alex."

He walked off to find the drinks and returned a minute later to hover near the edge of the action as though he was enjoying the scene. Thirty minutes afterward as the final john left the table, leaving Ziv with no customers, Alex struck up a conversation with the lad who had stolen fifty bucks from him already.

"You aware of anywhere else a guy can play cards?"

"What do you mean, Alex?"

"I was wondering if there were private tables for people who have a little more money to wager."

"You one of them guys, Alex?"

"I reckon so, Ziv. You know of any private gaming in this town?"

Ziv stopped tidying up his station and stared into the barrel of both Alex's eyes. In that split second of judgment, Ziv sealed his fate.

"There's a hotel suite nearby where high rollers can go, but you need an invitation."

"Would you be able to get me in, Ziv? I'd sure appreciate it."

Alex smiled and flashed a note between his knuckles so Ziv understood there was money to be made by hooking Alex up.

"Stay there and let me see what I can do, Alex. I won't be long."

In the time it took Ziv to go to the lobby, place a call and return to the table, Alex had picked out at least three other dealers who were palming cards. He ignored that issue and followed Ziv out of the Lucky Nugget and away from the boardwalk.

ZIV LED ALEX two blocks along the street and then ducked into an alleyway. Although he was only ten feet behind the boy, Alex couldn't see quite what was around the corner and knew to be ready.

As he turned into the alley, Ziv was visible at the far end—perhaps he was straighter than he appeared. Alex caught up with him and grabbed Ziv by the sleeve.

"What's with the rear entrance?"

"Let's just say that the fellas at the front won't welcome a guy like you to a game like this."

"But the players will be all right?"

Ziv blinked twice before answering.

"Yeah, they are stand-up guys in the room. It's just the goons in the lobby aren't too welcoming of strangers."

Alex knew that anyone dumb enough to follow Ziv into an alleyway was sufficiently stupid to believe his nonsense, but he carried on walking behind the boy as they entered the back of the building at the end of the alleyway.

Down a corridor and into the kitchen of what looked like a hotel—some of Ziv's story was true, then. Out of the cooking area and off to a service elevator and up to the sixth floor. By now, Alex was intrigued to find out with what action Ziv had got himself involved.

Ziv patted Alex on the shoulder when he explained to a suit on the door that this stranger was with him. The goon checked Alex for weapons and found nothing, so they stepped aside and allowed him in.

Much to Alex's relief, he didn't recognize anybody—all local guys, but judging by the color of the chips, they were all high rollers; the pot held at least ten thousand when they walked in.

Ziv introduced the assembled throng to Alex and he waited for Alex to show his appreciation before sitting down at the back of the room. Gaming etiquette demanded Ziv hang around for a while so as not to mess with anyone's concentration.

Alex also stuck to the side of the room until he was invited to join the table. He swapped out a bundle of green for chips and played out at least a dozen hands. The game was straight and he created some inroads into profit, but he needed to keep some of his attention on Ziv.

Sure enough, two hours later the boy prepared to leave. Alex apologized and explained that his losses meant he should quit before he was in too big a hole. He had ensured he'd slowly lost ground after his earlier good fortune.

He and Ziv took the same route out of the joint as they'd entered and they closed the door to the alleyway on their way out.

"Wait a minute, I've got something in my shoe."

Alex feigned trying to balance on one foot and beckoned for Ziv to stand near so he could lean on the boy and sort out his footwear. As soon as the kid had positioned himself as Alex's resting post, he pulled out a shiv from his ankle that the goon hadn't even bothered to check properly and stuck it deep into Ziv's stomach.

The boy fell to the ground in an instant and Alex towered over him, looking to the entrance of the alleyway in case some nosey citizen looked the wrong way in that instant. Nobody. Alex bent down and removed the blade from Ziv's gut. Blood gushed out—Alex was careful not to be on the receiving end of the mess.

"Listen to me. I have a message from Enoch Johnson: do not steal from him. Do you understand?"

Ziv couldn't verbalize his response but attempted to nod amid his whimpering. Alex grabbed the boy's right hand and sliced a finger clean off.

"No one likes a thief," he hissed as he slashed Ziv's throat wide open. Before he left A.C., Alex popped back to the Lucky Nugget and asked to speak with the manager.

9

THE SYNDICATE RARELY met as an entire group, but the senior members would get together to discuss important matters as the need arose. With the demise of Prohibition on the horizon, this was one such time and a private room at the Waldorf Astoria had been reserved in a fictitious name. Charlie chose the venue in remembrance of Rothstein's New Year parties, but frivolity was far from the minds of the attendees.

Along with Charlie and Alex were Meyer Lansky and Benny Siegel. Meyer had positioned himself as the primary financier for the group, always eager to have several fingers in as many different pies as he could manage. He wasn't the Big Bankroll, but he had gained sufficient financial acumen thanks to the profits generated by bootlegging and his other illegal pursuits.

Benny was the flightiest of the group, but he was not to be underestimated. A steely yet impatient figure, he had gained a reputation as a killer and cemented that with his focus on gaming operations in Manhattan and Brooklyn. Before it had a formal name, Benny had worked with Charlie to set up Murder Corporation and continued to take contracts when they were big enough to warrant his attention.

The men sprawled across a number of easy chairs, reminiscent of their times in Arnold's apartment. Alex had known them for over a decade and they were comfortable in each other's company. Meyer and Benny had been friends since childhood—Charlie had done business with Lansky when they were teenagers.

"There's only one thing I want us to talk about and that is the impending demise of our bootlegging operations."

"Charlie, we need to figure out what we will do with the trucks, the warehouses and the speakeasies."

"Benny, you are right that we will need to dismantle what we have in place, but more important is to work out where we go from here. When the booze money dries up, we will still have men who expect to get paid and who will want to dip their beaks in the trough."

Charlie nodded at Alex's words, as they all did, but there was little consensus on where next. Meyer was the first to break the silence.

"Perhaps we just need to do more of what we do. We should also check our profit margins. Shaving a few cents here and there will make a substantial difference to our bottom line."

"Spoken like a true accountant."

The group chuckled as Meyer scowled at Benny's quip, who realized he may have overstepped the mark.

"I mean, you are correct, Meyer. We must certainly improve on the money we make on existing ventures, but I doubt if we'll replace all the bootlegging revenues that way. Right, Charlie?"

"Damn straight. We need something new. Yes, we must keep everything ticking over, but that won't be sufficient. The good news is that we are not alone. Everyone is in the same boat and we are all looking around to find the next big thing. We just need to be the first to get there."

"Whoever is in early gets to control the business."

"Right, Meyer. Spoken like a true businessman."

Smiles all round as Charlie echoed Benny's words, but without the edge.

THE FELLAS TOOK a break to order in some food and to grab yet another coffee. This also gave everybody a chance to chat among themselves. The mix of pasta and latkes appeared strange on the table but nobody commented as they had all ordered precisely what they wanted and each individual was too powerful to be questioned on their culinary decisions by any member of the waitering staff.

"Anyone heard how Alfonse is getting on behind bars?"

"Not me, Charlie. Amazing how they managed to hit him without raising a fist."

"You're right, Meyer. It was the lack of paperwork that did him in. He had no evidence to show the prosecution were lying."

"What would you have done, Benny?"

"If I didn't have the receipts, then I'd have created them. Given what the Feds could have taken into court, a small amount of falsification of evidence would have been nothing."

Alex pondered the rights and wrongs of the situation. Charlie had cabinet after cabinet filled with a record of every legitimate purchase he'd ever made —along with some others which were still tax deductible should the need arise.

In contrast, Alex followed the Rothstein model and kept all the details in his head and nowhere else. The solitary filing cabinet in his study was singularly empty—a piece of office furniture only used to store an occasional bottle of Scotch.

"Charlie, do you think I should keep records?"

"Alex, why start now? Besides, if they ever come calling, I've got enough receipts to sink a battleship—you can always borrow a couple of crates of mine."

Benny laughed out loud and Meyer sniggered briefly, but Alex knew that Charlie was serious. Without receipts you lose because you can't defend yourself. With paperwork it shows you how much tax you should have paid and Uncle Sam calculates the size of your illicit earnings, so you lose. Neither option was great and both would send you straight to the slammer.

Alex considered another aspect of the situation, "The difference between Alfonse and those of us in this room is that he courted publicity. Most here are shy of the press."

"Don't look at me," intoned Charlie, "because the last thing I want is newspaper attention. My problem is that my name has become associated with a bunch of unsavory characters."

They laughed at that remark as he looked around the room and eyeballed each of them. While Charlie wasn't as brash as Alfonse had been, he still gave the occasional interview or comment if a member of the press came calling. Meyer refused to say anything on the record and Benny, along with Alex, was unknown outside of his personal circle.

To clear his head, Alex walked down to the lobby with the excuse of buying a packet of cigarettes, even though he knew he could call down for someone to bring them up to him.

ON THE FIRST floor, Alex bought his smokes and lit one before dropping into a nearby armchair in the hotel lobby. He was worried about what would happen to him and his friends. If the Feds were prepared to take Alfonse down, then it was only a matter of time before they came after Charlie and the rest of the group.

He took an enormous drag on his cigarette and watched the plume of exhaled smoke hang in the air above his head until it dissipated, while he pondered Charlie's heroin smuggling proposition again. If not opium, then where were they going to make their money?

Back up with the fellas, Alex had a suggestion: "Unless any of us can conceive of a fresh business line, we must do more than just squeeze what we've got left once we lose booze."

"What are you saying?"

"Meyer, it's not that you were wrong to think like an accountant. We should be more forensic than that. If prostitution has been good for us, then we must find new ways to generate money out of the oldest profession. Same with narcotics, gaming, and union bashing."

"Okay, so why don't we each take one of them and come back at the end of the month with some concrete approaches to double profit."

They all nodded in agreement to Charlie's proposal, in part because they all felt there would be no lightbulb moment. Before Prohibition started, none of them could have predicted how much gelt they would have made out of it. The smart ones saw that selling liquor would be good as the old bars went out of business, but only Arnold Rothstein envisaged how they could industrialize the transportation, storage, and distribution of the product to make some healthy money out of the Protestant desire for the purity of their souls.

Meyer volunteered to focus on the unions, Benny took gaming, and Charlie put his name down against narcotics, so that left Alex with the short straw. The oldest profession was also the one where most people had spent much time finessing into the streamlined factories that made up most cathouses. Nonetheless, he agreed to find fresh ways to generate new gelt out of old nafkas.

10

ALEX SPENT HIS life traveling from one diner to the next, a nomad in New York. He used to have a base in a seemingly innocuous office block downtown, but after too many attacks on himself and his family, Alex gave up on that and decided to only see business associates in public locations.

As for his friends, he would meet them in the privacy of their homes or hotel suites—whatever was most appropriate and the same was true for Sarah. With her, the problem was more that she tried to avoid meeting him at all and preferred to let the boys act as a social barrier between them.

He knew there must be something serious to discuss when she asked if they could meet up and offered to go into the city to make the schlep more convenient for him. So they sat opposite each other in Lindy's, which was as good a choice as any other joint in Manhattan.

Although he arrived some fifteen minutes early, Sarah was already there at their booth. She smiled briefly when she saw him and maintained that positivity in her expression until he sat down and ordered a coffee and some cheesecake.

"Thanks for seeing me, Alex."

"You're welcome. I'm surprised you were prepared to come all the way into the city just to see me. I hope you had some other errands to do today too."

"Sure, yeah…"

Sarah's eyes dipped down to her Key lime pie, which she mushed round her plate with a fork. Her hesitation piqued Alex's interest—she usually said exactly what she thought to him without batting an eyelid.

"Did you get here okay?"

"Yes, thanks."

"And are the boys all fit and well, Sarah?"

"I got the maid to keep an eye on them today. They are perfectly safe."

"Good. I wasn't trying to imply they weren't—just asking as a pleasantry, as their father. I know you always have their best interests at heart every waking moment."

Sarah switched on a smile again, but it flicked off almost as soon as it formed. Alex waited because whatever needed to be said was stuck in the back of her throat.

He settled into the seat and consumed three forkfuls of cake. It was perfectly baked and the base had a crunch to it. Every mouthful reminded him of Arnold and the rear table where he'd held court for so many years.

"We haven't been together for quite a while now, Alex."

"I know. I drove you away from me with my behavior and my not confronting the truth."

"You lied to me, yes, but I'm not trying to start an argument with you, so you shouldn't feel the need to defend yourself. That's not why I wanted us to meet up."

"Then what is the reason, Sarah?"

She took a glug of her drink, inhaled, and spoke, all the while gripping the cup as though it might fly away at any minute.

"Like I said, we have been living apart for over two years and I think it would be sensible for both of us if we were to, you know, make it official."

"Official?"

"Get the paperwork to catch up on our lives."

She looked right at him, not understanding his lack of comprehension. For Sarah had rehearsed this conversation in her head so many times, she thought she had imagined exactly how it would play out, but she had forgotten that Alex was incredibly smart in business but really dumb with women.

"The paperwork. What paperwork?"

"I've been speaking with a lawyer who says I should ask you if you'd agree to a divorce."

"We've only been separated for a brief time and, besides, I thought we might get back together…"

His voice trailed off—as soon as the words left his mouth, Alex realized how foolish they sounded even to him.

"Alex, it has been two long years and we are no nearer reconciling now than the day I walked out on you. I don't mean to sound harsh—it's just how it is, right?"

"I guess so… yeah. From that time I thought you would change your mind and come back to me at some point. I dunno. I suppose I just assumed."

"Well, Alex. I can't see that happening and I think it would be best for all of us if you agreed to divorce me. We could go to Reno for a few weeks perhaps."

"Spend six weeks away from business?—not now."

Even Alex knew New York had stringent divorce laws which required Sarah to provide evidence of his adultery. Clearly she figured this would be easier with his cooperation than without, especially as he hardly spent any time with his mistress and was too discreet to be seen out and about with a girlfriend. A trip to Nevada was common nowadays as that state would let you divorce if you were resident for a handful of weeks.

"Will you at least think about it some more, please? It's what's best for us all."

"So you keep telling me. I'll consider your request—you are the mother of my children and I respect you greatly—but I can't pretend to like the idea. Just one thing—are you seeing anybody?"

Sarah's cheeks reddened for a second. "Why no. This isn't about me but what's the proper thing to do for the boys."

THE NEXT DAY, Alex met up with Ezra and Massimo back at Lindy's. This time he positioned himself in a rear booth facing the front. The red in Sarah's cheeks raised a query mark in his head.

"I have a job for one of you, but it involves Sarah, so I understand if you don't want to touch it."

Both men shifted uncomfortably in their seats—they were fiercely loyal to their boss but had also seen his relationship with her in the best and worst of times. Neither wanted to stand between the man and his wife. Ezra broke rank first.

"If you think I can help…"

"I may be paranoid but there's something I want you to check up on for me. Massimo, as this is a discreet matter, you need not stick around for the next part of the discussion."

The Italian shrugged, swigged back his coffee and slunk off, wishing he had been faster to respond, but he knew Alex felt no ill will toward him. That's not how the guy operated.

With Massimo near the door, Alex leaned forward, lowered his voice, and spoke directly to Ezra, staring at him throughout the rest of their conversation.

"I think Sarah might be having an affair and I want you to find out if that is true."

"An affair? You haven't lived together since…"

The truth was it had been so long, Ezra couldn't place the last time the two of them had slept under the same roof.

"…the first syndicate meeting. That was when she left me."

"I don't know how to ask my next question without making you angry."

"There are no secrets between us."

"Do you really think she's sleeping with someone else because you said you might be paranoid."

"I'm not too sure. When we spoke yesterday, she hesitated and looked embarrassed at only one point. She's not a person to feel ashamed, so..."

"I see. Let me have a dig around and see what I turn up."

"Find out all you can, but do nothing to the man—if there is a guy to do anything to. It's facts I am looking for, not some foolish revenge on a stranger."

"I understand. Once I've gone fishing, I shall report back to you but I will not share with Massimo. This is private between you and I."

"Damn straight. We live together, we love together..."

"...but we die alone."

TWO WEEKS LATER, Ezra met up with Alex at his favorite booth in Lindy's. He sat still while his boss fussed about the menu and ordering coffee and cake. After the displacement activity came the inevitable question: "What did you find out, Ezra?"

"Short answer: you were right, there is another man. How much do you want to know about him?"

"Tell me what you got."

"He's a lawyer; works in a local firm in Hoboken. Lives around the corner and has spent nights over with your wife."

"Does he spend time alone with my boys?"

"Sarah has gone out and left them with him."

Alex sighed and sipped from his cup. Ezra moistened the inside of his mouth because he knew this was far from over. He cleared his throat, "Would you like me to kill him?"

"Oh no. This is personal, not business. There's no need for him to die— not at my instigation at least."

"Whatever you say."

"Besides, if he were to meet an untimely end then Sarah would immediately suspect me and I would never be forgiven. How long has he been in her life?"

"Six months. That's when they started going steady and he stayed over with her."

"The boys have said nothing to me. Zilch."

"And now they spend two to three days a week together plus weekends."

Alex ground his molars and ceased listening to Ezra's comments. Lost in his thoughts, Alex vowed not to give that woman her divorce. While he had hoped they might get back together at some point, the one thing he was certain about was that if he couldn't have her then no other man would have her either. If they wanted each other that much, they could skulk around until the day they died. Then Alex mulled over the irony that Sarah was dating a lawyer.

"I should have the guy disbarred."

11

WITH THOUGHTS RICOCHETING around his head about Sarah and her paramour, Alex did his best to focus on the job at hand—a trip to Detroit on company business and a chance to speak with Abe Bernstein, the boss of the Sugar Hill gang. They'd worked with each other since the start of Prohibition and had profited greatly from each other's endeavors.

On this occasion, Alex popped over to the City of Champions with Ezra and Massimo. Sat in their private compartment at the rear of the train, the three men could have a comfortable ride without interference from any Joe citizen. Alex lost himself inside his own thoughts for most of the journey while the other two played pinochle. Luckily for his fellas, Alex was totally in focus by the time they arrived at Abe's joint to talk business.

"Good to see you, Abe. I hope you remember Massimo and Ezra."

"How could I forget either of these mensches from our glory days bootlegging and hauling liquor across the country?"

"Well said. With a bit of luck those happy days will return to us shortly."

Abe spat three times for luck, as was the Jewish superstition.

"Please God next year in Jerusalem," he intoned, although none of the men assembled in the back of the speakeasy had any desire to travel to the Middle East any time soon. This was just a saying passed down from the older generation to the following one, which had lost its meaning along the way.

"So to business, Abe. I don't need to tell you we are here with a contract and we are seeking your cooperation in this matter."

"And you shall have it, Alex, of course. One of my men stole from a syndicate member when he was on a trip to Little Italy and that is unacceptable."

"Can you give us an itinerary so we can find this thief?"

"I'll do one better than that and arrange for you to meet him. Name the location and we shall send him there within the hour. I don't want this *schnook* to walk the streets any longer than he has to."

"Abe, I admire your sentiment and desire to see justice done, but we have been sat on a train for I've forgotten how long. Would you mind if we rested a while first and had a meal without the table shaking and our forks wobbling in front of our faces with the movement of the carriage on the tracks?"

"Sorry, I forgot. The *gonif* can wait. You fellas relax and we will deal with the *meeskait* tomorrow. Would you like any companionship tonight?"

Both Ezra and Massimo expressed interest with a simple nod of the head and Alex shrugged, not sure whether he cared about his answer.

Abe took the four men to a family-run restaurant where they had all the Yiddish cooking comforts. Once they had finished their meal and returned to their hotel, three women were waiting in the lobby for them.

"Which one would you like, Alex?"

"You two take whoever you want and I'll have what's left."

"Sure?"

"Yes, Ezra. I really don't care."

THE BRUNETTE FOLLOWED Alex into the elevator and read the situation well. Her girlfriends were pawing Ezra and Massimo before the doors slammed shut to take them up to the fifth floor, but Alex's broad stood near him without touching. She let her hand float toward his, but picked up on the fact that he wasn't grabbing and mauling her like his companions.

In his suite, she sat down on a couch as Alex sloped into his bedroom to put away his overcoat. Realizing he hadn't been followed, he popped his head round the door of the living room.

"Do you have a name, doll?"

"What do you want to call me?"

"Rebecca. And if you are going to earn any money tonight, I think you should join me."

A brief smile flickered across her face as she rose and headed toward him. When she neared him, Alex turned and walked back to the bedroom and on to the en suite bathroom. Just before he brushed his teeth, he muttered instructions for Rebecca to get into bed, which she dutifully obeyed.

He undressed and slipped under the sheets, aware of Rebecca's body for the first time. In the elevator, he hadn't bothered to pay her much attention but now, up close, he saw she was an attractive woman. Ezra and Massimo had left the best for last—for him.

He switched off the bedside light, curled into a ball with his back to the nafka and Rebecca spooned him until he fell asleep. In the morning, he placed a wad of green in her purse and thanked her for her understanding.

NOY YARDEN HAD been given a simple task by Abe Bernstein—to visit Little Italy, collect a package and return home with no fuss. Abe gave him sufficient funds to afford to stay in a reasonable hotel overnight and to keep himself in clover while in the Big Apple. Noy traveled coach on the train and negotiated his way across town until he arrived on Mulberry.

This was when a tiny error of judgment on his part created a massive difference to his life chances, because he took most of his remaining funds and used them to get into the back room of a nearby speakeasy. Emboldened by the ease with which he gained access to the high stakes game, Noy tried an all-or-nothing strategy.

He pulled out a gun and stole all the money that was on the table and anything lying inside the patrons' wallets. Then Noy did the only sensible thing and scarpered, picked up the package and headed straight for the station and the first train to Detroit.

Within ten minutes of this happening, and several hours before Noy arrived back home, Abe received a call from Johnny Torrio explaining that one of his men had just entered a Torrio gaming house and committed grand larceny. The following day, Johnny asked permission from the syndicate to whack Yarden and the guy's fate was sealed with a unanimous verdict. Nobody likes a thief, especially other thieves.

ALEX, MASSIMO, AND Ezra paid a visit to Noy to check on his welfare. He answered the door of his apartment wearing his pants and a tee shirt. He looked like he'd thrown the clothes on straight from getting out of bed, although it was late morning by the time they'd had breakfast and headed over to Noy's pad.

"Noy Yarden?" inquired Alex.

"Who wants to know?"

"We're friends of Abe's. Didn't he mention we might visit?"

"Nah, but he doesn't tell me everything. Come in and give me two minutes to get dressed."

"You got company, kid?"

Alex asked the question with a light air to his voice, but Ezra glanced at Massimo as the answer was given. A dame in the place would add an unnecessary complexity to their day.

"Not this morning, Mac."

"You kick her out early?"

Massimo grinned at the implication that Noy was a player, but maybe the Italian tried a little too hard or perhaps the three men gave off a suspicious air. Whatever the reason, Noy looked between them all and bolted back inside. Massimo chased him and Ezra pelted down the stairs because he thought he'd spotted Noy glance at the fire escape in his bedroom through the open living room.

Alex remained still, sighed, and sauntered into the apartment and closed the front door. At this point, Noy approached the bedroom window, flung the sash down and put one foot out onto the fire escape.

Massimo reached him in time to grab an arm, but Noy wriggled free and squeezed his body through the crack made by the window. With a thump and a dash, he scrambled down the fire escape. Massimo banged and scratched at the window until the gap was big enough for him to fit through.

Meanwhile Ezra stormed down the central stairway and reached the first-floor lobby in record time. He shot out of the entrance and looked left then right, trying to see if Noy had reached the street.

With nothing to see and no one to chase, Ezra stood still, not certain what to do next. He craned his head up, hoping to spot Noy's apartment, but he wasn't even sure he knew which side of the building Noy's was facing. The answer fell from the sky twenty seconds later, when he appeared in the periphery of Ezra's vision about four hundred feet away as he landed on the sidewalk, having leaped from the fire escape ladder.

Ezra ran toward him and once Noy had stood up and seen Ezra lunging at him, he flew at full pelt in the opposite direction. Ten seconds later, Massimo appeared from the sky and joined Ezra as they sped to catch up with the lad.

Noy attempted to zigzag around the sidewalk, but there were too many people on the street to make that a quick journey. Thinking they couldn't see him, Noy ducked into an alleyway and the two men slowed down, knowing they had him trapped.

Massimo and Ezra strolled into the alley and watched as Noy tried to climb a wall at the far end. Massimo jogged over, grabbed a leg, and yanked the guy onto the ground. As soon as he landed, Ezra booted him in the kidneys to make sure he didn't get up.

Then Massimo kicked him twice—once between the legs and once in the head. While the first blow made Noy squeal, the second stopped him breathing and he lay still, one leg twitching in a death throe. They picked the body up and carried him over their shoulders as though he was drunk. On the street, they waited until a truck sped past and threw the carcass in front of the moving vehicle.

In the apartment, Alex had watched his lieutenants follow Noy into the alley. Then he turned his back on proceedings and walked through each room to ensure there was no evidence of their passing through the place. He pulled the door shut on his way out and met up with Massimo and Ezra before they left the vicinity and popped by Abe's before returning to New York.

12

BACK IN THE city, Alex spent some time with Ezra and Massimo thinking about how they could make more money out of prostitution, just as Alex had promised the fellas he would.

"We might force the nafkas to work harder and reduce the minutes they spend with the johns."

"Yes, Ezra, but I wouldn't say we encourage the men to hang around as it is—and if they do, we make them pay for it."

"Why not just double the number of working girls. Wouldn't that double profit?"

"More or less, but where would we get all these extra women and how would we afford to house and feed them?"

"Dunno, Alex."

Massimo knew his suggestion was far from perfect, but they were throwing ideas around and he reckoned it was as good as anything the others would come up with. The three men fell into silence for ten minutes or more as each tried to figure out a system to make even more money out of sex than they currently did.

"We should use high-class call girls and extort rich johns."

"Ezra, would you say that is in any way different from what we already do? When was the last time one of your nafkas refused to exploit the situation with a police captain or politician?"

"You're right, Alex. That's just business as usual."

"Expansion is a possibility, though, Ezra. If we either find some untrammeled territory or take over somebody else's patch…"

"Alex, the whole point of the syndicate was to stop that sort of thing from happening."

"Yes, Massimo. Back to the drawing board."

More silence and blank expressions, occasionally punctuated with a raised eyebrow when some bright idea sprung into a head, which would lower as the fella realized the flaw in the plan before he'd pitched it to the other guys.

"Booze was great because it came as part of a package. Johns would come to the speakeasy for a gin-soaked coffee and stay for the entertainment, play a few hands or try their hand at a roulette wheel…"

"…and if we were lucky, they'd nip upstairs for thirty minutes with a girl. Alex, without the lure of liquor, why will people come to our bars?"

"Good question, Ezra. Couples turned up for a show and a drink. Men appeared later in the evening and headed straight for the second floor."

"You think it was just being in the right place at the right time? There'll never be a moment like that again?"

"Maybe. I hope not, but perhaps. For now, we have to assume we can repeat that success once beer is no longer the bait to lure in the johns."

"Can I suggest the obvious, Alex?"

"I'm all ears, Massimo. No suggestion is too stupid, given what we've come up with this evening."

"Well, people enjoy a drink—that was why Prohibition was so great for us. And when it is legal, they will still want to knock back a beer or a shot of whiskey."

"Right."

"And men like to have sex."

Everyone chuckled and nodded.

"So why are we overthinking this? We keep the speakeasies open on the first floor and use the same locations for the nafkas on the second. That's what happened before Uncle Sam banned booze. It can be the same when they repeal the act."

Alex swallowed hard, looked at Ezra and back to Massimo, who grabbed at his glass and consumed the remains of his Scotch.

"Do you reckon we'll make as much money?"

"It'll be cheaper without having to bribe the cops or worry about security on the door."

"Good point, Massimo, although I guess some citizens liked to go to a speakeasy because it was criminal but not viewed in a bad way."

"Sure, perhaps there might be fewer drinkers, but that doesn't mean the volume of booze will reduce. Some people didn't trust the quality of our hooch. The joints were called blind pigs for a reason. They might consume more when they don't suspect the alcohol has been brewed in a bathtub."

Ezra tapped the table to attract the others' attention.

"I disagree—we'll see a big drop in the numbers coming to our drinking holes and should expect to close a stack of them down. But the ones that survive will make a load more gelt for us. Besides, when booze goes back to being legitimate, breweries will want a piece of the action and they'll get it. Perhaps the smartest thing is to let them in on the game."

"Why is that?"

"Alex, it's simple—when businesses move into an area, we provide them protection, offer to solve any problems they might have with any unions and sell them product. The way I see it: without Prohibition, it is business as usual, only with more opportunities than before because we have the capital to invest."

"Ezra, next thing you'll tell me to buy stock in General Motors."

"Not a bad plan, Alex. I might do that myself."

ALEX'S OLD FRIENDS gathered again at the rear of Linsky's—the same booth every time, no matter how short the notice of their arrival. Several lieutenants were rammed at the front of the restaurant to keep an eye on all the other patrons. Charlie, Meyer, Benny, and Alex relaxed over their coffees and cake.

"I've been trying to come up with something creative around prostitution, but it has not been easy, Charlie."

"I understand. Is there anything you have been able to think of to replace our lost profits?"

"We've played with loads of ideas but nothing will generate enough gelt to be worth talking about here—extortion of wealthy johns, protection money from businesses that move into our old speakeasy locations. These are the cream of the crop."

Benny laughed at the suggestions, knowing they wouldn't get close to the amount of money the fellas were seeking to make.

"And what's your bright idea, Benny?"

Benny cleared his throat and stared into Alex's eyes for dramatic effect.

"Gambling."

"I'm glad we're sat on these seats otherwise we'd have fallen on the floor, Benny. We are sitting in the midst of a genius, gentlemen."

"Less with the sarcasm, Alex. Benny, what are you proposing because we already have extensive gaming operations."

"Charlie, if we can't make more money here, we must go somewhere else to generate the gelt. It stands to reason and there are plenty of places where we have no foothold. We should go to one of them and repeat what we've done here but in new territories. We know what we need to do and we must search for the real estate where we can do it."

"And you think gaming is the answer?"

"Meyer, it is part of the answer and one of the easiest things to start from scratch. You give me a piece of green baize, a pack of cards and some chips. I'll have a casino up and running within a week."

"If it was that easy, every fool would do it. And before you get on your high horse, Benny, I'm not accusing you of being a fool—just saying that we both know it is more complicated than you state."

"Alex, no offense taken, but is it that difficult? If we have the strength of our own conviction, we could be raking in the money within a month."

The other three looked at each other. While they hadn't agreed with Alex, the men believed he was right. Gambling was a profitable enterprise for sure, but organizing a gaming house was complex if you wanted it to survive interest from the Feds, the cops, and other gangs—let alone managing the sort of john who rocks into a casino. If they have any money on them worth taking then they need feeding and watering, along with tending to their other, more private needs.

"If the economy was in a better shape, then we could squeeze more out of the unions."

"Don't hold your breath, Meyer."

The conversation died again until Charlie spoke a minute later.

"There is an opportunity we have yet to examine, which promises to offer us substantial returns on our investment. It involves the importing of goods, for which we already have a significant transportation network. Then we need to repackage the item and sell it on the street. The profit margin is ten— a hundred—times bigger than liquor."

Alex could see the pay-off a mile away and wondered whether Charlie had pitched each of the men here with his private offer.

"Narcotics. I have contacts in Sicily who can obtain the heroin we'd need and we have enough warehouses going spare in the city. We could turn some of them into laboratories to cut the drug into something we could put on the streets. Then we use our fellas to move it at a vast profit."

"In the morning they deal with the numbers and in the evening they sell dope."

"That's the idea, Meyer."

"And do you think we'd keep the politicians we need for the rest of our activities?"

"Why not, Alex? Since when has Tammany Hall cared about anything other than who is lining their pockets and that their money keeps flowing? Provided they get their weekly payments, no politician will care what happens to a bunch of poor Jews and Italians."

"You think we should sell to our own, Charlie?"

"Yes, Benny. If we do this, we mustn't stray too far from what we know— at least not at the start. It'll be easier for us to keep control."

More cake and cups of coffee were consumed until all the details were ironed out. Only Benny seemed unconvinced about the power of heroin to save their asses—he continued to believe they should head west somewhere and pitch tent in a new location.

13

ALBERT, LOUIS, AND Alex sat around a table in what was the closest thing to a board meeting of Murder Corporation. The three men had taken a position in a Mulberry Street restaurant at Albert's insistence.

"You should try the calamari marinara."

"I'm trying to avoid shellfish."

Albert smiled because he'd known this would be Alex's response. The Italian was just hoping to annoy him into reacting, but Alex was better than that. Louis remained silent and allowed the two others to play their games. He had learned to let Albert have his say and not to admonish him in public. The fella was quick to temper and liable to lash out without considering the implications of his actions.

"Contracts appear to continue to be flowing well and Abe Reles can still supply men for the jobs, right?"

"Sure thing, Albert. He's a good guy. I've been relying on him for years."

"That right, Louis?"

"Alex, he and I met years ago. I can't remember a point when I didn't know him."

"Same with you, Albert?"

"We go back some ways, but not as long as with Louis."

The waiter arrived to take their order and departed as quickly as he was able—he saw Anastasia, recognized Louis and was learning Alex's face too. It had only taken him a couple of years, but to be fair to the guy, the three directors of Murder Corporation were more likely to meet midtown or out in Brownsville rather than in the heart of Little Italy.

"So, is there anything we should discuss?"

"Good question, Alex. There is one matter I'd like to raise."

"What's that, Albert?"

"We have been delivering what I can only describe as an excellent service to the syndicate and have done so from the moment we were formed. The three of us might not have conducted business together before then, but all has been running pretty smoothly between us ever since. Wouldn't you agree?"

"Yep."

Louis nodded, too.

"So one reason everything has been so peachy for us is that the rest of the syndicate has bought our services at a very reasonable rate."

"We agreed at the outset that there should be no bickering among ourselves over the cost of goods and services bought and sold between syndicate members."

"Yeah, Louis, but agreed by whom? I mean, did you negotiate the price we charge or did Luciano and Torrio impose that amount on us? Back in '29, that is."

"Shortly after the meeting in Atlantic City, we sat down and hammered out our fees."

"Alex, perhaps your head has got cloudy but I recall a price being named by Charlie and us nodding in agreement. There was no real negotiation—no discussion about the value of our services and the level of appreciation that would be shown for them. Just a number which we consented to with no other words being said."

"Albert, the conversation was brief, but I don't remember any of us feeling like we were being shortchanged."

"That's the difference between you and me then, Alex, because I maintain we are leaving money on the table and have done so from the time when the first contract was assigned to us."

Louis and Alex looked at each other and then turned their respective gazes on Albert, who stared both of them down. The man's mind appeared made up. Clearly this issue had been brewing for quite a while, but Alex had had no idea that Albert felt so aggrieved. Judging by Louis' expression, he was as surprised as Alex.

"Have you spoken to Charlie about this, Albert?"

"Not yet, because I wanted us to talk about it first."

Alex sighed because he had no desire to go behind Charlie's back on anything as important as this, but he also understood how powerful Albert was in the Italian gangs.

"What do you think, Louis?"

Alex figured the smart thing at this point was to throw the ball into Louis' court—he understood better than most how to handle Anastasia.

"I will never say that I don't want more money, Alex. And with all due respect to you, Albert, that doesn't mean I think now is the best time to broach this topic."

"You realize the syndicate has more pressing issues than giving us a price rise?"

"Alex, I'm pointing out that the end of Prohibition will throw up tremendous opportunities for us and that different gangs may well come into conflict with each other…"

"And we'll mop up the consequences of those disagreements?"

"Yeah. Chances are we shall make more money because there will be more bloodshed. If we ask for a bigger slice now, we might appear as though we are trying to have our cake and eat it. This may be true but it is not how we wish to appear, I would suggest."

Albert laughed and Alex smiled at Louis' remarks.

"This is why you and I have been friends for so long. I like the way you think, Louis Buchalter."

THE NEXT DAY, Alex made it his business to hook up with Louis in Brownsville. He predicted Buchalter would be more comfortable talking on home ground and that was what was necessary given the topic at hand.

"Do you reckon Albert is right to hike our prices?"

"There's nothing like getting straight to the point, Alex."

"I know but the look you gave me yesterday made me think you weren't keen on the idea and we should talk about it sooner rather than later. So, what are your thoughts?"

"I'm not sure my opinion counts for much."

"Don't be coy, Louis. There's only you and me here—you can be honest with me."

"Albert is a made man in the Italian mob—that means something much more than being a syndicate member. It's a Sicilian thing."

"Charlie has explained the inner workings of the Little Italy gangs to me. They have a deep sense of history and hierarchy. I get it and even if there was no syndicate, Albert would be a highly regarded and influential man, but do you think he is right?"

Louis looked into the middle distance and exhaled. Alex knew the conversation would be difficult, but he underestimated Louis' reticence—the man just didn't want to express an opinion out loud. Alex tried to give him the chance to consider his words carefully hoping something would come out of his mouth. After two long minutes of silence, Alex got his wish.

"Now is not the time to demand a pay rise."

"You said that yesterday. Why not today while business is good for us?"

"Because times are about to get very tough and I don't think the other syndicate members will appreciate a shakedown. Not now. Not anytime, really."

"You've known him way longer than me. How do we stop Albert?"

"Good question. I could try to have a quiet word with him and see if I can soften his position."

"Soften? If he goes to Charlie and the rest of the fellas, we'll be tarred with the same brush. All three of us will seem like gonifs."

"Alex, I might get him to reconsider his attitude, but it'll be a miracle if I could actually prevent him from demanding more money from the fellas."

"You think I should speak with Charlie and explain the situation before Albert makes a move?"

"If you do that and he finds out then he will never forgive you for going behind his back and dishonoring him."

"He blows hot and cold though, doesn't he? I don't know if it is his Italian blood or just that he's a *schmendrick*."

"Never make the mistake of underestimating him, Alex. He blusters away most of the time, but he got to the top of his family by being a formidable leader. His temper might be his weakness, but it is also his towering strength."

He listened to Louis' words and took counsel. Anastasia had the potential to ruin the golden goose of Murder Corporation, but his desire to seize on an opportunity was one that Alex recognized in himself.

14

DUTCH SCHULTZ HAD built his empire off the back of bootlegging, like so many other members of the syndicate, but he had spread his wings considerably and included the numbers and union racketeering in his arsenal. Over the years, he had seen his fair share of trouble, especially when one of his own lieutenants had tried to take control of Dutch's domain through force.

Nobody was surprised when Vincent Coll, the Irish hitman in question, was gunned down in a telephone booth one February night three years earlier. Now Dutch had a problem and had asked Alex to visit him for a quiet word in his penthouse apartment at the Lexington Hotel, which Dutch kept for daytime business meetings and nighttime assignations.

The decor was pleasant enough inside this plush hotel but nothing of any note, thought Alex. The pattern of the wallpaper reminded him of Sarah's room in the Oregon, which, given the contrast in the two locations, raised a smile in the corner of Alex's mouth.

"Something amuse you, Alex?"

"Nope, just reminiscing, Dutch. This room reminds me of a place I used to visit."

"Try to keep your attention on our current troubles, if you don't mind."

Alex listened as Dutch explained how Shea Coll, Vincent's half-brother, had appeared in town two nights before, asking for Dutch's whereabouts.

"I don't bear the guy any ill will, but I am concerned he might have turned up in the city intending to do me harm."

"That sounds like a genuine concern given the bad blood between you and Vincent."

"And this brings me to why I wanted us to have a discreet conversation. While I am thrilled to deal with this matter myself, I don't want this to get out of hand. Where there is one half sibling, there could be more waiting to come out of the woodwork like roaches."

"Are you in need of an exterminator?"

"I can kill my own insects, thank you, but I want everyone to see that this is not some stupid vendetta. If you are with me on this, people will conclude this Coll got whacked because of some syndicate business."

"As I understand the situation, this is not a syndicate hit, though, is it?"

"Oh no. This is a private contract between the two of us and nobody else must know about the arrangement."

"I can certainly remove this man permanently and his mortal remains will never be found."

"Alex, you need not go to that much trouble. All I want you to do is to accompany me on the hit so that if anyone recognizes us, then they'll see it is not just me with a piece and a hot head."

Alex smiled for the second time in their conversation—Dutch was a tremendous syndicate member who generated considerable income for all with whom he worked, but he was famed for his uneven temper. He and Albert had much in common.

THERE COMES A point in every man's life that he draws heavily on the third cigarette in a row, stood outside a theater, watching a news booth on the other side of the street. Dutch had been given a tipoff from one of his guys that Shea was staying in a nearby fleapit and was in the habit of walking down this drag in the early evening before crashing out in his crib for the rest of the night. Mostly he was alone, but occasionally there was a moll with him.

Alex received Dutch's elbow in his ribs just as he spotted the same guy in a black trench coat with a brunette on his arm. Alex threw his smoke onto the ground and squished it with his foot. Shea bought the late edition from the booth and walked his skirt a block east, all the while shadowed by Alex and Dutch, one on each side of the street.

Shea turned right and Alex found himself within feet of the guy as he shuffled along with his girl in tow. The guy didn't notice him and carried on along the sidewalk as if Alex weren't there. Another block and Shea crossed over and Alex let Dutch take the lead as he was now nearer the guy.

Instead, Alex trailed the three blocks until Shea came to a halt outside a tenement building, no more interesting than any other nearby. Dutch kept on walking past the couple as they talked and Alex watched as Shea leaned into the girl, who giggled a few times and allowed the man to flirt with her a while on her stoop.

As they stood rooted to the same spot for over five minutes, Alex did his best to blend into the night and he propped himself up against the wall of a building near the junction, smoking a cigarette and pretending that this looked normal. Luckily, Dutch circled back and caught up with Alex a minute later.

"Any idea what we'll do next, Alex?"

"We could run across the street, all guns blazing and blast a cap in each of them."

"Okay, are you packing enough heat?"

"I was joking, Dutch. There are easier ways to deal with Coll than waking up the neighborhood."

Dutch looked at him quizzically, as if to show that Alex's suggestion was perfectly fine as far as he was concerned and there was no need to confuse matters with humor.

"The biggest issue is what will happen with that broad, Dutch."

"I don't mind if we whack her too."

"That may well be so, but I care. In our line of work, we try not to hit civilians and if possible, we avoid calling attention to ourselves. If Coll goes up to the skirt's apartment then we should wait for another time when he is alone."

"Alex, I want this situation dispensed with tonight and that is the end of the matter. This is not a discussion."

As if to emphasize Dutch's point, as soon as he finished uttering his words, the couple entered the building. Alex thought for a spell, trying to figure out how they would even find Shea now he was hidden inside the tenement.

"You know which is her nest, Dutch?"

"Not a clue."

"Looks like we've got a problem on our hands then."

Coincidence abounded because that was when a light popped on in a third-floor apartment on the right-hand corner as the two men aimlessly stared at the building.

"Must have been them, right?"

Alex nodded and threw the remains of his cigarette on the ground.

"At least we have a location, although I haven't figured out how we can eliminate him without taking out the skirt."

"Alex, that's your problem, not mine—provided Coll is dead before dawn, I don't give a damn how many women you kill."

This was no longer a simple hit and Dutch's desire to get the job done this evening ran counter to all that Alex thought was sensible, but Dutch was paying for the contract and he had agreed to the deal. There was no backing out of it now. Alex sighed, put his hands in his pants pockets and sidled across the street, just as Shea appeared out of the entrance and hurtled past him with no flicker of recognition or acknowledgement that he had nearly knocked Alex over in his rush to leave the building.

Alex glanced up and the corner light remained on—looked like Coll had been sent out on an errand because the dame was staying put. Or he'd been thrown out on his ass and was heading home. Either way, Alex counted to ten and followed Shea at a respectful distance, leaving Dutch to stare at the glow of the apartment.

His route zigzagged from one corner to the next, all the while his path across town formed a large figure of eight. Fifteen minutes of what appeared to be mindless wandering later and Shea reached a small diner, the first place open since he'd left the tenement. You'd have thought it'd be easier to find a food joint in this city.

Shea went inside and Alex hustled to a position where he could see what was going on without standing immediately in front. There was a takeout counter and an old couple who occupied one of the three tables. The guy who must have been the owner stood behind the bar and appeared to be counting the day's takings.

A handful of muffled words and the boss beckoned toward the back of the joint and Shea tipped his hat and strode to the phone booth. An all-too-brief call later and he returned to the counter and bought some smokes. Alex decided now was the time to act.

He pushed through the door, eyed the seated couple who were too busy ignoring each other behind raised newspapers to give him any attention, and stepped toward Shea. The owner took one look at Alex, knew there was trouble ahead and ducked down, still clutching the notes from the day's earnings.

Alex whipped out his pistol and with a straight arm, fired two shots into Shea—one in the heart and the other to his head. The couple dropped their papers, glanced at each other and, with no comment or fuss, slipped out of the front and vanished into the night. They were so fast that they almost bumped into Alex on his way through the door.

Nobody stopped him or halted his progress along the deserted sidewalk. The sound of the gunfire must have been heard by some locals, but no sirens appeared and no cops had been called. Alex bet on the fact that the owner would plead ignorance when the flatfeet eventually came calling. If not, he was a dead man.

15

ATLANTIC CITY WAS the traditional home of meetings comprising the entire syndicate board. Once, it had taken place in the Catskills, but Charlie knew the fellas preferred a location where there was betting rather than borscht. There were more choices for female companionship in A.C. too.

The great and the good sat around an enormous boardroom table, each flanked by at least one of their lieutenants. Charlie, Meyer, Benny, Albert— the list was long and if you were responsible for any significant piece of criminal activity on the East Coast or parts of the Midwest, then you were in that hotel room, sipping your coffee or stroking the side of your water glass. As leader of the syndicate, Charlie began proceedings by tapping the back of a spoon on the side of his glass until there was silence.

"Thank you all for coming and taking time out of your busy schedules. As you know, we only meet when there is something significant to discuss or decide and today is one of those days."

Many nods and assenting murmurs from the assembled throng. Alex was impressed by how quickly these men had gathered together—Charlie had only issued the invitations on Friday and it was Monday now. They all understood how serious the situation would become.

"There are two issues we must agree on and they are intertwined. First, there is the question of what we shall do once the Volstead Act is repealed across the country. Second, we have benefitted from the fact that the Feds have been spread very thin across the land dealing with Prohibition violations. Soon, we won't have that luxury and we should expect them to come down on us hard—real hard."

Further murmuring ensued until Charlie called them to order. The number of people who had died as a result of the actions of the men in this room was countless and potentially unknown, but they still dutifully waited for each other to finish and even raised their hands to get attention and acknowledgement from the chair before they spoke. Sugar House gang leader Abe was the first to deal with their problems head on.

"Fellas, we are about to lose somewhere between a quarter and one half of our revenue and, Charlie is right, the cops will hit us with all their might. Doing nothing is not an option. In Detroit, we have already made plans— increasing our grip on the unions, edging other gangs not part of the syndicate out of town. But I can guarantee you that this will not be enough when the money from booze floats away."

"Joe Citizen won't want to go to our speakeasies," Meyer added. "An illegal drink was seen as a harmless pleasure, so our establishments were tolerated when the Federal government failed to give the people what they wanted. As soon as they can get a beer in a bar without any of us stood near them, they'll grab that opportunity with both hands. And no offense to anybody sat in this room. I am just giving my opinion of the average john."

Everyone knew that the syndicate's banker described their world perfectly and nobody was so foolish to believe that good citizens visited blind pigs because of the quality of the hooch or the owners of the joints. Cheap booze was all they cared about and they would go somewhere more comfortable and legal as soon as the opportunity arose.

Many of the syndicate members stood up to describe the problem of losing bootlegging from their perspectives, but there were no answers and no fresh ideas. Even though he didn't feel he had much to say, Alex didn't want to be left out from the roster—being seen to contribute on this stage might be useful to how these men viewed him. He changed topic so that his words would be more memorable. "Whatever we do, we need to address the issue of the cops."

"Let's hit them now before they have time to attack us," thundered Benny Siegel's voice above the noise of the general discussion. Trust Benny to take the direct approach, although no one was surprised because this was his usual carrion cry.

"We should stop talking and do it now." Dutch Schultz's response was less predictable and the rest of the group hushed to silence as Benny's suggestion received such vocal support.

"Benny, who do you think we should hit and how do you think it would help?"

Charlie looked at him with the corner of his mouth curled up, as though he was doing his best to show Benny respect, but he thought the idea was absurd. Alex knew this because he'd had a similar conversation with Charlie only four days ago.

"Hoover. Let's cut off the head of the snake."

"Benny, do you not think such an action might call attention to us? Are we not better to be more nuanced and perhaps look at ways of taking advantage of the inherent vulnerability of the flatfeet rather than hit the chief of the Bureau of Investigation?"

"If we act now, then they'll think twice about doing anything attacking us later."

This comment caused everybody in the room to express their views loudly and all at the same time. Charlie's attempt to quieten down the throng simply using a spoon and a glass was doomed to failure and he stopped trying within two seconds of starting.

AN HOUR LATER, everyone had calmed down and many had walked out to get away from the arguments taking place in the room. Nobody wanted to be the one to start any fight, but Benny and Dutch were both razor-thin close to getting their throats cut.

Alex kept himself calm by remaining near his crew—Ezra and Massimo were attending too, like many other lieutenants. With them being there, Alex let his attention wander briefly from the main stage to make sure their heads were in the right place.

"Dutch is an interesting guy."

"You can say that again, Ezra."

"Alex, you worked with him recently. Is he always like this?"

"Far be it from me to badmouth a member of the syndicate, but he is quick to reach conclusions—that's for certain, Massimo."

"Do you think we should kill Hoover?"

"No, Ezra. I had an opportunity to assassinate Eliot Ness, back in the day, and I let him live. No good comes from killing police officers. They are like cockroaches—as soon as you squash one, ten more appear out of the skirting and then a hundred more. Leave them alone and hope they'll pass you by—that's the best to expect."

"And if that doesn't work, bribe them?"

"Sure thing, Massimo, but keep your dignity. Those vermin will chew through your arm if you show them your hand."

BEFORE ANYONE COULD respond to Alex's dim view of law enforcement, Charlie called for everyone to sit down, which the attendees dutifully did. Those who were still outside were brought in by their lieutenants. Charlie stood up and the room fell silent with no clanging against any glass—the fire in his eyes spoke volumes.

"Gentlemen, we might not have consensus on how to handle inquisitive cops—although most of you agree with me—but this does not change the fact that we must shift out of bootlegging and into an altogether fresh line of business."

"Many of us have spent sleepless nights wrestling with this problem and we have only found one area ripe for exploitation."

"Meyer, explain to us your findings."

"We all know that we have a second-to-none transportation network and considerable storage facilities. To say we control vast swathes of retail space is also an understatement. The question is, what product can we fill it with?"

"Get on with it!" called out Benny, and Meyer scowled at his friend.

"What substance can we buy cheaply and sell for maximum profit that sits outside the law otherwise Rockefeller would have invested in it already?"

"Heroin," Charlie replied almost as if the speech had been rehearsed. "With my Sicilian connections, we could start shipping the opiate in a large scale into the country within a matter of weeks. We turn warehouses into laboratories to cut the stuff into street-grade heroin and then use our guys to sell it on the sidewalks."

"And the profit is so huge we'll ask ourselves why we ever bothered with booze," Meyer noted.

A million conversations broke out all at once, but Charlie let them happen —he and Meyer had lit a fire in everyone's belly and he didn't want it to go out. Ten minutes later, Alex could see that most debate had died down and Charlie took control of the room again.

"So we can all benefit from this opportunity, we need to get organized for the new business. And we must also make sure we keep an eye on all our existing activities. There's no point making money peddling heroin if we lose our regular payments from unions or protection money from local businesses."

Charlie nodded at Albert who was keen to speak.

"Some of us have concentrated our attention on other matters and are not best placed to take advantage of this new opportunity. How are we going to do this fairly, because whenever there's a vast amount of money being made, there are differences of opinion that Murder Corporation will have to tidy up? We won't have the time to build supply lines for heroin."

"That is what we are here to ensure, Albert. Every one of us should dip their beaks and benefit from the good fortune presented to us today. We will all contribute to the success of the heroin trade and we shall get paid a fair amount—once those who have expenses have those costs covered. After all, we are not communists."

A ripple of laughter and rueful smiles floated across the hotel room.

"Let's have a show of hands—who is in favor of moving into the heroin business?"

Nearly every arm was raised and Charlie announced the motion carried almost unanimously. Then he outlined his plan to bring in one shipment and to follow its progress from boat to Brownsville street corner. They would sell to their own for the time being and iron out all the wrinkles before expanding the operation.

They'd learned much in the early days of bootlegging and knew they would achieve more through a stealthy increase in production which the cops might not notice until they were completely set up. Then it would be too late. Alex was pleased Charlie had included him on the inside track those weeks before—he'd had no surprises today apart from Benny and Dutch's desire to attack law enforcement. Thoughts of heroin drew his mind to Ida for a second, but Massimo confronted him with more immediate issues.

"You going back tonight, Alex, or will you stay with us and party?"

JULY 1935

16

HEROIN FLOWED FROM Palermo through the Eastern Seaboard and onto the streets of New York, just as Charlie had promised. The profit margin was incredible and all syndicate members enjoyed the collective wealth generated from the brown powder.

As everybody got fatter on the tremendous opportunity that heroin dealing afforded, there was an inevitable heightening in tension between different parts of the organization. The leaders of Murder Corporation had earned their salaries since that syndicate meeting.

Now Albert, Louis and Alex sat for the umpteenth time in Albert's restaurant on Mulberry for another bowl of pasta and a discussion.

"We need to raise our rates."

No sooner had the words left Albert's lips than Alex's heart sank. Apart from greed, he saw no reason for the Italian to open this ancient conversation again. Hadn't this been resolved years ago?

"Do you not think we are making enough at the moment?"

"Alex, our outfit has always been almost pure profit because of what we do," interjected Louis, "But that doesn't mean we are being paid the appropriate rate by the syndicate."

"Sure, but equally it doesn't mean we are being underpaid either, does it?"

All three chewed on their food and mulled the issue over in their minds. Alex was the first to break cover.

"The price for killing a man has increased every year and payments are always made on time—within a day or two of the event occurring. With business booming and everything going as well as it is, I don't think we should seek any extra payments—at least not now. If the contracts dry up then by all means let's increase the amount we charge so we still end up with the same income. These suits don't grow on trees."

Alex flicked a bit of fluff off his sleeve to stress his point and brushed the wool material down where it had been momentarily shifted by his fingers. It was a beautiful piece of *schmatta*.

"Alex, forgive me—you are right. There are more important things for us to do than argue with Luciano over money."

"Absolutely. We should talk about the unions instead, at the very least."

Louis spoke as though Alex was meant to know what he was talking about, but he had no idea at all. Albert pounced on the silence created by this strange statement.

"You're right, Louis. While we have guys waiting for a call from Reles to make a hit, we could use their muscle for other activities."

"And that involves the unions?"

"Why not, Alex? There are many businesses in Midtown that are unionized but we have no influence either with the workers or their bosses. That's gelt we are leaving on the table."

"Have you been scouting around looking for easy pickings, Louis?"

"No, he hasn't, but I have instead."

"And what have you found, Albert?"

"There's not much opportunity downtown or even Midtown. Our outfits have worked this territory for thirty or more years by now, but if we go up to East Harlem, then there are many businesses whose workers need to be protected from the likes of us or require support from us to support their fight against the evil capitalist masters."

"Surely there are already gangs offering these services?"

"There are, Alex, but they are local and have yet to get affiliated with any syndicate member and that is where we can step in and help them."

Alex pondered Albert's words over two mouthfuls of linguini and wondered why the Italian would mention this now—and more interestingly, why was Louis so keen? Had they hatched a plan between them and were hoping to get a nod from Alex and then push him out before the game had even begun?

This made no sense as the two men could set themselves up to take over East Harlem territory without even mentioning it to Alex, because it was none of his business. However, Alex didn't want to come across as negative and chose his reply with the utmost care.

"I'm perfectly happy to get involved in some union bashing—I earned my spurs doing the same thing a lifetime ago under Waxey Gordon."

"Excellent news. We hoped that would be the case. Are you prepared to head north a few blocks and slam heads?"

"That I can do, but I assume we will all three need to encourage the locals to pay us for the right to carry on their daily duties."

"We thought that as you were so successful on the waterfront that you'd like to repeat that performance on dry land."

Alex swallowed hard as his heart sank at the implications of Albert's suggestion.

THE ENTHUSIASM SHOWN by Albert and Louis for Alex to get his hands dirty in the business of union racketeering was noticeable. He hoped it was only his imagination, but a gnawing doubt remained whispering in his ear like a weevil on his shoulder.

"We've all had experience hammering the unions, surely? Albert, I can't believe you got to where you are without cracking a few convener heads."

"That's not the point, Alex. The issue is, who of us is best placed to work on the ground in East Harlem. Louis and I have several other business interests beyond Murder Corporation and I don't believe you are so encumbered, right?"

"I have interests outside of our contracts. I might not talk about them, but they are there."

Louis eyed Albert and then cast his gaze over to Alex, whose spine was stiff with indignation. They were both treating him like their lieutenant and not their equal. He couldn't understand why they were behaving this way.

"I don't want to get into any chest-beating competition with you, but our activities are considerable—I'm sure you'll agree, Alex."

"No contest, Albert, but that is not my point. As we all three are busy men, if we wanted to, we could get some of our fellas to the donkeywork."

Alex stared at Louis, wondering why he was allowing Albert to behave this way—or perhaps the situation was reversed. Albert had influenced or instructed Louis to follow his lead—there was more gelt for Louis with Anastasia than with this Cohen.

Then Alex's thoughts turned to a darker place and he considered the possibility that the reason they wanted him on the street was that would increase his chances of getting attacked or killed. Why else were they so eager for him to take personal charge of a campaign that Ezra, Massimo, or a whole host of guys could run? Not for the first time during this meeting, he swallowed hard. Was this the beginning of the end?

17

THE MEETING ENDED with no real conclusion. Alex's intransigence prevented him from committing to take to the streets and strong-arm union officials and Albert was too hungry with the desire to seize territory and screw down the unions even further. In the end, they agreed to work together, which in practice meant Albert would encourage Louis to use his men instead of Alex. Meantime, Charlie and Meyer kept Alex close as they dealt with information gleaned from Lansky's informers.

"We said it would happen and we were not wrong."

"What are you talking about, Meyer?"

"A special prosecutor has been named, whose job it is to hit organized crime, Alex."

"We're disorganized most of the time so we've got nothing to worry about, right?"

"I wish. Thomas Dewey's been told to root out extortion, prostitution, and racketeering. He'll have us squarely in his sights."

"Are you really worried, Charlie?"

"Better believe it. This guy has a reputation for being cleaner than clean and Mayor Lehman will hand him more than sixty of New York City's finest to help him make arrests and get convictions. This is serious."

"And only four months ago, Hoover renamed his flatfeet to the Federal Bureau. The men in suits are getting mighty feisty."

Alex contemplated Meyer's words.

"Surely if we grease the right palms, they'll find someone else to pick on."

"Perhaps, Alex. I mean, if we can. From what I've heard from our inside contact, these guys are squeaky upright."

"Yes, Meyer, but the office cleaners, the stenographers, the girls in the typing pool—they are much more easily bought. And for less money."

Alex smiled at Charlie's comment but couldn't help wondering if they would survive until fall. With Anastasia nipping at his heels and potentially

Dewey biting at their ankles, what chance did he have for a peaceful few months?

WITHIN A WEEK of Dewey's task force getting an office, the special prosecutor sent his men out to hit the streets—and attack every operation they could find. Any fella who ran a significant angle in New York was on the receiving end of a visit from the gumshoes and their baseball bats. If they had been crooks, then heads would have been cracked.

As it was, doors were smashed, nefarious property bagged and removed. Worst of all, no one put their hand out to be taken care of—every man jack of them was on the up and up. One of Albert's guys tried to offer a Dewey officer a small token of his appreciation to leave the premises and was promptly arrested. Nobody could remember times quite like this.

"What are we going to do about this special prosecutor?"

"Charlie, are you saying you want me to whack Dewey?"

"Alex, that couldn't be further from my thoughts. Please don't even joke about such matters."

Meyer, Charlie, Benny, and Alex sat in the usual booth at the back of Lindy's. Four coffees and three slices of cake were on the table in front of them—Benny wasn't hungry.

"What are we going to do about this menace then, Charlie?"

"That is a question in desperate need of an answer."

Benny chuckled for far too long—so much so that Meyer glared at him to stop. For Alex, the problem of Dewey was already hitting his bank balance.

"Contracts have reduced with the Corporation."

"The crackdowns are making everyone cautious—so there is less friction between fellas as their activities are slowing down."

"Right, Meyer."

Benny laughed again and wouldn't stop.

"What is so goddamn funny?"

"Alex, can't you see that he's doing his job even when Dewey's not breaking down our doors? By attacking a handful of us and making a big deal about it, the cop's reach is far bigger than the fifty chumps he's put on the street."

"That's not funny—it is pitiful and that is costing us gelt, Benny."

"I know, Meyer, but you have to laugh otherwise you cry."

"I am not amused."

"Charlie, no disrespect but I am not changing who I am."

"I understand, Benny. I am not asking you to change, but to remain silent and not distract us as we wrestle with this problem. If this carries on then by the end of the year, you will have less money in your wallet and then you'll be laughing on the other side of your face, *boychik*."

Benny raised his eyebrows high because he couldn't remember the last time he had heard Charlie Luciano use Yiddish. This really was serious and they all fell silent, eating cake and occasionally slurping their coffees. Charlie broke the spell.

"For now, all we can do is tread carefully and not give Dewey any excuses to arrest any of us. Just because he's hitting warehouses today doesn't mean he won't look at our record keeping tomorrow."

"You think he'll copy Ness and hit our tax filings?"

"Why not? If they can take down Alfonse with a pile of paper, do you believe we are any more safe, Alex?"

"I have always ensured I operate through a legitimate company and have a trail of invoices to justify some of my income."

"You're a shrewd cookie, Meyer. I don't have a single document to my name. All the details are in my head."

"Alex, I've got oodles of sales and purchase dockets. You have some of mine if you like."

"Thanks, Charlie. I might take you up on that offer."

"You're welcome. Now, back to business. Until we can get some concrete information from our rat in Dewey's offices, we must also be very careful what we say and who we say it in front of. Loose talk will cost us our lives."

JERVIS MCCRACKEN SAUNTERED into Lindy's restaurant two days later and sat in the rearmost booth, much to the distress of the waitering staff. He only had to wait ten minutes before Charlie walked in and headed to his usual location, followed by Alex thirty seconds afterward. They both stopped in their tracks when they saw McCracken at their table.

"You seem to have been given the wrong table, Mac."

"I'm at the right place—and my name's not Mac."

Charlie sat down opposite the guy and twirled a match around his thumb and first finger, never taking his eyes off the stranger in front of him. Alex perched next to Charlie because he had no desire to be on the same side of the table as this unknown operator to get stabbed if the fella unleashed a temper.

"What do you want, little man?"

"I'm here to give you a piece of friendly advice and I hope you listen well to what I have to say."

"Go on."

Alex remained *schtum* and left Charlie to do all the talking. Just as Jervis was about to respond, Meyer arrived, five minutes late for their meeting. He looked at the situation, swallowed and caught Alex's eye, turned tail, and promptly exited the building.

"You and your people have two options and we really don't mind which one you choose. You can cease your criminal activities with immediate effect or we will come after you and take you down."

"Thanks for sharing your opinions. Who do you think you are exactly and why should I pay any attention to some shriveling lump of nothing who sits in restaurants and tries to threaten men before they even order a coffee...?"

"...and a piece of cake."

McCracken looked at Alex and back at Charlie—then he laughed.

"I work for Thomas Dewey. You will have heard of him because he has made it his sworn duty to convict every single last pond scum like you two breathing in New York City."

Charlie cracked his knuckles and smiled at Alex, who smirked back. He leaned forward a few inches, encouraging Jervis to mirror his body language. He stared at the cop, holding his gaze for five, ten seconds. When he spoke, his voice was barely a whisper.

"Now you listen to me and you listen real careful. Nobody comes to my restaurant and threatens me, you capiche? We told you before, we are here for some light refreshments and yet you accuse us with nothing to back you up. No evidence, no proof, and no bodyguard. That makes you a very foolish man. The next time you loudly attack me for being a criminal, you'd better have more to show for yourself than an ill-fitting suit and a sanctimonious grin on your face, you odious string of piss."

The corners of McCracken's mouth dropped and he gulped. Maybe he wasn't used to being spoken to with such disrespect—perhaps he felt the fear that ordinary men experienced in the presence of Charlie Luciano.

"Now it is your turn to listen to me. I came here in the spirit of friendship to let you know that you have a choice and that you do not have to end up behind bars. If you turf me out of this establishment, then you will have made your decision. And that is fine with me, because what we want is to rid this town of crime—we don't care how, just so long as it happens. The next time I come in here, I'll have a warrant in my hand or a subpoena in my pocket. Either way, you'll be walking out in handcuffs."

Jervis popped his hat on his head, thrust his hands in his pants pockets and waltzed out of Lindy's, whistling a tune, never looking back.

THE NEXT DAY, hell descended on the streets of the five boroughs. Dewey's men hit at least one significant operation of every member of the syndicate who was based in New York—almost as if they had mapped out the entire criminal fraternity in the city. Over the following two weeks, it felt as if each cathouse, gaming den and heroin facility had been raided.

Alex's transportation network was in tatters—many of his vehicles had been confiscated, pending proof they had been used in criminal activities. He wasn't too worried because most trucks were not actually owned by him in the first place so most of the mud would not stick.

Other syndicate members were not as relaxed about the situation. Meanwhile, others took advantage of the attention given by the cops to the Big Apple and focused their aim on other places like Boston. So Alex was not surprised when he received a call, and grabbed a train to carry out a contract for Murder Corporation.

18

FRANK MORELLI HAD made the request to the syndicate for a hit on Charles Solomon's son. The youth had been snapping at his heels ever since Frank assassinated the boy's father two years before. Then he didn't waste time seeking permission and asked for forgiveness after he'd consolidated his power base from his North End headquarters in Boston.

On this occasion, Alex held a contract on Hayim because Frank couldn't be bothered to carry out his own dirty work. The boy—twenty years old—was more a thorn in Frank's side than anything else and the boss of Boston could wait an extra day to rid himself of this nuisance with the minimum of fuss.

Whenever Alex spent time in Puritan City, he noticed how calm the place felt compared to New York. There was still a hustle and bustle as people made their way about their daily tasks, but the edge was missing—that feeling you always had to be on your toes when you walked the Midtown streets.

A cab ride from South Station on Summer Street to Charter Street took no time at all, and soon Alex sat opposite Frank to discuss the reason for his journey.

"There is a boy who has made threats, spouted big talk to his friends in public and generally showed me disrespect."

"Frank, you need not justify the hit to me—the syndicate has authorized it and here I am."

"Sure, Alex, but I knew him when he was growing up—I held him in my arms as a newborn."

"Sometimes they fail to come out of the oven properly."

"And you don't think it has anything to do with the fact I had his papa whacked?"

"Occasionally, Frank, the bread gets misshapen when it is dropped on the floor and trodden on."

They both smiled because Alex was correct on both counts. Why Hayim was in this situation was entirely because of his father's hit and the fact he complained about it rather than take matters into his own hands. Now the syndicate had sanctioned the killing, Frank's justifications were in the past— Hayim Solomon had to die and it was Alex's job to see that it happened before his return to New York.

"What information can you give me about the kid's whereabouts?"

"There are a number of cafés where he goes during the day when he's not making his collections. And in the evenings there are a thousand dives he drinks and cavorts in."

"Is he always with his crew during his daytime exploits?"

"Yeah, I mean apart from one or two visits he makes to special clients, but in the evening he's hanging around with the kids in his neighborhood. They go to all different joints—whichever place is in fashion that night. The Cotton Club was good enough back in my day, but the world has changed."

Alex nodded, although he hadn't gone to a nightclub to dance ever since he started owning them. He guessed Frank was cut from the same cloth.

"Let me watch his movements and then I can decide the best course of action. From now on, I will only contact you if there is something specific I need. I'll drop a dime before I leave town so you know it is done. Apart from that, is there anybody you could lend me while I am here?"

"For the job or for evening companionship?"

"The hit. I don't mix business with pleasure."

"And here was me thinking you find eternal happiness in your work."

"It has its moments, but no skirt to recognize me in a line-up, thanks all the same."

Both men shared a laugh, shook hands and Frank introduced Alex to Savio Altimari—tall, thin, eyes that would shoot bullets given half a moment.

ALEX ASKED SAVIO to walk the streets with him—it gave the out-of-towner an opportunity to get to know North End a little and to pick the local's brain.

"You worked with Frank long?"

"Long enough."

"How well would you say you know Junior?"

"Who?"

"Hayim Solomon."

"Oh, since before his father met with an untimely end."

"What do you make of him?"

"The guy has a chip on his shoulder and who can blame him? If I were him though, I'd have kept my mouth shut and done something about it instead."

"Really? That'd be what you'd have done?"

"Well, if I'd been the son of a gang boss, I'd have done it."

Alex smiled at Silvio, who showed tremendous understanding of the hierarchy in play in their world. The lieutenants did the bidding of their bosses and the bosses behaved however they wanted.

"So where's the best place to find Hayim right now?"

"He'll be looking after his special clients along Snow Hill Street."

"What makes them special? Frank described them like that too."

"Let's head over there and you can see for yourself."

WHEN THEY ARRIVED, Alex saw the usual mix of stores, apartment blocks and a variety of people on the sidewalks. Nothing and nobody appeared that unusual, but he minded himself and waited with Silvio, as they leaned against a wall and lit a cigarette each.

Ten minutes later, Silvio nudged Alex as a young man sauntered along the sidewalk on the opposite side of the street, heading left. At the third entrance, Hayim stopped, put a hand on the door handle, looked both ways up and down the street, and entered the building.

"What gives?"

"One of his specials."

"Looks like any other apartment block to me."

"It does, doesn't it?" Silvio said with a wry smile on his face.

Thirty long minutes and Hayim reappeared, adjusted his jacket, and carried on in the same direction as before. Two blocks later and the same thing happened—into a nondescript building, remained for more minutes than any human might need to collect a wad of gelt and then back out onto the street. After the third time, one block farther on, Alex was tired of watching and waiting.

"Am I going to follow the kid in to find out what's occurring or will you just tell me?"

"No mystery. These are cathouses and Hayim likes to taste the product when he picks up the day's takings. There are four more joints further down this street and two more around the corner. Hayim'll be busy for the rest of the afternoon."

Alex nodded and conjured with the viable ways he could attack Hayim on his route, but either he'd be highly visible on a sidewalk or he would be seen in one of the bordellos. Neither option sounded great.

"If you like, Alex, we could go for a bowl of pasta and meet up with the kid in two hours' time. I know the location of his last port of call. That way, we can rest our shoe leather."

THEIR TABLE WAS at the rear of the Italian restaurant which Silvio took them to and, judging by his reception when they arrived, the owners knew him well. Alex ensured he kept his fedora down over his eyes until they were ensconced at the back. Even then, he made sure he sat in the shadows, not wanting anybody to identify him as being in Boston should the unfortunate occasion arise.

"Relax, you are safe here. Nobody knows anyone or sees anything in this place."

"How can you be so certain?"

"Frank owns the joint. If anyone blabs, then they'll float in the Charles River by dusk."

With those words, Alex relaxed and ordered linguini with salmon and a coffee. Once the food had been delivered and the waiter had walked out of earshot, their conversation continued.

"What about the evenings? Frank said how Hayim never visited the same joint twice."

"Not quite. He is right that every few days there's a new venue for the kids to be seen in, but there are two points where you can guarantee you know the whereabouts of our hero."

"And?"

"Hayim returns to his crib to change into his nightclub threads—around six or so, depending on how busy he's been on Snow Hill Street. The creature of habit returns to his own bed at night. If there's a skirt with him then he never goes to her place, always brings her back to his lair. And usually throws her out onto the street by the early hours. It would appear our boy likes to sleep alone."

Alex smiled at the possibilities this news offered and checked his watch—four twenty. He could polish off the linguini, whack the guy and still make it back home tonight.

SILVIO TOOK ALEX over to Hayim's apartment block and gave him the door number. Then he shook hands and walked away–a job well done. Alex moved round the rear of the building and shimmied up the fire escape three floors and jimmied open the sash window with a knife he carried for this purpose. He scooted inside and ensured the frame was completely closed again, before checking out the place.

It was a simple affair—bedroom, bathroom, living room and kitchen all leading off from the hallway. Nothing fancy and the kind of accommodation suitable for a single man in his twenties. Another look at his watch and Alex reckoned the guy should appear some time in the next forty minutes.

Alex positioned himself behind the living room door. From this vantage point, he could see through the crack near the hinge, into the hallway and the apartment entrance. He leaned against the wall, knowing this was about to be the difficult, tedious phase of any campaign. Five minutes later his boredom was cut short as he heard a key being pushed into the lock and there stood Hayim, fiddling to remove the key. Alex held his breath and waited.

Finally, the boy wrestled the metal free and closed the door, heading straight for the bathroom. He swung the door to, but it didn't shut completely. The sound of liquid landing in the toilet bowl meant Alex understood exactly what to do next.

He ran through the hallway and kicked the door open so he'd have both hands free. Hayim turned round, but he was too late. Alex seized the back of his neck and pushed him sideways so his head slammed into the side of the shower. Crunch. Blood dribbled out of his skull and Hayim screamed.

Alex's spare palm covered the kid's mouth and he smashed Hayim's head twice into the ceramic floor of the shower unit. Muffled yelps, but the boy got his bearings and struggled to get out of Alex's clutches. With one hand round the back of Hayim's neck and the other still clasped over his mouth, Alex yanked him up and dragged him toward the sink.

A sharp motion forwards and Hayim's head smacked into the faucets. Once, twice, three times. Blood was streaming out of his mouth, an eye, and his forehead, and yet he wouldn't die. As much as Alex wanted this to be a silent kill, sometimes matters can get out of hand and this ox didn't want to lie down and die. So he pulled out his pistol, threw him with both hands into the back of the shower and shot him in the heart. Hayim slumped down, one leg twitching for fifteen seconds and then nothing.

Alex checked himself in the mirror above the sink and cleaned off Hayim's blood from his face and fingers. Luckily, there was no red on his clothes. He listened by the front door in case anyone was on the stairway, but nothing. Alex exited the building and walked four blocks before hailing a cab and asking to go to Beacon's Hill. From there he strolled two blocks and hailed a second taxi to take him to the station. Before he boarded his train, Alex popped into a phone booth and dropped a dime to Frank, as promised.

19

"HOW'S TRICKS?"

Charlie and Alex were spending an evening together in the back of one of Charlie's gaming joints, near Mulberry and Canal.

"Been better, but I won't complain."

"You never do, Charlie."

"I make more than enough money to keep me in clover. Why should I grouse when I can still afford three square meals and a roof over my head? You only have to look at the chumps on the street for a minute to know you're doing better than every single one of them."

"Murder Corporation revenue is down on last year, but we too are sitting pretty."

"Is that why Albert has been pushing into East Harlem without permission?"

"He's a made man and does what he thinks best."

"You didn't answer my question, Alex."

"You're right—and I'm not going to respond to it now. We both know that Louis and I can do nothing if Albert mops up some territory going spare. He doesn't need our permission to harangue Italian gangs on the up-and-up."

"Enough said. You heard from Benny recently?"

"Nah, he's a loner. Pops out from under his rock to break occasional bread with us, laugh at what we say, then go back into the soil. I like the guy, but he is strange."

"And no mistake. He and Meyer go way back. Besides, the guy knows how to handle himself and has a creative imagination. Sometimes that turns into little gold mines. You heard about Dutch?"

"Only what I read in the papers. Dewey is after him."

"And some. That cop has a hard-on for our boy."

"Anything we can do to help him?"

"He's got himself a lawyer—a good one—but the fella is a hothead and that means he's shot his mouth off in public one too many times. There are several witnesses, from what I hear, that tie Dutch's paperwork to income he hasn't declared or got a reason why."

"Tax evasion, Charlie, look what it did to Alfonse and see what it will do to Dutch."

"Tell me about it, Alex. It's funny because years ago we talked about the same subject and Meyer convinced me to run a legitimate shell company and now I feel a lot more secure. Having Meyer as my accountant helps too, of course. You?"

"Still no paperwork, no shell, bupkis."

"Alex, while Dewey is in New York, you'd better get yourself something to justify your income—otherwise you're on a one-way ticket to Sing Sing."

Alex stared coldly at Charlie because he knew his friend was right. Dewey would not go away just by ignoring him. He made a mental note to speak to Meyer and get some advice from the syndicate's consigliere.

THREE WEEKS LATER and Dutch's trial began. A stream of witnesses spoke of how the fella had not been where he said he was at the time when his paperwork showed he was out working at his clerical job. Then the IRS representatives walked the jury through all the details of each line of every invoice. Dewey ensured that the twelve good men and true could join the dots between the false claims made by the accused and the reality of what Dutch owned and earned.

Naturally, none of his allies could attend court and show any direct support, but in the evenings they'd meet up with him and discuss the day's events.

"I'm no Capone."

"You certainly kept a lower profile than Alfonse, but that doesn't mean you will walk away from this beef."

"Don't talk like that, Meyer. They aren't going to put me behind bars."

"I admire your spunk, Dutch, but if the newspaper reports are anything to go by, the evidence is building against you. It doesn't matter what those of us here believe—it is the jury that counts."

"Alex, that's easy for you to say as I'm the one looking at hard time."

"I'm only pointing out that you might want to think about how to give yourself an edge, Dutch."

Charlie smiled and Meyer tilted his head at Alex, deep in thought.

"What are you suggesting?"

"Have you considered an indirect route to a not guilty verdict if your lawyer can't get it for you the usual way?"

"You're talking like you got an idea, Alex."

"I was wondering what would happen if we could change the opinion of a juror—or two."

Dutch swallowed hard and considered Alex's proposal.

THE BEDROCK OF the American judicial system is that any man accused of a crime will be listened to by twelve of his equals. The prosecution and defense attorneys do their best to present evidence and argument to sway the opinion of the members of the jury, but the simple truth is this: what goes on inside the jury room, stays in the jury room and no one knows but those twelve.

And that was what Alex was banking on because he understood that the entire process operated on the basis that everyone is essentially good, whereas all the people he had ever met in his life demonstrated to him that every single person on this planet has a price and the trick is to find out what that amount is and offer just a little more to sweeten the deal further.

Alex sent Ezra out to the courthouse on the second day of the proceedings to check out the lay of the land. That night, he reported back.

"There are three potential John Does we could impress. One is rich—quality suits, the way he speaks. Number two is an obvious mark—he has turned up in the same shirt both days and would do anything for a buck."

"And the third?"

"He is quiet, doesn't mix with the other jurors. Any time someone talks, he scribbles away in a little notebook—takes himself seriously."

"That's the one we want. Follow him tomorrow and find out where we can bump into him on the way home."

"YOU GOT A light, Mac?"

"Sure. Here you go."

Alex thanked Matt Knowles and inhaled on his cigarette for a moment. The man smiled briefly and tried to push on down the street—he was only a block away from the bar where he consumed a single beer before going home. Alex blocked his route by leaning to one side—only a knowing eye would have spotted the move.

"I don't suppose you know a comfortable drinking place nearby?"

"Why, yes. As it happens, I'm heading that way myself."

"Mind the company?"

"Not at all."

There was a momentary hesitation which betrayed Knowles' instinct to be alone, but he had little choice, given Alex's friendly and innocent tone.

When they arrived at the tavern, Alex followed Matt to the bar and bought them both a beer. Matt thanked him for his generosity and turned to sit at what Alex knew to be his usual seat based on what Ezra had said.

Alex took a few sips of his drink from where he stood and then headed in Knowles' direction, much to his surprise.

"Mind if I share the table?"

"Well, I…"

Before Matt could express his actual opinion, Alex sat down and spread himself out opposite the hapless juror.

"What do you do for a living?"

"I'm an accounts clerk but I doubt I'll see the inside of my office for a while."

"Oh?"

"Yes, I am otherwise occupied at the moment."

"Doing what?"

Alex sipped his beer, indicating only a sociable interest in the response.

"I shouldn't say—we're not meant to talk about it."

"You a spy?"

"No, I'm on a jury—started this week."

"Juicy case?"

"Interesting enough. It's tax evasion."

"That doesn't sound too exciting. Anyone I've heard of?"

"Some Jew gangster, Dutch Flegenheimer."

Alex let the conversation twist around Schultz's situation until he took Matt's attention away from the unusual position of sharing a drink with a stranger who'd asked for a match.

"You think he's guilty?"

"What? I can't talk about the case—they were very clear about that."

"Sure, but you reckon he did it?"

Matt's eyes shifted right, then left. He shuffled on his chair and leaned in toward Alex as all conspirators do.

"There's no smoke without fire and you know what those people are like, right?"

"Are you certain? I mean, the trial's only been running two days. The defense might have something up their sleeve."

"Like stolen money?"

Knowles laughed at his own joke, but Alex stared straight at him without a glimmer of a smile.

"Let's not make light of a thing as important as this. The guy will be sent away for a long time if he's found guilty."

"And what if he was? Why do you care?"

"You like your apartment?"

"What? Sure. It's small, but I can afford the rent."

"Would you want to have a bigger place?"

"Sure, who wouldn't?"

"I could help you with that, if you'd like."

Matt put his beer down on the table and now it was his turn to look as serious as a heart attack at Alex.

"What d'you mean?"

"I have some friends who would show their appreciation if Dutch Schultz walks free."

"Friends?"

"Yep, and if that happened then you could afford a new apartment—with more space."

"I really don't think…"

"…and the other advantage of helping my associates is that you'd be alive to enjoy your new crib."

Matt stared at Alex and gulped.

"How can you be sure I won't go straight to the cops and turn you in?"

"I don't know that for sure, but there is one thing of which I am absolutely certain—if between now and the end of the trial, you visit a precinct station or talk to a cop about anything apart from to get directions then I guarantee you'll be dead before sunset. And then you'd need to think about how you would go about protecting your daughter—from your first marriage…"

Alex picked up his beer and downed what remained of the brew. He wiped his lips on the sleeve of his jacket and looked back at Matt, who had acquired tiny beads of sweat dripping off his cheeks and onto the table.

"Do we have an understanding?"

Matt Knowles nodded and Alex tipped his hat and walked out of the bar. They never met again, but on the day after the trial, Knowles discovered a brown paper bag in his mailbox that contained enough gelt to keep him in clover—and silent—for the rest of his days.

OCTOBER 1935

20

DESPITE ALL HIS fine words about ridding himself of the failed Yiddish actress, Ida Grynberg, Alex had done nothing about acting on those syllables for over five years. There were many months when he hardly visited her at all and later, whenever the mood descended on him, he would spend a week or two in her company before returning to his own suite and bed.

Ida never appeared to mind about his absences, wrapped as she was in her own theatrical world. When he turned up, she smiled and let him in and if he didn't show again, she carried on as though he was not in her life.

Following Alex's conversation with Knowles, he wanted to change his routine and spend a night with Ida. It wasn't the lure of sex, which was lackluster after all these years, but the desire for companionship, no matter how shallow that might be between them.

When he rang the doorbell, Alex had to wait an eternity for Ida to haul ass and open up for him. He had called before he left so he would be certain she was in and to give her a chance to get rid of any other guest, should any be in attendance. Alex didn't judge what she did when they weren't together— he had no high moral ground in this respect either.

When she eventually let him in, she smiled at him and pecked Alex on the cheek before twirling around and heading back to the apartment living room where she flopped onto the chaise longue.

"So glad to see you after all this time, Alex, darling."

"It has been a while—how are you doing, Ida. All well?"

"I have been absolutely divine, thank you for asking. How has the world of extortion and racketeering been to you?"

"No need to be like that, Ida. Business has been good, which is one reason it's been such a long time since we've been together. I'm hoping you'll be okay with me spending a few days with you now."

"Darling, that is absolutely priceless news."

ALEX WOKE UP next to Ida and did a double-take because he forgot where he was for a second. Then he shook off the sleep in his head and focused on his whereabouts until he recognized his location. Then he sighed inside when he recalled who he was with and why he was in Ida's bed.

He remained where he lay and enjoyed the silence of the early morning until his companion stirred ten minutes later. Alex had spent at least half that time staring at her naked back, trying to decide how much he still yearned for her physically. His conclusion was simple: while she wasn't unattractive, there was not enough about her to make him desire her anymore.

Not for the first occasion, Alex considered finding a fresh squeeze—one he might want to spend time with—but he knew himself sufficiently well to be aware that he wasn't really prepared to put in the required effort to sustain a relationship. If he was going to do that, then he would spend his energy trying to get Sarah back. And that had not happened since she walked out.

Ida stirred and rolled over to face him. She smiled and touched his chest briefly. Then she returned her arm under the covers to keep it warm.

"Good morning, darling. Be a love and light me a cigarette."

Alex nodded and hopped out of bed long enough to grab a packet of smokes and to rummage around until he found a book of matches. He lit two cigarettes and passed one to Ida. Then they lay next to each other, soaking in the warmth of each other's bodies. He wanted to find some kind of conversation with her, but no ideas sprang to mind until...

"Have you been in any productions recently?"

"Me, dear? No. There hasn't been a sniff of work for months. Sometimes I wonder if directors look at me and think I am too old for the lead roles."

"Really? I might not know much about the theater but how could anyone say you are mature?"

"You are sweet, but acting is a young girls' game. Nobody in the audience will look at me on stage and believe I could end up as a blushing bride when the curtain goes down."

"I still think it's crazy talk. Besides, you're a singer too."

"That I am, although my voice has seen better days. Too much smoking and living the high life have put paid to my vocal chords."

Alex found that hard to argue against—from the moment he saw her in the Richardson speakeasy, a blind pig he'd owned and run at the start of Prohibition, Ida's career had been going downhill and this period between roles was just the latest in a long line of tales she had offered him over the years.

AFTER THEY'D LAZED around for quite some time, Alex threw on his clothes while Ida sauntered to the kitchen and attended to their breakfast. She remembered he preferred a cup of strong coffee and maybe a slice of lightly buttered toast, but not much else.

Her idea of the opening meal of the day was a cigarette, so it didn't take her long to prepare the repast. Alex appreciated that she was trying as he tucked into the burned bread lying stiffly on his plate. At times like this, he wished he liked cereal—pouring milk on top of some flakes was less prone to culinary error.

They sat at the circular kitchen table, which stood by a window, to soak in as much of the natural light as possible. As he glanced at Ida, bathed in the sun's glow, Alex saw how haggard she appeared—the seasons had not been kind to her. She looked at least thirty years older than him, but he knew there were only ten separating them—he had been a late teenager when she was in her twenties. Now you would never believe that to be the case.

Once he'd swallowed the last vestige of toast and washed the crumbs down with the remains of his drink, Alex rose and fished out his hat from the pile of clothes in the hallway cupboard.

"I'll see you tonight if it's all the same to you."

"Darling, that would be absolutely divine."

GOOD TO HIS word, Alex returned that night and was received with the same warmth as Ida had offered him twenty-four hours earlier. The effusive words didn't quite match how she behaved towards him.

She slumped back on her chaises longue and picked up her pipe, inhaled deeply and then promptly lost herself in an opium haze for two or three hours. The first while, Alex just sat there and enjoyed the tranquility that Ida's intoxication offered, but soon he got bored. The whole point of being with Ida was to share some words and to steal a few moments of joy under the bedclothes.

Thirty minutes into her reverie, Alex grabbed his coat and hit the streets, determined to find a place to eat and to overhear other people's conversations if he wasn't able to engage in talk with his paramour. Perhaps that was the heart of the dilemma—Alex still thought of Ida as a mistress rather than as a girlfriend. Deep down he knew the problem between them couldn't be resolved by changing the name he used to describe her.

Alex wandered the streets for about five minutes before settling on a joint with a line of ten people waiting to get a seat. If nothing else, it showed it was popular—and judging by the decor, the food would be what was selling the restaurant and not its potted plants.

He walked to the front of the line and ignored the scowls from the johns who had been standing for quite some time ahead of him.

"I'm looking for a table."

"Aren't they all, Mac?"

The maître d' was busy scribbling away at his paperwork and failed to look at his customer for their first interaction. Then his eyes moved up Alex's torso until he saw his face.

"Oh, sir, forgive me. I didn't see you standing there."

With a flourish, Benito undid the rope which separated the line from his restaurant interior and Alex stepped through. Although they had never met, the guy recognized Alex on sight. He had purposefully headed toward the outskirts of Little Italy and anyone who valued their business knew who he was—and Anastasia and Louis too.

"I'm afraid there isn't a great selection of tables at present. If you'd been able to book ahead, then we could have been better prepared for you."

"No matter. I am interested in a simple bowl of pasta and then I'll be out of your hair. No need to go to any special effort on my account."

They both knew this was a lie and each man pretended they believed him. When a gang boss enters your establishment, only a fool would treat him like any other customer. So Alex enjoyed a sumptuous three-course meal along with a demi-bottle of red wine. He left a generous tip after Benito waived all charges and went back to the apartment to find Ida was still unconscious.

Alex hovered over her for a minute, trying to decide what he should do. He stared at the burned crumbs around the edge of her pipe and reminded himself of the pleasant hours he had spent lying in a soporific haze with an opium pipe when he was a young man. Those days were long gone and all he saw before him was an addled woman being eaten away from the inside by the opium she smoked. A shell of a person.

He shuddered uncontrollably and turned to leave. That was the moment Ida came to and reached out a hand.

"Get me a drink will you, darling?" she whispered hoarsely and then let her arm flop down again.

He acceded to her request but had no interest in spending much more time with her. Ida was part of his past and he should stop himself from looking back. If he did it too often, then he would turn into a pillar of salt.

21

THE AMERICAN LEGAL system is a wonderful thing and in time-honored tradition, Matt Knowles did exactly what was expected of him—he swung the jury around and Dutch walked free from court. Dewey was none too impressed with the outcome, but he couldn't argue with the decision made by twelve good men and true. Well, eleven and Knowles.

For Dutch, the news was bittersweet—he was pleased to be found not guilty but he wanted revenge on the prosecutor for trying to take him down. Schultz did the only sensible thing that a man in his position could do—he called an extraordinary meeting of the inner circle of the syndicate, with only one item on the agenda.

"Gentlemen, thank you all for coming. I understand this is out of the ordinary, but we live in unusual times."

Charlie offered a benign smile, Meyer stared blankly out of the suite window and the others shuffled papers, inhaled cigarettes, and sipped at their various refreshments. Alex was prepared to listen to the fella, although Albert and Louis seemed disinterested—hard for him to tell for certain.

"Dutch, I am sure I speak for everyone when I say how pleased I am that you have evaded justice and continue to walk free along these hallowed streets in New York. I'd have thought you would want to get back to your business interests rather than sit around and chat with us old men."

This generated a chuckle from the assembled group—all but Dutch, that is.

"Charlie, breathing air as a free man is a wonderful thing, but sometimes that is not enough. Besides, you flatter yourself if you think you are an *alte kaker*. None of you are over the hill—in contrast, you control this city and territories way beyond here too. Don't undersell yourself."

"Dutch, we all know how fortunate we have been in our business enterprises, but unfortunately, I have not been as successful predicting what's in people's minds. Why have you brought us here today?"

"I have a proposal for you all to consider."

Schultz looked around the room in Luciano's hotel suite to gauge the reaction, but these were the hardest men to read in the country. Meyer's bored expression was noticeable, but anyone who knew the man understood he didn't like to let fellas know what he was thinking, so it all could have been a bluff.

"There is a menace in our city and unless we do something, we will be destroyed by it. Maybe not today or tomorrow, but someday and that time is soon."

"It's too late to build an ark and wait for the flood."

Benny's derision oozed out of every syllable, and even Meyer raised an eyebrow before returning to his neutral countenance.

"I don't get why you are all being so flippant. First, they came for Alfonse and we did nothing and they locked him up and threw away the key. Then they put me in their sights and the jury saw fit to dismiss the charges."

Dutch glanced at Alex, but he didn't return the eye contact.

"So the next thing that'll happen is that they come after me again with some more trumped-up accusations or one of you will be taking your turn at the courthouse."

"What are you suggesting, Dutch?"

"We need to kill that cockroach, Thomas Dewey. If we don't slam him under our boots now, that roach'll scurry back again and again until he takes us all down, one after the other."

For the first time since he entered the room, Meyer's expression altered.

"Let me get this straight, you want to hit a special prosecutor because he charged you with tax evasion of which you were wholly guilty?"

"Yes, Meyer."

"And from what I understand, you are only at liberty to come to this meeting due to some help from your friends."

Alex felt Meyer's eyes bear down on him and ignored the implication of the attention he was receiving. Now was not the time to admit in front of witnesses he'd been jury tampering. Not that he had trust issues with any of the fellas in the room—although Louis and Anastasia were on his watch list —but that private matter should remain just that.

"This isn't anything personal—this is business. The longer Dewey sticks around, the more he'll uncover and the harder it will be for us to continue operating as we do. When Prohibition came in, we adapted to take account of the new circumstances. Now Prohibition is ending, we must be prepared to do the same again. Only this time, we need to alter what we do to protect our wealth. I won't remind any of you we are discussing way more than mere chump change."

Charlie's back stiffened and Meyer turned his head and body to face Dutch. Benny continued to slump down in his seat, twiddling a nickel around his fingers. Alex glanced at Albert and Louis and they too had leaned forward now that gelt was being discussed.

"There is nothing wrong in killing a cop if collectively his death is worth millions to us," intoned Dutch.

Albert nodded slowly but Louis tilted his head to one side as Schultz continued. "Why do you think this whack job won't move on to other parts of the country if he doesn't get a big win soon? You know what these federal gumshoes are like."

"The fact he is a cop makes matters difficult but not impossible," Charlie interjected. "But this is not an ordinary policeman on the beat. We can't offer this guy a handful of green and send him on his way. This is a person who has been nominated by Hoover and is a special prosecutor. Correct me if I'm wrong, but nobody has ever put a contract out on a bureau man before. Meyer?"

Lansky shook his head in the negative. "Not to my recollection, Charlie. Besides which, a special prosecutor isn't the same as a district attorney. Those we influence indirectly with our politicians. Dewey is clean. I wouldn't say he's untouchable, but a simple bribe will not work with his sort."

Dutch sighed heavily. "I am not saying we should give him money and tell him to go away. I'm saying we should bury the *goy*—no offense intended."

The Italians in the room were visibly rankled by Schultz's offensive term for non-Jews. Judging by their expressions, Alex couldn't decide if Dutch had got bound up in his own anger and passion or whether he had revealed his genuine distaste for those of other faiths.

Alex broke the tension in the room because everybody's attention had been diverted by Dutch's outburst and he for one needed them to reach a conclusion. He wanted to pop over to Ida on his way home to hand back his key and call it quits with her. He'd finally had enough of that opium head.

"You still haven't explained why Murder Corporation should get a new contract."

"Alex, the situation is very simple. Dewey has attacked me and I demand revenge on him and his family."

Meyer agreed with Alex. "Leave his wife and kids out of this, Dutch. If your complaint is business and nothing personal, then there is no need for citizens to get hurt."

"All right, don't touch the wife and kids, but kill the cop."

"Dutch, I understand you are angry and that is normal," commented Charlie, "but murdering a special prosecutor so soon after he tried to lock you up. Don't you think the cops will come running to your front door before the body is even cold?"

"You seem to believe if we hit Dewey that law enforcement won't take a sharp intake of breath before they do anything like respond. I'm not so sure. If you are right, and hitting a special prosecutor is such a big deal, don't you think they'll hold back from retaliating—they will want to appear all high and mighty."

"And your plan would be to skip town until the heat dies down and leave us to pick up the pieces?" Benny laughed again, even more so when Dutch's expression dramatically shifted to reflect that this was his actual intention.

"After we show what happens to senior cops when they poke their noses in our business, they'll back off. Surely, between us we have enough lawmakers in our pay to see that the squeaky Dewey is sent packing to shove his snout somewhere else, Charlie."

"The politicians who do our bidding are local—Tammany Hall has power, but it's taken a beating since the elections. Besides, with La Guardia as mayor, you know how he will only win more supporters if he uncovers a racket and shuts it down."

Meyer uncrossed his legs and poured himself another glass of water. Tempers were frayed and Alex knew Lansky preferred a calm atmosphere in which to discuss business. The others remained silent to give the financier time to gather his thoughts.

"Dutch, you are right to bring this matter to the syndicate and I commend you for showing this respect. And you are also correct to say that our takings will go up if Dewey leaves us alone or goes away and finds some other itch to scratch."

Dutch smiled, but Meyer raised his palm before adding, "But you are mistaken if you think assassinating the cop will make any difference. These are troubled times for everybody, with La Guardia and Dewey breathing down our necks. You are right to call Dewey a cockroach and like that insect, if you crush one of them then others will appear in their place."

Charlie rose, then paced up and down to stretch his legs.

"Let's put this to a vote. Those in favor of taking out Dewey?"

Dutch's solitary arm rose.

"Those against?"

Every other hand in the room showed opposition to the motion.

"Then we are decided—Dewey lives to fight another day."

As Charlie sat down, Dutch sprang to his feet and stormed out the door. As he turned the handle, they all heard him mutter under his breath, "I'm gonna kill that cockroach."

22

"DID I HEAR him straight?" Charlie looked round the room because he couldn't believe the words he'd just heard.

"Reckon so, and while I don't think now is the right time, Dutch has a point."

All eyes turned to Anastasia, who shrugged at the attention and quizzical expressions on everybody else's faces and took a drag on his cigarette.

"Are you serious?"

"I'm just saying Dewey is bad for business and it is better to rid ourselves of the current problem sooner rather than later. If they send another prosecutor after us, so be it. Meanwhile, it'll take ages for Hoover to appoint a different guy he can trust as much and we should use that time to prepare for the arrival."

Meyer shook his head. "We had a vote and decided. Do we have to rake over the coals again?"

"Who's raking? I am stating that La Guardia might not be so quick to send cops into our neighborhoods if there's a real possibility of a bullet heading in his direction."

"Albert, you started by reminding us you agreed with the decision," hissed Charlie, "So let it go. Now is not the time to attack the police and if Dutch keeps his word, he will take matters into his own hands."

"And that will be bad for business," added Meyer.

"What are we going to do about it?"

Alex's question was well-timed because it was what everyone was asking themselves.

"Shall I run after him and try to change his mind?"

"Thanks for the offer, Louis. Although that hothead might go home now, it doesn't mean he won't hit Dewey tomorrow instead."

"What are you suggesting?"

"Nothing at the moment—only that he needs to be stopped."

Charlie sat back in his chair and allowed the others to burst into conversation. Each man had a viewpoint and wanted to express it there and then. Luciano was smart and let them vent until their initial energy had dissipated and a calm descended in the room.

During this time, Alex checked out the decor of Charlie's suite. The penthouse was vast and the boardroom table shone with its recent polishing. Three paintings hung on the walls—all bright colors and country scenes. The furniture comprised leather upholstery and Alex imagined the bedroom contained a four-poster bed.

He was brought back to reality by Charlie's voice. His friend had brought matters to order otherwise they'd have spent the rest of the day jawing and achieving nothing.

"Sounds to me we agree that we should not allow Dutch to take out the prosecutor."

Nods all round, although Albert's head appeared the most reluctant.

"What do you propose we do about it, Charlie?"

"Albert, that is for us to discuss and then decide."

"Then let's give him a well-deserved break. Send him to Florida for a vacation. The weather might not be great, but he could spend some time in the casinos, meet some new girls—he'll be away from all this *tsoris* and we deal with Dewey in a more mature way."

"Meyer, a few weeks out of the city will do Dutch some good—but will it be enough to stop him?"

"What do you mean, Alex?"

"Assuming we can get Dutch to agree to pack up and leave Manhattan for a month, do you really think that would prevent him getting Abe Landau or Bernard Rosenkrantz to do his dirty work? They are fiercely loyal as his lieutenants should be."

"You saying we should force them on vacation too?"

"Meyer, that isn't realistic. We can't send the top tier of Dutch's crew away. How would his business survive?"

"So what are you suggesting, Alex?"

"Albert, I'm not sure—I am concerned that Meyer's suggestion won't work, but I don't have a solution to our problem."

"Meanwhile, he could march over to Dewey's office to put a bullet through his brains."

Albert uttered their biggest fear. If Dutch carried through with his threat —and everyone expected he would, sooner or later—then the heat that would rain down on them would be intense. Alex gathered his thoughts and followed the logic of Albert's statement.

"So we need to prevent Dutch from taking action—in the short term at the very least—and a vacation is not the answer."

"Do you think he's on his way over to Dewey as we sit here and yak?"

"Benny, if he is then we have no way to stop him at all—and this talk will cost us dear. If not then we must do something, if only we could agree what that was."

Charlie was right. Better they spend time and reach a sensible conclusion than behave like hotheads with itchy trigger fingers.

"Should we take him and offer him a forced vacation—as a guest of one of us out of town?"

"You mean kidnap him, Meyer?"

"Yes, Albert, if you must put it that way."

"Kidnapping will not work. At some point, we'll have to release him and then he will hit Dewey, anyway. I should know—I've worked with him longer than any of you."

Louis was right. Dutch would never let this go—it would chew up his insides until he burst.

"What's left?"

Louis looked straight into Charlie's eyes.

"There is only one option—Dutch must die."

FOR THE FIRST time that anyone could remember, somebody suggested killing one of their own. That the words fell out of Louis' lips made the moment even more poignant. He and Dutch had grown up together, played together, robbed together, strong-armed and assaulted together until they became bosses and members of the syndicate.

"Is there any need for bloodshed?"

"Meyer, your desire to solve all problems through discussion and contemplation is admirable, but sometimes a drop or two of blood has to flow."

Louis went silent, staring into his lap, adjusting himself to the possibility that Dutch Schultz would be killed by a man in the room. Alex tried to think if there was any other way out of this mess.

"It's us or him," noted Benny with no trace of emotion in his voice. He swallowed, and Alex wondered whether Siegel was hoping to have the honor of killing the fella. Him rather than me, determined Alex at the prospect of gunning down a commissioner in the syndicate. Albert sighed, sipped at his drink, and leaned back in his chair, mimicking Charlie.

"What other choice do we have? I think Dewey should be offed, only not now. We cannot be seen to allow fellas to fly around and do whatever they want. We have organizations to run and can't afford to have guys doing whatever they feel like. Even though the man has a point, he is going about this the wrong way and we need to stop him—and fast."

Louis continued to stare at his knees, refusing to acknowledge the discussion taking place around him. Meyer scratched his head, hoping an alternative might spring to mind. "I'd still like us to consider holding him against his will until he sees reason."

Benny laughed. "And how many years do you think it'll take before we can set him free? Get real. Dutch isn't a fella to change his opinion when he has fixed on an idea. Right, Louis?"

Louis looked up and nodded.

"His head is never for turning. Once he's decided, that's it until the day he dies."

"An unfortunate choice of words. Are you telling us we must kill him?"

Louis stared into Albert's eyes until he looked no more. He knew the answer and despite Meyer's hopes for a peaceful settlement, there was no way out that any of them could see.

"Any other proposals on the table?" Charlie asked, more as a formality than in the belief that anybody would step forward with a better suggestion. "Then let's put it to a vote, unless anyone wants to say anything first?"

Silence.

"Those in favor of clipping Dutch Schultz?"

Every hand rose—even Louis' because it was the right thing to do.

Charlie nodded without verbalizing what they had witnessed. "Let's break for a bite to eat. We all could do with getting out of the place and settling our stomachs."

THEY WALKED DOWN to the restaurant and into a private dining room. Albert, Louis, and Alex were only too aware they had a new contract and someone would have to follow through with it. Alex just hoped it wasn't going to be him.

A steak and fries later and he hadn't changed his mind. Charlie ensured the conversation didn't linger on Schultz all the time, but he was never far from any of their thoughts. Benny seized the opportunity to be the center of attention and cracked a series of funny gags, which made everyone laugh.

"We normally leave you guys to manage your own business but this isn't a usual hit. Which Murder Corporation executive will do the deed?"

The three men glanced at each other—no one wanted to volunteer.

"You two have known him far longer than me…"

"Does that mean it should be you as you have a weaker connection with him, Alex?"

"Albert, I did a favor for Schultz recently, so let's not play that game."

Anastasia shrugged and chewed on his chicken. Louis stuffed himself with his pastrami sandwich and refused to be so rude as to talk with his mouth full. Benny chuckled, shook his head, and enjoyed the scene. Everyone understood he'd happily whack the fella if anybody bothered to ask him, but this discussion wasn't so much about getting the job done as seeing who would be prepared to clip the guy. Finally Albert broke the silence. "It should be Louis. They go back and we can trust he'll do it decently—with respect."

"Only if I have Alex as a witness. I don't want any bums telling me I didn't follow through on my word."

Before Alex had a chance to complain, the matter was settled.

23

LOUIS AND ALEX told their respective lieutenants they wanted to know when anybody spotted Schultz and the next day Massimo reported he'd been seen in Newark, so the two headed off through the tunnel and hoped they'd figure out a plan before they met up with him.

Once in New Jersey, they switched cars so no one would look twice at their local plates—not that a New York vehicle was such a rare sight in the neighboring state. Caution was the word and using the same getaway car all the way into the city would have been a monumental mistake.

They drove round town randomly switching from street to street in case they bumped into Schultz, but after fifteen minutes they stopped and Alex hopped out to place a call.

"Massimo, any more news about our target?"

"Nothing certain, but his favorite Chinese restaurant can't be far from you. I don't know if you've noticed the time but I reckon you'll find Dutch at the Palace Chop House."

"You got an address for me? Newark is not my town."

"It's on East Park Street. Be careful because the joint is popular and there could be several citizens in there."

"Thanks for the warning."

Back in the limousine, Louis knew the place and, with a squeal, he lurched the vehicle toward Schultz's demise.

"WHAT'S YOUR PLAN?"

Louis parked the car around the corner from the restaurant and Alex relaxed into his seat, while Louis gripped the steering wheel like it was about to fly out of the window. Alex needed the guy to be much calmer before the hit could begin.

"My mind's blank, Alex. I can't imagine a single thing to do to murder my friend."

"You could burst through the entrance and blast your way to his table?"

"And shoot Dutch in the face while he's eating? What kind of person do you think I am?"

"You're a fella with a hit to carry out. It is not about how you feel that matters, but what you have been contracted to do."

"Easy for you to say."

"I've killed my fair share of friends, Louis—you have no idea."

They were both quiet for a spell as Louis remained locked to the wheel and Alex's mind flitted briefly to Sammy, the guy who'd introduced him to Waxey Gordon.

A truck backfired in the distance and Alex bounced back into the present day. He turned to check out Louis and saw the fella frozen to the spot—unmoved from the minute he pulled the car over and parked. Alex sighed because he experienced a sinking feeling in his stomach as he realized what would happen.

"Are you able to go through with this?"

"Maybe… I don't know. Honestly, I'm not sure I can do it."

"What are you saying?"

Louis exhaled and swallowed before responding.

"Will you carry out the job for me?"

Alex had figured this moment would come and deep within he didn't want to admit to himself that he had known from before they left Midtown.

"I guess I must."

Louis nodded, still unable to look Alex square in the face.

"Then I shall."

As soon as Louis heard Alex's agreement, he released his grip on the steering wheel and the tension seemed to ebb from his shoulders. They remained in the car for five minutes until Alex decided he'd had enough and resolved to walk around the block.

ALEX KEPT HIS hands in his pants pockets and his head down as he wandered the Newark streets. He couldn't stay in the same cage with Louis for another moment. After a few minutes air, he didn't so much have a plan as he'd cleared his mind enough to know that the best way was to try for a rear entrance and play it by ear from that point on. The only thing he was certain of—Louis would not be joining him and he hoped the guy could function as a getaway driver otherwise he was a total waste of space.

When Alex arrived back by the car, he looked round to get his bearings, nodded at Louis who was enjoying a cigarette, and vanished into the evening as he took a long arc before arriving at the rear of the Palace Chop

House. There were two large dumpsters six feet away from a rear glass door. As he approached, Alex saw there were also boxes next to the wall between the nearest dumpster and the doorway. In the dim light, he thought he made out some movement by the entrance, but couldn't see well enough to know exactly what was going on inside.

ALEX SIDLED FORWARD until his back slammed against the brickwork with the door to his left. He pulled out his pistol but kept it by his side. There was no point having a gun fight if all he had seen was a citizen heading for the john. He waited thirty seconds, ears pricked keenly, hoping to make out what was happening indoors. There were two muffled voices inches away from him, but he couldn't make out a single thing they said to each other.

A big exhalation and Alex edged closer to the handle and reached out just as the door swung open and a man in a tall white cylindrical hat walked out and strode six paces forward. The door remained still for a moment, shutting slowly to reveal Alex, but the cook hadn't seen him because the guy hadn't looked around. He stood, legs apart, inhaling his cigarette without a care in the world.

With his pistol returned to his jacket pocket, Alex strode four giant steps and put one palm over the guy's mouth, dragging him back toward the wall. A punch to the kidneys with his free hand and the cook scrunched into a little ball. A kick in the head as he lay on the ground and the man stopped moving. Alex checked his pulse—still alive—and opened the nearest dumpster and tipped the slumped body out of the way. He'd be fine when he eventually came to, although the stench of his surroundings would not be to his pleasing.

Back to the entrance and Alex could tell there was nobody on the other side, so he twisted the handle and pulled the door ajar. There were still no sounds nearby, so he opened the door fully and whipped inside.

He was in a corridor. At the far end was the main restaurant—he made out some white tablecloths with diners seated around them. Between him and the customers were two doors either side by the exit, clearly labeled as the washrooms for men and women. Five feet further up were another pair of doors. One was only an archway which led into the kitchen and the other was closed and marked as private for office staff only.

Alex considered checking it out, but Dutch was most unlikely to be there —and that was who he was after. So he darted past the kitchen, hustled to the end of the corridor, and peered around the joint. A moment's glance told him that Schultz was not in view, but the space was L-shaped which meant the fella was round the other leg, near the front entrance, out of sight for now.

Another check across the room and still there was nobody Alex recognized. As Schultz would not be dining alone, there must be a welcoming party round the corner and Alex wondered whether he should get Louis to double up the firepower.

He noticed a john stare at him and beckon him over. Alex grabbed a white napkin and draped it over his lower arm. Then he stepped forward.

"Another bottle of wine, waiter."

"Same as before, sir?"

"Yeah, the house red."

"Straight away, sir."

Now he was squarely in the room, Alex made his way forward ostensibly on the hunt for some vino. He reached the corner and returned his pistol to his palm. Deep breath and walk… into nothing. There were six tables in front of him, but Schultz sat at none of them.

Luckily, Alex spotted three faces he'd seen before so he went straight up to Abe Landau, Bernard Rosenkrantz and Otto Berman. The first two fellas would pack heat and the third one was a pencil pusher and was harmless. Bernard looked up at Alex and his jaw dropped open.

"Any of you birds seen Dutch around?"

"What the…?"

Otto responded but noticed the other two were stony silent, so he halted in mid-sentence. His eyes glanced back in the direction Alex had just come, while the others said nothing and very visibly kept their hands on the table, silverware down, palms facing the tablecloth. As passive and as calming as they could be.

Abe was the first to make a move and tried to stand up and pull a gun from out of his jacket. More fool him, because Alex squeezed a bullet into his right lung before both legs were straight. Bernard lurched sideways and tried to roll onto the floor, but Alex was too quick for him and pulled the trigger a second time, grazing Bernard's leg with the slug.

Like everybody else in the restaurant, Otto let out a scream but was the only person in the joint to stay perfectly still. Despite being an accountant, his desperate desire to live forced him to do the only sensible thing—remain motionless so he couldn't be hit by any stray bullet.

Alex pulled their table out of his way, causing chow mein to fly in all directions. This gave him the opportunity to fire a second shot into Abe at even closer range—this time in the head. Bernard tried to squirm around, but Alex fired at his kneecap.

With the room in uproar, Alex stood up straight and ensured every civilian got a good look at his piece—nobody would make the mistake of trying to be a hero.

"Everybody onto the ground."

This simple instruction was followed by half the johns and the rest sat and stared, not sure what to do, unable to believe they were sitting amid a gun battle when all they had been expecting was crispy fried duck.

Alex worked his way back toward the rear of the joint until he reached the corridor. Still no sign of Schultz. A quick check in the kitchen revealed nothing but scared chefs and waiters. He used the barrel of his gun to show that everyone needed to stay where they were—and no one looked like they had any other plans.

Then it struck him—there were two places Alex hadn't tried. He stormed down the corridor and into the men's washroom. Nothing. He kicked open the two cubicles, but there was nobody to be found.

Back to the office and inside was a solitary man, cowering behind his desk. The manager had stayed put—Alex couldn't tell if it was out of fear or good sense. Alex placed a finger in front of his lips to insist on silence and ripped the phone cord out of its socket and left.

Perhaps Schultz had somehow doubled back on him and escaped out the rear while Alex searched in the front. If so, he was wasting his time creating all this mayhem and needed to get out before the cops came flying in. Good job Alex had the presence of mind to put a kerchief over his face before firing the first shot.

Alex was about to leave when he discerned a noise from the women's washroom. He smiled because he knew what he would find even before he'd opened the door. But when he did, there was nobody there and just a bar of soap languishing on the otherwise clean floor. An empty room with two washbasins and three cubicles with all the partition doors closed.

He padded in and bent down to peek below the bottom of each of the cubicle doors. There was nothing but a toilet base to be seen in two of them, but the middle booth contained a pair of shoes. Men's shoes. Alex grinned, quietly entered one of the other cubicles and stepped up onto the toilet. There was Schultz, sat down, ear craning forward, trying to hear whatever was going on outside that cubicle space.

Alex let out a sigh which made Schultz turn round, but he failed to glance up. Alex fired twice at the fella until he fell off his perch and smashed onto the floor—his body wedged between the door and the toilet base. Alex dropped a third shot into Schultz's torso just to be certain he wouldn't survive. Then he exited the building and ran a block south before circling back to reach Louis' car.

"Get out of here."

"Thanks, Alex."

"Just drive, will you?"

24

THAT WEEKEND, ALEX made sure to spend some time with his boys. He felt as though he hadn't seen them for months, which was probably true. Funny thing was that he genuinely wanted to be there for them, although he found it hard to keep his word.

He called them boys because that was the age they were fixed in his head —and this reflected how little he actually saw of them. But the eldest were in their teens and beginning to get pimply. Moishe had grown himself a squarish man-jaw and David's limbs were barely under his control right now.

Asher, Elijah, and Arik were still prepared to play childish games with him, but Alex knew that within the next year or two, they would tire of this also and morph into young men. He had bought an apartment near to where they lived so they would have somewhere solid to come to when they were visiting him.

This was his New Jersey crash pad, but he tried to maintain it solely for the family. When he was entertaining out of town, he'd stay in a hotel rather than use this place for female company. It was almost as though he sensed the spirit of Sarah inside these walls, channeled by his four sons.

The irony was not lost on Alex that despite this, Sarah never came up into the apartment itself—the concierge would always call up for her and Ezra or Massimo would walk them out to the elevator and take them safely to the lobby.

This Sunday it was getting late—heading toward five in the evening, and Alex was wondering when he could head return to the city. The two eldest were becoming tetchy because the other three were proving insufferable—he should have listened to himself an hour ago and taken them out to the park to run them ragged. Instead they needed feeding–Alex knew there was not nearly enough food in the icebox to satisfy all these hungry mouths.

He was about to ask if they'd like to go for a Chinese when the buzzer rang. Alex let Ezra check who it was and, to his surprise, in walked Sarah. She smiled and headed toward him, landing a peck on the cheek.

"Good to see you, Sarah."

"Likewise, Alex. How have the boys been?"

"A bundle of fun—but I don't have to tell you that."

"Well they can be a riot, but I'm the one who has to set the rules and make them follow them."

"You do a fabulous job with the kids. They need to have a strong guiding hand so they grow up with a solid moral compass."

"Given who their parents are, I can't see that happening."

They chuckled because a nafka and a gangster were not everybody's idea of role models.

"We haven't done so bad by them, all things considered."

"Maybe not, Alex. Even so…"

Alex couldn't face a conversation which would take them on a journey through their failings as parents. He'd experienced this dialog before and he always finished up on the receiving end of Sarah's rebuking tongue—he didn't want that to be how his day with the boys finished. Besides, how often had Sarah been to the apartment?

"Would you like to be taken on the grand tour—I don't think you've seen this place before, have you?"

"That'd be nice. And yes, this is my first time here."

"Well, the children have always been able to pop down when you rang, haven't they?"

Sarah nodded, although they both understood she could have done the same thing this evening, only there must be a reason for her change in behavior.

Alex took her from one room to the next—the five bedrooms, spacious living area, kitchen and three bathrooms. Few men could afford a place as big as this, she thought.

Sarah had never judged Alex poorly for the manner in which he earned his money but resented his dishonesty over Ida and the way his business had put her and, more importantly, the children in danger. There was no excuse for either of those things.

They returned to the living room to find the younger boys in tears and the two oldest sat on the couch in abject silence.

"I'd better get these fellas fed."

"We could all go to a restaurant, if you fancied?"

"That's kind, Alex, but I'll say no thank you."

He must have showed how his hopes had been let down because Sarah added an unusual question.

"I don't suppose you might be free one evening this week? I'd like to talk to you about something and not have the children running around."

"Sure, pick a day. Any is good for me."

Alex wondered what was so important that she was prepared to meet up with him without the excuse of the boys, but deep down he knew the reason.

"I WANT A divorce, Alex."

He sat opposite her for their second meal together since she'd walked out on him all those years ago. It was like it had been yesterday, or rather that's how it seemed to him. Sarah clearly had a different experience of the intervening time.

Alex pretended not to have heard her, but they both knew this was not the case. He continued to chew his salmon, although Sarah had put her silverware down.

"This is good, don't you think?"

"Please don't change the subject on me, Alex. If what we had together meant anything to you, I deserve better than to be ignored."

She was right and he swallowed and stopped pretending to focus on his plate.

"What do you expect me to say?"

"Yes, of course. We have been apart for quite a while now."

Five and a half years, he thought, without needing to count.

"And I hate to break it to you, but there are no signs we are getting back together soon."

Alex clenched his molars because that was probably the only sentence in the world he didn't want to hear. Despite all he had done—and not done—he'd harbored the belief that one day, somehow, he and Sarah would live together again. That her departure was a blip and that he would someday sleep under the same roof as his boys. Now Sarah had uttered those words, the chances of his fervent wish coming true seemed as distant as the moon.

"I thought one day…"

"Really, Alex? Would you say anything has changed between us since I left?"

"I don't lie to you anymore. I have only spoken the truth. That much I owed you and you made it clear to me that was the reason you had to leave."

"Alex, babe. Yes, you have kept your word to me—about who you spend your time with. And I appreciate it—I do, but…"

She looked into his doleful eyes and realized how much she was hurting him, so she paused. Alex grabbed his water glass and took a few sips to quench his parched lips. Then he swiped his right eye with the back of his palm.

"...but we need to move on. You will always be the boys' father—and you are a wonderful provider even though they don't spend time with you as regularly as they would like."

"Or as often as I'd want too," Alex interjected.

"As adults we have drifted apart and that is only natural under the circumstances."

"I still feel close to you, Sarah."

"Huh? We've spoken only a handful of times and almost every time it has been about a kid."

"Maybe, I figured..."

"You figured wrong, Alex. We have both moved on and I'd like to make it official."

The word stuck in his craw. Raised a flag in his mind, although he was fighting back emotions he had stifled for so long now. He thought for a minute and understood the entire picture. What a fool he had been.

"Do you want to marry someone else?"

"Don't you want to settle down with somebody and not spend all your effort on those *shayner maidel* half your age I read about in the papers?"

"They've meant nothing to me. I was waiting for you to come back to me and just wanted some warmth in my bed."

"And I don't suppose Ida is still on the scene, is she?"

"Yes and no. I hardly see her and every time I do, I ask myself why I bother. It's laziness on my part—and punishment in equal measure."

"I'm not coming back to you, Alex. Divorce me and set me free, please."

Suddenly there was an edge to Sarah's voice—like she had tried to play nicely and now she just wanted to get the job done. It was the tone he imagined she would use on the children. Commanding. Assertive.

Precisely the approach which made him react with disgust that she should try that on him. He might have skulked about behind her back with that actress, but he had always treated Sarah with respect. He'd gone from tipping her ten bucks for a night under the covers to giving her five strapping sons. And this was how she would treat him.

"No divorce, Sarah. And no further discussion on the matter. We either finish our meal or you can walk away now. The choice is yours, but we will remain married. Do you hear?"

25

ALEX WAS STILL recoiling from the previous night's dinner conversation the following morning when Albert asked him to handle a job in Bed-Stuy, which was much closer to his beloved Midtown than Alex might have expected.

"The location might be local but the target is not—he's over from Philadelphia, hiding from a bunch of problems he hopes will go away by the time he returns..."

"...but, Albert, when he arrives home he'll be in a wooden box."

"Nicely put, Alex."

"You're welcome. Tell me more about the contract as I don't remember us discussing this one at our last meeting."

"The situation was urgent so Charlie, Louis, Meyer and Benny voted it through over the weekend. You were out of town, as I understand."

Alex nodded, concerned about what else had happened in his absence that he had no idea about. Was Albert scheming behind his back? That thought had no time to roost while Anastasia explained the situation.

"Huxley Cole left his hometown on Friday evening after a disagreement with a lieutenant."

"What was the nature of their discussion?"

"Luca Marchesi had a difference of opinion with Huxley over how he treated the girls he dated."

"I didn't think lieutenants bothered themselves over such matters."

"I never did, but we might change our minds if we'd found out that the boy Cole was messing around with was our daughter."

"How old?"

"Eighteen, but still..."

"So Luca wanted Huxley to leave the apple of his eye alone."

"And then some. If they'd been on a date or two behind her father's back then that would have been the end of it. The trouble was that they had got intimate and our boy Cole had yet to discover how to be gentle and caring with the women he slept with."

"You mean he got rough?"

"And some, from what we understand. The girl's a mess and Luca wants blood."

"The fact he is holed up in Brooklyn shows he knows how much trouble he's put himself in."

"My sources tell me he is staying with friends. Two troublemakers who've been a thorn in my side in their time."

"So why don't you deal with this situation, instead of dragging me into it?"

"Simple, really, Alex. If either of the other pair are caught in the crossfire, I can't be seen to have pulled the trigger. Don't get me wrong, I'll sleep easy tonight if both of the other guys get theirs."

Then Albert shrugged, not needing to explain to Alex how he wanted the other two hit as a favor as well as Huxley Cole, which was business.

A QUICK DRIVE around the neighborhood and Alex found the right apartment—Albert had supplied him with the address. There were at least three guys inside he could be sure of, maybe more—along with Huxley was Piero Buffone and Samuele Gallo.

Alex parked his stolen car around the corner and checked the number at the entrance before he walked in and went up the two flights to reach apartment D, Gallo's joint. He knocked on the door and readied himself for anything that might happen. As always in these situations, a lifetime later a guy in a bathrobe appeared at the threshold, stood with his hand on the handle. Alex eyed him up and down, trying to judge the measure of him and attempting to figure out why he answered the door at all.

"The landlord sent me. I need to check the windows."

"We're kinda busy, pop. Can't you come back later?"

"Nah, I have to get this done today. Landlord said so."

"If you have to then make yourself at home."

The boy sniggered slightly as he spoke and Alex wondered what was so funny. He followed the guy into the living room and got the joke. There were two other men and three women in various states of undress lying on top of or squatting near each other. It might have only been the middle of the afternoon, but the partying had definitely started before lunch.

Alex tipped his hat—he couldn't think of anything else to do—and zigzagged around the limbs and torsos until he got to the window and pushed and pulled at the sash, pretending to know something about fenestration. Even the guy with the robe had stopped watching him and had returned to more fleshy pursuits.

Still with his back to the group, Alex looked out on the street and noticed a pretzel and hotdog booth but not much else of interest down below. The fire escape came into focus as his near vision kicked in and he thought about how he would get the job done. He shut his eyes for a second and wished there were fewer people in the apartment.

When he opened them two seconds later, the same number of bodies lay in the living room, but at least Alex knew what he would do. He swiveled round and used the time to whip out his gun. He raised his arm and wielded the piece at Huxley. Just as he squeezed the trigger, a breast appeared in the periphery of his vision and he lost concentration. The bullet whizzed past Huxley's ear and lodged in the wall behind him.

The boy ducked down, pushing the woman kneeling in between his legs onto her back on the ground. She hit her head on a nearby table and called out in pain. Gallo and Buffone looked up at the commotion and only saw the girl lying on the floor.

Alex swallowed and stared straight at Huxley and fired three bullets into his torso, causing his body to flail against the wall and then slump back onto the armchair he had originally been sitting on. The two remaining living men stood up and searched around to find their pieces, but wherever they were, both guys realized their clothes were all jumbled up in their girls' underwear with their guns buried somewhere in that mess.

As Alex had moved into the center of the room to guarantee he hit Huxley, Gallo bolted for the window and Buffone headed for the exit. Watching their men fly in different directions, the girls remained on the floor for a moment before experiencing that deep pit of dread and fear that launched them upwards, screaming. Both women fled for the door knowing they needed to create as much distance as possible between themselves and the stranger with the gun.

They reached the entrance at exactly the same time as Buffone. He yanked one head out of the way and pushed the other girl onto the floor. The gentleman then ran the three paces across the hallway, almost ripped the front door off its hinges and hustled down the stairs. Once they got to their feet, the girls followed him out.

Meantime, Gallo had flung open the sash window and was out on the fire escape. Luckily for him, New York was experiencing a warm fall because Alex watched him fly downwards, as naked as the day he was born. Alex swore under his breath because he knew he couldn't walk away from the nude mayhem he had sent out onto the streets of Brooklyn.

He popped his head out of the window to see that Gallo was still on the fire escape, slowed down by the rough surface of the metal steps on the soles of his bare feet. Alex sighed and followed the boy onto the ladder and down.

◆ ◆ ◆

GALLO REACHED THE second floor by the time Alex was out on the fire ladder. The boy heard Alex's arrival on the metal steps—looked up, stared down—and leaped to the sidewalk rather than take the slower route of descending the steps farther. Despite his best intentions, Gallo landed badly and gripped his ankle, giving Alex the chance to catch up.

Before the boy could rise to his feet, Alex hurried down the ladder and dropped onto the sidewalk next to the guy. Revolver out, Alex put one slug in his chest and another between the eyes, then he reloaded from a bunch of loose slugs in his jacket pocket.

A noise made him swivel round. The apartment block entrance burst open and Buffone appeared, took a look at Alex, and hightailed it in the opposite direction. Four seconds later and the two girls emerged, whimpering and yelping, onto the street.

Alex thought about dropping them there and then, but they hugged each other, halted by the entranceway. Instead, Buffone needed to be stopped. Setting off at a trot, Alex followed the naked guy round the corner and reckoned he spotted a bare heel vanish into an alleyway.

Cornered, his quarry attempted to scramble up a fence at the far end of the alley. Finding a firm foothold was tricky as Buffone took four attempts to launch himself to a point where one hand got purchase on the top of the railing. Alex held his gun in both hands and aimed squarely in the middle of the back. Three shots and Buffone fell onto the dirt.

Alex checked his pistol and put a palm up to his mouth. Then he slapped his cheek—the kerchief he usually used to hide his face was still in his pants. He needed to find the two girls before they escaped.

He sprinted back to the apartment block and was lucky—the women hadn't had time to get to their senses and run off. Alex was only fifteen feet away when he shot both of them, one slug each. After they dropped to the ground, he continued to walk toward them and when he was stood right by them, he put two more bullets in both their bodies.

A quick check in both directions and Alex ensured there were no witnesses on the street—except for the pretzel and hotdog concession. He couldn't make out anyone there at first, but as he stared a little more and walked in its direction, Alex reckoned he spotted someone cowering behind the wooden structure.

"Give me a pretzel, will you?"

"Wh... what?"

"You heard me. Can I buy one?"

"Sure thing, mister."

The vendor scooped up a breaded ring and handed it over to Alex, who thanked him and offered a dollar bill as payment. The guy lowered his head to find the correct change and that was the moment Alex planted a bullet in the only witness to his slaughter. He chewed on his snack, headed over to his car and left Bed-Stuy, always traveling below the speed limit. Today was not the day to be stopped by some dumb traffic cop. Despite the vows he'd made to himself, Alex decided the best place for him to be right now was in Ida's suite—a hideout with room service and a warm body in the bed.

26

FOUR DAYS LATER, Alex left the confines of Ida's apartment and spent another week in Hoboken to be near his boys—and to be out of the state should any flatfeet come calling. The furore over the bloodshed had died down in the press—there are only so many times you can put tasteful pictures of naked corpses on your front page. Besides, the syndicate applied pressure on the newspaper owners to give it a rest. There were more important matters for Joe Citizen to worry about than the slaying of a rapist caught in the middle of an orgy, surely?

Alex returned to the city and hunkered down, keeping out of the public eye. He resented the attention the hit received and couldn't decide who he blamed more: Anastasia for putting him onto the gig in the first place or Sarah's request for a divorce that meant his head wasn't in the game when it should have been.

New York moved toward Thanksgiving and the world forgot all about Huxley Cole. Not Alex, but everyone else.

"Charlie, what you think about Albert?"

They had just sat down in the back row of the 44th Street Picture Palace watching a Western because Charlie wanted to see the latest *Hopalong* movie. The film had yet to start and they'd begun munching through their popcorn.

"Can't we simply enjoy the show?"

"Seriously, Charlie. I know he's got Sicilian protection, but don't you think he…?"

"Leave it be, Alex. He is who he is and nothing will change that. The man has a certain way about him—when he gets an idea in his skull, he is like a bull."

"Do you trust him?"

Charlie turned to look at Alex in the flickering light offered by the film projector.

"You kidding me? I count my fingers every time we shake hands."

Alex nodded and settled into his seat as the opening credits burst onto the screen and William Boyd appeared in glorious black and white.

LATER THEY WENT round the corner to a local diner to get a bite to eat. How were they able to walk so freely and safely around Midtown? Bodyguards flanked them the entire evening. A burger and fries each, and the two men sipped at their coffees.

"Alex, I've got a proposition for you."

"What gives?"

"I'd like to make you a fifty-fifty partner in some of my heroin interests in Brooklyn."

"Thank you, but why bestow this honor on me when you don't appear to need any help working this business. Besides, I thought we were focused on East Harlem and Midtown?"

"We are right now, but you always gotta look ahead. You should play checkers—it helps you think about your move after next. If I was smart enough, I'd learn chess."

"We're going to sell to our own in Brownsville?"

"That's not what I said. I'm offering you a half stake in the territory."

"It's filled with hard-working Jews. They don't have time to visit a crummy street corner and buy a packet of dope."

"No, but as they get richer, they'll move away from those street corners and another group of immigrants will arrive instead. Recall what's happened to the Bowery in our lifetimes. Before we arrived, there were the Germans and the Irish. Now the Jews and Italians and who knows who'll turn up next. My point is that we need to be ready when they do."

"And why now?"

"Well, to be honest I must liquidate some assets."

"Huh?"

"Meyer thinks it best for me to have some spending money available at short notice. So I'm asking for you to pay for your stake upfront."

"You want me to give you gelt to sell heroin to people who haven't even moved into the neighborhood yet?"

"That's the short of it, Alex."

"You're *meshugge*."

"I'm not crazy. This is a brilliant opportunity to invest a million dollars into the future."

"How much?" Alex's speedy retort reflected his surprise at the size of the number.

"A million."

"That's a lot of tomorrows you need me to buy today."

"It's an investment—like on Wall Street, only with those shysters the chances are you won't get your money back, let alone receive any return."

"And I suppose they will always want heroin in Bed-Stuy?"

"There's been a steady set of customers ever since I brought the powder into the country a decade ago."

Alex hadn't considered that point before—Charlie had seen the opportunity in heroin before anybody else. It had only just been criminalized when he first talked to Alex about it. The fella sure was good at seeing the move after next.

"We live together, we work together. Right?"

"I'm no Albert Anastasia. When have I ever offered you a bum steer?"

"You've always been true, Charlie. Where did the number of a million spring from?"

"That's all Meyer's doing. I will need to take care of some other affairs of mine and he estimates that'll cost me a seven-digit sum."

"If you don't mind me asking, who's the beef with that you won't use Murder Corporation to sort out?"

"Dewey."

Alex's blood ran cold at the sound of that name.

"We've only heard bupkis from him since the Schultz business."

"That doesn't mean he's put his feet up and stayed at home, Alex. He and his squad have been working through paperwork—Dutch's tax was only the first on their list. My informants tell me that Dewey has his eye on me next."

"And who else?"

"All of us, ultimately. Nobody will escape his attention, Alex."

"Are you paying somebody from out of town to hit him for a million bucks? I'll do it for half that."

Charlie laughed and allowed the mirth to ebb from his body over the course of thirty seconds.

"I'm not going to take Dewey down, but I will pay someone to make the problem go away—I am buying me a top-notch lawyer."

Alex whistled because that was a colossal amount of money for a fella in a suit to earn just by talking.

"And they call *us* robbers, Charlie."

"Yeah, but this guy, Mendy Greenberg reckons he can get me off with no jail time, no matter what I have done."

"That is worth a million of anybody's gelt—and it looks like it will be mine."

"Thank you, Alex. I won't forget this."

◆ ◆ ◆

THEY LEFT THE diner and headed to Charlie's place for a nightcap. Their entourage stood waiting by the curb before either man stepped onto the sidewalk and into the building.

At the back of the first floor Waldorf Astoria bar, they sat at Charlie's table nursing a Scotch on the rocks each. Massimo, Ezra, and Charlie's people surrounded them, but only drank coffee—they were on duty and had to keep their wits about them. Besides, drinking heavily was for saps—they all knew that.

"So what's the catch, Charlie? Apart from handing over a vast amount of money."

"Nothing, Alex. Why do you insult me by acting as though I am out to get you in some manner?"

"No disrespect intended, Charlie. I've received many gifts from you over the years and you have only ever treated me swell, but other fellas I have worked with in the syndicate have made me cautious, perhaps unnecessarily so."

"Not everybody is like Albert. He's one of a kind. No, the only thing I want you to do is to carry on working with the fella."

"Keep with Murder Corporation, you mean?"

"Yes, right now I need everything to be as calm as possible. If I am correct and Dewey guns for us, then we must all be focused on that threat and not spend any energy having to watch our backs. This is a time for unity."

"You trust him enough for me to believe he won't wake up one morning and cut my throat?"

"There are no certainties in this world, Alex. All we know is that we live together, we work together…"

"…and we die alone."

APRIL 1936

27

THE SAME REAR table in the same bar in the same hotel, but when Alex and Charlie met six months later, the atmosphere had changed—not with Alex, but Charlie's demeanor had altered. The fella was downcast, shoulders sagged and eyes looked like needle points.

"How are you holding up, Charlie?"

"Soon I'll have my day in court."

"You expected Dewey to hit you for tax fraud, not this."

"Yeah, pandering. What the hell is that supposed to be?"

Dewey hadn't bothered going after Charlie over misgotten gelt because there was an easier way to put him behind bars. Like so many other members of the syndicate, Charlie owned a string of cathouses across several boroughs.

Each of them generated income and operated within a strict hierarchy— from nafka to timekeeper, from the brothel owner up through the ranks to Charlie. He might have tried to create a shield between himself and the rest of the operation, but it didn't take Dewey very long to follow the trail and build a case against him.

"They let you out on bail?"

"Mendy worked his magic in front of the judge so I wouldn't have to spend time in Rikers."

"And you think he'll be able to get you off?"

"He's good, but I don't know if he's that good. I can be sure I'm paying him enough to guarantee the guy is focused on my trial and no one else's."

Alex shot a glance directly at Charlie, because they both knew where the funding for the legal eagle had come from.

"How long have you got before the case begins?"

"Two weeks. It's ridiculous. I have all these business matters to attend to but every time I walk out of a joint, there's another gumshoe putting out his cigarette and following me down the road."

"Surely your guys can convince the cops to beat it."

"These are special operations cops—hired by Dewey personally—they are beyond reproach. I haven't been able to bribe one of them since the start of this whole caper. Not one."

"If a detective died in mysterious, violent and public circumstances, that'd send a message."

"Alex, do not even think about joking over such a thing. You don't get it. I am under constant surveillance—as is everyone I come into contact with. They are bound to be watching you and every other member of the syndicate who's in New York. While we have been building our empire, Dewey has set up a massive operation to bring us down. That is all he exists to do—destroy everything we have worked hard to create."

"What if I were to intercede on your behalf with a member of the jury?"

Luciano's eyes darted left and right, then he ducked down even lower in his seat, before whispering, "Don't talk like that in front of me, Alex. You can't trust anyone nowadays—Dewey has his hooks into too many people."

"But it is possible."

"Anything can be done—the question is whether it will achieve the required outcome."

"What do you mean, Charlie?"

"Of course, I do not want you to tamper with the jury." Then in a lower voice, "If you bribe one member then that's just something else Dewey will hit you with when he arrests you. My informant tells me they intend to guard the jury members day and night so you wouldn't be able to get near to any one of them, even if you wanted to. This isn't Dutch's tax trial—this is much more serious. Dewey will use me to send a warning across the syndicate. I'm too high profile for him not to take me down."

"What do you want me to do?"

"You've done enough. Your investment capital makes sure Mendy is kept in new suits and either way, I'll go down fighting."

Alex considered Charlie's comments and wondered how to explain the difference between the bold words and his physical presence. The Italian was a deflated man, limbs limp by his side, face gaunt—the pocks on his cheeks almost appearing to want to leave his skin. Luciano talked a good talk but the threat of this trial was draining his life force away before Alex's eyes.

HE VISITED CHARLIE the following day, but this time the venue was his penthouse. Alex always felt at home here. Charlie had spent his money wisely on comfortable furniture and pleasant surroundings. Also, he'd been to the place so many times, there was nothing unusual about anything to do with the suite. Then a stranger walked into the room, causing Alex's eyebrows to rise.

"This is Arianna. I sent my family away to Florida, so they didn't have to run the gauntlet of the press hounds and I can concentrate on the work I have to do."

The explanation fell short of giving Alex a clue what Arianna's role was until she sat down next to Charlie and draped an arm around his neck while he leaned forward. He shrugged her off, grabbed a bunch of notes from his wallet and instructed her to go to Fifth Avenue and buy something nice. She grinned and didn't need to be told twice to skedaddle. When she was out the door, the men began their conversation.

"Back so soon, Alex. You must like my company."

"You know I do, Charlie, but that's not the main reason why I'm here."

The Italian sat on his couch and crossed his legs, a sign of how relaxed he was this morning compared to yesterday, but also it was the pose he adopted when it was time to talk business.

"I've been thinking about our arrangement regarding your heroin interests. Have you given much thought to what will happen if the worst comes to the worst?"

"If someone whacks me?"

"No, if Dewey convinces twelve men you are guilty of offering women to men who want to pay to sleep with them."

"I'm trying not to fill my head with those kinds of ideas. That's a loser's strategy."

"I understand, but, you shouldn't be caught off guard. Meyer is the cautious fella who must have spoken to you about planning for the unthinkable."

"You two been talking behind my back?"

"No, funnily enough I haven't seen him for two months. I have been looking at ways to prepare for my own future and the bigger stake I have in the heroin trade."

"What have you come up with, Alex?"

Now it was Alex's turn to sink back into his armchair and ready himself for his pitch to the most powerful gangster in America, the man who refused to call himself the boss of bosses.

"If Dewey gets his way, you must control your various interests while you're doing time."

"That's right."

"And you'll probably want fellas you can trust."

"That I would, Alex."

"So if you'd like to bear me in mind for the narcotics trafficking, that'd be mighty fine of you."

Charlie chuckled and Alex squirmed. This was as close as he would get to asking Luciano for a piece of the national heroin trade as he could utter. Every other time he'd got to enhance his empire thanks to one of the syndicate members, he had been offered and hadn't needed to ask.

"Sorry, Alex, but I can't help myself. Over the last month, countless guys have come to me offering to support me by taking my business from me before the gavel has even been struck and my sentence pronounced. You are the first fella to offer to borrow heroin trafficking and to give it back later."

Alex cleared his throat.

"What's yours is yours, Charlie. What else was I going to suggest?"

"Fellas like Albert Anastasia see my imminent jail time as an opportunity to seize what they do not have but want."

"We live together, we work together, Charlie."

"I agree, but not everyone sees things our way."

The two men fell quiet as they mulled over the conversation for a minute until Alex broke the silence.

"So have you figured out what you will do if Dewey gets his wish?"

"You, Meyer and Benny are my closest friends. We have been together off and on for as long as I can remember. I can't think of any bunch of fellas I trust more in this world and I will look to the three of you to run things on my behalf while I am away—if I am away."

"Thank you, Charlie."

"Don't mention it. You guys'll work hard to keep all the operations alive if I go down, but hopefully Mendy can weave a magic spell and save me from a lengthy stay at Sing Sing."

28

ALEX RECKONED SOMETHING was wrong the minute he hit the sidewalk outside his apartment. Ezra and Massimo had beckoned him out of the entrance and as he looked up and down, he noticed three men two hundred feet away just hanging around.

Nothing unusual in that, apart from their identical haircuts and impeccably polished shoes—the hallmark of a cop. One on his own would have been a coincidence because detectives hang out on street corners too. Two together wasn't a good sign but, again, they can be out to get donuts. Three was a team aiming to follow someone around the city, taking turns as the point man.

His lieutenants didn't seem to notice and opened the door to his vehicle. Alex tested out his theory and shook his head. "I'll walk the first few blocks —I need to clear my thoughts," he explained and Ezra hopped behind the wheel to slow-follow him, while Massimo hovered four paces back.

"Give me some space, Massimo. I'm going to pound the pavement and I don't want you scuffling at my heels."

Massimo remained silent but his eyes scrunched up in a quizzical expression—something was up.

Alex belted along the street until he reached the first corner and swiftly swung right and ducked into a storefront. Ten seconds later, Massimo walked past, barely shifting his head to acknowledge his boss and carried on half a block until he felt the overwhelming need to stop and tie a shoelace.

Thirty seconds more and a flatfoot hurried by, pretending to scratch his neck at the moment he passed Alex to force himself to turn his head in Alex's direction. Cheap theatricals—Ida could have done better.

He waited and shifted over one store to give the impression he was idly walking along and some items had caught his attention. Almost exactly on cue, if he had been counting, another gumshoe went past him thirty seconds later. At least Alex wasn't paranoid—these guys were following him for certain. He considered doubling back on them just to cause confusion, but that would have meant he'd signal to them he was onto them.

Instead, he resumed his journey at a slightly faster pace to force the cops up ahead to change gear and scatter, while the third unseen detective would need to jog to keep up.

Two blocks later and the cat-and-mouse game progressed with the detectives finally able to let Alex pass by, waiting near street corners so he wouldn't notice the same guys on the streets repeatedly showing up.

Alex switched left at the next corner and the gumshoes continued to keep up, while Massimo tailed him from only two hundred feet—following his orders to the letter. Ezra had given up running curbside and he parked on the same side as Alex, waited until he was at the end of a block and caught up.

At this point, Alex decided to lose the cops—he'd grown tired of this game and now he was just toying with them. Besides, he had some business to attend to which shouldn't be conducted in front of the prying eyes of law enforcement officials. He waited for Ezra's car to get to him and bent down to lean into the window.

"Any traffic we should know about?"

"None I've seen. You expecting company?"

"No questions, Ezra. When I jump into the back, I want you to hit the gas as fast as you can in one direction for at least fifteen blocks. Afterwards make a turn, I don't care where. Got it?"

Ezra nodded and followed his instructions as soon as Alex slammed the door shut. The car screeched forwards and Alex twisted his head to watch what was happening behind him. He saw Massimo stand still and at least two of the cops lurched forward for no good reason.

For the duration of their straight stretch, Alex kept checking all the lanes to the rear to make sure they hadn't missed any tail. By the time Ezra took a right, Alex was certain he could get to his meet with Meyer without hindrance.

Once he'd secured the financing he needed, he took an early lunch at Lindy's where he sat in his usual booth. Less than five minutes later, Alex gave his order for coffee and a pastrami on rye. He lit a cigarette and a clean-shaven suit, placed himself in the seat opposite and removed his hat, dangling it on the corner of his chair.

"Do you know who I am?"

"I read the newspapers, although you are uglier up close than on the front page, Thomas Dewey."

"Alex Cohen, do not make the mistake of treating me like a fool—and don't believe that you will escape my clutches like Dutch Schultz."

◆ ◆ ◆

ALEX STARED THROUGH his eyes and into Dewey's soul to see the man intent on his downfall and that of his friends—because he'd sworn to uphold the law and did that to the best of his ability.

"Can I offer you a coffee or a cookie?"

"I won't take a single thing from you, Cohen, until I get the satisfaction of seeing you behind bars."

"Dewey, if you had anything on me, we wouldn't be having this conversation in Lindy's as you'd have dragged me over to some precinct and slammed me in cuffs. Sorry, threaten me a little less, tell me what you feel you need to say, and leave."

Dewey's cheeks tinged crimson but he continued.

"I want you to know that the grand jury investigating your tax affairs will reach its verdict soon and it's not looking good for you. If you have any sense, you'd spend less time eating pastrami and more time with a lawyer. You will need one."

"Thanks for the legal advice—where should I send my payment: to the Police Benevolence Fund?"

"Are you trying to bribe an officer of the law?"

"Dewey, you think too much of yourself. What makes you believe you are worth spending gelt on? To me, you are just another Fed with a badge and a desire to drag down hard-working guys who have made some money over the years. Your words make you sound like a Democrat, but the suits you wear shriek pure Republican."

"You'd know all about Tammany, wouldn't you, Cohen?"

"If you were right, my politician buddies who live in my back pocket would have hauled you off my case months ago. They haven't because they don't exist. I am just a guy who works for a living and earns some gelt to get by."

"It's your money the grand jury has been focused on. How you get it and what you report."

"I'm no Capone."

"The only difference between you and that Chicago shyster is that you are walking free—for the moment."

Alex ground his molars at the flippant way Dewey spoke about his friend —not that he'd seen or spoken with him since his last visit to the Windy City just before Alfonse was dragged down to the cells. He sighed and chewed on another bite of his sandwich.

"Dewey, were you bullied when you were a child?"

The special prosecutor moved his back in reaction to this pivot in the conversation.

"What do you mean, Cohen?"

"As a kid—did the other children in your class wait until you'd got past the school gate on your way home and push you and shove at you and knock you over? Later when you were in high school, if you were lucky enough to get a girl, would she choose the captain of the football team over you because he was more attractive than you?"

"Well, really."

"No, I'm sorry, I've got it all wrong, haven't I? You were the football captain and every girl flocked round you like flies to a shit heap."

"Cohen, I was team captain, but that is none of your business and has nothing to do with the predicament you are in now."

"You should get your story straight. I thought the grand jury's verdict hadn't come in yet. Today, I've got nothing to worry about apart from strangers interrupting my lunch. That's the trouble with New York—you are never more than six feet away from vermin."

Alex stared at Dewey again, his eyelids narrowing his eyes as he looked through the cop, whose cheeks were redder than before. He reached inside his jacket and Alex instinctively reached for his piece, hidden in his pants. Dewey froze, his hand still in plain sight.

"Cohen, I am about to reach in my jacket to give you my business card, should you want to talk. Judging by your stance, you might be carrying a concealed weapon. If I saw it, you'd be in the back of a meat wagon by now."

Dewey pulled the card out and threw it on the table, causing it to spin a half turn before landing by Alex's coffee cup. Then he stood up and took off. Ten minutes after Dewey departed, Alex left Lindy's to pay a visit to Mendy Greenberg and hire him as his lawyer.

29

WITH DEWEY NEVER far from the forefront of his mind, Alex continued to run Charlie's heroin supply operation into Brooklyn, as well as East Harlem with Buchalter and Anastasia. He also had his own territory running from the Bowery up to Midtown in which to sell those folded pieces of paper containing brown powder and an intense feeling of ecstasy.

An investment of three thousand dollars bought him a sack of processed heroin from overseas. This was more than the average criminal might earn in over a year of stick-ups in some hick town. But this was the Five Boroughs and Alex was a member of the syndicate, so the sacks were taken to one of the many warehouses they still owned from days spent bootlegging and was cut up with other powder to generate hundreds of hits, each carefully placed inside a piece of paper and folded twice. After, it was distributed to crews who stood on street corners and sold the narcotics at competitive rates.

There were many potential weaknesses in this chain of events—the arrival of the heroin by boat, its storage in the warehouses, the cutting up of the narcotic into sellable units and the transportation of the hits onto the street. This was a complex set of tasks and needed careful management, but the sack that cost Alex a few thousand netted close to half a million retail.

Charlie had the smarts to see the potential for this business when heroin was still legal back in the early twenties, but he had watched and waited and seized the moment when it finally appeared. He was a great checkers player.

A week after Dewey had interrupted Alex's lunch, Ezra called him from a warehouse in Brownsville.

"The last shipment hasn't arrived and I have men sitting around with nothing to do. Massimo said there was some kind of delay. I can't get hold of him and I'm hoping you know what's happening."

"I thought this had all been taken care of. Charlie's contact in Palermo sent me a telegram to say the boat sailed two days late, but they expected to make up the time on the journey."

"No such luck, Alex. It's way overdue and I have no idea what's going on."

"Leave it with me, Ezra. Send your boys home on a full day's pay. Let's keep them sweet today, at any rate."

A QUICK TRIP to Massimo's and the explanation was simple.

"The ship vanished."

"What do you mean, Massimo?"

"You heard me—straight up. There was radio communication with the boat three days ago. It met strong winds during its crossing so hadn't made up any time that was lost with the troubles in Sicily."

"And?"

"Nothing. Zilch. It's like God picked up the vessel and took it we don't know where."

"This will be no divine hand, Massimo. Someone got to the ship before it could land. Accidents do not happen to shipments worth six figure sums."

"Who?"

"That I can't say, but either the captain joined somebody else's payroll, or the boat was hijacked. Neither is good for us because it means we are down one boatload of heroin."

Massimo gulped as he imagined his profit floating out of the window in his apartment where they sat.

"If it wasn't the gods, whose hand was it?"

"Massimo, that is an excellent question and I need to identify the person as soon as possible. Tell your crews to sniff around and find out. Before the end of the day, I want the name of the person who stole my heroin."

As the sun vanished behind the skyline, Massimo phoned Alex at his apartment.

"I have the answer to your question."

"Good. Who?"

"Anastasia. He issued the order and my men tell me he has already unloaded the ship and is processing it with his people. By tomorrow the first consignment will reach the streets."

Alex let out a lengthy breath. If it had been some young Turk, he would have been able to handle the situation himself—a little local difficulty requiring a visit from his lieutenants, a dose of retribution and the return of his property. That this had been sponsored by Albert Anastasia created considerably more complications and meant everything was a lot more dangerous—when a made man muscles into your turf, there can only be trouble ahead.

"SO, WHAT I'M asking is if you'd have any issues if Albert met with an accident?"

Meyer, Benny, and Alex were sitting in Meyer's suite at the Benjamin Hotel on Fiftieth having a conversation instigated by Alex. It had been twenty-four hours since Anastasia had stolen the heroin, and Alex was the only person who seemed the least bit perturbed—and that was making him angry.

Benny rotated his hat around a stretched-out finger, as was his habit during these meetings, and sniggered at Alex's question. Both Meyer and Alex scowled at him, but for different reasons. Meyer loved Benny like he was a brother, although a sibling who didn't take matters seriously enough for his liking. Alex just did not appreciate being laughed at by Siegel.

"And what is the likelihood of Albert being knocked down by a passing car, Alex?"

"Much higher than two days ago, Meyer."

The fedora continued to twirl and Benny said nothing—choosing to concentrate on the rotating headgear instead.

"I have proof he has stolen half a million of my assets and that needs to be resolved."

"What assets?"

"Uncut heroin, Meyer."

"And what is the evidence?"

"A missing ship, Anastasia's men crammed into a processing plant. His guys hitting my streets with my heroin and not paying me a dime."

Meyer crossed his legs and picked a piece of fluff off his knee, flicking it onto the ground. His expression showed he was mulling over what Alex had said. Given the scale of the deal, this was a serious matter despite the whimsy Benny saw in everything.

"Alex, how do you know that a third party didn't steal the ship and merely passed on the goods to Albert?"

"I cannot be certain—not like in a court of law—but who are you suggesting had the capability to steal a boat in the middle of the Atlantic Ocean and transport the narcotic ashore and shift it into Anastasia's warehouse? The only people I can think of in this city are sat in this room."

"Or Charlie."

"What Benny?"

"Charlie has the muscle for this."

Alex exhaled loudly.

"It was Charlie's dope in the first place, Benny. Why would he steal his own heroin from himself? You're not making any sense, man."

"Just saying, that's all."

"If you have nothing positive to contribute, perhaps it would be better for you to remain silent, Benny."

"All right, Meyer. Only trying to help."

Alex and Meyer eyed each other in exasperation—Benny was acting more strangely than normal, and neither understood why. He did this now and again—it was one of the reasons he worked alone because of his difficult behavior when mixing with people, even his friends.

"Back to the situation at hand, Alex. How certain are you that Albert is behind this?"

"As sure as I can be. If you are asking me if I saw him instruct his men to take over the boat then no, I didn't."

"That's what I thought, Alex."

"But, Meyer, despite Benny's sense of humor, he has a point. The only other person who'd have the resources to do this would be Charlie and as that's not possible, we are left with Albert Anastasia."

"This is circumstantial evidence, Alex. You can't tell the difference between Albert carrying out this deed or someone from Philadelphia or Chicago coming over here, pushing their way into our business and then selling the heroin on to your Murder Corporation partner."

"Are you telling me you really believe that's what's happened, Meyer?"

"Of course not, but it doesn't matter what I think. Do you reckon you can convince the others you are right?"

"Meyer, that is not what I am asking. I want to know how you two feel about this. If you aren't behind me then there's no point calling a syndicate meeting because I would lose the vote—when your friends don't believe you then others are unlikely to side with you either."

"There's no need to be like that, Alex. I just know we have to be watertight before the syndicate will agree to a hit on a made man."

"Then I'll get the proof you require, because Albert is trying to destroy my world."

30

NOT FOR THE first time in his life, Alex stood in an empty warehouse with Ezra and Massimo for company. There was another guy in the place, but he had his wrists and ankles tied and muslin stuffed into his mouth. Willis Tanzi wasn't going anywhere for a while.

Alex paced around—when he reached one wall, he turned and pounded the floor until he got to the other side. Meanwhile, Massimo stood next to Tanzi while Ezra sat opposite him, staring him down. Beads of sweat had formed on Tanzi's forehead and breathing was far from easy, judging by the snorting sounds squeezing out of his nostrils.

The three fellas talked loudly over the snorts and acted as though Tanzi wasn't sat in front of them, bruises forming around his cheeks where the lieutenants had slapped him about long enough for him to understand the seriousness of his situation. Alex began the interrogation with a calm voice and relaxed posture.

"Willis, do you know why you are here?"

A shake of his head and Tanzi's breathing increased a notch.

"You were overheard discussing a matter close to my heart. Have you any idea what that might be?"

Another snort, another shake of the head. Several of the beads of sweat flew from their resting place on his forehead and landed like miniature salty raindrops onto the floor.

"You are here because of a shipment which never made it to port."

Eyes widened as Tanzi realized what was going on. He shook his head repeatedly as if to emphasize what little information he had to offer.

"Would you be so kind as to take that cloth out of his mouth? Willis appears to want to tell us something."

Alex looked at Ezra when he said this, but Massimo was the one to carry out the instruction. His friend remained sat, staring at Tanzi with pure menace. Massimo threw the rag onto the floor and Tanzi choked for a minute, pleased to be released from the suffocating taste of the material

645

jammed to within spit of his tonsils. Alex raised a hand and pointed to a spot beyond where Tanzi could see.

Massimo sauntered over and returned with an open bottle of beer, which he gingerly put against the man's lips to let him take two sips—just enough to moisten his mouth and the back of his throat. Then Massimo walked away again with the bottle, out of Tanzi's line of sight.

"I don't know nothing. You gotta believe me."

"Willis, you are wrong, my friend. First, you spoke loudly in a bar about how you had been on board a ship at precisely the time when my vessel was being snatched from me. Second, I do not trust a word that comes out of your mouth—part of your job is to convince me you speak the truth. So please don't tell me you are innocent and haven't been involved in the robbery, because everybody in this room knows you have."

Tanzi swung his head round right then left, to catch sight of the three men's location. Massimo had positioned himself in the guy's blind spot.

"Sorry. Yes. Sure. I was in the crew on the tugboat that grabbed your shipment, but I was only operating under orders."

"Willis, I know you are not the mastermind behind this scheme—don't worry about that."

Tanzi's shoulders wilted slightly as though some weight had been lifted from his torso. Alex's voice stayed softly spoken and he ensured his body remained as relaxed as he could make it to keep Tanzi at his ease.

"So tell me, what were the orders you were instructed to follow—if you were the monkey and not the organ grinder?"

"Just to sail the tug out to meet the boat, climb aboard and get the captain to take it to the shore where trucks would be waiting."

"What were you instructed to do with my men?"

"No one said to do anything, but we knew what was expected of us."

"And what was that, Willis?"

Tanzi glanced at Ezra and turned his attention back to Alex.

"There were to be no survivors. Once we had unloaded the cargo, we were to scuttle the ship. Either we shot them when we boarded or they drowned."

Alex ground his molars and breathed through his nose for twenty seconds until the wall of anger within him had subsided enough to speak again.

"Thank you for your honesty, Willis. Lesser men would have spun a story, but you have spared yourself the embarrassment of untruths."

"I figure the only chance I have is to be straight up with you guys. If you detect a lie on my lips, then you'll torture me, then kill me and I really don't want that to happen."

"I reckon you do not—and I would much rather find out what I need without asking either of my friends here to do you harm. Violence has no place in business. It stops men thinking clearly—they panic and tell you what they think you want to be told. To prevent that, you must cause them immense pain and that takes time and effort."

Tanzi blinked the sweat out of his eyelashes and absorbed the underlying threat behind Alex's statement. His panting increased and Alex waited for the man to wade through the panic attack. This was difficult—he needed the guy to be fearful enough to respond but not so scared that he'd admit to killing Abraham Lincoln.

"So can you tell me who issued the orders you followed?"

"I don't know."

"Willis, you disappoint me. I would have been sure you'd remember the name of the person who instructed what to do and when. Surely, that's something hard to forget, especially when you've been hustled off the street with a sack over your head and taken into this warehouse for a conversation with me."

"No one told me anything."

"Now that is a lie, Willis, because you said earlier that you were following orders. Who gave them to you?"

An edge had entered Alex's voice and he leaned forward two inches in his seat. Not sufficient to appear menacing, but enough of a change to imply that worse was to come if Tanzi didn't toe the line.

"My friend Paulie told me the scoop—I wasn't in the room when it happened."

"Who is this Paulie? Do we need to bring him in here?"

"Jeez, no. He has a wife and a family."

"So do I, Willis, but if I had received instructions like your pal Paulie, I'd expect to be hauled into this warehouse to explain my actions."

"He heard it from another guy. You know how these things work. Nobody knows anything and that way the bosses stay safe."

"Willis, unless you tell me something more useful, you will force me to invite Paulie to join us and he has a wife and kids, you say, which means he is far more likely to spill what he has than you appear to be."

"I... All I know is that this kind of operation wasn't cheap and paid very well. They needed guys who would keep their cool when the going got rough and were professional, y'know?"

"And that means Paulie won't talk?"

"He knows about as much as I do. And I'm sure of that because we talked about it, him and me. We wanted to know who was paying our wages. It's only natural."

Massimo shifted his weight behind Tanzi, although the guy had no way of knowing that had happened. The glass bottle slipped out of the lieutenant's fingers and landed on the floor with a smash of glass, causing Tanzi to visibly jump.

"Just the beer—fell out of his hand. An accident, Willis. Don't worry about it. Go on."

"Yeah, like I was saying, we didn't know who was running the gig, but we got an idea who was backing it."

"What do you mean?"

"The money man. I told you it was an expensive operation and word was that Buchalter was funding it."

"Louis Buchalter?"

"That's what I said. Louis was the financier."

"Thank you, Willis, you have been most helpful."

Alex signaled a motion with his hand again and Ezra continued to stare at Tanzi, only this time the corners of his lips moved upwards. Meanwhile, Massimo stepped forward and grabbed Tanzi by the chin, whipping his head back. Holding the neck of the beer bottle in the other hand, he swiped across Willis Tanzi's throat with the naked shard of glass, sharp as a blade. Sliced him from ear to ear and let him droop down, blood spurting out of his throat like a kosher chicken in its death throes.

"Throw this one into the Hudson and then pay a call on Paulie. Find out if he knows anything of any use and kill him too. Chances are Tanzi told us the truth."

31

FOR THE NEXT three nights, Alex woke at four and couldn't get back to sleep. The following evening he walked the streets of Hoboken after he spent the evening hiding in plain sight. If nothing else, he figured Dewey's men wouldn't be able to follow him out of the state—they followed all the rules.

Then he paid a nafka to spend the night with him hoping their exploits would be enough to tire him out and make him snore through until morning, but no dice. She was merely a warm body to curl up next to as he had no interest in doing anything sexual with her, despite the girl's beauty and his hope that this would save him from himself.

By the end of the week, Alex didn't know which way to turn. There was now a heroin supply drought in New York—no matter how hard he tried, there was no source to buy from in the city or along the entire Eastern Seaboard. No one would trade with him and they wouldn't say why.

To make matters worse, every time he stepped out onto a sidewalk, Alex was being surveilled by the cops. The only good thing was that he wasn't paranoid, but that didn't decrease the stress of the situation at all for him.

Alex stayed away from Charlie until Friday—at this point he hadn't slept a wink the last two nights at all. He had held back because he knew that the pandering trial started on Monday and he had been trying not to bother his friend so close to the beginning of his day in court.

"THANKS FOR SEEING me, Charlie."

"Always a pleasure to break bread with a friend such as you, Alex."

Charlie had chosen Lindy's as the venue for their rendezvous mainly out of nostalgia and because he couldn't be sure he'd be able to take a trip to the restaurant again in the near future. Alex reckoned this was the reason but didn't want to ask—he had no desire to remind Charlie of how likely he was to face prison time under Dewey's prosecution.

"Are you still certain you don't need me to have a conversation with a jury member?

"Alex, you are very kind but my answer remains no. If Mendy can't get me off, then there is no point crippling a juror—Dewey will only come back smelling more blood and want to find out who nobbled his jury."

"You are not the only one to be at the wrong end of his sights. His guys have been tailing me for weeks."

"And you brought them here?"

"No, Charlie. Whenever I have any actual business to do, I ditch them. You should know me better than that. Although, there is nothing criminal about two men eating lunch together."

"True, but you did just offer to tamper with a jury which is a federal crime, Alex."

Alex laughed. "You can't prove nothing, cop." Then it was Charlie's turn to grin and they settled into their food. By the time they finished their meal, Alex was feeling relaxed, if tired.

"These have been some fabulous years, Charlie, wouldn't you say?"

"Sure have and it's not over yet. Don't forget that."

"I appreciate this isn't the greatest time, Charlie, but I need to ask a favor of you."

"Tell me and I'll do my best to help."

Alex stirred the spoon in his coffee for too long before responding because he wasn't sure of Charlie's reply.

"Albert and Louis are closing in on the dope trade—with you keeping your eye on Dewey, they have attacked our heroin transportation into the country. They've stolen the latest cargo from Sicily and there is nothing I can do."

"What do you want from me?"

"Authorize a hit on Anastasia. Let me whack the guy—Buchalter is only supplying the gelt—nothing more.

CHARLIE SMILED, LICKED the pad of his first finger and picked off the last crumb of cheesecake from his plate. A sip of coffee and he replaced the cup on its saucer.

"Alex, you never cease to amaze me. What went down between you and Albert to make you want him dead so much?"

"Nothing happened—he's been trying to cut into our rackets for a long time. I have tried to contain the problem and not bother you with it, but now your interests are aligned with mine and I'm hoping you will see what needs to be done. And soon, before we lose any more money or worsen our reputation."

"From the moment I introduced you to Albert and Louis at the first syndicate meeting, I could tell from the way you stood that you were not comfortable with them. This request of yours has nothing to do with whether you get on as people—it has to be tied to business."

"Charlie, this isn't anything personal—it is all business. He has attacked our drug supply line into New York. He has stolen our ship, taken our heroin and killed our men. This is business."

"And do you have proof for this allegation?"

"Suddenly everyone's a lawyer. No, I don't have witnesses who heard Anastasia issue the order, but there is a smoking gun—we have no heroin to sell and his boys are hitting our streets and selling the only powder available in the city. And I had a guy admit he was in the crew that assailed the boat."

"That's not enough, Alex, and you know it, otherwise you'd have put the proposal to the syndicate."

"I'm not asking the syndicate—it's you, Charlie."

"There are two problems—even if I wanted to help, my hands are tied. Albert is a made man—and that means I can't touch him, you can't touch him. No one can without permission from Sicily—and you won't get that as a Jew in New York. No disrespect, but that is the way the old-timers think. It is almost at the point when they only talk to guys born on the island. Everyone else they judge as an outsider."

"That's ridiculous."

"It is the reality of the situation. Like I say, it isn't down to me. I will not touch a hair on the head of a boss without approval."

"Would you ask on my behalf then. You're Sicilian, aren't you?"

"I am, but that is only half the issue. I said there were two difficulties and the old country dons are one thing. The other is that I'm not sure you have enough to make your allegation stick."

"But…" Charlie raised a finger to stop Alex in his tracks.

"I understand you spoke with a guy who'd stolen your boat and the most he gave up which was certain was that Louis had been the money behind the deal. Your man only heard rumors after that."

"Sure, but there was another…"

"Let me finish, Alex. There was indeed another of the gang, but when Massimo interrogated him, you got bupkis. Like every good gang member, he refused to give up a name. There is a vow of omertà for a reason."

"So you won't help me then."

"Less of the won't and more of the can't. Show me something concrete and I'll put the word out in a flash, but right now you've got nothing to hang your hat on—and do not misunderstand me; I would happily take Anastasia out because I also don't like the way he conducts his business."

They continued in silence for a minute while they both finished their coffees. When the waiter asked if they wanted anything else, they both declined and Alex ensured he was the one who paid for what they both feared might be Charlie's last lunch in Lindy's for quite some time. When they left, they shook hands and hugged, Alex patting Charlie repeatedly on the back as if to show how much he cared for his friend through the act of slapping him firmly. Charlie mirrored the gesture and then they separated on the sidewalk and Alex walked briskly away.

32

TO SAY THAT Alex was dissatisfied with his time with Charlie was an understatement. The disquiet idled in his gut all afternoon so that by the evening, he yearned for some company he could rely on and to sleep at night again. In the absence of any other ideas, he made his way over to Ida, up through the service elevator and into her suite.

"Darling, how fabulous to see you again. Come through, you have arrived just in time to mix me a martini."

He nodded, threw his jacket onto an empty chair, undid his tie, and sauntered over to the drinks trolley and whipped out the cocktail shaker in the shape of a penguin—Ida liked to add quirky touches to her surroundings.

Meanwhile, she languished on her chaise longue, allowing the split in her ankle-length skirt to reveal the side of her leg above her knee. Alex couldn't decide if she was being coquettish or just careless in how she sat. The woman's mind was addled by the narcotics she'd been inhaling the past two decades and she behaved erratically at times.

Alex walked over with a pair of wide-brimmed glasses and passed one to Ida, who took it graciously in a long-fingered hand and clinked the sides before taking a long sip.

"Marvelous. You make a fabulous martini, darling."

"You're welcome. How have you been?"

She started by regaling him with a meandering tale of woe that commenced with her adventure in the elevator the day before and pursued a trajectory that Alex found hard to follow. To take his mind off her prattling, he absentmindedly stroked the stretch of her leg which had become visible when she sat down.

His beau continued her story as he played with her knee, occasionally taking another mouthful of her cocktail, but not seeming to stop until the narrative and her glass had run dry. She held out the receptacle and Alex collected it from her, poured two more glasses from the shaker and returned to where he had been sitting.

For the first time in a week, Alex relaxed—as though Ida's prattling was a soothing tonic that blotted out the callings from the rest of the world invading his head. A hunger in the pit of his stomach bore inside of him in a way he had not experienced for more years than he cared to remember.

By the late afternoon, Ida wanted a fix, so she took out her pipe and Alex consumed another martini while she was flaked out. He made sure he remained focused only on what was going on inside the room. Maybe it was the effect of the opium smoke floating in the atmosphere or maybe he was just plain tired, but either way, when she roused herself, he grabbed her by the hand and led her into the bedroom.

WHEN ALEX WOKE up a few hours later, Ida was stroking his chest—the reason he'd regained consciousness, perhaps. He placed his palm on hers to stop the motion of her fingers.

"Thanks for being here for me."

"I had no plans for today anyway, darling."

"No, Ida, I meant over the years."

"You really are too kind. I am the one who should thank you—I live in this marvelous hotel suite because you are precious enough to pay for it. You buy me pretty things and cover the lodging fees every month. Few guys would have done that for a girl like me."

"The gravy train might come into the station fairly soon."

"What do you mean, Alex?"

"There are several men who are coming after me and I don't know how long I can fend them all off."

"I have every faith that good will prevail."

"Ida, one of the men is a prosecutor. He won't stop until he has me in chains."

"Then, darling, get rid of the tiresome fellow. You might not talk to me about your business, but I read the newspapers. If half of what is printed is true, then you know what you must do."

"Don't think I haven't considered whacking Dewey," Ida's eyes opened wider, reflecting that she didn't have a clue which cop Alex had been referring to. "But nobody'll support me. They're all turning their backs on me."

"If you deal with this ruffian, will you be able to resolve the other matters more easily?"

"With Dewey gone, the rest of the fellas would be so transfixed in fear, I could take care of other matters with no one able to stop me."

"There's the solution to your problems then. You and I should talk business more often."

Alex smiled and put his hands behind his head while Ida planted kisses all over his body until he lapsed back into unconsciousness.

ALEX OPENED HIS eyes again to find himself in Ida's bed—he had slept like a baby all night long. Bliss. She had rolled over and taken all the sheets, leaving him cold and naked, so he got up, grabbed his shorts, and padded over to the kitchen to make a coffee. Still Ida didn't stir.

He sat in an easy chair overlooking the bed and lit a smoke, cupping his drink in one hand and flicking the ash off the end of his cigarette with the other. The chink of light through the curtains landed on Ida's feet, which were poking out from the bottom of the sheets.

The tranquility of this moment soaked through him and Alex allowed himself the luxury of staring at Ida, drinking and smoking. As he put the cup down on a nearby side table, Ida awoke, turned over to see him better and smiled. She raised an arm for Alex to bring over a lit cigarette for her. He clambered over her body to lie next to her, inhaling her warm scent and enjoying the calm they inhabited.

"So will you kill him then?"

The question seemed to come from nowhere and Alex recoiled from Ida just on hearing the words.

"What are you talking about?"

"Dewey, darling. Are you going to do him in?"

The ceiling spun around him and Alex was glad he was lying down, otherwise he would have surely found himself sprawled on the ground. He blinked hard and tried to breathe normally despite the pounding in his chest. An acid taste burst into his mouth and Alex realized he had to stop this from happening. He hadn't been thinking straight when he shared what he was considering with her the night before.

He sat up and rolled on top of Ida with a smile on his face and a gentle touch to her cheek. One knee either side of her torso, Alex grabbed both her wrists, pulling them above her head. Ida glanced at both hands, a flash of concern on her face, while Alex bent down and planted a long kiss on her lips.

"I never wanted to leave you," he whispered as he leaned back slightly and moved one wrist to his other hand so he grasped both arms in a palm, freeing up the other hand to grab at the pillow behind her head. Before Ida knew what was going on, Alex had ripped the pillow out from under her and placed it over her face and mouth.

She tried to clutch at the pillow, but he held onto her wrists like a vice. Besides, he had her pinned down with the weight of his body so there wasn't much she could do. Ida only took two minutes to stop struggling and for her arms to go limp. Alex waited another thirty seconds just in case and eased the pressure off the pillow, but nothing.

He got off her and stood on the floor to survey the scene. Alex replaced the pillow under her head, threw the sheets over her body and maneuvered Ida's limbs so you could be forgiven for thinking she had died in her sleep.

Then he picked out his cigarette butts from the ashtrays scattered around the suite and cleaned his martini glass and coffee cup. With no obvious trace of his existence in the room that night, Alex put on his clothes and left the building using the service elevator.

While he might not have wanted to end things that way, Alex knew he was never going to leave her because she was never going to be worth the effort of saying, "It's time we called it quits, babe."

33

A MEETING OF the syndicate took place, only without Charlie as he was otherwise engaged spending his first day in court on the pandering changes brought by Dewey. Everyone agreed how sorry they were that he was so indisposed, but they also noted that life must go on and agreed Johnny Torrio should chair the discussions in Charlie's place.

Torrio was a square-headed fella and a smart Italian who had come over to America when he was two and made his fortune through hard work and an unceasing use of his muscles. He might have taken a back seat in New York the last few years, but he was as much the brains behind the creation of the syndicate as Charlie. When he asked everybody to come to order, they did so as promptly as if Luciano had been in the room.

"Thank you everybody for coming today. I appreciate that we all lead busy lives and a day trip to Ithaca was not high on everyone's priority list."

Various nods and mumbling to denote agreement from the twenty men assembled around the boardroom table in the no-name hotel which had been selected for the meeting. The first few minutes were spent with each boss describing issues they were having with local and federal cops. Where appropriate, others chimed in with suggestions on how to join forces to resolve these difficulties.

Eventually, the lead returned to Torrio, who invited Buchalter to start the next item on the agenda.

"Thank you, Johnny. I stand here before you with a simple request. I want permission for us to hit Joe Rosen."

His statement was met with complete and utter silence. Louis looked around the room, trying to understand the response he was receiving. Torrio offered him a clue.

"Louis, explain who Rosen is, as most of us have not heard of him before."

"Sure, sorry. Rosen is a trucker in the garment industry."

"Schmatta. Now I know all about that," Benny interjected and chuckles rippled across the room from all the Jewish attendees. Louis waited for the ripple to die down and then he continued.

"The situation is very simple. I have asked Rosen to leave town and yet he remains in Brooklyn and refuses to depart."

"I'm not sure we should kill someone just for ignoring a polite request." Meyer made the comment with no hint of irony in his voice, even though he knew the polite request should have been more assertive than that.

"You seem to ignore the reason I sent him out of town in the first place, Meyer."

"Then describe it to us, Louis. You haven't explained yourself very well. I think I speak for everyone here when I say we are happy to condemn the man to death, if only we understood why he must die."

"Forgive me, Meyer. I seem to have started in the middle. Let me go back to the beginning and try again."

Meyer nodded consent and, judging by the response in the room, the others agreed—Alex clenched his jaw, not wanting to side with Buchalter given this man stood in front of the syndicate had financed the hijacking of his heroin shipment.

"Around six months ago, we muscled in on the National Garment Workers of America, a relatively peaceful union which had more money than its members needed. All was good in that we convinced the leadership to either step aside or take an income from us. Roll forward four months and the union was a regular money earner and we fomented the occasional murmur of disquiet to shake down the odd factory owner to increase revenues further. Some members were less enthusiastic with our presence and they either got on the bus or stood in front of it. Joe Rosen did not ride on the public transport."

"Socialist," Benny whispered, but this time he didn't get his desired response as the group had been hooked into Louis' story.

"I didn't make a big deal over this—inevitably, some people can't get used to change, especially when it turns up in suits, fedoras and with loaded guns. So Joe Rosen left the union and stopped hauling clothing for a living."

"Can you skip to the part why you need him dead, please, Louis?" Meyer was nervous how long this tale would take as he wanted to get back to Manhattan before nightfall—he had an appointment he did not want to miss.

"That is when Rosen talked with Thomas Dewey."

The name caused the room to erupt as people banged on the tables, shouted, and generally allowed their tempers to run high at the mere mention of the special prosecutor.

◆ ◆ ◆

"LET ME GET this straight, Louis. You are telling us that this Rosen squealed to the cops."

Anastasia looked Buchalter square in the eye because the Italian operated under a simple policy—give nothing to the police even if they ask for the time of day.

"I reckon so."

"Believe or know? The difference is very important." Meyer had leaned in and taken his chin out of his hand.

"The guy lost his job because he wouldn't stay in the union. He visited Manhattan three times in one week. What else was the chump doing apart from spilling his guts to Dewey?"

"Perhaps he had a sick aunt at Mount Sinai."

Louis gave Benny a disdainful sideways glance and ignored him beyond that, even though he had generated a few smiles around the room.

"Did you have Rosen tailed? Do you know where he actually went in Manhattan?"

"Meyer, no I don't. He was one of a group of truckers who refused to pay their new union dues. We didn't mind because, as we all appreciate, when you take over a labor union, some old members leave. But it doesn't matter because you've still got everyone else putting up and shutting up. There's natural wastage."

"Then you are asking us to agree to a hit based on your belief that he's a rat? You don't know for sure."

"Meyer, I keep saying to you I can't offer you any hard evidence. All I am certain is that Rosen lost his job, before he left the union, and for a while afterwards, he complained to anybody who'd listen about how the union had gone to seed and that the likes of me were having undue influence, as he called it. The next thing you know he is going to Manhattan for entire days and not telling people where he'd been when he returned. Not even his wife knows what he's up to."

"In that case, it isn't an aunt he's visiting—it's a Midtown madam or a mistress."

"Benny, these asides really aren't helping." Torrio used a stage whisper so Benny understood he had received a public admonishment—his interventions were bordering on the childish.

"As I was saying, the only reason a person is secretive is because he has something to hide. Rosen is talking to the cops and it won't be about the intricacies of the Talmud."

"This is not meant to be the least bit flippant," Benny spoke, "but our problem isn't with Rosen but with Dewey. I understand this matter has come before this group before, but why don't we hit Dewey? We may or may not be sure that Rosen is a rat, but we know for certain that the special prosecutor needs to be taken down a peg or two. Let's deal with the bigger fish."

Torrio stepped in before anybody else could respond.

"Benny, your suggestion is not without merit as some in this room will no doubt agree, but as a point of order, right now we are addressing the question of whether Rosen should meet his maker sooner rather than later. After that, we can return to the problem of Thomas Dewey."

Siegel parted his lips as if he was about to say something, then thought better of it and shut his mouth and shrugged instead. Alex hoped the idea wouldn't get lost in this Rosen nonsense—Louis clearly didn't have sufficient proof to support his desire to see the guy dead, whereas Dewey needed to be taken care of.

Torrio continued to hold the floor.

"It seems to me that there are two issues with Rosen. First is that he appears to be squealing and second that people believe he is squealing and see that we are doing nothing about it. The first is subject to doubt, but the second point is an absolute certainty. Whatever happens, everybody must know that we will not tolerate dropping a dime to the cops. Who votes for the hit on Rosen to take place?"

Unanimous decision.

"That's agreed then. All I counsel is that we do not rush into the hit. Unless Louis receives any hard evidence, then I am happy for us to wait a month or two. When he drops to the sidewalk in a pool of blood, it will be more dramatic that we took our time and responded as cold as stone."

34

MENDY GREENBERG OCCUPIED a compact room in a midtown Park Avenue office block, so at least Alex knew the money he paid him wasn't wasted on swanky furniture and marble flooring. The level of discomfort you felt when you sat in one of his chairs emphasized the sense of disquiet many of his clients experienced as they discussed with him their battles with the law. ┏

Some lawyers specialized in fighting injustice, operating on a no-win, no-fee basis to enable the downtrodden masses the opportunity to have their day in court and to get back at the man. Mendy's moral compass operated in a different direction—he preferred to represent those who generally were guilty before being presumed innocent, but still didn't want to go to jail or pay a fine.

For him, growing up in the Bowery was simply another way to build up trust with his clientele as he came from the same stink hole as they did, only he had studied at night until he got himself a certificate to practice law in the state of New York.

"So what are my chances, Mendy?"

"I'd say there are very strong odds that you will do time—unless Dewey drops dead, that is."

Alex stared at him and crossed his legs, resting both palms on his uppermost knee. He tilted his head slightly to one side before responding.

"Are you suggesting that if Dewey were to be six feet under then my problem would go away?"

"Even with client confidentiality, there is no way I would ever recommend that you commit a crime to reduce your prospects for hard time. The New York City Bar Association would take a very dim view of that suggestion without a shadow of a doubt."

"So you are advising me that if Dewey were dead, then my situation would improve but you are not telling me to do anything about it."

"Exactly. I knew you'd understand."

"And yet you think I will be in jail before the end of the year."

"Dewey's case is strong. My understanding is that they have a paper trail connecting you and your income to a variety of revenue streams and you haven't paid a dime in tax since you came to this country."

"I kept no documents—it was all in my head. It's only in the last few years that Charlie suggested I should have some paperwork to show the cops if they came snooping."

"Alex, I will not make any statements about the quality of the advice you received from another of my clients, especially one as powerful as Charlie. Suffice to say, you should have got a second opinion."

"What's done is done, though. From where I am now, you'd say I'm on a one-way ticket up the river?"

"Yep. The most we can hope for is a lenient judge so you don't get the maximum sentence."

"Which is?"

"You don't want to know—more years than Alfonse received."

"And what do you advise me to do?"

"These are your options—don't shoot the messenger but you asked me the question. First, proclaim your innocence but say nothing and take the full force of the law. Take the fifth on anything and everything they ask—that way, your friends will know that you looked after their interests and they will look after you when you go inside. Second, you cut a deal with Dewey. Plead guilty to the tax evasion charges. The difference with the first option is that you'll spend next to no time in court and the judge will give you a shorter sentence because we will negotiate the duration with Dewey. Third, we throw ourselves at the mercy of the court—go to trial and convince a jury you're innocent of all charges."

"Is that all I got?"

"Alex, I can pretend to you we have a watertight case and that as soon as I explain to the jury they'll roll over and play ball—but how you have no discernible legal income apart from working at a union for a year or two before the war and yet you own a string of establishments and real estate, as well as possessing enough money to afford your lavish lifestyle?"

"How about jury tampering?"

"Again, I cannot tell you in too strong a form how I am not suggesting you should do this. In your situation, I'd bear in mind that if a jury heard the evidence Dewey has against you and then voted not guilty, even a senile judge would have to demand a mistrial or get the cops to arrest the twelve of them. It is not a wise option, Alex."

"What would you do if you were in my shoes?"

"Alex, that's not for me to say. It is your decision as it's your life."

ALEX DIDN'T SLEEP for a minute that night and when he opened his newspaper which was delivered every morning to his door, he found a note hidden in between the pages so that none of his guys would see it. There was a time and an address—and it was signed Thomas Dewey.

His instincts told him to either take the first train to Florida or plain ignore it. Then Alex thought some more and realized that he would have to deal. Just because he didn't want Dewey on his back, the truth was the special prosecutor was clinging to his neck and would not go away. He put a call through to Mendy.

"I know I've asked this before, but with whom would you share what we discuss?"

"Nobody under ordinary circumstances."

"And what happens in extraordinary circumstances?"

"If you tell me you are about to commit a crime, then I am supposed to inform the police. I try not to have good hearing sometimes."

"What if something I plan to do will impact another of your clients?"

"Whatever you tell me, stays with me. I will not disclose to Charlie what we discuss—just as I do not inform you what Charlie and I say. That's no way to conduct business."

Alex maintained a silence on the line as he mulled this over. Mendy was right—with the people he had as clients, if the lawyer broke client privilege then he'd be dead within a week.

"I've been summoned to meet with Dewey this afternoon and I need you there."

"Do you know how you will respond when he offers you a deal?"

"Depends what's on the table. If I can avoid jail time, that'd be good."

"Alex, Dewey will want his photo on the front pages with you being led away in handcuffs."

"Then I'll take the smallest jail term that's on offer."

"Which means you'll be expected to admit to your criminal activities, lose your money and, dare I say it, most likely your friends shall walk away."

"Because I'll have to name them as protagonists in my business dealings?"

"Yes. While you have protected yourself relatively well over the years by not keeping any records, there are still going to be witnesses to conversations. The good news for you is that you have been very careful around syndicate members, but you will throw your lieutenants to the wolves."

"And we can't be certain that somebody didn't hear something over all these years."

"Exactly right. Don't forget that Dewey has a small army of cops who can spend months harassing people until they find a shred of evidence, because from that they build a case against any of your work associates."

"Can we not hem Dewey in? Make him keep to my tax affairs and not go stomping all over everybody else's business?"

"You wish. Look, Alex, if you cooperate over the tax evasion, you'll get a light sentence and pay a hefty fine. If you plead not guilty, then it'll be down to a jury to decide and Dewey has the proof to send you away for a very long time and strip you of all the money you have ever earned."

"If I cut a deal, I must leave the country. Everyone'll think I spilled my guts."

"They will only expect you sang like a canary if you walk down the streets humming."

◆ ◆ ◆

ALEX TOLD EZRA and Massimo not to bother going with him as he had some private business to attend to and they shrugged and left him at the door of the Lexington Hotel on Forty-eighth Street where Alex had lived ever since Sarah walked out. He hopped in a taxi and went straight to the address on the piece of paper.

When he got out of the cab, Alex saw the rundown fleapit of a hotel that Dewey had chosen for their rendezvous. There was no one at the front desk and Alex headed up. Mendy was already there, waiting outside the room for his client.

"Anything I should know before we go in?"

"Alex, let me do as much of the talking as possible. Don't say a word directly to them without clearing it with me first."

He opened the door and the two men walked in to see a space with a desk and several chairs, but none of the usual hotel furniture. This was an interview room and nothing more. Alex spotted a refrigerator in the corner and noticed the smell of freshly brewed coffee. Dewey and Jervis McCracken sat at the table, and they both rose when Alex and Mendy arrived.

Two seats had been arranged on the other side of the table to the cops, and Dewey's hand indicated for them to sit down.

"I am glad you came today."

Alex glanced at Mendy, but said nothing as he had been instructed.

"My client is coming here of his own free will to assist the police in any way that he can."

"Well, counselor. Let's hope what you say is true."

Jervis took out a notebook and started scribbling, much to Alex's annoyance.

"You have been evading your fiscal duties from the day you arrived in this country, Mr. Cohen. That is a federal crime and, worse than that, your business dealings have been entirely illegal. I intend to prosecute you to the full extent of the law, do y'hear?"

"My client has conducted himself in an exemplary manner all his life—he's a war hero for goodness' sake—and has never been arrested or even charged with any crime."

"Notwithstanding his record, Mr. Cohen has been leading a crooked life and now he must pay the price."

"What are you offering?"

"If he gives us details of his criminal dealings, then he will walk free—no prison term and no fine."

"You want me to spill my guts about my friends?" Alex burst out. Mendy placed a hand gently on his client's arm and leaned towards Alex's ear. "He wants to make you respond. Don't give him the satisfaction. Let me speak for you."

Then he sat back, patted Alex's arm, and took over.

"As you can see, my client finds the consequences of what you are offering unpalatable. What else do you have for us?"

"We can still get him for racketeering."

"Mr. Dewey, you mistake me for an imbecile. You know as well as I do that to make a racketeering charge stick, you will need considerably more than a bunch of invoices and income statements. And if you had that kind of evidence, then we would meet downtown and not in some hovel like this. So let's be realistic, shall we? A wise man knows his reach."

Dewey's cheeks reddened and his partner continued to scratch away at his notepad.

"Your client has stolen money from the US Government and he must be punished for that crime. I demand justice for the American people."

"You want a big name to drag into the mud and anything else is a cherry on the top."

"Three million in back tax and a year in jail."

"My client has no desire to mix with criminals—he fought in the Great War—and the amount of damages you seek is punitive. Mr. Cohen isn't made of gelt."

Alex leaned over to Mendy. "Is this it? I lose most of my money?"

"Dewey wants your head on a spike so I can try to get you to pay less but you must hand something over otherwise there is no deal. Besides, if you don't pay a significant sum then Dewey won't be satisfied and will investigate you more—you and your business partners. And that is not advisable."

"Mendy, to do that means I must admit I am guilty, but all I have done is work hard all my life."

"Are you telling me you don't want me to cut you a deal?"

A thousand thoughts zoomed through Alex's mind. He wanted rid of Dewey, but his pride wouldn't let him be convicted of this crime. He couldn't rat out his friends, and that was the only way to free himself from Dewey's grasp now and in the future.

"No deal, Mendy. The *farbissener momzer* can *zoygn meyn hon.*"

JUNE 1936

35

THERE WAS SOMETHING Alex needed to resolve before he faced Dewey in court. He traveled out to his Hoboken apartment before placing a call with Sarah. He'd told Mendy of his plans because the last thing he wanted was to be stopped by the cops because he was crossing the state line when he was trying to see his family again.

The boys responded in their predictable manner, which Alex had accepted was normal several years ago. No matter what he thought, children were honest in their behavior—always—and he could pretend to himself that his absence made no difference to them and he could turn up whenever he wanted, but it was not true.

Instead, they visited him in the apartment and the oldest two did their best to ignore the fact that he existed. Massimo and Ezra were kind enough to join him and to help with the kids, but they had grown accustomed to the tykes so it wasn't that bad a day for these hardened killers.

At Alex's suggestion, Sarah arrived early to pick up the kids and he used the time to speak with her while the children were in the park.

"Thank you for letting me see the boys at such short notice, Sarah. I know my appearing in their lives is inconvenient at best. I have not been a good father to them and not an adequate husband to you."

Sarah walked to the other side of the living room and stared out of the window, arms crossed. Alex had hoped for a different reaction—silence was not how she was supposed to respond.

"I might be able to do something about becoming a better father, although we both know that is unlikely. But I sure can do something about being a better husband."

Sarah spun round, anger in her eyes.

"If you think I will take you back…"

"That's the last thing in the world I was thinking. Sarah, we can't relive our past, but I can offer you a better future. You deserve a divorce from me and that is what I want to give you."

A tear fell from her left eye, which she rubbed off with the back of her palm, and then she ran toward Alex and gave him a hug.

"Thank you, Alex Cohen."

A fire in Alex's stomach ignited as soon as he felt her touch, so he held on to the embrace far longer than he should have, although Sarah did not try to pull away either. It was almost like they both realized this was the last moment they would have together—their final time as a couple, even though they'd stopped living with each other years before. This moment in the Hoboken apartment room was the end of their relationship and, whether they recognized it or not, they both hurt.

She kissed him on the cheek and they separated. To extinguish the fluttering in his belly, Alex offered a coffee which Sarah gladly accepted. They wandered into the kitchen and he made their drinks.

"I'm not sure whether it's hit the New Jersey papers yet, but I will be on trial soon—for tax evasion."

"What are your chances?"

"Not great, according to my lawyer, and he should know."

"Is that why you're agreeing to the divorce?"

"I might be gone some time and you probably don't want the boys to be Cohens while I am away. I understand entirely."

"That's sweet of you."

"And as I have an attorney on retainer—I got Mendy to put together the paperwork for us."

Alex took a glug of his drink and sped into the hallway where he'd left his case. He opened it, removed a brown envelope, and returned to the kitchen table.

"This is for you, Sarah."

She squinted at the package, trying to imagine what it contained and then ripped it open to find the divorce papers inside.

"It's only fair that we get this sorted now. I don't want to have it hanging over me when I'm facing Dewey in court."

He pulled out a pen and placed it on the table.

"Shouldn't I hire a lawyer to check these over?"

"Of course, but it's a fair settlement. You get a million and there's another million in total held in trust for our sons. Sign today and I'll move the cash on Monday—then we hop over to Reno to make it legit."

Sarah picked up the documents and started to read the legal prose.

"I have always been straight with you, Sarah, with money. I only ever lied to you about where I was and who I was with."

She glanced up and carried on reading. Two seconds later, she stopped, put the papers down and picked up the pen.

"Where do I sign?"

Alex rifled through the sheets and showed her where to place her signature. Sarah's hand shook throughout the whole process, but she wrote her name in all the correct places. She placed the pen on the table and Alex picked it up and signed himself.

"I'll ask Ezra and Massimo to be our witnesses. Mendy will file everything the same day you get the money."

"You understand it was never about money."

"Gelt is only important if you don't have any. As soon as you do, there's always more significant things to worry about."

Sarah squeezed his hand and another tear dribbled out of her eye. Then a second and a third until she was crying full pelt. Alex collected her in his arms and did his best to soothe her pain.

"You are a free woman now. I hope you find happiness—and that you'll let me still be a part of your life somehow."

"There's the boys. I never want you to stop being with your sons."

"If I'm not in jail, I'll do my very best."

"I love you, Alex Cohen."

"And I love you too, Sarah Fleischman."

36

"DEWEY DUG UP a bunch of whores to testify against me. The jury believed that I collected envelopes from the madams myself. Then they were told I ran the biggest prostitution ring in New York. How does that add up, Alex?"

"He nailed you over tax, Charlie. Your paper income and your lifestyle didn't tally. That's what did for you."

The two men were sat in a cubicle at the heart of Sing Sing—Charlie's power and wealth had secured him a more pleasant jail experience than an ordinary Joe. He had dismissed the prison guard who had entered the room to accompany them during their conversation.

"Alex, if you are visiting just to harangue this panderer then leave me now."

"Not at all—forgive me. I have been spending a lot of time recently trying to understand how Dewey thinks and figure out what happens in tax evasion trials."

Charlie laughed out loud and raised a hand to show there was no disrespect.

"Sorry, Alex. I ignored Dewey until it was all too late. I see that you are doing your best not to make the same mistake."

"My day in court is around the corner."

"It always boils down to taxation in this country. They talk about streets paved with gold, but Uncle Sam wants you to pay for the privilege."

"We should have taken notice of what happened to Alfonse—he was on top of the world and was brought to his knees by not listening to his accountant. You know how he's doing?"

"Not really. Last I heard he was keeping his head down and doing his time like a model prisoner."

"How the mighty fall, Alex."

"That's not you, Charlie. Capone kept a high profile, and they clipped his wings when he flew too close to the sun. You are not him."

"Damn straight."

"So how can I help you keep running the syndicate?"

Charlie leaned in like the conspirator he was, and Alex mimicked the move.

"As much as I would want you to be my contact, that cannot be allowed to happen—not just because of your present difficulties, but because you need some plausible deniability and visiting me once a month is too dangerous for you if you do get off the current rap."

"I understand. What would you want me to do in the meantime, Charlie?"

"Contact my lieutenant, Vito Genovese. He will be responsible for day-to-day operations until I leave this place."

"The judge gave you a minimum of thirty years—you digging a tunnel?"

"Not me: Mendy. We have several lines of appeal he's working on. If everything goes to plan then I'll be out before Christmas and we can all celebrate New Year at the Waldorf Astoria Ball."

Alex wasn't convinced by Charlie's optimism. If Mendy was as direct with his friend as he was with Alex, the chances were that Luciano was not dealing with the information he was being told. Anyway, the fella was in jail and needed some hope on the horizon otherwise he'd die trapped inside these four walls. His sentence was ridiculously long—Dewey really had a point to prove, and the judge had helped him all the way.

While he wanted to be the kingpin in Charlie's plan, he understood that Genovese was the better choice—the man had been with Charlie since the start of Prohibition, could be trusted to the end of the world and wasn't about to stand trial for tax evasion.

"Is there anything else you'd like me to do for you?"

"Alex, it is kind of you to offer, but you need to focus on your own problems. Whatever you do, listen to Mendy's advice—he's a standup guy and knows what he's doing. If he gets you off, then sure you can help me some more and hopefully we'll be back at Lindy's in a few months having coffee and cheesecake. And if they put you behind bars or I don't get out on appeal, then none of this matters because we won't see each other again."

Charlie Luciano stared at Alex, inhaled, and let out a deep sigh. This was one hell of a way to say goodbye and that was how it felt like to Alex. They shook hands and hugged briefly. Then Charlie patted him on the shoulder. They separated and Alex walked out of Sing Sing, not knowing if he would ever see his friend again.

SEPTEMBER 1936

37

ALBERT HAD CALLED for a meeting of the heads of Murder Corporation, which was unusual as they normally only got together to assign contracts and not much else. Alex agreed as he wanted to gain a better idea of what was going on inside the man's head. Also, at the back of his mind was the notion he should confront both Anastasia and Buchalter over their assault on his heroin business.

The chosen location was Louis' Brownsville office and while he would have usually preferred to remain Midtown, secretly Alex was pleased to leave his old stomping ground for a few hours. When he arrived, there was something afoot—not one person was on the sidewalk and no other car was on the street. The entire block was deserted apart from a lone foot soldier standing in front of the building.

"What gives?"

"Park around the corner, please, Alex. We just want to make sure that you fellas can have a private meeting."

While that explanation made little sense, Alex did as he was asked and entered the joint from the service access at the rear. Although he had been doing this since he joined the syndicate, the irony was lost on Alex that men as powerful as he was used the same entrance as the janitor.

Stood outside the doorway was another of Anastasia's guys who frisked him before he could make his way inside. This had never happened before.

"What's with the extra security? You expecting trouble?"

"I just figured we should all be certain that everybody is safe here, that's all, Alex."

"Albert, you've brought your people here to keep Louis' building secure? What are you playing at?"

"This is no game, Alex. We have some serious matters to discuss. Let's not worry about the hired hands."

Alex shrugged and sat down opposite Anastasia and Buchalter, who offered him a coffee before proceedings began.

"There are two items on the agenda. The first is your court case, Alex."

"Dewey wants to take me down for tax evasion. My attorney says I have an excellent chance of beating the rap, so what is there to discuss?"

"I admire your optimism, Alex, and the fact that you still retain Mendy Greenberg as your attorney after what he did with Charlie."

"He's a good lawyer—the best money can buy."

"He is a shiny suit and a smile who has a certificate in a frame on his wall. Don't be fooled by his smooth talking and arrogant swagger—he's just another tinpot hack, soaking up the fees. When the government has taken all your money, you won't see him for dust."

"Thanks for the legal advice, Albert. I'll bear that in mind."

Louis broke the ensuing silence by regaling his companions with a tale of how he shot a lawyer in the *tuches* for a reason that Alex didn't care to listen to because he was wondering why Anastasia felt the need to undermine his choice of Mendy.

By the time the story had fizzled out with no one laughing at the punchline, Alex had mentally returned to the room and Albert had taken back control of the conversation.

"Your situation means we must make some changes at Murder Corporation."

"Why is that, Albert?"

"With all due respect, you are about to spend several weeks if not months embroiled in a court case and throughout that time, you won't be able to fulfill your duties—nor would we expect you to. Beating the cops is more important, right, Louis?"

"Of course, Albert."

"So we think it best if you were to temporarily step down from running the operation until all this Dewey business is behind you. After, you can come back just as before. It's for your own good."

"Kind of you to be so concerned about my welfare, again."

Alex created a pause by sipping his coffee before continuing.

"And will I still receive my compensation while I am no longer on active duty?"

Anastasia glanced at Louis and turned his attention back to Alex.

"Why, of course. This isn't about money—it's giving you the best chance to get through this legal difficulty you face and for the rest of us to know there's nothing you do that will catch the eye of Dewey or any of the other cops."

"If you want to pay me for doing absolutely nothing, how could I refuse?"

"Good, that's settled."

The door opened and Abe Reles appeared, mumbled something, and headed to the kitchen area. The noise of the boiling kettle rumbled through the room, but everybody ignored it.

"Albert, you said there were two items for us to discuss. What was the second?"

"We need to mop up the Joe Rosen business. Alex, would you mind sorting this out because everyone has been patient. He might not have spilled anything to Dewey." A quick glance at Louis to acknowledge all his disquiet, who picked up the conversation. "But we still need to show that his behavior has been unacceptable."

"You want me to handle this matter before I step down, Louis?"

"Think of it as a last hurrah, Alex."

"You said this was only for a few months."

"You know what I meant, I'm sure."

"Yes, I'll organize the Rosen hit."

Reles walked through the room and out the door.

"MEYER, THEY'VE TAKEN Murder Corporation away from me, and Albert has stolen Charlie's narcotics trafficking and nobody is doing anything to stop them."

"There's concern about you, Alex."

"Who?"

"They think you might cut a deal with Dewey to save yourself from jail."

"What do you reckon, Meyer?"

"I trust you, Alex. You know I do, I hope."

"Why isn't anyone else showing me the same courtesy?"

"It's not like that, Alex. Not everyone knows you as well as Charlie, Benny and me. The rest of them see a man who has been cornered by Dewey, and Charlie is looking at thirty to fifty years in jail. Are you prepared for that stretch? The only thing holding Charlie together is the belief that Mendy will get him out on appeal."

"I'm not in the same league as Charlie."

"It doesn't matter if it is true—people act on what they believe, Alex."

"And they expect me to squeal."

"Many of us would be tempted. Nobody wants to spend the rest of their lives in jail—even doing gangster time. The bars still won't go away."

"Just between you and me, Meyer, I considered it—of course I did. But I've chosen to face Dewey in court. I can't bring myself to plead guilty and take a plea because the prosecutor will have me under his thumb from now until the day I die. So I'm going to fight Dewey and convince the jury and the judge not to convict."

"Pleased to hear that, Alex. For some, that is enough, but for the likes of Anastasia, your pleading not guilty merely counts as a good start."

"So the only way Anastasia will trust me again is if I go to jail?"

"Pretty much. The longer the sentence, the more you'll be safe in their eyes."

"Do you know how crazy that sounds?"

"We live in a strange world, Alex. What can I tell you?"

Alex glanced round Meyer's suite and thought back on all the conversations which had taken place here with his friends—the hours spent with Arnold Rothstein, Charlie and the rest. And he wondered if he would see the Benjamin Hotel interior again.

38

ALEX KEPT THE Rosen hit nice and simple, so he asked Ezra if he'd like to take a ride and make some money along the way. The trip to Brooklyn took no time at all and soon they had parked in a dark corner of town and were agreeing how to handle the situation.

"The hardest part will be to find him and then wait until he is alone. This must not become a bloodbath. In, shoot, out. Got it, Ezra?"

"Sure thing. You have much on him?"

"He used to drive a truck and now he doesn't. We can't be sure, but he probably isn't packing a gun. That's all I got."

Ezra nodded at the acknowledgment of their collective ignorance.

"We'd better take a walk and see who we find, boss."

They hopped out of the black saloon, pushed their hats down over their eyes and turned up their collars. Then they headed to the corner of Brooklyn that Rosen called home—his candy store in Brownsville.

The frontage was nothing much to look at—Rosen Candy Store written in large letters on a sign running the front of the place, a window filled with trays of confection and a glass door. Everything was open to the light, hoping to entice passers-by to pop in and make a purchase. Alex and Ezra hung back across the street fifty feet along so that Rosen wouldn't notice two men staring at his store and not coming in.

"He spends almost all his time alone, which is great, but if anyone walks past, they will see us while we are in there."

"I agree, Ezra. Why don't we wait to see where he goes after he shuts up the joint this afternoon?"

FOR THE NEXT three hours, they took it in turns to skulk around in the shadows near the store. This gave the other an opportunity to grab a bite to eat and hide in their vehicle.

Alex watched the joint and glanced at his watch for the hundredth time that afternoon. For a fella whose only life skill was to drive from one city to another, Rosen had a surprisingly thriving little candy store—not exactly rammed with customers lining up and down the street, but a handful of people an hour to keep the wolf from the door. Alex guessed that the guy made most of his money after school and at weekends. His watch told him there would be a surge of youthful activity in the next ten minutes—and he wasn't wrong.

By six, Rosen seemed to pack up and eventually the lights went out. The trucker appeared at the door, locked up and headed down the sidewalk. Ezra had just arrived a minute before, so they agreed to split up and tail the candy guy hoping to find an opportunity that evening. Rosen walked one street south and then another east until he reached an apartment block and entered.

"He'll be in the bosom of his family now, Alex."

"Yep. Let's stick around for a short while in case he has to pop out for something, otherwise we're stuck until morning."

They smoked and waited fifteen long minutes, but nobody appeared.

"We could enter his apartment and take him out."

"Ezra, we really don't want any witnesses. That is the last thing I need— to be implicated in a homicide just before my tax evasion trial. It's bad enough that Anastasia has put me on this job without you getting us both tried for murder."

"I was merely trying to run through the options we got if we want to do for him this evening like you said you wanted. I thought I was helping."

"Sorry, Ezra, but in future only voice ideas you think will work out. I keep my dumbass thoughts to myself."

Another ten minutes and they had both spent more than enough time for one day in Brownsville.

"I have an idea, Ezra. Pick me up at five. Don't look at me like that—I know it's early. If everything works the way I hope then I'll buy you a slap-up breakfast at Lindy's."

EZRA HALTED HIS stolen vehicle around the rear of Rosen's candy store. The car was different from yesterday's and had been in an underground parking lot controlled by Ezra at least four weeks and had only seen the light of day when Ezra drove it to Alex's place and out to Brownsville. Needless to say, the plates had been boosted from another car a week before.

At eight, they heard a rustling inside the store and a minute later, Rosen opened the back door and stood by the entrance to enjoy a cigarette. Having drained the last vestige of tobacco from his smoke, Rosen threw the butt on the ground and returned to his work indoors.

"Shall we take him now?"

"Ezra, let's wait a short while. I figure a guy like Rosen is used to hard work but would still prefer to stay in bed than open up this early. My guess is that there will be a delivery soon and we don't want to get caught by an eyewitness."

Alex's patience bore fruit as five minutes after their conversation, a delivery truck drew up and Rosen signed for two enormous boxes of candies, taking them inside. When the vehicle had gone around the corner and vanished from sight, Alex nudged Ezra and both men got out of the saloon and edged toward the rear entrance of the place.

They waited fifteen seconds and Alex popped his head inside the joint, opened the door fully, and Ezra followed him in. They reached the front of the store and found Rosen behind the counter, bent down, unpacking his merchandise with the shades pulled down in the front door and windows. Their footsteps must have been louder than intended because he stood up and turned round.

"What can I do for you guys? You know we're not open yet."

Alex shrugged, looked at Ezra who copied his boss, then both men pulled out their revolvers and shot the former trucker in the chest, two slugs each. Alex stepped forward, careful not to walk in the ever-growing pool of blood to check the guy was dead.

"Let's get out of here. Once we've dumped the pieces and the car, we can take a cab in Manhattan over to Lindy's. I owe you a mighty breakfast."

39

THE DAY BEFORE the start of his trial, Alex paid a nafka to spend the evening with him. He informed her he would call her Rebecca, as he did on the rare occasion he hired female companionship. To make sure he gave himself a good night's sleep, he consumed most of a bottle of Scotch—Rebecca preferred a cosmo but Alex wasn't focused on keeping her happy.

After they ate steak and fries in his suite, he took her to bed but the only intimacy between them was that he curled round her and the two naked people fell asleep. The following morning, he slapped her ass to wake her and encouraged her to leave so he could have breakfast alone. Then downstairs and out to the waiting car wearing his finest suit.

The camera flashes popped in his face when he arrived at the courthouse; the press asking questions he had no intention of answering. Alex did his best to hide behind his fedora as he didn't want to be seen on the front page of the late editions. When he found the courtroom, Mendy smiled as he walked towards the lawyer.

"Let's go to a meeting room so we can have a private conversation."

Alex nodded and followed Mendy out of the court, filled with oak and the musty aroma of piles of paper, and headed over the corridor about twenty feet to the left.

"To work, then, Alex. All I want you to do is to keep your hands visible on the table, don't scowl at anything you hear or at anything that Dewey does. Finally, every so often glance at the jury. If you never make eye contact with them, you'll behave like a guilty man and that is not the impression we are trying to convey, right?"

"I am only guilty of being an industrious American."

"Save it for the jury."

A WEEK LATER and Alex had done his best to follow Mendy's instructions and at least held back from delivering an outburst like the one that erupted out of his lips when he last met Dewey. In the meantime, the special prosecutor laid out the lavish apartments, hotel suites and other real estate under Alex's control. By the time the court had waded through all that detail, it was Friday afternoon.

Then he worked his way through Alex's tax affairs, such as they were. Thirty minutes later and there was nothing more to say and the case for the prosecution rested, so the judge called for a recess until Monday. Before they left for the night, Mendy and Alex scooted back to their room down the corridor to take stock.

"What do you think, Mendy?"

"The evidence has piled high and it felt like Dewey found anyone who has seen you spend a dime and put them on the stand."

"We knew this would happen—you warned me the first day we met."

"Yes Alex, but I've been keeping my eye on the jury and the way they look at you. I can assure you this isn't going well. Most of them don't bother turning to see your reaction to the evidence anymore. That is not a good sign."

"So how do we counter Dewey?"

"Would you like me to see if he'll cut you a deal?"

"No. If I do that then no syndicate member'll trust me again. They will always assume that I spilled my guts to Dewey—which is what he wants me to do anyway, right?"

"Alex, if we fight to the bitter end, I cannot guarantee you won't do hard time."

"I'd rather accept that risk then wind up stabbed on the street on my way home one night—or worse."

"Dewey has taken the jury's heads. Why don't we try to grab at their hearts? Would you be prepared to take the stand, Alex?"

"Whatever you think will work."

"We can present you as an upright fella with a wife and family—and some commercial interests on the side."

"I signed the divorce papers last week."

"Until a trip to Reno they are just bits of paper. You, on the other hand, are a family guy who runs a small business—work with me here."

ON MONDAY, FIRST thing, Alex was sworn in and took the stand. Mendy got Alex to describe his domestic situation.

"Mr. Cohen. Where do you live?"

"In a hotel suite in midtown."

"And is that your only residence?"

"No, sir. I also have a small place in Hoboken."

"Why do you need a second home? Most New Yorkers aren't lucky enough to have two."

"My wife and children are there and I try to spend as much time with them as I possibly can. I work late in the city so I have somewhere to sleep here too."

"So you don't acquire real estate like toys in a box?"

"No, I am just a guy trying to get by."

"Thank you, Mr. Cohen. I'm sure your sons appreciate your care. What age are they?"

"Objection!"

"Sustained. Keep your questions relevant, Mr. Greenberg."

"Are your children old enough to visit you on their own in Manhattan?"

"No, I must go to them. They are aged between nine and fourteen years."

"Alex, the prosecution's contention is that you are a criminal who has never paid his taxes. Have you filed tax returns?"

"Of course I have. I am a good American, but I am no accountant. When I came to this country I was only fifteen and couldn't even speak the language. I didn't have a trade, but I learned fast and have earned enough to take care of my family. If my tax filings have been a few cents out, then I ask that the jury forgives me. I was more worried about feeding my kin than recording items in a ledger."

"Thank you. No further questions."

Mendy took a while to sit down and gave Alex time to relax before Dewey's cross-examination. He eyeballed as many jurors as he could. Perhaps if they saw Alex as a human and not as a bunch of papers and numbers then he might have a chance. The wily prosecutor raised off his haunches and pounded straight to the witness box, standing inches away from Alex's face.

"How many residences do you own, Mr. Cohen?"

"Two."

"That's not true. The court has already seen that your name is on the deeds of four properties. You know the evidence put before the jury, same as them."

"But…"

"And what is your business?"

"I import a variety of goods."

"What kind?"

"Food, drink, that sort of thing in the main."

"And have you ever been paid to carry out any criminal activity?"

"Of course, not. I am a respectable American."

"So you keep saying, Cohen."

"You have made many claims about me, Mr. Dewey. Just because you say something does not make it so. A good American looks after his family, helps his friends, and supports his country. I went to fight in Europe and survived while you were still playing ball in high school."

"This trial isn't about your war record. This is about whether you have paid your taxes. Did you file them last year?"

"Yes."

"But where are the documents? There are no records to support what you say."

"I know I filed them and I supplied you with a copy many months ago."

The eyes of the jury switched from Alex to Dewey—the first chink in Dewey's armor despite an onslaught that had lasted a week.

MENDY AND ALEX sat with a coffee in their private room that lunchtime, knowing that closing arguments would commence in the afternoon.

"Did we do well this morning, Mendy?"

"You scored a few points against Dewey but I don't know if it has been enough. I still recommend you let me speak to him right now and get a deal lined up."

"I've told you before and I will say it again: no. That cannot happen."

While they waited, Alex and Mendy remained in their room, drinking and eating. Mendy had ordered a takeout from Lindy's so at least Alex could enjoy a piece of cheesecake.

Then an officer of the court knocked politely and told them the jury had reached a verdict, so they trundled back into the courtroom. As Alex rose to hear the pronouncement, the foreman announced that yes, they had reached a verdict upon which they all agreed.

"How say you in this matter?"

"We find the defendant guilty."

Alex didn't hear another word anyone in court spoke that afternoon. Everything became a blur in his head.

A month later when they came back to the courthouse for sentencing, Mendy told him that five years was not as bad as it could have been and Dewey grinned before leaving the court to pontificate to the press outside.

Ida was dead; after a trip to Nevada, Sarah was no longer his wife. Meyer, Benny, and the rest of the syndicate had turned their backs on him. Anastasia and Louis had stolen the heroin trafficking racket from under him and no one had done anything to stop them. Not even Charlie, who hadn't lifted a finger to intervene.

When those five long years were over, Alex wouldn't be able to stay on the East Coast because none of the syndicate would speak to him. Despite serving time, there would be the suspicion that he had given some of them up to Dewey. After all, why had he only received such a short sentence when

Alfonse had received ten and Charlie was looking at spending the rest of his life in jail.

As he was led onto the waiting bus to take him to Rikers, Alex was alone —no wife, no mistress, no friends, no family. Not even the promise that his business partners would look after him while he was behind bars or when he came out. All that remained was the memory of the scent of a woman he called Rebecca and the lingering taste of cheesecake under his breath.

THE END

THANK YOU FOR READING!

Get a free novella

Building a relationship with my readers is the very best thing about writing. I send weekly newsletters with details of new releases, special offers and other bits of news relating to the Lagotti Family and Alex Cohen series, as well as information about my stand-alone novels.

And if you sign up to the mailing list I'll send you a copy of the Alex Cohen prequel, The Broska Bruiser. Just go to www.leob.ws/signup and we'll take it from there.

Of course, if you prefer to jump right into the next book in the series then go to www.leob.ws/chiseler to grab your copy of Casino Chiseler now.

Enjoy this book? You can make a difference

Reviews are the most powerful tools in my arsenal when it comes to getting attention for my books. Much as I'd like to, I don't have the financial muscle of a New York publisher. I can't take out full page ads or put posters on the subway.

(Not yet, anyway).

But I do have something much more powerful and effective than that, and it's something that those publishers would kill to get their hands on.

A committed and loyal bunch of readers.

Honest reviews of my books help bring them to the attention of other readers.

If you've enjoyed this book I shall be very grateful if you would spend just five minutes leaving a review (it can be as short as you like) on the book's page. You can jump right to the page by clicking www.books2read.com/alex1-3.

Thank you very much.

Leo

SNEAK PREVIEW

In book four, Casino Chiseler…

Bulbs popped and whizzed round his head as the crime reporters swarmed around him, hoping to catch the best photo of Alex for their front page noon editions. Local cops lined his route from the kerbside to the court entrance. Perhaps for the first time in his life, he was grateful to a bunch of flatfeet.

The crowd thickened at the bottom of the courthouse steps, forcing Mendy and Alex to pause their attempts to proceed.

"What you going to tell Kefauver?"

"Are you naming any names today?"

"How does it feel to be back in court?"

A thousand questions whirred around his ears as each reporter did their best to get their quote for their editor, but Alex followed Mendy's instructions and said nothing.

Although a handful of reporters stayed with them as they entered the hallowed portals of the courthouse building and Mendy asked a nearby court official where they needed to go. The answer delivered them to a wide corridor packed with men and women standing around, looking like they had as much idea what was going on as Alex did.

"Brace yourself, the world and his wife is watching us."

Into the courtroom and an usher took them to the front right-hand benches. Alex surveyed the joint: an arc of seats for the senators to question their witnesses, sat opposite with a bank of tables and chairs for them and their lawyers. Behind them, the auditorium packed with a mixture of concerned citizens, members of the press and court ghouls who'd turn up to the opening of a paper bag if it took place in this building.

To the wings, either side of the tables in front of the politicians' pews were enormous boxes on wheels—the TV cameras. Alex swallowed hard. Mendy nudged him and leaned in.

"Don't worry about the television crew. They are not your enemy —the senators are the ones who'll question you. Everything else is fluff. Stick to the script and if you think you will deviate from the plan, then stop and speak with me."

A hush entered the room and Alex twisted round to see what was happening. If he had bothered to remain facing forwards, he would have seen a side door open and a stream of men gush into the courtroom and take their seats in the arc in front of him. No sooner had they appeared than the lights on the top of the television cameras glowed red, showing they were live on air across the country.

After an interminable wait for everyone to sit down, open their cases, shuffle their papers and settle into their seats, the first witness was called. Alex stood up and sat down in the center of the tables with Mendy by his side.

A court official stepped toward him and asked Alex to swear to tell the truth, the whole truth and pretty much only the truth before his God. When this activity started, the TV cameras swung round and focused their rays on him. Despite being unsettled by this mechanical response, Alex sat down, leaning forward so that his elbows rested on the table and he interleaved the fingers of one hand in between those on the other. Then he exhaled and stared forwards and the cockroach immediately in front of Estes Kefauver.

"Let's keep this simple shall we, gentlemen?"

Those beady eyes bore inside him and Alex swallowed hard again.

"Mr. Cohen, let me remind you that you are under oath. Are you, or have you ever been, an active participant in the organized crime syndicate known as the mafia?"

To grab your copy, go to www.books2read.com/chiseler.

OTHER BOOKS BY THE AUTHOR

Alex Cohen

The Bowery Slugger (Book 1)
East Side Hustler (Book 2)
Midtown Huckster (Book 3)
Alex Cohen Books 1-3
Casino Chiseler (Book 4)
Cuban Heel (Book 5–Due 2021)
Hollywood Bilker (Book 6–Due 2021)
The Mensch (Book 7–Due 2021)
Alex Cohen Books 4-7 (Due 2022)

Stand Alone

The Case

The Lagotti Family

The Heist (Book 1)
The Getaway (Book 2)
Powder (Book 3)
Mama's Gone (Book 4)
The Lagotti Family Complete Collection (Books 1-4)

All books are available from www.leob.ws and all major eBook and paperback sales platforms.

ABOUT THE AUTHOR

Leopold Borstinski is an independent author whose past careers have included financial journalism, business management of financial software companies, consulting and product sales and marketing, as well as teaching.

There is nothing he likes better so he does as much nothing as he possibly can. He has travelled extensively in Europe and the US and has visited Asia on several occasions. Leopold holds a Philosophy degree and tries not to drop it too often.

He lives near London and is married with one wife, one child and no pets.

Find out more at LeopoldBorstinski.com.

Made in the USA
Las Vegas, NV
01 July 2023